William Roscoe

The Life of Lorenzo the Magnificent

Vol.1

William Roscoe

The Life of Lorenzo the Magnificent
Vol.1

ISBN/EAN: 9783743435636

Printed in Europe, USA, Canada, Australia, Japan

Cover: Foto ©Raphael Reischuk / pixelio.de

More available books at **www.hansebooks.com**

THE

LIFE

OF

LORENZO DE' MEDICI,

CALLED

THE MAGNIFICENT.

BY WILLIAM ROSCOE.

THE THIRD EDITION, CORRECTED.

VOL. I.

LONDON:

PRINTED FOR A. STRAHAN; T. CADELL JUN. AND W. DAVIES (SUCCESSORS TO MR. CADELL) IN THE STRAND; AND J. EDWARDS IN PALL MALL.

1797.

PREFACE.

THE close of the fifteenth, and the beginning of the sixteenth century, comprehend one of those periods of history which are entitled to our minutest study and inquiry. Almost all the great events from which Europe derives its present advantages, are to be traced up to those times. The invention of the art of printing, the discovery of the great western continent, the schism from the church of Rome, which ended in the reformation of many of its abuses, and established the precedent of reform, the degree of perfection attained in the fine arts, and the final introduction of true principles of criticism and taste, compose such an illustrious assemblage

assemblage of luminous points, as cannot fail of attracting for ages the curiosity and admiration of mankind.

A complete history of these times has long been a great desideratum in literature; and whoever confiders the magnitude of the undertaking will not think it likely to be foon supplied. Indeed, from the nature of the transactions which then took place, they can only be exhibited in detail, and under separate and particular views. That the author of the following pages has frequently turned his eye towards this interesting period is true, but he has felt himself rather dazzled than informed by the survey. A mind of greater compass, and the possession of uninterrupted leisure, would be requisite to comprehend, to select, and to arrange the immense variety of circumstances which a full narrative of those times would involve; when almost every city of Italy was a new Athens, and that favoured country could boast its historians, its poets, its orators, and its artists, who may contend with the great names of antiquity for the palm of mental excellence. When Venice, Milan, Rome,

Florence, Bologna, Ferrara, and several other places, vied with each other, not in arms, but in science, and in genius; and the splendor of a court was estimated by the number and talents of learned men who illustrated it by their presence; each of whose lives, and productions, would, in a work of this nature, merit a full and separate discussion.

From this full blaze of talents, the author has turned towards a period, when its first faint gleams afford a subject, if not more interesting, at least more suited to his powers. When, after a night of unexpected darkness, Florence again saw the sun break forth with a lustre more permanent, though perhaps not so bright. The days of Dante, of Boccaccio, and of Petrarca, were indeed past; but under the auspices of the House of Medici, and particularly through the ardour and example of Lorenzo, the empire of science and true taste was again restored.

After the death of Boccaccio, the survivor of that celebrated triumvirate who had carried their native tongue to an high pitch of refinement,

ment, and endeavoured, not without success, to introduce the study of the ancient languages into Italy, a general degradation of letters again took place; and the Italian tongue in particular was so far deteriorated, and debased, as, by the acknowledgment of the best critics, to have become scarcely intelligible. The first symptoms of improvement appeared about the middle of the fifteenth century; when Cosmo de' Medici, after having established his authority in Florence, devoted the latter years of a long and honourable life to the encouragement, and even the study of philosophy, and polite letters. He died in 1464; and the infirm state of health of his son Piero, who was severely afflicted by the gout, did not permit him to make that progress in the path which his father had pointed out, that his natural disposition would otherwise have effected. After surviving him only about five years, the greater part of which time he was confined to a sick-bed, he died, leaving two sons; to the elder of whom, Lorenzo, the praise of having restored to literature its ancient honours is principally due. In succeeding times, indeed, that praise has been almost exclusively bestowed on

Giovanni de' Medici, afterwards Leo the tenth, the second son of Lorenzo, who undoubtedly promoted the views, but never in any degree rivalled the talents of his father.

Certain it is that no man was ever more admired and venerated by his contemporaries, or has been more defrauded of his just fame by posterity, than Lorenzo de' Medici. Possessed of a genius more original and versatile than perhaps any of his countrymen, he has led the way in some of the most estimable species of poetic composition; and some of his productions stand unrivalled amongst those of his countrymen to the present day. Yet such has been the admiration paid by the Italians to a few favourite authors, that they have almost closed their eyes to the various excellencies with which his works abound. From the time of his death no general collection was made of his writings for upwards of sixty years, and after their first publication by Aldus in 1554, upwards of two centuries elapsed without a new edition. Neglected in Italy, they seem to have been unknown to the rest of Europe. A

French historian (*a*), in whose narrative Lorenzo makes a conspicuous figure, assures his readers that the writings of this great man, as well in verse as prose, are irrecoverably lost; and that he would no longer be known as an author, were it not from the commendations bestowed upon him by his friends, and the attention paid to him by Paulus Jovius, who has assigned a place to his memory in his eulogies on the modern writers of Italy.

But we are not to consider Lorenzo de' Medici merely in the character of an author, and a patron of learning. As a statesman he was without doubt the most extraordinary person of his own, or perhaps of any time. Though a private citizen and a merchant of Florence, he not only obtained the decided control of that state, at a period when it abounded with men of the greatest talents and acuteness, but raised himself to the rank of sole arbiter of Italy, and operated with considerable effect upon the politics

(*a*) Varillas, Anecdotes de Florence, ou l'histoire secrete de la Maison de Medicis. *p.* 149. *Ed. La Haye*, 1687.

ties of Europe. Without attempting to subjugate his native place, he laid the foundation of the future greatness of his family. His son, and his nephew, were at a short interval successively raised to the pontifical dignity; and in the succeeding centuries his descendants became connected by marriage with the first European sovereigns. The protection afforded by him to all the polite arts, gave them a permanent foundation in Italy. In the establishment of public libraries, schools and seminaries of learning, he was equally munificent, indefatigable, and successful; and these objects were all accomplished, by a man who died at the early age of forty-four years.

It is not however the intention of the author of the following work, to confine himself merely to the relation of the life of an individual, however illustrious. Of a family of whom so much has been said, and so little with certainty known, a more particular account cannot be uninteresting. In aiming at this purpose, he has been unavoidably led to give some account of the rise of modern literature; and particularly to notice many contemporary authors, whose reputation, at least in this country, has not yet been adequate to their merits. In an age when long and dangerous expeditions are undertaken to develope the manners of barbarians, or to discover the source of a river, it will surely not be thought an useless attempt, to endeavour to trace some of those minute and almost imperceptible causes, from which we are to deduce our present proficiency in letters, in science, and in arts.

Of the several narratives of the life of Lorenzo de' Medici hitherto published, the most ancient is that of Niccolo Valori a Florentine, eminent for his rank and learning, the contemporary and friend of Lorenzo. This account, written not inelegantly in Latin, and which composes a small octavo volume of sixty-seven pages, remained in manuscript, till Laurentius Mehus gave it to the public in 1749. An Italian translation had indeed been published at Florence, as early as the year 1560. The principal events in the Life of Lorenzo are here related with accuracy and fidelity: but upon the whole it it gives us too distant and indistinct a view of him. Though sensible in some respects of the magnitude of his subject, Valori seems not to have been sufficiently aware of the distinguishing characteristic of Lorenzo—the strength, extent, and versatility of his mind. Hence he has exhibited him only in one principal point of view; either wholly omitting, or at most slightly noticing, his many other endowments; closely adhering to his purpose, he confines himself to too small a circle, and enters not into those discussions respecting collateral events and circumstances, which a full display of the character of Lorenzo requires. The work of Valori may however be considered, not only as a well-written and authentic piece of biography, but as the foundation of all subsequent efforts on the same subject; although it wants that interest which it would have derived from a closer and more intimate examination of the temper, the character, and the writings of Lorenzo.

By what strange fatality it happened, that the reputation of the most eminent man of his own age should have fallen into almost absolute neglect

neglect in the course of that which immediately succeeded, it is difficult to discover; particularly when we consider that the Italians have been by no means inattentive to their national glory, and that the memoirs of the lives of many of the contemporaries of Lorenzo, who were inferior to him in every point of view, have been fully, and even ostentatiously set forth. Whatever was the cause, it is certain that from the publication of the work of Valori in its Italian dress, till the year 1763, no professed account of Lorenzo de' Medici made its appearance in public; although few authors have touched upon the history of those times, without paying him the passing tribute of their applause. This is the more extraordinary, as the materials for enlarging, and improving the narrative of Valori, were obvious. In the year last mentioned, the poems of Lorenzo were reprinted at Bergamo; and a new account of the life of the author was prefixed to the work (*a*). From this, however,

(*a*) Poesie del Magnifico Lorenzo de' Medici, con alcune Memorie attenenti alla sua vita, Testimonianze, &c. Bergamo, 1763, appresso Pietro Lancellotti.

however, little is to be expected, when it is understood, that the biographer, in his introduction, acknowledges that it is entirely founded on that of Valori; upon whose authority he solely relies, and protests against being answerable for any fact alledged by him, further than that authority warrants. To an exertion of this kind, as he justly observes, neither the deep research of criticism, nor the assistance of rare books, was necessary. In the few attempts which he has made to afford additional information, he has resorted principally to Negri (*a*), and Varillas (*b*), whose authority, nevertheless, he has himself deservedly impeached; and whose inaccuracy renders their testimony of little weight, when not expressly confirmed by other writers.

About twenty years since, several learned Italians united in drawing up memoirs of such of their countrymen as had distinguished themselves in

(*a*) Istoria degli scrittori Fiorentini, opera postuma del P. Giulio Negri. *Ferrara*, 1722.

(*b*) Anecd. de Florence. ut sup.

in different branches of science, and arts (*a*); and the life of Lorenzo, amongst others, fell to the pen of P. Bruno Bruni, professor of divinity in Florence. Unfortunately however it was executed without any new researches, being entirely compiled from previous publications; and it must be owned that the work derives no advantages from the professional prejudices or opinions of its author. The conspiracy of the Pazzi is one of the most striking events that ever engaged the attention of the historian, and the circumstances which accompanied it, compose a body of evidence as accurate and authentic, as history can produce. But the delicacy of the biographer shrunk from the relation of an incident, that involved in the guilt of premeditated assassination, the Vicar of Christ upon earth! This event is accordingly passed over with a general reference to previous relations; and an annotation is subjoined, tending to impeach the evidence of one who was an eye-witness of the transaction, and whose narrative was laid before the public immediately

(*a*) Elogj degli Uomini illustri Toscani. *In Lucca*, 1771, &c. 4 *vol.* 8vo.

diately after the event took place (*a*). No extraordinary number of pages was devoted to the work; and it may be enough to remark, that the resemblance of Lorenzo de' Medici does not well associate with a set of petty portraits, hung up by way of ornament, in frames of equal sizes. In order to do justice to such a subject, a larger canvass is necessary.

In enumerating the labours of my predecessors, it may not be improper more particularly to notice the singular work of Varillas, to which I have before had occasion to refer. This book, written in a lively style, with great pretensions to secret information from manuscripts in the French king's library, has more the resemblance of a romance than of an authentic narrative; and if we may judge of the author's private anecdotes, from his misrepresentations and

(*a*) Angeli Politiani Conjurationis Pactianæ anni 1478 Commentarium, in eodem anno excusum, *in 4to sine loci et typographi nominibus*, iterum typis impressum Neapoli anno 1769, curâ et studio Joannis Adimari ex Marchionibus Bumbæ.

and mistakes in matters of more general notoriety, we shall frequently be compelled to consider them rather as the offspring of his own imagination, than as substantiated facts. The absurdities of this author have frequently been exposed by Bayle (*a*), who has in many instances pointed out his glaring perversions of the relation of Paulus Jovius, the veracity of whom as an historian is itself sufficiently equivocal. The accuracy of Varillas may in some degree be determined by the singular list of books and manuscripts from which he professes to have derived his information, the very existence of some of which yet rests on his own authority.

Such, however, being the attempts that had been made to exhibit to the public the life and labours of Lorenzo de' Medici, I conceived that there could be no great degree of arrogance in endeavouring to give a more full and particular account of them: Nor was I deterred from this undertaking by the consideration, that Providence

(*a*) Dictionnaire Historique et Critique, *Art. Politien*, &c.

dence had placed my lot beyond the limits of that favoured country,

"Ch' Appenin parte, e'l mar circonda, e l'Alpe."

The truth is, that in a remote part of this remote kingdom, and deprived of the many advantages peculiar to seats of learning, I saw no difficulty in giving a more full, distinct, and accurate idea of the subject than could be collected from any performance I had then met with. For some years past, the works of the Italian writers had amused a portion of my leisure hours; a partiality for any particular object generally awakens the desire of obtaining further information respecting it; and from the perusal of the Italian poets, I was insensibly led to attend to the literary history of that cultivated nation. In tracing the rise of modern literature, I soon perceived that every thing great and estimable in science and in art, revolved round Lorenzo de' Medici, during the short but splendid æra of his life, as a common centre, and derived from him its invariable preservation and support.— Under these impressions I began to collect such scattered notices respecting him as fell in my way; and the Florentine histories of Machiavelli, and Ammirato, the critical labours of Crescimbeni, Muratori, Bandini, and Tiraboschi, with other works of less importance, of which I then found myself possessed, supplied me with materials towards the execution of my plan. I had not however proceeded far, before I perceived that the subject deserved a more minute inquiry; for which purpose it would be necessary to resort to contemporary authorities, and if possible to original documents. The impracticability of obtaining in this country the information of which I stood in need, would perhaps have damped the ardour of my undertaking, had not a circumstance presented itself in the highest degree favourable to my purpose. An intimate friend, with whom I had been many years united in studies and affection, had paid a visit to Italy, and had fixed his winter residence at Florence. I well knew that I had only to request his assistance, in order to obtain whatever information he had an opportunity of procuring, from the very spot which was to be the scene of my intended history. My inquiries were particularly directed towards the Laurentian and Riccardi libraries, which

which I was convinced would afford much original and interesting information. It would be unjust merely to say that my friend afforded me the assistance I required; he went far beyond even the hopes I had formed, and his return to his native country was, if possible, rendered still more grateful to me, by the materials he had collected for my use. Amongst these I had the pleasure to find several beautiful poems of Lorenzo de' Medici, the originals of which are deposited in the Laurentian library, although the former editors of his works appear not to have had the slightest information respecting them. These poems, which have been copied with great accuracy, and, where it was possible, collated with different manuscripts, will for the first time be given to the public at the close of the present work. The munificence of the late Great Duke Leopold, and the liberality of the Marquis Riccardi, had laid open the inestimable treasures of their collections to every inquirer; and under the regulations of the venerable Canonico Bandini, to whose labours the literary history of Italy is highly indebted, such arrangements have been adopted in the Laurentian library, that

that every difficulty which might retard research is effectually removed. Unlike the immense, but ill-digested and almost prohibited collections of the Vatican, the libraries of Florence are the common property of the learned of all nations; and an institution founded by Cosmo, and promoted by Lorenzo de' Medici, yet subsists, the noblest monument of their glory, the most authentic depository of their fame.

Amongst a number of printed volumes, immediately or remotely connected with my principal subject, which were supplied by the attention of my friend, were two works of which he had given me previous information. These were the life of Lorenzo de' Medici, written in Latin, by Monsignor Fabroni, a learned Italian prelate, and published in the year 1784, in two volumes in quarto; and the life of his grandfather Cosmo, by the same author, published in one volume in quarto in the year 1789. On receiving these extensive productions, it became a subject of consideration, whether it might not be advisable to lay aside my own narrative, although it was then far advanced, and satisfy myself with

a trans-a translation of the former of these works, adding such remarks as my previous researches had enabled me to make. The perusal of these volumes, whilst it afforded me considerable gratification, soon however convinced me that the purpose I had in view could not be obtained by a translation. The leading object of Fabroni is to illustrate the political, rather than the literary life of Lorenzo. It appeared to me, that the mere historical events of the fifteenth century, so far as they regarded Italy, could not deeply interest my countrymen in the eighteenth; but I conceived that the progress of letters and of arts would be attended to with pleasure in every country where they were cultivated and protected: many other motives, some of which will appear in the course of the work, determined me to prosecute my original plan; and the history now presented to the public bears no more resemblance to that of Fabroni, than his does to that of his predecessor Valori. The general incidents in the life of Lorenzo are indeed nearly the same in all; but for most of the sentiments and observations that may occur in the ensuing volume, and for a considerable part of the narrative,

rative, particularly such as relates to the state and progress of letters and of arts, the responsibility must fall on myself.

But although I have not thought it eligible to rest satisfied with a mere translation of the works of Fabroni, I have derived from them very important assistance and information. The numerous and authentic documents which he obtained by diligent researches through the archives of Florence, and which occupy two-thirds of his work, are a treasure with which, in the infancy of my undertaking, I little expected to be gratified. The assistance derived from these sources did not however supersede my exertions in procuring such additional information as other parts of the continent and this country could supply. The Crevenna library, lately exposed to sale at Amsterdam, and the Pinelli, in London, furnished me with several publications of early date, for which I might otherwise long have inquired throughout Europe to no purpose. The rich and extensive catalogues published by Edwards, Payne, and other London booksellers, who have of late years diligently sought for and

and imported into England whatever is curious or valuable in foreign literature, have alſo contributed to the success of my inquiries; and I may justly say, that I have spared neither trouble nor expence in the acquisition of whatever appeared to be necessary to the prosecution of my work.

I am not, however, arrogant enough to conceive, that, even with these advantages, I have been able to do justice to so extensive and so diversified a subject. Precluded by more serious and indispensable avocations from devoting a continued attention to it, I am apprehensive that facts of importance may either have escaped my diligence, or may be yet imperfectly related. The difficulties attending a critical examination of works of taste, written in a foreign language, contribute to render me diffident of the success of my labours. In the few attempts to translate or imitate the poetical pieces of Lorenzo and his contemporaries, I must regret my inability to do them more complete justice; an inability of which I am fully sensible, but for which

which I do not mean to trouble my reader with any further apology. Such as it is, I submit this performance to the judgment of the public; ready to acknowledge, though not pleased to reflect, that the disadvantages under which an author labours are no excuse for the imperfections of his work.

POSTSCRIPT.

Liverpool, Dec. 1795.

WHEN the first of these volumes was nearly printed, and the materials arranged for the second, I had the satisfaction of obtaining a copy of a very singular and interesting work, in three volumes octavo, intitled *Mémoires Généalogiques de la Maison de Médici*. For this performance I am indebted to the MARQUIS OF LANSDOWN; a nobleman who has conferred the most important benefits on his country, and whose attention has been invariably directed to the encouragement of those studies, which can only produce their proper fruits in that state of public tranquillity, which his distinguished talents have been uniformly exerted to secure.

The work above mentioned is the production of Mr. Tenhove of the Hague, a near relation of the late Greffier of the states of Holland, Mr. Fagel, to whose memory it is inscribed in the following affectionate terms:

A l' heureuse mémoire de François Fagel,
Greffier de leurs hautes puissances les Etats Generaux
des Provinces-unies:
Heritier des vertus et des talens de ses ancetres,
Collegue et ami du venerable vieillard son pere,
Favori des peuples et des grands,
Fragile espoir de la patrie,
Ami zelé des lettres et des arts,
Arbitre sur de l' elegance et du gout,
Et meilleure moitié de moi-meme.

But,

But, alas! the monument which affection had devoted to the memory of a friend, was itself destined to remain unfinished; and the accomplished author, by a fatality which will perhaps remind my readers of the events related in the last chapter of this history, whilst he lamented the loss of his patron, was called to join him, in the society of the wise, the learned, and the good of former ages—in that of Scipio and of Lælius, of Politiano and of Lorenzo de' Medici.

Inter odoratum Lauri nemus, unde superne
Plurimus Eridani per silvam volvitur amnis.

Of such part of his work as was printed before his death, a copy had been presented by him to the learned and venerable Dr. Macleane of the Hague, the well-known translator of Mosheim's ecclesiastical history, with whom he had lived for many years in the most friendly intimacy. At the kind request of the Marquis of Lansdown, Dr. Macleane transmitted these volumes to England; and a probability having since occurred, of his obtaining another copy, he has obligingly relinquished them to his lordship, by whose liberality I have now the pleasure of calling them my own.

Although these volumes appear to be rather the amusement of the leisure hours of a polite scholar, than the researches of a professed historian, yet they display an acquaintance with the transactions of Italy, seldom acquired except by a native. To a great proficiency in the literature of that country, Mr. Tenhove united an indisputable taste in the productions of all the fine arts, and a general knowledge of the state of manners, and the progress of science, in every period of society. The fertility of his genius, and the extent of his information, have enabled him to intersperse his narrative with a variety of interesting digressions, and brilliant observations; and the most engaging work that has perhaps ever appeared, on a subject of literary history, is written by a native of one country, in the language of another, on the affairs of a third.

Excellent however as the work of Mr. Tenhove certainly is, I have not derived from it any very important assistance; which will be more readily credited, when it is understood that it commences with the history of the family of the Medici in remote antiquity, and adverting to every member of it, of whom any historical notices remain, was intended to be continued down to the present century. The interval of time which I have undertaken to illustrate, extending only to the life of an individual who died at an early age, must consequently form a small portion in a work intended to embrace such an extent of time, yet not upon the whole more voluminous than my own. The character of Lorenzo is indeed finely conceived, and faithfully drawn by Mr. Tenhove; and his accomplishments are celebrated with a warmth of expression, which proves that the author was fully sensible of his genius and his merits. But it was not consistent with the plan that he had adopted, to enter into those particular inquiries, and more minute discussions, which the duty of a professed biographer requires. From this circumstance, and the advanced state of my work, I was not induced to make any alteration either in its arrangement or in the manner of its execution. After having proceeded so far in the character of a simple relater of facts, it would indeed ill become me to aim at the higher ornaments of composition.

Servetur ad imum
Qualis ab incepto processerit.

Unwilling,

Unwilling, however, to possess such a treasure as the volumes in question, without enabling my readers to share it with me in some degree, I have frequently taken occasion, in the notes to the second volume, to cite the sentiments of Mr. Tenhove, on the subject of our mutual inquiry. I am aware, that by this conduct I am inducing a comparison by no means favourable to my own performance; but having executed it to the best of my ability, I have not been led by that consideration to suppress any thing which I thought might tend to authenticate or illustrate my work. The motives which have encouraged me to persevere in this undertaking, amidst numerous avocations and duties, which connect me with society by almost every tie, have been a high admiration of the character of Lorenzo de' Medici, the singular pleasure which I have enjoyed in tracing his history, and the earnest desire which I feel, to place him in that rank in the estimation of my countrymen, to which he is so eminently entitled.

CHAP. I.

ORIGIN *of Florence—Government—Family of the Medici—Salvestro de' Medici—Giovanni de' Medici—Cosmo de' Medici—Influence of that family in Florence—Cosmo seized and imprisoned—Is banished to Padua—Allowed to reside at Venice—Ambrogio Traversari—Cosmo is recalled from banishment—Encourages men of learning—Leonardo and Carlo Aretino—Researches after the writings of the ancients—Poggio Bracciolini—Guarino Veronese—Giovanni Aurispa—Francesco Filelfo—Council of Florence—Revival of the Platonic Philosophy—Marsilio Ficino—Cosmo establishes the Laurentian Library—Niccolo Niccoli founds the Library of S. Marco—The Vatican Library founded by Pope Nicholas* V.*—Invention and progress of the art of printing—Capture of Constantinople by the Turks—Cosmo applies himself to study—Marriage of Piero de' Medici—Birth of Lorenzo and Giuliano—Celebrity of Cosmo—Antonio Beccatelli—Literary quarrels—Bessarion and George of Trebisond—Poggio and Filelfo—Death and character of Cosmo de' Medici.*

CHAP. I.

FLORENCE has been remarkable in modern history for the frequency and violence of its internal dissentions, and for the predilection of its inhabitants for every species of science, and every production of art. However discordant these characteristics may appear, they are not difficult to reconcile: The same active spirit that calls forth the talents of individuals for the preservation of their liberties, and resists with unconquerable resolution whatever is supposed to infringe them, in the moments of domestic peace and security seeks with avidity other objects of employment. The defence of freedom has always been found to expand and strengthen the mind; and though the faculties of the human race may remain torpid for generations, when once roused into action they cannot speedily be lulled again into inactivity and repose.

Origin of Florence.

Of the rise of Florence little can be traced with certainty, although much research has been employed on the subject. If we give credit to its historian Machiavelli (*a*) it derives its origin from the ancient and venerable city of Fiesole, whose walls yet remain at the distance of about three miles from Florence. The situation of Fiesole, on the summit of a steep hill, induced its inhabitants, many of whom were early devoted to commerce, to erect habitations for the convenience of traffic on the plain below, between the river Arno and the foot of the mountain. During the continuance of the Roman republic this infant establishment was reinforced by colonists from Rome. The popular tradition of the place, countenanced by Landino (*b*) and Verini (*c*), refers this event to the times of the

---

(*a*) *Mac. Istoria Fiorentina, lib.* ii.

(*b*) " Sed Florentinæ canerem primordia gentis;
" Nobile Syllanum tempus in omne genus;
" Syllanum genus Romana stirpe colonos
" A patribus nunquam degenerasse suis."
Landinus de laudibus Cosmi,
ap. Bandinii Specimen Literaturæ Florentinæ, vol. i. *p.* 200.

" Syllanus primus fugiens asperrima montis
" Purgavit nostros arte colonus agros;
" Atque Arnum recta, contractis undique lymphis,
" Obice disrupto compulit ire via."
Land. de primordiis urbis.
Ibid. v. i. *p.* 167.

(*c*) " Felici Comites Syllæ de marmore templum,
" Mavorti posuere suo."
Ugolinus Verinus de illustratione Urbis Florentiæ.
Flor. 1636, *lib.* i. *p.* 9.

the dictatorship of Sylla, whilst Politiano places it under the triumvirate of Octavius, Antonius, and Lepidus (*a*).

In the frequent irruptions of the northern nations that subverted the Roman state, Florence followed the fate of the rest of Italy; but about the year 1010 it had acquired some degree of strength and independence, which was first exerted in attacking and demolishing the place from which it sprung (*b*). Fiesole retains few traces of its former importance; but its delightful situation and pure air still render it an agreeable and healthy residence.

Government.

For some centuries previous to the commencement of the present history, the government of Florence had fluctuated between an aristocratic and a popular form. The discord and animosity that arose from this instability may well be conceived. When either of the contending factions had obtained the ascendency, the leaders of it soon disagreed

---

(*a*) "Deduxere igitur Florentiam coloniam triumviri Cajus Cæsar qui deinde "Augustus, Marcus Antonius, et Marcus Lepidus etiam pontifex maximus." For many curious observations and learned conjectures on the origin of Fiesole and Florence, *v. Politiani Ep. lib.* I. *Ep.* 2.

(*b*) "Ast ubi Syllanos felix concordia cives
"Altius evexit, Fesulæ venere redactæ
"Sub juga, tunc populi crevit numerosa propago.
"Urbs inimica, potens, vicinaque mœnibus olim
"Martigenæ, ulterius fines efferre negabat.
"Ac veluti quondam veteres auxere Sabini
"Sub Tatio Romam: sic urbs Fesulana relicto
"Vertice victricem tandem migravit in urbem."

Verinus de illustr. Urbis Flor. lib. i.

CHAP. I.

disagreed in the exercise of their power; and the weaker party, attaching themselves to the body of the people, speedily effected a revolution. The frequency of electing their magistrates, at the same time that it was favourable to the preservation of their liberties, fomented a continual spirit of opposition and resentment. A secret enmity, even in the most tranquil days of the republic, subsisted among the leaders of the different factions, and the slightest circumstance, whether of a foreign or domestic nature, was sufficient to kindle the latent spark into an open flame. The contests between the *Ghibellini* and the *Guelfi* (*a*), and between the *Bianchi* and the *Neri* (*b*), were entered into by the Florentines with an eagerness beyond that of any other people in Europe. For a great length of time Florence

(*a*) This distinction began about the twelfth century. In the dissentions between the pope and the emperor, the partizans of the former were denominated Guelphs, and those of the imperial faction Ghibelines; but in succeeding times these appellations conveyed other ideas, and the name of Guelphs was applied to those who, in any popular commotion, espoused the cause of the people, whilst that of Ghibelines became synonymous to the *optimates* of the Romans, or Aristocrates. Ammirato, without being able to trace the origin, pathetically laments the unhappy consequences of these distinctions to his country. *Istoria Fiorentina, v. i. p.* 55, 132. But the particular circumstances which introduced them into Florence are related at considerable length by Nerli. *Commentarii de' fatti civili di Firenze. Augs.* 1728. *p.* 2. *&c.*

(*b*) For these factions Italy was indebted to the city of Pistoia, where a disagreement took place between two young men of the family of Cancellieri, one of whom is called by Machiavelli, Geri, and the other, Lore. In this contest Geri received a slight blow from his relation, who immediately afterwards, at the command of his father Guglielmo, went to the house of Bertuccio, the father of Geri, to apologize for the offence. Bertuccio, exasperated at the indignity, seized the young man, and with the assistance of two of his

Florence was at continual war with itself; and a number of citizens under the name of *Fuorusciti*, or absentees, were constantly employed in attempting to regain their native residence, for which purpose they scrupled not, by all possible means, to excite the resentment of other powers against it. If their attempts proved successful, the weaker party left the city, till they in their turn could expel their conquerors.

These disadvantages were however amply compensated by the great degree of freedom enjoyed by the ctizens of Florence, which had the most favourable effects on their character, and gave them a decided superiority over the inhabitants of the rest of Italy. The popular nature of the government, not subjected to the will of an individual, as in many of the surrounding states, nor restricted like that of Venice to a particular class, was a constant incitement to exertion. Nor was it on the great body of the people only that the good effects of this system were apparent; even those who claimed the privileges of ancestry felt the advantages

servants, cruelly cut off his hand on a manger. This atrocious deed roused the resentment of Guglielmo, who took up arms to revenge the injury. Cancellieri the common ancestor of the family had two wives, from one of whom descended the line of Guglielmo, from the other that of Bertuccio. One of these wives was named Bianca, whence that branch of their family and their adherents were named *Bianchi*, and their opponents, by way of distinction, obtained the name of *Neri*. The whole city espoused the part of one or other of these factions, and the contagion soon spread to Florence, where it received fresh vigour from the ancient dissentions of the *Cerchi* and the *Donati*. The quarrel shortly became tinctured with political enmity, and the Bianchi were considered as Ghibelines, the Neri as Guelphs. *Mac. Ist. Fior. lib.* ii. *Amm. Ist. Fior.* v. i. *p.* 204.

advantages of a rivalship, which prevented their sinking into indolence, and called upon them to support by their own talents the rank and influence which they had derived from those of their ancestors. Where the business of government is confined to a few, the faculties of the many become torpid for want of exercise; but in Florence, every citizen was conversant with, and might hope, at least, to partake in the government; and hence was derived that spirit of industry, which in the pursuit of wealth, and the extension of commerce, was, amidst all their intestine broils, so conspicuous, and so successful (*a*). The fatigues of public life, and the cares of mercantile avocations, were alleviated at times by the study of literature or the speculations of philosophy. A rational and dignified employment engaged those moments of leisure not necessarily devoted to more important concerns; and the mind was relaxed

---

(*a*) The beneficial effects of their government were not unobserved by the Florentines, and are well adverted to by Verini.

——Semperque aliquid novitatis in urbe est
Stat tamen incolumis majestas publica; causa est
Præclaris quoniam ingeniis Florentia favet,
Festinosque libens virtuti impendit honores.
Ex quo si linguæ vitæque industria major
Concessa est cuiquam, nostram demigrat in urbem;
Ut magis eniteat virtus ubi præmia prompta:
Æquarique sibi fert ægre prisca colonos
Nobilitas, oriturque trucis discordia belli;
Fitque minor census, patrimoniaque hausta tributis,
Reddunt attonitum qui stemmate fulget avito.
Contra autem solers et cedere nescius, instat
Fortunæ, summosque animo molitur honores.

Ver. de illust. Urb. lib. iii.

relaxed without being debilitated, and amused without being depraved. The superiority which the Florentines thus acquired was universally acknowledged; and they became the historians, the poets, the orators, and the preceptors of Europe.

CHAP. I.

Family of Medici.

The family of the *Medici* had for many ages been esteemed one of the most considerable in the republic; nor have there been wanting authors who have derived its eminence from the age of Charlemagne: but it must be remembered, that these genealogies have been the production of subsequent times, when the elevation of this family to the supreme command in Florence, made it necessary to impress on the minds of the people an idea of its antiquity and respectability (*a*). It appears however from authentic monuments,

(*a*) In a *M.S.* of the Riccardi library at Florence, of which I have obtained an ample extract, intitled "*Origine e descendenza della casa de' Medici,*" the origin of the family greatness is romantically referred to Averardo de' Medici, a commander under Charlemagne, who, for his valour in destroying the gigantic plunderer *Mugello*, by whom the surrounding country was laid waste, was honoured with the privilege of bearing for his arms six *palle*, or balls, as characteristic of the iron balls that hung from the mace of his fierce antagonist, the impression of which remained on his shield. Verini had before this accounted for the family name and arms by another hereditary tale.

Est qui Bebryaca Medices testetur ab urbe
Venisse; et Toscam sobolem delesse superbam
Asserat: hinc Medicis meruit cognomen habere
Quod Medicus Tosci fuerit, sic ore venenum
Dixerunt patrio: factique insignia portet
Senis in globulis flaventem sanguine peltam.
Ver. de illust. Urbis, lib. iii.

It required some ingenuity to invalidate so strong a presumption of the

CHAP. I.

monuments, that many individuals of this family had signalized themselves on important occasions. Giovanni de' Medici (*a*) in the year 1251, with a body of only one hundred Florentines, forced his way through the Milanese army, then besieging the fortress of Scarperia, and entered the place with the loss of twenty lives.

Salvestro de' Medici.

Salvestro de' Medici acquired great reputation by his temperate, but firm resistance of the tyranny of the nobles (*b*), who, in order to secure their power, accused those who opposed them of being attached to the party of the Ghibelines, then in great odium at Florence. The persons so accused were said to be admonished, *ammoniti*, and by that act were excluded from all offices of government. This custom was at length carried to such an extreme, as to become insufferable. In the year 1379, Salvestro, being chosen chief magistrate, exerted his power in reforming this abuse; which was not however effected without a violent commotion, in which several of the nobility lost their lives. After the death of Salvestro, his son, Veri de' Medici, continued to hold a high rank in the republic, and, like the rest of this family, was always in great favour with the populace.

The

---

ancient family profession, as arises from the name of *Medici*, and the six pills borne as their device.

(*a*) *Amm. Ist. Fior.* i. 531.

(*b*) *Ranni vita di Salvestro de' Medici. Flor.* 1580. *Amm. Ist. Fior.* ii. 716, 717.

CHAP. I.

Giovanni de' Medici.

The person, however, who may be said to have laid the foundation of that greatness which his posterity enjoyed for several ages, was Giovanni de' Medici, the great grandfather of Lorenzo, the subject of our present history (*a*). By a strict attention to commerce, he acquired immense wealth; by his affability, moderation, and liberality, he ensured the confidence and esteem of his fellow-citizens. Without seeking after the offices of the republic, he was honoured with them all. The maxims, which, uniformly pursued, raised the house of Medici to the splendor which it afterwards enjoyed, are to be found in the charge given by this venerable old man on his death-bed to his two sons, Cosmo and Lorenzo (*b*); "*I feel,*" said he, "*that I have lived the time prescribed me. I die content; leaving you, my sons, in affluence and in health, and in such a station, that whilst you follow my example, you may live in your native place, honoured and respected. Nothing affords me more pleasure, than the reflection that my conduct has not given offence to any one; but that, on the contrary, I have endeavoured to serve all persons to the best of my abilities. I advise you to do the same. With respect to the honours of the state, if you would live with security, accept only such as are bestowed on you by the laws,*

(*a*) Giovanni nacque nel 1360, ebbe per moglie Piccarda di Nannino di Odoardo Bueri nel 1386. Fu principe nella republica Fiorentina, Ambasciatore al Papa, a Ladislao, e a Venegia. Morì il dì 20 di Febrajo del 1428. *Origine e descendenza, MS.*

(*b*) *Mac. Ist. Fior. lib.* v.

laws, and the favour of your fellow-citizens; for it is the exercise of that power which is obtained by violence, and not of that which is voluntarily given, that occasions hatred and contention." He died in the year 1428, leaving two sons, Cosmo, born in the year 1389, and Lorenzo in 1394 (*a*), from the latter of whom is derived the collateral branch of the family, that in the beginning of the sixteenth century obtained the absolute sovereignty of Tuscany (*b*).

Cosmo de' Medici.

1414.

Even in the life-time of his father, Cosmo had engaged himself deeply, not only in the extensive commerce by which the family had acquired its wealth, but in the weightier concerns of government. Such was his authority

---

(*a*) *Origine e discendenza, MS.*

(*b*) At the instance of the two brothers, Donatello the sculptor erected a monument to the memory of their father Giovanni de' Medici, and their mother Picarda, which yet remains in the church of S. Lorenzo at Florence, on one side of which is the following inscription:

"Si merita in patriam, si gloria, sanguis et omni
"Larga manus, nigra libera morte forent,
"Viveret heu! patriæ casta cum conjuge felix,
"Auxilium miseris, portus et aura suis,
"Omnia sed quando superantur morte, *Johannes*
"Hoc mausoleo, tuque *Picarda*, jacet:
"Ergo senex mœret, juvenis, puer, omnis et ætas
"Orba parente suo patria mœsta gemit."

On the other side:

"Cosmus et Laurentius de' Medicis, viro clarissimo, Johanni Averardi "filio et Piccardæ Adovardi filiæ carissimis parentibus hoc sepulcrum faciendum curarunt. Obiit autem Johannes x. Kal. Martii. MCCCCXXVIII. Piccarda vero XIII. Kal. Maii quinquennio post e vita migravit."

rity and reputation, that in the year 1414, when Balthasar Cossa, who had been elected pope, and had assumed the name of John XXIII. was summoned to attend the council of Constance, he chose to be accompanied by Cosmo de' Medici, amongst other men of eminence, whose characters might countenance his cause. By this council, which continued nearly four years, Balthasar was deprived of his pontifical dignity, and Otto Colonna, who took the name of Martin V. was elected pope. Divested of his authority, and pursued by his numerous adversaries, Balthasar endeavoured to save himself by flight. Cosmo did not desert in adversity the man to whom he had attached himself in prosperity. At the expence of a large sum of money, he redeemed him from the hands of the duke of Bavaria, who had seized upon his person; and afterwards gave him an hospitable shelter at Florence during the remainder of his life. Nor did the successful pontiff resent the kindness shewn to his rival; on the contrary, he soon afterwards paid a public visit to Florence, where, on the formal submission of Balthasar, and at the request of the Medici, he created him a cardinal, with the privilege of taking the first place in the sacred college. The new-made cardinal did not long survive this honour. He died in the year 1419 (*a*), and it was supposed, that the Medici at his death possessed themselves of immense riches, which he had acquired during his pontificate (*b*). This notion was afterwards encouraged,

(*a*) *Amm. Ist. Fior.* 2. 985.

(*b*) " Si crede che Cosmo de' Medici, del danaro di Baldassare accrescesse
" in modo le sue facoltà che fù poi tenuto il più ricco cittadino di Fiorenza, anzi

couraged, for malevolent purposes, by those who well knew its falsehood (*a*). The true source of the wealth of the Medici, was their superior talents and application to commerce: for the property of the cardinal was scarcely sufficient to discharge his legacies and his debts.

After the death of Giovanni de' Medici, Cosmo supported and increased the family dignity. His conduct was uniformly marked by urbanity and kindness to the superior ranks of his fellow-citizens, and by a constant attention to the interests and the wants of the lower class, whom he relieved with unbounded generosity. By these means he acquired numerous, and zealous partizans, of every denomination; but he rather considered them as pledges for the continuance of the power he possessed, than as instruments to be employed in extending it to the ruin and subjugation of the state. "*No family,*" says Voltaire, "*ever obtained its power by so just a title* (*b*)."

The

"che in Italia, e fuori d'Italia fosse." *Platina in vita di Martino* V. But this tale is confuted by Ammirato, who has cited the testament of Balthasar, by which it appears that he was doubtful whether his property would extend to pay the legacies he had bequeathed. To the altar of St. John the Baptist he gave a *finger of that saint*, which he had long carried secretly about his person. *Amm. Ist. Fior.* 2. 1047.

(*a*) The malice and virulence of Filelfo led him to accuse the Medici of having poisoned Balthasar, in order to obtain possession of his property; but this is sufficiently refuted by the slightest acquaintance with the characters of the accuser and the accused, to say nothing of the irrefragable testimony of Balthasar's will above referred to, of which Giovanni de' Medici was one of the trustees.

(*b*) *Essai sur les Mœurs*, &c. *vol.* ii. *p.* 282. 4*to. ed. Gen.*

CHAP. I.

Influence of the Medici in Florence.

The authority which Cosmo and his descendants exercised in Florence, during the fifteenth century, was of a very peculiar nature; and consisted rather in a tacit influence on their part, and a voluntary acquiescence on that of the people, than in any prescribed or definite compact between them. The form of government was ostensibly a republic, and was directed by a council of ten citizens, and a chief executive officer called the *Gonfaloniere*, or standard bearer, who was chosen every two months. Under this establishment the citizens imagined they enjoyed the full exercise of their liberties; but such was the power of the Medici, that they generally either assumed to themselves the first offices of the state, or nominated such persons as they thought proper to those employments. In this, however, they paid great respect to popular opinion. That opposition of interests so generally apparent between the people and their rulers, was at this time scarcely perceived at Florence, where superior qualifications and industry were the surest recommendations to public authority and favour. Convinced of the benefits constantly received from this family, and satisfied that they could at any time withdraw themselves from a connexion that exacted no engagements, and required only a temporary acquiescence, the Florentines considered the Medici as the fathers, and not as the rulers of the republic. On the other hand, the chiefs of this house, by appearing rather to decline than to court the honours bestowed on them, and by a singular moderation in the use of them when obtained, were careful to maintain the character of simple citizens of Florence, and servants of the state. An interchange of

 reciprocal

reciprocal good offices was the only tie by which the Florentines and the Medici were bound, and perhaps the long continuance of this connexion may be attributed to the very circumstance of its being in the power of either of the parties, at any time, to have dissolved it.

Cosmo seized and imprisoned.

But the prudence and moderation of Cosmo, though they soothed the jealous apprehensions of the Florentines, could not at all times repress the ambitious designs of those who wished to possess or to share his authority.

1433.

In the year 1433 (*a*) Rinaldo de' Albizi, at the head of a powerful party, carried the appointment of the magistracy. At that time Cosmo had withdrawn to his seat at Mugello, where he had remained some months, in order to avoid the disturbances that he saw were likely to ensue (*b*); but at the request of his friends he returned to Florence, where he was led to expect that an union of the different parties would be effected, so as to preserve the peace of the city. In this expectation he was however disappointed. No sooner

(*a*) *Amm. Ist. Fior.* 2. 1088.

(*b*) For some time before the close of the 14th century, it became a custom amongst the chiefs of this family, to keep private memorials of the circumstances attending it. These memorials, or Ricordi, were begun by Filigno de' Medici, who in the year 1373 entered, in a book yet extant, and intitled "*Notizie della famiglia de' Medici,*" some information respecting its wealth, population, and respectability. (*Appendix*, No. I.) Cosmo continued the practice, and in particular has left a very minute account of the circumstances attending his banishment and return, which greatly differs in many respects from the narrative of Machiavelli. (*Appendix*, No. II.) The Ricordi of Lorenzo also remain, and afford much indisputable information on the principal events of his life.

sooner did he make his appearance in the palace, where his presence had been requested, on pretence of his being intended to share in the administration of the republic, than he was seized upon by his adversaries, and committed to the custody of Federigo Malavolti. He remained in this situation for several days, in constant apprehension of some violence being offered to his person; but he still more dreaded that the malice of his enemies might attempt his life by poison. During four days, a small portion of bread was the only food which he thought proper to take.

Is banished to Padua.

The generosity of his keeper at length relieved him from this state of anxiety. In order to induce him to take his food with confidence, Malavolti partook of it with him (*a*). In the mean time, his brother Lorenzo, and his cousin Averardo, having raised a considerable body of men from Romagna and other neighbouring parts, and being joined by Niccolo Tolentino, the commander of the troops of the republic, approached towards Florence to his relief; but the apprehensions that in case they resorted to open violence, the life of Cosmo might be endangered, induced them

(*a*) The address of Malavolti to Cosmo on this occasion, as related by Machiavelli, is full of kindness and humanity. "Tu dubiti Cosimo di non "essere avvelenato, et fai te morire di fame, e poco honore à me, credendo "ch'io volessi tener le mani à una simile sceleratezza. Io non credi che tu "habbi à perdere la vita, tanti amici hai in palagio, et fuori; ma quando pure "avessi a perderla, vivi sicuro che pigliaranno altri modi che usar me, per "ministro à tortela: perche io non voglio bruttarmi le mani nel sangue d' "alcuno, e massime del tuo che non mi offendesti mai," &c.

Mac. Ist. Fior. lib. iv.

CHAP. I.

them to abandon their enterprise. At length Rinaldo and his adherents obtained a decree of the magistracy against the Medici and their friends, by which Cosmo was banished to Padua for ten years, Lorenzo to Venice for five years, and several of their relations and adherents were involved in a similar punishment. Cosmo would gladly have left the city pursuant to his sentence, but his enemies thought it more advisable to retain him till they had established their authority; and they frequently gave him to understand that if his friends raised any opposition to their measures, his life should answer it. He also suspected that another reason for his detention was to ruin him in his credit and circumstances; his mercantile concerns being then greatly extended. As soon as these disturbances were known, several of the states of Italy interfered in his behalf. Three ambassadors arrived from Venice, who proposed to take him under their protection, and to engage that he should strictly submit to the sentence imposed on him. The Marquis of Ferrara also gave a similar proof of his attachment. Though their interposition was not immediately successful, it was of great importance to Cosmo, and secured him from the attempts of those who aimed at his life. After a confinement of near a month, some of his friends, finding in his adversaries a disposition to gentler measures, took occasion to forward his cause by the timely application of a sum of money to Bernardo Guadagni the Gonfaloniere, and to Mariotto Baldovinetti, two of the creatures of Rinaldo. This measure was successful. He was privately taken from his confinement by night, and led out of Florence. For this piece of service Guadagni received

received one thousand florins, and Baldovinetti eight hundred. "*They were poor souls*," says Cosmo in his Ricordi, "*for if money had been their object, they might have had ten thousand, or more, to have freed me from the perils of such a situation* (a)."

Is allowed to reside at Venice.

From Florence, Cosmo proceeded immediately towards Venice, and at every place through which he passed, experienced the most flattering attention, and the warmest expressions of regard. On his approach to that city he was met by his brother Lorenzo, and many of his friends, and was received by the senate with such honours as are bestowed by that stately republic, only on persons of the highest quality and distinction. After a short stay there, he went to Padua, the place prescribed for his banishment; but on an application to the Florentine state, by Andrea Donato the Venetian ambassador, he was permitted to reside on any part of the Venetian territories, but not to approach within the distance of one hundred and seventy miles from Florence. The affectionate reception which he had

(a) Machiavelli ascribes the liberation of Cosmo to the interference and assistance of Fargonaccio, a buffoon, who was admitted by Malavolti to visit Cosmo during his confinement, and was employed by him in negotiating with the chiefs of the opposite faction for his deliverance. Varillas has ornamented the same story, according to his manner, with an infinite number of particulars. To judge from his narrative, this author might not only have been a contemporary, but intrusted with the most secret transactions of the negotiation, and the confidant of the most private thoughts of the parties concerned. *Var. Mem. de Flor. p.* 9, &c. In the narrative that I have given I have thought proper to discard these dubious accounts, and to adhere to the authentic relation of Cosmo himself; who adverts to no such circumstance, but on the contrary expressly states by whose assistance the money was paid. *v. Ricordi di Cosmo in App.*

CHAP. I.

had met with at Venice induced him to fix his abode there, until a change of circumstances should restore him to his native country.

Amongst the several learned and ingenious men that accompanied Cosmo in his banishment, or resorted to him during his stay at Venice, was Michellozzo Michellozzi, a Florentine sculptor and architect, whom Cosmo employed in making models and drawings of the most remarkable buildings in Venice, and also in forming a library in the monastery of St. George (*a*), which he enriched with many valuable manuscripts, and left as an honourable monument of his gratitude, to a place that had afforded him so kind an asylum in his adversity (*b*).

Ambrogio Traversari.

During his residence at Venice, Cosmo also received frequent visits from Ambrogio Traversari, a learned monk of Camaldoli near Florence (*c*), and afterwards superior of

(*a*) *Vasari Vite de' Pittori, vol.* i. *p.* 339. *Ed. Flor.* 1568.

(*b*) This library existed till the year 1614, when in consequence of the monastery being rebuilt, it was destroyed, and the books it contained are supposed to have perished.

Tiraboschi, Storia della Letteratura Italiana, vol. vi. *parte* 1. *p.* 102.

(*c*) Ambrogio was born in 1386, and was a native of Forli, but is usually ranked amongst the eminent men of Florence, where he was educated and where he principally resided. "In Firenze benchè fu educato Ambrogio: In Firenze "vestì l'abito monacale: In Firenze riposano le sue ossa; e però in tal qual "modo può Fiorentino appellarsi." *Zeno, Dissertazioni Vossiane, vol.* i. *p.* 75. So complete was his knowledge of the Greek language, that in the council of Florence he acted as interpreter between the Italians and the Greeks. His translation

of the monastery at that place. Though chiefly confined within the limits of a cloister, Traversari had, perhaps, the best pretensions to the character of a polite scholar of any man of that age. From the letters of Traversari, now extant, we learn that Cosmo and his brother not only bore their misfortunes with firmness, but continued to express on every occasion an inviolable attachment to their native place (*a*).

Cosmo is recalled from banishment.

The readiness with which Cosmo had given way to the temporary clamour raised against him, and the reluctance he had shewn to renew those bloody rencounters that had so often disgraced the streets of Florence, gained him new friends. The utmost exertions of his antagonists could not long prevent the choice of such magistrates as were known to be attached to the cause of the Medici; and no sooner did they enter on the execution of their office, than Cosmo and his brother were recalled, and Rinaldo, with his adherents, were compelled to quit the city.

of Diogenes Laertius, inscribed by him to Cosmo de' Medici, and first printed at Venice, by Nicolas Jenson, in 1475, has been several times reprinted. Traversari has had the good fortune to meet with a biographer and annotator in the learned Mehus, who has done justice to the subject, and made his life and writings the vehicle of much curious and useful information. It is only to be regretted that this extensive and valuable work is not better arranged. *Amb. Traversarii Lat. Ep.* &c. 2 *vol. fo. Flor.* 1759.

(*a*) "Cosmus et Laurentius, fratres, viri amicissimi, valent optimè; magnaque constantia animi ferunt calamitatem suam; et, quod his majus est, eo adfectu in patriam sunt ut illam majore constantia quam antea diligant," &c.
Trav. Ep. lib. viii. *Ep.* 53.

CHAP. I.

city. This event took place about the expiration of twelve months from the time of Cosmo's banishment (*a*).

Encourages men of learning.

From this time the life of Cosmo de' Medici was an almost uninterrupted series of prosperity. The tranquillity enjoyed by the republic, and the satisfaction and peace of mind which he experienced in the esteem and confidence of his fellow-citizens, enabled him to indulge his natural propensity to the promotion of science, and the encouragement of learned men. The study of the Greek language had been introduced into Italy, principally by the exertions of the celebrated Boccaccio (*b*), towards the latter part of the preceding century, but on the death of that great promoter of letters it again fell into neglect. After a short interval, another attempt was made to revive it by the intervention of Emanuel Chrysoloras, a noble Greek, who, during the interval of his important embassies, taught that

---

(*a*) The attachment of the populace to the Medici is strikingly described by Poggio. "Itaque indicta populi concione, quanta alacritate, Dii boni, quanta "exultatione, quanto gaudio, quanto studio, etiam infirmorum concursus est "ad Palatium factus, omnium ætatum, ordinum, nationum! Nemo non solum civem se, sed ne hominem quidem arbitrabatur, qui non huic causæ interesset, qui non manu, voce, vultus denique ac gestus significatione faveret. "Existimabant omnes non de tua, sed de publica salute agi, non [illegible] "unius domo, sed de communi omnium causa certari."

Poggii Ep. 340. *Ed. Basil.* 1538.

(*b*) Boccaccio is not only entitled to the honour of having introduced into Italy the study of the Greek language, but of having preserved and restored what constitutes its greatest glory—The writings of Homer—Thus he boasts of his meritorious labours: "Fui equidem ipse insuper, qui primus meis sumptibus Homeri libros, et alios quosdam grecos in Hetruriam revocavi, ex qua "multis ante seculis abierant, non redituri. Nec in Hetruriam tantum sed in "patriam deduxi." *Bocc. Genealogia Deorum, lib.* xv. *cap.* 7. *Ed.* 1481.

that language at Florence and other cities of Italy, about the beginning of the fifteenth century. His disciples were numerous and respectable. Amongst others of no inconsiderable note, were Ambrogio Traversari, Leonardo Bruni (*a*), Carlo Marsuppini (*b*), the two latter of whom were

Leonardo and Carlo Aretino.

(*a*) The life of this eminent scholar and promoter of science is prefixed to his *Epistolæ*, published by Mehus in 2 *vols*. 8*vo Flor*. 1741.—Many particulars may also be found in the *Dissert. Voss. of Zeno*. He was born at Arezzo in 1370, "de honestis quidem sed non admodum generosis parentibus." For several years he was one of the secretaries of the Roman court, but afterwards fixed his residence at Florence, where he held an office which had been long enjoyed only by men of the first character for learning and abilities, that of secretary to the republic. His history of Florence, written in Latin, was translated into Italian by Donato Acciajuoli, and published in Venice 1476. Flor. 1492. A considerable number of his works yet remain in MS. amongst which are many translations from the Greek. His Latin translation of the Epistles of Plato is inscribed to Cosmo de' Medici, and as the dedication is illustrative of his character, and has not hitherto been printed, I shall give it in the Appendix, from a MS. copy of the fifteenth century. (*Appendix*, No. III.)

(*b*) Carlo Marsuppini the elder, succeeded his countryman Leonardo Bruni in the office of secretary to the republic of Florence. Whilst he held this employment, a circumstance occurred in some degree unfavourable to his reputation as a scholar. On the emperor's arrival at Florence, it was the office of Carlo to address him in a Latin oration which he required two days to prepare, and by which he obtained no small share of applause: but Æneas Sylvius, the secretary to the emperor, and who afterwards became Pope Pius the II. having replied in the name of the emperor, and made some requisitions to the Florentines that demanded an extempore answer, Carlo requested time to prepare himself, and could not be induced to proceed. The interview was therefore concluded by Gianozzo Manetti, who, by the specimen he gave of his talents on this occasion, rose to great reputation amongst his countrymen.

We need not hesitate in attributing this event rather to an untimely diffidence, than to any want of talents in Carlo, as may be judged, not only from the numerous suffrages of his countrymen, but from his own works, some of which yet survive, although few have undergone the press. He is however improperly

were natives of Arezzo, from whence they took the name of Aretino, Poggio Bracciolini, Guarino Veronese, and Francesco Filelfo, who, after the death of Chrysoloras in 1415, strenuously vied with each other in the support of Grecian literature, and were successful enough to keep the flame alive till it received new aid from other learned Greeks, who were driven from Constantinople by the dread of the Turks, or by the total overthrow of the eastern empire. To these illustrious foreigners, as well as to the learned Italians, who shortly became their successful rivals, even in the knowledge of their national history and language, Cosmo afforded the most liberal protection and support. Of this the numerous productions inscribed to his name, or devoted to his praise, are an ample testimony (*a*). In some of these he is commended for his attachment to his country, his liberality to his friends, his benevolence to all. He is denominated the protector of

---

placed by *Vossius* amongst the writers of history, as *Apostolo Zeno* has fully shewn. The numerous errors of the *Oltramontani* in treating on the Literati of Italy ought to operate as a perpetual caution to those who follow them in so hazardous a track. Of his poetry, the only piece that has been printed is a translation of the Batrachomyomachia of Homer, first published at Parma in 1492, and afterwards at Florence by Bernardo Zucchetti 1518, with this distich in the place of a title.

" Accipe Mæonio cantatas carmine ranas,
" Et frontem nugis solvere disce meis."

(*a*) To Cosmo de' Medici Argyropylus addressed his translation of several tracts of Aristotle; Lapo Castellionchio his life of Themistocles from Plutarch; and Benedetto Accolti, his dialogue " de viris illustribus." A great number of other learned works, inscribed to Cosmo, remain in the Laurentian library, and are particularly cited in the catalogue of Bandini. *Flor.* 1774. &c.

of the needy, the refuge of the oppressed, the constant patron and support of learned men. "*You have shewn,*" says Poggio (*a*), "*such humanity and moderation in dispensing the gifts of fortune, that they seem to have been rather the reward of your virtues and merits, than conceded by her bounty. Devoted to the study of letters from your early years, you have by your example given additional splendor to science itself. Although involved in the weightier concerns of state, and unable to devote a great part of your time to books, yet you have found a constant satisfaction in the society of those learned men who have always frequented your house.*" In enumerating the men of eminence that distinguished the city of Florence, Flavio Blondo adverts in the first instance to Cosmo de' Medici (*b*). "*A citizen, who, whilst he excels in wealth every other citizen of Europe, is rendered much more illustrious by his prudence, his humanity, his liberality, and what is more to our present purpose, by his knowledge of useful literature, and particularly of history.*

Researches after the writings of the ancients.

That extreme avidity for the works of the ancient writers which distinguished the early part of the fifteenth century, announced the near approach of more enlightened times. Whatever were the causes that determined men of wealth and learning to exert themselves so strenuously in this pursuit, certain it is that their interference was of the highest

(*a*) *Poggii opera, p.* 312. *Ed. Basil.* 1538.

(*b*) *ap. Tiraboschi, Storia della Lett. Ital. v.* vi. *p.* 1. *p.* 27.

highest importance to the interests of posterity; and that if it had been much longer delayed, the loss would have been in a great degree irreparable; such of the manuscripts as then existed, of the ancient Greek and Roman authors, being mouldered away in obscure corners, a prey to oblivion and neglect. It was therefore a circumstance productive of the happiest consequences, that the pursuits of the opulent were at this time directed rather towards the recovery of the works of the ancients, than to the encouragement of contemporary merit; a fact that may serve in some degree to account for the dearth of original literary productions during this interval. Induced by the rewards that invariably attended a successful inquiry, those men who possessed any considerable share of learning, devoted themselves to this occupation, and to such a degree of enthusiasm was it carried, that the discovery of an ancient manuscript was regarded as almost equivalent to the conquest of a kingdom.

The history of the vicissitudes which the writings of the ancients have experienced, is little less than the history of literature itself, which has flourished or declined in proportion as they have been esteemed or neglected. A full and accurate detail of these circumstances, whilst it would be highly interesting to the scholar, would discharge in some degree the debt of gratitude due to those who have devoted their labours and their fortunes to this important service. In relinquishing an inquiry too extensive for the nature of the present work, it may here be allowed to advert to such remains of the ancient authors as were brought to light during the period in question, by the

munificence

munificence of Cosmo de' Medici, and the industry of those who so earnestly seconded his endeavours.

CHAP. I.

Poggio Bracciolini.

Of all the learned men of his time, Poggio (*a*) seems to have devoted himself the most particularly to this employment, and his exertions were crowned with ample success.

(*a*) This extraordinary man, whose writings throw considerable light on the history of the age, and whose Latin stile pleases by its unaffected simplicity; was born in the year 1381, of the noble family of *Bracciolini*, originally of Florence, and having spent his youth in travelling through different countries of Europe, settled at length at Rome. He remained in this city as secretary in the service of *eight* successive popes, till he was invited to Florence in the year 1452, being then upwards of seventy years of age, to succeed Carlo Marsuppini as secretary to the republic. After his return to Florence he began to write the history of that state, but dying before he had brought it to a conclusion, it was afterwards compleated by his unfortunate son Giacopo. His numerous works have been several times reprinted; the most general collection of them is that of *Basil*, 1538. Of all his productions his *Liber Facetiarum* is the most singular. The gross indecency of some of his tales can only be equalled by the freedom in which he indulges himself respecting the priesthood. It is difficult to conceive how he escaped in those times the resentment of that order; but we must remember that this work was produced in the bosom of the church, and was probably an amusement for the learned leisure of prelates and of cardinals. In a short preface Poggio explains the motives that led him to this composition, and attempts to excuse its licentiousness.

Although Poggio was an ecclesiastic, he had several children whom he openly acknowledged. His friend the cardinal of S. Angelo having remonstrated with him on the irregularity of his conduct, Poggio, in his reply, acknowledges his fault, but at the same time attempts to extinguish the glare of it in the general blaze of licentiousness that involved the age. His letter on this occasion affords a striking proof of the depravity of the times. (*Poggii, Hist. de varietate Fortunæ*, &c. *p.* 207, *Ed. Par.* 1723.) He afterwards divested himself of his clerical character, and married a young and handsome wife; in justification of which measure he thought it necessary to write a treatise,

success. The number of manuscripts discovered by him in different parts of Europe, during the space of near fifty years, will remain a lasting proof of his perseverance, and of his sagacity in these pursuits. Whilst he attended the council of Constance in the year 1415, he took an opportunity of visiting the convent of S. Gallo, distant from that city about twenty miles, where he had been informed that it was probable he might find some manuscripts of the ancient Roman writers. In this place he had the happiness to discover a compleat copy of Quintilian, whose works had before appeared only in a mutilated and imperfect state. At the same time he found the three first books, and part of the fourth, of the Argonautics of Valerius Flaccus. Some idea may be formed of the critical state of these works from the account that Poggio has left. Buried in the obscurity of a dark and lonely tower, covered with filth and rubbish, their destruction seemed inevitable (*a*). Of this fortunate discovery he gave immediate notice to his friend Leonardo Aretino, who, by representing to him the importance and utility of his labours, stimulated him to fresh exertions. The letter addressed by Leonardo to Poggio on this occasion is full of the highest commendations, and the most extravagant expressions of joy (*b*). By his subsequent researches through France and Germany,

---

which he intitled "*An seni sit uxor ducenda*," and which he addressed to Cosmo de' Medici. This *important* dissertation yet remains, though it has not hitherto been printed. *Zeno, Diss. Voss.* i. 36, &c.

(*a*) "Non in bibliothecâ ut eorum dignitas postulabat, sed in teterrimo quo-" dam et obscuro carcere, fundo scilicet uniùs turris, quo ne vitâ quidem "damnati detruderentur." *Pog. ap. Zeno, Diss. Voss.* i. 44.

(*b*) *Leonardi Bruni Ep. lib.* iv. *Ep.* 5.

many, Poggio also recovered several of the orations of Cicero (*a*). At that time only eight of the comedies of Plautus were known. The first compleat copy of that author was brought to Rome at the instance of Poggio, by Nicholas of Treves, a German monk, from whom it was purchased by the cardinal Giordano Orsini, who was afterwards with great difficulty prevailed upon to suffer Poggio and his friends to copy it; and even this favour would not have been granted without the warm interference of Lorenzo, the brother of Cosmo de' Medici. The monk had flattered the Italian scholars that he also possessed a copy of the work of Aulus Gellius, and of the first book of Quintus Curtius; but in this they were disappointed (*b*). From a Latin elegy by Christoforo Landino, on the death of Poggio, we are fully authorized to conclude that he also first discovered the beautiful and philosophic poem of Lucretius, that of Silius Italicus, and the valuable work of Columella (*c*): and from a memorial yet existing in the hand-writing of Angelo Politiano, it appears that the poems of Statius were brought into Italy by the same indefatigable investigator. In the opinion of Politiano these poems were indeed inaccurate and defective,

(*a*) *Trav. Ep. v.* i. *præf. p.* 36.

(*b*) *Trav. Ep. v.* i. *præf. p.* 40, 41. 43.

(*c*) " Quin etiam, ut veterum erueret monimenta virorum,
" Nec vinceret turpem tot bona ferre situm,
" Ausus barbaricos populos penitusque reposta
" Poscere Lingonicis oppida celsa jugis.

defective, yet all the copies which he had seen were derived from this manuscript (*a*).

Poggio had once formed the fullest expectations of obtaining a copy of the Decades of Livy, which a monk had assured him he had seen in the Cistercian monastery of Sora, comprized in two volumes in large Lombard characters (*b*). He immediately wrote to a friend at Florence, requesting him to prevail on Cosmo de' Medici to direct his agent in that neighbourhood to repair to the monastery, and

" Illius ergo manu nobis, doctissime Rhetor,
" Integer in Latium, *Quintiliane*, redis;
" Illius atque manu, divina poemata *Sili*
" *Italici* redeunt, usque legenda suis:
" Et ne nos lateat variorum cultus agrorum,
" Ipse *Columella* grande reportat opus:
" Et te, *Lucreti*, longo post tempore, tandem
" Civibus et Patriæ reddit habere tuæ.
" Tartareis potuit fratrem revocare tenebris
" Alterna Pollux dum statione movet;
" Conjugis ac rursus nigras subitura lacunas
" Euridice sequitur fila canora sui.
" *Poggius* at sospes nigrà e caligine tantos
" Ducit ubi æternum lux sit aperta viros."

Land. Eleg. ap. Band. Spec. Lit. Flor. vol. i. *p.* 93.

(*a*) " Incidi in exemplar Statii Silvarum, quod ex Gallia *Poggius*, gallicâ " scriptum manu, in Italiam adtulerat; a quo videlicet uno, licet mendoso " depravatoque, et (ut arbitror) etiam dimidiato, reliqui omnes codices qui " sunt in manibus emanarunt."

Pol. ap. Band. Cat. Bib. Laur. Plut. xxxii. *Cod.* 10.

(*b*) " Duo sunt volumina magna, oblonga, literis Longobardis in monas- " terio de Sora ordinis Cisterciensium prope Roschild, ad duo milliaria " Theutonica, quo adiri potest a Lubich biduo amplius. Cura ergo ut Cos-

and to purchase the work. Some time afterwards Poggio addressed himself to Leonello de' Este, marquis of Ferrara, on the same subject, but apparently without any great hopes of success (*a*). His attempts to recover the writings of Tacitus, were equally fruitless (*b*). After long inquiry, he was convinced that no copy of that author existed in Germany; yet at the distance of nearly a century, the five books of his history were brought from thence to Rome, and presented to Leo. X. In prosecution of his favourite object, Poggio extended his researches into England, where he resided some time with the cardinal bishop of Winchester (*c*); and from whence he transmitted to Italy the Bucolics of Calphurnius, and a part of the works of Petronius (*d*).

The

" mus scribat quamprimum diligenter ad Gherardum de Bueris, ut si opus " sit, ipse eo se conferat, imo omnino se conferat ad monasterium, nam si " hoc verum est, triumphandum erit de Dacis."

Poggii Ep. ap. Trav. Ep. v. i. *praef. p.* 46.

(*a*) *Poggius de Var. For. p.* 215.

(*b*) *Trav. Ep. v.* i. *praef. p.* 47.

(*c*) Poggio has given a picture of the English nobility somewhat different from that of the present times—" Hos (Gallos) Britanni sequuntur, Angli " hodie vocitati, qui nobiles in civitatibus morari ignominiae loco putant, rura, " sylvis ac pascuis seclusa inhabitant; nobiliorem ex censu judicant; rem " rusticam curant, vendentes lanam et armentorum faetus; neque turpe " existimant admisceri quaestui rusticano."

Poggius de Nobilitate, in Op. Bas. 1538. *p.* 69.

(*d*) At least there is reason to conjecture so, from a passage in a letter from Poggio to Niccolo Niccoli: " Mittas ad me oro Bucolicam Calphurnii " et partiunculam Petronii quas misi tibi ex Britannia," &c.

Trav. Ep. v. i. *praef. p.* 29.

CHAP. I.

The researches of Guarino Veronese (*a*), of Giovanni Aurispa, and of Francesco Filelfo were directed towards another quarter. For the purpose of procuring ancient manuscripts, and of acquiring a competent knowledge of the Greek language, they visited Constantinople and other parts of the east, where their perseverance was repaid by the acquisition of many valuable works. Guarino on his return to Italy was shipwrecked, and unfortunately for himself and the world, lost his treasures. So pungent was his grief upon this occasion, that if we may believe the relation of one of his countrymen, his hair became suddenly white (*b*). Aurispa was more successful; he arrived at Venice in the year 1423, with two hundred and thirty-eight manuscripts, amongst which were all the works of Plato, of Proclus, of Plotinus, of Lucian, of Zenophon, the histories of Arrian, of Dio, and of Diodorus Siculus, the geography of Strabo, the poems of Callimachus, of Pindar, of Oppian, and those attributed to Orpheus. In one of his epistles to Traversari, many other works are particularly enumerated, some of which are not at present known, and have most probably perished.

Guarino Veronese.

Giovanni Aurispa.

(*a*) Many particulars respecting Guarino may be collected from the poems of his pupil Janus Pannonius, printed at *Basil* by Frobenius, in 1518, and which are possessed of considerable merit. Guarino was born in 1370, and was the first native Italian who publicly taught the Greek tongue in Italy. He is more celebrated as a preceptor than as an author. Almost all the learned men of the 15th century have profited by his instructions, but his diction is considered by Cortesi as harsh and inelegant.

Cort. de hom. doctis. Flor. 1734.

(*b*) Pontico Virunio, Scrittore dei primi anni del secolo xvi.

ap. Tirab. Storia della Lett. Ital. v. vi. *p.* 1. *p.* 89.

perished (*a*). The large sums of money which Aurispa had expended in purchasing so considerable a number of books, and the charges of conveying them to Venice, had exhausted his finances, and he was obliged to apply to Traversari to procure him the sum of fifty florins to relieve him from his embarrassments. This was readily supplied by Cosmo de' Medici and his brother Lorenzo, to whom Aurispa expresses his obligations with great warmth, and apparent sincerity (*b*).

Francesco Filelfo.

Filelfo was about twenty years of age when he undertook his expedition to Constantinople, where he remained about seven years, and married the daughter of the noble and learned John Chrysolotas. In the year 1427 he returned to Italy with a great number of manuscripts which he had collected; and made a conspicuous figure amongst the literati there during the chief part of the fifteenth century, having been successively engaged as professor of different branches of science, at most of the universities and seminaries of education throughout that country. With all his learning, Filelfo had not acquired the art of controlling his own temper, which was in a high degree petulant, suspicious, and arrogant. His whole life was passed in quarrels and dissensions. At some times he narrowly escaped the public punishment due to his excesses;

(*a*) *Aurispa Ep. in Epistolis Amb. Trav. lib.* xxiv. *Ep.* 53.

(*b*) "Volui ego Cosmo et Laurentio pro tot eorum erga me beneficiis gra-"tias agere in Epistolis quas ad eos scribo, sed non poteram calamo prosequi "quantum eis obligari videor. Quamobrem id officium linguæ tuæ reliqui."

Aurispa Ep. in Trav. Epistolis. lib. xxiv. *Ep.* 57.

excesses; at others, the effects of the private resentment of those whom he had offended. He was even accused of having conspired against the life of Cosmo de' Medici, and of having engaged a Greek assassin to murder him. Their disagreement seems to have taken place during the exile of Cosmo at Venice. Amongst the letters of Filelfo there are some to Cosmo, in which he falls greatly short of the respect which he owed him for his patronage; and wherein he inveighs with much rancour against Niccolo Niccoli and Carlo Aretino, the particular friends of Cosmo (*a*). From several of these letters he appears to have had frequent apprehensions of assassination; and even affects to accuse Cosmo of favouring the attempt (*b*). How much Cosmo was superior to such imputations, appeared in the moderation of his conduct, which at length overcame even the arrogance and resentment of Filelfo himself;

(*a*) Nicolaum Nicolum nosti; hic loquacior est, et levior; at Carolus Aretinus, ut est versuto occultoque ingenio, et eo plane improbo, ita mihi maxime inimicus. Is apud Medices plurimum potest. And the character he gives of Cosmo in a letter to the Cardinal of Bologna, dated 1432, is sufficiently invidious: "Cosmus quamquam videtur amantissimus mei, ejusmodi "tamen virum esse animadverto qui et simulet et dissimulet omnia. Estque "usque adeo taciturnus ut ne ab intimis quidem familiaribus ac domesticis "queat intelligi." *Phil. Ep. p.* 18, 19. *Ed.* 1501.

(*b*) By a letter of Filelfo to Lapo Castellionchio, which came to the sight of Ambrogio Traversari, it appeared that he expressed himself in terms of resentment against both Traversari and Cosmo de' Medici. Traversari upbraided him with his duplicity, and Filelfo attempted to justify it by accusing Cosmo, in his reply, of a design on his life. "De Cosmi Medices in me animo "nihil est quod minus credam. Nam quam me sit exosus jam pridem exper- "tus sum. Istius in me benevolentiam Philippus sicarius declaret—itaque de "reconcillanda gratia mihi posthac verbum nullum facito. Sicis ipse vene- "nisque utatur. Ego autem ingenio et calamo." *Phil. Ep. p.* 26.

himself; who lived to receive innumerable favours from him and his descendants; and died at Florence in the year 1481, in the eighty-third year of his age.

The productions of Filelfo are very numerous, and in almost every branch of literature (*a*). His industry in collecting manuscripts was however of more indisputable service to the cause of learning. Of the particular works brought by him into Italy he has not left a very explicit account, but it appears that he had sent a considerable number to his friend Leonardo Giustiniani at Venice, from whom he found some difficulty in obtaining them after his return. The letters of Filelfo contain indeed innumerable complaints of the injustice of his friends, in withholding the books which he had lent for their use, or intrusted to their care. Perhaps, says Tiraboschi, they acted upon the same principle as the enthusiasts of the darker ages, who considered the stealing the relicks of a saint, not as a theft, but as a pious and meritorious act. Such was the high estimation in which these works were held, that a manuscript of the history of Livy, sent by Cosmo de' Medici to Alfonso king of Naples, with whom he was at variance, conciliated the breach between them, and although the king's physicians insinuated that the book was probably poisoned,

---

(*a*) A very extensive catalogue of them may be found in the *Dissert Voss.* of Apostolo Zeno. The character of Filelfo is well given by Paolo Cortesi (*De hom. doctis. p.* 32.): "Habebat a natura ingenium vagum, multiplex, volubile. "Exstant ab eo scripta, et poemata, et orationes; sed ut vita, sic erat in toto "genere varius. Erat vendibilis sane scriptor, et is, qui opes, quam scribendi "laudem consequi malebat."

CHAP. I.

poisoned, Alfonso disregarded their suspicions, and began with great pleasure the perusal of the work.

Council of Florence.

1438.

In the year 1438 a general council was held by Eugenius IV. at Ferrara, for the purpose of settling some contested points, both of doctrine and discipline, between the Greek and Roman churches, preparatory to their proposed union; but the plague having made its appearance at that place, the council was in the following year transferred to Florence. On this occasion, not only the pope and several of his cardinals, the Greek patriarch and his metropolitans, but the emperor of the east, John Paleologus, attended in person. Shortly before their arrival, Cosmo had been invested a second time with the office of Gonfaloniere, and the reception that he gave to these illustrious visitors, whilst it was highly honourable to his guests, was extremely gratifying to the citizens of Florence, who were as remarkable for the magnificence of their public exhibitions, as for their moderation and frugality in private life. As the questions agitated at this council would not admit of illustration from reasoning, and could only be argued from authority, the longer the dispute continued, the more were the parties at variance; but the critical situation of the eastern empire, then closely attacked by the Turks, and the expectations which the emperor had formed of procuring succours from the pope, and from other European princes, reconciled what the efforts of the schoolmen had only served to perplex. The proposed union accordingly took place; and the pope was acknowledged by the whole assembly as the legitimate successor of St. Peter. Little advantage was

 however

however derived by either of the parties from this remarkable transaction. The emperor was disappointed in his expectations of support, and with respect to the supremacy of the Roman church over the Greek, the ecclesiastics of the latter refused to obey the decree; and even many, who had been present and signed it at the council, publicly retracted at Constantinople (*a*).

Revival of the Platonic Philosophy.

For the purpose of conducting these important debates, each of the parties had selected six disputants, eminent for their rank and learning. Amongst those chosen on the part of the Greeks, was Gemisthus Pletho, who was then at a very advanced period of a life which had been devoted to the study of the platonic philosophy (*b*). As often as his public avocations afforded him an opportunity, he employed himself in the propagation of his opinions, which were not only new to the scholars of Italy, but were greatly at variance with those doctrines which had long obtained an uninterrupted ascendancy in all the public schools and seminaries of learning. So powerful was the effect which the discourses of Gemisthus had upon Cosmo de' Medici, who was his constant auditor, that he determined to establish an academy at Florence, for the sole purpose

(*a*) A full and interesting account of the visit of the Greek emperor to Italy, and of the proceedings and consequences of the council of Florence, may be found in Gibbon's history of the decline and fall of the Roman empire, c. 66.

(*b*) Pletho, though living in 1439, had been the preceptor of Emanuel Chrysoloras, the great promoter of Grecian literature in Italy, whom he however long survived, having lived to the extended age of one hundred years.
Hodius de Græcis illustribus, p. 22. Ed. Lond. 1741.

pose of cultivating this new and more elevated species of philosophy. For this purpose he selected Marsilio Ficino, the son of his favourite physician, and destined him, though very young, to be the support of his future establishment. The education of Ficino was, as he has himself informed us, entirely directed to the new philosophy (*a*). The doctrines and precepts of the Grecian sage were assiduously instilled into his infant mind, and as he increased in years, he applied himself to the study, not of the works of Plato only, but also of those of Plotinus, a distinguished promoter of the doctrines of that philosopher in the third century. Nor were the expectations which Cosmo had formed of Ficino disappointed. The Florentine academy was some years afterwards established with great credit, and was the first institution in Europe for the pursuit of science, detached from the scholastic method then universally adopted. It is true, the sublime and fanciful doctrines of Plato were almost as remote from the purposes of common life, and general utility,

---

(*a*) Thus he speaks of his education in his proeme to his translation of the works of Plotinus, addressed to Lorenzo de' Medici: "Magnus Cosmus, senatus consulto patriæ pater, quo tempore concilium inter græcos atque latinos, sub Eugenio pontifice, Florentiæ tradabatur; philosophum Græcum nomine Gemisthum, cognomine Plethonem, quasi Platonem alterum, de mysteriis platonicis disputantem frequenter audivit. E cujus ore fervente, sic afflatus est protinus, sic animatus, ut inde *academiam* quandam alta mente conceperit, hanc opportuno primo tempore pariturus. Deinde cum conceptum tantum magnus ille Medices quodamodo parturiret, me, electissimi Medici sui filium, adhuc puerum tanto operi destinavit," &c. *Plotini op. Flor.* 1492. *per Ant. Miscomimum magnifico sumptu Laurentii Medicis patriæ servatoris.*

lity, as the dogmatic opinions of Aristotle: but the introduction of the former was nevertheless of essential service to the cause of free inquiry, and substantial knowledge. By dividing the attention of the learned, they deprived the doctrines of Aristotle of that servile respect and veneration which had so long been paid to them: and by introducing the discussion of new subjects, they prepared the way for the pursuit of truths more properly within the sphere of the human intellect.

Cosmo establishes the Laurentian Library.

As the natural disposition of Cosmo led him to take an active part in collecting the remains of the ancient Greek and Roman writers, so he was enabled by his wealth, and his extensive mercantile intercourse with different parts of Europe, and of Asia, to gratify a passion of this kind beyond any other individual. To this end he laid injunctions on all his friends and correspondents, as well as on the missionaries and preachers who travelled into the remotest countries, to search for and procure ancient manuscripts, in every language, and on every subject (*a*). Besides the services of Poggio and Traversari, Cosmo availed himself

---

(*a*) "The example of the Roman pontiff was preceded or imitated by a "Florentine merchant, who governed the republic without arms, and without "a title. Cosmo of Medici was the father of a line of princes, whose name "and age are almost synonymous with the restoration of learning: His credit "was ennobled into fame; his riches were dedicated to the service of mankind; he corresponded at once with Cairo and London, and a cargo of Indian spices and Greek books were often imported in the same vessel."

Gibbon's Hist. of the Decline and Fall of the Roman Empire, c. 66.

himself of those of Cristoforo Buondelmonti, Antonio da Massa, Andrea de Rimino, and many others. The situation of the eastern empire, then daily falling into ruins by the repeated attacks of the Turks, afforded him an opportunity of obtaining many inestimable works in the Hebrew, Greek, Chaldaic, Arabic, and Indian languages (*a*). From these beginnings arose the celebrated library of the Medici, which, after having been the constant object of the solicitude of its founder, was after his death further enriched by the attention of his descendants, and particularly of his grandson Lorenzo; and after various vicissitudes of fortune, and frequent and considerable additions, has been preserved to the present times under the name of the *Bibliotheca Mediceo-Laurentiana.*

Niccolo Niccoli founds the Library of S. Marco.

Amongst those who imitated the example of Cosmo de' Medici was Niccolo Niccoli, another citizen of Florence, who devoted his whole time and fortune to the acquisition of ancient manuscripts; in this pursuit he had been eminently successful, having collected together eight hundred volumes of Greek, Roman, and Oriental authors; a number in those times justly thought very considerable. Several of these works he had copied with great accuracy, and had diligently employed himself in correcting their defects and arranging the text in its proper order. In this respect he is justly regarded by Mehus as the father of this species of criticism (*b*). He died in 1436, having by his

(*a*) *Bandini, Lettera sopra i principj e progressi della Biblioteca Laurenziana. Firenze*, 1773.

(*b*) *In praef. ad Ep. Trav. p.* 50.

his will directed that his library should be devoted to the use of the public, and appointed sixteen Curators, amongst whom was Cosmo de' Medici. After his death it appeared that he was greatly in debt; and that his liberal intentions were likely to be frustrated by the insolvency of his circumstances. Cosmo therefore proposed to his associates, that if they would resign to him the right of disposition of the books, he would himself discharge all the debts of Niccolo, to which they readily acceded. Having thus obtained the sole direction of the manuscripts, he deposited them for public use, in the Dominican monastery of S. Marco, at Florence, which he had himself erected at an enormous expense (*a*). This collection was the foundation

---

(*a*) From the funeral oration of Niccolo Niccoli, by Poggio, we learn, that the most celebrated collections that had been formed in Italy, before that of Niccolo, were those of Petrarca, of Lodovico Marsilio an Augustine monk, of Boccaccio, and of Colucio Salutati. The first of these was sold and dispersed after the death of its possessor. Marsilio and Boccaccio bequeathed their collections to the library of the Augustine monastery at Florence; and that of Colucio, which almost equalled in number the library of Niccolo, was sold by his children after his death. To Niccolo Niccoli we must therefore attribute the honour of having set the first example of forming in Italy an institution so favourable to the interests of learning, as a *public library*.—" Id " egit vir egregius, doctorum virorum amantissimus, quod nullum multis " antea seculis fecisse, neque memoria hominum constat, neque ullæ literæ " prodiderunt. Rem sane statuit temporum omnium ac seculorum laudibus " celebrandam. Ex libris, quos homo nequaquam opulentus, & rerum per- " sæpe inops, supra octingentos codices, summo labore ac diligentia compa- " ruerat, decrevit testamento fieri per amicos publicam bibliothecam, ad uti- " litatem hominum sempiternam. O preclarissimum omnium quem unquam " condita sunt et utillissimum testamentum! quo non unum aliquem, aut al- " terum, sed tam Græcas, tum latinas musas, hujus preciosissimi thesauri " reliquit hæredes." *Poggius in funere Nic. in op. Basil*, 277.

CHAP. I.

ation of another celebrated library in Florence, known by the name of the *Bibliotheca Marciana*; which is yet open to the inspection of the learned, at the distance of three centuries (*a*).

In

(*a*) Tiraboschi suspects that the books collected by Cosmo and by Niccolo Niccoli, were united together in the library of S. Marco, and that Lorenzo was the first of his family who began a collection under his own roof. (*Storia della Lett. Ital. vol.* vi. *parte* i. *p.* 98.) But ample evidence remains of the establishment of a domestic library by Cosmo. To say nothing of the authority of the modern Florentine bibliographers, and particularly of Bandini (*Lettera sopra i principj*, &c.), I may cite the explicit testimony of Alberto Avogradi, a contemporary of Cosmo, who addressed to him a poem in two books, intitled, *De religione & magnificentia Illustris Cosmi Medices Florentini*, which has been published by Lami (*Deliciæ Erudit.* v. 12.), in which these two collections are distinctly adverted to. Speaking in his first book of the public buildings erected by Cosmo, and particularly of the monastery of S. Marco, he adds,

"Post cellas gravis iste labor numerare libellos
"Quos duplici linguâ bibliotheca tenet:
"Ista tenet *nostros*, servat pars altera *Graecos*,
"Quis poterit quot sunt enumerare libros?"

But in his second book, when he describes the palace of Cosmo, he expatiates largely on his library.

"Iste colit musas, colit hic quoque verba soluta:
"O mira in *tectis bibliotheca suis*!
"Nunc legit altisoni sparsim pia scripta *Maronis*,
"Nunc *Augustini* sacra notata pii.
"Aut ea quæ *Cicero*; *Senecæ* moralibus atque
"Insudat, memori mente notanda notans.
"Interdum ne fors semper sua pectora curis
"Repleat, adveniant dulcia scripta jubet,
"Et quando accedit *Naso*, vel quando *Tibullus*;
"Aut priscis lectis sæpe moderna legit,
"Atque novas laudat musas, nova carmina spectans
"Dicit, habet faciles hæc nova musa modos."

The Vatican Library founded by Pope Nicholas V.

In the arrangement of the library of S. Marco, Cosmo had procured the assistance of Tomaso Calandrino, who drew up a scheme for that purpose, and prepared a scientific catalogue of the books it contained. In selecting a coadjutor, the choice of Cosmo had fallen on an extraordinary man. Though Tomaso was the son of a poor physician of Sarzana, and ranked only in the lower order of the clergy, he had the ambition to aim at possessing some specimens of these venerable relicks of ancient genius. His learning and his industry enabled him to gratify his wishes, and his perseverance surmounted the disadvantages of his situation. In this pursuit he was frequently induced to anticipate his scanty revenue, well knowing, that the estimation in which he was held by his friends, would preserve him from pecuniary difficulties. With the Greek and Roman authors no one was more intimately acquainted, and as he wrote a very fine hand, the books he possessed acquired additional value from the marginal observations which he was accustomed to make in perusing them. By the rapid degrees of fortunate preferment, Tomaso was, in the short space of twelve months, raised from his humble situation to the chair of St. Peter (*a*), and in eight years, during which time he enjoyed the supreme dignity, by the name of Nicholas V. acquired a reputation that has increased with the increasing estimation of those studies which he so liberally fostered and protected. The scanty library of his predecessors had been nearly dissipated or destroyed by frequent removals between

(*a*) *Bart. Facius de viris illustribus. Flor.* 1745.

CHAP. I.

tween Avignon and Rome, according as the caprice of the reigning pontiff chose either of those places for his residence; and it appears from the letters of Traversari, that scarcely any thing of value remained. Nicholas V. is therefore to be considered as the founder of the library of the Vatican. In the completion of this great design, it is true, much was left to be performed by his successors; but Nicholas had before his death collected upwards of five thousand volumes of Greek and Roman authors, and had not only expressed his intention of establishing a library for the use of the Roman Court, but had also taken measures for carrying such intention into execution (*a*).

Invention of printing.

Whilst the munificence of the rich, and the industry of the learned, were thus employed throughout Italy in preserving the remains of the ancient authors, some obscure individuals in a corner of Germany, had conceived, and were silently bringing to perfection, an invention, which by means equally effectual and unexpected, secured to the world the result of their labours. This was the art of printing with moveable types; a discovery of which the beneficial effects have been increasing to the present day, and are yet advancing with accelerated progress (*b*). The

(*a*) *Trav. Ep. in præf. p.* 65.

(*b*) Of the numerous authors who have minutely inquired into the rise of this useful art, no one has had greater opportunities of obtaining information, or has pursued his inquiries with more accuracy than Mr. Heineken, who has clearly shewn, that the fabrication of cards for games of chance, was first practised in Germany, and was in use before the close of the fourteenth century. Not long afterwards, the same art that had at first been subservient to the amusement, was employed to gratify the superstition of the people, and it

The coincidence of this discovery with the spirit of the times in which it had birth, was highly fortunate. Had it been made known at a much earlier period, it would have been disregarded, or forgotten, from the mere want of materials on which to exercise it; and had it been further postponed, it is probable, that notwithstanding the generosity of the rich, and the diligence of the learned, many works would have been totally lost, which are now justly regarded as the noblest monuments of the human intellect.

Capture of Constantinople.

Nearly the same period of time that gave the world this important discovery, saw the destruction of the Roman empire in the east. In the year 1453 the city of Constantinople was captured by the Turks, under the command of Mahomet II, after a vigorous defence of fifty-three days. The encouragement which had been shewn to the Greek professors at Florence, and the character of Cosmo de' Medici as a promoter of letters, induced many learned Greeks to seek a shelter in that city, where they met with a welcome and honourable reception. Amongst these

1453.

became usual to cut upon blocks of wood the figures of saints, with inscriptions. Mr. Heineken has cited an indisputable specimen of the latter, so early as the year 1423. These inscriptions gave the first idea of printing with tablets of wood, which are well known to have led the way to the invention of moveable types. The first book printed with such types was a copy of the bible, which made its appearance between the years 1450 and 1452. This discovery is certainly to be attributed to the Germans, whether it consisted in printing with blocks of wood, or with types moveable at pleasure. John Guttenburg of Mayence, has the best claim to the honour of an invention which has so essentially contributed to enlarge the sphere of action of the human faculties. *Idée générale d'une collection complete d'estampes. Leipsic & Vienne*, 1771.

these were Demetrius Chalcondyles, Johannes Andronicus Calistus, Constantius and Johannes Lascaris, in whom the Platonic philosophy obtained fresh partizans, and by whose support it began openly to oppose itself to that of Aristotle (*a*). Between the Greek and Italian professors a spirit of emulation was kindled that operated most favourably on the cause of letters. Public schools were instituted at Florence for the study of the Greek tongue. The facility of diffusing their labours by means of the newly discovered art of printing, stimulated the learned to fresh exertions; and in a few years the cities of Italy vied with each other in the number and elegance of works produced from the press (*b*).

Towards

(*a*) The celebrated Johannes Argyropylus, though ranked by Dr. Hody amongst the learned Greeks who did not arrive in Italy until after the capture of Constantinople, had undoubtedly taken up his residence there before that event, as is fully shewn by Mehus. *Præf. ad Trav. Ep. v.* i. *præf.* 20.

(*b*) Although Italy has no pretensions to the invention of printing, it was the first country that followed the example of Germany, and that with such ardour, as not only to outvie the rest of Europe in the number of printed works, but even to give speedy perfection to the art. Much investigation has been employed in determining in what city of Italy it was first practised, and attempts have been made to shew that Venice produced the "*Decor Puellarum*," in 1461, and Milan, the "*Historiæ Augustæ Scriptores*," in 1465. The evidence of these is at least doubtful, but it is certain, that in the year last mentioned, the works of Lactantius were printed at the monastery of Sosbiaco, in the Campagna of Rome, and that the grammatical work of Donatus, had before issued from the same press. The character used by the German inventors was the *Gothic*, and those of the early Roman printers partook of the same form, but in a few years it was superseded by the character now in general use, which has therefore obtained the name of *Roman*. In the year 1471 this art was practised in Naples, Bolonga, Ferrara, and Florence, and in a short time there was scarcely a place of any note in Italy in which it was unattempted.

Cosmo applies himself to study.

Towards the latter period of his life, a great part of the time that Cosmo could withdraw from the administration of public affairs was passed at his seats at Careggi and Caffaggiolo, were he applied himself to the cultivation of his farms, from which he derived no inconsiderable revenue. But his happiest hours were devoted to the study of letters and philosophy, or passed in the company and conversation of learned men. When he retired at intervals to his seat at Careggi, he was generally accompanied by Ficino, where, after having been his protector, he became his pupil in the study of the Platonic philosophy. For his use Ficino began those laborious translations of the works of Plato and his followers, which were afterwards compleated and published in the life-time and by the liberality of Lorenzo. Amongst the letters of Ficino is one from his truly venerable patron, which bespeaks most forcibly the turn of his mind, and his earnest desire of acquiring knowledge, even at his advanced period of life (*a*). "*Yesterday*," says he, "*I arrived at Careggi—not so much for the purpose of improving my fields, as myself—let me see you, Marsilio, as soon as possible, and forget not to bring with you the book of our favourite Plato,* DE SUMMO BONO—*which I presume, according to your promise, you have ere this translated into Latin; for there is no employment to which I so ardently devote myself as to find*

The *Carattere Corsivo*, or running type, was the invention of the celebrated Aldo Manutio, and being first used in Italy, thence acquired the name of the *Italic*, or Aldine, character.

(*a*) *Ficini Ep. lib.* i. *Ep.* 1.

find out the true road to happiness. Come then, and fail not to bring with you the Orphean lyre." Whatever might be the proficiency of Cosmo in the mysteries of his favourite philosopher, there is reason to believe that he applied those doctrines and precepts which furnished the litigious disputants of the age with a plentiful source of contention, to the purposes of real life and practical improvement. Notwithstanding his active and useful life, he often regretted the hours he had lost. Midas was not more sparing of his money, says Ficino, than Cosmo was of his time.

Marriage of Piero de' Medici.

The wealth and influence that Cosmo had acquired, had long entitled him to rank with the most powerful princes of Italy, with whom he might have formed connexions by the intermarriage of his children; but being apprehensive, that such measures might give rise to suspicions that he entertained designs inimical to the freedom of the state, he rather chose to increase his interest amongst the citizens of Florence, by the marriage of his children into the most distinguished families of that place. Piero his eldest son married Lucretia Tornabuoni, by whom he had two sons, Lorenzo, the subject of our present history, born on the first day of January 1448, and Giuliano born in the year 1453. Piero had also two daughters, Nannina, who married Bernardo Rucellai, and Bianca, who became the wife of Guglielmo de' Pazzi. Giovanni, the younger son of Cosmo, espoused Cornelia de' Alessandri, by whom he had a son who died very young. Giovanni himself did not long survive. He died in the year 1461, at forty-two years of age.

Birth of Lorenzo and Giuliano.

Living

Living under the shade of paternal authority, his name scarcely occurs in the pages of history; but the records of literature bear testimony, that in his disposition and studies he did not derogate from that characteristic attachment to men of learning, by which his family was invariably distinguished (*a*).

Besides his legitimate offspring, Cosmo left also a natural son, Carlo de' Medici, whom he liberally educated, and who compensated the disadvantages of his birth by the respectability of his life. The manners of the times might

(*a*) In the Laurentian library are several manuscripts which appear to have been copied for his use. At the close of the works of Lactantius (Plut. xxi. Cod. 2.) is the following memorial—*Scriptus autem fuit manu mea Gerardi Johannis del Ciriagio civis & notarii Florentini pro Johanne Cosmi de Medicis optimo & primario cive Florentino de anno Domini* MCCCCLVIII. *Florentiæ, Laus Deo.*—Similar memorials occur in other instances. *(Bandinii, Cat. Bib. Laur.)* Nicolo Tignosio inscribed to Giovanni de' Medici his treatise *De laudibus Cosmi patris ejus.* On his death Naldo Naldio addressed a Latin poem to his father, which is printed in the *Carmina illust. Poet. Ital. v. 6. p.* 451. The same work contains other testimonies of the regret that attended his loss. I shall content myself with giving one of the several epitaphs that Peregrino Allio wrote upon this occasion.

Hic sita magnanimi *Medicis* sunt ossa *Joannis*
  Quanto heu privata est urbsque, domusque viro!
Fratre Petro, patriæque bonis, Cosmoque parente
  Ac tanto rerum culmine dignus erat.

The death of Giovanni de' Medici may afford a useful lesson: and I shall not conceal from my readers, that in the manuscript I have before cited, intitled, *Origine e descendenza della casa de' Medici*, this event is said to have been attributed to *high living*, "Molti vogliono che tal morte di Giovanni derivasse "dal soverchio bere e mangiare, perche era di natura caldissimo, e bevendo "e mangiando tutte robe calde furono poi la cagione della sua morte."

might be alledged in extenuation of a circumstance apparently inconsistent with the gravity of the character of Cosmo de' Medici; but Cosmo himself disclaimed such apology, and whilst he acknowledged his youthful indiscretion, made amends to society for the breach of a salutary regulation, by attending to the morals and the welfare of his illegitimate descendant. Under his countenance Carlo became canon of Prato, and one of the apostolic notaries, and as his general residence was at Rome, he was frequently resorted to by his father and brothers, for his advice and assistance in procuring ancient manuscripts and other valuable remains of antiquity (*a*).

The death of Giovanni de' Medici, on whom Cosmo had placed his chief expectations, and the weak state of health that Piero experienced, which rendered him unfit for the exertions of public life, in so turbulent a place as Florence, raised great apprehensions in Cosmo, that at his decease, the splendor of his family would close. These reflections embittered the repose of his latter days. A short time before his death, being carried through the apartments of his palace, after having recently lost his son, he exclaimed with a sigh, "*This is too great a house*

(*a*) Plures extant in tabulario Mediceo Caroli Epistolæ, tum ad patrem tum ad fratres, in quibus de rebus suis, et emendis Græcis et Latinis codicibus scribit. Cetera inter mandatum habuit a Cosmo, ut Phalaridis Epistolas, e Græco, in Latinum convertendas curaret. Inter Protonotarios Apostolicos relatus fuit, ac demum collegio Canonicorum Pratensium præfuit. Extat in principe æde prope sacrarium, marmoreum ejus monumentum, a Dantio Aretino scalptum, cum hoc titulo. CAROLO MEDICES COSMI FILIO PRÆPOSITO QUI OBIT MCDXCIIII. *Fabronius, in vita Cos.* 2, 213.

house for so small a family." These apprehensions were in some degree realized by the infirmities under which Piero laboured during the few years in which he held the direction of the republic; but the talents of Lorenzo soon dispelled this temporary gloom, and exalted his family to a degree of reputation and splendor, of which it is probable that Cosmo himself had scarcely formed an idea.

Celebrity of Cosmo de' Medici.

The kindness and attention shewn by Cosmo to men of learning were not without their reward. His virtues and his liberality were their most frequent topic. In every event of his life they were ready to attend him, to participate with him in his prosperity, and to sympathize with him in his misfortunes. The affectionate epistles addressed to him by Poggio on his banishment to Padua, and on his recall to Florence, exhibit not only a proof of the sincere esteem, but of the high admiration of their author (*a*). Of the continued attachment of Leonardo Aretino to his great patron, innumerable evidences remain. Amongst the eminent men of the time who endeavoured to console him for the untimely loss of his son, was Pius II. who addressed to him a Latin epistle, to which Cosmo replied with great propriety and dignity, and in a style not inferior to that of this learned pontiff (*b*). To the poem of Alberto Avogradi,

(*a*) *Poggii Ep. in Op. p.* 312. 339. *Ed. Basil.*

(*b*) These letters will be found in the Appendix, No. IV.

CHAP. I.

Avogradi, we have before had occasion to refer (*a*). A considerable number of works, as well in verse as in prose, inscribed to him on different occasions, were, after his death, collected together by Bartolomeo Scala, and are yet preserved in the Laurentian Library, under the name of *Collectiones Cosmianæ* (*b*).

But

(*a*) "*De religione et magnificentia Illustris Cosmi Medices Florentini.*" By which however the author only means to celebrate the buildings erected by Cosmo for public and private use. Accordingly, in his first book he adverts to the churches of S. Marco and S. Lorenzo, the dormitory of the convent of S. Croce, the chapels of Boschetti and Monte Averno, and the monastery of Fiesole, of each of which he gives a description. He also alludes to the intention which Cosmo had then formed, and which he afterwards executed, of erecting at Jerusalem a house of reception for poor and infirm pilgrims, in which it seems he had to contend with the prejudices of the Saracens.

——" Domini tu sancta sepulchra,
" Quæ sunt *Jerusalem* condecorasse paras,
" Magna parat Cosmus, sed tu, Saladine, recusas,
" O rapiant sensus, ista negata, tuos."

In the second book Avogradi recounts, in similar language, the magnificence of the palaces and other buildings erected by Cosmo for secular purposes.

(*b*) Plut. liv. Cod. 10. This manuscript consists of *seventy-two* distinct pieces, composing a large volume in quarto, with the portrait of Cosmo prefixed to the work, which is also preceded by the following short introductory epistle from Scala to Lorenzo de' Medici.

" Bart. Scala, Laurentio Medici, urbis spei, S. D. Collegi, Laurenti " charissime, scripta compluria & omnia fere in quæ manus inciderunt, ubi " nomen Cosmi Avi tui, Patris hujus urbis legeretur. Ea redegi in volumen, " quod mitto nunc ad te. Velim ut tantum otii subtrahas maximis tuis oc" cupationibus, ut mira et legendi et intelligendi divini ingenii tui solertia " omnia percurras; & si tibi videbuntur digna quæ legantur ab hominibus, " alicui ex bibliothecis Cosmi ut inserantur curabis. Vale."

Antonio Beccatelli.

But perhaps the most extraordinary production that solicited the patronage of Cosmo, was the *Hermaphroditus* of Antonio Beccatelli, or as he is usually called from Palermo, the place of his birth, Antonio Panhormita (a). When the respectability and situation of Beccatelli are considered, our surprize must be excited on finding him the avowed author of a production so grossly indecent as the Hermaphroditus; when we advert to the age and character of Cosmo de' Medici, it is no less extraordinary that he should be the patron to whom it is inscribed.

Beccatelli did not however escape without reprehension, for thus indulging, at an advanced age, a pruriency of imagination not excusable at any time of life. Amongst others, Filelfo and Lorenzo Valla exclaimed against his licentiousness. Invectives against the author were likewise poured out from the pulpit, and he was burnt in effigy at Ferrara and afterwards at Milan. Valla had the charity

(a) Beccatelli was born of a respectable family, in 1394, and was for some years a public professor of history and letters at Pavia, where he enjoyed the protection of Filippo Visconti, duke of Milan, and a salary of eight hundred gold crowns. After having received the laurel by favour of the emperor Sigismund, he went to the court of Alfonso, king of Naples, in whose employ he passed the remainder of his days, honoured with the office of his secretary and counsellor, and the constant companion both of his studies and his military expeditions. His "*Dicta et facta Alphonsi Regis Arragoniæ*," in four books, were commented on by Æneas Sylvius (pope Pius II.), and have been frequently printed. His epistles and orations were published at Venice in 1553. His *Hermaphroditus* is divided into two books, containing short epigrammatic poems on a variety of subjects. Some of the least exceptionable may be found at the end of his "*Epistolæ & Orationes*." (*Ven.* 1553.) And others in the "*Carmina illustrium Poetarum Italorum*." (*Vol.* ii. *p.* 109.) The remainder have been strictly confined within the limits of the Laurentian Library.

rity to hope, that the third time the author might be burnt in his proper person (*a*). Even Poggio, who in his *Facetiæ* had not confined himself within the strict limits of decorum, thought it necessary to remonstrate with his friend Beccatelli on the indecency of his work, though he highly commends its elegance and latinity (*b*). Beccatelli attempted to excuse his performance by the authority of the ancient Greek and Roman writers, but his reply may rather be considered as a repetition than as a justification of his offence (*c*). On the contrary, there were men of known talents who expressed their thorough approbation of this performance. A commendatory epistle of Guarino Veronese, is prefixed to the manuscript copy of it in the Laurentian

---

(*a*) "Declamarono contra di esso, insino dal pulpito, *Bernardino da Siena*, "e *Roberto da Lecce*, che in Bologna, in Ferrara, e in Milano lo fecero abbruc- "ciare nelle pubbliche piazze. Se dobbiam credere al *Valla (In Facium Invect.* "II. *p.* 543. *Ed. Basil*, 1540). Non solo due volte fu abbruciato il libro, ma il "ritratto ancora del *Panormita: Certe bis in celeberrimis Italiæ locis, primum* "*Ferrariæ cum Papa Synodo adesset, iterum Mediolani omnium populorum frequentia* "*inspectante, per imaginem chartaceam crematus est. Tertio per se ipsum cremandus* "*ut spero.*" *Zeno Dissert. Voss. v.* i. *p.* 316.

(*b*) "Delectatus sum mehercle, varietate rerum, & elegantia versuum, si- "mulque admiratus sum res adeo impudicas, adeo ineptas, tam venuste, tam "composite a te dici: atque ita multa exprimi turpiuscula, ut non enarrari, "sed agi videantur; nec ficta à te jocandi causa ut existimo, sed acta extimari "possint. Laudo ego doctrinam tuam, jocunditatem carminis, jocos ac sales, "tibique gratias ago pro portiuncula mea, qui latinas musas, quæ jamdudum "nimium dormierunt à somno excitas. Pro charitate tamen, qua omnibus "debitores sumus, unum est quod te monere & debeo & volo, ut scilicet dein- "ceps graviora quædam mediteris." "Scis enim non licere idem nobis, qui "Christiani sumus, quod olim poetis qui deum ignorabant."

Poggii Op. Ed. Bas. p. 49.

(*c*) *Beccatelli Epist. lib.* 4. *p.* 80.

Laurentian Library, in which he defends Beccatelli, by alledging the example of St. Jerome.

Literary Quarrels.

One of the most striking, though not the most pleasing features, in the history of the fifteenth century, is exhibited in the frequent and violent dissensions which took place amongst the learned. In some instances these disputes arose between the chiefs of the two leading sects of philosophy; whilst in others the contest was more personal, and originated in the high opinion entertained by the disputants of their own respective merits. The controversy between cardinal Bessarion, and George Trapezuntius, or of Trebisond, was of the former kind. A Greek by birth, Bessarion had early imbibed the doctrines of Plato. Having attained the dignity of Bishop of Nice, he attended in his public capacity the council of Florence, and was one of the disputants on the part of the Greeks. Whether Bessarion was alarmed at the disorderly state of his own country, or whether he found himself influenced by the arguments of his opponents, is uncertain; but soon after his return to Constantinople, he paid another visit to Italy, where he passed the remainder of his days. His learning and his integrity recommended him to Eugenius IV. who in the year 1439 honoured him with the purple; and it has been said, that a mistake made by his secretary prevented him from obtaining the pontifical dignity; but the futility of this tale of Jovius has been sufficiently exposed by Hody (*a*). That he had nearly arrived at that honour

Bessarion and George of Trebisond.

(*a*) *Hodius de Græcis illustribus, Lond.* 1741. *p.* 146. It is however related by Mr. Gibbon, v. xii. c. 66.

honour is however certain; and his more fortunate competitor Pius II. endeavoured to console him for his disappointment by bestowing upon him the empty title of Patriarch of Constantinople. In the year 1468, Bessarion gave a striking proof of his munificence and love of literature, by presenting his very valuable collection of Greek and Latin manuscripts to the state of Venice, to be deposited in the church of St. Mark. His letter to the senate on this occasion, gives us a most favourable idea of his temper and character (a). George, though called of Trebisond, was a Cretan by birth, who, after having taught in different parts of Italy, was at length called to Rome by Nicholas V. and nominated one of the apostolic secretaries. His arrogant and haughty temper soon offended the Pope, and he was compelled to spend the remainder of his days in seeking a precarious subsistence in different parts of Greece and Italy. The dispute between him and Bessarion was occasioned by Theodore Gaza, who published a treatise against the Platonic philosophy, and in commendation of the opinions of Aristotle, to which Bessarion opposed a temperate and well-written reply. Gaza, overpowered by the arguments, or the authority of his adversary, declined any further controversy; but George of Trebisond boldly came forwards to the relief of the declining cause of Aristotle, and in several invectives against the Platonists, endeavoured to throw an odium on their doctrines and their morals; insomuch, that there is scarcely a crime with which he hesitates to charge them, nor a public calamity which he does not contend

(a) *Lettere di Principi*, v.i. p. 2.

contend to be the consequence of their system. This attack again called forth Bessarion, who, in his treatise "*In Calumniatorem Platonis* (a)," is considered as having obtained a complete victory over his opponent. Other learned Greeks then in Italy, joined in the debate. The Italians were indeed silent spectators of the controversy; but the eloquence of Bessarion, and the example and patronage of the Medici, overpowered the partizans of Aristotle; and the Platonic academy instituted by Cosmo, acquired additional strength, till by the countenance and support of his grandson Lorenzo, it arrived at its highest pitch of eminence.

Poggio and Filelfo.

A debate of this nature, on an important subject, if kept within the bounds of decorum, affects not the disputants with any degree of opprobrium, except so far as it may attach to the erroneousness of their opinions, or the futility of their arguments; but this applies not to the other kind of controversy to which I have before alluded; and of which the age in question produced frequent instances. The turbulent and vindictive temper of Filelfo has already been animadverted on. Unwearied in soliciting the favours of the great, he often extorted promises which were never meant to be performed, but the breach of which infallibly brought down the weight of his resentment. Almost all the sovereigns of Italy were successively the subject of his indecent satire, or his exaggerated

(a) First printed by Sweynheim and Pannartz at Rome about 1470, and several times afterwards, particularly by Aldus in 1516.

CHAP. I.

gerated complaints. He did not however escape without full retribution for the abuse which he so liberally dealt around him. In Poggio he met with an antagonist, that, if possible, exceeded him in rancour and scurrility. Their dispute commenced in an attack made by Filelfo on the character of Niccolo Niccoli, which, if we give credit even to his friend Leonardo Aretino, was not perfectly immaculate (*a*). This gave occasion to the *invectivæ* of Poggio against Filelfo. If we for a moment suppose there could have been the slightest foundation for the charges exhibited against Filelfo in these pieces, he must have been a monster of depravity. After reproaching him with the meanness of his birth, Poggio pursues his track from place to place, successively accusing him of fraud, ingratitude, theft, adultery, and yet more scandalous crimes. The voyage of Filelfo to Constantinople, was undertaken to shelter himself from punishment. The kindness of Chrysoloras, who received him destitute and friendless into his house, he repaid by debauching his daughter, whom Chrysoloras was therefore obliged to bestow upon him in marriage. Not satisfied with serious invective, Poggio has also introduced his adversary in his *Facetiæ*; and Filelfo will long be remembered as the original Hans Carvel of Prior, and La Fontaine (*b*). The contentions of Poggio with Lorenzo

---

(*a*) For a curious instance of this, see *Leonardi Aretini Ep. tom.* ii. *p.* 17.

(*b*) Mr. Warton (*Essay on Pope, v.* ii. *p.* 68.) traces the genealogy, as he calls it, of this curious tale from Poggio to Rabelais, "Who," says he, "inserted it in his eighth book, and thirty-third chapter; it was *afterwards* "related in a book called the *Hundred Novels*. Ariosto finishes his fifth satire

renzo Valla were carried on with an equal degree of rancour and licentiousness; and even his debate with Guarino Veronese on the comparative excellence of Scipio and Julius Cæsar, was sufficiently acrimonious. By these quarrels the learned were divided into factions, and Leonardo Aretino, Poggio, Niccolo Niccoli, and Beccatelli, were opposed to Valla, Niccolo Perotti, and others; but the leaders of these parties often disagreed amongst themselves, and scrupled not at times to accuse each other of the most scandalous enormities. As these imputations were however attended by no very serious consequences, charity would lead us to conclude that they were mutually understood to be rather contests of skill between these literary gladiators, than proofs of real criminality in their respective antagonists. The life of a scholar is seldom stained by atrocious crimes; but that almost all the learned men of the age should have disgraced themselves by so shameless a degree of moral turpitude, is surely a supposition beyond the bounds of credibility.

Cosmo

" with it. Malespini also made use of it. Fontaine, who imagined Rabelais " to be the inventor of it, was the sixth author who delivered it, as our Prior " was the last, though perhaps not the least spirited." If this be worth relating, it is worth correcting.—Mr. Warton had his information from the *Menagiana*; but he has mistaken his authority, in placing the writings of Rabelais *before* the well-known work of the *Cent Nouvelles Nouvelles*, which is more ancient by nearly a century. Even Ariosto was prior to Rabelais, who was only the *fourth* amongst these *Hogs of Westphaly*. Of this Menage was well aware. *Menag*. i. 369

CHAP. I.

Death and character of Cosmo de' Medici.

Cosmo now approached the period of his mortal existence, but the faculties of his mind yet remained unimpaired. About twenty days before his death, when his strength was visibly on the decline, he entered into conversation with Ficino, and, whilst the faint beams of a setting sun seemed to accord with his situation and his feelings, began to lament the miseries of life, and the imperfections inseparable from human nature.—As he continued his discourse, his sentiments and his views became more elevated, and from bewailing the lot of humanity, he began to exult in the prospect of that happier state towards which he felt himself approaching. Ficino replied by citing corresponding sentiments from the Athenian sages, and particularly from Xenocrates; and the last task imposed by Cosmo on his philosophic attendant, was to translate from the Greek the treatise of that author on death (*a*). Having prepared his mind to wait with composure the awful event, his next concern was the welfare of his surviving family, to whom he was desirous of imparting in a solemn manner, the result of the experience of a long and active life. Calling into his chamber his wife Contessina and his son Piero, he entered into a narrative of all his public transactions; he gave a full account of his extensive mercantile connexions, and adverted to the state of his domestic concerns. To Piero he recommended a strict attention to the education of his sons, of whose promising talents he expressed his hopes

(*a*) This information we derive from the introduction of Ficino to his translation of that work, inserted in the *Collectiones Cosmianae*.

hopes and his approbation. He requested that his funeral might be conducted with as much privacy as possible, and concluded his paternal exhortations with declaring his willingness to submit to the disposal of Providence whenever he should be called upon. These admonitions were not lost on Piero, who communicated by letter to Lorenzo and Giuliano, the impression which they had made upon his own mind (*a*). At the same time, sensible of his own infirmities, he exhorted them to consider themselves not as children, but as men, seeing that circumstances rendered it necessary to put their abilities to an early proof. *A physician*, says Piero, *is hourly expected to arrive from Milan, but, for my own part, I place my confidence in God.* Either the physician did not arrive, or Piero's distrust of him was well founded, for, about six days afterwards, being the first day of August 1464, Cosmo died, at the age of seventy-five years, deeply lamented by a great majority of the citizens of Florence, whom he had firmly attached to his interest, and who feared for the safety of the city from the dissensions that were likely to ensue (*b*).

The character of Cosmo de' Medici exhibits a combination of virtues and endowments rarely to be found united in

(*a*) This letter yet remains, and gives us a very interesting account of the conduct of Cosmo shortly before his death. I have therefore inserted it in the Appendix, from the collection of Fabroni. *App. No.* V.

(*b*) In the Ricordi of Piero de' Medici is a particular account of the death of his father, a character of whom is there given, drawn with great truth and simplicity by the hand of filial affection. It is with pleasure I illustrate my work with these authentic documents. The family of the Medici thus become their own historians. *App. No.* VI.

in the same person. If in his public works he was remarkable for his magnificence, he was no less conspicuous for his prudence in private life. Whilst in the character of chief of the Florentine republic, he supported a constant intercourse with the sovereigns of Europe, his conduct in Florence was divested of all ostentation, and neither in his retinue, his friendships, or his conversation, could he be distinguished from any other respectable citizen. He well knew the jealous temper of the Florentines, and preferred the real enjoyment of authority, to that open assumption of it, which could only have been regarded as a perpetual insult, by those whom he permitted to gratify their own pride, in the reflection that they were the equals of Cosmo de' Medici.

In affording protection to the arts of architecture, painting, and sculpture, which then began to revive in Italy, Cosmo set the great example to those, who by their rank, and their riches, could alone afford them effectual aid. The countenance shewn by him to those arts, was not of that kind which their professors generally experience from the great; it was not conceded as a bounty, nor received as a favour; but appeared in the friendship and equality that subsisted between the artist and his patron (*a*). In the erection

(*a*) Of this nature was the intercourse between Cosmo and Donatello. The treasures of the citizen were applied under the direction of the sculptor in the acquisition of the most beautiful specimens of ancient art. Donatello survived his patron, but Cosmo on his death recommended him to the attention of Piero his son, who amply provided for the wants of his age. Donatello died in 1466, and was buried in the church of S. Lorenzo, adjoining to

erection of the numerous public buildings in which Cosmo expended incredible sums of money, he principally availed himself of the assistance of Michellozzo Michellozzi and Filippo Brunelleschi; the first of whom was a man of talents, the latter of genius (*a*). Soon after his return from banishment, Cosmo engaged these two artists to form the plan of a mansion for his own residence. Brunelleschi gave scope to his invention, and produced the design of a palace which might have suited the proudest sovereign in Europe; but Cosmo was led by that prudence which, in his personal accommodation, regulated all his conduct, to prefer the plan of Michellozzi, which united extent with simplicity, and elegance with convenience (*b*). With the consciousness, Brunelleschi possessed also the irritability of genius, and in a fit of vexation, he destroyed a design which he unjustly considered as disgraced by its

---

the sepulchre of Cosmo, according to his own directions, for which he alleged as a reason, that as his soul had always been with Cosmo whilst living, so he desired their bodies might be near each other when dead.

(*a*) Before the time of Brunelleschi, the Italians had imitated in their public buildings the Gothic structures of their German neighbours. He was the first who attempted to restore the Grecian orders of architecture, and under his control this important branch of art attained a degree of perfection which it had not known from the times of the ancients.

(*b*) This venerable edifice is now the residence of the noble family of Riccardi, who, in the year 1659, purchased it from the grand duke Ferdinand II. Under the auspices of its present owner, the marquis Riccardi, whose extensive collection of manuscripts and antiquities are open to public inspection, this mansion yet emulates its ancient glory. In the year 1715 an inscription was placed in one of the façades of the inner court, which will be found in the Appendix, No. VII.

its not being carried into execution (a). Having compleated his dwelling, Cosmo indulged his taste in ornamenting it with the most precious remains of ancient art; and in the purchase of vases, statues, busts, gems, and medals, expended no inconsiderable sum. Nor was he less attentive to the merits of those artists which his native place had recently produced. With Masaccio a better style of painting had arisen, and the cold and formal manner of Giotto, and his disciples, had given way to more natural and expressive composition. In Cosmo de' Medici this rising artist found his most liberal patron and protector. Some of the works of Masaccio were executed in the chapel of the Brancacci, where they were held in such estimation, that the place was regarded as a school of study by the most eminent artists who immediately succeeded him. Even the celebrated Michelagnolo, when observing these paintings many years afterwards, in company with his honest and loquacious friend Vasari, did not hesitate to express his decided approbation of their merits. The reputation of Masaccio was emulated by his disciple Filippo Lippi, who executed for Cosmo and his friends many celebrated pictures, of which Vasari has given a minute account. Cosmo however found no small difficulty in controlling the temper and regulating the eccentricities of this extraordinary character (b). If the efforts

(a) Cosmo had employed Brunelleschi in compleating the church of S. Lorenzo, and in erecting the church and monastery of S. Bartolomeo, and acknowledged him on all occasions as the first architect of his time; after his death Cosmo also raised a monument to his memory.

Fab. in vitâ Cos. v. i. p. 155.

(b) His attachment to women was extreme, and if the favourite object

efforts of these early masters did not reach the true end of the art, they afforded considerable assistance towards it; an whilst Masaccio and Filippo decorated with their admired productions the altars of churches and the apartments of princes, Donatello gave to marble a proportion of form, a vivacity of expression, to which his contemporaries imagined that nothing more was wanting; Brunelleschi raised the great dome of the cathedral of Florence; and Ghiberti cast in brass the stupendous doors of the church of St. John, which Michelagnolo deemed worthy to be the gates of paradise.

In his person Cosmo was tall; in his youth he possessed the advantage of a prepossessing countenance; what age had taken from his comeliness, it had added to his dignity, and in his latter years, his appearance was so truly venerable as to have been the frequent subject of panegyric (*a*). His

resisted his assiduities, he found some consolation in painting her likeness. By this unconquerable propensity his labours were often interrupted, and an expedient adopted by Cosmo to remedy it, nearly cost Filippo his life. Having engaged the painter to compleat a piece of work for him, Cosmo made him a prisoner in his chamber, but a confinement of two days exhausted the patience of the artist. At the risque of his life he made his escape through the window, and devoted himself for several days to his pleasures, nor did he return till sought out and solicited by Cosmo, who heartily repented of a proceeding which, however friendly in its motive, was certainly somewhat too arbitrary.

(*a*) Thus Bartolomeo Scala, on a portrait of Cosmo, painted when he was young:

"Quæ vera est Cosmi facies, haud vera videtur;
"Dissimiles adeo longa senecta facit;
"Talis erat quondam, quem nunc perfectior ætas,
"Ex homine, incœpit fingere velle deum."

Carm. illust. Poet. Ital. v. 8. *p.* 489.

His manner was grave and complacent, but upon many occasions he gave sufficient proofs that this did not arise from a want of talents for sarcasm; and the fidelity of the Florentine historians has preserved many of his shrewd observations and remarks (*a*). When Rinaldo de' Albizi, who was then in exile, and meditated an attack upon his native place, sent a message to Cosmo, importing that the hen would shortly hatch, he replied, *She will hatch with an ill grace out of her own nest.* On another occasion, when his adversaries gave him to understand that they were not sleeping, *I believe it*, said Cosmo, *I have spoiled their sleep.—Of what colour is my hair?* said Cosmo, uncovering his head to the ambassadors of Venice, who came with a complaint against the Florentines, *White*, they replied; *It will not be long*, said Cosmo, *before that of your senators will be so too.* Shortly before his death, his wife inquiring why he closed his eyes, *That I may perceive more clearly*, was his reply.

If, from considering the private character of Cosmo, we attend to his conduct as the moderator and director of the Florentine republic, our admiration of his abilities will increase with the extent of the theatre upon which he had to act. So important were his mercantile concerns, that they often influenced in a very remarkable degree the politics of Italy. When Alfonso king of Naples leagued with the Venetians against Florence, Cosmo called in such immense debts from those places, as deprived them of resources for carrying on the war (*b*). During

(*a*) *Mac. Ist. Fior. lib.* vii. (*b*) *Ibid.*

During the contest between the houses of York and Lancaster, one of his agents in England was resorted to by Edward IV. for a sum of money, which was accordingly furnished, to such an extraordinary amount, that it might almost be considered as the means of supporting that monarch on the throne, and was repaid when his successes enabled him to fulfil his engagement (*a*). The alliance of Cosmo was sedulously courted by the princes of Italy, and it was remarked that by a happy kind of fatality, whoever united their interests with his, were always enabled either to repress, or to overcome their adversaries. By his assistance the republic of Venice resisted the united attacks of Filippo duke of Milan, and of the French nation, but when deprived of his support, the Venetians were no longer able to withstand their enemies. With whatever difficulties Cosmo had to encounter, at home or abroad, they generally terminated in the acquisition of additional honour to his country and to himself. The esteem and gratitude of his fellow-citizens were fully shewn a short time before

(*a*) La Maison de Medicis estoit la plus grande, que je croy que jamais ait esté au monde: car leurs serviteurs & facteurs ont eu tant de credit soups couleur de ce nom de Medicis, que ce seroit merveilles à croire à ce que j'en ay veu en Flandres & en Angleterre. J'en ai veu un appelé Guerard Quanvese presque etre occasion de soutenir le Roy Edouard le quart en son etat, estant guerre en son royaume d'Angleterre, & fournir par fois au dit roy plus de six vingt mille escus: où il fit peu de profit pour son maitre: toutes fois il recouvra ses pieces a la longue. Un autre ay vu nommé e appelé Thomas Portunary, estre pleige entre le dit roy Edouard & le duc Charles de Bourgogne, pour cinquante mille escus, & une autre fois en un lieu, pour quatre vingt mille. *Mem. de P. de Comminas, ap. Fabr. in vitâ Laurentii, v.* ii. *p.* 224.

before his death, when by a public decree he was honoured with the title of *Pater Patriæ*, an appellation which was inscribed on his tomb, and which, as it was founded on real merit, has ever since been attached to the name of Cosmo de' Medici.

CHAP. II.

*EARLY accomplishments of Lorenzo—Education—Lorenzo visits different parts of Italy—Conduct of Piero—Conspiracy of Luca Pitti—Frustrated by Lorenzo—The exiles instigate the Venetians to attack the Florentines—Battle near Bologna—Piero promotes the interests of learning—Leo Battista Alberti—Cristoforo Landino—Piero patronizes other eminent scholars—Giostra of Lorenzo and Giuliano—Poem of Luca Pulci—Poem of Angelo Politiano—*DISPUTATIONES CAMALDULENSES—*Lorenzo's description of his mistress—Sonnets in her praise—Lucretia Donati the object of his passion—Lorenzo marries Clarice Orsini—Visits the duke of Milan—Death of Piero de' Medici.*

CHAP. II.

Early accomplishments of Lorenzo.

LORENZO de' Medici was about sixteen years of age when Cosmo died, and had at that time given striking indications of extraordinary talents. From his earliest years he had exhibited proofs of a retentive and vigorous mind, which was cultivated, not only by all the attention which his father's infirmities would permit him to bestow, 1464.
but by a frequent intercourse with his venerable grandfather. He owed also great obligations in this respect to his mother Lucretia, who was one of the most accomplished women of the age, and distinguished herself not only as a patroness of learning, but by her own writings. Of these some specimens yet remain, which are the more

entitled

entitled to approbation, as they were produced at a time when poetry was at its lowest ebb in Italy (*a*). The disposition of Lorenzo which afterwards gave him a peculiar claim to the title of *magnificent*, was apparent in his childhood. Having received as a present a horse from Sicily, he sent the donor in return a gift of much greater value, and on being reproved for his profuseness, he remarked, that there was nothing more glorious than to overcome others in acts of generosity. Of his proficiency in classical learning, and the different branches of that philosophy which was then in repute, he has left indisputable proofs. Born to restore the lustre of his native tongue, he had rendered himself conspicuous by his poetical talents before he arrived at manhood. To these accomplishments he united a considerable share of strong natural penetration and good sense, which enabled him, amidst the many difficulties that he

(*a*) Several of her *Laudi*, or hymns, are printed in the collection of sacred poems by the Medici family, published by *Cionacci* at Florence, 1680, and since reprinted at Bergamo in 1763; but a much more favourable specimen of her talents is given by *Crescimbeni* (*Della volgar poesia*, *v.* iii. *p.* 377.) who is of opinion that she excelled the greater part of, not to say all, the poets of her time. Her versifications of scripture history are noticed by *Luigi Pulci*, in his *Morgante*, which poem he was induced to compleat by her encouragement, and in which he thus adverts to the writings of his patroness.

"Quivi si legge della sua *Maria*
"La vita, ove il suo libro è sempre aperto;
"E di *Esdram* di *Judith* e di *Tobia*
"Quivi si rende giusto premio e merto;
"Quivi s' intende hor l' alta fantasia
"A descriver *Giovanni nel deserto*;
"Quivi cantano hor gli angeli i suoi versi,
"Dove il ver d' ogni cosa può vedersi."

Morgante. Ed. Ven. per Comin de Trino, 1546.

he was involved in, to act with a promptitude and decision which surprized those who were witnesses of his conduct; whilst the endowments which entitled him to admiration and respect, were accompanied by others that conciliated, in an eminent degree, the esteem and affection of his fellow-citizens.

Tall in his stature, robust in his form, Lorenzo had in his person more the appearance of strength than of elegance. From his birth he laboured under some peculiar disadvantages; his sight was weak, his voice harsh and unpleasing, and he was totally deprived of the sense of smell (*a*). With all these defects his countenance was dignified, and gave an idea of the magnanimity of his character; and the effects of his eloquence were conspicuous on many important occasions. In his youth he was much addicted to active and laborious exercises, to hawking, horsemanship, and country sports. Though not born to support a military character, he gave sufficient proofs of his courage, not only in public tournaments, which were then not infrequent in Italy, but also upon more trying occasions. Such was the versatility of his talents, that it is difficult to discover any department of business, or of amusement, of art, or of science, to which they were not at some time applied; and in whatever he undertook, he arrived at a proficiency which would seem to have required the labour of a life much longer than that which he was permitted to enjoy.

Under

(*a*) *Valerius, in vitâ Laur. Med. p.* 9.

CHAP. II.

Education of Lorenzo.

Under the institution of Gentile d'Urbino, who afterwards, by the patronage of his pupil, became bishop of Arezzo, Lorenzo received the first rudiments of his education, and from the instructions of his tutor, aided perhaps by the exhortations of his pious mother, acquired that devotional temper which is so conspicuous in some of his writings (*a*). This disposition was however only occasional, nor was the mind of Lorenzo overshaded with the habitual gloom of the professed devotee. In his hours of seriousness, or of sickness, the impression made upon him by his early instructors became sufficiently apparent; but the vivacity of his temper often hurried him to a contrary extreme; and the levity, not to say the licentiousness, of some of his writings, is strikingly contrasted with the piety and seriousness of his other productions. The vigour of his intellect seems to have thrown an indiscriminate lustre on every object that presented itself. So various, yet so extensive were his powers, that they are scarcely reconcileable to that consistency of character with which the laws of human nature seldom dispense (*b*).

In

(*a*) Valori dwells with apparent satisfaction on his early piety. "Audivi," says he, "sæpius a Gentile ejus preceptore, cum quo et in Gallia, quum ibi legatum ageret, & in patria familiarissime vixi, Laurentium a latere suo discessisse nunquam. Die in Templo, donec res divina perageretur, permansisse semper: nocte etiam secum ire solitum ad divi Pauli societatem, quo conveniebant plurimi, Immortali Deo in sobrietate et vigiliis ac precibus gratias agentes: obvios Christi pauperculos eleemosynis prosequi ad unum omnes: nihil in eo puerile, nihil delicatum apparuisse" *Val in vitâ Laur. p.* 5.

(*b*) This peculiarity in the character of Lorenzo was not unobserved by his contemporaries. "Jam vero quo unquam in homine tam diversæ inter se fu-

In superintending the subsequent progress of Lorenzo, several other persons eminent for their learning concurred. In the year 1457, Cristoforo Landino was appointed by the magistracy of Florence to the office of public professor of poety and rhetoric in that city, and was soon afterwards intrusted by Piero de' Medici with the instruction of his two sons. Between Landino and his pupil Lorenzo a reciprocal attachment took place, and such was the opinion that the master entertained of the judgment of his scholar, that he is said frequently to have submitted his various and learned works to his perusal and correction (*a*). In the Greek language, in ethics, and in the principles of the Aristotelian philosophy, Lorenzo had the advantage of the precepts of the learned Argyropylus (*b*), and in those of the Platonic sect he was sedulously instructed by Marsilio Ficino, for whom he retained through life an unalterable friendship; but for many of his accomplishments he was not indebted to any preceptor. That exquisite taste in poetry, in music, and in every department of the fine arts, which enabled him to contribute so powerfully towards their

" eruut partes virtutum maximarum? Quid enim longius abest quam a gravi-
" tate facilitas? Quis tamen te constantior? Contra vero quis elementior aut
" lenior? Quid tam mirabile quam magnitudinem istam animi humanitatis
" condimentis temperari?" &c. *Pauli Cortesii Ep. ad Laur. Med. ad Dial. de Hominibus doctis praef. Ed. Flor.* 1734. vide et *Val. in vità Laur. p.* 14.

(*a*) *Band. Spec. Lit. Flor. v.* i. *p.* 183.

(*b*) Argyropylus Byzantius insigni fuit & auctoritate & gratia apud Cosmum Medicem, hujus filium Petrum, nepotemque Laurentium, quem non modo Græcis literis sed et dialecticis imbuit, eaque philosophiæ parte qua de moribus præcipitur. *Politian. in Proœm. ad Miscell.*

CHAP. II.

their restoration, was an endowment of nature, the want of which no education could have supplied.

1465.

With such qualifications Lorenzo, soon after the death of his grandfather, entered on the stage of public life; for it was the laudable custom of the Florentines early to habituate their youth to serious and important occupations. Besides, the infirmities of Piero de' Medici rendered such a coadjutor as Lorenzo was likely to prove, of great importance to him. Having therefore completed his domestic education, his father judged it expedient for him to visit some of the principal courts of Italy; not so much for the purpose of gratifying an idle curiosity, as to conciliate, by a personal intercourse, the friendship of those with whom he was in future to maintain a correspondence on matters of great moment, and to inform himself of such local circumstances as might enable him to transact the affairs of the republic with every possible advantage. In the year 1465, he had an interview at Pisa with the son of Ferdinand king of Naples, Federigo, who after the death of his eldest brother Alfonso, and his nephew Federigo, succeeded to the crown. This prince was then on his journey to Milan, to escort Ippolita, the daughter of Francesco Sforza, from thence to Naples, where she was to marry his elder brother Alfonso, duke of Calabria (*a*). At this interview some instances of mutual respect and attachment took place between Federigo

(*a*) *Muratori, Annali d'Italia. v. ix. p.* 493.

Federigo and Lorenzo, which we shall hereafter have occasion to relate.

In the following year Lorenzo made a visit to Rome, where he was kindly received by Paul II. one of the most arrogant pontiffs that ever sat in the chair of St. Peter. A few months afterwards he proceeded through Bologna and Ferrara to Venice, and thence to Milan. During his absence he had frequent letters from his father, several of which yet remain, and sufficiently evince the confidence that Piero placed in his son, with whom he enters into a detail of all political occurrences, and to whom he transmits such letters of importance as were received on public affairs during his absence (*a*). That the respect paid by Piero to the judgment of Lorenzo, did not arise from a blind partiality, may appear from the intercourse that already subsisted between Lorenzo and some of the most celebrated scholars of the age; several of whom, on his occasional absence from Florence, addressed themselves to him by letter, as their acknowledged patron and warmest friend (*b*).

The

(*a*) *App. No.* VIII.

(*b*) Some specimens of these, which have been preserved in the *Palazzo Vecchio* at Florence, and not before published, are given in the Appendix, No. IX. The first is an extract of an Italian letter from the celebrated Luigi Pulci, the author of the Morgante, and is as strongly marked by affection for Lorenzo, as by the whimsical peculiarities of its author's character. The second is from Peregrino Allio, whose Latin poems in the *Carmina Illust. Poet. v.* i. *p.* 11, are a better testimony of his abilities than the exaggerated account

CHAP. II.

Conduct of Piero de' Medici.

The death of Pius II. who had preceded Paul II. in the pontifical chair, happened a few days after that of Cosmo de' Medici, and not long afterwards died Francesco Sforza, duke of Milan, who had governed that state with great ability for the space of sixteen years (*a*). This event gave no small alarm to Piero de' Medici, whose family had long supported a close intimacy with that of Sforza, from which they had mutually derived important advantages. Lorenzo was then at Rome, where his father addressed to

of *Negri* (*Scrittori Fiorentini*, *p.* 450.) "Fu mostrato non dato al mondo questo "mostro d' ingegno e di memoria; affinche si vedesse che nel secolo de' Ficini, "de' Mirandolani, de' Benevieni, de' Barbari, de' Poliziani, ingegni tutti portentosi e grandissimi, poteva ancora far qualche cosa di piu maraviglioso la "natura." This author is mistaken in placing the death of Allio in 1458, although the accurate Bandini has in this instance adopted his authority. (*Negri* 450. *Band. Spec. Lit. Flor. p.* 204.) I have before cited the epitaph by Allio on John de' Medici, the son of Cosmo, who died in 1463; and amongst the letters which I have procured from the *Palazzo Vecchio*, is one from him to Lorenzo, dated the 25th of May 1466. That he died young may however be inferred from Verini. (*De illustr. Urbis, p.* 34.)

"Te pariter juvenem tetricæ rapuere sorores:
"Aequasses priscos, Alli Peregrine, poetas."

(*a*) The Sforza were a family of adventurers. Sforza degli Attendogli, the father of Francesco, from the condition of a peasant, acquired such a high degree of military reputation, as enabled his son, who was also a soldier of fortune, to obtain in marriage the daughter of Filippo Maria Visconti, duke of Milan, and the Milanese territory, at that period one of the most extensive in Italy, as her portion. According to tradition, Sforza was employed in turning the soil, when he was invited by some of his companions to enter into the army. His determination was a matter of difficulty, for the solution of which he resorted to his spade—Throwing it into an oak, he declared that if it fell to the ground he would continue his labours, if it hung in the tree, he would pursue his fortunes. (*Murat. Ann. vol.* ix. *p.* 2.) He became the father of a line of princes who were regarded as the most splendid sovereigns of Italy, and formed alliances with the chief families in Europe.

to him several letters, in some of which his anxiety for the peaceable establishment of the widow and children of Francesco in the government of Milan is strongly expressed. By the death of so many of the Italian princes within so short a space of time, the minds of men began to be turned towards new commotions, particularly in Florence, where the bodily imbecility of Piero gave grounds to hope that a vigorous attempt to deprive the house of Medici of its influence, might be crowned with success. Nor was the conduct of Piero, on his succession to the immense inheritance of his father, calculated to strengthen the friendship of those whom Cosmo had attached to his interest. Apprehensive that his commercial concerns were too widely extended, and prompted by the treacherous advice of Dietisalvo Neroni, a man of ability and intrigue, who owed his fortunes to the protection and generosity of Cosmo, he began indiscriminately to collect the sums of money which his father had advanced to the citizens of Florence. The result was such as Neroni expected. Those who were friends of the father became enemies of the son; and had not Piero discovered the snare, and desisted from such rigorous proceedings, he might too late have found, that in supporting the character of the merchant, he had forgotten that of the statesman.

Conspiracy of Luca Pitti.

1466.

Amongst the number of opulent and aspiring citizens who had reluctantly submitted to the superior talents of Cosmo de' Medici, was Luca Pitti, whose name has been transmitted to posterity as the founder of the magnificent palace which has for some centuries been the residence of of the sovereigns of Tuscany. The death of Cosmo, and the infirmities of Piero, afforded an opportunity that Luca conceived to be highly favourable to his ambitious purposes (*a*). Having formed a combination with the powerful family of the Acciajuoli, he attempted in conjunction with them, to supplant the authority and destroy the influence of the Medici, with the magistrates and council of Florence. Being defeated in their exertions, they resorted to more violent methods, and resolved upon the assassination of Piero de' Medici; believing, that if they could succeed in such a project, his sons were too young to occasion any formidable opposition to their views. Debilitated by the gout, Piero was generally carried in a chair by his domestics from his house at Careggi to his residence at Florence. Having received intimation of an intended commotion, and being alarmed at the sudden approach of Ercole d'Este, brother of Borso, marquis of Ferrara, whom the conspirators had engaged to enter the territories of the republic, at the head of 1300 cavalry, he conceived his presence to be necessary in Florence, and accordingly set out from Careggi, accompanied only by a few attendants (*b*). Lorenzo, who had left Careggi a short time before his father, was surprized to find the road to the city beset by armed men, and immediately suspecting their purpose, dispatched one of his followers to him with directions to proceed by a more retired and circuitous path, whilst taking

(*a*) *Amm. Ist. Fior.* v. iii. *p.* 93.

(*b*) *Val. in vitâ Laur. p.* 10.

taking himself the direct road, he informed those who inquired with apparent anxiety for his father, that he was following at a short distance; by which means Lorenzo rescued his father from the impending danger, and gave a striking proof of that promptitude of mind which so eminently distinguished him on many subsequent occasions.

The suspicions that fell upon Luca Pitti and his party, induced the conspirators to abandon their design of open violence; and the intrigues of the politician were again substituted for the dagger of the assassin. Encouraged by the support of the marquis of Ferrara, they daily increased in numbers and audacity, but when an open contest between the opposite parties was hourly expected, and the citizens apprehended a renewal of those sanguinary commotions, from which, under the guidance of the Medici, they had been a long time exempted, Luca suddenly withdrew himself from his party, and effected a reconciliation with the Medici. Several of the malcontents followed his example, and their desertion gave a decided superiority to the cause of Piero, which was also most opportunely strengthened by the appearance of a body of two thousand Milanese troops, that kept in awe the army of the insurgents, and frustrated the hopes founded on its assistance. The friends of the Medici failed not to take advantage of this favourable concurrence; Piero Acciajuoli and his two sons, Dietisalvo Neroni, and two of his brothers, and Niccolo Soderini, with his son Geri, were declared enemies of the state, and condemned to banishment (*a*). The archbishop of Florence,

(*a*) *Amm. Ist. Fior. v.* iii. *p.* 99.

rence, who had taken a decided part against the Medici, retired to Rome. A few other citizens, unable to support their disgrace, adopted a voluntary exile; but the kindness of Lorenzo allayed the apprehensions of the greater part of the conspirators, and rendered them in future more favourable to his interests.—*He only knows how to conquer*, said Lorenzo, *who knows how to forgive* (*a*).

Though exempted from the fate of the other leaders of the faction, Luca experienced a punishment of a more galling and disgraceful kind. From the high estimation in which he had before been held, he fell into the lowest state of degradation. The progress of his magnificent palace was stopped; the populace who had formerly vied with each other in giving assistance, refused any longer to labour for him; many opulent citizens who had contributed costly articles and materials, demanded them back, alledging that they were only lent. The remainder of his days was passed in obscurity and neglect, but the extensive mansion which his pride had planned, still remains to give celebrity to his name (*b*).

The

(*a*) *Val. in vitâ, p.* 11. *Fabr. in vitâ Laur. v.* i. *p.* 28.

(*b*) It is deserving of remark that Machiavelli is mistaken not only in the period he assigns for the commencement of this building, but in the motives that led to it. After relating the successful interposition of Luca Pitti in the affairs of the republic, in the year 1453, by which he rose to great eminence, and obtained a reward from his fellow citizens, which was supposed to amount to 20,000 ducats, he adds, (*Hist. lib.* vii.) "Donde egli salì in tanta riputa-"tione che non Cosimo ma Messer Luca la Città governava. Da che egli "venne in tanta confidanza, ch' egli incominciò due edificii, l'uno a Firenze; "l'altro a Ruciano, luogo propinquo un miglio alla città, tutti superbi &

Frustrated by Lorenzo.

The defection of Luca Pitti, and the consequent establishment of the authority of the Medici in Florence, have been uniformly attributed by the Florentine historians to the abilities and prudence of Lorenzo; who, instead of resorting to forcible opposition, employed his own eloquence, and the influence of his friends, in subduing the resentment of his adversaries, and particularly of Luca Pitti, whose versatile disposition fluctuated a long time between the remonstrances of his associates, and the pacific representations of Lorenzo. A short time previous to this contest, Lorenzo had paid a visit to Naples, probably with a view of influencing the king to countenance his cause, in case the dissensions at Florence, which were then a subject of alarm, should terminate in an open rupture. The magnanimity of his conduct, as well in defeating this formidable conspiracy, as in his lenity towards his enemies, extended his reputation throughout Italy. No sooner was the result known at Naples, than Ferdinando addressed to him a letter strongly expressive of admiration and esteem; which being the testimony of a monarch whose character for sagacity and

" regii; ma quello della Città al tutto maggiore che alcun' altro che da pri-" vato cittadino fino à quel giorno fusse stato edificato." It is however certain, that both these palaces were designed, and in part executed by Filippo Brunelleschi, who died in 1446, seven years before the event related by Machiavelli took place. (*Vasari in vita di Filippo.*) " Ordinò ancor Filippo à M. " Luca Pitti, fuor della porta à S. Niccolo di Fiorenza, in un luogo detto " Ruciano un ricco e magnifico palazzo; ma non già à gran pezza simile à " quello che per lo medesimo cominciò in Firenze, e condusse al secondo " finestrato, con tanta grandezza & magnificenza, che d' opera Toscana, non " si è ancor veduta il più raro, ne il più magnifico." This palace was afterwards purchased by Leonora of Toledo, wife of Cosmo I. duke of Florence, and was compleated under the directions of Bartolomeo Ammanati.

CHAP. II.

and political knowledge was superior to that of any other potentate in Europe, must have been highly gratifying to the youthful ambition of Lorenzo (*a*). The success of Lorenzo in this critical business increased also the confidence which his father had before placed in him, and from this time he was intrusted with a considerable share in the conduct of the republic, as well as in the management of the extensive private concerns of the family. But if the prudence of Lorenzo was conspicuous in defeating his adversaries, it was more so in the use he made of his victory. He well knew that humanity and sound policy are inseparable, and either did not feel, or wisely suppressed, that vindictive spirit which civil contests seldom fail to excite. " I have heard from my brother Filippo," says Valori, " that upon his introducing to Lorenzo, for the purpose of " reconciliation, Antonio Tebalducci, who had by different " means attempted his ruin, Lorenzo, observing that my " brother hesitated in requesting his indulgence towards " an avowed enemy, said to him with great kindness, " *I should owe you no obligation, Filippo, for introducing to* " *me a friend; but by converting an enemy into a friend, you* " *have done me a favour, which I hope you will as often as* " *possible repeat.*"

The exiles instigate the Venetians to attack the Florentines.

The exiled party, which consisted principally of men of abilities and intrigue, soon began to stir up new commotions. But Agnolo Acciajuoli, who had retreated only to Sienna, was desirous, before he engaged in further opposition,

(*a*) This letter will be found in App. No. X.

position, of trying whether a reconciliation with the Medici yet remained practicable. His letter to Piero on this subject, and the answer it occasioned, are yet extant (*a*). Many of the other conspirators retired to Venice, where they exerted their utmost endeavours to exasperate that formidable state against their countrymen. This attempt might have failed of success, had they not, in seeking to gratify their private resentment, flattered the ambitious aims of the Venetians on the rest of Italy. With this view they insinuated to the senate, that the support given by the Florentines, under the influence of Cosmo de' Medici, to Francesco Sforza, had enabled him to defend his states against their pretensions, and prevented their possessing themselves of all Lombardy. These representations had their full effect. Under the command of Bartolomeo Coglione, one of the most celebrated commanders of the time, a considerable army was collected for the purpose of attacking the states of Florence. Several of the Italian princes joined in person the standard of Bartolomeo, and amongst others Ercole d'Este, Alessandro Sforza prince of Pesaro, the lords of Forli, of Faenza, and Mirandula; insomuch that this army was not more formidable for its numbers, than respectable for the rank and the talents of its leaders.

Battle near Bologna.

Nor were the Florentines in the mean time ignorant of the intended hostilities, or inattentive to their own defence. Besides

(*a*) Machiavelli informs us that Agnolo withdrew to Naples, and professes to cite the particulars of the letters between him and Piero. The accuracy of this historian may appear by comparing the authentic letters published in the Appendix, from the collection of Fabroni, with the recital of them by Machiavelli in the 7th book of his history. *App. No. XI.*

Besides the support derived from the duke of Milan, the king of Naples sent his son Federigo with a powerful reinforcement to their assistance. Galeazzo, the young duke of Milan, joined the army in person, as did also Giovanni Bentivoglio, prince of Bologna; and the command of the whole was intrusted to Federigo count of Urbino (*a*), whose character as a soldier was not inferior to that of Coglione. The adverse forces approached each other near Bologna, but no great alacrity was shewn on either side to begin the engagement. Wearied with apprehensions, and sinking under the expence of supporting so numerous an army, the Florentines began to complain of the indecisive conduct of their general, which they at length understood was chiefly to be attributed to the duke of Milan, who reserving to himself great authority, and having little experience in military affairs, threw continual obstacles in the way of the chief commander. A message was therefore dispatched to the duke, requesting his presence in Florence, where he soon after arrived, and took up his residence in the palace of the Medici (*b*). The count of Urbino being freed from this restraint, or having no apology for longer delay, attacked the advanced guard of the enemy, under

---

(*a*) "Principe di accorgimento e di valore non ordinario; per cui da tutti "i più potenti sovrani d'Italia, era a gara richiesto per condurre le loro "truppe, e accolto co' i più singolari onori."

Tirab. Storia della Lett. Ital. v. vi. *parte* i. *p.* 13.

(*b*) L'anno 1467 di Luglio, ci venne il duca Galeazzo di Milano, ch' era in campo contro Bartolomeo da Bergamo, in Romagna, che vessava lo stato nostro, e alloggiò in casa nostra, che così volle, benchè dalla signoria gli fusse stato apparecchiato in Santa Maria novella. *Ricordi di Lorenzo, in App. No.* XII.

1467.

under the command of Alessandro Sforza. The engagement soon became general, and continued from noon till evening. Machiavelli assures us, that at the close of the battle both parties kept the field, that not a soldier lost his life, and that only a few horses were wounded, and some prisoners taken; but historians of more veracity have given a different relation (*a*). It is however certain, that no important consequences resulted from a contest that had excited so much expectation. The troops shortly afterwards withdrew into their winter quarters, which afforded the Florentines an opportunity, by the mediation of the marquis of Ferrara, of negociating for a peace. This was accordingly effected without any stipulation being introduced on the part of the exiles; and thus the storm which seemed for a while to threaten the destruction of the Florentine state, after having been repressed in its first fury, gradually abated, and at length settled in a perfect calm.

Piero promotes the interests of learning.

Although Piero de' Medici was inferior in talents both to his father Cosmo and his son Lorenzo, yet he gave repeated proofs of a strong attachment to the cause of letters, and continued an hereditary protection to those men of learning

(*a*) Platina, (I quote the Italian translation,) in reference to this battle, says, "Quelli, ch' in questa battaglia si retrovarono, dicono che nel età nostra la "maggior non si vedesse, e vi morirono molti." (*Plat. v.* i. *p.* 448. *Ven.* 1744.) And Ammirato expressly informs us, in direct contradiction to Machiavelli, who, says he, "schernendo, come egli soul far, quella milizia, dice che non vi "mori niuno," that both armies fought with great courage; that according to the most moderate accounts 300 men and 400 horses were killed; that another account stated the loss at 800, and another at 1000 men. He also cites the Venetian history of Sabellico, who denominates this a very bloody engagement. "Cosi," says he, "siamo trascurati à saper la verità delle cose."

Amm. v. iii. *p.* 102.

learning who, under the patronage of his father, had arisen in, or been attracted to Florence. In the year 1441 he had been engaged in promoting a literary contest in that city, by proposing a premium for the best poem on a given subject. The reward of the victor was to be a coronet of silver imitating a laurel wreath. The secretaries of the pope were appointed to decide upon the merits of the candidates. Splendid preparations were made. Several competitors appeared, and publicly recited their poems; but the laudable intentions of Piero were defeated by the folly or the knavery of the ecclesiastics, who gave the prize to the church of S. Maria, pretending that the merits of the pieces were so nearly equal that a decision was impossible. This absurd determination occasioned great dissatisfaction to the Florentines, and was probably considered not only as obliquely satirizing the candidates, but the city itself (*a*).

Leo Battista Alberti.

The coadjutor of Piero de' Medici on this occasion was the celebrated Leo Battista Alberti, who, independent of his extraordinary talents as an artist, deserves particular notice as one of the earliest scholars that appeared in the revival of letters (*b*). He first distinguished himself by

(*a*) These poems are however yet preserved in the Laurentian library, Plut. xc. cod. xxxviii. The subject is *Friendship*. The derided candidates were Michele di Noferi, Francesco Altobianco, Antonio Allio, afterwards bishop of Fiesole, Mariotto Davanzati, Anselmo Calderoni, and Francesco Malecarni. Pozzetti, somewhat unfortunately, denominates this contest *The triumph of literature*. (*v. L. B. Alberti, laud. a Pompilio Pozzetti*, 4to. *Flor.* 1789.)

(*b*) Alberti was of a noble family of Florence, but was born at Venice in 1404. In his youth he was remarkable for his agility, strength, and skill in bodily exercises. An unquenchable thirst of knowledge possessed him from his

by his Latin comedy intitled *Philodoxios*, copies of which he distributed amongst his friends, as the work of Lepidus, an ancient Roman poet. The literati were effectually deceived, and bestowed the highest applauses upon a piece which they conceived to be a precious remnant of antiquity. It first appeared about the year 1425, when the rage for ancient manuscripts was at its height, and Lepidus for a while took his rank with Plautus and with Terence (*a*). As Alberti advanced in years, he turned his attention to practical knowledge, and the present times are indebted to him for many useful and amusing inventions (*b*). In his Latin treatises, which have been translated into Italian by Cosimo Bartoli, and published under the name of *Opuscoli Morali*, he appears as an author on a great variety of subjects, but he is better known by his treatise on architecture, which has been translated into many languages. Nor ought it to be forgotten, that Alberti made an attempt to reconcile the measure of the Latin distich with the genius of his native

earliest years. In the learned languages he made a speedy and uncommon proficiency, and had perhaps a more general acquaintance with the sciences than any man of that age. Of all the fine arts he had a thorough and practical knowledge; and as a painter, a sculptor, but particularly as an architect, obtained no small share of celebrity.

Vasari, vita di Alberti. L. B. Abl. laud. à Pozzetti, ut sup.

(*a*) This piece was written by Alberti during the confinement of sickness, occasioned by too close an application to study. It was printed in the succeeding century by the younger Aldo Manutio, who had procured a manuscript copy, and not aware of the deception, gravely confesses in the proeme his ignorance of *Lepidus* the Roman poet.

(*b*) On the authority of Vasari we may attribute to Alberti the discovery of the *Camera oscura*, though that invention is generally given to Giambattista Porta in the succeeding century. " L'anno 1437 trovò per via d'uno stru-

CHAP. II.

tive tongue, in which he has been followed by Claudio Tolomei, and other writers (*a*).

The reputation of Alberti as an architect, though it deservedly stands high in the estimation of posterity, must however be considered as inferior to that of Filippo Brunelleschi, who is the true father of the art in modern times. Vasari expresses his disapprobation of some part of the labours of Alberti. His paintings were not numerous, nor on a large scale; nor did he in this branch of art arrive at great practical perfection, which, as Vasari observes, is not much to be wondered at, as his time was mostly devoted to other studies. His principal merit is certainly to be sought for in his useful discoveries, and his preceptive writings. He was the first author who attempted practical treatises on the arts of design, all of which, but more particularly his treatise on architecture, are allowed to exhibit

---

" mento il modo di lucidare le prospettive naturali et diminuire le figure," &c. (*Vasari, in vita di Alberti, da Bottari, Fir.* 1771.) The invention of the optical machine for exhibiting drawings so as to imitate nature, is indisputably due to him. " Opera ex ipsa arte pingendi effecit inaudita, & spectatoribus " incredibilia, quæ quidam parva in capsa conclusa pusillum per foramen " ostenderet. Vidisses illic montes maximos," &c.

Alb. vita, ab Anonymo. ap. Vasari. ut sup.

(*a*) Of this Vasari has preserved the following specimen:

" Questa per estrema miserabile pistola mando,
" A te, che spregi miseramente noi."

Some of the sonnets of Alberti are yet extant, and are printed with those of Burchiello, with whom he seems to have been on terms of intimacy; and Pozzetti, who has lately favoured the public with a very full account of this extraordinary man, has also pointed out several of his poetical pieces, which are yet preserved in different libraries of Italy.

hibit a profound knowledge of his subject, and will long continue to do honour to his memory.

Cristoforo Landino.

Had all the other professors of letters been silent as to the merits of Piero de' Medici, the applauses bestowed on him by Cristoforo Landino would alone be sufficient to rescue his memory from neglect. Landino had indeed every motive of gratitude to the family of his patron. He was born a Florentine, and being early disgusted with the study of the civil law, devoted himself to that of poetry and polite letters. In pursuing his inclinations he had the good fortune to find the road that led him to honour and to affluence. The bounty of a private friend supported him through the early part of his education, to which the finances of his family were inadequate, and the munificence of Cosmo de' Medici compleated what the kindness of Angelo da Todi had begun. His proficiency in the Greek language was remarkable, even at a period when the study of it was in its highest vigour, and immediately supplied from its native fountain. The philosophy of Aristotle, and the dogmas of the stoics, had early engaged his attention; but from his intercourse with the Medici, and his intimacy with Ficino, he afterwards became a decided partisan of the new philosophy, and was among the few learned men whom Ficino thought proper to consult on his translation of the works of Plato. The Latin elegies of Landino (*a*) bear

(*a*) To these poems Landino prefixed the name of *Xandra*, being the diminutive of *Alessandra*, the appellation of his poetical mistress. This work has not been published; but the Canonico Bandini has given us some extracts from it in his *Spec. Lit. Flor.* v. i. p. 110, &c. The prefatory verses to his second book, addressed to Piero de' Medici, are given in the Appendix, No. XIII.

CHAP. II.

bear ample testimony to the virtues, the liberality, and the accomplishments of Piero de' Medici, whom he constantly honours with the appellation of his Mæcenas, and seems to have selected from the other individuals of that illustrious family, as the object of his particular affection and veneration.

Piero patronises other eminent scholars.

If we consider the numerous testimonies that remain of the liberality of Piero de' Medici to men of learning, and advert at the same time to the infirm state of his health, and the short period during which he enjoyed the direction of the republic, we shall not hesitate in allotting to him a distinguished rank amongst the early promoters of letters. To Piero, Benedetto Accolti addressed, in terms of high commendation, his history of the wars between the christians and the infidels (*a*), a work of considerable historical credit, and which, in the succeeding century, served as a guide to Torquato Tasso, in his immortal poem the *Gerusalemme liberata* (*b*). An uninterrupted friendship subsisted

(*a*) This work, written in Latin, was first printed at Venice in 1532; again, at Basil, 1544, and at Florence, 1623; the last-mentioned edition being accompanied by the annotations of Thomas Dempster, a Scotchman, and professor of humanity in the college of Bologna. It was translated into Greek by Irone Ducas, and printed at Paris in 1620; and into Italian by Francesco Baldelli, and published by Giolito at Venice in 1549.

Zeno. Diss. Voss. v. i. p. 163.

(*b*) Accolti is not less celebrated as a civilian than as a polite scholar. He was born at Arezzo, in 1415, whence his usual appellation of Benedetto Aretino. Having been sent on an embassy from that place to Florence, he took up his residence there, and in the year 1459 succeeded Poggio Bracciolini as secretary to the republic, in which office he continued till his death, in 1466. Besides his history, he is the author of a dialogue, intitled, *De præstantia virorum sui ævi*, inscribed to Cosmo de' Medici, which was first printed in 1689. Paulo

sisted between Piero and the celebrated Donato Acciajuoli, who inscribed to him several of his learned works (*a*). The Laurentian library contains many similar instances of the gratitude and observance of the scholars of the time. Amongst those deserving of more particular notice is Francesco Ottavio, who dedicated to Piero his poem *De cœtu poetarum*, in which he hesitates not to represent his patron as surpassing the example of his father, in his attention to the cause of literature, and in his kindness to its professors (*b*).

Giostra of Lorenzo and Giuliano.

No sooner was the city of Florence restored to peace, and the dread of a foreign enemy removed, than the natural disposition of the inhabitants for splendid exhibitions began to revive. Amongst other amusements, a tournament was held, in which Lorenzo de' Medici bore away the prize, being a helmet of silver, with a figure of Mars as the crest. In another encounter Giuliano had equal success with his brother. This incident is the more entitled to our notice, as it has given rise to two of the most celebrated Italian poems of the fifteenth century, the *Giostra of Lorenzo de' Medici*, by Luca Pulci; and the *Giostra of Giuliano de' Medici*, by Angelo Politiano.

1468.

At

Cortesi, a severe censor, allows that his history is a work of great industry, and that it throws considerable light on a very difficult subject.

Zeno. Diss. Voss. v. i. *p.* 164. *Cortes. de hom. doct. p.* 22.

(*a*) *Band. Cat. Bib. Laur. v.* ii. *p.* 554, 748.

(*b*) This poem is published in the *Carmina Illustr. Poetar. Ital. v.* vii. *p.* 1.

CHAP. II.

At what particular time this event took place, and whether the two brothers signalized themselves on the same, or on different occasions, has been rendered doubtful by the inattention and discordant relations of different writers, who have directly or incidentally adverted to this subject. Amongst these, Machiavelli has misinformed (*a*), and Paulus Jovius confused his readers (*b*). Of the authors who have followed them, some have employed themselves

(*a*) If we believe Machiavelli, this exhibition took place in 1465, (at which time Lorenzo was only seventeen years of age,) and was intended merely to turn the attention of the people from the affairs of state. " Per tor via adunque questo otio, e dare che pensare à gli huomini qualche cosa che levassero " i pensieri dello stato, sendo già passato l' anno che Cosimo era morto, presero occasione, da che fusse bene rallegrar la città, e ordinarono due feste " (secondo l' altre che in quella città si fanno) solennissime. Una che rappresentava quando i tre magi vennero d' oriente dietro alla stella che dimostrava la natività di Christo; la quale era di tanta pompa & si magnifica, " che in ordinarla e farla, teneva più mesi occupata tutta la città. L' altra " fù uno torniamento dove i primi giovani della città si essercitarono insieme " coi più nominati cavallieri d' Italia; e tra i giovani fiorentini il più riputato " fu Lorenzo, primo genito di Piero, il quale non per gratia, ma per proprio " suo valore ne riportò il primo honore." *Mac. Hist. lib.* vii.

(*b*) In his elogies Jovius adverts to the Giostra of Lorenzo, as prior to that of Giuliano. " Politianus à prima statim juventa admirabilis ingenii " nomen adeptus est: cum novo illustrique poemate, Juliani Medicis equestres " ludos celebrasset; Luca Pulcio nobili poeta omnium confessione superato, " qui Laurentii fratris ludicrum equestris pugnæ spectaculum, iisdem modis " & numeris decantarat," &c. *In Elog. vir. doct.* But in his life of Leo X. he directly contradicts his own evidence. Speaking of the tournament of Giuliano, he says: " Ejus gloriosi laboris premium fuit triumphus Politiani " divini poetæ carminibus celebratus. Nec multo post Laurentius, ut fraternis laudibus æquaretur, novum spectaculum periculocissimæ pugnæ edidit. " Hujus quoque speciocissimi certaminis memoriam Pulcius ipse, Politiani " æmulus, perjucundo edito poemate sempiternam fecit."

Jovius, in vitâ Leonis X. lib. i.

selves in comparing or contesting these various authorities (*a*), whilst others have gone a step further, and ingrafted their own absurdities on the errors of their predecessors (*b*). Even amongst those who are entitled to a greater share of attention, Fabroni has decided wrong (*c*), and Menckenius, after a full inquiry into all previous testimony, confesses his inability to decide at all (*d*). In solving this difficulty, it might have been expected that recourse would have been had, in the first instance, to the internal evidence of the poems themselves, by which all doubts on the subject would have been effectually removed; but Menckenius had never seen even the poem of Politiano, though it is of much more common occurrence than that of Pulci (*e*); and Fabroni, with the poem of Pulci before him, has suffered himself to be betrayed into an anachronism by the authority of Machiavelli. In the poem last mentioned,

---

(*a*) Bayle cites these different passages of Jovius, but, as usual, leaves his reader to form his own judgment upon them. *Dict. Hist. Art. Politien.* Vide *Boissardum in Elog. vir. doct. & Jo. Mich. Brutum in Hist. Flor. lib.* ii. *ap. Bayle.*

(*b*) Varillas and Baillet. The former of whom gives an account of the poem of Politiano, sufficiently absurd to afford amusement to the reader, the substance of which has been adopted by the latter. *Anec. de Flor. p.* 194. *Jugemens des Savans, v.* v. *p.* 29.

(*c*) Fabroni places this event before the conspiracy of Luca Pitti, and the attempt on the life of Piero de' Medici. *Laur. Med. vita, v.* i. *p.* 20.

(*d*) "Scriptorem qui hunc exsolvat nodum, ego quidem scio nullum. Certi "adeo hac in re nihil definire audeo," &c. *Menck. in vitâ Politiani, p.* 44.

(*e*) "Compertum mihi est per Italos, mei studiosissimos, atque hujus "carminis probe gnaros, duobus illud libris distingui, nec ad finem perductum "esse alterum," &c. *Menck. in vitâ Pol. p.* 43.

CHAP. II.

mentioned, not only the year, but the precise day on which the tournament took place is particularly specified. This appears to have been the seventh of February 1468 (*a*), at which time Lorenzo was in his twentieth year, to which the poet also expressly adverts (*b*), as well as to the attack lately made upon the Florentines by Bartolomeo Coglione, called of Bergamo (*c*). The circumstance that gave rise to this solemnity was the marriage of Braccio Martello, an intimate friend of Lorenzo (*d*). The second prize of honour was adjudged to Carlo

(*a*) " L'anno correva mille quattro cento
" Et sessant'octo dall' incarnazione,
" Et ordinossi per mezzo Gennaio,
" Ma il septimo dì fessi di Febraio."

Giostra di Lor.

It must be observed that the year, according to the Florentine computation, did not terminate till the 25th day of March.

(*b*) " Ch' era al principio del ventesimo anno,
" Quando e' fu paziente à tanto affanno."

Ib.

(*c*) " Ma poi che in tutto fu l'orgoglio spento
" Del furor bergamasco: al fier leone
" Venne la palma, et ciascun fu contento
" Di far la giostra nel suo antico agone."

Ib.

(*d*) " E' si faceva le nozze in Fiorenza
" Quando al ciel piacque, di Braccio Martello,
" Giovane ornata di tanta eccellenza
" Ch'io non saprei chi comparare à quello," &c.

Ib.

Carlo Borromei (*a*). At this time Giuliano was only in his fifteenth year; but he made his appearance on horseback among the combatants (*b*), and obtained a prize during the same festival; it being evident from the poem of Pulci, that he was to try his courage on a future day (*c*). The poem of Politiano contains also sufficient proof that the tournament of Giuliano is to be placed at no very distant period from that of Lorenzo, as it appears Lorenzo was not then married, although that event took place within a few months after he had signalized himself in this contest (*d*). If further confirmation were necessary, it may be found in the Ricordi of Lorenzo, who defrayed the expence of this exhibition, which cost ten thousand florins, and was held in the place of S. Croce. In this authentic document

(*a*) " Trassonsi gli elmi i giostranti di testa
" E posto fine à si lungo martoro:
" Fu data al giovinetto con gran festo
" Il primo honor di Marte, con l' alloro,
" Et l' altro a Carlo Borromei si resta."

Giostra di Lor.

(*b*) " Poi seguitava il suo fratel Giuliano,
" Sopra un destrier tutto d' acciaio coperto."

(*c*) " Digli, che sono per Giuliano certi squilli
" Che deston come Carnasciale il corno,
" Il suo cor magno all' aspettata giostra;
" Ultima gloria di Fiorenza nostra."

Ib. in fine.

(*d*) *Giostra di Giuliano de' Med. lib.* ii. *stan.* 4.

document Lorenzo speaks with becoming modesty of these his youthful atchievements (*a*).

Poem of Luca Pulci.

It must be confessed that the poem of Pulci derives its merit rather from the minute information it gives us respecting this exhibition, than from its poetical excellence (*b*). A considerable part of it is employed in describing the preparations for the tournament, and the habits and appearance of the combatants. The umpires were, Roberto da Sanseverino, Carlo Pandolfini, Tomaso Soderini, Ugolino Martelli, Niccolo Giugni, and Buongianni Gianfigliazzi. The candidates for the prize were eighteen in number. The steed upon which Lorenzo made his first appearance was presented to him by Ferdinand king of Naples. That on which he relied in the combat, by Borso marquis of Ferrara. The duke of Milan had furnished him with his suit of armour. His motto was *Le tems revient.* His device, the *fleurs de lys*, the privilege of using the arms of France having shortly before been conceded to the Medici by Louis XI. by a solemn act (*c*). His first conflict was with Carlo Borromei; his next with Braccio

(*a*) *Ric. di Lor. in App. No.* XII.

(*b*) Of this poem I have seen only two editions; the first printed without note of date or place, but apparently about the year 1500, under the title of LA GIOSTRA DI LORENZO DE' MEDICI MESSA IN RIMA DA LUIGI DE' PULCI ANNO, M.CCCC.LXVIII. in which it is to be observed, that this work is erroneously attributed to *Luigi*, the author of the *Morgante*, instead of *Luca*, his brother. The other edition is printed in Florence by the Giunti, in 1572, accompanied by the *Ciriffo Calvaneo*, and the *Epistole* of *Luca Pulci*, and is there attributed to its proper author.

(*c*) The grant of this privilege yet remains. *v. App.* No. XIV.

Braccio de' Medici, who attacked him with such strength and courage, that if the stroke had taken place, Orlando himself, as the poet assures us, could not have withstood the shock. Lorenzo took speedy vengeance, but his spear breaking into a hundred pieces, his adversary was preserved from a total overthrow. He then assailed Carlo da Forme, whose helmet he split, and whom he nearly unhorsed. Lorenzo then changing his steed, made a violent attack upon Benedetto Salutati, who had just couched his lance ready for the combat.

Vedestu mai falcon calare a piombo,
E poi spianarsi, e batter forte l' ale,
C' ha tratto fuori della schiera il colombo?
Così Lorenzo Benedetto assale;
Tanto che l' aria fa fischiar pel rombo,
Non va si presto folgor, non che strale;
Dettonsi colpi che parvon d'Achille,
Et balza un mongibel fuori di faville.

Hast thou not seen the falcon in his flight,
When high in air on balanced wing he hung,
On some lone straggler of the covey light?
—On Benedetto thus Lorenzo sprung.
Whistled the air, as ardent for the fight,
Fleet as the arrow flies he rushed along;
Achilles' rage their meeting strokes inspires,
Their sparkling armour rivals Etna's fires.

Poem of Politiano.

The poem of Politiano is of a very different character, and though produced about the same period of time is a

 century

century posterior in point of refinement (*a*). The age of Politiano when he wrote it scarcely exceeded fourteen years, and it must not be denied that the poem bears upon the face of it the marks of juvenility—but what a manhood does it promise?—From such an early exuberance of blossom what fruits might we not expect? The general approbation with which it was received, must have been highly flattering both to the poet and the hero; nor has posterity appealed from the decision. On the contrary, it has been uniformly allowed that this was one of the earliest productions in the revival of letters, that breathed the true spirit of poetry; and that it not only far excelled the Giostra of Pulci, but essentially contributed towards the establishment of a better taste in Italy.

It may seem strange, that although this poem be of considerable length, containing about fourteen hundred lines, it is left unfinished, and breaks off even before the tournament begins. Instead of giving us, like Pulci, a minute

(*a*) The *Stanze* of Politiano on the *Giostra* of Giuliano de' Medici have been frequently printed. In the earliest edition I have seen, they are accompanied by his Fable of Orfeo, *stampate in Firenze, per Giannstephano di Carlo da Pavia, a stanza di Ser Piero Pacini da Pescia, questo dì* XV. *d' Ottobre* M. D. XIII. This, however, is not the first edition, they having been printed in the lifetime of Politiano, though without his concurrence, as appears by the dedication from Alessandro Sartio to Galeazzo Bentivoglio, reprinted in the edition of 1513, wherein Sartio alludes to their having been printed by Plato de Benedictis, one of the best printers of the fifteenth century, and adds, "Credo "ancora che se alquanto al Politiano dispiacerà che queste sue Stanze dallui "già disprezzate, si stampino; pur all incontro gli piacerà che havendosi una "volta a divulgare, sotto el titolo e nome di tua signoria si divulghino." Many subsequent editions have been published; at Venice, 1521, 1537, &c. and at Padua, by Comino, 1728, 1751, and 1765.

nute description of the habillments of the combatants, the poet takes a wider circuit, and indulges himself in digressions and episodes of great extent. The express purpose for which it was written would not indeed be very apparent, were it not for the information afforded us in the commencement; and even here the author does not propose to confine himself to one subject in particular, but professes to celebrate the feats of arms and pomps of Florence, and the loves and studies of Giuliano de' Medici (*a*). Although Giuliano be the subject, the poem is addressed to Lorenzo, whose favour Politiano earnestly supplicates.

E tu, ben nato LAUR', sotto il cui velo
Fiorenza lieta in pace si riposa,
Nè teme i venti, o'l minacciar del cielo,
O Giove irato in vista più crucciosa;
Accogli al ombra del tuo santo ostelo
La voce umil, tremante, e paurosa;
Principio, e fin, di tutte le mie voglie,
Che sol vivon d' odor delle tue foglie.

Deh sarà mai che con più alte note,
Se non contrasti al mio voler fortuna,
Lo spirto delle membre, che divote
Ti fur da' fati, insin già dalla cuna,
Risuoni te dai Numidi a Boote,
Dagl' Indi, al mar che'l nostro ciel imbruna,
E, posto'l

(*a*) " Le gloriose pompe, e i fieri ludi
" Della città che 'l freno allenta e stringe
" A' magnanimi Toschi: e i regni crudi
" Di quella dea che'l terzo ciel dipinge:
" E i premj degni a gli onorati studi."

CHAP. II.

E, posto'l nido in tuo felice ligno,
Di roco augel diventi un bianco cigno?

High born LORENZO, laurel—in whose shade
Thy Florence rests, nor fears the lowering storm,
Nor threatening signs in heaven's high front display'd,
Nor Jove's dread anger in its fiercest form;
O to the trembling muse afford thine aid,
—The muse that courts thee, timorous and forlorn,
Lives in the shadow of thy prosperous tree,
And bounds her every fond desire to thee

Ere long the spirit that this frame inspires,
This frame, that from its earliest hour was thine,
If fortune frown not on my vast desires,
Shall spread to distant shores thy name divine,
To lands that feel the sun's intenser fires,
That mark his earliest rise, his last decline;
Nurs'd in the shade thy spreading branch supplies,
Tuneless before, a tuneful swain I rise.

The poet then proceeds to describe the youthful employments and pursuits of Giuliano de' Medici, and particularly adverts to his repugnance to surrender his heart to the attacks continually made upon it by the fair sex.

Ah quante Ninfe per lui sospirorno!
Ma fu sì altero sempre il giovinetto,
Che mai le Ninfe amanti lo piegorno,
Mai potè riscaldarsi 'l freddo petto.
Facea sovente pe' boschi soggiorno;
Inculto sempre, e rigido in aspetto;

Il

Il volto diffendea dal solar raggio
Con ghirlanda di pino, o verde faggio.

E poi, quando nel ciel parean le stelle,
Tutto gioioso a suo magion tornava;
E'n compagnia delle nove sorelle,
Celesti versi con disio cantava:
E d' antica virtù mille fiammelle,
Con gli alti carmi ne' petti destava:
Così chiamando amor lascivia umana,
Si godea con le Muse, e con Diana.

For Julian many a maiden heav'd the sigh,
And many a glance the tender flame confest;
But not the radiance of the brightest eye,
Could melt the icy rigour of his breast.
Wild thro' the trackless woods the youth would hie,
Severe of aspect, and disdaining rest:
Whilst the dark pine, or spreading beech supplied
A wreathe, from summer suns his head to hide.

When evening's star its milder lustre lends,
The wanderer to his cheerful home retires,
There every muse his lov'd return attends,
And generous aims, and heavenly verse inspires:
Deep thro' his frame the sacred song descends,
With thirst of ancient praise his soul that fires;
And Love, fond trifler, mourns his blunted dart,
That harmless flies where Dian shields the heart.

After some beautiful verses, in which Giuliano reproaches the weakness of those who devote themselves to the

the tender passion, he goes to the chace, which gives the poet an opportunity of displaying his talent for description, in which he particularly excels. Love, who feels his divinity insulted, employs a stratagem to subdue the obdurate heart of Giuliano. A beautiful white hind crosses his way, which he pursues, but which perpetually eludes his endeavours to wound it, and leads him far distant from his companions. When his courser is almost exhausted with fatigue, a nymph makes her appearance, and Giuliano, astonished at her beauty, forgets the pursuit, and accosts her with trepidation and amazement. Her answer compleats her triumph. Evening comes on, and Giuliano returns home, alone and pensive. The poet then enters upon a description of the court of Venus in the iſland of Cyprus, which extends to a considerable length, and is ornamented with all the graces of poetry. Cupid, having compleated his conquest, returns thither to recount his success to his mother; who, in order to enhance its value, is desirous that Giuliano should signalize himself in a tournament. The whole band of loves accordingly repairs to Florence, and Giuliano prepares for the combat. In a dream sent by Venus, he seems to come off with victory. On his return, crowned with olive and laurel, his mistress appears to him, but is soon enveloped in a thick cloud, and carried from his sight; which incident the poet applies to the sudden death of the beautiful Simonetta, the mistress of Giuliano (*a*). Some consolatory verses are applied to the

(*a*) On this lady we have an epitaph by Politiano, (the substance of which is said to have been suggested to him by Giuliano,) printed amongst his smaller

the lover, who awaking, invokes Minerva to crown his attempt with glory. But here the narrative is interrupted, nor does it appear that the author resumed his taſk at any subsequent period, having thrown the work aside as a production of his younger years, scarcely deserving of his riper attention.

Disputationes Camaldulenses.

The proficiency made by Lorenzo and Giuliano in active accomplishments, did not however retard their progress in the pursuits of science, or the acquisition of knowledge. About the year 1468, Landino wrote his *Disputationes Camaldulenses*, which, at the same time that they open to us the means of instruction, adopted by him in the education of his pupils, give us the fairest evidence of their proficiency (*a*). In the infancy of science, particular departments of knowledge are frequently cultivated with great success; but it is only in periods of high improvement that men are accustomed to comprehend the general

---

poems, in *Opp. Ald.* 1498. And Bernardo Pulci has also left an elegy on her death, published by Miscomini at Florence in 1494.

(*a*) This work was first published without note of place or date, but, as Bandini supposes, about the year 1472, (*Spec. Lit. Flor. v.* ii. *p.* 5.) or 1475. (*Ib. v.* ii. *p.* 192.) De Bure conjectures it was printed about the year 1480. (*Bibliographie Instructive, v.* iv. *p.* 272. *Ed.* 1763.) This edition is extremely scarce. Bandini could not find a copy in the Vatican library, although it appears in the catalogue. It was reprinted at Straſburg in 1508. The title of this last edition, now before me, is CHRISTOPHORI LANDINI FLORENTINI LIBRI QUATTUOR. *Primus de vita activa et contemplativa. Secundus de summo bono. Tertius et quartus in Publii Virgilii Maronis Allegorias*; and at the close, "*Has Camaldulenses Disputationes pulcherioribus typis Mathias Schürerius, artium doctor excussit in officina sua litteratoria Argentoraci die* XXVI *Augusti. Anno Christi* M.D.VIII. *Regnante Caesare Maximiliano Augusto.*"

L

general plan of human life, and to allot to every occupation and pursuit its proper degree of importance. The *Disputationes Camaldulenses* afford us sufficient proof that the Florentines had, at this early period, arrived at that mental elevation, which enabled them to take a distinct view of the various objects by which they were surrounded, and to apply all that was then known of science to its best uses. In the introduction to this work Landino informs us, that having, in company with his brother Piero, made an excursion from his villa in Casentina to a monastery in the wood of Camaldoli, they found that Lorenzo and Giuliano de' Medici had arrived there before them, accompanied by Alamanni Rinuccini, and Piero and Donato Acciajuoli; all men of learning and eloquence, who had applied themselves with great diligence to philosophical studies. The pleasure of their first meeting was enhanced by the arrival of Leo Battista Alberti, who, returning from Rome, had met with Marsilio Ficino, and had prevailed upon him to pass a few days, during the heat of autumn, in the healthful retreat of Camaldoli. Mariotto, abbot of the monastery, introduced to each other his learned friends, and the remainder of the day, for it was then drawing towards evening, was passed in attending to the conversation of Alberti, of whose disposition and accomplishments Landino gives us a most favourable idea (*a*). On the following day, after the performance

---

(*a*) Erat enim vir ille, omnium quos plura jam secula produxerint, omni humanitatis, ac salium genere cumulatissimus; nam quid de litteris loquar? cum nihil omnino extet, quod quidem homini scire fas sit, in quo ille scienter, prudenterque, non versaretur. *Land. Disput. Camal. p.* 7. *Ed.* 1508.

formance of religious duties, the whole company agreed to ascend through the wood towards the summit of the hill; and in a short time arrived at a solitary spot, where the extended branches of a large beech overhung a clear spring of water. At the invitation of Alberti, a conversation here takes place, which he begins by observing, that those persons may be esteemed peculiarly happy, who, having improved their minds by study, can withdraw themselves at intervals from public engagements and private anxiety, and in some agreeable retreat indulge themselves in an ample range through all the objects of the natural and moral world. "But if this be an occupation "suitable for all men of learning, it is more particularly "so for you," continued Alberti, addressing himself to Lorenzo and Giuliano, "on whom the direction of the "affairs of the republic is likely, from the increasing in-"firmities of your father, soon to devolve (*a*). For al-"though, Lorenzo, you have given proof of such virtues "as would induce us to think them rather of divine than "human origin; although there seems to be no under-"taking so momentous as not to be accomplished by that "prudence and courage which you have displayed, even "in your early years; and although the impulse of youth-"ful ambition, and the full enjoyment of those gifts of for-"tune

(*a*) *Land. Disput. Camal. p.* 7. Bandini conjectures that Landino composed this work about the year 1460, (*Spec. Lit. Flor. v.* ii. *p.* 2.) at which time Lorenzo was only twelve years of age. But from the above passage it is evident that it was written towards the latter part of the life of Piero de' Medici, and probably about the year 1468, when Lorenzo had already distinguished himself by his successful interference in public affairs.

" tune which have often intoxicated men of high expect-" ation and great virtue, have never yet been able to im-" pel you beyond the just bounds of moderation; yet, both " you, and that republic which you are shortly to direct, " or rather which now in a great measure reposes on your " care, will derive important advantages from those hours " of leisure, which you may pass either in solitary medi-" tation, or social discussion, on the origin and nature of " the human mind. For it is impossible that any person " should rightly direct the affairs of the public, unless he " has previously established in himself virtuous habits, and " enlightened his understanding with that knowledge, " which will enable him clearly to discern why he is called " into existence, what is due to others, and what to him-" self." A conversation then commences between Lorenzo and Alberti, in which the latter endeavours to shew, that as reason is the distinguishing characteristic of man, the perfection of his nature is only to be attained by the cultivation of his mind, and by a total abstraction from worldly pursuits. Lorenzo, who is not a mere silent auditor, opposes a doctrine which, if carried to its extreme, would separate man from his duties, and contends, that no essential distinction can be made between active and contemplative life, but that each should mutually assist and improve the other; and this he illustrates in such a variety of instances, that although it is evidently the object of Landino, through the medium of Alberti, to establish the pure Platonic dogma, that abstract contemplation can alone constitute the essence of human happiness, yet Lorenzo appears to have raised objections, which the ingenuity of the philosopher in the sequel of the dispute seems

scarcely

scarcely to have invalidated (*a*). On the following day the same subject is pursued, and Alberti fully explains the doctrine of Plato respecting the true end and aim of human life; illustrating it by the opinions of many of the most celebrated followers of that philosopher. The third and fourth days are spent in a commentary by Alberti on the Æneid, in which he endeavours to shew, that under the fiction of the poem are represented the leading doctrines of that philosophy which had been the subject of their previous discussion. Whatever may be thought of the propriety of such a construction, certain it is that there are many passages in this poem which seem strongly to countenance such an opinion; and at all events, the idea is supported by Alberti with such a display of learning, and such a variety of proofs, as must have rendered his commentary highly amusing and instructive to his youthful auditors.

Lorenzo's description of his mistress.

It must not however be supposed, that amidst his studious avocations, Lorenzo was insensible to that passion which has at all times been the soul of poetry, and has been

(*a*) Alberti appears, from the following passage, to have almost given up the contest: "Nam quod aiebas maximum idcirco inde provenire reipublicæ "detrimentum quod occupatis excellentioribus ingeniis circa veri cognitionem, "ipsa a deterioribus regatur, nunquam profecto cessabit sapiens, quin se de "rebus arduis consulentes recta semper moneat; unde si non opera, consilio "tamen juvabit." (*Quæst. Camal. p.* 28.) Thus the philsopher is obliged to stoop from his celestial height, and to disturb the calm repose of his mind with the cares of this grosser world.—Beautiful, but impracticable system of philosophy! which must perhaps wait for its completion till another state of being!

been so philosophically, and so variously described in his own writings. To this subject he has indeed devoted a considerable portion of his works; but it is somewhat extraordinary that he has not thought proper, upon any occasion, to inform us of the name of his mistress; nor has he gratified our curiosity so far as to give her even a poetical appellation. Petrarca had his Laura, and Dante his Beatrice; but Lorenzo has studiously concealed the name of the sovereign of his affections, leaving it to be ascertained by a thousand brilliant descriptions of her superlative beauty and accomplishments. In the usual order of things it is love that creates the poet; but with Lorenzo, poetry appears to have been the occasion of his love. The circumstances, as related by himself, are these (a)—" A young lady of great personal at-" tractions happened to die in Florence; and as she had " been very generally admired and beloved, so her death " was as generally lamented. Nor was this to be won-" dered at, for independent of her beauty, her manners " were so engaging, that almost every person who had " any acquaintance with her, flattered himself that he had " obtained the chief place in her affections. This fatal " event excited the extreme regret of her admirers; " and as she was carried to the place of burial, with " her face uncovered, those who had known her when " living pressed for a last look at the object of their " adoration,

(a) *Commento di Lor. de' Medici sopra alcuni de' suoi Sonetti nel fine delle sue Poesie volgari, p.* 123, 129, *&c. Ed. Ald.* 1554.

" adoration, and accompanied her funeral with their
" tears (a).

" Whilst death smil'd lovely in her lovely face."

Morte bella parea nel suo bel volto.

PETR.

" On this occasion all the eloquence and the wit of
" Florence were exerted in paying due honours to her
" memory, both in prose and in verse. Amongst the
" rest, I also composed a few sonnets; and in order to give
" them greater effect, I endeavoured to convince myself
" that I too had been deprived of the object of my love,
" and to excite in my own mind all those passions that
" might enable me to move the affections of others. Un-
" der the influence of this delusion, I began to think how

" severe

(a) From this singular circumstance, compared with the evidence of one of the epigrams of Politiano, we are enabled to determine that this lady was the beautiful Simonetta, the mistress of Giuliano de' Medici, to whose untimely death we have before adverted.

" *In Simonettam.*

" Dum pulchra effertur nigro Simonetta feretro,
" Blandus et exanimi spirat in ore lepos,
" Nactus amor tempus quo non sibi turba caveret,
" Jecit ab occlusis mille faces oculis:
" Mille animos cepit viventis imagine risus;
" Ac morti insultans est mea dixit adhuc;
" Est mea dixit adhuc, nondum totam eripis illam
" Illa vel exanimis militat ecce mihi.
" Dixit—et ingemuit—neque enim satis apta triumphis
" Illa puer vidit tempora—sed lachrymis."

Pol. lib. Epigram. in Op. Ald. 1498.

CHAP. II.

"severe was the fate of those by whom she had been beloved; and from thence was led to consider, whether there was any other lady in this city deserving of such honour and praise, and to imagine the happiness that must be experienced by any one whose good fortune could procure him such a subject for his pen. I accordingly sought for some time without having the satisfaction of finding any one, who, in my judgment, was deserving of a sincere and constant attachment. But when I had nearly resigned all expectations of success, chance threw in my way that which had been denied to my most diligent inquiry; as if the god of love had selected this hopeless period, to give me a more decisive proof of his power. A public festival was held in Florence, to which all that was noble and beautiful in the city resorted. To this I was brought by some of my companions (I suppose as my destiny led) against my will, for I had for some time past avoided such exhibitions; or if at times I attended them, it proceeded rather from a compliance with custom, than from any pleasure I experienced in them. Amongst the ladies there assembled, I saw one of such sweet and attractive manners, that whilst I regarded her I could not help saying, *If this person were possessed of the delicacy, the understanding, the accomplishments of her who is lately dead—most certainly she excels her in the charms of her person.*"

* * *

"Resigning myself to my passion, I endeavoured to discover, if possible, how far her manners and her conversation agreed with her appearance, and here I found such

" such an assemblage of extraordinary endowments, that " it was difficult to say whether she excelled more in her " person, or in her mind. Her beauty was, as I have be- " fore mentioned, astonishing. She was of a just and " proper height. Her complexion extremely fair, but not " pale; blooming, but not ruddy. Her countenance was " serious, without being severe; mild and pleasant, without " levity or vulgarity. Her eyes were lively, without any " indication of pride or conceit. Her whole shape was " so finely proportioned, that amongst other women she " appeared with superior dignity, yet free from the least " degree of formality or affectation. In walking, in danc- " ing, or in other exercises which display the person, every " motion was elegant and appropriate.—Her sentiments " were always just and striking, and have furnished ma- " terials for some of my sonnets; she always spoke at " the proper time, and always to the purpose, so that " nothing could be added, nothing taken away. Though " her remarks were often keen and pointed, yet they were " so tempered as not to give offence. Her understanding " was superior to her sex, but without the appearance of " arrogance or presumption; and she avoided an error too " common among women, who when they think themselves " sensible, become for the most part insupportable (a).

" To

(a) Let it not be thought that I should hazard such a sentiment without the full authority of my author, who has indeed expressed it in more general terms.—" Lo ingegno," says he, " maraviglioso e ciò senza fasta o presun- " zione, e fuggendo un certo vitio commune à donne, à quali parendo d'inten- " dere assai, divengono insupportabili; volendo giudicare ogni cosa, che vol- " garmente le chiamiamo Saccenti."—But we must recollect that Lorenzo de' Medici wrote in the fifteenth century!

CHAP. II.

"To recount all her excellencies would far exceed my "present limits, and I shall therefore conclude with affirm- "ing, that there was nothing which could be desired "in a beautiful and accomplished woman, which was not "in her most abundantly found. By these qualities I was "so captivated, that not a power or faculty of my body or "mind remained any longer at liberty, and I could not "help considering the lady who had died, as the star of "Venus, which at the approach of the sun is totally "overpowered and extinguished." Such is the description that Lorenzo has left us of the object of his passion, in his comment upon the first sonnet which he wrote in her praise; and if we do not allow great latitude to the partiality of a lover, we must confess that few poets have been fortunate enough to meet with a mistress so well calculated to excite their zeal, or to justify the effects of their admiration.

Sonnets in her praise.

The first poetical offspring of this passion was the following

SONETTO.

Lasso a me, quando io son là dove sia
  Quell' angelico, altero, e dolce volto,
  Il freddo sangue intorno al core accolto
  Lascia senza color la faccia mia:
Poi mirando la sua, mi par sì pia,
  Ch'io prendo ardire, e torna il valor tolto
  Amor ne' raggi de' begli occhi involto
  Mostra al mio tristo cor la cieca via;

E par-

E parlandogli alhor, dice, io ti giuro
  Pel santo lume di questi occhi belli
  Del mio stral forza, e del mio regno honore,
Ch'io sarò sempre teco; a ti assicuro
  Esser vera pietà che mostran quelli:
  Credogli lasso! & da me fugge il core.

Alas for me! whene'er my footsteps trace
  Those precincts where eternal beauty reigns,
  The sanguine current from a thousand veins
  Flows round my heart, and pallid grows my face:
But when I mark that smile of heavenly grace,
  Its wonted powers my drooping soul regains;
  Whilst Love, that in her eyes his state maintains,
  Points to my wandering heart its resting place;
And stooping from his beamy mansion swears,
  " By all that forms my power and points my dart,
  " The living lustre of those radiant eyes,
" I still will guide thy way; dismiss thy fears;
  " True are those looks of love." My trusting heart
  Believes th' insidious vow—and from me flies.

The effects of this passion on Lorenzo were such as might be expected to be produced on a young and sensible mind. Instead of the glaring exhibitions to which he had been accustomed, the hurry of the city, and the public avocations of life; he found in himself a disposition for silence and for solitude, and was pleased in associating the ideas produced by every rural object with that of the mistress of his affections. Of these sentiments he has afforded us a specimen in the following sonnet:

CHAP. II.

SONETTO.

Cerchi chi vuol, le pompe, e gli alti honori,
Le piazze, e tempii, & gli edificii magni,
Le delicie, il tesor, qual accompagni
Mille duri pensier, mille dolori:
Un verde praticel pien di bei fiori,
Un rivolo, che l'herba intorno bagni,
Un augelletto, che d' amor si lagni,
Acqueta molto meglio i nostri ardori:
L' ombrose selve, i sassi, e gli alti monti,
Gli antri oscuri, e le fere fuggitive,
Qualche leggiadra ninfa paurosa;
Quivi veggo io con pensier vaghi, e pronti,
Le belle luci, come fossin vive.
Qui me le toglie hor una, hor altra cosa.

Seek he who will in grandeur to be blest,
Place in proud halls, and splendid courts, his joy;
For pleasure, or for gold, his arts employ,
Whilst all his hours unnumbered cares molest.
—A little field in native flow'rets drest,
A rivulet in soft murmurs gliding by,
A bird whose love-sick note salutes the sky,
With sweeter magic lull my cares to rest.
And shadowy woods, and rocks, and towering hills,
And caves obscure, and nature's free-born train,
And some lone nymph that timorous speeds along,
Each in my mind some gentle thought instills
Of those bright eyes that absence shrouds in vain;
—Ah gentle thoughts! soon lost the city cares among.

Having

Having thus happily found a mistress that deserved his attention, Lorenzo was not negligent in celebrating her praises. On this, his constant theme, he has given us a considerable number of beautiful sonnets, canzoni, and other poetical compositions, which, like those of Petrarca, are sometimes devoted to the more general celebration of the person, or the mind of his mistress, and sometimes dwell only on one particular feature or accomplishment; whilst at other times these productions advert to the effects of his own passion, which is analyzed and described with every possible illustration of poetic ingenuity, and philosophic refinement.

Lucretia Donati the object of his passion.

But having thus far traced the passion of Lorenzo, we may now be allowed to ask who was the object of so refined a love; adored without being defined, and celebrated without a name? Fortunately the friends of Lorenzo were not in this respect equally delicate with himself. Politiano, in his Giostra of Giuliano, has celebrated the mistress of Lorenzo by the name of Lucretia. And Ugolino Verini, in his Fiametta, has addressed to her a Latin poem in elegiac verse, in which he shews himself a powerful advocate for Lorenzo, and contends, that whatever might be her accomplishments, he was a lover deserving of her favour (*a*). Valori affords us more particular information; from him we learn that Lucretia was a lady of the noble family of the Donati, equally distinguished by her beauty and her virtue; and a descendant of Curtio Donato, who had rendered

(*a*) v. *App.* No. XV.

rendered himself eminent throughout Italy by his military atchievements (*a*).

Whether the assiduities of Lorenzo, and the persuasions of his friends, were sufficiently powerful to soften that obduracy, which there is reason to presume Lucretia manifested on his first addresses, yet remains a matter of doubt. The sonnets of Lorenzo rise and fall through every degree of the thermometer of love; he exults and he despairs—he freezes and he burns—he sings of raptures too great for mortal sense, and he applauds a severity of virtue that no solicitations can move. From such contradictory testimony what are we to conclude? Lorenzo has himself presented us with the key that unlocks this mystery. From the relation which he has before given, we find that Lucretia was the mistress of the poet, and not of the man. Lorenzo sought for an object to concentrate his ideas, to give them strength and effect, and he found in Lucretia a subject that suited his purpose, and deserved his praise. But having so far realized his mistress, he has dressed and ornamented her according to his own imagination. Every action of her person, every motion of her mind, is subject to his control. She smiles, or she frowns: she refuses, or relents; she is absent, or present; she intrudes upon his solitude by day, or visits him in his nightly dreams, just as his presiding fancy directs. In the midst of these delightful visions Lorenzo was called upon to attend to the dull realities of life. He had now attained his twenty-first year, and his father conceived that it was time

(*a*) *Valor. in vitâ Laur.* p. 8.

Lorenzo marries Clarice Orsini.

time for him to enter into the conjugal state. To this end he had negotiated a marriage between Lorenzo and Clarice, the daughter of Giacopo Orsini, of the noble and powerful Roman family of that name, which had so long contended for superiority with that of the Colonna. Whether Lorenzo despaired of success in his youthful passion, or whether he subdued his feelings at the voice of paternal authority, is left to conjecture only. Certain however it is, that in the month of December 1468, he was betrothed to a person whom it is probable he had never seen, and the marriage ceremony was performed on the fourth day of June 1469 (*a*). That the heart of Lorenzo had little share in this engagement is marked by a striking circumstance. In adverting to his marriage in his Ricordi, he bluntly remarks that he took this lady to wife, *or rather*, says he, *she was given to me* on the day before mentioned (*b*). Notwithstanding this apparent indifference, it appears from indisputable documents, that a real affection subsisted between them; and there is reason to presume that Lorenzo always treated her with particular respect and kindness. Their nuptials were celebrated with great splendor. Two military spectacles were exhibited, one of which represented

(*a*) Bayle is mistaken in supposing that the marriage of Lorenzo took place in 1471. Speaking of Machiavelli, he says; " Il ne marque pas l' annee de " ce mariage ce qui est un grand defaut dans un Ecrivain d' histoire, mais on " peut recueillir de sa narration que ce fut l' an 1471." *Dict. Hist. Art. Politien.* In correcting Bayle, Menckenius falls into a greater error, and places this event in 1472. *Menck. in vitâ Pol. p.* 48.

(*b*) *Ricordi di Lor. App. No.* XII.

CHAP. II.

Visits the duke of Milan.

1469.

represented a field battle of horsemen, and the other the attack and storming of a fortified citadel.

In the month of July following, Lorenzo took another journey to Milan, for the purpose of standing sponsor, in the name of his father, to Galeazzo, the eldest son of Galeazzo Sforza, the reigning duke. In this expedition he was accompanied by Gentile d' Urbino, who gave a regular narrative of their proceedings to Clarice. A letter from Lorenzo himself to his wife is also yet preserved, written upon his arrival at Milan, which, though very short, and not distinguished by any flights of fancy, exhibits more sincerity and affection than the greater part of his amorous sonnets (a).

Lorenzo de' Medici to his wife Clarice.

" *I arrived here in safety, and am in good health. This*
" *I believe will please thee better than any thing else except*
" *my return: at least so I judge from my own desire to be*
" *once more with thee. Associate as much as possible with*
" *my father and my sisters. I shall make all possible speed*
" *to return to thee, for it appears a thousand years till I*
" *see thee again. Pray to God for me. If thou want any*
" *thing from this place write in time. From Milan, twenty-*
" *second July* 1469.

" *Thy Lorenzo de' Medici.*"

From the Ricordi of Lorenzo and the letters of Gentile, it appears that Lorenzo was treated at Milan with great

(a) *Fabr. in vitâ Lor. Adnot. & Mon.* v. ii. p. 56.

great distinction and honour. *More indeed*, says he, *than were shewn to any other person present, although there were many much better entitled to it.* On his departure he presented the duchess with a gold necklace, and a diamond which cost about three thousand ducats, *whence*, says he in his Ricordi, *it followed, that the duke requested that I would stand sponsor to all his other children.*

Death of Piero de' Medici.

Piero de' Medici did not long survive the marriage of his son. Exhausted by bodily sufferings, and wearied with the arrogant and tyrannical conduct of many of those who had espoused his cause, and which his infirmities prevented him from repressing, he died on the third day of December 1469, leaving his widow Lucretia, who survived him many years. His funeral was without ostentation; "perhaps," says Ammirato, "because he had in his lifetime given directions to that effect; or because the parade of a magnificent interment might have excited the envy of the populace towards his successors, to whom it was of more importance to be great, than to appear to be so (*a*)."

Before Piero was attacked by the disorder which for a long time rendered him almost incapable of attending to public business, he had been employed in several embassies of the greatest importance, which he had executed much to his own honour, and the advantage of the republic. Even after he was disabled from attending in the council, he continued to regulate the affairs of Florence, and to discuss with

(*a*) *Amm. Ist. Fior. v.* iii. *p.* 106.

with the principal citizens the most important subjects, in such a manner as to evince the solidity of his judgment and the integrity of his heart. He possessed a competent share of eloquence, some specimens of which are given by Machiavelli, who asserts that the extortions and abuses practised by his friends and adherents were so flagitious, and so hateful to his temper, that if he had lived it was his intention to have recalled the exiled citizens; for which purpose he had an interview, at his seat at Caffagiolo, with Agnolo Acciajuoli; but the numerous errors of this celebrated historian give us just reason to doubt on those points which have not the concurrent testimony of other writers. "It is "probable," says Tiraboschi, "that had Piero enjoyed "better health and longer life, he might have done more "for the interests of literature; but if he had only been "known as the father of Lorenzo de' Medici, it would have "been a sufficient title to the gratitude of posterity."

CHAP. III.

POLITICAL state of Italy—Venice—Naples—Milan—Rome—Florence—Lorenzo succeeds to the direction of the republic—Giuliano de' Medici—Attack on Prato—League against the Turks—Riches of the Medici—Their commercial concerns—Other sources of their revenue—The duke of Milan visits Florence—Lorenzo devotes his leisure to literature—Angelo Politiano—His temper and character—Death of Paul II.*—A persecutor of learned men—Succeeded by Sixtus* IV.*—Lorenzo deputed to congratulate him—Revolt and saccage of Volterra—Lorenzo establishes the academy of Pisa—Negotiation for a marriage between the dauphin and a daughter of the king of Naples—The king declines the proposal—Ambition and rapacity of Sixtus* IV.*—League between the duke of Milan, the Venetians, and the Florentines—The king of Denmark at Florence—Progress of the Platonic academy—Poem of Lorenzo intitled* ALTERCAZIONE*—Platonic festival—Effects of this institution—Number and celebrity of its members.*

CHAP. III.

1469.

Political state of Italy.

AT the time of the death of Piero de' Medici, the republic of Florence was not engaged in any open war. The absentees were however a cause of continual alarm, and the situation of the Italian states was such, as to give just grounds of apprehension that the tranquillity of that country would not long remain undisturbed. Of these the most powerful was that of Venice, which aspired to nothing less than the dominion of all Lombardy, and the supreme control of Italy itself. The superiority which it had acquired was in a great degree derived from the extensive commerce then carried on by the Venetians to different parts of the East, the valuable pro-

Venice.

Q 2 ductions

CHAP. III.

ductions of which were conveyed by way of Egypt into the Mediterranean, and from thence distributed by the Venetians throughout the rest of Europe. In this branch of commerce the Genoese and the Florentines had successively attempted to rival them; but although each of these people, and particularly the latter, had obtained a considerable portion of this lucrative trade, the Venetians maintained a decided superiority, until the discovery of a new and more expeditious communication with India, by the Cape of Good Hope, turned the course of eastern traffic into a new channel. The numerous vessels employed in transporting their commodities to different countries, rendered the state of Venice the most formidable maritime power in Europe. Ever intent on its own aggrandizement, it has only been restrained within its limits by formidable leagues between the Italian sovereigns, and by the seasonable intervention of foreign powers. Its internal tranquillity is remarkably contrasted with the turbulence of Florence; but the Venetian nobility had erected their authority on the necks of the people, and Venice was a republic of nobles, with a populace of slaves. In no country was despotism ever reduced to a more accurate system. The proficiency made by the Venetians in literature has accordingly borne no proportion to the rank which they have in other respects held among the Italian states. The talents of the higher orders were devoted to the support of their authority, or the extension of their territory; and among the lower class, with their political rights, their emulation was effectually extinguished. Whilst the other principal cities of Italy were daily producing works of genius, Venice was content

with

with the humble, but more lucrative employment of communicating those works to the public by means of the press. Other governments have exhibited a different aspect at different times, according to the temper of the sovereign, or the passions of the multitude; but Venice has uniformly preserved the same settled features, and remains to the present day a phenomenon in political history.

Naples.

The kingdom of Naples was at this time governed by Ferdinand of Arragon, who had in the year 1458 succeeded his father Alfonso. Under his administration that country experienced a degree of prosperity to which it had long been a stranger. At the same time that Ferdinand kept a watchful eye on the other governments of Italy, and particularly on that of Venice, he was consulting the happiness of his own subjects by the institution of just and equal laws, and by the promotion of commerce and of letters; but the virtues of the monarch were sullied by the crimes of the man, and the memory of Ferdinand is disgraced by repeated instances of treachery and inhumanity. Galeazzo Maria, son of the eminent Francesco Sforza, held the states of Milan, which were then of considerable extent. Of the virtues and talents of the father little however is to be traced in the character of the son. Immoderate in his pleasures, lavish in his expences, rapacious in supplying his wants, he incurred the contempt and hatred of his subjects. Like another Nero, he mingled with his vices a taste for science and for arts. To the follies and the crimes of this man, posterity must trace the origin of all those evils which, after the death of Lorenzo de Medici, depopulated and laid waste the most flourishing governments of Italy.

Milan.

The

CHAP. III.

Rome.

The pontifical chair was filled by Paul II. the successor of Pius II. A Venetian by birth, he had been educated in the profession of a merchant. On his uncle Eugenius IV. being promoted to the papacy, he changed his views, and betook himself to study, but too late in life to make any great proficiency. To compensate for this defect, Paul assumed a degree of magnificence and splendor before unknown. His garments were highly ornamented, and his tiara was richly adorned with jewels. Of a tall and imposing figure, he appeared in his processions like a new Aaron, and commanded the respect and veneration of the multitude. His dislike to literature was shewn by an unrelenting persecution of almost all the men of learning who had the misfortune to reside within his dominions. In the pontifical government, it may with justice be observed, that the interests of the prince and the people are always at variance with each other. Raised to the supremacy at an advanced period of life, when the claims of kindred begin to draw closer round the heart, the object of the pope is generally the aggrandizement of his family; and as he succeeds to the direction of a state whose finances have been exhausted by his predecessor, under the influence of similar passions, he employs the short space of time allowed him, in a manner the most advantageous to himself, and the most oppressive to his subjects. Such is nearly the uniform tenor of this government; but in the fifteenth century, when the pope by his secular power held a distinguished rank among the sovereigns of Italy, he often looked beyond the resources of his own subjects, and attempted to possess himself by force, of some of the smaller independent states which bordered upon his dominions, and over

over which the holy see always pretended a paramount claim, as having at some previous time formed a part of its territory, and having been either wrested from it by force, or wrongfully granted away by some former pontiff. These subordinate governments, though obtained by the power of the Roman state, were generally disposed of to the nominal nephews of the pope, who frequently bore in fact a nearer relationship to him; and were held by them until another successor in the see had power enough to dispossess the family of his predecessor, and vest the sovereignty in his own.

Florence.

With any of these governments, either in extent of territory, or in point of military establishment, the city of Florence could not contend; but she possessed some advantages that rendered her of no small importance in the concerns of Italy. Independent of the superior activity and acuteness of her inhabitants, their situation, almost in the center of the contending powers, gave them an opportunity of improving circumstances to their own interest, of which they seldom failed to avail themselves; and if Florence was inferior to the rest in the particulars before mentioned, she excelled them all in the promptitude with which she could apply her resources when necessity required. The battles of the Florentines were generally fought by *Condottieri*, who sold, or rather lent their troops to those who offered the best price; for the skill of the commander was shewn in these contests, not so much in destroying the enemy, as in preserving from destruction those followers on whom he depended for his importance or his support. The Florentines were collectively and individually

CHAP. III.

dividually rich; and as the principal inhabitants did not hesitate, on pressing emergencies, to contribute to the credit and supply of the republic, the city of Florence was generally enabled to perform an important part in the transactions of Italy, and if not powerful enough to act alone, was perhaps more desirable as an ally than any other state of that country (*a*).

Such was the situation of the different governments of Italy at the time of the death of Piero de' Medici; but, besides these, a number of inferior states interfered in the politics of the times, and on some occasions with no inconsiderable

(*a*) Of the population and finances of Florence, in the fifteenth century, I am enabled to give some interesting particulars, from a manuscript of that period, hitherto unpublished, intitled *Inventiva d' una impositione di nuova gravezza*, or " A proposition for a new mode of taxation," by Lodoviço Ghetti. In this document the projector calculates the number of Florentine citizens capable of bearing arms at 80,000 men, which, by computing four persons with each, so as to include infirm people, women, and children, he estimates as a population of 400,000 inhabitants. He then calculates the amount of the consumption, by this number of inhabitants, of the necessary articles of life, of which he proposes to take a tenth part in one general tax upon the produce of the soil and the labour of the country, amounting to 475,815 florins, which, after making all due allowances, would be sufficient to support the military establishment of the republic, and to discharge the other necessary expences of the government. Many other particulars, respecting the ancient state of Florence, may be found in this piece, which I have given in the Appendix, as accurately as the state of the manuscript will admit. *v. App. No.* XVI.

The florin is no longer a current coin in Tuscany; it may therefore be proper to observe, that the value of the ancient florin, or *Fiorino d' oro*, was about two shillings and sixpence, having been of the value of three lire and ten soldi. *Amm. Ist. Fior. v.* ii. *p.* 753.

considerable effect. Borso d' Este, marquis of Ferrara, although of illegitimate birth, had succeeded to the government on the death of Leonello, to the exclusion of his own legitimate brothers, and administered its affairs with great reputation (*a*). Torn by domestic factions, the Genoese were held in subjection by the duke of Milan, whilst Sienna and Lucca, each boasting a free government, were indebted for their independence rather to the mutual jealousy of their neighbours, than to any resources of their own.

Lorenzo succeeds to the direction of the republic.

We have already seen, that during the indisposition of Piero de' Medici, Lorenzo had frequently interfered in the administration of the republic, and had given convincing proofs of his talents and his assiduity. Upon the death of his father, he therefore succeeded to his authority as if it had been a part of his patrimony. On the second day after that

(*a*) The family of Este may be considered as powerful rivals of the Medici in the encouragement of learning and arts. This taste seems to have arisen with Leonello, who had studied under Guarino Veronese, (*Tirab. v.* vi. *p.* 2. *p.* 259.) and is not less entitled to a place in the annals of letters than in those of political events. Under his protection the university of Ferrara was splendidly re-established and endowed. His court was resorted to by men of learning from all parts of Italy. Of his own poetical productions some specimens yet remain which do honour to his memory. "Principe," says Muratori, "d' immortale memoria; perchè, secondo la Cronica di Ferrara, "fu amatore della pace, della giustitia, e della pietà; di vita onestissima, "studioso delle divine scritture, liberale massimamente verso i poveri; nella "avversità paziente, nelle prosperità moderato, e che con gran sapienza go- "vernò e mantenne sempre quieti i suoi popoli; di modo che si meritò il pregia- "tissimo nome di Padre della Patria." (*Mur. Ann. v.* ix. *p.* 459.) His successor was not inferior to him as a patron of learning; and Ercole I. who succeeded Borso in 1471, continued his hereditary protection of literature to the ensuing century.

that event, he was attended at his own house by many of the principal iuhabitants of Florence, who requested that he would take upon himself the administration and care of the republic, in the same manner as his grandfather and his father had before done (*a*). Had Lorenzo even been divested of ambition, he well knew the impossibility of retiring with safety to a private station, and without long hesitation complied with the wishes of his fellow-citizens (*b*). Sensible however of the difficulties which he

(*a*) *Ricor. di Lor. in App. No.* XII.

(*b*) If we give implicit credit to Machiavelli, Lorenzo was in a great degree indebted for this high distinction to Tomaso Soderini, who (as that author informs us) had, after the death of Piero de' Medici, obtained such influence in the city, that he was consulted on all affairs of importance, and was even addressed by foreign powers as the principal person in the republic. On this trying occasion, Tomaso, we are told, gave a striking proof of his moderation and fidelity. He assembled by night the principal citizens in the convent of S. Antonio, when Lorenzo and Giuliano were present, to take into consideration the state of the republic; where, by many arguments, he convinced his auditors of the expediency of continuing the Medici in the elevated station which their ancestors had so long enjoyed. (*Mac. Ist. lib.* 7.) This account, though so circumstantially related, and adopted even by Ammirato and Fabroni, I am led to reject, on the simple narrative of Lorenzo in his Ricordi. If Lorenzo was in fact called upon to take the direction of the republic two days after the death of his father, there seems to have been but little time allowed for the honours paid by the citizens, and by foreign powers, to Tomaso Soderini. And if Lorenzo accepted this honourable distinction in his own house, as he expressly informs us was the case, there was no occasion for his attendance in the convent of S. Antonio, whilst the citizens debated whether he should preserve the rank which his family had so long held in Florence. His continuance in this rank was not owing to the favour or the eloquence of an individual, but to the extensive wealth and influence of his family, its powerful foreign connexions, and above all, perhaps, to the remembrance of the many benefits which it had conferred upon the republic.

he had to encounter, he took every precaution to obviate the ill effects of envy and suspicion, by selecting as his principal advisers, such of the citizens as were most esteemed for their integrity and their prudence, whom he consulted on all occasions of importance. This practice, which he found so useful to him in his youth, he continued in his maturer years; but after having duly weighed the opinions of others, he was accustomed to decide on the measures to be adopted, by the strength of his own judgment, and not seldom in opposition to the sentiments of those with whom he had consulted. Letters of condolence were addressed to him on the death of his father, not only by many eminent individuals, but by several of the states and princes of Italy, and from some he received particular embassies, with assurances of friendship and support.

Giuliano de' Medici.

Between Lorenzo and his brother Giuliano there subsisted a warm and uninterrupted affection. Educated under the same roof, they had always participated in the same studies and amusements. Giuliano was therefore no stranger to the learned languages, and in his attention to men of talents, emulated the example and partook of the celebrity of his brother. He delighted in music and in poetry, particularly in that of his native tongue, which he cultivated with success; and by his generosity and urbanity gained in a great degree the affections of the populace, to which it is probable his fondness for public exhibitions not a little contributed. At the death of his father, Giuliano was only about sixteen years of age, so that the administration of public affairs rested wholly on Lorenzo, whose constant

CHAP. III.

attention to the improvement of his brother may be considered as the most unequivocal proof of his affection (*a*).

Attack on Prato.

1470.

A hasty and ill-conducted attempt by Bernardo Nardi, one of the Florentine exiles, to surprise and possess himself of the town of Prato, a part of the Florentine dominions, was one of the first events that called for the interposition of the republic. A body of soldiers was dispatched to the relief of the place, but the intrepidity of Cesare Petrucci, the chief magistrate, assisted by Giorgio Ginori a Florentine citizen and knight of Rhodes, had rendered further assistance unnecessary; and Bernardo being made prisoner, was sent to Florence, where he paid with his life

(*a*) " Gaudeo mirum in modum Julianum nostrum se totum literis tradi-" disse; illi gratulor, tibique gratias ago, quod eum ad hæc prosequenda " studia excitaveris." *Laur. Med. ad Pol. in Ep. Pol. lib.* 10.

" Julianus tuus verè frater, hoc est ut docti putant ferè alter, ipse sibi in " studiis est non modo jam mirificus hortator, sed et preceptor; nihilque no-" bis ad summam voluptatem deest nisi quod abes," &c. *Pol. ad Laur. Med. ib.*

If we may admit the evidence of a poet, the two brothers exhibited a striking example of fraternal affection.

In Laurentium, Julianumque Petri F. Fratres piissimos.

" Nec tanta Ebalios tenuit concordia fratres,
" Nec tanto Atridas fœdere junxit amor,
" Implicuit quanto *Medicum* duo pectora nexu
" Mitis amor, concors gratia, pura fides;
" Unum velle animis, unum est quoque nolle duobus,
" Corque sibi alterna dant capiuntque manu:
" Esse quid hoc dicam *Juli*, et tu maxime *Laurens*,
" Anne duos una mente calere putem!"

Pol. lib. Epigram. in Op. Ald. 1498.

life the forfeit of his folly (*a*). Being interrogated previous to his execution, as to his motives for making such an attempt with so small a number of followers, and such little probability of success, he replied, that having determined rather to die in Florence than to live longer in exile, he wished to ennoble his death by some splendid action (*b*). No sooner had this alarm subsided, than apprehensions arose of a much more formidable nature. Pursuing his destructive conquests, the Turkish emperor, Mahomet the II., had attacked the island of Negropont, which composed a part of the Venetian territory, and after a dreadful slaughter of both Turks and Christians, had taken the capital city by storm, and put the inhabitants to the sword (*c*). Encouraged by success, he vowed not to lay down his arms until he had abolished the religion of Christ, and extirpated all his followers. A strong sense of common danger is perhaps of all others the most powerful incentive to concord, and the selfish views of the Italian states were for a short time lost in the contemplation of this destructive enemy, whose success was equally dreaded by the prince, the scholar, and the priest. In the month of December 1470, a league was solemnly concluded, for the common defence, between the pope, the king of Naples, the duke of Milan, and the Florentines, to which almost all the other states of Italy acceded (*d*). In the same month Lorenzo de' Medici received a further proof of the confidence of his fellow-citizens, in being appointed syndic of

League against the Turks.

(*a*) *Amm. Ist. Fior.* v. iii. *p.* 107.

(*b*) *Mach. Hist. lib.* 7.

(*c*) *Murat. Ann.* v. ix. *p.* 507.

(*d*) *Ib. p.* 508.

of the republic, by virtue of which authority he bestowed upon Buongianni Gianfiliazzi, then Gonfaloniere, the order of knighthood in the church of S. Reparata (*a*).

Riches of the Medici.

The multiplicity of his public concerns did not prevent Lorenzo from attending to his domestic affairs, and taking the necessary precautions for continuing with advantage those branches of commerce which had proved so lucrative to his ancestors. Such were the profits which they had derived from these sources, that besides the immense riches which the family actually possessed, the ancestors of Lorenzo had in a course of thirty-seven years, computing from the return of Cosmo from banishment in 1434, expended in works of public charity or utility upwards of 660,000 florins; a sum which Lorenzo himself justly denominates incredible, and which may serve to give us a striking idea of the extensive traffic by which such munificence could be supported (*b*). In relating this circumstance, Lorenzo gives his hearty sanction to the manner in which this money had been employed. *Some persons would perhaps think*, says he, in his private Ricordi, *that it would be more desirable to have a part of it in their purse, but I conceive it has been a great advantage to the public, and well laid out, and am therefore perfectly satisfied.* Of this sum the principal part had been acquired and expended by Cosmo de' Medici, who had carried on, in conjunction with his brother Lorenzo, a very extensive trade,

(*a*) *Amm. Ist. Fior. v.* iii. *p.* 107.

(*b*) *Ricordi di Lor. de' Med. in App. No.* XII.

trade, as well in Florence as in foreign parts. On the death of Lorenzo, in the year 1440, his proportion of the riches thus obtained, which amounted in the whole to upwards of 235,000 florins, was inherited by his son Pier Francesco de' Medici, for whose use Cosmo retained it until the year 1451, when a distribution took place between the two families. From that time it was agreed, that the traffic of the family should be carried on for the joint benefit of Pier Francesco, and of Piero and Giovanni, the sons of Cosmo, who were to divide the profits in equal shares of one-third to each, and immense riches were thus acquired (*a*); but whilst Cosmo and his descendants expended a great part of their wealth in the service of the country, and supported the hereditary dignity of chiefs of the republic, Pier Francesco preferred a private life, and equally remote from the praise of munificence or the reproach of ostentation, transmitted to his descendants so ample a patrimony, as enabled them, in concurrence with other favourable circumstances, to establish a permanent authority in Florence, and finally to overturn the liberties of their native place.

Their commercial concerns.

Of the particular branch of traffic by which the Medici acquired their wealth little information remains; but there is no doubt that a considerable portion of it arose from the trade which the Florentines, in the early part of the fifteenth century, began to carry on to Alexandria for the productions of the east, in which they attempted to rival the states

(*a*) *Ricordi di Lor. de' Med. in App. No.* XII.

CHAP. III.

states of Genoa and of Venice. To this they were induced by the representations of Taddeo di Cenni, who having resided at Venice, and being apprized of the advantages which that city derived from the traffic in spices and other eastern merchandize, prevailed upon his countrymen, in the year 1421, to aim at a participation in the trade. Six new officers were accordingly created, under the title of maritime consuls, who were to prepare at the port of Leghorn (the dominion of which city the Florentines had then lately obtained by purchase) two large galleys and six guard-ships (*a*). In the following year the Florentines entered on their new commerce with great solemnity. A public procession took place, and the divine favour, which had always accompanied their domestic undertakings, was solicited upon their maritime concerns. At the same time the first armed vessel of the republic was fitted out on a voyage for Alexandria, in which twelve young men of the chief families in Florence engaged to proceed, for the purpose of obtaining experience in naval affairs. Carlo Federighi and Felice Brancacci were appointed ambassadors to the sultan, and were provided with rich presents to conciliate his favour. The embassy was eminently successful. Early in the following year the ambassadors returned, having obtained permission to form a commercial establishment at Alexandria, for the convenience of their trade, and with the extraordinary privilege of erecting a church for the exercise of their religion (*b*). In this branch of traffic, which was of

---

(*a*) *Amm. Ist. Fior.* v. ii. *p.* 994.

(*b*) *Ib. p.* 999.

of a very lucrative nature, and carried on to a great extent; the Medici were deeply engaged, and reciprocal presents of rare or curious articles were exchanged between them and the sultans, which sufficiently indicate their friendly intercourse.

Other sources of their revenue.

Besides the profits derived from their mercantile concerns, the wealth of the Medici was obtained through many other channels. A very large income arose to Cosmo and his descendants from their extensive farms at Poggio-Cajano, Caffagiolo, and other places, which were cultivated with great assiduity, and made a certain and ample return. The mines of allum in different parts of Italy were either the property of the Medici, or were hired by them from their respective owners, so that they were enabled almost to monopolize this article, and to render it highly lucrative. For a mine in the Roman territory it appears that they paid to the papal see the annual rent of 100,000 florins (*a*). But perhaps the principal sources of the riches of this family arose from the commercial banks which they had established in almost all the trading cities of Europe, and which were conducted by agents in whom they placed great confidence. At a time when the rate of interest frequently depended on the necessities of the borrower, and was in most cases very exorbitant, an inconceivable profit must have been derived from these establishments, which, as we have before noticed, were at times resorted to for pecuniary assistance by the most powerful sovereigns of Europe.

In

(*a*) *Fabr. in vitâ Laur. v.* i. *p.* 39. 181.

CHAP. III.

The duke of Milan visits Florence.

1471.

In the month of March 1471, Galeazzo Sforza, duke of Milan, accompanied by his dutchess Bona, sister of Amadeo, duke of Savoy, paid a visit to Florence, where they took up their residence with Lorenzo de' Medici, but their attendants, who were very numerous, were accommodated at the public charge (*a*). Not sufficiently gratified by the admiration of his own subjects, Galeazzo was desirous of displaying his magnificence in the eyes of the Florentines, and of partaking with them in the spectacles and amusements with which their city abounded. His equipage was accordingly in the highest style of splendor and expence (*b*); but notwithstanding this profusion, his wonder, and perhaps his envy, was excited by the superior magnificence of Lorenzo, which was of a kind not always in the power of riches to procure. Galeazzo observed with admiration the extensive collection of the finest remains of ancient art, which had been selected throughout all Italy for a long course of years with equal assiduity and

(*a*) They consisted of one hundred men at arms, and five hundred infantry as a guard, fifty running footmen richly dressed in silk and silver, and so many noblemen and courtiers, that, with their different retinues, they amounted to two thousand horsemen. Five hundred couple of dogs, with an infinite number of falcons and hawks, compleated the pageantry. *Amm. Ist. Fior. v.* iii. *p.* 108.

(*b*) Muratori, (*Annali d' Italia, v.* ix. *p.* 511.) after Corio, (*Ist. di Milano,*) informs us, that this journey was undertaken by Galeazzo under the pretext of the performance of a vow. Valori supposes that the motive of the duke was to confirm the authority of Lorenzo in Florence. Galeazzo was not remarkable either for his piety or his prudence, and it seems more probable that this excursion was undertaken merely to gratify his vanity, which he did at the expence of 200,000 gold ducats. In tracing the motives of conduct, historians frequently forget how many are to be sought for in the follies of mankind.

and expence. He examined with apparent pleasure the great variety of statues, vases, gems, and intaglios, with which the palace of Lorenzo was ornamented, and in which the value of the materials was often excelled by the exquisite skill of the workmanship; but he was more particularly gratified by the paintings, the productions of the best masters of the times, and owned that he had seen a greater number of excellent pictures in that place, than he had found throughout the rest of Italy. With the same attention he examined the celebrated collection of manuscripts, drawings, and other curious articles of which Lorenzo was possessed; and notwithstanding his predilection for courtly grandeur, had the taste, or the address, to acknowledge, that in comparison with what he had seen, gold and silver lost their value. The arrival of the duke at Florence seems to have been the signal for general riot and dissipation. Machiavelli affects to speak with horror of the irregular conduct of him and of his courtiers; and remarks, with a gravity that might well have become a more dutiful son of the church, that this was the first time that an open disregard was avowed in Florence of the prohibition of eating flesh in lent (*a*). For the amusement of the duke and his attendants three public spectacles were exhibited; one of which was the annunciation of the virgin, another the ascension of Christ, and the third the descent of the holy spirit. The last was exhibited in the church of the S. Spirito; and as it required the frequent use of fire, the building caught the flames, and was entirely consumed—a circumstance

(*a*) *Mac. Hist. lib.* 7.

circumstance which the piety of the populace attributed to the evident displeasure of heaven.

Lorenzo devotes his leisure to literature.

There is however abundant reason to believe that Lorenzo was induced to engage in the avocations and amusements before mentioned, rather by necessity than by choice; and that his happiest hours were those which he was permitted to devote to the exercise of his talents, and the improvement of his understanding; or which were enlivened by the conversation of those eminent men who sometimes assembled under his roof in Florence, and occasionally accompanied him to his seats at Fiesole, Careggi, or Caffagiolo. Those who shared his more immediate favour, were Marsilio Ficino, the three brothers of the family of Pulci, and Matteo Franco; but of all his literary friends, Politiano was the most particularly distinguished. It has been said that this eminent scholar was educated under the protection of Cosmo de' Medici; but at the death of Cosmo he was only ten years of age, having been born on the fourteenth day of July 1454. Politiano was indebted for his education to Piero, or rather to Lorenzo de' Medici, whom he always considered as his peculiar patron, and to whom he felt himself bound by every tie of gratitude (*a*). The place of his birth was Monte Pulciano, or *Mons Politianus*, a small town in the

Angelo Politiano.

(*a*) Ficino, addressing himself to Lorenzo, denominates Politiano "Angelus Politianus noster, *alumnus tuus*, acerrimo vir judicio." And Politiano himself says, "Innutritus autem *penè à puero* sum catissimis illis penetralibus magni viri, et in hac sua florentissima republica principis Laurenti Medicis."

Pol. Ep. ad Johannem Regem Portugalliæ in Ep. lib. x. Ep. 1.

the territory of Florence, whence he derived his name, having discontinued that of his family, which has given rise to great diversity of conjecture respecting it (*a*). The father of Politiano, though not wealthy, was a doctor of the civil law, which may be an answer to the many invidious tales as to the meanness of his birth. On his arrival at Florence he applied himself with great diligence to the study of the Latin language under Cristoforo Landino, and of the Greek, under Andronicus of Thessalonica. Ficino and Argyropylus were his instructors in the different systems of the Platonic and Aristotelian philosophy; but poetry had

(*a*) Some authors have given him the name of *Angelus Bassus*, but more modern critics have contended that his real name was *Cini*, being a contraction of *Ambrogini*. (*Menage Antibaillet*, *lib.* i. *c.* 14. *Bayle Dict. Hist. Art. Politien.*) Menckenius, in his laborious history of the life of this author, employs his first chapter in ascertaining his real name, and constantly denominates him *Angelus Ambroginus Politianus*. The Abate Serassi, in his life of Politiano, prefixed to the edition of his Italian poems by Comino, (*Padua*, 1765,) is also of opinion, that the name of *Bassus* is supposititious, and endeavours, on the authority of Salvini, to account for the rise of the mistake. Notwithstanding these respectable authorities, indisputable evidence remains, that in the early part of his life Politiano denominated himself by the Latin appellation of *Bassus*. Not to rely on the epigram "*ad Bassum*," printed amongst his works, and certainly addressed to him, which Menckenius supposes led Vossius into his error, we have the most decisive evidence on this subject from different *memoranda* in the hand-writing of Politiano, yet remaining in the Laurentian library, which I shall hereafter have occasion more particularly to state, and in which he subscribes his name *Angelus Bassus Politianus*. Bandini, who has had every possible opportunity of information on this subject, accordingly gives him that denomination. (*Spec. Lit. Flor.* *v.* i. *p.* 172.) That *Bassus* was an academical name, assumed by Politiano in his youth, might be contended with some degree of probability. De Bure has given him the name of *Jean Petit*, (*Bibliogr. Instr.* *v* iv. *p* 271.) in which absurdity he was preceded by another of his countrymen, Guy Patin.

had irresistible allurements for his young mind, and his *stanze* on the Giostra of Giuliano, if they did not first recommend him to the notice of Lorenzo, certainly obtained his approbation, and secured his favour (*a*). The friendship of Lorenzo provided for all his wants, and enabled him to prosecute his studies free from the embarrassments and interruptions of pecuniary affairs (*b*). He was early inrolled among the citizens of Florence, and appointed secular prior of the college of S. Giovanni. He afterwards entered into clerical orders, and having obtained the degree of doctor of the civil law, was nominated a canon of the cathedral of Florence. Intrusted by Lorenzo with the education of his children, and the care of his extensive collection of manuscripts and antiquities, he constantly resided under his roof, and was his inseparable companion at those

(*a*) Etenim ego tenera adhuc ætate sub duobus excellentissimis hominibus, Marsilio Ficino Florentino et Argyropulo Bizantino Peripateticorum sui temporis, longe clarissimo, dabam quidem philosophiæ utrique operam, sed non admodum assiduam; videlicet ad Homeri poetæ blandimenta natura et ætate proclivior. *Pol. in fine Miscell.*

(*b*) Omnia tibi ad ingenue philosophandum adjumenta suppeditat favor ac gratia Laurentii Medices, maximi hac tempestate studiorum patroni: qui missis per universum terrarum nunciis, in omni disciplinarum genere libros conquirit, nulli sumptui parcit, quo tibi ac reliquis præclaris ingeniis, bonarum artium studia æmulantibus, instrumenta abundantissima paret. (*Nic. Leonicenus ad Pol. in Pol. Ep. lib.* ii. *Ep.* 7.) Nor did Politiano hesitate upon occasion to trouble his patron with his personal wants. From one of his epigrams it appears that his inattention to dress had rendered it necessary for him to request immediate assistance from Lorenzo's wardrobe: and from another we find that such assistance was not denied him. These epigrams merit a place in the Appendix, *vide No.* XVII.

those hours which were not devoted to the more important concerns of the state.

His temper and character.

Respecting the temper and character of Politiano, his epistles afford us ample information. In one of these, addressed to Matteo Corvino king of Hungary, a monarch eminently distinguished by his encouragement of learned men, he hesitates not, whilst he pays a just tribute of gratitude to the kindness of Lorenzo, to claim the merit due to his own industry and talents (*a*). *From a humble situation*, says he, *I have, by the favour and friendship of Lorenzo de' Medici, been raised to some degree of rank and celebrity, without any other recommendation than my proficiency in literature. During many years I have not only taught in Florence the Latin tongue with great approbation, but even in the Greek language I have contended with the Greeks themselves—a species of merit that I may boldly say has not been attained by any of my countrymen for a thousand years past*. In the intercourse which Politiano maintained with the learned men of his time, he appears to have been sufficiently conscious of his own superiority. The letters addressed to him by his friends were in general well calculated to gratify his vanity; but although he was in a high degree jealous of his literary reputation, he was careful to distinguish how far the applauses bestowed upon him were truly merited, and how far they were intended to conciliate his favour. If he did not always estimate himself by the good opinion entertained of him by others, he did not suffer himself to be depressed

(*a*) *Pol. Ep. lib.* ix. *Ep.* 1.

depressed by their envy or their censure (*a*). *I am no more raised or dejected*, says he, *by the flattery of my friends, or the accusation of my adversaries, than I am by the shadow of my own body; for although that shadow may be somewhat longer in the morning and the evening than it is in the middle of the day, this will scarcely induce me to think myself a taller man at those times than I am at noon.*

The impulse which Lorenzo de' Medici had given to the cause of letters soon began to be felt, not only by those who immediately surrounded him, but throughout the Tuscan territories, and from thence it extended itself to the rest of Italy. By the liberal encouragement which he held out to men of learning, and still more by his condescension and affability, he attracted them from all parts of that country to Florence; so that it is scarcely possible to name an Italian of that age, distinguished by his proficiency in any branch of literature, that has not shared the attention or partaken of the bounty of Lorenzo.

Death of Paul II.

Paul the II. between whom and the family of the Medici there subsisted an irreconcileable enmity, died on the 26th day of July 1471, leaving behind him the character of an ostentatious, profligate, and illiterate priest. This dispute, which took place in the lifetime of Piero de' Medici, though Fabroni supposes it arose after his death (*b*), was occasioned by the ambition of Paul, who under the

---

(*a*) *Pol. Ep. lib.* iii. *Ep.* 24.

(*b*) *Fabr. in vitâ Laur. v.* i. *p.* 29.

the influence of motives to which we have before adverted, was desirous of possessing himself of the city of Rimini, then held by Roberto, the natural son of Gismondo Malatesti, whose virtues had obliterated in the eyes of the citizens the crimes of his father (*a*). Finding his pretensions opposed, Paul attempted to enforce them by the sword, and prevailed upon his countrymen the Venetians to afford him their assistance. Roberto had resorted for succour to the Medici, and by their interference the Roman and Venetian troops were speedily opposed in the field by a formidable army, led by the duke of Urbino, and supported by the duke of Calabria and Roberto Sanseverino. An engagement took place, which terminated in the total route of the army of the pope, who, dreading the resentment of so powerful an alliance, acceded to such terms as the conquerors thought proper to dictate; not however without bitterly inveighing against the Medici for the part they had taken in opposing his ambitious project.

Paul a persecutor of learned men.

During the pontificate of Paul II., letters and science experienced at Rome a cruel and unrelenting persecution, and their professors exhibited in their sufferings a degree of constancy and resolution, which in another cause might have advanced them to the rank of martyrs. The imprisonment of the historian Platina, who, on being arbitrarily deprived of a respectable office to which he was appointed by Pius II., had dared to thunder in the ears

(*a*) *Amm. Ist. Fior.* v. iii. p. 105. *Murat. Ann.* v. ix. p. 505.

ears of the pope the dreaded name of a general council, might perhaps admit of some justification; but this was only a prelude to the devastation which Paul made amongst the men of learning, who, during his pontificate, had chosen the city of Rome as their residence (*a*). A number of these uniting together, had formed a society for the research of antiquities, chiefly with a view to elucidate the works of the ancient authors, from medals, inscriptions, and other remains of art. As an incitement to, or as characteristic of their studies, they had assumed classic names, and thereby gave the first instance of a practice which has since become general among the academicians of Italy. Whilst these men were employing themselves in a manner that did honour to their age and country, Paul was indulging his folly and his vanity in ridiculous and contemptible exhibitions (*b*); and happy had it been if he had confined his attention to these amusements; but on the pretext of a conspiracy against his person, he seized upon many members of the academy, which he pretended to consider as a dangerous and seditious assembly, accusing them of having by their adoption of heathen names, marked their aversion to

(*a*) *Platina nella vita di Paolo* II. *Muratori Ann. v.* ix. *p.* 508.

(*b*) Correvano i vecchi, correvano i giovani, correvano quelli che erano di mezza età, correvano i giudei, e li facevano ben saturare prima, perchè meno veloci corressero. Correvano i cavalli, le cavalle, gli asini, e i buffali con piacere di tutti, che per le risa grandi potevano appena star le genti in pie. Il correre che si faceva, era dall' arco di Domiziano sino alla chiesa di S. Marco, dove stava il papa, che supremo gusto e piacere di queste feste prendeva; e dopo il corso usava anche a fanciulli, lordi tutti di fango, questa cortesia, che ad ogni uno di loro faceva dare un carlino. *Plat. ut sup.*

to the Christian religion. Such of them as were so unfortunate as to fall into his hands he committed to prison, where they underwent the torture, in order to draw from them a confession of crimes which had no existence, and of heretical opinions which they had never avowed. Not being able to obtain any evidence of their guilt, and finding that they had resolution to suffer the last extremity rather than accuse themselves, Paul thought proper at length to acquit them of the charge, but at the same time, by a wanton abuse of power, he ordered that they should be detained in prison during a compleat year from the time of their commitment, alledging that he did it to fulfil a vow which he had made when he first imprisoned them (*a*).

Succeeded by Sixtus IV.

To Paul II. succeeded Francesco della Rovere, a Franciscan monk, who assumed the name of Sixtus IV. His knowledge of theology and the canon law had not conciliated the favour of the populace, for during the splendid ceremony of his coronation, a tumult arose in the city, in which his life was endangered (*b*). To congratulate him on his elevation, an embassy of six of the most eminent citizens was deputed from Florence, at the head of which was Lorenzo de' Medici. Between Lorenzo and the pope mutual instances of good-will took place, and Lorenzo, who under the direction of his agents had a bank established at Rome, was formally invested with the office of treasurer of

Lorenzo deputed to congratulate him.

(*a*) *Platina nella vita de Paolo* II.—*Zeno. Dissert. Voss. Art. Platina*—*Tirab. Storia della Lett. Ital. v.* vi. *par.* 1. *p.* 82.

(*b*) *Muratori Ann. v.* ix. *p.* 511.

of the holy see, an appointment which greatly contributed to enrich his maternal uncle, Giovanni Tornabuoni, who, whilst he executed that office on behalf of Lorenzo, had an opportunity of purchasing from Sixtus many of the rich jewels that had been collected by Paul II. which he sold to different princes of Europe to great emolument (*a*). During this visit Lorenzo made further additions to the many valuable specimens of ancient sculpture, of which, by the diligence of his ancestors, he was already possessed. On his return to Florence he brought with him two busts in marble, of Augustus and Agrippa, which were presented to him by the pope, with many cameos and medals, of the excellence of which he was an exquisite judge (*b*). In the warmth of his admiration for antiquity, he could not refrain from condemning the barbarism of Paul, who had demolished a part of the Flavian amphitheatre in order to build a church to S. Marco (*c*). At this interview it is probable that Lorenzo solicited from Sixtus the promise of a cardinal's hat for his brother, and it is certain that he afterwards used his endeavours to obtain for Giuliano a seat in the sacred college, through the medium of the Florentine envoy at Rome; but the circumstances of the times, and the different temper of the pope and of Lorenzo, soon put an end to all friendly intercourse between them, and an enmity took place which was productive of the most sanguinary consequences.

Soon

(*a*) *Fabr. in vitâ Laur. v.* i. *p.* 38.

(*b*) *Ricordi di Lor. in App. No.* XII.

(*c*) *Fabroni in vitâ Laur. v.* i. *p.* 40.

Revolt and sacrage of Volterra.

Soon after the return of Lorenzo to Florence, a disagreement arose between that republic and the city of Volterra, which composed a part of its dominions. A mine of allum had been discovered within the district of Volterra, which being at first considered as of small importance, was suffered to remain in the hands of individual proprietors; but it afterwards appearing to be very lucrative, the community of Volterra claimed a share of the profits as part of their municipal revenue. The proprietors appealed to the magistrates of Florence, who discountenanced the pretensions of the city of Volterra, alledging that if the profits of the mine were to be applied to the use of the public, they ought to become a part of the general revenue of the government, and not of any particular district. This determination gave great offence to the citizens of Volterra, who resolved not only to persevere in their claims, but also to free themselves, if possible, from their subjection to the Florentines. A general commotion took place at Volterra. Such was the violence of the insurgents, that they put to death several of their own citizens who disapproved of their intemperate proceedings. Even the Florentine commissary, Piero Malegonelle, narrowly escaped with his life. This revolt excited great alarm at Florence, not from the idea that the citizens of Volterra were powerful enough to succeed in an attempt which they had previously made at four different times without success, but from an apprehension that if a contest took place, it might afford a pretext for the pope or the king of Naples to interfere on the occasion. Hence a great diversity of opinion prevailed amongst the magistrates and council of Florence, some of whom, particularly Tomaso Soderini, strongly recommended conciliatory

CHAP. III.

liatory measures. This advice was opposed by Lorenzo de' Medici, who, from the enormities already committed at Volterra, was of opinion that the most speedy and vigorous means ought to be adopted to repress the commotion. In justification of this apparent severity, he remarked, that in violent disorders, where death could only be prevented by bold and decisive measures, those physicians were the most cruel, who appeared to be the most compassionate. His advice was adopted by the council, and preparations were made to suppress the revolt by force. The inhabitants of Volterra exerted themselves to put the city in a state of defence, and made earnest applications for assistance to the neighbouring governments. About a thousand soldiers were hired and received within the walls, to assist in supporting the expected attack; but the Florentines having surrounded the place with a numerous army (*a*), under the command of the count of Urbino, the citizens soon surrendered at discretion. The Florentine commissaries took possession of the palace, and enjoined the magistrates to repair peaceably to their houses. One of them on his return was insulted and plundered by a soldier, and notwithstanding the utmost exertions of the duke of Urbino, who afterwards put to death the offender, this incident led the way to a general saccage of the city, the soldiers who had engaged in its defence uniting with the conquerors in despoiling and plundering the unfortunate inhabitants. Lorenzo was no sooner

(*a*) Ten thousand foot and two thousand horse, according to Machiavelli, (*lib.* 7.) but Ammirato, with more probability, enumerates them at five thousand of the former and five hundred of the latter. *Ist. Fior. v.* iii. *p.* 3.

sooner apprized of this event than he hastened to Volterra, where he endeavoured to repair the injuries done to the inhabitants, and to alleviate their distresses by every method in his power (*a*). Although the unhappy termination of this affair arose from an incident, which as the sagacity of Lorenzo could not foresee, so his precaution could not prevent, yet it is highly probable, from the earnestness which he shewed to repair the calamity, that it gave him no small share of regret. Nor has he on this occasion escaped the censure of a contemporary historian, who being himself an inhabitant of Volterra, probably shared in those distresses of which he considered Lorenzo as the author, and has therefore, on this and on other occasions, shewn a disposition unfriendly to his character (*b*).

1472.

Lorenzo establishes the academy of Pisa.

About the close of the following year, great apprehensions of a famine arose in Florence, and five citizens were appointed to take the necessary precautions for supplying the place. The dreadful effects of this calamity were however obviated, principally by the attention of Lorenzo, who shortly afterwards took a journey to Pisa, where he made a long residence (*c*). The object of this visit was the re-establishment and regulation of the academy of that place,

---

(*a*) *Fabr. in vitâ*, v. i. p. 45.

(*b*) *Raffaello da Volterra, in Commentar. Urban. Geogr. lib.* 5. p. 138. *Ed. Lugd.* 1552.

(*c*) The coincidence of these circumstances is adverted to in an epigram of Politiano, whose poems illustrate almost all the principal incidents in the life of Lorenzo.

" Cum commissa sibi tellus malefida negasset
" Semina, et agricolæ falleret herba fidem,

place, which after having existed nearly two centuries, and having been celebrated for the abilities of its professors, and the number of its students, had fallen into disrepute and neglect. An institution of a similar nature had been founded in Florence in 1348—a year rendered remarkable by the dreadful pestilence of which Boccacio has left so affecting a narrative; but Florence was on many accounts an improper situation for this purpose. The scarcity of habitations, the high price of provisions, and the consequent expence of education, had greatly diminished the number of students, whilst the amusements with which that place abounded were unfavourable to a proficiency in serious acquirements. Sensible of these disadvantages, the Florentines, who had held the dominion of Pisa from the year 1406, resolved to establish the academy of that place in its former splendor. Lorenzo de' Medici and four other citizens were appointed to superintend the execution of their purpose (*a*); but Lorenzo, who was the projector of the plan,

" Protinus optatas patriæ tua dextera fruges
" Obtulit, et celerem jussit abire famem.
" Nec mora, Piscis commutas sedibus urbem
" Servatam, et nimio tempore lentus abes.
" Heu quid agis? Patriæ *Laurens* te redde gementi.
" Non facta est donis lætior illa tuis.
" Mœsta dolet, malletque famem perferre priorem,
" Quam desiderium patria ferre tui."

Pol. in lib. Epigr.

(*a*) The other deputies were Tomaso de' Ridolfi, Donato degli Acciajuoli, (after whose death his place was supplied by Piero Minerbetti,) Andrea de' Puccini, and Alamanno de' Rinuccini. *Fabron. in vitâ Laur. p.* 50. This author, who was lately, and perhaps is yet, at the head of the Pisan academy, has, in his life of Lorenzo, given a very full account of its renovation, and of the different professors who have contributed towards its celebrity.

plan, undertook the chief direction of it, and in addition to the six thousand florins annually granted by the state, expended, in effecting his purpose, a large sum of money from his private fortune. Amongst the professors at Pisa were speedily found some of the most eminent scholars of the age, particularly in the more serious and important branches of science. At no period have the professors of literature been so highly rewarded (*a*). The dissensions and misconduct of these teachers, whose arrogance was at least equal to their learning, gave Lorenzo no small share of anxiety, and often called for his personal interference (*b*). His absence from his native place was a frequent cause of regret to Politiano, who consoled himself by composing verses

(*a*) The teachers of the civil and canon law were Bartolommeo Mariano Soccini, Baldo Bartolini, Lancelotto and Filippo Tristano, Pier Filippo Corneo, Felice Sandeo, and Francesco Accolti; all of whom had great professional reputation. In the department of medicine we find the names of Albertino de Chizzoli, Alessandro Sermoneta, Giovanni d' Aquila, and Pier Leoni. In philosophy, Nicolo Tignosi. In polite letters, Lorenzo Lippi and Bartolommeo da Prato. In divinity, Domenico di Flandria and Bernardino Cherichini. Of these the civilians had the highest salaries—that of Soccini was 700 florins annually; that of Baldo 1050, and that of Accolti 1440.

(*b*) Forgetful of the *jus gentium* which it was his province to teach, Soccini made an attempt to evade his engagements at Pisa, and to carry off with him to Venice sundry books and property of the academy entrusted to his care, which he had artfully concealed in wine casks. Being taken and brought to Florence, he was there condemned to death, but Lorenzo exerted his authority to prevent the execution of the sentence, alledging as a reason for his interference, that *so accomplished a scholar ought not to suffer an ignominious death*. An observation which may shew his veneration for science, but which will scarcely be found sufficient to exculpate a man whose extensive knowledge rather aggravated than alleviated his offence. Soccini however not only escaped punishment, but in the space of three years was re-instated in his professorship, with a salary of 1000 florins.

verses expressive of his affection for Lorenzo, and soliciting his speedy return (*a*). To this circumstance we are however indebted for several of the familiar letters of Lorenzo that have reached posterity, many of which have been published with those of Ficino, and perhaps derive some advantage from a comparison with the epistles of the philosopher, whose devotion to his favourite studies is frequently carried to an absurd extreme, and whose flattery is sometimes so apparent as to call for the reprehension even of Lorenzo himself (*b*).

1473.

Negociation for a marriage between the dauphin and a daughter of the king of Naples.

The increasing authority of Lorenzo, and his importance in the affairs of Europe, now began to be more apparent. In the year 1473 he took part in a negociation, which, had it been successful, might have preserved Italy from many years of devastation, and at all events must have given a different complexion to the affairs not only of that country, but of Europe. Louis XI. of France, who laid the foundation of that despotism, which, after having existed for three centuries, was at length expiated in the blood of the most guiltless of his descendants, and whose views were uniformly directed towards the aggrandizement of his dominions, and the depression of his subjects, was desirous of connecting his family with that of Ferdinand king of Naples, by the marriage of his eldest son with a daughter

(*a*) I give the following for its conciseness rather than its merit:

"Invideo Pisis Laurenti nec tamen odi,
"Ne mihi displiceat quæ tibi terra placet."

Pol. in lib. Epigr.

(*b*) "Scribis ut in te laudando posthæc parcior esse velim," &c.

Fic. ad Laur. in Ep. Fic. p. 34. Ed. 1502.

daughter of that prince. To this end he conceived it necessary to address himself to some person, whose general character, and influence with Ferdinand, might promote his views, and for that purpose he selected Lorenzo de' Medici. The confidential letter from Louis to Lorenzo on this occasion is yet extant, and affords some striking traits of the character of this ambitious, crafty, and suspicious monarch (*a*). After expressing his high opinion of Lorenzo, and his unshaken attachment to him, he gives him to understand, that he is informed a negociation is on foot for a marriage between the eldest daughter of the king of Naples and the duke of Savoy, upon which the king was to give her a portion of 300,000 ducats. Without apologizing for his interference, he then mentions his desire that a connexion of this nature should take place between the princess and his eldest son the dauphin, and requests that Lorenzo would communicate his wishes to the king of Naples. To this proposal Louis stipulates as a condition, that Ferdinand should, in consequence of such alliance, not only assist him in his contest with the house of Anjou, but also against the king of Spain, and his other enemies; alluding to the duke of Burgundy, whom he was then attempting to despoil of his dominions. After making further arrangements respecting the proposed nuptials, he requests that Lorenzo would send some confidential person to reside with him for a time, and to return to Florence as often as might be requisite, but with particular injunctions that he should have no intercourse with any of the French nobility

(*a*) For this letter, first published by Fabroni, *v. App. No.* XVIII.

CHAP. III.

bility or princes of the blood. The conclusion of the letter conveys a singular request: conscious of his guilt, Louis distrusted all his species, and he desires that Lorenzo would furnish him with a large dog, of a particular breed, which he was known to possess, for the purpose of attending on his person and guarding his bed-chamber (*a*). Notwithstanding the apparent seriousness with which Louis proposes to connect his family by marriage with that of the king of Naples, it is probable that such proposal was only intended to delay or prevent the marriage of the princess with the duke of Savoy. Whether Ferdinand considered it in this light, or whether he had other reasons to suspect the king of France of sinister or ambitious views, he returned a speedy answer (*b*), in which, after the warmest professions of personal esteem for Lorenzo, and after expressing his thorough sense of the honour he should derive from an alliance with a monarch, who might justly be esteemed the greatest prince on earth, he rejects the proposition on account of the conditions that accompanied it; declaring that no private considerations should induce him to interrupt the friendship subsisting between him and his ally the duke of Burgundy, or his relation the king of Spain; and that he would rather lose his kingdom, and even his life, than suffer such an imputation upon his honour and his character. If in his reply he has alledged the true reasons for declining a connexion apparently so advantageous

Ferdinand declines the proposal.

(*a*) —— Vigilum canum
Tristes excubiæ. Hor.

(*b*) *v. App. No.* XIX.

advantageous to him, it must be confessed that his sentiments do honour to his memory. The magnanimity of Ferdinand affords a striking contrast to the meanness and duplicity of Louis XI. It is scarcely necessary to add that the proposed union never took place. The dauphin, afterwards Charles VIII., married the accomplished daughter of the duke of Bretagne, and some years afterwards expelled the family of his once intended father-in-law from their dominions, under the pretence of a will, made in favour of Louis XI. by a count of Provence, one of that very family of Anjou, against whose claims Louis had himself proposed to defend the king of Naples.

Ambition and rapacity of Sixtus IV.

Sixtus IV. at the time he ascended the pontifical chair, had several sons, upon whom, in the character of nephews, he afterwards bestowed the most important offices and the highest dignities of the church. The indecency of Sixtus, in thus lavishing upon his spurious offspring the riches of the Roman see, could only be equalled by their profuseness in dissipating them. Piero Riario, in whose person were united the dignities of cardinal of S. Sisto, patriarch of Constantinople, and archbishop of Florence, expended at a single entertainment in Rome, given by him in honour of the duchess of Ferrara, 20,000 ducats, and afterwards made a tour through Italy with such a degree of splendor, and so numerous a retinue, that the pope himself could not have displayed greater magnificence (*a*). His brother Girolamo was dignified with the appellation of count;

(*a*) *Muratori Ann.* v. ix. *p.* 515.

count; and that it might not be regarded as an empty title, 40,000 ducats were expended in purchasing from the family of Manfredi the territory of Imola, of which he obtained possession (*a*), and to which he afterwards added the dominion of Forli. The city of Castello became no less an object of the ambition of Sixtus; but instead of endeavouring to possess himself of it by compact, he made an attempt to wrest it by force from Niccolo Vitelli, who then held the sovereignty; for which purpose he dispatched against it another of his equivocal relations, Giuliano della Rovere, who afterwards became pope under the name of Julius the II. and who, in the character of a military cardinal, had just before sacked the city of Spoleto and put the inhabitants to the sword. Niccolo Vitelli, having obtained the assistance of the duke of Milan and of the Florentines, made a vigorous defence, and though obliged at length to capitulate, obtained respectable terms. The long resistance of Niccolo was attributed by the pope, and not without reason, to Lorenzo de' Medici, who, independent of his private regard for Niccolo, could not be an indifferent spectator of an unprovoked attack upon a place which immediately bordered on the territories of Florence, and greatly contributed towards their security (*b*). These depredations, which were supposed to be countenanced by the king of Naples, roused the attention of the other states of Italy, and towards the close of the year 1474, a league was

(*a*) *Muratori Ann. v.* ix. *p.* 516.

(*b*) *Amm. Ist. Fior. v.* iii. *p.* 113.

was concluded at Milan, between the duke, the Venetians, and the Florentines, for their mutual defence, to which neither the pope nor the king were parties; liberty was however reserved for those potentates to join in the league if they thought proper, but this they afterwards refused, probably considering this article of the treaty as inserted rather for the purpose of deprecating their resentment, than with the expectation of their acceding to the compact (*a*).

League between the duke of Milan, the Venetians, and the Florentines.

In this year, under the magistracy of Donato Acciajuoli, a singular visitor arrived at Florence. This was Christian, or Christiern, king of Denmark and Sweden, who was journeying to Rome, for the purpose, as was alledged, of discharging a vow. He is described by the Florentine historians as of a grave aspect, with a long and white beard, and although considered as a barbarian, they admit that the qualities of his mind did not derogate from the respectability of his external appearance. Having surveyed the city, and paid a ceremonial visit to the magistrates, who received their royal visitor with great splendor, he requested to be favoured with a sight of the celebrated copy of the Greek Evangelists, which had been obtained some years before from Constantinople, and of the Pandects of Justinian, brought from Amalfi to Pisa, and thence to Florence. His laudable curiosity was accordingly gratified, and he expressed his satisfaction by declaring, through the medium of his interpreter, that these were the real treasures of princes, alluding, as was supposed, to the conduct

The king of Denmark visits Florence.

1474.

(*a*) *Amm. Ist. Fior.* v. iii. p. 113. *Muratori Ann.* v. ix. p. 518.

conduct of the duke of Milan, who had attempted to dazzle him with the display of that treasure of which he had plundered his subjects, to gratify his vanity and his licentiousness; on which occasion Christian had coldly observed, that the accumulation of riches was an object below the attention of a great and magnanimous sovereign. Ammirato attempts to shew that this remark is rather specious than just, but the authority of the Roman poet is in favour of the Goth (*a*). It was a spectacle worthy of admiration, says the same historian, to see a king, peaceable and unarmed, pass through Italy, whose predecessors had not only overthrown the armies of that country, and harassed the kingdoms of France and of Spain, but had even broken and overturned the immense fabric of the Roman empire itself.

Progress of the Platonic academy.

If we do not implicitly join in the applauses bestowed by Landino on the professors and the tenets of the Platonic, or new philosophy (*b*), we must not, on the contrary, conceive that the study of these doctrines was a mere matter of speculation and curiosity. From many circumstances, there is great reason to conclude that they were applied to practical use, and had a considerable influence on the manners and the morals of the age. The object towards which mankind have always directed their aim, and in the acquisition of which every system both of religion and philosophy proposes to assist their endeavours, is the *summum bonum*, the greatest possible degree of attainable happiness; but

---

(*a*) *Hor. lib.* ii. *Ode* 2.

(*b*) Land. in proem. ad lib. 1. de vera nobilitate ad magnum vereque nobilem *Laurentium Medicem, Petri. F. ap. Band. Spec. Lit. Flor.* v. ii. *p.* 38.

but in what this chief good consists has not been universally agreed upon, and this variety of opinion constitutes the essential difference between the ancient sects of philosophy. Of all these sects there was none whose tenets were so elevated and sublime, so calculated to withdraw the mind from the gratifications of sense, and the inferior objects of human pursuit, as that of the Platonists; which by demonstrating the imperfection of every sensual enjoyment, and every temporal blessing, rose at length to the contemplation of the supreme cause, and placed the ultimate good in a perfect abstraction from the world, and an implicit love of God. How far these doctrines may be consistent with our nature and destination, and whether such sentiments may not rather lead to a dereliction than a completion of our duty, may perhaps be doubted; but they are well calculated to attract a great and aspiring mind. Mankind, however, often arrive at the same conclusion by different means (*a*), and we have in our own days seen a sect rise up, whose professors, employing a mode of deduction precisely opposite to the Platonists of the fifteenth century, strongly resemble them in their sentiments and manners. Those important conclusions which the one derived from the highest cultivation of intellect, the other has found in an extreme of humiliation, and a constant degradation and contempt of all human endowments. Like navigators who steer

(*a*) Sono infinite vie e differente,
E quel che si ricerca solo è uno.

Poesie di Lor. de' Medici, p. 33. Ed. 1554.

steer a course directly opposite, they meet at last at the same point of the globe. And the sublime reveries of the Platonists, as they appear in the works of some of their followers, and the doctrines of the modern Methodists, are at times scarcely distinguishable in their respective writings.

Poem of Lorenzo entitled *Altercazione.*

In this system Lorenzo had been educated from his earliest years. Of his proficiency in it he has left a very favourable specimen in a poem of no inconsiderable extent. The occasion that gave rise to this poem appears from a letter of Ficino, who undertook to give an abstract of the doctrines of Plato in prose, whilst Lorenzo agreed to attempt the same subject in verse (*a*). Lorenzo completed his tafk with that facility for which he was remarkable in all his compositions, and sent it to the philosopher, who performed the part he had undertaken by giving a dry and insipid epitome of the poem of Lorenzo (*b*). What seems yet more extraordinary is, that Ficino, in a letter to Bernardo Rucellai, (who had married one of the sisters of Lorenzo,) transmits to him a prosaic paraphrase of the beautiful address to the deity at the conclusion of the

(*a*) Cum ego ac tu nuper in agro Careggio multa de felicitate ultro citroque disputavissemus, tandem in sententiam eandem, duce ratione, convenimus. Ubi tu novas quasdam rationes quod felicitas in voluntatis potius quam intellectus actu consistat subtiliter invenisti. Placuit autem tibi, ut tu disputationem illam carminibus, ego soluta oratione conscriberem. Tu jam eleganti poemate tuum officium implevisti. Ego igitur nunc, aspirante deo, munus meum exequar quam brevissime. *Fic. Ep. lib.* 1. *p.* 38. *Ed.* 1497.

(*b*) Lege feliciter, Laurenti felix, quæ Marsilius Ficinus tuus; hic breviter magna ex parte a te inventa, de felicitate perstrinxit. *Ib. p.* 41.

the poem, affirming that he daily made use of it in his devotions, and recommending it to Bernardo for the like purpose. At the same time, instead of attributing the composition to its real author, he adverts to it in a manner that Bernardo might well be excused from understanding (*a*). It is needless to add, that this subject appears to much greater advantage in the native dress of the poet, than in the prosaic garb of the philosopher (*b*). The introduction is very pleasing. The author represents himself as leaving the city, to enjoy for a few days the pleasures of a country life.

Da più dolce pensier tirato e scorto,
  Fuggito avea l' aspra civil tempesta,
  Per ridur l' alma in più tranquillo porto.
Così tradutto il cor da quella, a questa
  Libera vita, placida, e sicura,
  Che è quel po del ben ch' al mondo resta:
E per levar da mie fragil natura
  Mille pensier, che fan la mente lassa,
  Lassai il bel cerchio delle patrie mura.
E pervenuto in parte ombrosa, e bassa,
  Amena valle che quel monte adombra,
  Che'l vecchio nome per età non lassa,

La

(*a*) Audivi Laurentium Medicem nostrum, nonnulla horum similia ad lyram canentem, furore quodam divino ut arbitror concitum. *Fic. Ep. lib.* i. *p.* 41.

(*b*) Printed without date, apparently about the close of the fifteenth century, and not since reprinted, nor noticed by any bibliographer. It is entitled ALTERCATIONE OVERO DIALOGO COMPOSTO DAL MAGNIFICO LORENZO DI PIERO DI COSIMO DE' MEDICI *nel quale si disputa tra el cittadino el pastore quale sia più felice vita o la civile o la rusticana con la determinatione facta dal philosopho dove solamente si truovi la vera felicità.* In 12°.

La ove un verde laur' facea ombra,
  Alla radice quasi del bel monte,
  M'assisi ; e'l cor d' ogni pensier si sgombra.

Led on by pensive thought, I left erewhile
  Those civil storms the restless city knows,
Pleased for a time to smooth my brow of toil,
  And taste the little bliss that life bestows.
Thus with free steps my willing course I sped
  Far from the circle of my native walls ;
And sought the vale with thickest foliage spread,
  On whose calm breast the mountain shadow falls.
Charmed with the lovely spot, I sat me down
  Where first the hill its easy slope inclined,
And every care that haunts the busy town,
  Fled, as by magic, from my tranquil mind.

Whilst the poet is admiring the surrounding scenery, he is interrupted by a shepherd, who brings his flock to drink at an adjacent spring ; and who, after expressing his surprize at meeting such a stranger, inquires from Lorenzo the reason of his visit.

Dimmi per qual cagion sei quì venuto ?
  Perchè i theatri, e i gran palazzi, e i templi
  Lassi, & l' aspro sentier ti è più piaciuto ?
Deh ! dimmi in questi boschi hor che contempli ?
  Le pompe, le richezze, e le delitie,
  Forse vuoi prezzar più pe' nostri exempli ?
—Ed io a lui—Io non so qual divitie,
  O qual honor sien più suavi, & dulci,
  Che questi, fuor delle civil malitie.

Tra

Tra voi lieti pastori, tra voi bubulci,
  Odio non regna alcuno, o ria perfidia,
  Nè nasce ambition per questi sulci.
Il ben quì si possiede senza invidia;
  Vostra avaritia ha piccola radice;
  Contenti state nella lieta accidia.
Quì una per un altra non si dice;
  Nè è la lingua al proprio cor contraria;
  Che quel ch' oggi el fa meglio, è più felice,
Nè credo che gli avvengha in sì pura aria,
  Che'l cuor sospiri, e fuor la bocca rida;
  Che più saggio è chi 'l ver più copre, e varia.

Thy splendid halls, thy palaces forgot,
  Can paths o'erspread with thorns a charm supply;
Or dost thou seek from our severer lot,
  To give to wealth and power a keener joy?
—Thus I replied—I know no happier life,
  No better riches than you shepherds boast,
Freed from the hated jars of civil strife,
  Alike to treachery and to envy lost.
The weed ambition midst your furrowed field
  Springs not, and avarice little root can find;
Content with what the changing seasons yield,
  You rest in cheerful poverty resigned.
What the heart thinks the tongue may here disclose;
  Nor inward grief with outward smiles is drest.
Not like the world—where wisest he who knows
  To hide the secret closest in his breast.

Comparing

Comparing the amusements of the city, with the more natural and striking incidents of the country, he has the following passage:

S' advien ch' un tauro con un altro giostri,
   Credo non manco al cuor porgha diletto,
   Che feri ludi de' theatri nostri.
E tu giudicatore, al più perfetto
   Doni verde corona, ed in vergogna
   Si resta l' altro, misero, ed in dispetto.

If chance two bulls in conflict fierce engage,
   And stung by love maintain the doubtful fight;
Say can the revels of the crowded stage
   In all its pomp afford a nobler sight?
Judge of the strife, thou weav'st a chaplet gay,
   And on the conqueror's front the wreathe is hung:
Abash'd the vanquish'd takes his lonely way,
   And sullen and dejected moves along.

The shepherd however allows not the superior happiness of a country life, but in reply represents, in a very forcible manner, the many hardships to which it is inevitably liable. In the midst of the debate the philosopher Marsilio approaches, to whom they agree to submit the decision of their controversy. This affords him an opportunity of explaining the philosophical tenets of Plato; in the course of which, after an inquiry into the real value of all subordinate objects and temporal acquisitions, he demonstrates, that permanent happiness is not to be sought for either in the exalted station of the one, or in the humble condition

condition of the other, but that it is finally to be found only in the knowledge and the love of the first great cause.

Platonic festival.

In order to give additional stability to these studies, Lorenzo and his friends formed the intention of renewing, with extraordinary pomp, the solemn annual feasts to the memory of the great philosopher, which had been celebrated from the time of his death to that of his disciples Plotinus and Porphyrius, but had then been discontinued for the space of twelve hundred years. The day fixed on for this purpose was the seventh of November, which was supposed to be the anniversary not only of the birth of Plato, but of his death, which happened among his friends at a convivial banquet, precisely at the close of his eighty-first year (*a*). The person appointed by Lorenzo to preside over the ceremony at Florence was Francesco Bandini, whose rank and learning rendered him extremely proper for the office. On the same day another party met at Lorenzo's villa at Carreggi, where he presided in person. At these meetings, to which the most learned men in Italy resorted, it was the custom for one of the party, after dinner, to select certain passages from the works of Plato, which were submitted to the elucidation of the company, each of the guests undertaking the illustration or discussion of some important or doubtful point. By this institution, which was continued for several years, the philosophy of Plato was supported not only in credit but in splendor, and its professors were considered as the most respectable

(*a*) *Ficini Ep. lib.* 1. *Band. Spec. Lit. Flor. v.* ii. *p.* 60.

respectable and enlightened men of the age. Whatever Lorenzo thought proper to patronize became the admiration of Florence, and consequently of all Italy. He was the *glass of fashion*, and those who joined in his pursuits, or imitated his example, could not fail of sharing in that applause which seemed to attend on every action of his life.

Effects of this institution.

Of the particular nature, or the beneficial effects of this establishment, little further is now to be collected, nor must we expect, either on this or on any other occasion, to meet with the transactions of the Florentine academy in the fifteenth century. The principal advantages of this institution seem to have been the collecting together men of talents and erudition, who had courage to dissent from established modes of belief, and of supplying them with new, rational, and important topics of conversation. From these discourses it was not difficult to extract the purest lessons of moral conduct, or the sublimest sentiments of veneration for the deity, but good sense was the only alembic through which the true essence could be obtained, and this was not at hand on all occasions. The extravagancies of some of the disciples, contributed to sink into discredit the doctrines of their master. Even Ficino himself, the great champion of the sect, exhibits a proof, that when the imagination is once heated by the pursuit of a favourite object, it is difficult to restrain it within proper bounds. Habituated from his earliest youth to the study of this philosophy, and conversant only with Plato and his followers, their doctrines occupied his whole soul, and appeared in all his conduct and conversation. Even his epistles breathe

 nothing

nothing but Plato, and fatigue us with the endless repetition of opinions which Lorenzo has more clearly exhibited in a few luminous pages. Ficino was not however satisfied with following the track of Plato, but has given us some treatises of his own, in which he has occasionally taken excursions far beyond the limits which his master prescribed to himself (*a*). We might be inclined to smile at his folly, or to pity his weakness, did not the consideration of the follies and the weaknesses of the present times, varied indeed from those of past ages, but perhaps not diminished, repress the arrogant emotion.

Number and celebrity of its members.

Of those who more particularly distinguished themselves by the protection which they afforded to the new philosophy, or by the progress they made in the study of it, Ficino has left a numerous catalogue in a letter to Martinus Uranius, in which he allots the chief place to his friends of the family of the Medici (*b*). Protected and esteemed by Cosmo, the same unalterable attachment subsisted between the philosopher and his patrons for four successive generations. If ever the love of science was hereditary, it must have been in this family. Of the other eminent men whom Ficino has enumerated, Bandini has given us some interesting particulars (*c*), to which considerable additions might be

(*a*) In his treatise *de vita cœlitus comparanda*, we have a chapter, *de virtute verborum atque cantus ad beneficium cœleste captandum*, and another, *de astronomica diligentia in liberis procreandis*, with other disquisitions equally instructive.

Fic. de vita. Ven. 1548, 8°.

(*b*) *Fic. Ep. lib.* xi. *Ep.* 30. *Ed.* 1497. *v. App. No.* XX.

(*c*) *Band. Spec. Lit. Flor. passim.*

be made, but the number is too great, and the materials are too extensive, to be comprized in the limits necessarily allotted to this department of our subject; and of many of them, some particulars will be found in other parts of the work. In perusing the catalogue of the disciples of this institution, we perceive that the greatest part of them were natives of Florence, a circumstance that may give us some idea of the surprising attention which was then paid in that city to literary pursuits. Earnest in the acquisition of wealth, indefatigable in improving their manufactures and extending their commerce, the Florentines seem not however to have lost sight of the true dignity of man, or of the proper objects of his regard. A thorough acquaintance as well with the ancient authors as with the literature of his own age, was an indispensable qualification in the character of a Florentine; but few of them were satisfied with this inferior praise. The writers of that country, of whose lives and productions some account is given by Negri, amount in number to upwards of two thousand, and among these may be found many names of the first celebrity. In this respect the city of Florence stands unrivalled. A species of praise as honourable as it is indisputable.

CHAP. IV.

ASSASSINATION of the duke of Milan—Ambition of Lodovico Sforza—Conspiracy of the Pazzi—Parties engaged in it—Family of the Pazzi—Origin of the attempt—Arrangements for its execution—Giuliano assassinated, and Lorenzo wounded—The conspirators attack the palace—Repulsed by the Gonfaloniere—Punishment of the conspirators—Conduct of Lorenzo—Memorials of the conspiracy—Lorenzo prepares for his defence against the pope and the king of Naples—Latin ode of Politiano—Kindness of Lorenzo to the relatives of the conspirators—Violence of Sixtus IV.*—He excommunicates Lorenzo and the magistrates—Singular reply of the Florentine synod—Sixtus attempts to prevail on the Florentines to deliver up Lorenzo—Danger of his situation—Conduct of the war—Lorenzo negociates for peace—Death of Donato Acciajuoli—Various success of the war—Lorenzo resolves to visit the king of Naples—His letter to the magistrates of Florence—He embarks at Pisa—Concludes a treaty with the king—Sixtus perseveres in the war—The Turks make a descent upon Italy—Peace concluded with the pope.*

CHAP. IV.

WHILST Lorenzo was dividing his time between the cares of government and the promotion of literature, an event took place that attracted the attention of all Italy towards Milan. This was the death of the duke Galeazzo Maria, who was assassinated in a solemn procession, and in his ducal robes, as he was entering the church of S. Stefano. This daring act, which ſeems to have originated partly in personal resentment, and partly in an aversion to the tyranny of the duke, was not attended with the consequences expected by the perpetrators; two of whom were killed on the spot; and the third, Girolamo Olgiato, a youth of twenty-three years of age, after having been refused

Assassination of the duke of Milan.

1476.

fused shelter in his father's house, died upon the scaffold. On his execution he shewed the spirit of an ancient Roman (*a*). The conspirators undoubtedly expected to meet with the countenance and protection of the populace, to whom they knew that the duke had rendered himself odious by every species of cruelty and oppression. The delight he seemed to take in shedding the blood of his subjects, had rendered him an object of horror—his insatiable debauchery, of disgust (*b*);—he was even suspected of having destroyed his mother, who, as he thought, interfered too much in the government of Milan; and who suddenly died as she was making her retreat from thence to Cremona. But no commotion whatever took place in the city, and Giovan Galeazzo, a child of eight years of age, peaceably succeeded his father in the dukedom (*c*). The imbecility of his youth tempted the daring spirit of his uncle, Lodovico, to form a systematic plan for obtaining the government of Milan, in

(*a*) Ne fu nel morire meno animoso, che nell' operare si fusse stato; perche trovandosi ignudo, e con il carnefice davanti, che aveva il coltello in mano per ferirlo, disse queste parole in lingua Latina, perche litterato era, "*Mors* "*acerba, fama perpetua, stabit vetus memoria facti.*" *Mac. Hist. lib.* vii.

It appears however from the ancient chronicle of Donato Bossi, that more than one of the conspirators suffered the horrid punishment which he there relates:—"Post questionem de participibus conjurationis, in vestibulo arcis, "urbem versus, in quaterna membra vivi discerpti sunt."

Chronic. Bossiana. Ed. Mil. 1492.

(*b*) Era Galeazzo libidinoso, e crudele; delle qual due cose gli spessi esempi l'havevano fatto odiosissimo; perche non solo non gli bastava corrompere le donne nobili, che prendeva ancora piacere di publicarle; ne era contento fare morire gli huomini, se con qualche modo crudele non gli ammazzava. *Mac. lib.* vii.

(*b*) *Murat. Ann. v.* ix. *p.* 522.

in the execution of which he drew ruin upon himself, and entailed a long succession of misery upon his unfortunate country.

Ambition of Lodovico Sforza.

The connexion that had long subsisted between the houses of Sforza and of Medici, rendered it impossible for Lorenzo to be an indifferent spectator of this event. At his instance Tomaso Soderini was dispatched to Milan, to assist by his advice the young prince and his mother, who had taken upon herself the regency during the minority of her son. The ambitious designs of Lodovico soon became apparent. Having persuaded his three brothers, Sforza duke of Bari, Ottaviano, and Ascanio, to second his views, he began to oppose the authority of the dutchess, and attempted to divest her of the assistance of her faithful and experienced counsellor Cecco Simoneta, a native of Calabria, whose integrity and activity had recommended him to the patronage of the celebrated Francesco Sforza (*a*). Simoneta, aware of his design, endeavoured to frustrate it, by imprisoning and punishing some of his accomplices of inferior rank. The four brothers immediately resorted to arms, and of this circumstance Simoneta availed himself to obtain a decree, that either banished them from Milan or prohibited their return. Ottaviano, one of the brothers, soon

(*a*) Cecco was brother to the historian Simoneta, whose elegant Latin history of the life of Francesco Sforza has furnished future historians with some of the most interesting particulars of that period. This work was first published at Milan in 1479, and reprinted there in 1486. The Italian translation, by Cristoforo Landino, was also published at Milan in 1490, under the title of *La Sforziada*.

soon afterwards perished in attempting to cross the river Adda. These rigorous measures, instead of depressing the genius of Lodovico, gave a keener edge to his talents, and superadded to his other motives the desire of revenge. Nor was it long before his resentment was gratified by the destruction of Simoneta, who expiated by his death the offence which he had committed against the growing power of the brothers (*a*). No sooner was the dutchess deprived of his support, than Lodovico wrested from her feeble hands the sceptre of Milan, and took the young duke under his immediate protection; where, like a weak plant in the shade of a vigorous tree, he languished for a few miserable years, and then fell a victim to that increasing strength in which he ought to have found his preservation.

Conspiracy of the Pazzi.

1478.

The public agitation excited by the assassination of the duke of Milan had scarcely subsided, before an event took place at Florence of a much more atrocious nature, inasmuch as the objects destined to destruction had not afforded a pretext, in any degree plausible, for such an attempt. Accordingly we have now to enter on a transaction that has seldom been mentioned without emotions of the strongest horror and detestation; and which, as has justly been observed, is an incontrovertible proof of the practical atheism of the times in which it took place (*b*).—A transaction in which a pope, a cardinal, an archbishop, and several other ecclesiastics, associated themselves with a band of ruffians, to destroy two men who were an honour to their

(*a*) *Murat. Ann.* v. ix. p. 532.

(*b*) *Voltaire Essai sur les moeurs, &c. des nations*, v. ii. p. 283. *Ed. Genev.* 1769. 4°.

their age and country; and purposed to perpetrate their crime at a season of hospitality, in the sanctuary of a Christian church, and at the very moment of the elevation of the host, when the audience bowed down before it, and the assassins were presumed to be in the immediate presence of their God.

Parties engaged in it.

At the head of this conspiracy were Sixtus IV. and his nephew Girolamo Riario. Raffaello Riario, the nephew of this Girolamo, who, although a young man then pursuing his studies, had lately been raised to the dignity of cardinal, was rather an instrument than an accomplice in the scheme. The enmity of Sixtus to Lorenzo had for some time been apparent, and if not occasioned by the assistance which Lorenzo had afforded to Niccolo Vitelli, and other independent nobles, whose dominions Sixtus had either threatened or attacked, was certainly increased by it. The destruction of the Medici appeared therefore to Sixtus as the removal of an obstacle that thwarted all his views; and by the accomplishment of which the small surrounding states would soon become an easy prey. There is however great reason to believe that the pope did not confine his ambition to these subordinate governments, but that if the conspiracy had succeeded to his wish, he meant to have grasped at the dominion of Florence itself (a). The alliance lately formed

(a) At least Ferdinand of Naples, the ally of Sixtus in the contest that ensued, assured the Florentine ambassador that such was the intention of the pope, "che sapeva lui, che Sisto non tenne meno fantasia in capo d' occupare "e farsi signore di Firenze, che il presente sommo pontefice si habbi tenuta di "occupare questo regno."—Alluding to the subsequent attack made by Innocent VIII. upon the kingdom of Naples. *Fabr. in vitâ Laur. v. ii. p. 107.*

CHAP. IV.

formed between the Florentines, the Venetians, and the duke of Milan, which was principally effected by Lorenzo de' Medici, and by which the pope found himself prevented from disturbing the peace of Italy, was an additional and powerful motive of resentment (*a*). One of the first proofs of the displeasure of the pope, was his depriving Lorenzo of the office of treasurer of the papal see, which he gave to the Pazzi, a Florentine family, who as well as the Medici had a public bank at Rome, and who afterwards became the coadjutors of Sixtus in the execution of his treacherous purpose.

Family of the Pazzi.

This family was one of the noblest and most respectable in Florence; numerous in its members, and possessed of great wealth and influence. Of three brothers, two of whom had filled the office of gonfaloniere, only one was then living. If we may credit the account of Politiano (*b*), Giacopo de' Pazzi, the surviving brother, who was regarded as the chief of the family, and far advanced in years, was an unprincipled libertine, who having by gaming and intemperance dissipated his paternal property, sought an opportunity of averting, or of concealing his own ruin in that of the republic. Giacopo had no children; but his

(*a*) *Murat. Ann. v.* ix. *p.* 526.

(*b*) CONJURATIONIS PACTIANÆ COMMENTARIUM. This piece, written by a spectator, and printed in the same year in which the event took place, is as remarkable for the vehemence of its invective, as for the elegance of its style, and proves how deeply Politiano felt, and how keenly he resented the injury done to his great patrons. Not being republished with the other works of this author in 1498 or 1499, or in the Paris edition of 1519, it became extremely

his elder brother Piero had left seven sons, and his younger brother Antonio three; one of whom, Guglielmo de' Pazzi, had in the lifetime of Cosmo de' Medici married Bianca, the sister of Lorenzo. Francesco, the brother of Guglielmo, had for several years resided principally at Rome. Of a bold and aspiring temper, he could not brook the superiority of the Medici, which was supposed to have induced him to choose that place as his residence in preference to Florence.

Several of the Florentine authors have endeavoured to trace the reason of the enmity of this family to that of the Medici, but nothing seems discoverable, which could plausibly operate as a motive, much less as a justification of their resentment. On the contrary, the affinity between the two families, and the favours conferred by the Medici on the Pazzi, memorials of which yet remain in the hand-writing of Giacopo (*a*), might be presumed to have prevented animosity, if not to have conciliated esteem; and that they lived on terms of apparent friendship and intimacy is evident from many circumstances of the conspiracy.

---

rare, "tam rarum deventum quidem, ut inter doctos sæpe dubitatum est, an "unquam typis impressum fuerit, ac inter alios ignoratus etiam libri titulus." *Adimarius in præf. ad Pact. Conj. Comment. Ed. Nap.* 1769. Adimari having procured the ancient copy from the Strozzi library, and collated it with various manuscripts, republished it at Naples in 1769, with great elegance and copious illustrations, forming an ample quarto volume; from which accurate edition this piece is given in the Appendix, No. XXI.

(*a*) In letters from him to Lorenzo, two of which are given by Fabroni, and will be found in the Appendix, No. XXII.

CHAP. IV.

racy. Machiavelli relates a particular injury received by one of the Pazzi, which, as he informs us, that family attributed to the Medici. Giovanni de' Pazzi had married the daughter of Giovanni Borromeo, whose immense property upon his death should have descended to his daughter. But pretensions to it being made by Carlo, his nephew, a litigation ensued, in the event of which the daughter was deprived of her inheritance (*a*). There is however reason to believe that this decree, whether justifiable or not, and of which we have no documents to enable us to form a judgment, was made many years before the death of Piero de' Medici, when his sons were too young to have taken a very active part in it; and it is certain that it produced no ostensible enmity between the families. It is also deserving of notice, that this transaction happened at a time when Lorenzo was absent from Florence, on one of his youthful excursions through Italy (*b*).

Origin of the attempt.

This conspiracy, of which Sixtus and his nephew were the real instigators, was first agitated at Rome, where the intercourse between the count Girolamo Riario and Francesco de' Pazzi, in consequence of the office held by the latter, afforded them an opportunity of communicating to each other their mutual jealousy of the power of the Medici, and their desire of depriving them of their influence

(*a*) *Mac. Hist. lib.* 8.

(*b*) This fact is authenticated by the letter from Luigi Pulci to Lorenzo de' Medici, dated the twenty-second of April 1465, and now first published in the Appendix from the MS. in the Palazzo Vecchio at Florence. *App. No.* IX.

fluence in Florence; in which event it is highly probable, that the Pazzi were to have exercised the chief authority in the city, under the patronage, if not under the avowed dominion of the papal see. The principal agent engaged in the undertaking was Francesco Salviati, archbishop of Pisa, to which rank he had lately been promoted by Sixtus, in opposition to the wishes of the Medici, who had for some time endeavoured to prevent him from exercising his episcopal functions. If it be allowed that the unfavourable character given of him by Politiano is exaggerated, it is generally agreed that his qualities were the reverse of those which ought to have been the recommendations to such high preferment. The other conspirators were, Giacopo Salviati, brother of the archbishop, Giacopo Poggio, one of the sons of the celebrated Poggio Bracciolini, and who, like all the other sons of that eminent scholar, had obtained no small share of literary reputation (*a*); Bernardo Bandini, a daring libertine, rendered desperate by the consequences of his excesses; Giovan Battista Montesicco, who had distinguished himself by his military talents as one of the *Condottieri* of the armies of the pope; Antonio Maffei, a priest of Volterra,

(*a*) Giacopo not only translated the Florentine history of his father from Latin into Italian, but has also left a specimen of his talents in a commentary on the *Trionfo della Fama* of Petrarca, which was published in folio, without a date, but, as Bandini conjectures, about the year 1485 or 1487. It may however be presumed, from the dedication of this book, a copy of which is now before me, to Lorenzo de' Medici, that it was printed previous to the year 1478, when the author joined in this conspiracy to destroy a man, of whom, and of whose family, he had shortly before expressed himself in the following affectionate and grateful terms: " E perché charissimo Lorenzo io conosco quel " poco di cognitione è in me, tutto essere per conforto e acerrimo stimolo ne " miei teneri anni, da Cosimo tuo avolo, pari per certo a Camillo, o Fabritio, o

terra, and Stefano da Bagnone, one of the apostolic scribes, with several others of inferior note.

Arrangements for its execution.

In the arrangement of their plan, which appears to have been concerted with great precaution and secrecy, the conspirators soon discovered, that the dangers which they had to encounter were not so likely to arise from the difficulty of the attempt, as from the subsequent resentment of the Florentines, a great majority of whom were strongly attached to the Medici. Hence it became necessary to provide a military force, the assistance of which might be equally requisite whether the enterprize proved abortive or successful. By the influence of the pope, the king of Naples, who was then in alliance with him, and on one of whose sons he had recently bestowed a cardinal's hat, was also induced to countenance the attempt.

These preliminaries being adjusted, Girolamo wrote to his nephew cardinal Riario, then at Pisa, ordering him to obey whatever directions he might receive from the archbishop. A body of two thousand men were destined to approach by different routes towards Florence, so as to be in readiness at the time appointed for striking the blow.

Shortly

" Scipione, o qualunche altro, i quali appresso di noi sono in veneratione se
" fussi nato nella Romana republica, mi pare essere obligato e costretto ogni
" frutto producessi per alcun tempo le sue gravissime monitioni et exortationi,
" come persona grata, a te, vero e degno suo herede destinarlo; acciochè in-
" tenda quel tanto di lume d' alcuna virtù è in me, reconoscerlo dalla casa tua,
" alla quale tanto sono obligato quanto giudicherai sieno da stimare queste
" mie lettere." *Giac. Poggio in Proem.*

Shortly afterwards, the archbishop requested the presence of the cardinal at Florence, whither he immediately repaired, and took up his residence at a seat of the Pazzi, about a mile from the city. It seems to have been the intention of the conspirators to have effected their purpose at Fiesole, where Lorenzo then had his country residence, to which they supposed that he would invite the cardinal and his attendants. Nor were they deceived in this conjecture, for Lorenzo prepared a magnificent entertainment on this occasion: but the absence of Giuliano, on account of indisposition, obliged the conspirators to postpone the attempt (*a*). Disappointed in their hopes, another plan was now to be adopted; and on further deliberation it was resolved, that the assassination should take place on the succeeding Sunday, in the church of the Reparata, since called *Santa Maria del Fiore*, and that the signal for execution should be the elevation of the host. At the same moment the archbishop and others of the conspirators were to seize upon the palace, or residence of the magistrates, whilst the office of Giacopo de' Pazzi was to endeavour, by the cry of liberty, to incite the citizens to revolt.

The immediate assassination of Giuliano was committed to Francesco de' Pazzi and Bernardo Bandini, and that of Lorenzo had been intrusted to the sole hand of Montesicco. This office he had willingly undertaken whilst he understood that it was to be executed in a private dwelling, but he shrunk from the idea of polluting the house of God with

so

(*a*) *Valor. in vitâ Laur. p.* 23.

CHAP. IV.

so heinous a crime (a). Two ecclesiastics were therefore selected for the commission of a deed, from which the soldier was deterred by conscientious motives. These were Stefano da Bagnone, the apostolic scribe, and Antonio Maffei.

Giuliano assassinated, and Lorenzo wounded.

The young cardinal having expressed a desire to attend divine service in the church of the Reparata, on the ensuing Sunday, being the twenty-sixth day of April 1478, Lorenzo invited him and his suite to his house in Florence. He accordingly came with a large retinue, supporting the united characters of cardinal and apostolic legate, and was received by Lorenzo with that splendor and hospitality with which he was always accustomed to entertain men of high rank and consequence. Giuliano did not appear, a circumstance that alarmed the conspirators, whose arrangements would not admit of longer delay. They soon however learnt that he intended to be present at the church.— The service was already begun, and the cardinal had taken his seat, when Francesco de' Pazzi and Bandini, observing that Giuliano was not yet arrived, left the church and went to his house, in order to insure and hasten his attendance. Giuliano accompanied them, and as he walked between them, they threw their arms round him with the familiarity of intimate friends, but in fact to discover whether

(a) Disse che non gli bastarebbe mai l'animo, commettere tanto eccesso *in chiesa*, ed accompagnare il tradimento col sacrilegio; il che fu il principio della rovina dell' impresa loro. *Mac. lib.* 8.

ther he had any armour under his dress (*a*); possibly conjecturing from his long delay, that he had suspected their purpose. At the same time, by their freedom and jocularity, they endeavoured to obviate any apprehensions which he might entertain from such a proceeding (*b*). The conspirators having taking their stations near their intended victims, waited with impatience for the appointed signal (*c*). The bell rang—the priest raised the consecrated wafer—the people bowed before it—and at the same instant Bandini plunged a short dagger into the breast of Giuliano.—On receiving the wound he took a few hasty steps and fell, when Francesco de' Pazzi rushed upon him with incredible fury, and stabbed him in different parts of his body, continuing to repeat his strokes even after he was apparently dead. Such was the violence of his rage that he wounded himself deeply in the thigh. The priests who had undertaken the murder of Lorenzo were not equally successful. An ill-directed blow from Maffei, which was aimed at the throat,

(*a*) Condottolo nel tempio, e per la via e nella chiesa con motteggi, e giovenili ragionamenti l' intratenero. Ne mancò Francesco sotto colore di carezzarlo, con le mani e con le braccia strignerlo, per vedere se lo trovava o di corazza, o d' altra simile difesa munito. *Mac. lib.* 8.

(*b*) Giuliano was indisposed, and totally unarmed, having left at home even his dagger, which he was generally accustomed to wear. "Infirmus quidem, & qui ea die, præter morem, gladiolum, qui ei ulceratum crus quatiebat, domi reliquerat." *Synod. Flor. Act. ap. Fabr. v.* ii. *p.* 134.

(*c*) In the point of time fixed for the perpetration of this deed, historians are nearly agreed. "Cum Eucharistia attolleretur," says *Raffaello da Volt. Geogr.* 151. "Cum sacerdos manibus Eucharistiam frangeret." *Val. in vitâ, p.* 24. "Peracta sacerdotis communione," says *Politian.* "Post Eucharistiæ consecratione." *In Prov. Rep. Flor. ap. Fabr. v.* ii. *p.* 111. "Quandosi communicava il sacerdote." *Mac. lib.* 8.

throat, but took place behind the neck, rather roused him to his defence than disabled him (*a*). He immediately threw off his cloak, and holding it up as a shield in his left hand, with his right he drew his sword, and repelled his assailants. Perceiving that their purpose was defeated, the two ecclesiastics, after having wounded one of Lorenzo's attendants who had interposed to defend him, endeavoured to save themselves by flight. At the same moment, Bandini, his dagger streaming with the blood of Giuliano, rushed towards Lorenzo; but meeting in his way with Francesco Nori, a person in the service of the Medici, and in whom they placed great confidence, he stabbed him with a wound instantaneously mortal (*b*). At the approach of Bandini the friends of Lorenzo encircled him, and hurried him into the sacristy, where Politiano and others closed the doors, which where of brass. Apprehensions being entertained that the weapon which had wounded him was poisoned, a young man attached to Lorenzo sucked the wound (*c*). A general alarm and consternation took place in the church; and such was the tumult which ensued, that

---

(*a*) " Il primo colpo fu nella collotola, perchè non potè tenerlo pel braccio " per dargli nel petto, e cosi confessò." *Strinatus, ap. Adimar. in not. p.* 25.

(*b*) When Leo X. many years afterwards paid a visit to Florence, he granted an indulgence to all those who should pray for the soul of Francesco Nori, under the idea that his death had preserved the life of his father Lorenzo. *Adimar. in not. p.* 20.

(*c*) " Aggressus in eos factus fuit a Francisco de Pazzis, et aliis pluribus " suis sotiis armatis *armis veneno infectis*," says Matteo de Toscano, cited by Adimari, *Documenta Conj. Pact. p.* 142. I do not find that any other author mentions this circumstance. The young man who gave this striking proof of his affection to Lorenzo was Antonio Ridolfo, of a noble family of Florence.
Pol. Conj. Pact. Comment. in App.

that it was at first believed by the audience that the building was falling in (*a*); but no sooner was it understood that Lorenzo was in danger, than several of the youth of Florence formed themselves into a body, and receiving him into the midst of them, conducted him into his house, making a circuitous turn from the church, lest he should meet with the dead body of his brother.

The conspirators attack the palace.

Whilst these transactions passed in the church, another commotion took place in the palace; where the archbishop, who had left the church, as agreed upon before the attack on the Medici, and about thirty of his associates, attempted to overpower the magistrates, and to possess themselves of the seat of government (*b*). Leaving some of his followers stationed in different apartments, the archbishop proceeded to an interior chamber, where Cesare Petrucci, then gonfaloniere, and the other magistrates were assembled. No sooner was the gonfaloniere informed of his approach, than out of respect to his rank he rose to meet him. Whether the archbishop was disconcerted by the presence of Petrucci, who was known to be of a resolute character, of which he had given a striking instance in frustrating the attack of Bernardo Nardi upon the town of Prato, or whether his courage was not equal to the undertaking, is uncertain;

(*a*) "Qui in templo fuerant, clamoribus territi, huc atque illuc cursitantes "veluti attoniti, quidnam rei fuisset quæritabant. Fuere qui crederent templum ruere." *Valor. in vitâ Laur. p.* 25.

(*b*) "Con la sua compagnia, ch' erano circa persone ventotto," says Belfredello Strinato, *ap. Adimar. in not. p.* 17. Ammirato informs us, that the archbishop had about thirty followers, and that he left the church on the pretence of paying a visit to his mother. *Amm. Ist. v.* iii. *p.* 117.

uncertain; but instead of intimidating the magistrates by a sudden attack, he began to inform Petrucci that the pope had bestowed an employment on his son, of which he had to deliver to him the credentials (*a*). This he did with such hesitation, and in so desultory a manner, that it was scarcely possible to collect his meaning. Petrucci also observed that he frequently changed colour, and at times turned towards the door, as if giving a signal to some one to approach.—Alarmed at his manner, and probably aware of his character, Petrucci suddenly rushed out of the chamber, and called together the guards and attendants. By attempting to retreat, the archbishop confessed his guilt (*b*). In pursuing him, Petrucci met with Giacopo Poggio, whom he caught by the hair, and throwing him on the ground, delivered into the custody of his followers. The rest of the magistrates and their attendants seized upon such arms as the place supplied, and the implements of the kitchen became formidable weapons in their hands. Having secured the doors of the palace, they furiously attacked their scattered and intimidated enemies, who no longer attempted resistance. During this commotion they were alarmed by

Repulsed by the gonfaloniere and magistrates.

(*a*) Sub nomine & colore præsentandi cujusdam brevis papalis.
M. Tuscanus ap. Adimar. int. doc. p. 142.

(*b*) He was deprived of his expected support by a singular incident. Some of his followers had retired into an adjoining chamber to wait his signal. It was customary for every succeeding magistrate to make an alteration in the doors of that place, as a precaution against treachery; and Petrucci had so constructed them that they closed and bolted on the slightest impulse. The followers of the archbishop thus found themselves unexpectedly secured in the chamber, without the possibility of affording assistance to their leader.
Fabr. v. i. *p.* 67. *v.* ii. *p.* 108.

by a tumult from without, and perceived from the windows Giacopo de' Pazzi, followed by about one hundred soldiers, crying out liberty, and exhorting the people to revolt. At the same time they found that the insurgents had forced the gates of the palace, and that some of them were entering to defend their companions. The magistrates however persevered in their defence, and repulsing their enemies, secured the gates till a reinforcement of their friends came to their assistance. Petrucci was now first informed of the assassination of Giuliano, and the attack made upon Lorenzo. The relation of this treachery excited his highest indignation. With the concurrence of the state counsellors, he ordered Giacopo Poggio to be hung in sight of the populace, out of the palace windows; and secured the archbishop, with his brother and the other chiefs of the conspiracy. Their followers were either slaughtered in the palace, or thrown half alive through the windows. One only of the whole number escaped. He was found some days afterwards concealed in the wainscots, perishing with hunger, and in consideration of his sufferings received his pardon (*a*).

Punishment of the conspirators.

The young cardinal Riario, who had taken refuge at the altar, was preserved from the rage of the populace by the interference of Lorenzo, who appeared to give credit to his asseverations, that he was ignorant of the intentions of the conspirators (*b*). It is said that his fears had so violent an

(*a*) *Amm.* v. iii. *p.* 118.

(*b*) *Valor. in vitâ Laur. p.* 26.

an effect upon him that he never afterwards recovered his natural complexion (*a*). His attendants fell a sacrifice to the resentment of the citizens. The streets were polluted with the dead bodies and mangled limbs of the slaughtered. With the head of one of these unfortunate wretches on a lance the populace paraded the city, which resounded with the cry of *Palle*, *Palle* (*b*), *Perish the traitors* (*c*)! Francesco de' Pazzi being found at the house of his uncle Giacopo, where on account of his wound he was confined to his bed, was dragged out naked and exhausted by loss of blood, and being brought to the palace, suffered the same death as his associate. His punishment was immediately followed by that of the archbishop, who was hung through the windows of the palace, and was not allowed even to divest himself of his prelatical robes. The last moments of Salviati, if we may credit Politiano, were marked by a singular instance of ferocity. Being suspended close to Francesco de' Pazzi, he seized the naked body with his teeth, and relaxed not from his hold even in the agonies of death (*d*). Jacopo de' Pazzi had escaped from the city during

(*a*) "Tali tantoque metu arreptum, ut exinde nunquam naturalem co- "lorem acquisierit." *Ciacconius ap. Adimar. in not. p.* 26.

(*b*) The palle d' oro, or golden balls, the arms of the family of Medici.

(*c*) Un prete del vescovo fu morto in piazza, e squartato, e levatogli la testa, e per tutto il dì fu portata la detta testa in sur una lancia per tutto Firenze; e strascinato le gambe, e un quarto dinanzi con un braccio portato in su uno spiede per tutta la citta, gridando sempre MUOIANO I TRADITORI. *Landuccius ap. Adimar. in not. p.* 26. Tutti gridando VIVA LE PALLE, E MUOIANO I TRADITORI. *Chron. Caroli e Florentiola ap. idem.*

(*d*) In the opinion of Politiano, the crime of the archbishop was not expiated by his death. Amongst his poems, printed in the edition of Basil, are

during the tumult, but the day following he was made a prisoner by the neighbouring peasants, who regardless of his intreaties to put him to death, brought him to Florence, and delivered him up to the magistrates (*a*). As his guilt was manifest, his execution was instantaneous, and afforded from the windows of the palace another spectacle that gratified the resentment of the enraged multitude. His nephew Renato, who suffered at the same time, excited in some degree the commiseration of the spectators. Devoted to his studies, and averse to popular commotions, he had refused to be an actor in the conspiracy, and his silence was his only crime. The body of Giacopo had been interred in the church of Santa Croce, and to this circumstance the superstition of the people attributed an unusual and incessant fall of rain that succeeded these disturbances. Partaking in their prejudices, or desirous of gratifying their revenge, the magistrates ordered his body to be removed without the walls of the city. The following morning it was again torn from the grave by a great multitude of children, who in spite of the restrictions of decency, and the

---

several epigrams that strongly speak his unquenchable resentment. The following is a specimen :

Salviatus mitræ sceleratus honore superbit :
Et quemquam cœlo credimus esse deum?
Scilicet hæc scelera, hoc artes meruere nefandæ?
At laqueo en pendet. Estis io superi!

(*a*) *Amm. Ist. Fior.* v. iii. *p.* 119. "L' altro dì ne venne preso Messer "Jacopo de' Pazzi che era fuggito; e' fu preso in Romagna, che fu a di 27, "e fu isaminato, e di subito impiccato a detta finestra del palagio."

Strinat. ap. Adimar. in not. p. 27.

the interference of some of the inhabitants, after dragging it a long time through the streets, and treating it with every degree of wanton opprobrium, threw it into the river Arno (*a*). Such was the fate of a man who had enjoyed the highest honours of the republic, and for his services to the state had been rewarded with the privileges of the equestrian rank (*b*). The rest of this devoted family were condemned either to imprisonment or to exile (*c*), excepting only Guglielmo de' Pazzi, who, though not unsuspected, was first sheltered from the popular fury in the house of Lorenzo, and was afterwards ordered to remain at his own villa, about twenty-five miles distant from Florence.

Although most diligent search was made for the priests who had undertaken the murder of Lorenzo, it was not till the

---

(*a*) Quando furono all' uscio della sua casa, messono il capestro nella campanella dell' uscio, e lo tirarono sù, dicendo, *picchia l' uscio*. *Landuccius ap. Adimar. in not. p.* 43. Politiano, who seems to dwell with pleasure on the excesses of an enraged populace, relates more particularly their insults to the lifeless body of Jacopo.

(*b*) Machiavelli, who bore no partiality towards the Medici, gives us a more favourable idea of the character of Jacopo. "Narronsi de i suoi alcuni "vitii, tra i quali erano giuochi e bestemmie, più che a qualunque perduto "huomo non si converebbe; i quali vitii con le molte elemosine ricompen-"sava; perchè a molti bisognosi, e luoghi pii largamente sovveniva. Puossi "ancora di quello dire questo bene, che il sabbato davanti a quella Domenica "diputata a tanto homicidio, per non fare partecipe dell' aversa sua fortuna "alcun' altro, tutti i suoi debiti pagò, tutte le mercantie che' egli haveva in "dogana ed in casa, le quali ad altrui appartenessero, con maravigliosa sol-"lecitudine a i padroni di quelle consegnò." *Mac. lib.* 8.

(*c*) Furono presi Andrea di Piero de' Pazzi, Giovanni, e Nicolo, e Galeotto e Antonio de' Pazzi fratelli, trovati nell' orto de' Monaci degli Angeli. Nicolo, Giovanni, e Galeotto furono menati nella Torre di Volterra.

Cod. Abbatiæ Flor. ap. Adimar. in not. p. 36.

the third day after the attempt that they were discovered, having obtained a shelter in the monastery of the Benedictine monks. No sooner were they brought from the place of their concealment, than the populace, after cruelly mutilating them, put them to death; and with difficulty were prevented from slaughtering the monks themselves (*a*). Montesicco, who had adhered to the cause of the conspirators, although he had refused to be the active instrument of their project, was taken a few days afterwards, as he was endeavouring to save himself by flight, and beheaded, having first made a full confession of all the circumstances attending the conspiracy, by which it appeared that the pope was privy to the whole transaction (*b*). The punishment of Bernardo Bandini was longer delayed. He had safely passed the bounds of Italy, and had taken refuge at length in Constantinople; but the sultan Mahomet being apprised of his crime, ordered him to be seized and sent in chains to Florence, at the same time alledging as the motive of his conduct, the respect which he had for the character of Lorenzo

(*a*) *Pol. Conj. Pact. Comment. in App.*

(*b*) Montesiccus in ipsa fuga comprehensus, postquam omnia uti gesta erant, et non solum consilia, sed etiam dicta pontificis, et comitis Hieronymi de tota conjuratione aperuisset, reste suspenditur. *Fabr. in vitá Laur. v.* i. *p.* 69. But Adimari had before produced documents from the libraries of Florence, which shew that Montesicco was decapitated. " A dì 1. maggio " venne preso M. Gio. Bat. da Montesecco, e a dì 4. di detto mese, gli fu tag- " liato la testa al palazzo del podestà." *Bibl. Abbat. Flor. Cod. No.* 67. *ap. Adimar.* " Fu tagliato il capo sulla porta del podestà, a Gio Battista da Montesecco." *In not. ad lib. cui titulus,* Il Priorista, *ap. idem.*

CHAP. IV.

renzo de' Medici. He arrived in the month of December in the ensuing year. and met with the due reward of his treachery. An embassy was sent from Florence to return thanks to the sultan in the name of the republic (*a*).

Conduct of Lorenzo.

Throughout the whole of this just but dreadful retribution, Lorenzo had exerted all his influence to restrain the indignation of the populace, and to prevent the further effusion of blood. Soon after the attempt upon his life, an immense multitude surrounded his house, and not being convinced of his safety, demanded to see him (*b*). He seized the opportunity which their affection afforded, and notwithstanding his wound, endeavoured by a pathetic and forcible address to moderate the violence of their resentment. He entreated that they would resign to the magistrates the task of ascertaining and of punishing the guilty, lest the innocent should be incautiously involved in

(*a*) "Bernardo di Bandino Bandini ne venne preso da Constantinopoli, a "dì 14 Dicembre 1479, e disaminato che fu al Bargello, fu impiccato alle "finestre di detto Bargello, allato alla Doana, a dì 29 Dicembre 1479, che "pochi dì stette." *Strinatus ap. Adimar. in notis ad Conj. Pact. Comment. p.* 36. Adimari, on the authority of the Chronicle of Carlo a Florentiola, attributes the seizure of Bandini to the orders of the sultan Bajazet, but the capture of Bandini took place in the reign of his predecessor Mahomet II. whose death did not happen till the year 1481. *Murat. Ann. v. ix. p.* 537. *Sagredo, Mem. Istor. de' Monarchi Ottomani, p.* 95. *Ed. Ven.* 1688.

(*b*) "Jam ante Laurentianas aedes, populus ingens de illius salute sollicitus "convenerat, quibus ut animum confirmaret, quum se e fenestris vulneratum "quidem, sed alioqui incolumem ostendisset, tanto plausu, tantisque acclama- "tionibus exceptus est, ut exprimi non possit." *Valor. in vitâ, p.* 25.

in destruction (*a*). His appearance and his admonitions had a powerful and instantaneous effect. With one voice the people devoted themselves to the support of his cause, and besought him to take all possible precautions for his safety, as upon that depended the hopes and welfare of the republic. However Lorenzo might be gratified with these proofs of the affection of his fellow-citizens, he could not but lament that inconsiderate zeal which was so likely to impel them to a culpable excess. Turning to some of the Florentine nobility by whom he was attended, he declared that he felt more anxiety from the intemperate acclamations of his friends, than he had experienced even from his own disasters (*b*).

The general sorrow for the loss of Giuliano was strongly marked. On the fourth day after his death his obsequies were performed, with great magnificence, in the church of S. Lorenzo. It appeared that he had received from the daggers of Bandini and Francesco de' Pazzi no less than nineteen wounds (*c*). Many of the Florentine youth changed their dress in testimony of respect to his memory. In the predilection of the Florentines for Giuliano, historians are agreed. Even Machiavelli allows, that he possessed all the humanity and liberality that could be wished for in one born to such an elevated station, and that his funeral was honoured by the tears of his fellow-citizens (*d*). Tall of stature—strong in his person—his breast prominent—his

(*a*) *Amm. Ist. v.* iii. *p.* 118.

(*b*) *Valor. in vitâ Laur. p.* 17.

(*c*) *Pol. Conj. Pact. Com. in App.*

(*d*) *Mac. Hist. lib.* 8.

his limbs full and muscular—dark eyes—a lively look—an olive complexion—loose black hair turned back from his forehead :—such is the portrait given of Giuliano by his intimate associate Politiano, who to these particulars has further added, that he excelled in active exercises, in horsemanship, in wrestling, in throwing the spear: that he was habituated to thirst and to hunger, and frequently passed a day in voluntary abstinence: possessed of great courage, of unshaken fortitude, a friend to religion and order, an admirer of painting, music, and other elegant arts (*a*).— From the same author we also learn, that Giuliano had given proofs of his poetical talents in several pieces remarkable for their strength of diction, and plenitude of thought, but of these no specimens now remain. Shortly after this transaction, Lorenzo received a visit from Antonio da San Gallo, who informed him that the untimely death of Giuliano had prevented his disclosing to Lorenzo a circumstance, with which it was now become necessary that he should be acquainted (*b*). This was the birth of a son, whom a lady of the family of Gorini had born to Giuliano about twelve months before his death, and whom Antonio had held over the baptismal fount, where he received the name of Giulio. Lorenzo immediately

(*a*) *Pol. Conj. Pact. Com. in App.*

(*b*) "Antonio da S. Gallo andò allora a trovar Lorenzo, dicendo, che es-"sendo morto Giuliano, ei non aveva potuto far noto, come aveva avuto da "una donna de' Gorini, sua amica, un figlio, già un anno, quale aveva tenuto "egli a battesimo, e stava al rincontro della sua casa antica, nella via di "Pinti. Il detto Lorenzo l' andò a vedere, e dettolo alla cura del medesimo "Antonio, dove stette fino al settimo anno."

Cod. Abbat. Flor. ap. Adimar. in notis ad Conj. Pact. Com. p. 40.

diately repaired to the place of the infant's residence, and taking him under his protection, delivered him to Antonio, with whom he remained until he arrived at the seventh year of his age. This concealed offspring of illicit love, to whom the kindness of Lorenzo supplied the untimely loss of a father, was destined to act an important part in the affairs of Europe. The final extinction of the liberties of Florence; the alliance of the family of Medici with the royal house of France; the expulsion of Henry VIII. of England from the bosom of the Roman church; and the consequent establishment of the doctrines of the reformers in this island, are principally to be referred to this illegitimate son of Giuliano de' Medici, who, through various vicissitudes of fortune, at length obtained the supreme direction of the Roman see, and under the name of Clement VII. guided the bark of St. Peter through a succession of the severest storms which it has ever experienced (*a*).

The

(*a*) Machiavelli, who wrote his history in the pontificate of Clement VII. informs us, that this pontiff was born a few months after the death of his father, in which he has been generally followed by succeeding writers. "Rimase di lui (Giuliano) un figliuolo, ilquale dopo a pochi mesi che fu morto, "nacque, e fu chiamato Giulio; il quale fu da quella virtù & fortuna ripieno, "che in questi presenti tempi tutto il mondo conosce." *Mac. lib.* 8. A full account of the political transactions of Clement VII. will be found in the Florentine history of Benedetto Varchi, written under the auspices of Cosmo I. grand duke of Florence, who granted the author access to all the archives of his family. The favour of an absolute sovereign did not seduce Varchi from the duty of an historian, but the extreme freedom with which he commented upon the events which led to the subjugation of his country, and animadverted on the characters of Clement VII. and others who contributed towards it, prevented for nearly two centuries the publication of his work, which first appeared at Cologne in 1721, in folio, and afterwards without date at Leyden, *ap. Pietro vander Aa.*

CHAP. IV.

Memorials of the conspiracy.

The public grief occasioned by the death of Giuliano was however mingled with, and alleviated by exultation for the safety of Lorenzo. Every possible method was devised to brand with infamy the perpetrators of the deed. By a public decree, the name and arms of the Pazzi were ordered to be for ever suppressed. The appellations of such places in the city as were derived from that family were directed to be changed. All persons contracting marriage with the descendants of Andrea de' Pazzi were declared to be *ammoniti*, and prohibited from all offices and dignities in the republic (*a*). The ancient ceremony of conducting annually the sacred fire from the church of S. Giovanni to the house of the Pazzi was abolished, and a new method was adopted of continuing this popular superstition (*b*). Andrea dal Castagno was employed, at the public expence, to represent the persons of the traitors on

---

(*a*) The descendants of Andrea de' Pazzi are thus accurately given by Adimari.

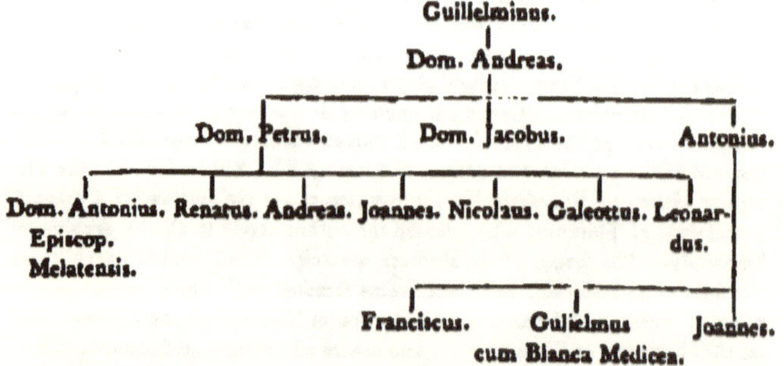

(*b*) The decree on this occasion appears amongst the documents published by Fabroni, and is given in the Appendix, No. XXIII.

on the walls of the palace, in the execution of which he obtained great applause, although the figures, as a mark of infamy, were suspended by the feet (*a*). On the other hand the skill of the Florentine artists was exerted in soothing the feelings, and gratifying the curiosity of the public, by perpetuating the remembrance of the dangers which Lorenzo had escaped. By the assistance of Andrea Verocchio, Orsini, a celebrated modeller in wax, formed three figures as large as the life, which bore the most perfect resemblance of the person and features of Lorenzo, and which were placed in different churches of the territory of Florence. One of these represented him in the dress which he wore when he received the wound, and as he appeared to the populace at the window of his palace (*b*). A more lasting memorial was devised by Antonio Pollajuoli, who struck a medal on this occasion, exhibiting in the ancient

---

(*a*) " L' anno 1478, quando dalla famiglia de' Pazzi & altri loro adhe-" renti & congiurati; fu morto in S. Maria del Fiore Giuliano de' Medici, e " Lorenzo suo fratello ferito, fu deliberato dalla Signoria, che tutti quelli della " congiura fussino, come traditori, dipinti nella facciata del palagio del podestà; " onde essendo questa opera offerta ad Andrea, egli, come servitore, ed obli-" gato alla casa de' Medici l'accetto molto ben volontieri, e messovisi, la fece " tanto bella, che fu uno stupore; ne si potrebbe dire quanta arte e giudizio " si conosceva in quei personaggi ritratti per lo più di naturale, ed impiccati " per i piedi in strane attitudini, e tutte varie e bellissime. La qual opera, " perchè piacque a tutta la citta, & particolarmente agli intendenti delle cose " di pittura, fu cagione che da quella in poi, non più Andrea dal Castagno, ma " Andrea degli Impiccati fusse chiamato."

Vasari, nella vita di Andrea dal Castagno.

(*b*) *V. Vasari, nella vita di Andr. Verocchio*, where a particular account is given of these figures, which were " tanto ben fatti, che rappresentavano non " più uomini di cera, ma vivissimi," one of them was placed in the church of the Chiariti " dinanzi al Crucifisso *che fa miracoli*." It appears they were all remaining at the time Vasari wrote.

ancient choir of the Reparata, the assassination of Giuliano, and the attack made upon Lorenzo. In this medal, the conspirators are all represented naked, not merely for the purpose of displaying the knowledge of the artist in the human figure, in which he excelled all his contemporaries, but, as some have conjectured, as being characteristic of the flagitious act in which they were engaged (*a*).

Lorenzo prepares for his defence against the pope and the king of Naples.

Although the body of troops destined to support the conspirators had kept aloof from the scene of action, and with difficulty effected their retreat from the Florentine dominions (*b*), yet Lorenzo was well aware of the storm that was gathering around him, and with equal prudence and resolution prepared to meet it. By the confession of Montesicco he was fully informed of the implacable hatred of the pope, which was inflamed almost to madness by the miscarriage of his designs, and the publicity of his treachery. Lorenzo also knew that the king of Naples, who was not less formidable to Italy from the ferocity and military reputation of his son Alfonso, duke of Calabria, than from the extent and resources of his own dominions, would most probably concur with the pope. His comprehensive eye saw at one glance the extent of the danger to which

(*a*) *Vasari vita di Ant. Pollaiuoli.*—" Fece il medesimo alcune medaglie " bellissime, e fra l' altre in una la congiura de' Pazzi; nella quale sono le " teste di Lorenzo e Giuliano de' Medici, e nel riverso il choro di S. Maria del " Fiore, & tutto il caso come passò appunto."

(*b*) " Adfuit eodem die e conjuratis Joannes Franciscus Tollentinas ex " agro Forocorneliensi, cum peditibus mille, totidemque Laurentius Tifernas " ex alia parte, qui, ubi rem infectam viderunt, magno se periculo domum " receperunt." *Raph. Volater. in Geogr. lib. 5.*

which he was exposed, and he accordingly adopted every measure that might be likely to oppose or to avert it. He addressed himself to all the Italian states, with strong representations of the conduct of the pope, and entreated them, by every motive which was likely to influence them, to shew their open disapprobation of a species of treachery, from which neither rank, nor talents, nor virtue, could afford protection. He adverted to the fatal consequences which must arise to Italy from the subjugation of the Florentine republic, and connected his cause with that of the country at large. In the same terms he wrote to the kings of France and of Spain, endeavouring to obtain their interference in his behalf, and to convince them of the injustice and criminality of his enemies, and of his own innocence and moderation (*a*). Nor was he negligent in the mean time in providing for his own defence. By every possible means he incited the citizens of Florence to make preparation for repelling their enemies. He procured from all quarters large supplies of provisions, with every other requisite for supporting an obstinate siege. The activity of Lorenzo infused a similar spirit into those around him, and the hopes of the people were supported by the early appearance, in Mugello, of Giovanni Bentivoglio, the firm ally of the Medici, with a chosen band of soldiers, which he led to the relief of Lorenzo as soon as he was apprized of his danger. Moved by his representations, or jealous of

(*a*) Louis XI. had anticipated his communication by a letter written to Lorenzo, immediately after the intelligence of the assassination had arrived at Paris, in which he expressed the warmest resentment against the authors of the treachery; these letters are yet extant, and are given from the documents of *Fabroni*, in the Appendix, No. XXIV.

CHAP. IV.

of the power of the pope and of the king of Naples, several other states of Italy warmly espoused the cause of the Florentines. Ercole d'Este, duke of Ferrara, attended in person with a powerful reinforcement. The Venetians, although cautious in their determination, displayed a manifest partiality to the Florentines, and even the kings of Spain, and of France, transmitted to Lorenzo the fullest assurances of their conviction of the rectitude of his conduct, and of their willingness to interpose with all their authority in his behalf (*a*). So favourable a concurrence of circumstances gave fresh spirits to the Florentines, and removed in a great degree the apprehensions of the friends of the Medici. At this juncture Politiano addressed to Gentile d' Urbino, bishop of Arezzo, a Latin ode, which is not less entitled to notice for its intrinsic merit, than as an authentic indication of the public opinion at the time it was written (*b*).

Ode of Politiano.

Ad

(*a*) Philip de Commines was sent by Louis XI. to Florence, from whence he afterwards went to Milan to request the Milanese to send a body of soldiers to the relief of the Florentines, with which he informs us they complied, "tant a la requete du Roi, que pour faire leur devoir;" speaking of the Florentines, he further adds, "La faveur du Roi leur fait quelque chose: mais "non pas tant que jeusse voulu. Car je n'avoye armée pour les aider; mais "seulement avoye mon train. Je demouray au dit lieu de Florence un an, "ou en leurs territoires, & bien traitté d'eux, & a leurs despens, & mieux le "dernier jour que le premier." *Mem. de P. de Commines, lib.* vi. *c.* 5. For this last assertion the French statesman had sufficient reason, for Ammirato informs us, that at his departure from Florence, the republic presented him with fifty-five pounds weight of wrought silver for the use of his table. *Amm.* iii. 126.

(*b*) Politiano afterwards sent this poem with the following address to Lorenzo de' Medici:

"Qua ode Gentilem nostrum nuper sum consolatus, eandem quoque ad

Ad Gentilem Episcopum.

Gentiles animi maxima pars mei,
Communi nimium sorte quid angeris?
Quid curis animum lugubribus teris,
Et me discrucias simul?

Passi digna quidem perpetuo sumus
Luctu, qui mediis (heu miseri) sacris
Illum, illum juvenem, vidimus, O nefas!
Stratum sacrilega manu!

At sunt attonito quæ dare pectori
Solamen valeant plurima, nam super
Est, qui vel gremio creverit in tuo,
LAURENS Etruriæ caput.

LAURENS quem patriæ cælicolum pater
Tutum terrifica gorgone præstitit;
Quem Tuscus pariter, quem Venetus Leo
Servant, et Draco pervigil.

Illi bellipotens excubat Hercules;
Illi fatiferis militat arcubus;
Illi mittit equos Francia martios,
Felix Francia regibus.

Circumstat

" te mittendam statui, visa est nam mihi res, quæ non minus ad te, quam ad " eum, atque ad meipsum pertineret. Omnia collegi quæ communem hunc " nostrum dolorem, etsi minus tollere, levare procul dubio aliqua ex parte " possint: Tu, cum tot videas tuæ saluti tam diligenter invigilare, potes ad- " moneri quam tibi necesse sit magni teipsum facere; neque tuam, hoc est " publicam totius (ita me deus amet) Italiæ salutem neglectam pati. Lege " et vale." *Pol. Op. Ed. Ald.* 1498.

Circumstat populus murmure dissono;
  Circumstant juvenem purpurei patres;
  Causa vincimus, et robore militum;
    Hac stat Juppiter, hac favet.

Quare, O cum misera quid tibi Nenia,
  Si nil proficimus? quin potius gravis
  Absterisse bono lætitiæ die
    Audes nubila pectoris.

Nam cum jam gelidos umbra reliquerit
  Artus, non dolor hanc perpetuus retro,
  Mordacesve trahunt sollicitudines,
    Mentis, curaque pervicax.

O Friend, whose woes this bosom shares,
Why ceaseless mourn our mutual cares?
Ah why thy days to grief resign,
With thy regrets recalling mine?

Eternal o'er the atrocious deed,
'Tis true our kindred hearts may bleed;
When He, twin glory of our land,
Fell by a sacrilegious hand!

But sure, my friend, there yet remains
Some solace for these piercing pains,
Whilst He, once nurtur'd at thy side,
Lorenzo lives, Etruria's pride.

Lorenzo, o'er whose favour'd head,
Jove his terrific gorgon spread;
Whose steps the lion-pair await,
Of *Florence*, and *Venetia*'s state.

For

For him his crest the dragon rears;
For him the *Herculean* band appears;
Her martial succour Gallia brings;
Gallia that glories in her kings!

See round the youth the purpled band
Of venerable fathers stand;
Exulting crowds around him throng
And hail him as he moves along.

Strong in our cause and in our friends,
Our righteous battle Jove defends;
Thy useless sorrows then represt,
Let joy once more dilate thy breast.

To animate the clay-cold frame,
No sighs shall fan the vital flame;
Nor all the tears that love can shed,
Recall to life the silent dead.

Kindness of Lorenzo to the relatives of the conspirators.

Notwithstanding the vigour and activity of Lorenzo in preparing for the war, he was anxiously desirous of preventing, if possible, such a calamity. By his moderation, and even kindness to the surviving relatives of the conspirators, he thought to obliterate the remembrance of past disturbances, and to unite all the citizens in one common cause. Upwards of one hundred persons had already perished, some by the hands of justice, and others by the fury of the populace (*a*). Many had absconded or concealed themselves

(*a*) In tal che la città tutto era sollevata per il rumore, furono tagliati a pezzi circa venti persone della famiglia del cardinale, ed altrettanti di quella del

themselves under apprehensions of being charged with a participation of the crime. Among the latter was Averardo Salviati, a near relation of the Archbishop of Pisa. Lorenzo being informed that he had secreted himself in his house, requested, by the mediation of a common friend, an interview with him, and on his arrival received him with such tokens of kindness and benevolence as drew tears from all who were present (*a*). Salviati was not ungrateful; a closer intimacy took place between them, and a few years afterwards Lorenzo gave one of his daughters in marriage to Giacopo Salviati, the nephew of Averardo, whose character and accomplishments merited such an honour. The cardinal Raffaello Riario was liberated as soon as the tumult had subsided, and was suffered to return to Rome (*b*). To Raffaello Maffei of Volterra, the brother of Antonio, one of the priests who had undertaken the assassination of Lorenzo, a man distinguished by his uncommon learning and indefatigable spirit of research, Lorenzo wrote a Latin letter, full of kindness and urbanity, which, on account of the

---

Arcivescovo; e tra le fenestre del palagio della Signoria e quelle del podestà furono impiccati circa sessanta persone, tutti congiurati, e molt' altri malconci dalle ferite. *Orig. e descend. della casa de' Med. M.S.*

(*a*) *Valori in vitâ, p.* 35.

(*b*) Whatever share the cardinal had in the conspiracy, he was by no means insensible of the lenity that had been shewn him. In a letter to the pope of the 10th of June 1478, some days after he was liberated, he expresses the strongest sense of his obligations to the Florentines, and in particular to Lorenzo de' Medici; he remonstrates with the pope in warm terms on the injustice of subjecting to ecclesiastical censures those persons to whom he is indebted for his preservation; and declares his resolution not to leave Florence until the sentence of excommunication issued by Sixtus be annulled. *v. App. No.* XXV.

the elegance of its diction, Maffei erroneously attributed to the pen of Politiano (*a*). Even the survivors of the Pazzi family, although they had at first been treated with great severity, were, by the interference of Lorenzo, in a short time restored to their former honours. The only public monument that remained of this transaction was the painting on the walls of the palace by Andrea dal Castagno, which was suffered to remain, long after the family of the Pazzi had been reinstated in their ancient rights and dignity.

Violence of Sixtus IV.

The generosity and moderation of Lorenzo, although they endeared him still more to his fellow-citizens, had no effect upon the temper of Sixtus, who no sooner heard of the miscarriage of his design, the death of the archbishop, and the restraint imposed upon the cardinal, than he gave a loose to his impetuosity, and poured out against Lorenzo the bitterest invectives. In the first paroxisms of his anger, he directed that the property of the Medici and of all Florentine citizens then in Rome should be confiscated, and the Florentines themselves imprisoned; and had he not entertained apprehensions respecting the fate of the cardinal, it is probable that he would have treated them with still greater severity. To appease his wrath the republic dispatched to Rome, Donato Acciajuoli, a person no less celebrated for his talents and his learning, than for the credit with which he had performed the most important embassies and filled the highest offices of the state. This measure,

(*a*) Mihi quoque quem Antonii supradicta fratris mei gravis causa, suspectum reddere debuerat, Epistolam humanitatis ac officii plenissimam scripsit adeoque elegantem, ut eam a Politiano scriptam omnino putaverim, nisi ille postea jurasset Laurentii ingenio dictatam, qui paucis, si quando a curis esset vacuus, in hoc genere cederet. *Raph. Vol. Com. Urb. p.* 153. *Ed. Lugd.* 1552.

measure, far from pacifying the pope, seemed to add fresh fuel to his anger. Instead of attending to the representations of the ambassador, he threatened to send him as a prisoner to the castle of S. Angelo, and would certainly have executed his purpose, had not the legates from Venice and from Milan interfered in his favour, and declared that they should consider such a breach of the faith of nations, as an insult to themselves. The resentment of Sixtus then burst forth through another channel. He attacked the Florentines with his spiritual weapons, and anathematized not only Lorenzo de' Medici, but the gonfaloniere and other magistrates of the republic. In the document which Sixtus issued on this occasion, Lorenzo is emphatically styled "the child of iniquity and the nurseling of perdition." After bestowing similar epithets on the magistrates, Sixtus proceeds to relate the manifold offences of Lorenzo against the holy see. Adverting to the gentleness and moderation of his own character, he then declares, that according to the example of our Saviour, he had long suffered in peace the insults and the injuries of his enemies, and that he should still have continued to exercise his forbearance, had not Lorenzo de' Medici, with the magistrates of Florence, and their abettors, discarding the fear of God, inflamed with fury, and instigated by diabolical suggestions, laid violent hands on ecclesiastical persons, *proh dolor et inauditum scelus!* hung up the archbishop, imprisoned the cardinal, and by various means destroyed and slaughtered their followers. He then solemnly excommunicates Lorenzo, the gonfaloniere, and other officers of the state, and their immediate successors; declaring them to be incapable of receiving or transmitting property

He excommunicates Lorenzo and the magistrates.

by

by inheritance or will; and prohibiting their descendants from enjoying any ecclesiastical employment. By the same instrument he suspended the bishops and clergy of the Florentine territories from the exercise of their spiritual functions (a).

Singular reply of the Florentine synod.

Whatever might have been the effect of this denunciation, if directed solely against the persons immediately concerned in the transactions to which the pope referred, it appears, that in extending his censures to the dignitaries of the church who were not personally implicated in the imputed guilt, Sixtus had exceeded his authority; and the exasperated ecclesiastics, availing themselves of his imprudence, retorted upon the pope the anathemas which he had poured out against them. The most eminent civilians of the time were consulted on this occasion, many of whom asserted the nullity of the prohibition. By the exertions of Gentile d' Urbino, bishop of Arezzo, a convocation was summoned in the church of the Reparata, and Fabroni has produced from the archives of Florence, a document yet remaining in the hand-writing of Gentile, which purports to be the result of the deliberations which there took place (b). The professed tendency of this piece is to criminate the

(a) Although this piece be of considerable length, I have thought proper to give it a place in the Appendix. First, because Sixtus, labouring under such imputations, ought to be allowed to relate his own story. Secondly, because this document will throw farther light on many of the facts before adverted to; and lastly, because it is one of the most extraordinary specimens of priestly arrogance that ever insulted the common sense of mankind.

v. App. No. XXVI.

(b) Fabroni conjectures that this convocation was not held; but for this opinion he adduces no reasons, and other historians have related it as a well-

CHAP. IV.

the pope as being the chief instigator of the enormities committed at Florence, and to exculpate Lorenzo de' Medici and the Florentines from the charges which Sixtus had brought against them; but this vindication would have lost nothing of its effect, if, in exposing the guilt of the pontiff, it had consulted the dignity of those he had injured, and exhibited a more temperate and dispassionate refutation. How so unmodified and daring an attack can be reconciled to the catholic idea of the infallibility of the holy see, it is not easy to discover. If it be acknowledged that the bull of Sixtus had exceeded all the limits of decorum, it must also be allowed that the reply of the synod is in this respect equally censurable; nor is it in the power of language to convey a more copious torrent of abuse, than was poured out upon this occasion by the Florentine clergy, on the supreme director of the Roman church.

Sixtus attempts to prevail on the Florentines to deliver up Lorenzo.

Sixtus did not however relax from his purpose. Whilst he brandished in one hand the spiritual weapon, which has impressed with terror the proudest sovereigns of Europe, in the other he grasped a temporal sword, which he now openly, as he had before secretly, aimed at the life of Lorenzo. At

known circumstance. Some doubt may perhaps remain whether the document, purporting to be the act of the synod, was in fact adopted there; or whether it was merely proposed for the approbation of the assembly; though the presumption is in favour of the former opinion. For producing a document addressed in such contumelious terms to the head of the church, Fabroni thinks it necessary to apologize: "Vererer reprehensionem prudentum, quod talia, "injuriosa sane Sixto pontifici ediderim, nisi historici munus esset referre "omnia quæ dicta et acta sunt." *Fabr. in vitâ Laur. v.* ii. *p.* 136. Happily I can lay this piece before my readers without a similar precaution.

v. App. No. XXVII.

At his instigation the king of Naples dispatched an envoy to Florence to prevail upon the citizens to deliver up Lorenzo into the hands of his enemies, or at least to banish him from the Tuscan territories. The alternative denounced to them was the immediate vengeance of both the king and the pope. These threats had not, however, the intended effect, but on the contrary produced another instance of the attachment of the Florentines to Lorenzo. They not only refused to comply with the proposition of the king, but avowed their firm resolution to suffer every extremity, rather than betray a man with whose safety and dignity those of the republic were so nearly connected. They also directed their chancellor Bartolomeo Scala to draw up an historical memorial of all the proceedings of the conspiracy (*a*); by which it clearly appeared, that throughout the whole transaction the conspirators had acted with the privity and assent of the pope (*b*).

Lorenzo

(*a*) *v. App. No.* XXVIII. Several eminent scholars also testified their readiness to transmit to posterity the memory of this transaction. Even Filelfo, the ancient adversary of the family, offered his pen to Lorenzo on this occasion. *v. App. No.* XXIX.

(*b*) As to the atrocity of the crime, and the turpitude of the authors of it, contemporary historians are agreed. It is only in our own days that an attempt has been made to transfer the guilt from its perpetrators, to those who suffered by it. The *Conspiracy of the Pazzi* has afforded a subject for a tragedy to a celebrated living author, who, in his various dramatic works, has endeavoured to accustom his countrymen to bolder sentiment, and to remove the idea, that the genius of the Italian language is not adapted to the purposes of tragedy. It must however be confessed, that in attempting to render this transaction subservient to the interests of freedom, by his *Congiura de' Pazzi*, he has fallen greatly short of that effect which several of his other pieces produce. The causes of this failure are not difficult to discover. In selecting a subject for tragedy, the author may either derive his materials from his own

CHAP. IV.

Danger of his situation.

1479.

Lorenzo was now fully apprized of the danger of his situation. It was sufficiently evident that this powerful league was not formed against the Florentines, but against him individually; and that the evils of war might be avoided by a compliance with the requisition of the king. Under these circumstances, instead of sheltering himself in the affections of his fellow-citizens, he boldly opposed himself to the danger that threatened him, and resolved either to fall with dignity, or to render his own cause that of the republic at large. He therefore called together about

fancy, or he may choose some known historical transaction. The first of these is the creature of the poet, the second he can only avail himself of so far as acknowledged historical credence allows. In the one the imagination is predominant; in the other, it is subservient to the illustration of truths previously understood, and generally admitted. What then shall we think of a dramatic performance in which the Pazzi are the champions of liberty? in which superstition is called in to the aid of truth, and Sixtus consecrates the holy weapons devoted to the slaughter of the two brothers? in which the relations of all the parties are confounded, and a tragic effect is attempted to be produced by a total dereliction of historical veracity, an assumption of falsehood for truth, of vice for virtue? In this tragedy Guglielmo de' Pazzi (there called Raimondi), who married Bianca the sister of Lorenzo, is the chief of the conspirators, and failing in his attempt, executes vengeance on himself; but Machiavelli expressly informs us, that "Gulielmo de' Pazzi, di "Lorenzo cognato, nelle case di quello, e per l' innocenza sua, e per l' aiuta "di Bianca sua moglie, si salvò;" *Hist. lib.* 8. Whereas Francesco the leader of the assassins, and who was not related to the Medici, died by a halter. If we are surprised at so extraordinary a perversion of incident and character, we are not less so in perusing the remarks with which the author has accompanied his tragedy, in which he avows an opinion, that Lorenzo would be too insignificant even to be the object of a conspiracy, if he had not lent him a fictitious importance! It is to be hoped that the better information, or the riper judgment of this feeling author, will induce him to form a more just estimation of the character of a man, whose name is the chief honour of his country; and to adopt the converse of the assertion with which he concludes his remarks on this tragedy, "che per nessuna cosa del mondo non vorrebbe "l' aver fatta." *Trag. del Conte Vittorio Alfieri. vol.* iv. *Paris, ap. Didot* 1788.

about three hundred of the principal citizens, whom he addressed in a striking and energetic harangue, at the close of which he earnestly besought them, that as the public tranquillity could not be preserved by other means, nor a treaty effected with their enemies unless it was sealed with his blood, they would no longer hesitate to comply with the terms proposed, nor suffer their attention to the safety of an individual to bring destruction upon the state. When Lorenzo had concluded, Giacopo de' Alexandri, with the concurrence of every person present, declared it to be the unanimous resolution of the assembly to defend his life at the hazard of their own (*a*).

All was now prepared for war, the approaching horrors of which were increased by the appearance of the plague at Florence. In this emergency, Lorenzo thought it advisable to send his wife and children to Pistoia. "I now "remove from you," said he to the citizens, "these ob-"jects of my affection, whom I would, if necessary, will-"ingly devote for your welfare; that whatever may be "the result of this contest, the resentment of my enemies "may be appeased with my blood only."

Conduct of the war.

Though the duke of Calabria and the count of Urbino were esteemed the most formidable commanders of Italy, the Florentines could boast of men of great eminence and experience in the military art; but the supreme command was intrusted to Ercole d' Este, duke of Ferrara. The enemy were now approaching towards Florence, and marked their

(*a*) *Mac. Hist. lib.* 8. *Amm.* v. iii. *p.* 123. *Fabr. in vitâ*, v. i. *p.* 87.

their way with devastation. After possessing themselves of several smaller places, they at length besieged Arezzo, but on the approach of the Florentine troops they prepared for an engagement. Notwithstanding the inferiority of the latter in the reputation of their generals, and in the number of their soldiers, they possessed such advantages as it was supposed would, in case of a general engagement, have ensured their success. The citizens of Arezzo by a vigorous defence had damped the spirit of the Papal and Neapolitan troops, who experienced also a scarcity of provisions, and were very disadvantageously posted; but after the two armies had regarded each other for some time with mutual apprehensions, a truce was proposed by the duke of Urbino, which was acceded to by the duke of Ferrara, to the great dissatisfaction of the Florentines, who conceived that their general had betrayed their cause. The two armies retired into their winter quarters; and the Florentines found themselves incumbered with great and increasing expence, without being relieved from their fears (*a*).

Lorenzo negotiates for peace.

This season, however, afforded Lorenzo another opportunity of trying the result of further negotiation; but whilst he endeavoured on the one hand to reconcile himself to the pope, on the other hand, he made preparation to meet his enemies, in case his negotiations should prove unsuccessful. From the connexion between his family and that of Sforza, he had promised himself powerful support from Milan, but the disagreement between the duchess and Lodovico

(*a*) *Mac. Hist. lib.* 8.

Lodovico Sforza, which terminated in the latter assuming the regency during the minority of the young duke, in a great degree disappointed his hopes. The Venetians had sent Bernardo Bembo, the father of the celebrated Pietro Bembo (*a*), as their ambassador to Florence, and professed themselves inimical to the proceedings of the pope and the king. They did not however yet think proper to engage in the war; but with that species of policy by which they were always distinguished, looked on for the purpose of taking advantage of any opportunity of aggrandizing themselves at the expence of their neighbours. In the course of the winter, different envoys arrived at Florence from the emperor and the kings of France and Bohemia, who repeated to Lorenzo their assurances of attachment and support, at the same time advising him once more to attempt a reconciliation with the pope, under the sanction of their names and influence. A deputation consisting of several of the most respectable citizens of Florence was accordingly sent to Rome; but Sixtus still remained inflexible, and paid no more regard to the recommendations of the European sovereigns, than he had before done to the intreaties and remonstrances of Lorenzo himself.

In

(*a*) On this occasion Bernardo was accompanied by his son, then only nine years of age. He remained there about two years, and to this circumstance his historian, Casa, attributes the proficiency he made in the Italian tongue, of which he was destined to be one of the brightest ornaments. "Nec vero patris consilium filii fefellit industria: sic enim excitatum puerile Bembi ingenium Florentiæ est, sic teneræ pueri aures, animusque, puro ac dulci illo Etruscorum sermone imbutus, ut jam inde a prima adolescentia, multa cum Latine, tum vero Tusce, a se scripta ediderit, quibus nihil hominum auribus politius, nihil omnino elegantius aut suavius accidere possit."

Joh. Casa in vitâ P. Bembi. in Op. Cas. v. iv. p. 46. Ed. Ven. 1728.

Death of Donato Acciajuoli.

In order to testify to the king of France the sense which they entertained of his interposition, the Florentines dispatched Donato Acciajuoli as their ambassador to Paris. Shortly after his departure, intelligence was received at Florence of his death, which happened at Milan as he was pursuing his journey. This circumstance was a subject of the sincerest grief to the Florentines, who well knew how to appreciate the virtues of their fellow-citizens, and omitted no opportunity of inciting the patriotism of the living, by the honours they bestowed on the memory of the dead. A sumptuous funeral was decreed to his remains; Lorenzo de' Medici and three other eminent citizens were appointed curators of his children, who were declared to be exempt from the payment of taxes, and the daughters had considerable portions assigned them from the public treasury (*a*).

Various success of the war.

Besides the duke of Ferrara, the Florentines had, during the course of the winter, prevailed upon several other experienced commanders, amongst whom were Roberto Malatesta, Constantino Sforza, and Rodolfo Gonzaga, to espouse their cause. The states of Venice also at length sent a reinforcement under the command of Carlo Montone and Deifebo d' Anguillari; by these powerful succours the Florentines found themselves enabled to take the field in the ensuing spring with great expectations of success. Emboldened by this support they determined to carry on a war not merely defensive. Their troops were divided into

(*a*) *Amm. Ist.* v. iii. p. 126.

into two bodies, one of which was destined to make an irruption into the territories of the pope, and the other to oppose the duke of Calabria. At the approach of Montone, who intended to attack Perugia, the troops of the pope made a precipitate retreat; but the unexpected death of that commander relieved them in some degree from their fears, and they at length ventured to oppose the further progress of the Florentines. The two armies met near the lake of Perugia, the ancient Thrasymenus, rendered remarkable by the defeat which the Romans experienced there from the arms of Hannibal. Struck with the similiarity of their situation, a sentiment of terror pervaded the papal troops, who were soon repulsed, and obliged to quit the field with considerable loss, whilst the successful army proceeded to invest Perugia. The other division of the Florentine troops was not equally successful. The mercenary views of the different commanders, who preferred plunder to victory, defeated the hopes which the Florentines had justly formed of their success. A disagreement took place among the leaders, in consequence of which the duke of Ferrara, with his own immediate followers, retired from the service of the republic. Availing himself of this opportunity, the duke of Calabria made an instantaneous attack upon the Florentines, who having lost all confidence in their commanders, pusillanimously deserted their standards, and consulted their safety by a shameful flight. The consternation occasioned at Florence by this disaster is scarcely to be described, as it was supposed that the duke of Calabria would immediately proceed to the attack of the city; and this distress was heightened by the ravages of the plague, and by impending famine. Happily, however, the

CHAP. IV.

the apprehensions of the Florentines on this occasion were not wholly realized. Instead of proceeding towards Florence, the duke rather chose to employ himself in plundering the surrounding country. The capture of the town of Colle, which made an obstinate resistance, and of some adjacent places of less importance, engaged his attention till the detachment that had been sent to the attack of Perugia, having suddenly raised the siege, returned towards Florence, and alleviated the fears of the citizens. An unexpected proposition made by the duke of Calabria for a truce of three months, was chearfully assented to by the Florentines, who thus once more obtained a temporary relief from a state of anxiety and a profusion of expence, which were become equally insupportable (*a*).

Lorenzo resolves to visit the king of Naples.

But although by this cessation of hostilities the tranquillity of the city was for a time restored, the situation of Lorenzo de' Medici was in the highest degree critical and alarming. He had witnessed the terrors of the populace on the approach of the Neapolitan army, and although he had great confidence in the affection of the citizens, yet as the war was avowedly waged against him as an individual, and might at any time be concluded by delivering him up to his enemies, he knew enough of human nature to be convinced that he had just grounds to dread the event. The rising discontents and murmurs of the people increased his suspicion; even the truce was unfavourable to him, as it gave the Florentines an opportunity of estimating the injuries

(*a*) *Mac. Hist. lib.* 8. *Amm.* v. iii. *p.* 142.

injuries they had sustained by the war, which, like wounds received by an individual in the ardour of action, were not fully felt till the heat of the contest had subsided (*a*). Complaints began to be heard that the public treasure was exhausted, and the commerce of the city ruined, whilst the citizens were burdened with oppressive taxes. Insinuations of a more personal nature were not always suppressed; and Lorenzo had the mortification of being told, that sufficient blood had been already shed, and that it would be expedient for him rather to devise some means of effecting a peace than of making further preparations for the war (*b*). Under these circumstances, Lorenzo resolved to adopt some measure which should effectually close the contest, although with the hazard of his life. In deliberating on the mode of accomplishing his purpose, his genius suggested to him one of those bold expedients, which only great minds can conceive and execute. He resolved secretly to quit the city of Florence, to proceed immediately to Naples, and to place himself in the hands of Ferdinand, his avowed enemy, determined either to convince him of the injustice and impolicy of his conduct, and thereby induce him to agree to a separate peace, or to devote himself to the preservation of his country.

His letter to the magistrates of Florence.

In the commencement of the month of December 1479, Lorenzo accordingly left the city, without having communicated his intentions to his fellow-citizens, and proceeded to San Miniato, a town in the Florentine state, whence

(*a*) *Mac. Hist. lib.* 8. (*b*) *Fabr. in vitâ Laur.* v. i. *p.* 100.

CHAP. IV.

whence he addressed a letter to the magistrates of Florence, which places the motives of his conduct in a very clear point of view (*a*).

Lorenzo de' Medici to the States of Florence.

"If I did not explain to you, before I left Florence, the "cause of my departure, it was not from want of respect, "but because I thought, that in the dangerous circum-"stances in which our city is placed, it was more necessary "to act than to deliberate. It seems to me that peace is be-"come indispensable to us; and as all other means of ob-"taining it have proved ineffectual, I have rather chosen to "incur some degree of danger myself, than to suffer the "city to continue longer under its present difficulties; I "therefore mean, with your permission, to proceed directly "to Naples; conceiving that as I am the person chiefly "aimed at by our enemies, I may, by delivering myself "into their hands, perhaps be the means of restoring "peace to my fellow-citizens. Of these two things, one "must be taken for granted; either the king of Naples, as "he has often asserted, and as some have believed, is "friendly to the Florentine state, and aims, even by these "hostile proceedings, rather to render us a service, than to "deprive

(*a*) It is somewhat surprising that this letter, so explicitly stating the purpose of Lorenzo, should have escaped the attention of Fabroni; who has, however, favoured us with the oration of Lorenzo to Ferdinand, on his arrival at Naples, the authority of which may perhaps be doubted; as well as that of Lorenzo to the magistrates of Florence before his departure for Naples, attributed to him by Ammirato. *Ist. v.* iii. *p.* 143. The efforts of imagination should not be substituted for the documents of history. This letter is published in the *Lettere di Principi, v.* i. *p.* 3. *Ed. Ven.* 1581.

" deprive us of our liberties; or he wishes to effect the " ruin of the republic. If he be favourably disposed towards " us, there is no better method of putting his intention to " the test, than by placing myself freely in his hands, and " this I will venture to say is the only mode of obtaining " an honourable peace. If, on the other hand, the views of " the king extend to the subversion of our liberties, we " shall at least be speedily apprized of his intentions; and " this knowledge will be more cheaply obtained by the " ruin of one, than of all. I am contented to take upon " myself this risque, because, as I am the person princi-" pally sought after, I shall be a better test of the king's " intentions; it being possible that my destruction is all " that is aimed at; and again, as I have had more honour " and consideration amongst you than my merits could " claim, and perhaps more than have in our days been be-" stowed on any private citizen, I conceive myself more " particularly bound than any other person to promote the " interest of my country, even with the sacrifice of my life. " With this full intention I now go; and perhaps it may be " the will of God, that as this war was begun in the blood " of my brother, and of myself, it may now by my means " be concluded. All that I desire is, that my life and my " death, my prosperity and my misfortunes, may contri-" bute towards the welfare of my native place. Should " the result be answerable to my wishes, I shall rejoice in " having obtained peace to my country, and security to my-" self. Should it prove otherwise, my misfortunes will " be alleviated by the idea that they were requisite for my " country's welfare; for if our adversaries aim only at my

" destruction,

CHAP. IV.

"destruction, I shall be in their power; and if their views "extend further, they will then be fully understood. In "the latter case, I doubt not that all my fellow-citizens will "unite in defending their liberties to the last extremity, "and I trust with the same success as, by the favour of "God, our ancestors have heretofore done. These are the "sentiments with which I shall proceed; entreating hea- "ven that I may be enabled on this occasion to perform "what every citizen ought at all times to be ready to do "for his country. *From San Miniato, the 7th December* "1479 (*a*)."

The departure of Lorenzo upon so novel and so dangerous an expedition, occasioned various opinions and conjectures at Florence. Those who were friendly to the Medici, or who were interested in the personal welfare of Lorenzo, could not regard this measure without great anxiety. Even those who entertained the highest opinion of his prudence, were inclined to consider his conduct in this instance as rash and inconsiderate, and as having resulted rather from the impulse of the monent, than from that mature deliberation which generally preceded his determinations (*b*). They remembered the fate of Giacopo Piccinini, who with more claims on the favour of Ferdinand than Lorenzo could pretend

(*a*) Valori informs us, that when the letter of Lorenzo was recited in the senate, not one of the assembly could refrain from tears. "Litteræ recitatæ "sunt in Senatu, assensu vario, ita tamen, ut nemo a lachrymis temperaret. "Movebat omnes tanti viri desiderium, qui pro salute patriæ nullis suis labo- "ribus, aut periculis parceret." *Val. in vitâ Laur. p.* 33.

(*b*) *Murat. Ann. v.* ix. *p.* 533.

pretend to, had, on a visit to him at Naples, in violation of all the laws of honour and hospitality, been thrown into a dungeon, and soon afterwards secretly murdered (*a*). Those who entertained better hopes, founded them on a conjecture that Lorenzo had previously obtained an assurance from Ferdinand of a welcome reception, and a safe return, which assurance was supposed to be sanctioned by the other states of Italy. In proportion as his friends were alarmed at the dangers that threatened him, those who feared, or who envied the authority which he had obtained in Florence, rejoiced in the probability of his destruction, and by affecting on all occasions to express their apprehensions of his ruin, and of a consequent change of government in Florence, endeavoured as far as in their power to prepare the way for those events (*b*).

He embarks at Pisa.

From San Miniato, Lorenzo went to Pisa, where he received from the magistrates of Florence their unlimited authority to enter into such conditions with the king as he might

(*a*) Piccinini was one of the most eminent *Condottieri* of his time, and by his valour had acquired the absolute sovereignty of several towns in Italy, and raised himself to such consideration as to obtain in marriage Drusiana, one of the daughters of the great Francesco Sforza duke of Milan. Soon after his marriage he was invited by Ferdinand, who had some secret cause of enmity against him, to pass a short time at Naples, whither he went, accompanied by his new bride, and fell an easy victim to the treachery of Ferdinand; who, not being able to alledge any plausible reason for this atrocious act, endeavoured to propagate a report that Piccinini had broken his neck by a fall from the window of the place of his confinement. *v. Murat. Ann. v.* ix. *p.* 493.

(*b*) *Mac. Ist. lib.* 8.

CHAP. IV.

might think advisable (*a*). Thence he embarked for Naples; and on his arrival there was surprised, but certainly not displeased, to find that the king had information of his approach, and had directed the commanders of his gallies to receive him with due honour. This token of respect was confirmed by the presence of the king's son Federigo, and his grandson Ferdinand, who met Lorenzo on his landing, and conducted him to the presence of the king (*b*). The Neapolitans testified their eagerness to see a man who had been the object of such contention, and whose character and accomplishments were the subject of general admiration. On his interview with Ferdinand, Lorenzo omitted nothing that was likely to conciliate his esteem, and attach him to his cause. Fully acquainted with the political state of Italy, and with the temper and intentions of its different potentates, he demonstrated to Ferdinand the impolicy of separating the interests of the Neapolitans from those of the Florentines. He reminded him of the dangers which the kingdom of Naples had repeatedly experienced from the pretensions of the holy see, and thence adverted to the imprudence of contributing to the aggrandizement of the papal power. Nor was he silent on that flagrant breach of divine and human laws, which had deprived him of a brother, and endangered his own life; from

(*a*) The instructions sent by the magistracy of Florence to Lorenzo on this occasion were drawn up by Bartolomeo Scala, the chancellor of the republic, who transmitted them to Lorenzo, accompanied by a private letter, strongly expressive of his anxiety for the success of his patron in this dangerous expedition. *v. App. No.* XXX.

(*b*) *Valori in vitâ Laur. p.* 34.

from which he justly inferred, that the perpetrators of such a crime could be bound by no engagements but such as suited their own interest or ambition. To representations thus forcibly urged, it was impossible that the king could be inattentive; and although he did not immediately comply with the wishes of Lorenzo, yet he gave him hopes of eventual success, and treated him with every distinction due to his character, expressing his approbation of him in the words of Claudian, "*vicit præsentia famam* (*a*)."

Lorenzo concludes a treaty with the king.

During the abode of Lorenzo at Naples, which was protracted by the cautious hesitation of the king, he rendered his liberality, his taste, and his urbanity, subservient to the promotion of his political views, and was careful that the expectations formed of him by the populace should not be disappointed. His wealth and his munificence seemed to be equally boundless, and were displayed, amongst other instances, in apportioning out in marriage, young women of the lower rank, who resorted to Naples from Calabria and Appulia to share his bounty (*b*). The pleasures which he experienced from thus gratifying his natural disposition were however counterbalanced by the anxiety of his solitary moments, when the difficulties which he had to encounter pressed upon his mind with a weight almost irresistible (*c*). The disposition of Ferdinand was severe and unrelenting; from

(*a*) *Val. in vitâ Laur. p.* 34. (*b*) *Val. in vitâ, p.* 35.

(*c*) Addebant, qui se in die omnibus hilarem, gratumque præbebat, eundem in nocte, quasi duas personas gereret, secum ad miserationem usque lamentari solitum, nunc suam ipsius, nunc patriæ vicem dolere. *Val. in vitâ, p.* 36.

from an appeal to his feelings little was to be expected; his determination could only be influenced by motives of policy or of interest. The conquests of his son Alfonzo had rendered him less favourable to the views of Lorenzo; and it was particularly unfortunate, that whilst the negotiation was depending, Alfonso broke the stipulated truce, and gained advantages over the Florentine troops. The pope had also received intelligence of the arrival of Lorenzo at Naples, and exerted all his interest with Ferdinand to prevail upon him either to detain Lorenzo there, or to send him to Rome, on pretence of accommodating his difference with the holy see, and effecting a general peace. Notwithstanding these unfavourable circumstances, Lorenzo did not relax in the pursuit of his object, nor exhibit in public the least appearance of dejection. He had already obtained the confidence of Caraffa, count of Metalonica, the minister of Ferdinand, and made daily progress in the affections of the king himself, who was at length induced seriously to weigh his propositions, and to consider the advantages that might result to himself and his family, by attaching to his interests a man of such talents and influence, now in the prime of life, and daily rising in the public estimation. Led by these considerations, and by the unwearied assiduities of Lorenzo, he at length gave way to his solicitations; and having once adopted a decided opinion, became as warmly devoted to Lorenzo, as he before had been inimical to him. The conditions of the treaty were accordingly agreed on (*a*); and Lorenzo,

(*a*) These conditions were, that the parties should mutually assist each other in the defence of their dominions. That the places which had been

Lorenzo, who had arrived at Naples not merely an unprotected stranger, but an open enemy, left that place at the end of three months, in the character of an ally and a friend.

Having thus accomplished his purpose, he instantly embarked for Pisa, notwithstanding the entreaties of Ferdinand, who wished to prolong his stay. His apology to the king for this apparent want of respect, was the desire that he had to communicate to his fellow-citizens, as speedily as possible, the happy result of his expedition; but the excuses of Lorenzo were urged with a levity and jocularity which he judged most likely to conceal his real motives, and to prevent the suspicions of Ferdinand. Shortly before his departure the king presented to him a beautiful horse, and Lorenzo returned his thanks by observing, *That the messenger of joyful news ought to be well mounted.* He had however more urgent reasons for his haste; every moment that delayed his return gave encouragement to his enemies, and endangered his authority at Florence; but above all, he was apprehensive that the repeated remonstrances of the pope might induce the king to waver in his resolution, or to change his opinion. The event proved that his distrust was not unfounded; Lorenzo had no sooner sailed from Naples, than a messenger arrived there from Rome,

1480.

taken from the Florentines should be restored at the discretion of the king. That the survivors of the Pazzi family should be liberated from the tower of Volterra; and that the duke of Calabria should receive a certain sum of money to defray the expences of his return. *Amm. Ist. v. iii. p. 145.*

Rome, with such propositions to the king, on the part of the pope, as would in all probability not only have defeated the treaty, but have led the way to the ruin of Lorenzo de' Medici. Such was the effect which this communication had on the mind of the king, that he dispatched a letter to Lorenzo, entreating him, in the most pressing language, that at whatever place he might receive it, he would immediately return to Naples, where the ambassador of Sixtus was ready to accede to the articles of pacification. Having once escaped from the jaws of the lion, Lorenzo did not think proper a second time to confide in his clemency; and his determination was probably confirmed by the tenor of the letter from Ferdinand, which discovers such an extreme degree of anxiety for the accomplishment of his purpose, as seems scarcely consistent with an open and generous intention (*a*).

After touching at Leghorn, Lorenzo returned to Pisa, where the event of his embassy being known, he was received with the utmost demonstrations of joy. Thence he hastened to Florence, where the exultation of the populace was unbounded. Secured from the storm that had so long threatened to burst upon their heads, and restored to tranquillity by the magnanimity of a single citizen, they set no limits to their applause. All ranks of people surrounded and congratulated Lorenzo on his return. His faithful associate Politiano, having struggled in vain to approach his patron, expressed his affection in a few extempore stanzas, in which is given a lively picture of this

(*a*) *v. App. No.* XXXI.

this interesting scene; where Lorenzo is represented as towering above his fellow-citizens, by his superior stature, and expressing his sense of their kindness by all the means in his power, by his smiles, his nods, his voice, and his hands (*a*).

Sixtus perseveres in the war.

The reconciliation which had thus been effected between the king of Naples and the republic of Florence, was a cause of vexation not only to the pope, but to the Venetians, who expressed great dissatisfaction that a measure of such importance should have been adopted without their previous concurrence. In order to excuse to the pope the step which he had taken, Ferdinand alledged his apprehensions from the Turks, who had long threatened a descent

(*a*) *Ad Laurentium Medicem.*

" O ego quam cupio reducis contingere dextram
" Laurenti! et læto dicere lætus, ave!
" Maxima sed densum capiunt vix atria vulgus,
" Tota salutantum vocibus aula fremit.
" Undique purpurei Medicem pia turba senatus
" Stat circum; cunctis celsior ipse pater.
" Quid faciam? accedam?—nequeo;—vetat invida turba
" Alloquar?—at pavido torpet in ore sonus.
" Aspiciam?—licet hoc, toto nam vertice supra est,
" Non omne officium, turba molesta, negas.
" Aspice sublimi quum vertice fundit honorem
" Sidereo quantum spargit ab ore jubar.
" Quæ reducis facies, lætis quam lætus amicis!
" Respondet nutu, lumine, voce, manu.
" Nil agimus: cupio solitam de more salutem
" Dicere, et officium persoluisse meum.
" Ite mei versus, Medicique hæc dicite nostro,
" Angelus hoc mittit Politianus, ave."

Pol. in Op. ap. Ald.

scent upon Italy. Sixtus did not however relinquish the prosecution of his favourite object, the destruction of Lorenzo de' Medici, in which he was constantly incited to persevere, by his nephew Girolamo Riario, whose hatred to Lorenzo was unalterable. To no purpose did the Florentines dispatch a new embassy to Rome to deprecate the wrath, and entreat the clemency of the pope. Riario began to make preparations for renewing the war; and at his instance the duke of Calabria, instead of withdrawing his troops from Tuscany, remained at Sienna; where he continued to exercise great authority, and to fill with apprehensions the surrounding country. But while the affairs of Florence remained in this state of suspense, a more general alarm took place, and speedily accomplished what the intercessions and humiliation of the Florentines might have failed of effecting. Mahomet II. the conqueror of Constantinople, was yet living, and meditated further victories. In turning his arms westward, he first attacked the island of Rhodes; but being delayed and irritated by a vigorous defence, he determined to retrieve his military credit by making a descent upon Italy, where he captured the important city of Otranto, and threatened the whole extent of that country with devastation and slavery.

Descent of the Turks upon Italy.

This alarming incident roused the adjacent states of Italy to their defence. So opportunely did it take place for the safety of Lorenzo, that it has given rise to an opinion that he incited and encouraged it (*a*). But if Mahomet had in

(*a*) *Albinus, p.* 35. de bello Etrusco. *Camillus Portius* la Conguira de' Baroni in fact any invitation upon this occasion, it was most probably from the Venetians, who were strongly suspected of having favoured his purpose; and this suspicion was afterwards strengthened by the reluctance which they shewed to unite with the other states of Italy in expelling the Turks from Otranto (*a*). Compelled to attend to the defence of his own country, the duke of Calabria suddenly withdrew his troops from Sienna, and the pope of his own motion gave the Florentines to understand, that, on a proper submission, he should now listen to terms of reconciliation. Twelve of the most respectable citizens were sent to Rome, as a deputation in the name of the republic; but although the pope expressed his desire that Lorenzo should be of the number, he wisely judged that such a measure would neither be consistent with his honour nor his safety. Francesco Soderini, bishop of Volterra, made the oration to the pope; who in his reply once more gave way to his anger, and, in very severe language, reproached the Florentines with their disobedience to the holy see. Having vented his rage, he received their submission;

Peace concluded with the pope.

di Napoli contro il Re Ferdinando I. et *Jannonius* ap. *Fabronium*. *v.* ii. *p.* 216. *v. also Swinburn's Travels in the Two Sicilies, p.* 377.

(*a*) "Sospettarono i Napolitani," says Muratori, "che Maometto, o pure "il suo Bassà Achmet, fosse stato mosso a questa impresa dai Veneziani, per "l'odio grande che portavano al Re Ferdinando." *Murat. Ann. v.* ix. *p.* 535. That Ferdinand did not suppose Lorenzo had any share in instigating Mahomet to this enterprize, is evident from his subsequent letters to him, several of which yet remain. Fabroni has also preserved a letter from Lorenzo de' Medici to Albino, who attended the duke of Calabria on his expedition to Otranto, in which he expresses his strong aversion to the *Cani Turchi*, as he denominates the invaders, and his extreme and perhaps courtly solicitude for the success and personal safety of the duke. *v. App. No.* XXXII.

mission; and in milder terms reconciled them to the church; at the same time touching their backs with a wand, according to the usual ceremony, and releasing the city from his interdict.

CHAP. V.

STUDIES of Lorenzo de' Medici—Rise of Italian literature in the fourteenth century—Its subsequent degradation—Revivors of it in the fifteenth century—Burchiello—The three brothers of the Pulci—Writings of Bernardo Pulci—Of Luca Pulci—Of Luigi Pulci—Of Matteo Franco—Early productions of Lorenzo—Inquiry into his merits as a poet—Object and characteristics of poetry—Description—Talents of Lorenzo for description—Poetic comparison—Instances of it from the writings of Lorenzo—Personification of material objects—Of the passions and affections—Comparative excellence of the ancients and moderns in the PROSOPOPEIA*—Instances of this figure in the writings of Lorenzo—Various species of poetry cultivated by him—Origin of the Italian sonnet—Character of the sonnets of Dante—Of Petrarca—Of Lorenzo de' Medici—*SELVE D' AMORE *of Lorenzo—His poem of* AMBRA*—On hawking—Moral pieces—Sacred poems—The* BEONI*—Rise of the jocose Italian satire—*STANZE CONTADINESCHE*—State of the Italian Drama—The musical drama—*CANTI CARNASCIALESCHI—CANZONE A BALLO*—Critique of Pico of Mirandula on the poems of Lorenzo—Opinions of other authors on the same subject—The poems of Lorenzo celebrated in the* NUTRICIA *of Politiano.*

CHAP. V.

THE establishment of peace was a blessing which Lorenzo felt in common with the rest of his fellow-citizens; but to him it was peculiarly grateful, as it left him at liberty to attend to the prosecution of those studies in which he had always found his most unembittered pleasures, and the surest alleviation of his cares. "When my mind is dis-"turbed with the tumults of public business," says he, writing to Ficino, "and my ears are stunned with the "clamours of turbulent citizens, how would it be possi-"ble for me to support such contention unless I found a "relaxation in science?" Nor was it to any particular study, in exclusion of all others, that he addicted himself during his hours of leisure, although poetry had in his

Studies of Lorenzo de' Medici.

younger years a decided preference. "So vigorous and "yet so various was his genius," says Pico of Mirandula, "that he seemed equally formed for every pursuit; but "that which principally excites my wonder is, that when "he is deeply engaged in the affairs of the republic, his "conversation and his thoughts should be turned to "subjects of literature as if he were perfect master of his "time (*a*)." Lorenzo was not however insensible that, amidst his serious and important avocations, the indulgence of a poetical taste might be considered as indicating a levity of disposition inconsistent with his character. "There "are some," says he (*b*), "who may perhaps accuse me "of having dissipated my time in writing and comment- "ing upon amorous subjects, particularly in the midst of "my numerous and unavoidable occupations; to this accu- "sation I have to reply, that I might indeed be justly con- "demned if nature had endowed mankind with the power "of performing, at all times, those things which are most "truly estimable; but inasmuch as this power has been "conceded only to few, and to those few the opportunity "of exercising it cannot often occur in the course of life, "it seems to me, that considering our imperfect nature, "those occupations may be esteemed the best in which "there is the least to reprove.—If the reasons I have be- "fore given," he afterwards adds, "be thought insuffi- "cient for my exculpation, I have only to confide in the "compassion of my readers. Persecuted as I have been "from

(*a*) *In Proem. ad tract. de ente et uno, ad Angelum Politianum in op. Pici. Ed. Ven.* 1498.

(*b*) *Commento di Lorenzo sopra alcuni de suoi sonetti, Ed. Aldo* 1554.

" from my youth, some indulgence may perhaps be allowed " me for having sought consolation in these pursuits." In the sequel of his commentary he has thought it necessary to touch more fully on the peculiarity of his situation. " It " was my intention," says he, " in my exposition of " this sonnet (*a*), to have related the persecutions which I " have undergone; but an apprehension that I may be " thought arrogant and ostentatious, induces me to pass " slightly over them. In relating our own transactions " it is not indeed easy to avoid these imputations. When " the navigator informs us of the perils which his ship has " escaped, he means rather to give us an idea of his own " exertions and prudence, than of the obligations which " he owes to his good fortune, and perhaps enhances the " danger beyond the fact, in order to increase our admira- " tion. In the same manner physicians frequently re- " present the state of their patient as more dangerous " than it is in reality, so that if he happen to die, the " cause may be supposed to be in the disorder, and not in " their want of skill, and if he recover, the greater is " the merit of the cure. I shall therefore only say, that " my sufferings have been very severe, the authors of " them having been men of great authority and talents, " and fully determined to accomplish, by every means in " their power, my total ruin. Whilst I, on the other hand, " having nothing to oppose to these formidable enemies, " but youth and inexperience, saving indeed the assistance " which I derived from divine goodness, was reduced to " such an extreme of misfortune, that I had at the same " time

(*a*) " *Se tra gli altri sospir ch' escon di fore.*"

" time to labour under the excommunication of my soul, " and the dispersion of my property, to contend with en- " deavours to divest me of my authority in the state, and " to introduce discord into my family, and with frequent " attempts to deprive me of my life, insomuch that I " should have thought death itself a much less evil than " those with which I had to combat. In this unfortunate " situation it is surely not to be wondered at, if I endea- " voured to alleviate my anxiety by turning to more agree- " able subjects of meditation, and in celebrating the charms " of my mistress sought a temporary refuge from my cares."

Rise of Italian literature in the fourteenth century.

In taking a retrospect of the state of letters in Italy, it is impossible not to be struck with the great superiority which that country possessed over the rest of Europe. " To the Commedia of Dante, the sonnets of Petrarca, " and the Decamerone of Boccaccio, three little books " written for the purposes of satire, of gallantry, and of " feminine amusement, we are to trace the origin of " learning and true taste in modern times (*a*)." Whether Dante was stimulated to his singular work by the success of his immediate predecessors, the provençal poets, or by the example of the ancient Roman authors, has been doubted. The latter opinion seems however to be the more probable. In his Inferno he had apparently the descent of Eneas in view. " Virgil is the guide of Dante " through these regions of horror (*b*)." In the rest of his poem

(*a*) *Andres, Dell' Origine progressi e stato attuale d' ogni letteratura, v. i. p.* 339.

(*b*) Landino considered Dante as a close imitator of Virgil. " Nonne è

poem there is little resemblance to any antecedent production. Compared with the Æneid, it is a piece of grand Gothic architecture at the side of a beautiful Roman temple. Dante was immediately succeeded by Boccaccio and by Petrarca, not as imitators, but as originals in the different branches to which their talents led them. Though they followed Dante, they did not employ themselves in cultivating the ground which he had broken up, but chose each for himself a new and an untried field, and reaped a harvest not less abundant. The merits of these writers have been frequently recognized and appreciated, but perhaps by no one with more accuracy than by Lorenzo himself. In attempting to shew the importance and dignity of the Italian tongue, he justly remarks, that the proofs of its excellence are to be sought for in the writings of the three authors before mentioned; "who," says he, "have fully "shewn with what facility this language may be adapted "to the expression of every sentiment." He then proceeds as follows (*a*): "If we look into the Commedia of "Dante,

---

"nostris Danthem, virum omni doctrina excultum, gravissimum auctorem "habemus? qui ejus itineris quo mundum omnem ab imis tartaris ad supremum usque cœlum peragrat, in eo sibi illum (Virgilium) ducem fingit. In "quo summum hominis bonum perquirens, miro quodam ingenio unicam "Æneida imitandam proponit; ut cum pauca omnino inde excerpere videatur, "nunquam tamen si diligentius inspiciemus ab ea discedat." *Land. Disput. Camal. lib.* 4. *Ed.* 1508. Even the form of his hell and his purgatory, the first of which resembled the cavity of an inverted cone, the other the exterior of an erect one, may perhaps be traced to the following passage:

"——— Tum Tartarus ipse
"Bis patet in præceps tantum, tenditque sub umbras
"Quantus ad æthereum cœli suspectus olympum."

Æn. lib. vi.

(*a*) *Com. di Lorenzo sopra alcuni de' suoi sonetti ap. Ald.* 1554.

" Dante, we ſhall find theological and natural subjects " treated with the greatest ease and address. We ſhall " there discover those three species of composition so " highly commended in oratory, the simple, the middle " style, and the sublime; and shall find in perfection, in " this single author, those excellencies which are dispersed " amongst the ancient Greek and Roman writers. Who " can deny that the subject of love has been treated " by Petrarca with more consistency and elegance than by " Ovid, Catullus, Tibullus, Propertius, or any other of " the Latin poets? The prose compositions of the learned " and eloquent Boccaccio may be considered as unrivalled, " not only on account of the invention which they dis- " play, but for the copiousness and elegance of the style. " If on pursuing the Decamerone we attend to the diver- " sity of the subjects, sometimes serious or tragical, at " others conversant with common life, and at othrs humor- " ous or ridiculous; exhibiting all the perturbations inci- " dent to mankind, of affection and of aversion, of hope " and of fear; if we consider the great variety of the " narrative, and the invention of circumstances which dis- " play all the peculiarities of our nature, and all the effects " of our passions, we may undoubtedly be allowed to deter- " mine, that no language is better adapted to the purposes " of expression than our own."

Its subsequent degradation.

But although the career of these first reformers of Italian literature was wonderfully rapid, the disciples they formed were few, and of those none maintained the reputation of their masters. Petrarca died in 1374, and Boccaccio in the year following. The clouds that had been awhile

awhile dispersed by the lustre of their abilities, again collected, and involved the world in their gloom. A full century elapsed without producing any literary work that can be ranked with the compositions of those great men (*a*). The attempt of Piero de' Medici, in the year 1441, to create a spirit of poetical emulation in Florence, while it serves as a proof of his munificence, sufficiently indicates the low degree of estimation in which this study was then held, and the insignificance of its professors. If philosophy in the fourteenth century went poor and naked, in the next she had changed her destiny with her sister poetry (*b*). The state of prose composition was equally wretched. No longer the vehicle of elegant or learned sentiment, the Italian language was consigned over to the use of the vulgar, corrupted by neglect, and debased by the mixture of provincial dialects. It was only on the most common occasions, or in the freedom of epistolary intercourse, that men of learning condescended to employ their native tongue; and even then, it appears to have been considered as inadequate to the purpose, and the assistance of the Latin language was often resorted to, and intermixed with it, in order to render it intelligible (*c*).

The

(*a*) The *Bella Mano* of Giusto da Conti, a Roman civilian by profession, but a poet by inclination, who wrote in the beginning of the fifteenth century, may perhaps be exempted from this general censure. It consists of a series of sonnets in praise of the author's mistress, some of which may contend in point of elegance with those of Petrarca, on the model of which they are professedly written. "Benchè pur," says Tiraboschi, not without reason, "vi abbia "molto di stentato e di languido." *Storia della Lett. Ital.* v. vi. *parte* ii. *p.* 146.

(*b*) *Povera e nuda vai Filosofia.* Petr.

(*c*) Some authors, who have taken too general and indistinct a view of this subject, would induce us to believe, that a continual improvement in Italian

CHAP. V.

Revivers of it in the fifteenth century.

Burchiello.

The only symptoms of improvement which had appeared in Italy, at the time that Lorenzo de' Medici first began to distinguish himself by his writings, are to be found in the productions of Burchiello, or in those of the three brothers of the family of Pulci, to some of which we have before adverted. Burchiello, who flourished about the middle of the fifteenth century, and who exercised in Florence a profession, in which, as he informs us,

"*The muses with the razor were at strife* (a),"

has left a great number of sonnets, which exhibit no inconsiderable

---

literature took place from the time of Petrarca, till it arrived at its summit in the sixteenth century; and have had influence enough to establish this as a popular opinion; but to say nothing of the evidence of the best Italian critics, by whom this singular degradation of their language is fully attested, it is yet capable of being ascertained by an appeal to facts. If the rise of literature had been gradual during this period, some memorials of it must have remained; but from the death of Petrarca to the time of Lorenzo de' Medici, Italy did not produce a single specimen of this boasted improvement; whilst on the other hand, innumerable instances remain, both in verse and prose, of the barbarous and degraded style then in use. Even the celebrity of Cosmo de' Medici, the great patron of letters, never gave rise to a panegyric in his native tongue that has any pretensions to the approbation of the present time, although there yet remain among the manuscripts of the Laurentian library, innumerable pieces in his praise, of which the two sonnets given in the Appendix (No. XXXIII.) are a fair, and perhaps will be thought a sufficient specimen. Voltaire indeed informs us, "that there was an uninterrupted succes-" sion of Italian poets, who are all known to posterity; that Pulci wrote " after Petrarca; that Bojardo succeeded Pulci; whilst in the fertility of his " imagination, Ariosto surpassed them all." *Essai sur les mœurs, &c.* v. ii. *p.* 163. Pulci, it is true, is the next author of popular estimation that followed Petrarca, but the period between them is precisely the time in question. The *Morgante* was not written till upwards of a century after the death of Petrarca. The errors into which many writers on this subject have fallen, have been occasioned by a want of discrimination between the progress of Italian and of classical literature; a distinction which I shall hereafter have occasion to develope more at large.

(a) "*La Poesia combatte col rasoio.*" BURCH.

considerable share of wit and vivacity, and occasionally display a felicity of expression, that might have done honour to better subjects than those which generally employed his pen; but it is to be regretted that the excellencies of these pieces are too often lost in their obscurity, and that although we may at times perceive the vivid sallies of imagination, it is only as we see coruscations from a cloud by night, which leave us again in total darkness. This obscurity has been the cause of great regret to his admirers, several of whom have undertaken to comment upon and illustrate his works. Crescimbeni is of opinion, that these extravagant productions were intended to satirize the absurdities of his poetical contemporaries, and the folly of their admirers; but satire too obscure to be generally understood is not likely to effect a reformation (*a*).

The three brothers of the Pulci.

The Pulci were of a noble family of Florence, but seem to have declined any participation in the offices of the republic, for the purpose of devoting themselves to their favourite studies. That a close intimacy subsisted between them and the Medici, is apparent from many of the works of these brothers, some of which are inscribed to their great patrons, and others entirely devoted to their praise.

(*a*) The sonnets of Burchiello were several times printed in the fifteenth century, generally without date. The earliest edition is supposed to be that of Bologna, 1475. In the following century they were commented by Anton Francesco Doni, and published at Venice, 1553; but the commentator stands no less in need of an interpreter than the author. This edition is inscribed by the editor to the celebrated artists Tintoretto and Romanelli, and is printed by Francesco Marcolini, in a singular but not inelegant type. Besides his

CHAP. V.

Writings of Bernardo Pulci.

praise. The earliest production of any of this family is probably the elegy by Bernardo, to the memory of Cosmo de' Medici, which he has addressed to Lorenzo. To his elegy on the death of the beautiful Simonetta, we have before assigned its proper date. He afterwards translated the Eclogues of Virgil, which he also inscribed to Lorenzo de' Medici (*a*). Bernardo is likewise the author of a poem on the passion of Christ, which is by no means devoid of poetical merit. It is preceded by a dedication to a pious nun, from which it appears, that the good sister had not only prescribed this subject to the poet, but that by her pressing instances he had been induced to compleat the work,

---

sonnets, Burchiello is also the author of a satire in *terza rima*, in which he has attempted to imitate the manner of Dante. The objects of his animadversion are the practitioners of what are called the liberal professions in Florence, amongst whom the physicians have their full share of ridicule. Of this poem, which has not been printed, a copy is preserved in the Gaddi library, now incorporated with that of the great duke of Florence. (*Band. Cat. vol.* v. *Plut.* xliv. *cod.* 30) Another transcript, of the fifteenth century, is in my possession; from which I shall give a short extract in the Appendix, whence the reader may be further enabled to judge of the state of Italian literature immediately previous to the time of Lorenzo de' Medici. *App. No.* XXXIV.

(*a*) This was the first attempt to translate the Eclogues of Virgil into the Italian language. From the dedication of these pieces, it is not difficult to determine that they were translated about the year 1470, as the author adverts to the recent death of Piero de' Medici, and at the same time mentions his translation as having been commenced in the year preceding his address to Lorenzo; that they are not to be referred to a much later period, is evident from his congratulating Lorenzo on his knowledge of the Latin tongue, which he asserts is far beyond his years. These translations were first published in 1481, and again at Florence in 1494. Tiraboschi is mistaken in supposing that the Eclogues of Bernardo, and his version of the Bucolics, are different works. (*Storia della Let. Ital. v.* vi. *parte* ii. *p.* 174.) In both these editions, the works of Bernardo are united with those of other writers, although in the latter some additional pieces are included. The title of

work, which he affirms had cost him many a tear (*a*). In the Laurentian library some other poems of this author are yet preserved, that have not hitherto been published (*b*).

Luca Pulci.

Of Luca Pulci, whose verses on the tournament of Lorenzo have before been noticed, we have two other poems. The first of these, intitled *Il Ciriffo Calvaneo*, is an epic romance, and was probably the first that appeared in Italy; it being certainly produced some years prior to the *Morgante* of Luigi Pulci, and to the *Orlando Innamorato* of Bojardo, two pieces which have generally been considered as the first examples of this species of poetry. In relating the wars between the Christians and the Infidels, the author seems to have prepared the way for the more celebrated works

---

this edition is as follows: BUCOLICHE ELEGANTISSIMAMENTE COMPOSTE DA BERNARDO PULCI FIORENTINO. ET DA FRANCESCO DE ARSOCHI SENESE ET DA HIERONYMO BENIVIENI FIORENTINO ET DA JACOPO FIORINO DE BONINSEGNI SENESE. At the close we read—*Finite sono le quattro Buccoliche sopra decte con una elegia della morte di Cosimo. Et una altra elegia della morte della diva Simonetta. Et una altra elegia di nuovo adgiunta. Impresse in Firenze per maestro* ANTONIO MIS-CROMINI ANNO MCCCCLXXXXIIII *a di* xviii *del mese Aprile.*

(*a*) This poem was published at Florence *per Franc. Bonaccursio, die* 3 *Novembris, anno* 1490, in 4to. (*Haym. Bibl. Ital. p.* 95.) But I conceive that the edition also printed at Florence without note of the year, or name of the printer, and having at the close only the mark *Florentiae impressum*, is of earlier date. The lady to whom it is inscribed is *Annalena de' Tanini nel monasterio delle murate*, who was probably sister of the author's wife, as it appears that he married a lady of the family of Tanini, who, as well as her husband, was distinguished by her talents for poetry.

(*b*) From these I shall give two sonnets addressed to Lorenzo de' Medici, which are followed by thirty-eight others, all on the exhaustless subject of love. At what time they were written is uncertain, but from their being addressed to Lorenzo, we may conjecture that he was then of manly age, before which time he had given some specimens of his own poetical talents. *App. No.* XXXV.

works on the same subject which soon afterwards followed (*a*). This poem was left unfinished by the author, but at the instance of Lorenzo de' Medici, was, after the death of Luca, compleated by Bernardo Giambullari (*b*). The *Driadeo*

(*a*) *Il Ciriffo Calvaneo*, and his companion *Il Povero Avveduto*, the heroes of the poem, are the illicit offspring of two unfortunate ladies, who, being abandoned by their lovers, are indebted to the shepherd *Lecore* for their preservation. As the young men grow up, they display their courage in pursuing wild beasts, and their generosity in giving away the old shepherd's cattle and effects; in consequence of which he breaks his heart. *Massima*, the mother of Il Ciriffo, then informs them of the nobility of their origin, and of the distress she has herself suffered; in consequence of which her son piously swears to accomplish the death of his father, which vow he accordingly fulfils. Repenting of his crime, he hastens to Rome, obtains Christian baptism and the remission of his sins. In the mean time Il Povero Avveduto is carried off by Epidoniffo, a pirate of Marseilles, who stood in fear neither of God nor his saints.

" Egli harebbe rubata quella nave
" Dove Christo a San Pier venne in ajuto;
" E se vi fusser stato su, le chiave
" Tolte, e poi l'oro e l'argento fonduto;
" E preso in terra l'angel che disse ave,
" Menato a fusta, e ne' ferri tenuto,
" E spogliato Gioseppe vecchiarello,
" Ma col baston prima scosso il mantello."

After many adventures, Il Povero Avveduto goes to the assistance of Tebaldo, sultan of Egypt, who was besieged by Luigi, king of France. The combatants on each side are particularly described. A battle takes place, after which Il Povero is made a cavalier by the sultan, for whose particular amusement he tilts with his newly-discovered brother Lionetto. Such is the heterogeneous mixture which composes this poem; the invention of which is not however to be wholly attributed to Luca. In the Gaddi library is a MS. anterior to his time by 150 years, intitled, by Bandini, "*Liber pauperis prudentis.*" (*Cat. Bibl. Laur. vol.* v. *Plut.* xliv. *cod.* 30.) From which it sufficiently appears, that, in this instance, Luca is only an imitator. It is to be regretted that his judgment did not lead him to select a better model.

(*b*) It was printed with the continuation of Giambullari at Florence, in 1535; and had probably been printed before, as it is dedicated to Lorenzo de'

Driadeo d' amore is a pastoral romance in *ottava rima*, and is dedicated by the author to Lorenzo de' Medici, for whose particular amusement he professes to have written it (*a*). The heroic epistles of Luca Pulci do credit to their author. These epistles are eighteen in number, and are composed in *terza rima*. The first is from Lucretia to Lauro; that is, from the accomplished Lucretia Donati to Lorenzo de' Medici. The others are founded on different incidents in the ancient Greek and Roman history (*b*).

Luigi Pulci.

Luigi Pulci, the youngest of these brothers, was born on the third day of December 1431, and appears from many circumstances, to have lived on terms of the utmost friendship with Lorenzo de' Medici, who in one of his poems mentions him with great freedom and jocularity (*c*). The principal work of this author is the *Morgante maggiore*, a poem

---

Medici, the grandson of Lorenzo the Magnificent, who died in the year 1519. It there consists of four books, of which the first only is the work of Pulci. The Ciriffo Calvaneo was reprinted with the Giostra of Lorenzo, and other works of Luca, by the *Giunti* at Florence, in 1572, but the continuation by Giambullari is there omitted.

(*a*) Printed at Florence in 1479. (*De Bure Bibliogr. Instruc. No.* 3411.) I have seen two other ancient editions of this poem, without date; at the close of one of which we read *Finito il Driadeo per Luca Pulci ad Petitione di ser Piero Pacini.* Haym erroneously attributes this poem to Luigi Pulci, and I conceive he is also mistaken in citing an edition of 1489. *Bibl. Ital. p.* 91.

(*b*) These epistles have been several times printed. Tiraboschi refers to an edition of 1481, and I have met with three others; the first, *Impresso in Firenze per ser Francesco Bonaccorsi et per Antonio di Francesco Venetiano nell' anno* MCCCCLXXXVIII, *a di* XXVIII *di Febraio*, the second at Florence in 1513, and the last in 1572.

(*c*) In his poem on hawking, intitled *La Caccia col Falcone*, first published at the close of the present work.

CHAP. V.

poem which has given rise to various opinions and conjectures, as to its tendency and its merits. Whether this poem, or the Orlando Innamorato of the count Bojardo was first written, has been a matter of doubt; certain it is, that in publication the *Morgante* had the priority, having been printed at Venice in 1488, after a Florentine edition of uncertain date, whilst the Orlando Innamorato did not appear till the year 1496 (*a*). Accordingly the Morgante is generally regarded as the prototype of the *Orlando Furioso* of Ariosto. It has been said that Ficino and Politiano had each a share in the composition of this work, but the poetry of Politiano is of a very different character, and there is no instance on record that Ficino ever attempted poetical composition (*b*). The same degree of credibility is

(*a*) It is evident from the following lines at the conclusion of the poem of Bojardo, that it was not finished when the French made an irruption into Italy, in the year 1494:

" Mentre ch'io canto, Ahime Dio redentore,
" Veggio l' Italia tutta a fiamma e a fuoco
" Per questi Galli, che con gran furore
" Vengon per rovinar non so che luoco."

Bojardo Orl. Inam. lib. 3. *Canto* 9. *Ed. Ven.* 1548.

(*b*) Limerno Pitocco (*Teofilo Folengi*) in his extravagant and licentious poem of *Orlandino*, ridicules the idea of Politiano being the author of the Morgante.

" Politian fu quello, ch' altamente
" Cantò del gran gigante dal bataio:
" Et a Luigi Pulci suo cliente
" L' honor diè senza scritto di notajo.
" Pur dopo si pentì; ma chi si pente
" Po'l fatto, pesta l' acqua nel mortajo.
" Sia o non sia pur cotesto vero
" So ben, chi credde troppo, ha del liggero."

Orlandino, Cap. i. *Ed. Ven.* 1550.

is due to the opinion, that Luigi Pulci was accustomed to recite his poem at the table of Lorenzo de' Medici, about the year 1450 (*a*); for it must be remembered that Lorenzo de' Medici was only born in 1448. It may further be observed, that although the Morgante was written at the particular request of Lucretia, the mother of Lorenzo, it was not finished till after her death, which did not happen till the year 1482 (*b*). This singular offspring of the wayward genius of Pulci has been as immoderately commended by its admirers, as it has been unreasonably degraded and condemned by its opponents; and whilst some have not scrupled to give it the precedence, in point of poetical merit, to the productions of Ariosto and of Tasso, others have decried it as vulgar, absurd, and profane; and the censures of the church have been promulged in confirmation of the latter part of the sentence (*c*). From the solemnity and devotion

(*a*) *Dr. Burney's History of Music*, *v.* iv. *p.* 14. For this the learned and ingenious author has cited the authority of Crescimbeni, (*vol.* ii. *part* ii. *p.* 273. *Ed. Ven.* 1730.) who informs us, as is probably the truth, that Pulci was accustomed to recite his poem in the manner of ancient rhapsodists, at the table of Lorenzo de' Medici, but does not fix this event at any particular period, though he afterwards informs us, that Luigi flourished about the year 1450.

(*b*) *Morgant. Magg. Cant.* xxviii. *Stan.* 124. *Ed.* 1546.

(*c*) Folengi, however, ranks the poem of Pulci as canonical, with those of Bojardo, Ariosto, Francesco Cieco, and himself; and freely condemns those of the other romances to the flames, as apocryphal.

——" Trabisonda, Ancroia, Spagna, e Bovo,
" Con l' altro resto al foco sian donate:
" Apocrife son tutte; e le riprovo
" Come nemighe d'ogni veritate.
" Bojardo, l' Ariosto, Pulce, e'l Cieco,
" Autenticati sono, ed io con seco."

Orlandin. cap. i.

tion with which every canto is introduced, some have judged that the author meant to give a serious narrative; but the improbability of the relation, and the burlesque nature of the incidents, destroy all ideas of this kind. By others, this author has been accused of a total want of elegance in his expressions, and of harmony in his verse; but this work yet ranks as classical in Italian literature, and, if it be not poetry of the highest relish, has a flavour that is yet perceptible (*a*).

Matteo Franco.

The sonnets of Luigi Pulci, printed with those of Matteo Franco, have the same capricious character as his other writings, and bear a resemblance to those of his predecessor Burchiello. Franco, the poetic correspondent of Pulci, was a canon of Florence, and was by no means inferior to him in pungency and humour. It is to be regretted that these authors so far exceeded at times the bounds of civility and decorum, that it is scarcely possible to suggest an expression

---

(*a*) A very judicious French critic has given the following just and accurate character of this work: "C'est un poeme en Rime octave, de 28 chants, "d'un goût original. L'auteur s'y est mis au dessus des régles, non pas de dessein, comme Vincent Gravina lui a fait l'honneur de le croire, mais parcequ'il "les a entiérement ignorées. Fort en repos du jugement des critiques, il a "confondu les lieux et les tems, allié le comique aux serieux, fait mourir burlesquement de la morsure d'un cancre marin au talon, le géant son héros, et "cela dès le 20 livre, en sorte qu'il n'en est plus parlé dans les huit suivans. "La naiveté de sa narration a couvert tous ces defauts. Les amateurs de la "diction Florentine font encore audjourd'hui leurs delices de la lecture de "Morgante, sur tout quand ils en peuvent rencontrer un exemplaire de l'edition de Venice 1546 ou 1550, accompagnée des explications de Jean Pulci "neveu de l'auteur." *M. de la Mounoye. v. Baillet Jugem. des Scav. v.* iv. *p.* 30. I must however add, that these explications amount to nothing more than a glossary of a very few words, placed at the end of each canto.

expression of reproach and resentment which is not to be found in their writings. The family name of Pulci (*Pulex*) affords an ample subject for the satirical powers of Franco (*a*). His person is a theme equally fertile. Famine, says his antagonist, was as naturally depicted in his countenance as if it had been the work of Giotto (*b*). He had made an eight days truce with death, which was on the point of expiring, when he would be swept away to *Giudecca* (the lowest pit of Dante), where his brother Luca was gone before to prepare him a place (*c*). Luigi supports this opprobrious contest by telling his adversary that he was marked at his birth with the sign of the halter, instead of that of the cross, and by a thousand other imputations, of which decency forbids a repetition (*d*). We are however informed by the editor of the ancient edition of these poems, that

(*a*) A che credi ch'io pensi, o ch'io balocchi
Tanti de' Pulci le persone stolte?
Perchè de' Pulci hai sol tre cose tolte,
Leggerezza, colore, e piccini occhi,
Ma il nome tuo e Gigi de' Pidocchi, &c.

Son. ix.

(*b*) E già la fame in fronte al naturale
Porti dipinta, e pare opra di Giotto.

Son. xxxvii.

(*c*) Tenuto hai con la morte,
Otto dì triegua; hor che sofferto ha troppo,
Con la falce fienaja vien di galoppa.
Tu n' andrai a piè zoppo,
A trovar Luca tuo, ladro di zecca,
Che per te serba un luogo alla Judecca.

Son. xxxvii.

(*d*) Tu nascesti col segno del capresto,
Come in Francia si dice della croce.

Son xxx.

that although for the amusement of their readers, these authors so lavishly abused and satirized each other, they continued in reality intimate friends (*a*); and this information is rendered highly probable, by their having equally shared the favour of Lorenzo de' Medici, whose authority would have suppressed the first indications of real dissension. The freedoms in which they indulged themselves called however for the interference of the inquisition, and a prohibition was issued against the further circulation of this work (*b*). But although the productions of the before-mentioned authors

---

(*a*) Et benchè M. Matteo & Luigi in questi loro sonetti dimonstrino esser poco amici l'uno dell' altro, niente di manco nel secreto erono amicissimi. Ma per dare piacere & dilectare altri, alcuna volta si mordevano & svillaneggiavono in tal modo come se proprio stati fussono nimici capitali.

(*b*) I have before me an edition of these poems, without note of date or place, but apparently printed about the close of the fifteenth century, and intitled, "SONETTI DI MISSERE MATTHEO FRANCO ET DI LUIGI PULCI JOCOSI ET "FACETI CIOE DA RIDERE." Many of these sonnets are addressed to Lorenzo de' Medici, for whose favour the rival poets seem to have contended, by endeavouring to surpass each other in eccentricity and scurrility. A new edition was published in the year 1759, by the marchese Filippo de' Rossi, who informs us, that they were three times printed in the fifteenth century; to which he adds, "Il S. S. tribunale dell' inquisizione gli fulminò una giustissima proi-"bizione, che avendone sempre meritamente impedita la ristampa, ha tal-"mente resi rari questi sonetti, che da ogn' uno oramai si cercano invano." If my readers be curious to know the style of these formidable compositions, which excited the vigilance of the holy tribunal, they may take as a specimen the following sonetto of Luigi Pulci:

LUIGI PULCI A UN SUO AMICO PER RIDERE.

Costor, che fan sì gran disputazione
Dell' anima, ond' ell' entri, o ond' ell' esca,
O come il nocciol si stia nella pesca,
Hanno studiato in su n' un gran mellone.

2

authors display some share of vivacity and imagination, and exhibit at times a natural and easy vein of poetry; yet upon the whole they are strongly tinctured with the rusticity of the age in which they were produced.

Early productions of Lorenzo.

That Lorenzo de' Medici had begun to exercise his talents for poetry at a very early age, there remains decisive proof. We have before adverted to his interview with Federigo of Naples, at Pisa, in the year 1465. On this occasion he was requested by that prince, to point out to him such pieces of Italian poetry as were most deserving of his attention. Lorenzo willingly complied with his request; and shortly afterwards selected a small volume, at the close of which he added some of his own sonnets and canzoni, addressing them to Federigo in a few prefatory lines,

---

Aristotile allegano, e Platone,
E voglion ch' ella in pace requiesca
Fra suoni, e canti, e fannoti una tresca,
Che t' empie il capo di confusione.
L' Anima è sol come si vede espresso
In un pan bianco caldo un pinnocchiato,
O una carbonata in un pan fesso.
E chi crede altro ha il fodero in bucato,
E que' che per l' un cento hanno promesso
Ci pagheran di succiole in mercato.
Mi dice un che v' è stato
Nell' altra vita, e più non può tornarvi
Che appena con la scala si può andarvi.
Costor credon trovarvi
E' beccafichi, e gli ortolan pelati,
E' buon vin dolci, e letti spiumacciati,
E vanno drieto a' Frati.
Noi ce n' andrem, Pandolfo, in val di buja,
Senza sentir più cantare: Alleluja.

CHAP. V.

lines, as a testimony of his affection and regard (*a*). Hence it appears, that at the age of seventeen, Lorenzo had attempted different kinds of composition, which may be considered not only as anterior to the celebrated poem of Politiano, on the *Giostra* of Giuliano, which we have before noticed, but probably to any of the writings of the Pulci. But, however the Pulci may contend with Lorenzo in priority, they fall greatly short of him in all the essential requisites of a poet; and whilst their productions bear the uniform character of a rude and uncultivated age, those of Lorenzo de' Medici are distinguished by a vigour of imagination,

(*a*) This singular circumstance, which so decisively ascertains the early period at which Lorenzo began to exercise his poetical talents, was first discovered by Apostolo Zeno, who having, in the year 1742, found in the possession of his friend Jacopo Facciolati, at Padua, a manuscript collection of ancient Italian poems, was, after mature deliberation, induced to conjecture that they were collected and arranged by Lorenzo de' Medici. To this supposition he was principally led by the introductory address to Federigo of Aragon, in which the compiler adverts to the visit of Federigo to Pisa, in the preceding year, and afterwards addresses that prince in the followng terms: *At the close of the book, (conceiving that it might afford you some satisfaction,) I have inserted a few of* MY OWN SONNETS AND CANZONI, *with the expectation, that when you peruse them they may recall to your remembrance the fidelity and attachment of their author*. On comparing the productions of the anonymous compiler, with the *Poesie Volgari* of Lorenzo, printed by Aldo, in 1554, the conjectures of the critic were amply confirmed: he having there discovered almost every poem which appeared in the manuscript, except five pieces, which he conceived might probably be inserted in the *Canzone a ballo* of Lorenzo and Politiano; but which in fact he could not then ascertain for want of that work. I shall give the letter of Zeno on this subject, in the Appendix, No. XXXVI. I must however observe, that the visit of Federigo to Pisa was not in 1464, as mentioned by Zeno, who has too hastily quoted Ammirato (*v.* iii. *p.* 93.), but in 1465, as will appear by a reference to the before-cited passage of the Florentine historian.

gination, an accuracy of judgment, and an elegance of style, which afforded the first great example of improvement, and entitle him, almost exclusively, to the honorable appellation of the restorer of Italian literature. Within the course of a few years Politiano, Benivieni, and others, imbibed the true spirit of poetry, and Florence had once more the credit of rekindling that spark which was soon to diffuse a lustre through the remotest parts of Europe.

Inquiry into his merits as a poet.

If in order to justify the pretensions of Lorenzo to the rank here assigned him, it were sufficient merely to adduce the authority of succeeding critics, this would be productive of little difficulty. But to form our opinion of an author whose works are yet open to examination, on that of others, however it may sooth our indolence, or gratify our curiosity, cannot inform our judgment. It is from the writings which yet remain of Lorenzo de' Medici that we are to acquire a just idea of his general character as a poet, and to determine how far they have operated in effecting a reformation in the taste of his countrymen, or in opening the way to subsequent improvements.

Object and characteristics of poetry.

The great end and object of poetry, and consequently the proper aim of the poet, is to communicate to us a clear and perfect idea of his proposed subject. What the painter exhibits to us by variety of colour, by light and shade, the poet expresses in appropriate language. The former seizes merely the external form, and that only in a given attitude; the other surrounds his object, pierces it, and discloses its most hidden qualities. With the former it is inert and motionless; with the latter it lives and moves, it is expanded

or

CHAP. V.

or compressed, it glares upon the imagination, or vanishes in air, and is as various as nature herself.

Description.

The simple description of natural objects is perhaps to a young mind the most delightful species of poetry, and was probably the first employment of the poet. It may be compared to melody in music, which is relished even by the most uncultivated ear. In this department, Virgil is an exquisite master (*a*). Still more lively are the conceptions of Dante, still more precise the language in which they are expressed. As we follow him, his wildest excursions take the appearance of reality. Compared with his vivid hues, how faint, how delicate, is the colouring of Petrarca! yet the harmony of the tints almost compensates for their want of force. With accurate descriptions of the face of nature the works of Lorenzo abound; and these are often heightened by those minute but striking characteristics, which, though open to all observers, the eye of the poet can alone select. Thus the description of an Italian winter, with which he opens his poem of *Ambra* (*b*), is marked by several appropriate and striking images.

Talents of Lorenzo for description.

The foliage of the olive appears of a dark green, but is nearly white beneath.

L'uliva

(*a*) How grateful to our sensations, how distinct to our imaginations, appear the

" Speluncæ, vivique lacus, ac frigida Tempe
" Mugitusque boûm, mollesque sub arbore somni."

(*b*) Published for the first time at the close of the present work.

L'uliva in qualche dolce piaggia aprica,
Secondo il vento par or verde, or bianca.

On some sweet sunny slope the olive grows,
Its hues still changing as the zephyr blows.

The flight of the cranes, though frequently noticed in poetry, was perhaps never described in language more picturesque than the following, from the same poem :

Stridendo in ciel, i gru veggonsi a lunge
  L'aere stampar di varie e belle forme ;
  E l' ultima col collo steso aggiunge
  Ov' è quella dinanzi alle vane orme.

Marking the tracts of air, the clamorous cranes
  Wheel their due flight, in varied lines descried ;
And each with out-stretched neck his rank maintains,
  In marshal'd order through th' etherial void.

The following picture from his *Selve d' amore* is also drawn with great truth and simplicity :

Al dolce tempo il bon pastore informa
  Lasciar le mandre, ove nel verno giacque :
  E 'l lieto gregge, che ballando in torma,
  Torna all 'alte montagne, alle fresche acque.
  L' agnel, trottando pur la materna orma
  Segue ; ed alcun, che pur or ora nacque
  L' amorevol pastore in braccio porta :
  Il fido cane a tutti fa la scorta.

Sweet spring returns; the shepherd from the fold
Brings forth his flock, nor dreads the wint'ry cold;
Delighted once again their steps to lead
To the green hill, clear spring, and flowery mead.
True to their mother's track, the sportive young
Trip light. The careful hind slow moves along,
Pleased in his arms the new-dropt lamb to bear;
His dog, a faithful guard, brings up the rear.

In the same poem is a description of the golden age, in which the author seems to have exerted all his powers, in selecting such images as are supposed to have been peculiar to that happy state of life.

Poetic comparison.

But the description of natural objects awakes in the poet's mind corresponding emotions; as his heart warms his fancy expands, and he labours to convey a more distinct or a more elevated idea of the impressions of his own imagination. Hence the origin of figures, or figurative language; in the use of which he aims at describing his principal subject, by the qualities of some other object more generally known, or more striking in its nature. These figures of poetry have furnished the philologists of ancient and modern times with a great variety of minute distinctions, but many of them consist rather in form than in substance; comparison, express or implied, will be found to be the essence of them all.

Instances from the writings of Lorenzo.

In the employment of comparative illustration, Lorenzo de' Medici is often particularly happy. An attentive observer of the works of nature, as well in her general appearances, as in her more minute operations, intimately

intimately acquainted with all the finer productions of art, and accustomed to the most abstruse speculations of philosophy, whatever occurred to his mind excited a profusion of relative ideas, either bearing a general resemblance to his immediate subject, or associated with it by some peculiar circumstance. The first of these he often employed for the purpose of explanation or of ornament in his more serious compositions, the latter with great wit and vivacity in his lighter productions. At some times one external object, or one corporeal action, is elucidated by another; at other times natural phenomena are personified, and illustrated by sensible images; and instances occur where abstract ideas and metaphysical sentiments are brought before the mind, by a comparison with the objects of the material world. Of the simplest mode of comparison the following is no inelegant instance:

Quando sopra i nevosi ed alti monti,
Apollo spande il suo bel lume adorno,
Tal i crin suoi sopra la bianca gonna.

Son. lxxiii.

——O'er her white dress her shining tresses flow'd;
Thus on the mountain heights with snows o'erspread,
The beams of noon their golden lustre shed.

In his pastoral of Corydon, the shepherd thus addresses his scornful mistress, elucidating one action by another:

Lasso quanto dolor io aggio avuto,
Quando fuggi da gli occhi col pie scalzo;
Et con quanti sospir ho già temuto

Che

Che spine, o fere venenose, o il balzo
Non offenda i tuoi piedi; io mi ritegno,
Per te fuggo i pie invano, e per te gli alzo:
Come chi drizza stral veloce al segno,
Poi che tratt' ha, torcendo il capo crede
Drizzarlo, egli è già fuor del curvo legno.

Ah nymph! what pangs are mine, when causeless fright
O'er hill o'er valley wings thy giddy flight,
Lest some sharp thorn thy heedless way may meet,
Some poisonous reptile wound thy naked feet.
Thy pains I feel, but deprecate in vain,
And turn, and raise my feet, in sympathetic pain.
So when the archer, with attentive glance,
Marks his fleet arrow wing its way askance,
He strives with tortuous act and head aside,
Right to the mark its devious course to guide.

The following sonnet affords an instance, not only of the illustration of one sensible object by another, but of the comparison of an abstract sentiment, with a beautiful natural image:

SONETTO.

Oimè, che belle lagrime fur quelle
Che'l nembo di disio stillando mosse!
Quando il giusto dolor che'l cor percosse,
Salì poi su nell' amorose stelle!
Rigavon per la delicata pelle
Le bianche guancie dolcemente rosse,
Come chiar rio faria, che'n prato fosse,
Fior bianchi, e rossi, le lagrime belle;

Lieto

Lieto amor stava in l'amorosa pioggia,
  Com' uccel dopo il sol, bramate tanto,
  Lieto riceve rugiadose stille (*a*).
Poi piangendo in quelli occhi ov' egli alloggia,
  Facea del bello e doloroso pianto,
  Visibilmente uscir dolce faville.

Ah pearly drops, that pouring from those eyes,
  Spoke the dissolving cloud of soft desire!

What

(*a*) Spenser has a similar passage in his *Mourning Muse of Thestylis*:

The blinded archer boy,
  Like larke in showre of rain,
Sate bathing of his wings,
  And glad the time did spend
Under those chrystall drops
  Which fell from her faire eyes,
And at their brightest beams,
  Him proyn'd in lovely wise.

Mr. Warton in his observations on the Fairy Queen (*v.* i. *p.* 223.) has traced this passage to Ariosto (*Canto* 11. *Stanza* 65.):

Così a le belle lagrime le piume,
Si bagna amore, e gode al chiaro lume.

Though he thinks Spenser's verses bear a stronger resemblance to those of Nic. Archias (or the count Nicolo d'Arco, a Latin poet of the 16th century):

Tum suavi in pluvia nitens Cupido,
  Insidebat, uti solet volucris,
  Ramo, vere novo, ad novus tepores
  Post solem accipere aetheris liquores
  Gestire et pluviæ ore blandiendo.

I have only to add, that as Lorenzo de' Medici is the earliest author who has availed himself of this beautiful idea, so his representation of it has not been surpassed by any of those who have since adopted it.

What time cold sorrow chill'd the genial fire,
" Struck the fair urns and bade the waters rise."
Soft down those cheeks, where native crimson vies
With ivory whiteness, see the chrystals throng;
As some clear river winds its stream along,
Bathing the flowers of pale and purple dyes.
Whilst Love, rejoicing in the amorous shower,
Stands like some bird, that after sultry heats
Enjoys the drops, and shakes his glittering wings;
Then grasps his bolt, and conscious of his power,
Midst those bright orbs assumes his wonted seat,
And thro' the lucid shower his living light'ning flings.

To examples of this kind I shall only add another, in which the poet has attempted to explain the mysterious intercourse of Platonic affection, by a familiar but fanciful comparison:

Delle caverne antiche
Trahe la fiamma del sol, fervente e chiara,
Le picciole formiche.
Sagace alcuna e sollecita impara,
E dice all' altre, ov' ha il parco villano
Ascoso astuto un monticel di grano;
Ond' esce fuor la nera turba avara:
Tutte di mano in mano
Vanno e vengon dal monte;
Porton la cara preda in bocca, e'n mano:
Vanno leggieri, e pronte,
E gravi e carche ritornon di fore.
Fermon la picciola orma
Scontrandosi in cammino; e mentre posa
L' una, quell' altra informa
Dell' alta preda; onde più disiosa

Alla

Alla dolce fatica ogn'or l'invita.
Calcata e spessa è la via lunga, e trita;
E se riporton ben tutte una cosa,
Più cara e più gradita
Sempre è, quant 'esser deve
Cosa, senza la qual manca la vita.
Lo ingiusto fascio è lieve,
Se'l picciol animal senz 'esso more.
Così li pensier miei
Van più leggieri alla mia Donna bella;
Scontrando quei di lei
Fermonsi, e l'un con l'altro allor favella.
Dolce preda s'è ben quanto con loro,
Porton dal caro ed immortal tesoro.

Canz. xii.

As from their wint'ry cells,
The summer's genial warmth impels
The busy ants—a countless train,
That with sagacious sense explore,
Where provident for winter's store,
The careful rustic hides his treasur'd grain;
Then issues forth the sable band,
And seizing on the secret prize,
From mouth to mouth, from hand to hand,
His busy task each faithful insect plies,
And often as they meet,
With scanty interval of toil,
Their burthens they repose awhile,
For rest alternate renders labour sweet.
The travell'd path their lengthened tracks betray,
And if no varied cates they bear,

Yet

Yet ever is the portion dear,
Without whose aid the powers of life decay.
Thus from my faithful breast,
The busy messengers of love,
Incessant towards my fair one's bosom move;
But in their way some gentle thought
They meet with kind compassion fraught,
Soft breathing from that sacred shrine,
Where dwells a heart in unison with mine,
And in sweet interchange delight awhile to rest.

Personification of material objects.

But the poet does not confine himself to the lively description of nature, or of the corresponding emotions of his own mind. His next attempt is of a bolder kind, and the inanimate objects by which he is surrounded seem to possess life and motion, consciousness and reason, to act and to suffer. The mountains frown, the rivers murmur, the woods sigh, and the fable of Orpheus is revived. In the use of this figure Petrarca is inexhaustible, and there are few rural objects that have not been called upon to share his emotions; the tenderness of the lover inspires the fancy of the poet, he addresses them as if they were conscious of his passion, and applauds or reproaches them as they are favourable or adverse to the promotion of it. The works of Lorenzo afford also frequent instances of the use of this figure, which more than any other gives action and spirit to poetry. In the following sonnet he not only animates the violets, but represents them as accounting, by a beautiful fiction, for their purple colour:

SONETTO.

SONETTO.

Non di verdi giardin, ornati, e colti
Del soave e dolce aere Pestano,
Veniam Madonna, in la tua bianca mano;
Ma in aspre selve, e valli ombrose colti;
Ove Venere afflitta, e in pensier molti,
Pel periglio d'Adon correndo in vano,
Un spino acuto al nudo piè villano
Sparse del divin sangue i boschi folti:
Noi sommettemmo allora il bianco fiore,
Tanto che'l divin sangue non aggiunge
A terra, ond' il color purpureo nacque.
Non aure estive, o rivi tolti a lunge
Noi nutrit' anno, ma sospir d'amore
L'aure son sute, e pianti d'Amor l'acque.

Not from the verdant garden's cultur'd bound,
That breathes of Pœstum's aromatic gale,
We sprung; but nurslings of the lonely vale,
'Midst woods obscure, and native glooms were found.
'Midst woods and glooms, whose tangled brakes around
Once Venus sorrowing traced, as all forlorn
She sought Adonis, when a lurking thorn
Deep on her foot impress'd an impious wound.
Then prone to earth we bow'd our pallid flowers,
And caught the drops divine; the purple dyes
Tinging the lustre of our native hue:
Nor summer gales, nor art-conducted showers
Have nursed our slender forms, but lovers sighs
Have been our gales, and lovers tears our dew.

 The

Of the passions and affections.

The province of the poet is not however confined to the representation, or to the combination of material and external objects. The fields of intellect are equally subject to his controul. The affections and passions of the human mind, the abstract ideas of unsubstantial existence, serve in their turn to exercise his powers. In arranging themselves under his dominion, it becomes necessary that they should take a visible and substantial form, distinguished by their attributes, their insignia, and their effects. With this form the imagination of the poet invests them, and they then become as subservient to his purpose as if they were objects of external sense. In process of time, some of these children of imagination acquire a kind of prescriptive identity, and the symbolic forms of pleasure, or of wisdom, present themselves to our minds in nearly as definite a manner as the natural ones of Ajax, or of Achilles. Thus embodied, they become important actors in the drama, and are scarcely distinguishable from human character. But the offspring of fancy is infinite; and however the regions of poetry may seem to be peopled with these fantastic beings, genius will ſtill proceed to invent, to vary, and to combine.

Comparative excellence of the ancients and moderns in the use of the prosopopœia.

If the moderns excel the ancients in any department of poetry, it is in that now under consideration. It must not indeed be supposed, that the ancients were insensible of the effects produced by this powerful charm, which more peculiarly than any other may be said

———To give to airy nothing,
A local habitation and a name.

But

But it may safely be asserted, that they have availed themselves of this creative faculty, much more sparingly, and with much less success, than their modern competitors. The attribution of sense to inert objects is indeed common to both, but that still bolder exertion which embodies abstract existence, and renders it susceptible of ocular representation, is almost exclusively the boast of the moderns (*a*). If, however, we advert to the few authors who preceded Lorenzo de' Medici, we shall not trace in their writings many striking instances of those embodied pictures of ideal existence, which are so conspicuous in the works of Ariosto, Spenser, Milton, and subsequent writers of the higher class, who are either natives of Italy, or have formed their taste upon the poets of that nation (*b*).

The

(*a*) If Virgil has given us a highly-finished personification of rumour, if Horace speak of his *atra cura*, if Lucretius present us with an awful picture of superstition, their portraits are so vague as scarcely to communicate any discriminate idea, and are characterised by their operation and effects, rather than by their poetical insignia. Of the ancient Roman authors, perhaps there is no one that abounds in these personifications more than the tragedian Seneca; yet what idea do we form of labour when we are told, that

> Labor exoritur durus, et omnes
> Agitat curas, aperitque domos.

Or of hope or fear from the following paſſage:

> Turbine magni, spes solicitæ
> Urbibus errant, trepidique metus.

The personification of hope by Tibullus (*Lib.* ii. *Eleg.* 6.), is scarcely worthy of that charming author; and if he has been happier in his description of sleep (*Lib.* i. *Eleg.* 1.), it is still liable to the objections before mentioned.

(*b*) One of the finest personifications of Petrarca, is that of liberty, in a

CHAP. V.

Instances of this figure.

The writings of Lorenzo afford many instances of genuine poetical personification; some of which will not suffer by a comparison with those of any of his most celebrated successors. Of this his representation of jealousy may afford no inadequate proof.

Solo una vecchia in un oscuro canto,
  Pallida, il sol fuggendo, si sedea,
  Tacita sospirando, ed un ammanto
  D'un incerto color cangiante havea:
  Cento occhi ha in testa, e tutti versan pianto
  E cent' orecchie la maligna dea:
  Quel ch'è, quel che non è, trista ode e vede;
  Mai dorme, ed ostinata a se sol crede.

Sad in a nook obscure, and sighing deep,
  A pale and haggard beldam shrinks from view;
  Her gloomy vigils there she loves to keep,
  Wrapt in a robe of ever-changing hue;
  A hundred eyes she has, that ceaseless weep,
  A hundred ears, that pay attention due.

Imagin'd

---

beautiful canzone; which, on account of its political tendency, has been excluded from many editions of his works.

Libertà, dolce e desiato bene!
  Mal conosciuto a chi talor no'l perde;
  Quanto gradito al buon mondo esser dei.
  Per te la vita vien fiorita e verde,
  Per te stato gioioso mi mantiene,
  Ch'ir mi fa somiglianti a gli alti dei:
  Senza te, lungamente non vorrei
  Ricchezze, onor, e cio ch'uom più desia,
  Ma teco ogni tugurio acqueta l'alma.

Yet the painter who would represent the allegorical form of liberty, would derive but little assistance from the imagination of the poet.

Imagin'd evils aggravate her grief,
Heedlefs of sleep, and stubborn to relief.

If his personification of hope be less discriminate, it is to be attributed to the nature of that passion, of which uncertainty is in some degree the characteristic.

È una donna di statura immensa,
La cima de' capelli al ciel par monti ;
Formata, e vestita è di nebbia densa ;
Abita il sommo de' più alti monti.
Se i nugoli guardando un forma, pensa
Nove forme veder d' animal pronti,
Che'l vento muta, e poi di novo figne
Così Amor questa vana dipigne.

Immense of bulk, her towering head she shews,
Her floating tresses seem to touch the skies,
Dark mists her unsubstantial shape compose,
And on the mountain's top her dwelling lies.
As when the clouds fantastic shapes disclose,
For ever varying to the gazer's eyes,
Till on the breeze the changeful hues escape,
Thus vague her form, and mutable her shape.

Her attendants are also highly characteristic.

Seguon questa infelice in ogni parte
Il sogno, e l' augurio, e la bugia,
E chiromanti, ed ogni fallace arte,
Sorte, indovini, e falsa profezia :
La vocale, e la scritta in sciocche carte,
Che dicon, quando è stato, quel che fia :

L'archimia,

L'archimia, e chi di terra il ciel misura,
E fatta a volontà la conjettura.

Illusive beings round their sovereign wait,
Deceitful dreams, and auguries, and lies,
Innumerous arts the gaping crowd that cheat,
Predictions wild, and groundless prophecies;
With wondrous words, or written rolls of fate,
Foretelling—when 'tis past—what yet shall rise;
And alchymy, and astrologic skill,
And fond conjecture—always form'd at will.

Though not perhaps strictly to be ranked in this department, I shall not deprive my readers of the following fanciful description of the formation of the lover's chain.

Non già così la mia bella catena
 Stringe il mio cor gentil, pien di dolcezza:
 Di tre nodi composta lieto il mena
 Con le sue mani; il primo fe bellezza,
 La pietà l'altro per sì dolce pena,
 E l'altro amor; nè tempo alcun gli spezza:
 La bella mano insieme poi gli strinse
 E di sì dolce laccio il cor avvinse.

• • •

Quando tessuta fu questa catena,
 L'aria, la terra, il ciel lieto concorse:
 L'aria non fu giammai tanto serena,
 Nè il sol giammai sì bella luce porse:
 Di frondi giovinette, e di fior piena
 La terra lieta, ov'un chiar rivo corse:

Ciprigna

Ciprigna in grembo al padre il dì si mise,
Lieta mirò dal ciel quel loco, e rise.

Dal divin capo, ed amoroso seno,
Prese con ambo man rose diverse,
E le sparse nel ciel queto e sereno:
Di questi fior la mia donna coperse.
Giove benigno, di letizia pieno,
Gli umani orecchi quel bel giorno aperse
A sentir la celeste melodia,
Che in canti, ritmi, e suon, dal ciel venia.

Dear are those bonds my willing heart that bind,
Form'd of three chords, in mystic union twin'd;
The first by beauty's rosy fingers wove,
The next by pity, and the third by love.
—The hour that gave this wonderous texture birth,
Saw in sweet union, heaven, and air, and earth;
Serene and soft all ether breath'd delight,
The sun diffus'd a mild and temper'd light;
New leaves the trees, sweet flowers adorned the mead,
And sparkling rivers gush'd along the glade.
Repos'd on Jove's own breast, his favorite child
The Cyprian queen, beheld the scene and smil'd;
Then with both hands, from her ambrosial head,
And amorous breast, a shower of roses shed,
The heavenly shower descending soft and slow,
Pour'd all its fragrance on my fair below;
Whilst all benign the ruler of the spheres
To sounds celestial open'd mortal ears.

From

CHAP. V.

Various species of poetry cultivated by Lorenzo.

From the foregoing specimens we may be enabled to form a general idea of the merits of Lorenzo de' Medici, and may perceive, that of the essential requisites of poetic composition, instances are to be found in his writings. The talents of a poet he certainly possessed. But before we can form a complete estimate of his poetical character, it will be necessary to inquire to what purpose those talents were applied, and this can only be done by taking a view of the different departments of poetry in which he employed his pen. In the execution of this task, we may also be enabled to ascertain how far he has imitated his predecessors, and how far he has himself been a model to those who have succeeded him.

Origin of the Italian sonnet.

The Italian sonnet is a species of composition almost coeval with the language itself; and may be traced back to that period when the Latin tongue, corrupted by the vulgar pronunciation, and intermixed with the idioms of the different nations that from time to time over-ran Italy, degenerated into what was called the *lingua volgare;* which language, though at first rude and unpolished, was, by successive exertions, reduced to a regular and determinate standard, and obtained at length a superiority over the Latin, not only in common use, but in the written compositions of the learned. The form of the sonnet, confined to a certain versification, and to a certain number of lines, was unknown to the Roman poets, who adopting a legitimate measure, employed it as long as the subject required it, but was probably derived from the Provençals; although instances of the regular stanza, now used in these compositions, may be traced amongst the Italians, as early as the thirteenth century (*a*). From that time to the present, the sonnet has retained its precise form, and has been the most favourite mode of composition in the Italian tongue. It may however be justly doubted, whether the Italian poesy has, upon the whole, derived any great advantage from the frequent use of the sonnet. Confined to so narrow a compass, it admits not of that extent and range of ideas which suggest themselves to a mind already warm with its subject. On the contrary, it illustrates only some one distinct idea, and this muſt be extended or condensed, not as its nature requires, but as the rigid laws of the composition prescribe. One of the highest excellencies of a master in this art consists, therefore, in the selection of a subject neither too long nor too short for the space which it is intended to occupy (*b*). Hence the invention is cramped, and the free excursions of the mind are fettered and restrained. Hence, too, the greater part of these compositions display rather the glitter of wit than the fire of genius; and hence they have been almost solely appropriated to the illustration of the passion of love: a subject which, from its various nature, and the endless analogies of which it admits, is more susceptible than any other, of being apportioned into those detached sentiments of which the sonnet is composed.

To

(*a*) For a learned and curious disquisition on the origin of the Sonetto, *v. Annotazioni di Francesco Redi, al suo ditirambo di Bacco in Toscana, p.* 99.

(*b*) The following remarks by Lorenzo de' Medici, on this kind of composition, are as judicious as they are pointed and concise: "La brevità del sonetto "non comporta, che una sola parola sia vana, ed il vero subietto e materia "del sonetto debbe essere qualche acuta e gentile sentenza, narrata attamente, "ed in pochi versi ristretta, e fuggendo la oscurità e durezza."

Comment. di Lor. de' Med. sopra i suoi Sonetti, p. 180. *Ed. Ald.* 1554.

CHAP. V.

To these restraints, however, the stern genius of Dante frequently submitted. In his *Vita Nuova* we have a considerable number of his sonnets, which bear the distinct marks of his character, and derogate not from the author of the *Divina Commedia* (*a*). These sonnets are uniformly devoted to the praises of his Beatrice; but his passion is so spiritualized, and so remote from gross and earthly objects, that great doubts have arisen among his commentators, whether the object of his adoration had a substantial existence, or was any thing more than the abstract idea of wisdom, or philosophy. Certain it is, that the abstruse and recondite sense of these productions seems but little suited to the comprehension of that sex to which they are addressed, and ill calculated to promote the success of an amorous passion. The reputation of Dante as a poet is not however founded on this part of his labours; but Petrarca, whose other works have long been neglected, is indebted to his sonnets and lyric productions for the high rank which he yet holds in the public estimation. Without degrading his subject

(*a*) If written in later times, some of these sonnets might have been thought to border on impiety. Thus the poet addresses the faithful—in love—

" A ciascun alma presa, e gentil core,
" Nel cui cospetto viene il dir presente,
" In ciò chè mi rescrivan suo parvente,
" Salute in lor signore—cioè Amore."

And again, in allusion to a well-known passage,

" O voi che per la via d'amor passate,
" Attendete e guardate,
" S'egli è dolore alcun quanto 'l mio grave."

Vita Nuova di Dante, Fir. 1723.

subject by gross and sensual images, he has rendered it susceptible of general apprehension; and, whether his passion was real or pretended, for even this has been doubted (*a*), he has traced the effects of love through every turn and winding of the human bosom; so that it is scarcely possible for a lover to find himself so situated, as not to meet with his own peculiar feelings reflected in some passage or other of that engaging author.

Without possessing the terseness of those of Dante, or the polish and harmony of those of Petrarca, the sonnets of Lorenzo de' Medici have indisputable pretensions to high poetical excellence. It is indeed to be regretted, that, like those of his two celebrated predecessors, they are almost all devoted to one subject—the illustration of an amorous passion; but he has so diversified and embellished them with images drawn from other sources, as to rescue them from that general censure of insipidity, which may properly be applied to the greater part of the productions of the Italians, in this their favourite mode of composition. These images he has sought for in almost all the appearances of nature, in the annals of history, the wilds of mythology, and the mysteries of the Platonic philosophy; and has exhibited them with a splendor and vivacity peculiar to himself. If the productions of Dante resemble the austere grandeur

(*a*) "Interpretabar olim nostri Petrarchæ Elegias, Lyricosque, quibus "Lauram canit; aderantque adversarii, qui Lauram fuisse negarent, as-"sererentque non illo nomine puellam a se amatam intelligi, sed aliud alle-"gorice ibi latere." (*Land. in Interp. Carm. Hor. lib. 2. ap. Band. Spec. Lit. Flor. v. i. p. 232.*) where it appears that Landino past a tolerable jest on these refined critics.

grandeur of Michael Agnolo, or if those of Petrarca remind us of the ease and gracefulness of Raffaello, the works of Lorenzo may be compared to the less correct, but more animated and splendid labours of the Venetian school. The poets, as well as the painters, each formed a distinct class, and have each had their exclusive admirers and imitators. In the beginning of the succeeding century, the celebrated Pietro Bembo attempted again to introduce the style of Petrarca; but his sonnets, though correct and chaste, are too often formal and insipid. Those of Casa, formed upon the same model, possess much more ease, and a greater flow of sentiment. Succeeding authors united the correctness of Petrarca with the bolder colouring of Lorenzo; and in the works of Ariosto, the two Tassos, Costanzo, Tansillo, and Guarini, the poetry of Italy attained its highest degree of perfection.

The sonnets of Lorenzo de' Medici are intermixed with *Canzoni*, *Sestine*, and other lyric productions, which in general display an equal elegance of sentiment, and brilliancy of expression. One of his biographers is however of opinion, that the merit of his odes is inferior to that of his sonnets (*a*); but it is not easy to discover any striking evidence of the propriety of this remark. It must not however be denied, that his writings occasionally display too evident proofs of that haste with which it is probable they were all composed; or that they are sometimes interspersed with modes of expression,

(*a*) Felicior mihi fuisse videtur in brevioribus epigrammatibus, quam in odis. *Fab. in vitâ Laur.* v. i. *p.* 10.

sion, which would scarcely have been tolerated among the more accurate and polished writers of the succeeding century. The language of Lorenzo de' Medici appears even more obsolete, and is more tinctured with the rusticity of the vulgar dialect, than that of Petrarca, who preceded him by so long an interval. But, with all these defects, the intrinsic merit of his writings has been acknowledged by all those who have been able to divest themselves of an undue partiality for the fashion of the day, and who can discern true excellence, through the disadvantages of a dress in some respects antiquated, or negligent. Muratori, in his treatise on the poetry of Italy, has accordingly adduced several of the sonnets of Lorenzo, as examples of elegant composition: "It is gold from the mine (*a*)," says that judicious critic, adverting to one of these pieces, "mixed "indeed with ruder materials, yet it is always gold (*b*)."

The

(*a*) E' oro di miniera, mischiato, con rozza terra, ma sempre è oro.
Murat. della perfetta poesia Italiana, v. ii. *p.* 376.

(*b*) In the general collection of the poems of Lorenzo, printed by Aldo in 1554, his sonnets are accompanied with a copious commentary, which exhibits many striking traits of his character, and is a very favourable specimen of his prose composition. This commentary has not been reprinted; and the copies of this edition have long been of such rare occurrence in Italy, that even Cionacci, the editor of the sacred poems of Lorenzo, and of others of the Medici family, in 1680, had never been able to obtain a sight of the book. "Di questi "due," says he, adverting to the *Selve d'amore*, and the *Libro di Rime, intitolato Poesie volgari*, "fa menzione il Poccianti, e il Valori, sopra citati; ma io non "ho veduto se non *il primo*, stampato in ottavo." *Cion. osserv.* 28. This volume is intitled "POESIE VOLGARI, NUOVAMENTE STAMPATE DI LORENZO "DE' MEDICI, CHE FU PADRE DI PAPA LEONE." *Col commento del medesimo sopra alcuni de' suoi sonetti. In Vinegia* M.D.LIIII. From the expression *nuovamente stampate*, we might infer, that these poems had before been printed, but I have not been able to discover any trace of a former impression; and Apostolo Zeno, in his notes on the *Biblioteca Italiana* of Fontanini, *v.* ii. *p.* 59. *Ed. Ven.* 1753,

The *Selve d'amore* of Lorenzo de' Medici is a composition in *ottava rima*, and, though it extend to a considerable length, deserves to be held at least in equal esteem with his sonnets and lyric productions (*a*). The stanza in which it is written is the most favourite mode of versification amongst the Italians, and has been introduced with great success into the English language. It was first reduced to its regular form by Boccaccio, who employed it in his heroic romances, the *Theseide* and the *Filostrato* (*b*); but

---

expressly informs us that this is the only edition known, "l'unica edizione "delle poesie del Magnifico." A variation however occurs in the copies: the sheet marked with the letter O having, in the greater part of the edition, been reduced from eight leaves to four, as appears by a defect in the numeration of the pages. This is generally understood to have arisen from the scrupulous delicacy of the printer, who, having discovered some indecent pieces inserted from the *Canzoni a ballo*, cancelled the leaves in such copies as remained unsold. Hence the copies which contain the sheet O compleat, have, in the perverse estimation of bibliographers and collectors, acquired an additional value. On an examination of the pieces thus omitted, I have however some doubts, whether the reason above assigned be the true motive for the caution of the printer; a caution which I conceive was rather occasioned by an apprehension of the censures of the inquisition, for having unaccountably blended in the same poem some pious stanzas, with others of a more terrestrial nature, without giving the reader the least notice of so unexpected a change of sentiment. The works of Lorenzo were reprinted, with the addition of several pieces, at Bergamo, in octavo, in 1763.

(*a*) This poem has been several times printed. The earliest edition which I have seen is "*Impresso in Pesaro per Hieronymo Soncino nel* M.CCCCCXIII *a di* XV "*di Luglio*," under the title of, STANZE BELLISSIME ET ORNATISSIME INTITULATE LE SELVE D'AMORE COMPOSTE DAL MAGNIFICO LORENZO DI PIERO DI COSIMO DE' MEDICI. It was again printed by *Matthio Pagan* at Venice, in 1554, and is also inserted in the Aldine and Bergamo edition of his works. In the last-mentioned edition it is however preceded by thirty *stanze*, which form a poem entirely distinct in its subject, though not inferior in merit; and the reader ought to commence the perusal of the *Selve d'amore* at the thirty-first stanza, "*Dopo tanti sospiri e tanti omei.*"

(*b*) *Crescim.* i. *v. p.* 200. *Manni Istoria del Decamerone*, *p.* 52.

but the poems of Ariosto and of Torquato Tasso have established it as the vehicle of epic composition (*a*). These *stanze* were produced by Lorenzo at an early age, and are undoubtedly the same of which Landino and Valori expressed such warm approbation (*b*). The estimation in which they were held may be determined by the many imitations which have appeared from Benivieni (*c*), Serafino d'Aquila (*d*), Politiano,

---

(*a*) Notwithstanding these illustrious authorities, it may perhaps be allowable to doubt, whether a series of stanzas be the most eligible mode of narrating an epic, or indeed any other extensive kind of poem. That it is not natural, must be admitted; for naturally we do not apportion the expression of our sentiments into equal divisions; and that which is not natural, cannot in general long be pleasing. Hence the works of Ariosto, of Tasso, and of Spenser, labour under a disadvantage which it required all the vigor of genius to surmount; and this is the more to be regretted, as both the Italian and the English languages admit of compositions in blank verse, productive of every variety of harmony.

(*b*) Legere memini opusculum ejus amatorium, cum eodem Gentile, lepidum admodum, et expolitum, multiplex, varium, copiosum, elegans, ut nihil supra. Christophorus certe Landinus per ea tempora poeta et orator insignis, viso carmine, in hoc, inquit, scribendi genere, ceteros hic sine controversia superabit: id quod etiam suis scriptis testatum reliquit. Nec mirum quum ingenium alioqui maximum, vis ingens amoris accenderit. *Val. in vitâ, p.* 8.

(*c*) *I dilettevoli amori di messer Girolamo Benivieni Fiorentino*, printed at Venice, by *Nicolo d'Aristotile di Ferrara, detto Zoppino*, 1537, with another poem intitled, *Caccia bellissima del Reverendissimo Egidio*, and several pieces of the count Matteo Bojardo. This piece of Benivieni is not printed in the general edition of his works. *Ven.* 1524.

(*d*) *Strambotti di Serafino d'Aquila*. This celebrated poet and improvvisatore, "A quo," says Paolo Cortese, "ita est verborum et cantuum conjunctio "modulata nexa, ut nihil fieri posset modorum ratione dulcius," was born in 1466, and died in 1500. *Tirab. Storia della Let. Ital. v.* vi. *parte* 2. *p.* 154. His works have been frequently printed, but the edition most esteemed is that

CHAP. V.

Politiano (*a*), Lodovico Martelli (*b*), and others; who seem to have contended with each other for superiority in a species of poetry which gives full scope to the imagination, and in which the author takes the liberty of expatiating on any subject, which he conceives to be likely to engage the attention, and obtain the favour of his mistress.

Among the poems of Lorenzo de' Medici, which have been preserved for three centuries in manuscript, in the Laurentian Library, and which are given to the public for the first time at the close of the present work (*c*), is a beautiful Ovidian allegory, intitled *Ambra*, being the name of a small island, formed by the river Ombrone, near Lorenzo's villa at Poggio Cajano, the destruction of which is the subject of the poem. This favourite spot he had improved and ornamented with great assiduity, and was extremely delighted with the retired situation, and romantic

of Florence, by the Giunti, in 1516. Zeno has cited no less than sixteen editions of the works of Serafino, the latest of which is in the year 1550. *Bib. Ital. v.* i. *p.* 429.

(*a*) Some of these *Stanze* of Politiano were first published in the edition of his works by Comino, *Padua*, 1765; but, being there left imperfect, I have given a compleat copy in the Appendix, as they have been preserved in the Laurentian Library. *v. Band. Cat. Bib. Laur. t.* v. *p.* 51. *App. No.* XXXVII.

(*b*) *Stanze in lode delle Donne*, printed in the works of this author. *Flor.* 1548.

(*c*) About a dozen copies of these poems were printed in the year 1791, chiefly for the purpose of regulating the text; which have since been distributed by the editor amongst his friends. This he thinks it necessary to mention, to prevent any misapprehension on the part of those into whose hands such volume may chance to fall.

mantic aspect of the place (a). He was not, however, without apprehensions that the rapidity of the river might destroy his improvements, which misfortune he endeavoured to prevent by every possible precaution: but his cares were ineffectual; an inundation took place, and sweeping away his labours, left him no consolation but that of immortalizing his *Ambra* in the poem now alluded to (b). The same stanza is employed by Lorenzo in his poem on hawking, now also first published under the title of *La Caccia col Falcone*. This piece is apparently founded on a real incident. The author here gives us a very circumstantial, and at the same time a very lively account of this once popular diversion, from the departure of the company in the morning, to their return in the heat of the day. The scene is most probably at Poggio-Cajano, where he frequently partook of the diversions of hunting and of hawking, the latter of which he is said to have preferred (c). In this poem, wherein the author has introduced many of his companions

Poem of Ambra.

Poem on hawking.

(a) Laurentius Medices—qui scilicet Ambram ipsam Cajanam, prædium (ut ita dixerim) omniferum, quasi pro laxamento sibi delegit civilium laborum. *Pol. ad Laur. Tornabonum in Op. ap. Ald.*

(b) This is not the only occasion on which *Ambra* has been celebrated in the language of poetry. Politiano has given the same title to his beautiful Latin poem devoted to the praises of Homer; in the close of which, is a particular description of this favourite spot, which was at that time thought to be sufficiently secured against the turbulence of the flood:

"Ambra mei Laurentis amor, quam corniger Umbro
"Umbro senex genuit, domino gratissimus Arno;
"Umbro, suo tandem non erupturus ab alveo."

(c) Circa quoque pretorium Cajanum, quod regali magnificentia a fundamentis erexit, prædia habuit proventus maximi, et amænitatis plurimæ, quibus in locis frequens esset venationibus deditus, sed multo magis falconum et ejusmodi avium volatibus. *Valor. in vitâ Laur. p. 39.*

CHAP. V.

panions by name, the reader will find much native humour, and a striking picture of the manners of the times.

Moral pieces.

Lorenzo has however occasionally assumed in his writings a more serious character. His *Altercazione*, or poem explanatory of the Platonic philosophy, has before attracted our notice; but notwithstanding this attempt has great merit, and elucidates with some degree of poetical ornament a dry and difficult subject, it is much inferior to his moral poems, one of which in particular exhibits a force of expression, a grandeur and elevation of sentiment, of which his predecessors had set him no example, and which perhaps none of his countrymen have since excelled. This piece, in which the author calls upon the faculties of his own mind to exert themselves to great and useful purposes, thus commences;

Destati pigro ingegno da quel sonno,
 Che par che gli occhi tuoi d'un vel ricopra,
 Onde veder la verità non ponno;
Svegliati omai; contempla, ogni tua opra
 Quanto disutil sia, vana, e fallace,
 Poi che il desio alla ragione è sopra.
Deh pensa, quanto falsamente piace,
 Onore, utilitate, ovver diletto,
 Ove per più s'afferma esser la pace;
Pensa alla dignità del tuo intelletto,
 Non dato per seguir cosa mortale,
 Ma perchè avessi il cielo per suo obietto.
Sai per esperienza, quanto vale
 Quel, ch' altri chiama ben, dal ben più scosto,
 Che l'oriente dall' occidentale.
Quella vaghezza, ch' a gli occhi ha proposto
 Amor, e cominciò ne' teneri anni,
 D' ogni tuo viver lieto t'ha disposto.

3 Brieve,

Brieve, fugace, falsa, e pien d' affanni,
  Ornata in vista, ma è poi crudel mostro,
  Che tien lupi e delfin sotto i bei panni.
Deh pensa, qual sarebbe il viver nostro,
  Se quel, che de' tener la prima parte,
  Preso avesse il cammin, qual io t' ho mostro,
Pensa, se tanto tempo, ingegno, o arte,
  Avessi volto al più giusto desio,
  Ti potresti hor in pace consolarte.
Se ver te fosse il tuo voler più pio,
  Forse quel, che per te si brama, o spera,
  Conosceresti me', s' è buono o rio.
Dell età tua la verde primavera
  Hai consumata, e forse tal fia il resto,
  Fin che del verno sia l'ultima sera;
Sotto falsa ombra, e sotto rio pretesto,
  Persuadendo a te, che gentilezza
  Che vien dal cuor, ha causato questo.
Questi tristi legami oramai spezza:
  Leva dal collo tuo quella catena
  Ch' avolto vi tenea falsa bellezza:
E la vana speranza, che ti mena,
  Leva dal cuor, e fa il governo pigli
  Di te, la parte più bella e serena:
Et sottometta questa a' suoi artigli
  Ogni disir al suo voler contrario,
  Con maggior forza, e con maggior consigli,
Sicchè sbattuto il suo tristo aversario,
  Non drizzi più la venenosa cresta.

Rise from thy trance, my slumbering genius rise,
That shrouds from truth's pure beam thy torpid eyes!
Awake, and see, since reason gave the rein
To low desire, thy every work how vain.

Ah

CHAP. V.

Ah think how false that bliss the mind explores,
In futile honours, or unbounded stores;
How poor the bait that would thy steps decoy
To sensual pleasure, and unmeaning joy.
Rouse all thy powers, for better use designed,
And know thy native dignity of mind;
Not for low aims and mortal triumphs given,
Its means exertion, and its object heaven.
Hast thou not yet the difference understood,
'Twixt empty pleasure, and substantial good?
Not more opposed—by all the wise confest,
The rising orient from the farthest west.
Doom'd from thy youth the galling chain to prove
Of potent beauty, and imperious love,
Their tyrant rule has blighted all thy time,
And marr'd the promise of thy early prime.
Tho' beauty's garb thy wondering gaze may win,
Yet know that wolves, that harpies dwell within.
Ah think, how fair thy better hopes had sped,
Thy widely erring steps had reason led;
Think, if thy time a nobler use had known,
Ere this the glorious prize had been thine own.
Kind to thyself, thy clear discerning will,
Had wisely learnt to sever good from ill.
Thy spring-tide hours consum'd in vain delight,
Shall the same follies close thy wintry night?
With vain pretexts of beauty's potent charms,
And nature's frailty, blunting reason's arms?
—At length thy long-lost liberty regain,
Tear the strong tie, and break the inglorious chain,
Freed from false hopes, assume thy native powers,
And give to Reason's rule thy future hours;
To her dominion yield thy trusting soul,
And bend thy wishes to her strong control;
Till love, the serpent that destroy'd thy rest,
Crush'd by her hand shall mourn his humbled crest.

The

Sacred poems.

The sacred poems of Lorenzo de' Medici, distinguished by the names of *Orazioni*, and *Laude* (*a*), have been several times printed in various ancient collections, from which they were selected and published (with others by different persons of the same family) by Cionacci at Florence, in the year 1680 (*b*). The authors of the other poems in this collection are Lucretia the mother of Lorenzo, Pier Francesco his cousin, and Bernardo d'Alamanni de' Medici; but the reputation of Lorenzo as a poet will not be much increased by our assigning to him a decided superiority over his kindred. The poems of Lorenzo need not, however, the equivocal approbation of comparative praise, as they possess a great degree of positive excellence. In the following beautiful and affecting address to the Deity, the sublimity of the Hebrew original is tempered with the softer notes of the Italian muse (*c*):

ORA-

(*a*) Of the union of poetry and music in the *Laude Spirituali*, or sacred songs, Dr. Burney has traced the origin in Italy, and has given a specimen of a hymn to the Trinity, with the music, so early as the year 1336, from the MS. which he had himself consulted in the Magliabechi Library. *v. Hist. of Music, vol.* ii. *pag.* 326.

(*b*) RIME SACRE *del Magnifico* LORENZO DE' MEDICI *il Vecchio, di Madonna* LUCREZIA SUA MADRE, *e d' altri della stessa famiglia. Raccolte e d' osservazioni corredate per Francesco Cionacci. In Firenze* 1680.

(*c*) Since the above was written, I have discovered this hymn to be a paraphrase of "*The Secret Song, or Hymn of Regeneration*," in the *Pymander* of Hermes Trismegistus; who is said to have been the lawgiver of Egypt, and the inventor of hieroglyphic writing, and to have lived sixteen centuries before Christ. In the Laurentian library (*Plut.* xxi. *Cod.* 8. *v. Band. Cat.* 1. 668.) is a translation of this work from the Greek by Ficino, bearing the date of 1463, and dedicated to Cosmo de' Medici; from which Lorenzo undoubtedly translated or imitated the ensuing poem. The translation by Ficino also ap-

ORAZIONE.

Oda il sacro inno tutta la natura,
    Oda la terra, e nubilosi e foschi
    Turbini, e piove, che fan l' aere oscura.
Silenzj ombrosi, e solitari boschi:
    Posate venti: udite cieli il canto,
    Perchè il creato il creator conoschi.
Il creatore, e 'l tutto, e l' uno, io canto;
    Queste sacre orazion sieno esaudite
    Dell' immortale Dio dal cerchio santo.
Il Fattor canto, che ha distribuite
    Le terre; e 'l ciel bilancia; e quel che vuole,
    Che sien dell' ocean dolci acque uscite
Per nutrimento dell' umana prole;
    Per quale ancor comanda, sopra splenda
    Il fuoco: e perchè Dio adora e cole.
Grazie ciascun con una voce renda
    A lui, che passa i ciel; qual vive e sente,
    Crea, e convien da lui natura prenda.
Questo è solo e vero occhio della mente,
    Delle potenzie; a lui le laude date,
    Questo riceverà benignamente.
O forze mie, costui solo laudate,
    Ogni virtù dell' alma questo nume
    Laudi, conforme alla mia voluntate.

Santa

---

pears in his printed works, *vol.* ii. *p.* 789. *ed. Par.* 1641. An English version of the same author, said to be from the Arabic, by Dr. Everard, was published at London by *Thomas Brewster*, 1657. I scarcely need observe, that the authenticity of this work is doubtful; it being generally regarded as a pious fraud, produced about the second century of the Christian æra.

Santa è la cognizion, che del tuo lume
Splende, e canta illustrato in allegrezza
D' intelligibil luce il mio acume.
O tutte mie potenzie, in gran dolcezza
Meco cantate, o spirti miei costanti,
Cantate la costante sua fermezza.
La mia giustizia per me il giusto canti:
Laudate meco il tutto insieme e intero,
Gli spirti uniti, e' membri tutti quanti.
Canti per me la veritate il vero,
E tutto 'l nostro buon, canti esso bene,
Ben, che appetisce ciascun desidero.
O vita, o luce, da voi in noi viene
La benedizion; grazie t' ho io,
O Dio, da cui potenzia ogn' atto viene.
Il vero tuo per me te lauda Dio;
Per me ancor delle parole sante
Riceve il mondo il sacrificio pio.
Questo chieggon le forze mie clamante:
Cantano il tutto, e così son perfette
Da lor l' alte tue voglie tutte quante.
Il tuo disio da te in te reflette;
Ricevi il sacrificio, o santo Re,
Delle parole pie da ciascun dette.
O vita, salva tutto quel ch' è in me;
Le tenebre, ove l' alma par vanegge
Luce illumina tu, che luce se'.
Spirto Dio, il verbo tuo la mente regge,
Opifice, che spirto a ciascun dai,
Tu sol se' Dio, onde ogni cosa ha legge.
L' uomo tuo questo chiama sempre mai;
Per fuoco, aria, acqua, e terra t' ha pregato,
Per lo spirto, e per quel che creato hai.
Dall' eterno ho benedizion trovato,

E spero,

E spero, come io son desideroso,
Trovar nel tuo disio tranquillo stato;
Fuor di te Dio, non è vero riposo.

All nature, hear the sacred song!
Attend, O earth, the solemn strain!
Ye whirlwinds wild that sweep along;
Ye darkening storms of beating rain;
Umbrageous glooms, and forests drear,
And solitary deserts hear!
Be still, ye winds, whilst to the Maker's praise
The creature of his power aspires his voice to raise.

O may the solemn breathing sound
Like incense rise before the throne,
Where he, whose glory knows no bound,
Great cause of all things, dwells alone.
'Tis he I sing, whose powerful hand
Balanc'd the skies, outspread the land;
Who spoke—from ocean's stores sweet waters came,
And burst resplendent forth the heaven-aspiring flame.

One general song of praise arise
To him whose goodness ceaseless flows;
Who dwells enthron'd beyond the skies,
And life, and breath, on all bestows.
Great source of intellect, his ear
Benign receives our vows sincere:
Rise then, my active powers, your task fulfil,
And give to him your praise, responsive to my will.

Partaker of that living stream
Of light, that pours an endless blaze,
O let thy strong reflected beam,
My understanding, speak his praise:

My

My soul, in stedfast love secure,
Praise him whose word is ever sure:
To him, sole just, my sense of right incline,
Join every prostrate limb, my ardent spirit join.

Let all of good this bosom fires,
To him, sole good, give praises due:
Let all the truth himself inspires,
Unite to sing him only true.
To him my every thought ascend,
To him my hopes, my wishes, bend.
From earth's wide bounds let louder hymns arise,
And his own word convey the pious sacrifice.

In ardent adoration join'd,
Obedient to thy holy will,
Let all my faculties combin'd,
Thy just desires, O God, fulfil.
From thee deriv'd, eternal king,
To thee our noblest powers we bring:
O may thy hand direct our wandering way,
O bid thy light arise, and chase the clouds away.

Eternal spirit! whose command
Light, Life, and being, gave to all;
O hear the creature of thy hand,
Man, constant on thy goodness call:
By fire, by water, air, and earth,
That soul to thee that owes its birth,
By these, he supplicates thy blest repose,
Absent from thee no rest his wandering spirit knows.

The Italian language had not yet been applied to the purposes of satire, unless we may be allowed to apply that

The Beoni of Lorenzo.

Rise of the jocose Italian satire.

name to some parts of the *Commedia* of Dante, or the unpublished poem of Burchiello before noticed. The *Beoni* (*a*) of Lorenzo de' Medici is perhaps the earliest production that properly ranks under this title; the *Canti Carnascialeschi*, or carnival songs, which we shall hereafter notice, and which are supposed by Bianchini to have set the first example of the jocose Italian satire, being a very different kind of composition (*b*). This piece is also composed in *terza rima*, and is a lively and severe reprehension of drunkenness. The author represents himself as returning, after a short

(*a*) The *Beoni*, or *Simposio* of Lorenzo, was first published by the Giunti, at Florence, 1568, with the sonnets of Burchiello, Alamanni, and Risoluto; and was afterwards inserted in the third volume of the collection of the *Opere Burlesche*, printed with the date of (London) 1723. In the former edition many of the objectionable passages are omitted, which are however restored in the latter. The editors of the poems of Lorenzo, published at Bergamo in 1763, have again mutilated this poem, having totally omitted the 8th capitolo, as *mancante e licenzioso*. In all the editions the work is left imperfect, and ends in the midst of the 9th capitolo; after which, in the edition of 1568, it is added, "*Dicon ch' el magnifico Autore lasciò l' opera così imperfetta.*"

(*b*) "Or questi *Canti Carnascialeschi*, fatti per intrattenere allegramente il "popolo, io gli considero come non solamente primi, ma grandi avanzamenti "altresì della giocosa satira Italiana; a quali aggiugnere dobbiamo *I Beoni*, e "*La Compagnia del Mantellaccio*, componimenti dello stesso Lorenzo de' Medici, "i quali furono scritti da quel grand' uomo per sollievo delle pubbliche gravose "occupazioni, e dagli studj piu sublimi delle scienze, &c." *Bianchini, della satira Italiana, p.* 33. *Ed. Fir.* 1729. *La Compagnia del Mantellaccio* was not however written by Lorenzo, though it has frequently been attributed to him. In the earliest edition I have seen of this poem, which is without a date, but was probably printed before the year 1500, it appears without the name of its author. A more complete copy is annexed to the sonetti of Burchiello, Alamanni, and Risoluto, by the Giunti in 1568, where it is attributed to Lorenzo de' Medici; but it is by no means possessed of those characteristic excellencies that distinguish the generality of his works.

a short absence, to Florence; when, as he approached towards the *Porta di Faenza*, he met many of his fellow-citizens, hastening along the road with the greatest precipitation. At length he had the good fortune to perceive an old acquaintance, to whom he gives the appellation of Bartolino, and whom he requests to explain to him the cause of this strange commotion.

Non altrimente a parete ugelletto,
  Sentendo d' altri ugelli i dolci versi,
  Sendo in cammin, si volge a quell' effetto;
Così lui, benchè appena può tenersi,
  Che li pareva al fermarsi fatica;
  Che e' non s' acquista in fretta i passi persi.

—As when some bird a kindred note that hears,
His well-known mate with note responsive cheers,
He recogniz'd my voice; and at the sound
Relax'd his speed; but difficult he found
The task to stop, and great fatigue it seem'd.
For whilst he spoke, each moment lost he deem'd;
Then thus:

Bartolino informs him that they are all hastening to the bridge of Rifredi, to partake of a treat of excellent wine,

——che presti facci i lenti piedi.

That gives new vigour to the crippled feet.

He then characterizes his numerous companions, who, although sufficiently discriminated in other respects, all agree

 in

in their insatiable thirst. Three priests at length make their appearance; Lorenzo inquires

Colui chi è, che ha rosse le gote?
  E due con seco con lunghe mantella?
  Ed ei: ciascun di loro è sacerdote;
Quel ch' è più grasso, è il Piovan dell' Antella,
  Perch' e' ti paja straccurato in viso,
  Ha sempre seco pur la metadella:
L' altro, che drieto vien con dolce riso,
  Con quel naso appuntato, lungo, e strano,
  Ha fatto anche del ber suo paradiso;
Tien dignità, ch'è pastor Fiesolano,
  Che ha in una sua tazza divozione,
  Che ser Anton seco ha, suo cappellano.
Per ogni loco, e per ogni stagione,
  Sempre la fida tazza seco porta,
  Non ti dico altro, sino a processione;
E credo questa fia sempre sua scorta,
  Quando lui muterà paese o corte,
  Questa sarà che picchierà la porta:
Questa sarà con lui dopo la morte,
  E messa seco fia nel monimento,
  Acciochè morto poi lo riconforte;
E questa lascerà per testamento.
  Non hai tu visto a procession, quand' elli
  Ch' ognun si fermi, fa comandamento?
E i canonici chiama suoi fratelli;
  Tanto che tutti intorno li fan cerchio,
  E mentre lo ricuopron co' mantelli,
Lui con la tazza, al viso fa coperchio.

With

With rosy cheeks who follows next, my friend,
And who the gownmen that his steps attend?
—Three pious priests—the chief in size and place,
Antella's rector—shews his vacant face;
He, who, with easy smile and pointed nose,
In social converse with the rector goes,
Of Fesulé a dignified divine,
Has wisely placed his paradise in wine.
The favourite cup that all his wants supplies
Within whose circle his devotion lies,
His faithful curate, Ser Antonio brings——
—See, at his side the goodly vessel swings.
On all occasions, and where'er he bends
His way, this implement its lord attends;
Or more officious, marches on before,
Prepares his road, and tinkles at the door;
This on his death-bed shall his thoughts employ,
And with him in his monument shall lie.
Hast thou not seen—if e'er thou chanc'd to meet,
The slow procession moving through the street,
As the superior issues his command,
His sable brethren close around him stand;
Then, whilst in pious act with hands outspread,
Each with his cassock shrouds his leader's head,
His face the toper covers with his cup,
And e'er the prayer be ended, drinks it up.

The fiery temperament of an habitual drunkard is described by the following whimsical hyperbole:

Come fu giunto in terra quell' umore,
  Del fiero sputo, nell' arido smalto,
  Unissi insieme l'umido e'l calore;

E poi quella virtù, che vien da alto,
Li diede spirto, e nacquene un ranocchio,
E inanzi a gli occhi nostri prese un salto.

He sneez'd; and as the burning humour fell,
The dust with vital warmth began to swell,
Hot, moist, and dry, their genial powers unite,
Up sprang a frog and leapt before our sight.

So expeditious was Lorenzo in his compositions, that he is said to have written this piece nearly extempore, immediately after the incident on which it was founded took place (*a*). Posterity ought to regard this poem with particular favour, as it has led the way to some of the most agreeable and poignant productions of the Italian poets, and is one of the earliest models of the satires and *capitoli* of Berni (*b*), Nelli,

(*a*) Ex Caregio suo in urbem rediens, Satyram in bibaces, argumento e re nato, inchoavit simul et absolvit; opus in suo genere consummatissimum, salibus plurimis et lepore conditum. Fuit enim in hoc homine cum gravitate urbanitas multa. Quum jocabatur, nihil hilarius; quum mordebat nihil asperius. *Valor. in vitâ Laur. p.* 14.

(*b*) Francesco Berni, availing himself of the examples of Burchiello, Franco, Luigi Pulci, and Lorenzo de' Medici, cultivated this branch of poetry with such success, as to have been generally considered as the inventor of it; whence it has obtained the name of *Bernesche*. The characteristic of this poetry is an extreme simplicity of provincial diction, which the Italians denominate *Idiotismo*. The most extravagant sentiments, the most severe strokes of satire, are expressed in a manner so natural and easy, that the author himself seems unconscious of the effect of his own work. Perhaps the only indication of a similar taste in this country appears in the writings of the facetious Peter Pindar; but with this distinction, that the wit of the Italians generally consists in giving a whimsical importance to subjects in themselves ridiculous or

Nelli (*a*), Ariosto (*b*), Bentivoglio (*c*), and others, who form a numerous class of writers, in a mode of composition almost peculiar to the natives of Italy.

Stanze Contadinesche.

Italy has always been celebrated for the talents of its *Improvvisatori*, or extempore poets. Throughout Tuscany, in particular, this custom of reciting verses has for ages been the constant and most favourite amusement of the villagers and country inhabitants. At some times the subject is a trial of wit between two peasants; on other occasions a lover addresses his mistress in a poetical oration, expressing his passion by such images as his uncultivated fancy suggests, and endeavouring to amuse and engage her by the liveliest sallies of humour. These recitations, in which the

---

contemptible, whilst that of our countryman is for the most part shewn in rendering things of importance ridiculous. The principal work of Berni is his *Orlando Innamorato*, being the poem of Bojardo, newly versified, or rather travestied; in the third book and 7th chapter of which he has introduced, without much ceremony, some particulars of his own history, which the reader may not be displeased to find in the Appendix, No. XXXVIII.

(*a*) The satires of Pietro Nelli were published under the name of Andrea da Bergamo. *Ven.* 1546, 1584.

(*b*) In the satires of Ariosto, the author has faithfully recorded his family circumstances and connexions, the patronage with which he was honoured, and the mortifications and disappointments which he from time to time experienced: whilst his independent spirit, and generous resentment of the oppressive mandates of his superiors, are exhibited in a lively and interesting style. In the *Orlando Furioso* we admire the poet; but in the satires of Ariosto we are familiarized with, and love the man.

(*c*) Ercole Bentivoglio was of the same family that for many years held the sovereignty of Bologna. His satires do him infinite credit as a poet, and are scarcely inferior to those of Ariosto his friend and contemporary.

the eclogues of Theocritus are realized, are delivered in a tone of voice between speaking and singing, and are accompanied with the constant motion of one hand, as if to measure the time and regulate the harmony; but they have an additional charm from the simplicity of the country dialect, which abounds with phrases highly natural and appropriate, though incompatible with the precision of a regular language, and forms what is called the *Lingua Contadinesca* (*a*), of which specimens may be found in the writings of Boccaccio (*b*). The idea of adapting this language to

---

(*a*) Few attempts have been made in England to adapt the provincial idom of the inhabitants to the language of poetry. Neither the *Shepherd's Calendar* of Spenser, nor the *Pastorals* of Gay, possess that native simplicity, and close adherence to the manners and language of country life, which ought to form the basis of this kind of composition. Whether the dialect of Scotland be more favourable to attempts of this nature, or whether we are to seek for the fact in the character of the people, or the peculiar talents of the writers, certain it is, that the idiom of that country has been much more successfully employed in poetical composition, than that of any other part of these kingdoms, and that this practice may there be traced to a very early period. In later times, the beautiful dramatic poem of *The Gentle Shepherd* has exhibited rusticity without vulgarity, and elegant sentiment without affectation. Like the heroes of Homer, the characters of this piece can engage in the humblest occupations without degradation. If to this production we add the beautiful and interesting poems of the Ayrshire ploughman, we may venture to assert, that neither in Italy nor in any other country has this species of poetry been cultivated with greater success. *The Cotter's Saturday Night* is perhaps unrivalled in its kind in any language.

(*b*) *Decam. Giorn.* viii. *Nov.* 2. Bentivegna del Mazzo being interrogated whither he went, replies *Guaffe, Sere, in buona verità io vo infino a Città per alcuna mia vicenda, e porto queste cose a Serre Bonaccorri di Ginestreto, che m'ajuti di non so che m'ha fatto richiedere per una comparigione del parentorio per lo pericolator suo il guidice del dificio.* That the ancient Romans had also a marked distinction between the written tongue, and the dialect of the country inhabitants, may be inferred from the following lines of Tibullus. *Lib.* ii. *Eleg.* 3.

Ipsa Venus laetos jam nunc migravit in agros,
Verbaque aratoris rustica discit amor.

poetry first occurred to Lorenzo de' Medici, who, in his verses intitled *La Nencia da Barberino* (*a*), has left a very pleasing specimen of it, full of lively imagery and rustic pleasantry (*b*). This piece no sooner appeared, than Luigi Pulci attempted to emulate it, in another poem, written in the same stanza, and called *La Beca da Dicomano* (*c*); but instead of the more chastised and delicate humour of Lorenzo, the poem of Pulci partakes of the character of his *Morgante*, and wanders into the burlesque and extravagant. In the following century, Michelagnolo Buonaroti, the nephew of the celebrated artist of the same name, employed this style with great success in his admirable rustic comedy, *La Tancia* (*d*); but perhaps the most beautiful instance

(*a*) *Nencia* is probably the rustic appellation of *Lorenza* or *Lorenzina*; thus from *Lorenzo*, in the same dialect, is formed *Nencio* and *Renzo*; and from the diminutive *Lorenzino*, *Nencino* and *Cencino*. In this poem, the rustic, Vallero, also addresses his mistress by the augmentative of *Nenciozza*. These variations are frequently used in the Florentine dialect to express the estimation in which the subject of them is held; thus *ino*, and *ina*, denote a certain degree of affection and tenderness, similar to that which is felt for infants; whilst the augmentatives of *uccio*, *uccia*, *one*, *ona*, usually imply ridicule or contempt.

(*b*) As the peculiar excellence of this poem consists in its being an exact transcript of the Tuscan idiom, I shall not attempt to exhibit it in another language; particularly in a language which, if we may judge from previous attempts, seems scarcely susceptible of this kind of composition. A few *stanzas* from the original will be found in the Appendix, No. XXXIX.

(*c*) Published with *La Nencia*, in the *Canzoni a ballo*. *Flor*. 1568.

(*d*) The learned Anton Maria Salvini has given an excellent edition of this comedy, with another by the same author, intitled *La Fiera*. *Firenz*. 1726. The annotations of Salvini upon these pieces are highly and deservedly esteemed.

instance that Italy has produced, is the work of Francesco Baldovini, who, towards the close of the last century, published his *Lamento di Cecco da Varlungo* (*a*); a piece of inimitable wit and simplicity, and which seems to have carried this species of poetry to its highest pitch of perfection.

State of the Italian drama.

If, during the darkness of the middle ages, the drama, that great school of human life and manners, as established among the ancients, was totally lost, it was not without a substitute in most of the nations of Europe, though of a very imperfect and degraded kind. To this factitious species of dramatic representation, which led the minds of the people from the imitation of the ancient Greeks and Romans, and closed their eyes to their excellencies, we are probably to attribute the slow progress which, in the revival of letters, took place in this important department. Innumerable attempts have indeed been made to trace the origin of the modern drama, and the Italians, the Germans, the Spaniards, the French, and the English (*b*), have

(*a*) An elegant edition of this poem was also published at Florence in 1755, in quarto, with copious notes and illustrations by Orazio Marrini; in which the editor has, with great industry and learning, traced the history of rustic poetry in Italy, from the time of Lorenzo de' Medici, to whom he attributes the invention of it (*Pref. p.* 10.), to that of his author Baldovini; and has illustrated the text in the most judicious and satisfactory manner.

(*b*) Several of our most celebrated critics have warmly contended for the antiquity of the English stage, which they suppose may be traced higher than the Italian by 150 years; in proof of which is adduced the miracle-play of St. Catherine, said to be written by Geoffry, abbot of St. Alban's, and performed at Dunstable in the year 1110. *v. Malone's Shakspeare, in Pref.* Hence we might be led to conclude that this miracle-play was composed in dialogue; but there is reason to conjecture that the whole consisted in dumb shew,

have successively claimed priority of each other. But questions of this kind scarcely admit of decision. Imitation is natural to man in every state of society; and where shall we draw the line of distinction between the polished productions of Racine, and the pantomimes of Bartholomew-fair? This propensity to imitation, operating upon the religious or superstitious views of the clergy, produced at length that species of exhibition which was formerly known throughout Europe by the name of Mysteries; but it is probable, that for a long time they were merely calculated to

and that the author's only merit lay in the arrangement of the incidents and machinery. Of the same nature were the grotesque exhibitions, well known in this country under the name of the harrowing of Hell. (*Tyrwhit's Chaucer, v.* iv. *p.* 243.) And the representations at Florence, mentioned by Villani (*lib.* viii. *c.* 10.) and Ammirato (*lib.* iv.), who inform us, that in the year 1304, the inhabitants of the district of S. Borgo publicly proclaimed that they would give an insight into the next world to those who would attend upon the bridge of Carrara. A great number of people were accordingly collected together to witness a representation of the infernal regions, which was displayed in boats or rafts upon the river. In this spectacle the damned appeared to be tormented by demons in various forms, and with dreadful shrieks struck the spectators with terror: when, in the midst of the performance, the bridge, which was of wood, gave way, and the unfortunate attendants became the principal actors in the drama. The interludes preserved among the Harleian MSS. said to have been performed at Chester in 1327, and adverted to by Mr. Malone, are manifestly antedated by nearly two centuries; nor do I conceive it possible to adduce a dramatic composition in the English language that can indisputably be placed before the year 1500; previous to which time they were common in Italy; though possibly not so early as Mr. Malone allows, when he informs us, on the authority of the Histriomastix, that pope Pius II. about the year 1416, composed, and caused to be acted before him on Corpus Christi day, a mystery, in which was represented the court of the kingdom of heaven. Æneas Sylvius, who assumed that title, was not raised to the pontifical dignity till the year 1458. In the extensive catalogue of his writings by Apostolo Zeno (*Dissert. Voss.*) I find no notice of any such composition.

to strike the eyes of the spectators. In the city of Florence they were often prepared at the public expence, and at times by rich individuals, for the purpose of displaying their wealth, and conciliating the public favour. Four days in the year were solemnly celebrated by the four districts of the city, in honour of their patron saints; but the feast of St. John, the tutelary saint of Florence, was provided, not at the expence of the particular district which bore his name, but of the city at large. The fabrication of these spectacles employed the abilities of the best artists and engineers of the time (*a*).

It was not, however, till the age of Lorenzo de' Medici that these ill-judged representations began to assume a more respectable form, and to be united with dialogue. One of the earliest examples of the sacred drama is the *Rappresentazione* of *S. Giovanni e S. Paolo* (*b*), by Lorenzo de' Medici. Cionacci conjectures that this piece was written at the time of the marriage of Maddalena, one of the daughters of Lorenzo, to Francesco Cibo, nephew of Innocent VIII. and that it was performed by his own children; there being many passages which seem to be intended as precepts for such as are intrusted with the direction of a state, and which

(*a*) *Vasari, vita di Cecca Ingegnere e di Filippo Brunelleschi.*

(*b*) Of this piece I have two ancient editions without date; one of which, printed at Florence by *Francesco Bonaccorsi*, bears sufficient evidence of its having been published during the life of the author. "Se errore alchuno," says the editor, "trovate nella impressa opera, quello non ascriviate alle occupazioni "del nostro magnifico Lorenzo; sed indubitatamente lo imputate allo impressore; perochè chi è solerte, che significa in omni re prudente, in nessuno "tempo è occupato; ma occupato è sempre che non è solerte." It is also republished by Cionacci amongst the sacred poems of Lorenzo and others. *Fir*, 1680.

which particularly point out the line of conduct which he and his ancestors had pursued, in obtaining and preserving their influence in Florence (*a*). The coadjutors of Lorenzo in this attempt to meliorate the imperfect state of the drama were Feo Belcari, Bernardo Pulci and his wife Madonna Antonia de' Tanini (*b*). That Lorenzo had it in contemplation to employ dramatic composition in other subjects is also apparent. Among his poems published at the end of the present work will be found an attempt to substitute the deities of Greece and Rome, for the saints and martyrs of the Christian church; but the jealous temper of the national religion seems for a time to have restrained the progress which might otherwise have been expected in this important department of letters. Some years after the death of

(*a*) Sappiate che chi vuol popol regere,
Debbe pensare al bene universale,
E chi vuol altri dalli error correggere,
Sforzisi prima lui di non far male;
Però conviensi giusta vita eleggere,
Perchè lo esemplo al popol molto vale;
E quel che fa il Signor, fanno poi molti,
Che nel Signor son tutti gli occhi volti.

It must be observed, that St. John and St. Paul, the heroes of this drama, are not the personages of those names mentioned in the sacred writings, but two eunuchs, attendant on the daughter of Constantine the Great, who are put to death by Julian the apostate for their adherence to the Christian religion.

(*b*) A considerable collection of the ancient editions of the *Rappresentazioni* of the fifteenth century, printed without date, and formerly in the Pinelli library, has fallen into my hands. I may say of them, with Apostolo Zeno, "trattone alquanti che hanno qualche suco di buon sapere, mescolato "però di agro & di spiacevole, son rancidumi ed inezie; cavate anche da le"gende apocrife, e da impure fonti, con basso e pedestre stile, e d'arte prive, "e di grazia poetica." *Annot. alla Bib. Ital. di Fontan.* v. i. p. 489.

of Lorenzo, a more decided effort was made by Bernardo Accolti, in his drama of *Virginia*, founded on one of the novels of Boccaccio (*a*); and this again was followed at a short interval by the *Sofonisba* of Trissino, and the *Rosmunda* of Giovanni Rucellai, two pieces which are justly considered as the first regular productions of the drama in modern times.

The musical drama.

The origin of the musical drama, or Italian opera, is by general consent attributed to Politiano, who gave the first example of it in his *Orfeo*. The idea of this species of composition seems to have been first suggested by the Eclogues of the ancient Greek and Roman authors; nor does there appear to have been any extraordinary exertion of genius in adapting to music the sentiments and language of pastoral life: but it should be remembered, that the intrinsic merit of any discovery is to be judged

(*a*) *Decam. Gior.* iii. *Nov.* 9. The argument of this piece is given by Accolti in the following sonetto, prefixed to the edition of Flor. 1514:

Virginia amando el Re guarisce, e chiede,
Di Salerno el gran principe in marito;
Qual costretto a sposarla, e poi partito
Per mai tornar fin lei viva si vede:
Cerca Virginia scrivendo, mercede,
Ma el principe da molta ira assalito
Gli domanda, s'a lei vuol sia redito,
Due condizion qual impossibil crede.
Però Virginia sola, e travestita,
Partendo, ogn' impossibil conditione
Adempie al fin con prudentia infinita.
Onde el principe pien d' amiratione
Lei di favore, e grazia rivestita
Sposa di nuovo con molta affectione.

judged of rather by the success with which it is attended, than by the difficulties that were to be surmounted. Of the plan and conduct of this dramatic attempt, a particular account has been given by a very judicious and amusing author (*a*). Little however is to be expected in point of arrangement, when we understand that it was the hasty production of two days, and was intended merely for the gratification of Gonzaga, cardinal of Mantua, before whom it was first represented. Accordingly, its principal merit consists in the simplicity and elegance of some of the Lyric pieces with which it is interspersed. From the early editions of this poem, it appears that the character of Orpheus was first exhibited by the celebrated *Improvvisatore* Baccio Ugolini, whose personal obligations to the cardinal occasioned the introduction of the beautiful Latin ode, in which, by a singular exertion of the *quidlibet audendi*, the Theban bard is introduced singing the praises of the cardinal, but which was afterwards superseded by the verses in praise of Hercules, generally found in the subsequent editions.

In a dedicatory epistle prefixed to this piece, and addressed to Carlo Canale, the author, whilst he professes himself willing to comply with the wishes of some of his friends by its publication, openly protests against the propriety of such a measure (*b*). A species of conduct which, in

(*a*) *v. Dr. Burney's Gen. Hist. of Music*, v. iv. *p.* 14.

(*b*) Viva adunque poi che così ad voi piace, ma ben vi protesto che tale pietà è una expressa crudeltà; e di questo mio giudizio desidero ne sia questa epistola testimonio. *Pol. in Pref.*

CHAP. V.

in modern times, might perhaps savour of affectation; but of this we may safely acquit Politiano, who, in the midst of his learned labours, certainly regarded a slight composition in the vulgar tongue as much below his talents and his character.

Canti Carnascialeschi.

During the time of carnival, it was customary to celebrate that festival at Florence with extraordinary magnificence. Among other amusements, it had long been usual to collect together, at great expence, large processions of people, sometimes representing the return of triumphant warriors with trophies, cars, and similar devices; and at other times some story of ancient chivalry. These exhibitions afforded ample scope for the inventive talents of the Florentine artists, who contended with each other in rendering them amusing, extravagant, or terrific. The pageantry was generally displayed by night, as being the season best calculated to conceal the defects of the performance, and to assist the fancy of the spectators. "It "was certainly," says Vasari (*a*), "an extraordinary sight, "to observe twenty or thirty couple of horsemen, most "richly dressed in appropriate characters, with six or eight "attendants upon each, habited in an uniform manner, and "carrying torches to the amount of several hundreds, after "whom usually followed a triumphal car with the trophies "and spoils of victory"—of imaginary victories indeed, but not on that account less calculated to display the ingenuity of the inventor, or less pleasing in the estimation of the philosopher.

(*a*) *Vasari, vita di Piero di Cosimo.*

philosopher. The promised gaiety of the evening was sometimes unexpectedly interrupted by a moral lesson, and the artist seized the opportunity of exciting those more serious emotions, which the astonished beholders had supposed it was his intention to dissipate. Thus Piero di Cosimo, a painter of Florence, appalled the inhabitants by a representation of the triumph of Death, in which nothing was omitted that might impress upon their minds the sense of their own mortality (*a*). Prior however to the time of Lorenzo de' Medici, these exhibitions were calculated merely to amuse the eye, or were at most accompanied by the insipid madrigals of the populace. It was he who first taught his countrymen to dignify them with sentiment, and add to their poignancy by the charms of poetry (*b*). It is true, the examples which he has himself given of these compositions in the *Canti Carnascialeschi*, or carnival songs, being calculated for the gratification of the multitude,

(*a*) Of this exhibition, which took place about the year 1512, Vasari has left a very particular account. (*vita di Piero di Cosimo.*) The same author has preserved the following lines of the *Carro della Morte*, sung upon this occasion, which was the composition of Antonio Alamanni ·

> " Morti siam come vedete,
> " Così morti vedrem voi,
> " Fummo già come voi siete,
> " Voi sarete come noi."

The whole piece is published in the *Canti Carnascialeschi*, *p*. 131. *Ed*. 1559.

(*b*) Questo modo di festeggiare fu trovato dal Mag. Lorenzo de' Medici, uno dei primi e più chiari splendori ch' abbia havuto non pure la illustrissima e nobilissima casa vostra, e Firenze, ma Italia ancora, e il mondo tutto quanto; degno veramente di non esser ricordato mai nè senza lagrime, nè senza riverenza.

Il Lasca, ad Sig. Francesco de' Medici. Canti Carnascialeschi in pref. Flor. 1559.

CHAP. V.

multitude, and devoted only to the amusement of an evening, exhibit not any great energy of thought, nor are they distinguished by an equal degree of poetical ornament with his other works. Their merits are therefore principally to be estimated by the purity of the Florentine diction, which is allowed to be there preserved in its most unadulterated state (*a*). The intervention and patronage of Lorenzo gave new spirit to these amusements. Induced by his example, many of his contemporaries employed their talents in these popular compositions, which were continued by a numerous succession of writers, till the middle of the ensuing century, when they were diligently collected by Anton Francesco Grazzini, commonly called *Il Lasca*, and published at Florence in the year 1559 (*b*).

The

(*a*) These pieces, as well as the other poems of Lorenzo de' Medici, are frequently cited by the academicians della Crusca, in their celebrated dictionary, as authorities for the Italian tongue; and consequently compose a part of those works, selected for the purity of their style, and known by the name of *Testi di lingua*.

(*b*) This was not however the first edition of the *Canti Carnascialeschi*. Zeno, in his notes on the *Bibl. Ital.* of Fontanini (*v.* ii. *p.* 83.), has cited two editions printed without note of date or place, but prior, as he thought, to the year 1500; the first entitled *Canzone per andare in Maschera*, the latter *Ballatette del Magnifico Lorenzo de' Medici, di M. Agnolo Poliziano, e di Bernardo Giamburlari*. The edition of 1559 is however the first general collection of these pieces, towards which a great number of the natives of Florence contributed. Of this edition the greater part of the copies are mutilated, having been deprived of 100 pages about the middle of the book; viz. from page 298 to page 398, in which space were contained the pieces of Battista dell' Ottonajo, whose brother Paolo having remonstrated against their publication in a surreptitious manner, and in an inaccurate state, had sufficient influence with the government of Florence to obtain an order that the printer, Torrentino, should deliver up all the copies in his hands, which appeared to be 495; after a year's

Canzoni a ballo.

The *Canzoni a ballo* are compositions of a much more singular and inexplicable kind. From their denomination it is probable, that they were sung by companies of young people, in concert with the music to which they danced; and the measure of the verse appears to be so constructed as to fall in with the different movements and pauses. It may perhaps be thought that the extreme licentiousness of some of these pieces militates against such an idea, but in the state of manners in Italy at that period, this objection can have but little weight. Indeed, if we trace to its source this favourite amusement, we shall probably discover, that a dance is in fact only a figurative representation of the passion of love, exhibited with more or less delicacy according to the character and state of civilization of those who practise it. To improve its relish, and heighten its enjoyment, seems to have been the intention of the *Canzoni a ballo*. From the known affability of Lorenzo de' Medici, and the festivity of his disposition; as well as from other circumstances,

litigation the poems of Ottonajo were ordered to be cut out from the book, and Paolo was left at liberty to publish another edition of them, which he accordingly did. This dispute has given rise to another contest during the present century, between the Canonico Biscioni, late librarian of the grand duke's library at Florence, and Sig. Rinaldo Maria Bracci, who published at Pisa, under the date of Cosmopoli 1750, a new edition of the *Canti Carnascialeschi*, in two volumes quarto, including those of Ottonajo, from the impression of his brother Paolo; in the introduction to which he justifies the decree that suppressed these pieces in the edition of 1559, contrary to the opinion of Biscioni, who considered it as severe and unjust. The dispute seems of little importance, but the result of it was unfavourable to the modern editor, whose elegant and apparently correct edition of these poems has never obtained that credit amongst the literati of Italy, to which, on many accounts, it appears to be entitled. I shall give one of these poems in the Appendix, being the Triumph of Bacchus and Ariadne, by Lorenzo de' Medici. *v. App. No.* XL.

stances (*a*), there is reason to conclude, that he was accustomed to mingle with the populace on these mirthful occasions,

(*a*) In the edition of the *Canzoni a ballo*, published at Florence in 1568, the title-page is ornamented with a print in wood, of which the above is a copy, representing twelve women dancing before the palace of the Medici, known by

sions, and to promote and direct their amusements. Nor are we to wonder that the arbiter of the politics of Italy should be employed in the streets of Florence, participating the mirth, and directing the evolutions, of a troop of dancing girls. On the contrary, this versatility of talent and of disposition may be considered as the most distinguishing feature in the character of this extraordinary man; who from the most important concerns of state, and the highest speculations of philosophy, could stoop to partake of the humblest diversions of the populace, and who in every department obtained by general consent the supreme direction and control.

Thus far we have taken a review of the chief part of the poems which yet remain of Lorenzo de' Medici, and have seen him by his own example stimulating his countrymen

---

the arms affixed to it, and singing, as we may presume, a dancing song. Towards the front of the print appears Lorenzo de' Medici; two females kneel before him, one of whom presents him with a garland taken from her head, of which he seems to decline the acceptance. Behind Lorenzo stands Agnolo Politiano, his associate in this work. This print seems to have a more particular reference to one of the songs written by Lorenzo, which became extremely popular by the name of *Ben venga Maggio*, and which the reader will find in the Appendix, No. XLI. In an ancient collection of *Laude*, or hymns, printed at Venice in 1512, I find that several of these devout pieces are directed to be sung to the air of *Ben venga Maggio*. From this collection it appears that it was then a general custom in Italy, as it now is, or lately was, the practice of a certain sect in this country, to sing pious hymns to the most profane and popular melodies, for the purpose of stimulating the languid piety of the performers, by an association with the vivacity of sensual enjoyments. Thus the hymn *Jesu sommo diletto*, is sung to the music of *Leggiadra damigella*; *Jesu sommi morire*, to that of *Vaga bella e gentile*; *Genetrice di Dio*, to that of *Dolce anima mia*; and *Crucifisso a capo chino*, to that of *Una Donna d'amor fino*, one of the most indecent pieces in the *Canzoni a ballo*.

CHAP. V.

men to the pursuit of literature. The restorer of the Lyric poetry of Italy, the promoter of the dramatic, the founder of the satiric, rustic, and other modes of composition, he is not merely entitled to the rank of a poet, but may justly be placed among the distinguished few, who, by native strength, have made their way through paths before untrodden. Talent may follow and improve; emulation and industry may polish and refine; but genius alone can break those barriers that restrain the throng of mankind in the common track of life.

Critique of Pico of Mirandula, on the poems of Lorenzo.

The poetical merits of Lorenzo de' Medici were perceived and acknowledged by his contemporaries. Were we to collect the various testimonies of respect and admiration that were produced in honour of him in different parts of Italy, they would form a very unreasonable addition to the present volume. We must not however omit to notice the opinion of Pico of Mirandula, who, in a letter addressed to Lorenzo, has entered into a full discussion of the character of his writings, comparing them with those of his predecessors Dante and Petrarca, and contending that they unite the vigour of thought apparent in the former, with the harmony and polish of the latter (*a*). Succeeding critics have however appealed against a decision, which seems to attribute to Lorenzo de' Medici a superiority over the great masters of the Tuscan poetry; and have considered the opinion of Pico, either as an instance of courtly adulation, or as a proof of the yet imperfect taste of the

(*a*) This letter, which has occasioned so much animadversion, is given in the Appendix, No. XLII.

the age (*a*). Without contending for the opinion of Pico in its full extent, we may be allowed to remark, that the temper and character both of him and of Lorenzo, are equally adverse to the idea, that the one could offer, or the other be gratified, with unmerited approbation and spurious praise; and that Pico was not deficient in the qualifications of a critic, may appear even from the very letter which has been cited as an impeachment of his taste. For although he there treats the writings of Dante and Petrarca with great severity, and asserts not only the equality, but, in a certain point of view, the superiority of those of Lorenzo, yet he clearly proves that he had attentively studied these productions, and by many acute and just observations demonstrates, that he was well qualified to appreciate their various merits and defects. Nor does Pico, in avowing this opinion, stand alone amongst his countrymen. Even in the most enlightened period of the ensuing century, the pretensions

---

(*a*) " A questo s'aggiunge che Giovanni Pico Conte della Mirandola, uomo " di singolarrissimo ingegno e dottrina, in una lettera latina, la quale egli " scrisse al Mag. Lorenzo de' Medici vecchio—non solo lo pareggia, ma lo pre- " pone indubitatamente così a Dante come al Petrarca, perchè al Petrarca " (dic' egli) mancano le cose, cioè i concetti, e a Dante le parole, cioè l' elo- " quenza; dove in Lorenzo non si desideremo nè l'une nè l' altre. Le quali " cose egli mal affermate così precisamente non arebbe, se i giudicj di quel " secol fossero stati sani, e gli orecchi non corrotti." *Varchi Ercolano, p.* 27. *Ed. Com.* 1744. The same author, however, after acquitting Pico of the charge of adulation, subjoins, " Nè sarebbe mancata materia al Pico di potere vera- " mente commendare Lorenzo, senza biasimare non veramente il Petrarca, e " Dante; perchè nel vero egli con M. Agnolo Poliziano, e Girolamo Bene- " vieni furono i primi i quali comminciassero nel comporre a ritirarsi e discos- " tarsi dal volgo, e, se non imitare, a volere, o parere di volere imitare il Pe- " trarca, e Dante, lasciando in parte quella maniera del tutto vile, e plebea, " la quale assai chiaramente si reconosce ancora eziandio nel *Morgante Mag-* " *giore* di Luigi Pulci, e nel *Ciriffo Calvaneo* di Luca suo Fratello."

CHAP. V.

Opinions of other authors on the same subject.

tensions of Lorenzo de' Medici to rank with the great fathers of the Italian tongue, are supported by an author whose testimony cannot be suspected of partiality, and whose authority will be acknowledged as generally as his writings are known (*a*). The most celebrated literary historians of Italy, in adverting to the age of Lorenzo, have acknowledged the vigour of his genius, and the success of his labours; Crescimbeni, in tracing the vicissitudes of the Tuscan poetry, informs us, that it had risen to such perfection under the talents of Petrarca, that not being susceptible of further improvement, it began, in the common course of earthly things, to decline; and in a short time was so debased and adulterated, as nearly to revert to its pristine barbarity. " But at this critical juncture," says the same well-informed author (*b*), " a person arose " who preserved it from ruin, and who snatched it from " the dangerous precipice that seemed to await it.—This " was Lorenzo de' Medici, from whose abilities it received " that support of which it then stood so greatly in need; " who, amidst the thickest gloom of that barbarism which " had spread itself throughout Italy, exhibited, whilst yet a " youth,

(*a*) Non so adunque come sia bene in luogo d' arrichir questa lingua, e darle spirito, grandezza, e lume, farla povera, esile, umile ed oscura, e cercare di metterla in tante angustie che ognuno sia sforzato ad imitare solamente il Petrarca e'l Boccaccio, e che nella lingua non si debba ancor credere al Poliziano, a *Lorenzo de' Medici*, a Francesco Diaceto e ad alcuni altri, che pur sono Toscani, e forse di non minor dottrina e giudicio, che si fosse il Petrarca e'l Boccaccio. *Castiglione Il Cortegiano, lib.* i.

(*b*) *Della volgar Poesia. v.* ii. *p.* 323.

" youth, a simplicity of style, a purity of language, a hap-" piness of versification, a propriety of poetical ornament, " and a fulness of sentiment, that recalled once more " the graces and the sweetness of Petrarca." If, after paying due attention to these authorities, we consider, that the two great authors with whose excellencies Lorenzo is supposed to contend, employed their talents chiefly in one species of composition, whilst his were exercised in various departments; that during a long life, devoted to letters, they had leisure to correct, to polish, and to improve their works, so as to bear the inspection of critical minuteness, whilst those of Lorenzo must in general have been written with almost extemporaneous haste, and, in some instances, scarcely perhaps obtained the advantages of a second revisal; we must be compelled to acknowledge, that the inferiority of his reputation as a poet has not arisen from a deficiency of genius, but must be attributed to the avocations of his public life, the multiplicity of his domestic concerns, the interference of other studies and amusements, and his untimely death (*a*). When therefore we estimate the number, the variety, and the excellence of his poetical works, it must be admitted, that if those talents, which, under so many obstacles and disadvantages, are still so conspicuous,

(*a*) Se la sua vita fosse più lungamente durata, e se quella ch' egli menò, fosse stata più sciolta dalle cure famigliari, e politiche, sto per dire, che avrebbe ancor quel secolo avuto il suo Petrarca.

Murat. della Perfetta Poesia Ital. v. i. *p.* 20.

ous, had been directed to one object, and allowed to exert themselves to their full extent, it is in the highest degree probable, that, in point of poetic excellence, Italy had not boasted a more illustrious name than that of Lorenzo de' Medici.

The poems of Lorenzo celebrated in the *Nutricia* of Politiano.

In dismissing this subject, it may yet be allowed to point out one tribute of respect to the poetical character of Lorenzo, which may serve at the same time to illustrate a passage in an author, who, though a modern, deserves the appellation of classical. This will be found at the close of the *Sylva* of Politiano, intitled *Nutricia*, which will scarcely be intelligible to the reader, without some previous acquaintance with the writings of Lorenzo, as the author has there, in a small compass, particularly celebrated most of the productions of his patron's pen.

Nec tamen ALIGERUM fraudarim hoc munere DANTEM,
Per Styga, per stellas, mediique per ardua montis
Pulchra BEATRICIS sub virginis ora volantem.
Quique cupidineum repetit PETRARCHA triumphum.
Et qui bis quinis centum argumenta diebus
Pingit, et obscuri qui semina monstrat amoris :

Nor ALIGHIERI, shall thy praise be lost,
Who from the confines of the Stygian coast,
As BEATRICE led thy willing steps along,
To realms of light, and starry mansions sprung ;
Nor PETRARCH thou, whose soul-dissolving strains
Rehearse, O love! thy triumphs and thy pains ;

Unde

Unde tibi immensæ veniunt præconia laudis,
Ingeniis, opibusque potens, FLORENTIA mater.

Tu verò æternum per avi vestigia COSMI,
Perque patris (quis enim pietate insignior illo?)
Ad famam eluctans, cujus securus ad umbram
Fulmina bellorum ridens procul aspicit Arnus,
Mæoniæ caput, O LAURENS, quem plena senatu
Curia, quemque gravi populus stupet ore loquentem,
Si fas est, tua nunc humili patere otia cantu,
Secessusque sacros avidas me ferre sub auras.
Namque importunas mulcentem pectine curas,
Umbrosæ recolo te quondam vallis in antrum
Monticolam traxisse deam; vidi ipse corollas
Nexantem, numerosque tuos prona aure bibentem:
Viderunt socii pariter, seu grata Dianæ

Nor HE, whose hundred tales the means impart,
To wind the secret snare around the heart,
Be these thy boast, O FLORENCE! these thy pride,
Thy sons! whose genius spreads thy glory wide.

And thou LORENZO, rushing forth to fame,
Support of COSMO's and of PIERO's name!
Safe in whose shadow Arno hears from far,
And smiles to hear, the thunder of the war;
Endow'd with arts the listening throng to move,
The senate's wonder, and the people's love,
Chief of the tuneful train! thy praises hear,
—If praise of mine can charm thy cultur'd ear;
For once, the lonely woods and vales among,
A mountain-goddess caught thy soothing song,

 Nympha

Nympha fuit, quamquam nullæ sonuere pharetræ:
Seu soror Aonidum, & nostræ tunc hospita sylvæ.
Illa tibi, lauruque tuâ, semperque recenti
Flore comam cingens, pulchrum inspiravit amorem,
Mox et Apollineis audentem opponere nervis
Pana leves calamos nemoris sub rupe Pheræi,
Carmine dum celebras (*a*), eadem tibi virgo vocanti
Astitit, & sanctos nec opina afflavit honores.
Ergo & nocticanum per te Galatea Corinthum (*b*)
Jam non dura videt: nam quis flagrantia nescit
Vota, Cupidineoque ardentes igne querelas?

As swelled the notes, she pierc'd the winding dell,
And sat beside thee in thy secret cell;
I saw her hands the laurel chaplet twine,
Whilst with attentive ear she drank the sounds divine.
Whether the nymph to Dian's train allied,
—But sure no quiver rattled at her side;
Or from th' Aonian mount, a stranger guest,
She chose awhile in these green woods to rest—
Thro' all thy frame while softer passions breathe,
Around thy brows she bound the laureate wreathe;
—And still—as other themes engaged thy song,
She with unrivall'd sweetness touch'd thy tongue;
To tell the contest on Thessalia's plains,
When Pan with Phœbus tried alternate strains (*a*),
Or Galatea, who no more shall slight
Corynthus' song, that sooths the ear of night (*b*).

Seu

(*a*) *Capitolo del Canto di Pan*, a dramatic pastoral.

(*b*) The address of the Shepherd Corynthus to Galatea, commencing,
"*La luna in mezzo alle minori stelle.*"

Seu tibi Phœbeis audax concurrere flammis (*c*)
Claro stella die, seu lutea flore sequaci
Infelix Clytie (*d*), seu mentem semper oberrans
Forma subit dominæ (*e*), seu pulchræ gaudia mortis (*f*),
Atque pium tacto jurantem pectore amorem (*g*),

—But who shall all thy varying strains disclose,
As sportive fancy prompts, or passion glows?
When to thine aid thou call'st the solar beams,
And all their dazzling lustre round thee flames (*c*),
Or sing'st of Clytie, sunward still inclined (*d*);
Or the dear nymph whose image fills thy mind (*e*);
Of dreams of love, and love's extremest joy (*f*);
Of vows of truth and endless constancy (*g*);

Atque

(*c*) *Sonetto* 66.

"*O chiara stella che co' raggi tuoi.*"

(*d*) *Sonetto* 67.

"*Quando il sol giù dall' oriente scende.*"

(*e*) *Sonetto* 103.

"*Lasso, or la bella donna mia che face?*"

(*f*) *Sonetto* 86.

"*O veramente felice e beata*
Notte."

(*g*) *Sonetto* 99.

"*Amorosi sospir, e quali uscite.*"

CHAP. V.

Atque oculos canis (*b*), atque manus (*i*), niveisque capillos
Infusos humeris (*k*), et verba (*l*), et lene sonantis
Murmur aquæ (*m*), violæque comas (*n*), blandumque soporem,
Lætaque quam dulcis suspiria fundat amaror (*o*);

Or of those eyes a thousand flames that dart (*b*);
That hand that binds in willing chains thy heart (*i*);
The tresses o'er those ivory shoulders thrown (*k*);
The secret promise, made to thee alone (*l*);
The stream's soft murmur (*m*), and the violet's glow (*n*),
And love's embittered joys and rapturous woe (*o*);

Quan tum

(*b*) *Sonetto* 88.

"*Ove Madonna volge gli occhi begli.*"

(*i*) *Sonetto* 78.

"*O man mia suavissima e divera.*"

(*k*) *Sonetto* 73.

"*Spesso mi torna a mente anzi giammai.*"

(*l*) *Sonetto* 91.

"*Madonna io veggo ne' vostri occhi belli.*"

(*m*) *Sonetto* 75.

"*Chiar' acque i sento del vostro mormorio.*"

(*n*) *Sonetto* 80.

"*Belle fresche e purpuree viole.*"

Or perhaps 114.

"*Non di verdi giardin ornati e colti.*"

(*o*) *Sonetto* 39.

"*Io son si certo amor di tua incertezza.*"

Quantum addat formæ pietas (*p*), quàm sæpe decenter
Palleat, utque tuum foveat cor pectore Nymphe (*q*).
Non vacat argutosque sales, Satyraque Bibaces
Descriptos memorare senes (*r*); non carmina festis
Excipienda choris, querulasve animantia chordas (*s*).
Idem etiam tacitæ referens pastoria vitæ
Otia (*t*), et urbanos thyrso extimulante labores;
Mox fugis in cœlum, non ceu per lubrica nisus,
Extremamque boni gaudes contingere metam (*u*).

How pity adds to beauty's brightest charms (*p*);
And how thy bosom beats with soft alarms (*q*);
Nor wants there sprightly satire's vivid beam,
Whose lustre lights th' inebriate fools to fame (*r*);
Nor choral songs whose animating sound
Provokes the smile, and bids the dance go round (*s*),
—Then free from babbling crowds, and city noise,
Thou sing'st the pleasures rural life enjoys (*t*);
Or with no faultering step, pursuest thy way,
To touch the confines of celestial day (*u*).

Quodque

(*p*) *Sonetto* 56.

"*Talhor mi prega dolcemente amore.*"

(*q*) *Sonetto* 141.

"*Dura memoria, perchè non ti spegni.*"

(*r*) The *Beoni*, or satire against drunkenness.

(*s*) *Canzoni a ballo.*

(*t*) *Altercazione*, or dialogue between a shepherd and a citizen.

(*u*) *Rime sacre, &c.*

Quodque alii studiumque vocant, durumque laborem,
Hic tibi ludus erit: fessus civilibus actis,
Huc is emeritas acuens ad carmina vires.
Felix ingenio, felix cui pectore tantas
Instaurare vices, cui fas tam magna capaci
Alternare animo, et varias ita nectere curas.

—These the delights thy happiest moments share,
Thy dearest lenitives of public care:
Blest in thy genius! thy capacious mind
Nor to one science, nor one theme confined,
By grateful interchange fatigue beguiles,
In private studies and in public toils.

APPENDIX.

APPENDIX.

N° I.

Ex adnotationibus & monumentis Ang. Fabronii ad vitam Laur. Medicis pertinentibus.

IN libro perantiquo inscripto: Notizie della Famiglia dei Medici: *haec in proemio leguntur.*

Al Nome di Dio MCCCLXXIII. di Gennajo.

Al nome di Dio e della sua Santissima Madre Madonna Santa Maria e di tutta la corte del Paradiso checcidia gratia di bene fare e di bene dire. N° I.

Io Filigno di Chonte de' Medici veggendo le passate fortune di guerre citanesche e di fuori, e le fortunose pistolenze di mortalità, che Domenidio a mandate in terra, e che si teme che mandi, vigiendole a nostri vicini, farò memoria delle cose passate chio vedrò, che possano essere di bisongno sapere a voi che rimarrete o verrete dietro amme, a ciò che voi le troviate, se bisongno fosse, per ciauno chaso: pregando voi che scriviate bene per loinanzi, e che conserviate quelle terre e chase, che troverete inscritte in quest' libro, la maggiore parte aquistate per la dengna memoria del nobile chavaliere Mess. Giovanni di Chonte meo fratello, dopo la di cui morte io formo questo libro, levando del suo e daltri, e priegovi, che questo libro guardiate bene, e tengniate en luogho segreto, sicchè ninvenisse a mano altrui, e si perchè vi potrebbe essere de bisongno per lonanzi, come ora bisongna a noi, che ci con-

 viene

N° I. viene trovare carte di c. anni per chagioni, che nanzi troverete inscritto, peroche gli stati si mutano, e non anno fermezza.

Ancora vi priego, che non solamente conserviate lavere, ma conserviate lo stato aquistato pe nostri passati, il quale è grande, e maggiore soleva essere, e comincia a manchare per carestia di valenti uomini chabbiamo, de' quale soleramo avere gran quantità.

Ed era tanta la nostra grandigia, che si dicea, tusse com uno de Medici, e ogni uomo ci temea; e anchora si dice, quando un cittidino fa una forza o ingiuria altrui, se gli el facesse uno de Medici, che si direbbe: anchora è grandissima e di stato d' amichi e di riechezza, piaccia a Dio conservarlaci.

E oggi in questo dì, lodato Idio, siamo uomeni intorno cinquanta.

E' nota poi chio naqqui, sono morti di casa nostra intorno a cento uomeni; e di pochi e famiglia, e oggi siamo male a fanciulli, cioè nabiamo pochi.

I scriverò in più parti questo libro, e prima metterò note di charte, quanto potrò sapere e dote, fini, compromessi e altre, poi metterò tutte le compere, e chi fece le charte, poi metterò tutte le case e terre confinate coggi possediamo, &c.

N° II.

Jo. Lamii. Deliciæ Eruditorum, v. xii. *p.* 169. *Flor.* 1742.

Copia di Parlamento dell' anno 1433. c. 34. levato da un libro di propria mano di Cosimo de' Medici, dove scriveva i suoi ricordi d' importanza; e fu levata detta copia da Luigi Guicciardini.

N° II. RICORDO come a dì primo di Settembre entrò all' Uffizio del Sig. Giovanni di Matteo dello Scelto, Donato di Cristofano Sannini, Carlo di Lapo Corsi, Iacopo Berlinghieri, Mariotto di Mess. Niccolò Baldovinetti, Bartolommeo di Bartolommeo Spini, Bernardo di Vieri Guadagni Gonfaloniere di Giustizia, e Berto di Messer Marco di Cenni Albergatore; e quando furono tratti si cominciò a mormorare, che al tempo loro si farebbe novità nella Terra; e fummi scritto in Mugello dove era stato più mesi per levarmi dalle contese, e divisioni, ch' erano nella città, ch' io tornassi, e così tornai a dì 4. Il dì medesimo visitai il Gonfaloniere, e gli altri, come insieme Giovanni

vanni dello Scelto, il quale, reputava molto amico, ed erami obligato, e il simile degli altri; e dicendo loro quello si deceva, ei prestamente tutti lo negarono, e che fussi di buon animo, che volevano lasciare la Terra, come l' avevano trovata. Ordinarono a' 5. una Pratica d' otto Cittadini, due per quartieri, dicendo volevano con il consiglio di questi fare ogni loro deliberazione, e furono questi, Messer Giovanni Guicciardini, Bartolommeo Ridolfi, Ridolfo Peruzzi, Tommaso di Lapo Corsi, Messer Agnolo Acciaioli, Giovanni di Messer Rinaldo Gianfigliazzi, Messer Rinaldo degli Albizi, ed io Cosimo. E benchè per la Terra, come si è detto, fusse sparso dovessino fare novità, pure avendo da loro quello aveva, e reputandoli amici, non vi prestassi fede. Seguì che a dì 7. la mattina soto colore di volere la detta Pratica, mandarono per me, e giunto in Palazzo trovai la maggior parte, de compagni, e stando a ragionare, dopo buono spazio mi fu comandato per parte de Signori, che io andassi su di sopra, e dal Capitano de' Fanti fui messo in una Camera, che si chiama la Barberia, e fui serrato dentro; e sentendosi, tutta la Terra si sollevò. Il dì fecero consiglio de' Richiesti, e per lo Gonfaloniere fu detto, che quello avevano fatto di ritenermi, era per buona cagione, come altra volta sarebbe loro noto; e che di questo non volevano consiglio, e licenziarono i Richiesti: e li Signori per le sei fave mi confinarono a Padova per un anno. Fatta questa azione fu subito avvisato Lorenzo mio fratello, ch' era in Mugello, e Averardo mio cugino, ch' era a Pisa, e così fu fatto intendere a Niccolo da Tolentino Capitano di Guerra del Comune, ch' era molto mio amico. Lorenzo venne il dì medesimo in Firenze, e mandarono i Signori per lui che andasse a Palazzo, gli fu significato il perchè, subito si partì, e ritornossi al Trebbio. Averardo si partì da Pisa presto, che avevano dato ordine farlo pigliare là, e così se ci avessero preso tutti a tre, ci facessero male arrivare. Niccolò da Tolentino sentito il caso a dì 8. venne la mattina con tutta la sua Compagnia alla Lastra, e con animo di fare novità nella Terra, perchè io fussi lasciato; e così subito che si sentì il caso nell' Alpe di Romagna, e di più altri luoghi, venne a Lorenzo gran quantità di fanti. Fu confortato il Capitano, e così Lorenzo a non fare novità, che poteva esser cagione di farmi fare novità nella persona, e così feciono; e benchè chi consigliò questo fussino parenti, e amici, e a buon fine, non fu buono consiglio; perchè se si fussino fatti innanzi, ero libero, e chi era stato cagione di questo, restava disfatto. Ma tutto si vuol dire fussi per lo meglio, perchè ne seguì maggior bene, e con più mio onore, come innanzi farò menzione. Non parendo agli amici miei si dovessi far novità, come ho detto, el Capitano si tornò indietro alle stanze, mostrando esser venuto per altra cagione, e Lorenzo se n' andò a Venezia coi miei figli, e portonne quello

N° II.

potè

Nº II. potè de' denari, e delle cos sottili. E Signori confinarono il detto Lorenzo per un anno Venezia, e me a Padova per 5. anni, e Averardo a Napoli per 5. anni. Dipoi a dì 9. feciono sonare a parlamento, e vennero in Piazza quelli ch' erano stati cagione della novità con fanti, avevano fatto venire de fuori ventitre Cittadini, e fu piccolo numero, e poco popolo vi si trovò, perchè in vero il forte de' Cittadini n' erano mal contenti.

Per Parlamento dierono Balìa a' Cittadini, come si costumava in tali casi, e confinarono me per anni 10. a Padova, Lorenzo per anni 5. a Venezia, Averardo per anni 10. a Napoli, Orlando de' Medici per anni 10. in Ancona, e Giovanni d' Andrea de Messer Alamanno e Bernardo d' Alamanno de' Medici a Rimini; e fecero la mia famiglia de' Medici de' Grandi, eccetto i figliuoli di Messer Veri, perchè Niccolò era Gonfaloniere; eccetto ancora i figliuoli d' Antonio di Giovenco de' Medici, perchè Bernardetto era molto amato dal Capitano della Guerra, e per contemplazione del Capitano mostrarono eccettuare il detto Averardo e fratelli; feciono più ordini contro a noi, e massime che io non potessi vendere possessioni, nè denari di monte; e ritennommi in Palazzo in sino a dì 3. d' Ottobre.

Sentendosi questo a Venezio, mandarono subito quì tre Ambasciatori, cioè Messer Luisi Storlando, Messer Tommaso Micheli, e . . . . li quali con ogni istanza proccurarono, e concordarono la mia liberazione con offerire tenermi a Venezia, e promettere non farei contro alla Signoria, e obbedirei a quello mi fussi commandato; e benchè non facessono ottenere fussi libero, pure la venuta loro giovò assai, perchè e' era di quelli confortavano fussi morto, e ebbono promissione non mi sarebbe fatto offensione nella persona. Per simil modo mandò qui il Marchese di Ferrara Ser Gherardino da Sabiglia al Capitano della Balìa, ch' era Messer Lodovico del Ronco da Modena, suddito del Marchese, a comandargli, che se io gli fussi messo nelle mani, non ne facessi altro conto, che se fussi Messer Lionardo suo figliuolo; e che se ne fuggisse meco, e non dubitasse di danno, nè di nessuna altra cosa.

Mi ritennero, siccome è detto, in sino a' 3. di Ottobre per due cagioni, la prima perchè potessero ottenere nella Balìa nell' ordinare la terra a loro modo; che quando non si riceva, minacciavano che mi farebbono morire, e per questa paura gli amici, e i parenti, che si trovavano nella Balìa, deliberavano quello era loro messo innanzi, La seconda fu, che credettono, che per tenermi in prigione, e aver fatto io non mi potessi valere del mio, farci fallire; il che non riuscì loro, che non per questo perdessimo credito; ma da molti

molti Mercatanti forestieri, e Signori, ci fu offerto, e mandato a Venezia gran somma di denari. In fine vedendo non riusciva loro il pensiero di farci fallire; Bernardo Guadagni, offertogli da due persone denari, cioè dal Capitano della Guerra fiorini 500. e dallo Spedalingo di S. Maria Nuova fiorini 500. i quali ebbe contanti, e Mariotto Balduinetti per mezzo di Baccio d' Antonio di Baccio fiorini 800. a dì 3. d' Ottobre la notte mi trassero di Palazzo, e menommi fuori della Porta a S. Gallo: ebbono poco animo, che se avessero voluto denari, l' arebbono avuti diecimila, o più, per uscir di pericolo.

A dì 4. di Ottobre il dì di S. Francesco arrivai a Cutigliano nella montagna di Pistoia, e fui accompagnato da due degli otto della Guardia, cioè Francesco Soderini, e Cristofano . . del Chiaro. Dagli uomini della montagna fui presentato di biada e cera, come se fussi Ambasciadore. A dì 5. mi partii, e venni a Fassano Terra del Marchese di Ferrara, e fui accompagnato da più di 20. uomini della montagna. A dì 6. arrivai a Modana, e il Governatore ch' era Messer Piero . . venne a me per parte del Signore, mi visitò, e presentò, e la mattina mi fe dare compagnia, e guida. A dì 7. arrivai al Bondeno, e l' altra mattina per acqua andai a Francolino; stetti due giorni per aspettare Antonio Uguccione d' Contrari, che per parte del Marchese mi fece molte offerte. A dì 11. arrivai a Venezia, dove mi venne incontro molti Gentiluomini nostri amici, insieme con Lorenzo; e fui ricevuto, non come confinato, ma come Ambasciadore. La mattina seguente visitai la Signoria, e ringraziaila di quello aveva operato per la mia salute, mostrando riconoscere la vita da quella: fui ricevuto con tanto onore e tanta carità, che non si potrebbe dire, dolendosi delli affanni mia, & offerendo la Signoria, la Città, l' entrata loro, per ogni mio contentamento, e la casa: da molti Gentiluomini fui visitato, e presentato. A dì 13. mi partj per andare a Padova, come m' era comandato, e in mia compagnia venne Messer Iacopo Donato, e m' alloggiò in una sua bella casa fornita di panni, e di letta, e di cose da mangiare per ogni gran maestro; e stette meco per infino ritornai a Venezia, che furono circa a dì 20. A Padova venne a casa a me a visitarmi per parte della Signoria di Venezia, offerendomi tutto quello potesse fare per loro in mia complacenzia. Ho voluto fare ricordo dell' onore che mi fu fatto per non essere ingrato in farne ricordo, e ancora perchè fu cosa da non credere, essendo cacciato di casa, trovar tanto onore, perchè si suol perdere gli amici con la fortuna; fu replicato a Lorenzo l' onore avevo ricevuto, e per via de mercanti, e per un mazzieri de' Signori, che venne meco insino a Padova, al quale fu comandato non ne dovesse parlare.

N° II. Dipoi del mese di Decembre chiedendo io di grazia a Signori di potere stare a Padova, e a Venezia, e per lo territorio della Signoria di Venezia essendo de' Signori Bartolommeo de Ridolfi Gonfalonieri di Giustizia, fu deliberato, e ottenni di potere stare per il territorio Veneziano, non m' appressando a Firenze più che 170. miglia; e questo fecero ancora a complacienzia della Signoria di Venezia, la quale per loro Ambasciatore, che fu Messer Andrea Donato, ne richieseno la Città; bene appiccorono questa grazia sotto gran pene, non si potessi più rimuovermi, o farmi grazia di confini, come appare per la declarazione fatta.

Al tempo di questi Signori fu confinato Puccio, e Giovanni d' Antonio di Puccio, i quali erano miei principali amici; e di poi al tempo de Priori seguenti, ch' era Gonfaloniere Mariotto Scambrilla, fu confinato Messer Agnolo Acciaioli, per certe novelle aveva scritto a Puccio e a noi; le quali in vero non erano d' importanza, nè da esserne cacciato.

Ricordo che a dì 1. Settembre 1434. entrarono de' Signori Gio. di Mico Cappone, Caca di Buonaccorso Pitti, Niccolo di Cecco Donati Governatore di Giustizia, Piero d' Antonio di Piero Felriano, Toto Martini per artefici, Simone di Francesco Guiducci, e . . . . di Tommaso Redditi, Baldassarri d' Antonio di Santi, Neri di Domenico Bartoleni; e come furono tratti tutti i buoni Cittadini, presero vigore, e conforto, parendo fusse tempo di uscire dal mal governo avevano, il che prima averebbono fatto, se avessero avuto Signori che avessono voluto attendere; perchè in vero tutto il Popolo, e tutti i buoni Cittadini, stavano mal contenti; e subito venne a me a Venezia Antonio di Ser Tommaso Masi, mandato da più Cittadini, perchè venissimo verso Firenze, offerendo, quando sentissono fussimo presi, si solleverebbono, e metterebbonci dentro; e così da molti parenti, e amici eravamo continuo sollecitati. Parveci volere intendere l' animo de' Signori con dire, non volevamo fare contro al volere della Signoria; e per questo mandammo da Venezia a Firenze Antonio Martelli, perchè sentisse da' Signori la loro intenzione, da' quali ebbe buona risposta che venissimo, e così per fante proprio ci avvisò per sua lettera; la quale avuta ci partimmo da Venezia 29. di Settembre Lorenzo e io Cosimo; e Averardo rimase a Venezia ammalato di febbre, che non poteva venire, e a' 30. arrivamo al Ponte a Lago. Stemmo in casa dell' Magnifico Uguccione, il quale insieme col Marchese, a nostra richiesta, aveva ordinato gran quantità di Fanti nella montagna di Modena, e del Frigano, e ancora 200. Cavalli aveva a suo soldo, perchè venissono con noi, com' era prima ordinato; e a

dì

dì 1. d'Ottobre essendo la mattina a udir Messa, avemmo un Corrieri d' Antonio Salutati con lettere, per le quali ci avvisava, come sentendosi per la Terra l'animo de Signori, e presentendosi la nostra venuta, i nostri nemici avevano preso l'armi a dì 26. cioè, Messer Rinaldo delli Albizi, Ridolfo Peruzzi, e più altri in numero di 600 persone: di poi la sera mancando loro l'animo, e essendo mezzano d'accordo per parte del Papa, Messer Giovanni Vitelleschi allora Vescovo di Recanati, e dipoi Arcivescovo di Firenze, e poi Cardinale, il quale era molto mio amico, si ridussono a S. Maria Novella dove abitava il Papa; e sentendo che gli amici nostri erano provvisti, e di gente, e d'armi, per tema di loro persone, Messer Rinaldo, e Ormanno suo figliuolo, e Ridolfo Peruzzi, si rimasero la notte là, e non vollero uscire; e chi era con loro si partì chi in quà, e chi in là, e andaronsi a disarmare. Il perchè i Signori fecero venire dentro gran numero di fanterie, che solo di Mugello, e dell' Alpe, e di quello di Romagna, venne a casa nostra, più di fanti 3000. e così fecero venire la compagnia di Niccolo da Tolentino; e a dì 29. il dì di S. Michele fecero parlamento in su la piazza, dove fu tutto il Popolo armato, che fu numero grandissimo e bene in punto, dettero la Balìa a . . . . Cittadini, e annullarono quello avevano fatto l'anno passato, e il primo partito e deliberazione che fecero, fu che Cosimo e Lorenzo fussero restituiti ne' primi onori, e annullato tutto quello fusse fatto contra di loro, che non vi fu 4. fave in contrario, confortandoci per parte di tutti a venire presto. E letta detta lettera subito la mandammo a Venezia, dove se ne fece gran festa, e noi andammo a visitare il Marchese, il quale dimostrò maggior allegrezza di noi; ringraziammolo de' favori, che ci aveva prestati, e a dì 2. ci partimmo di Ferrara, e a 3. fummo a Modana, dove fummo ricevuti con grand' onore in casa del Marchese, e venneci incontro il Governatore e il Podestà, e molti Cittadini di Modana. A dì 4. venimmo . . . . . e per la via sempre ci fu fatto le spese dal Marchese, e per tutto trovammo fanti, che erano ordinati a venire con noi, i quali licenziammo, perchè non era di bisogno; e a 5. venimmo a Cutigliano, e poi a Pistoia, e appunto in capo dell'anno in quel medesimo dì, cioè a 5. d' Ottobre, e in quella medesima ora, rientrammo in su quello del Commune, e in quel medesimo luogo. Di questo ho fatto ricordo perchè ci fu detto da più persone devote, e buone, quando fummo cacciati, che non passerebbe l'anno che saremmo restituiti, e torneremmo a Firenze. Per la via trovammo molti Cittadini, che ci venivano in contro, e a Pistoia tutto il Popolo si fece alla porta per vederci così armati, quando vi passammo, che non volemmo entrare dentro. Venimmo a dì 6. a desinare al nostro luogo a Careggi, dove fu gran gente; i Signori bi mandarono

N° II.

N° II. mandarono a dire non entrassimo dentro, se non ce lo facevano intendere, e così facemo; e tramontato il Sole mandarono a dire che venissimo, e così ci movemmo con gran compagnia, e perchè tutta la via, si stimava facessimo in sino a casa nostra, era piena d'uomini, e di donne, Lorenzo, ed io con un famiglio, e un mazziere volgemmo lungo le mura, e venissimo dietro a' Servi, e poi dietro a Santa Reparata, e dal Palazzo del Podestà, e dal Palazzo dell' esecutore entrammo nel Palazzo de' Signori, senza essere quasi veduti da persona, perchè tutto il popolo era nella via larga, e da Casa nostra a aspettarci, e per questa cagione non vollero i Signori entrassimo di dì per non far maggior tumulto nella Terra. Da Signori fummo ricevuti graziosamente, e ringraziatigli con quelle parole si richiedeva, vollero che insieme con più altri Cittadini rimanessimo in Palazzo con le loro Signorie, e così facemo.

Trovammo prima che giugnessimo, era stato confinato Messer Rinaldo, e Ormanno suo figliuolo, Ridolfo Peruzzi, e molti altri Cittadini; e la Terra era pacificata, benchè continuamente in Piazza, e in Palazzo stessono buon numero di fanti armati, per sicurtà del Palazzo.

Dipoi in Calendi Novembre si fecero i Priori a mano di là dall' acqua, Sandro di Giovanni Biliotti, Piero di Bartolommeo del Benino in Santa Croce, Andrea Nardi, e Lodovico da Verrazzano, in Santa Maria Novella; Giovanni Minerbetti Gonfaloniere di Giustizia, Brunetto Beccaio per Artefice in S. Giovanni, Ugolino Martelli, e Antonio di Ser Tommaso Masi. Questi Priori confinarono molti Cittadini, e così posarono a sedere molte famiglie sospette, e fecero molte cose in favore dello Stato; e a loro tempo spirò la Balìa data a più Cittadini, e finirono li squittini, e rimasero le borse per 5. anni in mano degli Accoppiatori, cioè le borse del Priorato; e potranno de' Priori e Gonfaloniere di Giustizia, quelle vorranno fare a loro piacimento. E del mese di Gennaio prossimo fui il primo tratto delle borse dello squittino per Gonfaloniere di Giustizia, e al mio tempo non si confinò, nè si fece male a persona. Ma Francesco Guadagni, e più altri, i quali trovai nelle mani del Capitano della Balìa, & avevano raffermo la . . . . Lo operai in forma non morirono, ma furono condennati in perpetua carcere, e così al mio tempo feci levare certi fanti armati, che stavano alla porta del Palazzo, ridurre il Palazzo, e la piazza come solevano stare innanzi alla novità, e feci prolungare la lega con la Signoria di Venezia per 10. anni.

N° III.

Ex M. S. sec. xv. penes auctorem.

Leonardi Aretini Epistola ad Cosmum Medicem de conversione Epistolarum Platonis e Græco in Latinum.

INTER clamosos strepitus negotiorumque procellas, quibus Florentina palatia, quasi Euripus quidam, sursum deorsumque assidue æstuant, cum singula non modo dicta, sed verba etiam interrumperentur, tamen, ut potui, Latinas effeci Platonis epistolas, quas nunc tibi dono dedo atque mitto; putans multo pretiosius quiddam ad te mittere quam si tantidem pondo auri dilargirer. A te certe longe carius gratiusque existimandum. Etenim aurum tibi abunde est, Sapientia vero nec tibi nec alteri cuiquam hominum abunde. Deinde quæ comparatio justa esse potest aurum inter ac sapientiam? Ad quam non solum opulentia ista privatorum eximia, verum etiam regum opes atque potentia, fascesque & imperia comparata vilescunt. Fragilia nempe bona, ac nescio an omnino bona sint existimanda, quæ auferri nobis atque eripi possunt, & quorum possessio usque adeo imbecilla est & incerta, ut nemo exploratum habere queat ad vesperas usque esse duraturam: sapientiæ vero ac virtutis stabilis est firmaque possessio. Neque enim eripi ab homine ulla vi possunt, neque fortunæ subjacent ictibus. Nec eas, ut philosophis placet, labefactat oblivio. Præterea cum homo constet ex animo & corpore ac utriusque particulæ bona & quasi dotes quædam existant, ut animi quidem sapientia, fortitudo, justitia, cæteræque virtutes, corporis autem valitudo, forma, firmitas, patientia laborum, pernicitas, et hujuscemodi alia, nemini dubium esse potest quanto animus corpori dignitate præstat, tanto bona animi bonis corporis antecellere. Divitiæ vero & opes, nec animi sunt neque corporis bona. Itaque ne nostra quidem illa dicuntur, sed externa & a corporis dignitate longe superantur. Itaque comparare divitias ad sapientiam, nihil est aliud quam infimi gradus bonum cum supremo conferre. Et de his quidem satis. Traductio autem harum epistolarum ita vehementer mihi jocunda fuit, ut cum Platone ipso loqui, cumque intueri eorum viderer. Quod eo magis in his mihi accidit quam in cæteris ejus libris, quia hic neque fictus est sermo, nec alteri attributus; sed procul ab ironia atque figmento, in re seria actionem exigente, ab illo summo ac sapientissimo homine perscriptus. Sæpe enim præstantes viri, doctrinam vivendi aliquam prosecuti, multa præcipiunt aliis, quæ ipsi dum agunt præstare non possunt. Ex quo fit un aliter loquantur, aliter vivant. N° III.

 Cerno

N° III. Cerno integritatem hominis incorruptam, libertatem animi, fidei sanctitatem. Inter hæc prudentiam eximiam, justitiam singularem, constantiam vero non protervam neque inhumanam; sed quæ & consuli sibi & suaderi permittat. In amicos vero tantam benevolentiam, ut commoda sua propria illorum commodis posthabere videatur. Ad hæc autem dii boni! quæ consiliorum suorum explicatio, quæ circumspectio, quæ observatio, quæ modestia, jam vero de adeunda republica quæ appetitio, quæ ratio, quæ consideratio, quæ religio! Fateor in his magnum & absolutum quendam virum bonum mihi ad imitandum proponi. Imitationes vero nonnunquam efficaciores sunt quam doctrinæ, ut in oratoribus & histrionibus intueri licet; quorum artes difficilius quidam addiscunt, facilius imitantur. Ego certe plus utilitatis lectione harum paucarum epistolarum percepisse me intelligo, quam ex multis voluminibus antea perlectis: ita mihi viva hæc quodammodo & spirantia, illa vero intermortua & umbratilia videbantur. Quæ enim in re agenda mihi ambiguitas esse queat, in quâ videam Platonem ita fecisse. Tu igitur has epistolas multum lege quæso, ac singulas earum sententias memoriæ commenda, præcipue vero quæ de republica monent. Intelliges vero quid dicam si cuncta diligenter triteque perlegeris. Nec eò ista scribo quod tuæ aut intelligentiæ aut voluntati diffidam, sed quod propositum tuum, auctoritate summi viri, confirmandum & corroborandum censeo. Vale, & munus hoc meum non tam verbis, quam lectione operibusque tibi non frustra collatum ostendas.

N° IV.

Ex Aug. Fabronii Monum. ad vitam Cosmi Med.

Pius PP. II. Cosmo Medici.

N° IV. DILECTE fili, Salutem & Apostolicam benedictionem. Mors bonae memoriae Johannis filii tui, quam modo intelleximus, molesta nobis plurimum fuit, non ob id solum, quia per naturam est immatura, sed quia aetati, & valetudini tuae multum adversa. Consolandus esses omnibus horis, & vita in dulcedine Spiritus protrahenda: sed hoc nos consolatur, quia sapiens es, & exercitatus in fortunae casibus, & moderari tuis sensibus potes. Ita rogamus te, Cosme, facias, & convertas ad Deum oculos, & illi benedicas, & in bonum omnia deputes. Neque enim scimus arcana Dei; novit ille solus quid nobis expediat, & quorum indigemus. Credamus nobiscum & cum illo

illo actum misericorditer esse. Venturorum nec tu eras conscius, nec ille. Hortamur tuam nobilitatem, Fili, ut voluntatem hanc Domini patienter feras, sicut te ferre audimus, neque dolori indulgeas. Aetati tuae moeror non convenit, & valetudini contrarius est. Expedit nobis, patriae tuae, & toti Italiae, ut quam diutissime vivas. Johannem filium bonis operibus, & piis prosequere. Aliud ex tota substantia tua non stetit, eleemosinae, devotio, & oratio sunt sua suffragia. Haec pauca ad te scripsimus, ut tristitiam nostram agnosceres, & de tua nos esse sollicitos intelligeres. Singula in partem caritatis accipito. Datum Romae apud Sanctum Petrum, sub anulo piscatoris die non. Novembris 1463. Pontificatus nostri anno sexto. N° IV.

Pio II. S. P. Cosmus Medices.

Videor te legens, Beatissime Pater, tanta est verborum vis, & sapientia, eum vere audire me consolantem, cujus tu vere vicem geris. Quid enim melius, aut sanctius, & plane divinus scribi potuit? Igitur hac consolatione tua, Beatissime Pater, id est effectum, ut qui prius utile esse, & laude dignum putarem quam minimum dolere, nam nihil haud possum, nunc etiam nefas aliter ac tu suadeas, facere existimem. Itaque do operam pro viribus, & pro infirmitate animi mei, ut feram aequo animo tam adversum casum, ut mihi quidem visum est. Sed Deus novit solus quid adversum sit. Nos nescimus, ut sapienter, religioseque scribis. Quanquam cum Johanne filio nunquam male actum putavi, qui non e vita, sed e morte migrasset ad vitam. Est enim mors haec, quam nos vocamus vitam. Illa vere vita est, quae aeterna est. Si quid in ejus obitu mali videbatur, nobis, qui ejus, ut opinamur, indigebamus, id evenisse judicavi. Sed nos nescimus quid petamus. Confido fore ut Deus misereatur etiam nostri, qui relicti sumus, secundum multitudinem miserationum suarum, quoniam suavis est Dominus, & multum misericors. De vita autem mea, quod Summus Pontifex Christi Vicarius sollicitus est, etiam felicitati ascribo. Curabo id quidem non his de causis, quibus tu pro divina humanitate tua curandam scribis. Quid enim jam nos possumus? Aut quid unquam potuimus? Sed ut Dei tam excellens vivendi munus non neglexisse, aut tot, tantorumque beneficiorum divina pietate susceptorum oblitus fuisse videar. Tu, quo id facere possim, Beatissime Pater, velim pro me filiolo tuae Sanctitatis ad Deum preces porrigas.

Extat

N° V.

Extat in Tabulario Mediceo: Copia d' una lettera scritta da Pietro di Cosimo, a Lorenzo e Giuliano de' Medici, da Carreggi a Casaggiolo il dì 26. Luglio 1464.

N° V. SCRIPSIVI jer l' altro, & avvisai come Cosimo era aggravato dal male, di poi mi pare che si vadi logorando, & questo pare a lui medesimo, in modo che Martedì sera volle che in camera non fossi, se non Monna Contessina et io. Cominciò da principio a dire tutta la sua vita, dipoi entrò sul governo della città, e poi seguitando a quello de' traffichi, di poi alla cura familiare delle possessione et di casa, et sopra e fatti di voi due, confortando, essendo voi di buono ingegno, io vi dovessi allevare bene, perchè mi levereste assai faticha, & che di due cose si doleva, l' una di non haver fatto quanto arebbe voluto & potuto fare, l' altra che essendo io mal sano mi lasciava con assai noia. Di poi disse non volere fare testamento alcuno, perchè mai non fu suo pensiero di farlo, eziandio vivente Giovanni, perchè sempre ci vide con buono amore & in buono accordo & stima, & che quando Iddio facesse altro di lui, non voleva alcuna pompa, nè dimostratione nell' esequie, & come in vita altra volta mi aveva detto, mi ricordava dove voleva la sepoltura sua in S. Lorenzo; & tutto disse con tanto ordine & con tanta prudentia, & con uno animo sì grande, che fu una maraviglia, soggiungendo che era vissuto lunga età, & in modo che si partiva molto ben contento, quando Dio lo volessi. Di poi jermattina di buon ora si fece levare, calzare & vestire di tutto, essendoci il Priore di S. Lorenzo, quel di S. Marco, e della Badia; si confessò dal Priore di S. Lorenzo & di poi fece dire la messa, alla quale tutta rispose come da sano. Dipoi domandato delli articoli della fede, a tutti rispose per lettera, fece la confessione lui medesimo, & prese il S. Sacramento con tanta devotione, quanto si potessi dire, havendo prima chiesto perdono a ciascuno. Le quali cose m' hanno fatto crescere l' animo & la speranza verso Messer Domenedio, & benchè secondo il senso, io non sia senza dolore, pure veduto la grandezza dell' animo suo, la dispositione buona, sono in gran parte contento, che viene a quel fine che tutti habbiamo a fare. Lui si stette jeri assai bene, & così questa nocte passata; pure rispetto all' età grave non posso sperar molto del suo guarire. Fate fare per lui orationi ai Frati del Bosco, & fate dar elemosina come pare ad voi, pregando Iddio ce lo lasci ancora per un tempo, sendo per lo meglio. Et voi pigliate exemplo, che siete

siete giovani, & con buono animo pigliate la parte vostra delle fatiche, poichè Messer Domenedio dispone così, & fate conto d' essere huomini, essendo garzoni, che così lo richiede lo stato vostro & il caso presente, & sopra tutto attendete a quello, che vi può fare onore & utile, perchè è venuto il tempo che bisogna che voi facciate sperientia di voi; et vivete col timor di Dio, & sperate bene. Quello che seguirà di Cosimo vi adviserò. Noi attendiamo ognora un medico di Milano, ma ho più speranza in Messer Domenedio, che in altri. Non altro al presente. Chareggi ai 26. Luglio 1464. N° V.

N° VI.

Ricordi di Piero de' Medici.

RICORDO che a dì 1. d' Agosto 1464. a ore XXII ½. Cosimo di Giovanni d' Averardo de' Medici passò di questa presente vita, essendo stato pel passato molto vexato da dolore di giunture, benchè d' ogni altro male fosse sano, salvo che in quest' ultimo fine della vita sua per spazio d' un mese fosse oppressato per difecto d' orina con alquanta febbre. Era d' età d' anni LXXVII. grande e bello uomo, e di perfecta natura, excepto e' mali sopradecti. Fu uomo di grandissima prudentia, e vie maggior bontà, el più riputato ciptadino, & di maggior credito che avesse la nostra ciptà per lunghi tempi; e quello che ebbe maggior fede, & più amato da tucto el popolo: nè si ricorda morire alcuno a questa età con migliore grazia e maggior fama, e di cui più dolesse a ciascuno; e meritamente, perchè non si trovò nessuno che con ragione si dolesse di lui: ma furono molti, e' quali da lui erano stati serviti, & sovvenuti, & ajutati; di che più si dilectò che alcun altro: e non solamente parenti e amici, ma gli strani, e ancora, che par difficile a crederlo, non che a farlo, chi non gli era amico: col quale laudabil modo si fece più e più persone, che per difecto loro e d' altri non gli erano amici, amicissimi. Fu molto liberale, caritativo, e misericordioso, e molte elemosine fece in sua vita; e non solamente nella ciptà e distretto, ma eziandio ne' luoghi molto lontani, in accrescimento di Religioni, e riparatione di Chiese, & generalmente d' ogni ragione di beni, che accadesse. Fu per sua sapientia molto extimato e creduto da tutti e' Signori e Potentie d' Italia, e fuori d' Italia. Fu onorato di tutti gli uficj degni nella nostra ciptà; di fuori non volle mai accettare alcuno oficio. Exercitò le più honorate et importanti legationi, che a' suoi N° VI.

Nº VI. a' suoi tempi accadessero alla nostra Repubblica: & nella ciptà fece ricchi molti uomini per mezzo de' traffichi suoi, oltre alla ricchezza che di lui rimase, nel quale esercizio fu non solamente savio, ma bene avventurato mercatante. Morì, come si dice, el dì sopra decto, nella casa e luogo nostro da Careggi, avendo prima ricevuti tutti e Sacramenti di Sancta Chiesa con grandissima divotione, e riverentia: non volle fare testamento, ma liberamente el tutto rimise in me. Fu seppellito el dì seguente nella Chiesa di S. Lorenzo in terra, e nella sepoltura innanzi per lui ordinata, senza alcuna honoranza, o pompa funebre, dove non volle altri che Calonaci & Preti di decta Chiesa, & Frati di S. Marco, e' Calonaci Regolari della Badia di Fiesole; nè con più e manco cera che a uno mediocre mortorio si richiede, perchè così dispose per l' ultima sua parola; affermando, le limosine e altri beni doversi fare in vita, che giovano più che di poi, come aveva facto lui. Il perchè non ostante questa, volendo io satisfare al debito filiale verso la pietà paterna, feci fare quanto si richiedeva, & era conveniente a chi restava; et ordinai le elemosine, & uficj, che nel presente libro seguiranno.

Nº VII.

H O S P E S.

Nº VII. ÆDES CERNIS FAMA CELEBERRIMAS. PULCHERRIMAS ATQUE MAGNIFICAS. A COSMO MEDICE PATRE PATRIÆ. MICHELOTIO ARCHITECTO ERECTAS A. S. PLUS MINUS CIↃ CCCC. XXX. IN QUIBUS MAGNUS ILLE SENEX SUCCESSORESQUE SUI IN R. P. FLORENTINA PRINCIPES. ET ALEXANDER DUX R. P. FLOR. PETRUS MEDICES COSMI I. TERTIUS FILIUS HABITARUNT. HIC A SENATU FLORENTINO COSMUS MEDICES DUX FLORENTIÆ PLENIS LIBERISQUE SUFFRAGIIS CREATUS AD QUINQUE ANNOS SEDEM SUAM HAC REGIAM HABUIT. CAPTIVOS MONTIS MURLI VICTORIÆ TESTES VIDIT. NUPTIAS CELEBRAVIT. REGIAM STIRPEM FELICITER HODIE REGNANTEM FUNDAVIT. VARIIS TEMPORIBUS ROMANI PONTIFICES. ROMANI IMPERATORES. REGES. REGINÆ ALIIQUE PRINCIPES. INNUMERIQUE PROCERES HOSPITIO EXCEPTI. LEO X. P.

P. M. IN ITU BONONIAM REDITUQUE CAROLUS V. IMPERAT. CUI ORATORES TUNETANI REGIS HIC SOLENNE TRIBUTUM SOLVERUNT. CAROLUS VIII. GALLIARUM REX. CARLOTA CYPRI REGINA, ET SARMATIÆ REGINA. THOMÆ REGIS FILIA. FRIDERICUS PRINCEPS SALERNI. FERRANDI REGIS NEAPOLITANI FILIUS ET MARIA HIPPOLYTA DUX CALABRIÆ. GALEATIUS MARIA SFORTIA MEDIOLANI DUX. HIC LITTERÆ LATINÆ GRÆCÆQUE RESTAURATÆ. MUTÆ ARTES EXCULTÆ. PLATONICA PHILOSOPHIA RESTITUTA. ACADEMIA FLORENTINA A COSMO I. VERNACULÆ ETRUSCÆ LINGUÆ CULTUI SACRATA. SEMPER HI PARIETES COLUMNÆQUE ERUDITIS VOCIBUS RESONUERUNT. ÆDES HASCE. TANTÆ GLORIÆ VIX CAPACES. GABRIEL CHIANNI ET RIVALTI MARCHIO. SENATORIS FRANCISCI RICCARDI F. A FERDINANDO II. M. E. D. A. CIↃ. IↃ C LVIIII. COMPARATAS. IN POSTICA PARTE AUXIT. FRANCISCUS MARCHIO. COSMI MARCHIONIS F. GABRIELIS SUPRADICTI. EX FRATRE N. ET HERES. VETUSTAM ÆDIUM MAGNIFICENTIAM ÆMULATUS. ILLAS SACELLO SACRIS RELIQUIIS REFERTO. BIBLIOTHECA. MUSEO. SIGNIS. SCALPTIS CÆLATISQUE GEMMIS. VETERIBUS NUMMIS. ANAGLYPHIS. PICTURIS INSTRUCTAS. INTUS FORISQUE DUPLO AMPLIAVIT. VETEREM PARTEM IN MELIOREM FORMAM REDEGIT. ORNAVIT. ORNAT. A. CIↃ. IↃCC. XV. Nº VII.

HOSPES

MEDICEAS OLIM ÆDES. IN QUIBUS NON SOLUM TOT PRINCIPES VIRI. SED ET SAPIENTIA IPSA HABITAVIT. ÆDES OMNIS ERUDITIONIS. QUÆ HIC REVIXIT. NUTRICES. NUNC ETIAM AD ERUDITUM LUXUM ANTIQUITATIS ET ELEGANTIARUM THESAURUM.

GRATUS VENERARE.

Nº VIII.

Ex Monum Ang. Fabronii.

Laurentio de' Medicis Filio Carissimo, Romae, Petrus Medices.
Florentiae die 15. Martii 1465.

Nº VIII. IO mi ritrovo in tanta afflictione & dispiacere pel mesto & doloroso caso della morte dell' Illmo Duca di Milano, che io non so dove mi sia, & per tua discretione puoi giudicare quanto cimporta & publice & privatim, & parmi col suo M. Oratore che costì si truova, te ne debba per mia parte con lui cordialmente dolere, & te conforto a pigliarne pensiero & non maninconia, la quale non giovaniente, & i pensieri alle volte sono utili, facendoli buoni. Io ancora che mi sia duro quanto puoi stimare, m' ingegno pigliarne partito meglio che posso, & spero, che quel che al presente non puole in me la ragione, ancorchè difficile sia, lo farà el tempo. E ci sono poi lettere da Milano de' 9. & de' 10. le quali mando, perchè tu intenda come le cose di là passano, che alla ventura andranne meglio che non era l' oppinione & credentia di molti. Io scrissi di principio a N. S., il quale come capo & guida non solamente della Lega, ma di tucti e Christiani, che facesse pensiero alla conserva di quello stato, che vi può fare più sua Beatitudine, che nessuno altro, & quando non fosse per altro rispecto per mantenere la pace & la quiete d' Italia, & benchè io creda Sua Beatitudine esserci optimamente disposta, pure accadendo farne ogni opportuna opera, perchè sai quel che richiede l' oficio & debito nostro verso la felicissima memoria del S. passato e della Excellentia di Madonna & de' suoi incliti figliuoli. Et appresso leverai via sonare d' instrumenti, o canti e balli, o simili altre cose d' allegrezza; & della cagione, perchè è venuto Malatesta, per ora lascia stare, & maxime in fino a Pasqua, & non ne ragionare, perchè credo bisognerà mutare proposito, & di quello che io delibererò saprai, & tu non ne parlare con nessuno, excepto non Giovanni & Malatesta.

Per l' ultima tua delli VIII. eri arrivato costì a salvamento che mi piace, & all' entrata tera stato facto grande honore, che tutto habbiamo a riconoscere & da Dio & dagli huomini del mondo, a chi siamo troppo obligati, & ni fa pensiero di satisfare in parte al debito coll' opere, & fare conto d' essere vecchio innanzi al tempo, che così richiede el bisogno.

Dell' altre cose che costì seguono alla giornata intenderati, come per altra to detto, con Giovanni (Tornabuoni) & infrallaltre metti el capo a intendere

tendere lo stato di cotesta regione, e ne' termini che ella si truova, acciò che al suo ritorno tu lo raporti chiaro ne' termini, in che si truova. Nè altro al presente: Christo ti guardi. N° VIII.

Erami scordato come jersera ci furono lettere da Mantova delli 11. & avvisono come quello Sig. avea capitolato & conchiuso, & restare soldato del Re Ferrando, & questo per un passo è grande & utile; così habbiamo questo dì lettere similmente delli 11. da Genova, & raccontano come quelli cittadini universalmente tutti come sono stati alla devozione della felice memoria del Signore passato, vogliono essere a Madonna & alli figliuoli; & haverano facto octo cittadini, che col Governatore insieme circa tale effecto facessono quanto fusse di bisogno.

Eidem.

A questi dì to scripto a bastanza. Ho di poi una tua de' 15, & per essa intendo, come costì era la nuova della morte del Duca di Milano, el quale Dio habbi ricevuto a gratia, e delle provisioni facte costì del mandare a Milano & scrivere altrove, & ultimamente della determinazione havea fatto N. S. della conserva di quello stato, che molto è piaciuto universalmente a ciascuno. Noi quì per lo simile siamo in disposizione far tanto per quella Illma. Madonna & pe' suoi incliti figliuoli quanto per la libertà nostra che non manco cimporta, & potrà essere che non sarà a fare altro che dimostrationi, perchè per infino a dì 17. del presente, che sono l' ultime, habbiamo da Milano, non v' era innovato cosa nessuna, & tutto passava in buona pace & quiete, & per quanto si sente a Vinezia, secondo le parole e le dimostrationi, quella Signoria mostrava volere vivere in buona pace & quiete con Madonna & con li figliuoli, come havevan fatto colla felice memoria del Padre. Io sono di quelli che lo credo, parendomi che la ragione lo persuada. Circa questa parte non mi distendo, havendotene per altra mia detto allungo, & perchè rimando le lettere chio ò di là ma a ogni modo conosco essere grande profitto & utilità, che la Sanctità di N. S. dimostri volere, che si conservi la pace & quiete d' Italia, & a questo effecto credo concorreremo tucti; & perchio sono certo Sua Beatitudine ce inclinata, & sempre na facto dimostratione, me ne passo di leggiere, sperando che per la gratia di Dio & l' opere di Sua Sanctità tucto habbi a succedere bene.

N° VIII. Resto avisato come colla Sanctità del Papa eri stato & parlato della faccenda di Stefano da Osimo, & come Sua Sanctità restava contenta, che così porta la ragione pel bene comune delle parti & l' universale della città, & parmi N. S. lantenda a buon verso & sapientissimamente che non si da tagliare, ma tenere in spalla, che non può stare, se non per giovare, e potrebbe essere, che la dispositione del tempo sarebbe mutare proposito pure a me; basta sentire che questo non sia motuproprio di Sua Beatitudine, ma daltri, & vedi sopra tucto di fare che resti satisfacto & contento, perchè quando fusse altrimenti, restarei mal quieto nell' animo.

Non sò quello harete eseguito dipoi circa la dispositeria dello allume, la quale, come per altra ho decto, son contento che accepti in mio nome, & non dubito ce ne governeremo in modo, che la S. di N. S. se ne terrà ben servita & contenta: circa di ciò ti ristrignerai con Giovanni Tornabuoni, & di questa & dell' altre cose ne determinerete quello che crederete sia el meglio.

Come per altra to decto dell' andare tuo più in là, mi pare da soprastare per insino facto la pasqua: in questo mezzo s' intenderà tanto innanzi che c' insegnerà deliberare el meglio. Facesti bene a incitare Messer Agnolo, el quale aspectiamo quì ogni giorno. Le lettere da Milano, ch' io ti mandai ne' dì passati, & quelle che ti si mandano al presente, rimandale indrieto. Quì si actende ognora sentire dell' entrata dell' Illmo. Galeazzomaria. El Conte d' Urbino a dì 18. fu alla Scarperia senza venire quì, che stimo lo facesse per non perder tempo: subitto doverrà essere a Milano; & simile el Sig. Alessandro: di quel che seguirà sarai avvisato. El Sig. Gismondo era arrivato a Vinegia.

Eglè el vero che l' Arcidiacono è stato in extremo di morte, di poi è migliorato in modo, che non si stima habbia a morire di questo male, e l' inpensiero, che avevi facto di Pellegrino, lodo sommamente, et essendo accaduto el bisogno glarei dimostrato quanto desidero conpiacerlo & servirlo: quando tu vedi el Vescovo di Raugia, raccomandami alla Sua Signoria, & simile a Messer Lionardo Dati. Nè altro. Christo ti guardi. A dì 22. di Marzo 1465.

Lettera

Nº IX.

Lettera di Luigi Pulci a Lorenzo de' Medici.
Tratto da testo a penna nel archivio del Palazzo Vecchio a Firenze.

AL nome di dio, a dì 22 Apr. 1465. Caro mio Lorenzo, tu ci lasciasti si sconsolati nel tuo partire, ch' io non credo ancora potere sostenere la penna a scriverti questa lettera. Ho bene intesto da Braccio dlligentemente del tuo cammino, et stimo al presente sia in Vinegia; et acciochè noi facciamo buono principio al mio scrivere, dico ch' io son tutto soletto, smarrito, afflitto senza te. D' altra parte io son molto contento della tua dipartita, però ch' io la riputo avventurata per molte ragioni. Tu vedrai cose degne et varie, di che suole volentieri pascersi il tuo ingegno, lo quale io extimo prestantissimo di tutti gli altri, excepto in una sola cosa, et cetera ceterorum. Et la tua consolazione non può per alcuno modo essere senza mio gaudio. Et ancora ho chiamata più volte felicissima questa tua partenza; acciochè tu non abbi commesso peccato, ad ajutare nella sua petizione nuovamente affermata, quello, con che l' amico di Valdarno del corno, voleva entrare nell' orto del Borromeo per le mura; overo con che egli pota le pergole, quando non v' agiugne dappie col suo pennatuzzo. Non domandare s' ella ci è alzata tre braccia più che quest' anno passato la neve; et io n' ho tanta havuta pel capo, e per gli occhi, che non sa se non a fare di me, come facemo in Mugello di pesci al salceto poi che furono morti. Et al tutto la mia buona diligenzia, la mia povera fatica in ricercare per ogni parte vocaboli accomodati al bisogno, per ritrovare l' origine vero, andando personalmente, è perduta, e cassa, "*Mai più non vo cantar com' io solea,*" &c. Se tu ci fussi io farei mazze di sonetti come di ciriege in questo calendo di maggio. Io direi cose ch' el sole et la luna si fermarebbono, come a Josue, per udirle. Tuttavia n' o tra denti qualcuno per uscir fuori; poi dico il mio Lorenzo non ci è, nel quale era veramente ogni mio refugio, et ogni speranza. Questo solo mi ripreme; ma sia felice e presto il tuo tornare, ch' io farò pure un tratto ridere il popolo tutto; poi me n' andrò in sul carre Delio; et la mia patria sarà dove lo stajo della farina valli pochi soldi, e dove s' infarinino i pesci, e funghi secchi, et le zucche, et non gl' huomini, &c. Vale— Nº IX.

Ex

N° IX. *Ex M. S. in Pal. vet. Florentiæ adservato.*

Nobilissimo atque optimo adolescenti Laurentio Medici Petri Filio tanquam fratri suavissimo — Peregrinus Allius S. D.

Ne fortè mireris hominem tibi deditissimum, in tuo a patria discessu, amicorum illa communia tibi minime præstitisse, reddam si potero rationem per litteras, quas ne multum differam facit incredibile desiderium tui, pietasque in te nostra singularis. Ut enim ii quibus forte vulnera resecantur vultus avertunt, neque Medici manus aspicere patiuntur, sic ego cum a me dimidium mei separatur, æquiore animo absens tui quam præsens extitissem. Accessit et alia cura quam nos dicendam in aliud tempus differemus; sed profecto hoc vero affirmare possum, inter tot calamitates quibus me fortuna vehementer exercuit, nihil mihi hac nostra disjunctione, his annis accidisse molestius. Neque tamen ego is sum ut aliquis forte putaret malignus alienæ voluntatis interpres, qui ut mel muscæ, cadavera corvi sequuntur, sic fœnerator amicitias proposita metiar utilitate; sed tanta certe ob singulares virtutes tuas et mores ingenuos exarsit in nobis benevolentiæ magnitudo, ut sine te ab ipsa pene humanitate destituti esse videamur. Et jam tam brevi paucorum dierum intervallo, tam diu videmur suavissima consuetudine tua caruisse, ut quin aliquid ad te demus litterarum quibus tecum quasi coram colloquamur facere nullo modo possimus. Qui enim aliter desiderium nostrum fallamus, atque orbitatem nostram consolemur? Atque in hoc illud nobis deesse sentimus, illud requirimus, illud omnibus votis expetimus, jocundissimas sermonum tuorum per litteras vices, quæ quidem si cogitationibus nostris accesserint, multum erit profecto de nostro desiderio diminutum. Videbimur enim nobis et tecum esse, et vivas ut ait Maro audire et reddere voces. Quam quidem rem facere tu profecto debes; sive ut amicitiæ satisfacias, sive ut hac exercitatione aliquam dicendi facultatem consequaris; est enim ut ait Cicero optimus ac præstantissimus dicendi effector ac magister stilus: quem præcipue adolescentes intermittere nullo pacto debent; Frequens namque a teneris annis faciendum periculum, atque altius agendæ radices eorum studiorum ex quibus postea in provectiore ætate maximam gratiam atque uberrimos fructus expectamus. Et quarum ut inquit idem Cicero laudum gloriam adamamus, quibus artibus eæ laudes comparentur in iis est potissimum certe ab adolescentiâ laborandum. Usus præterea et experientia omnibus in rebus dominatur, sine quibus profecto nedum res tam ardua, tam præclara, sed ne minimæ quidem et vilissimæ artium perdiscuntur. Quod si ulla res est quæ assidui usus ac sedulitatis indiget, ea certe stilus est: qui ut frequenti exercitatione

citatione alitur, ita desuetudine obsolescit, atque intercidit. Neque solum in iis qui nondum jecerunt dicendi fundamenta, sed et in iis qui multum in ea re perfecerunt, si intermittatur, scribendi languescit industria. Quare sive ob exercitationis utilitatem, sive ut amico tibi deditissimo rem gratam facias, scribe ad nos, quam sæpissime, neve nos suavissima verborum tuorum vicissitudine fraudes. Satis enim erit superque satis ejus aspectu carere, qui uno tantum obtutu (neque hoc te latet) ex maxima animi perturbatione ad summam tranquillitatem revocare potestatem habet. Vale et nos ama, nosque Gentili nostro commendato. Ex Florentia 4. Kalendas Novembris 1463. N° IX.

N° X.

Ex Monum. Ang. Fabronii.

Rex Siciliae Laurentio.

MAGNIFICE vir amice noster carissime. Amavamove prima sì per le virtute vostre, sì per li meriti paterni & aviti, ma nuovamente inteso con quanta prudentia virilità & animo vi siate portato in la reformatione del novo reggimento, & quanta demonstratione habiate data de vui liberamente, havete tanto adiuncto all' amore ve portavamo, che è stata una moltiplicatione infinita. Congratulomene dunque al Magnifico Piero, che abbia un sì digno figliolo: congratulomene etiam al populo Fiorentino, che habia sì notabile difensore de la sua libertà: & non mino ad nui medisimi, che abbiamo tale amico, in lo quale la virtute con gli anni insieme piglia ogne dì manifestissimo augmento. Apparteneria forse ad nui excitarve ad le opere laudabili, ma la natura vostra generosa et prona ad le cose digne non ha bisogno de excitatore. Ultra di questo la memoria del vostro nobilissimo avo et lo exemplo del patre, che havete avanti loechi, hanno in se tanta efficacia, che non rechedino exortatione ne conforto alcuno. Pur lamore, che ve portamo ne stringe a pregarve vogliate de continuo producere tali fructi, quali havete comenzato ad dare delle vostre digne opere con tanta laude de vui propri, gloria del vostro Magnifico Patre, & expectatione de la vostra città, & finalmente con laudabilissimo testimonio de Italia tutta, in notizia della quale è andata la virtù vostra. Seguitate dunque como havere comenzato, dando ogne dì de' vui ali cittadini, & amici vostri maior speranza dela virtù propria, & de haver ad esser digno successore della notabilissima casa vostra. Ad la qual cosa così como non ve mancano anche abundantemente, ve supn N° X.

 pliscono

Nº X. pliscono tutte facultate ad ciò necessarie, & de la cassa & de la cittate, così haverete etiam da lontano amici, che ve daranno vera & effectuoso evidentia de vera & perfecta amicitia, inter li quali haverete nui per precipui.

Datum in Castro novo Neapolis XXVIII. Sept. 1466.

Rex Ferdinandus.

Nº XI.

Lettera di Angelo Acciajoli a Pietro Medici.

Siena 17. *Settembre* 1466.

Nº XI. SPECTABILIS vir frater honorande. Io mi rido di quel ch' io veggio. Dio t' ha apparecchiato potermi cancellare tucte le ragioni che io ho teco, & non lo sai fare, e mi fu totla la patria & lo stato per tuo padre; tu se' in termine che me lo puoi rendere: io l' ajutai che non li fusse tolta la roba, ora e' tolgono a me & grani & certe miserie di masserizie; tu me le puoi salvare; non dormire più in dimostrare che tu non vuoi essere ingrato; io non dico questo per la roba, bench' io n' abbi bisogno, quanto io lo dico per rispetto tuo: raccomandomi a te.

Risposta di Pietro Medici ec.

Firenze 22. *Settembre* 1466.

Magnifice eques tanquam pater honorande. Il vostro ridere ha fatto che io non pianga, che pure avevo dispiacere di questa vostra fortuna. Ma voi usate el vostro consueto senno, che in simili casi è necessario. La vostra colpa, come per altra mia ve ho detto è manifesta & tale, che la mia o altra intercessione non gioverebbe. Io di mia natura volentieri dimentico & a voi & a ciascun altro, che contro di me ha havuto animo inimico & hostile. Io ho dimesso ogni ingiuria; la Repubblica non può e non debbe per lo exemplo così de leggiere perdonare, come voi sapete meglio di me, che solete di queste cose vedere assai, & in pubblico & in privato predicarle. Scrivete che fusti cacciato per mio padre, & per salvargli la roba; ricordate gli obblighi. Non niego essere stato sempre grande amicitia la vostra con mio padre, & con noi altri, la quale secondo ragione mi vi dovea fare figliuolo, come io sempre mi vi sono reputato. Fusti cacciato con mio padre, fusti eziandio richiamato

richiamato con lui, come piacque alla Repubblica, che di noi ha piena & libera potentia, nèc redo l' amicitia nostra con voi vi sia stata danno o vergogna alcuna, come chiaro si dimostra, & forse che la ragione oblighi & benefizj fra noi batte, e resta più del pari, che non vi pare secondo el vostro scrivere, benchè io certamente sempre mi vi riputai obligato; ma voi me avete, se bene examinate la coscientia vostra, assai disobligo; nientedimeno voglio restarvi obligato in quanto appartiene a me privatamente, che la ingiuria publica non posso, nè voglio, nè debbo perdonare, ed in privato dimenticare el tutto, & dimettere ogni ingiuria, & restare quel figliuolo che debbo essere in verso di voi tal padre. N° XI.

N° XII.

Ricordi del Magnifico Lorenzo di Piero di Cosimo de' Medici.

Cavati da due fogli scritti di sua propria mano.

ESTRATTI DA UN CODICE DELLA PUBBLICA LIBRERIA MAGLIABECHIANA.

E stampati nel nuovo Lunario della Toscana dell' anno 1775.

NARRAZIONE breve del corso di mia vita e d' alcune altre cose d' importanza degne di memoria per lume e informazione di chi succederà massimamente de' figli nostri cominciata questo dì 15. Marzo 1472. N° XII.

Trovo per libri di Piero nostro padre, che io nacqui a dì primo di gennaio 1448, ed ebbe detto nostro padre di Maria Lucrezia di Francesco Tornabuoni nostra madre sette figli, quattro, maschi, e tre femmine, dei quali restiamo al presente quattro due maschi e due femmine, cioè Giuliano mio fratello d' età d' anni . . . ed io d' anni 24. e la Bianca donna di Guglielmo de' Pazzi, e la Nannina donna di Bernardo Rucellaj.

Giovanni di Averardo, ovvero di Bicci dei Medici nostro bisavolo trovo che morì a dì 20. Febbraio 1428. a ore 4. di notte senza voler far testamento, lascio il valsente di Fiorini 178. mila 221. di suggello come appare per un ricordo di mano di Cosimo nostro avolo a un suo libro segreto di cuoio rosso a c. 7. visse detto Giovanni anni 68.

Nº XII. Rimase di lui due figli cioè Cosimo nostro avolo allora d' età d' anni 40. e Lorenzo suo fratello d' età d' anni 30.

Di Lorenzo nacque Pier Francesco a dì . . . nel 1430. che al presente vive.

Di Cosimo nacque Piero nostro Padre a dì . . e Giovanni nostro zio a dì . . .

A dì . . . di Settembre 1433. fu sostenuto in Palazzo Cosimo nostro avolo con pericolo di pena e supplicio capitale.

E a dì 9. di Settembre confinato e relegato a Padova lui, e Lorenzo suo fratello e a dì 11. confermato per la Balìa del 1433.

E a dì 16. di Dicembre 1433. allargato di potere stare in tutte le terre de' Veneziani, non più presso a Firenze che fusse Padova.

A dì 29. di Settembre 1434. per il consiglio della Balìa fu revocato nella Patria con grandissimo contento di tutta la Città, e quasi di tutta Italia, dove poi visse insino all' ultimo de' suoi giorni Principale nel governo della nostra Repubblica.

Lorenzo de' Medici fratello di Cosimo nostro avolo passò da questa vita a dì 20. di Settembre 1440. d' età di anni 46. in circa a Careggi a ore 4. di notte senza voler fare testamento, restò suo unico Erede Pier Francesco, suo figlio e trovossi alla sua morte il valsente di fiorini 235. mila 137. di suggello come appare a detto libro segreto di Cosimo a c. 13. del qual valsente Cosimo sopradetto tenne a utile a benefizio di detto Pier Francesco figlio del detto Lorenzo, come di Piero, e Giovanni suoi figli insino che fu d' età conveniente, come appare tutto particolarmente per i libri di detto Cosimo, dove è tenuto particolarmente conto di tutto.

A dì . . . di Dicembre 1451. sendo detto Pier Francesco in età si divise da noi per lodo dato M. Marcello degli Strozzi, e Alamanno Salviati, M. Carlo Marsuppini, Bernardo de' Medici, Amerigo Cavalcanti, e Giovanni Serristori, per il qual lodo gli fu consegnato la metà di tutti e nostri beni grassamente

samente dandoli il vantaggio, ed i migliori capi, e di tutto fu rogato Ser Antonio Pugi Notaro. N° XII.

E nel medesimo tempo lo ritirò compagno per il terzo in tutti e nostri traffichi, dove ha avanzato più di noi, per aver avuto manco spese.

Giovanni nostro zio sopradetto morì a di primo di Novembre 1463. nella nostra casa di Firenze senza fare testamento, perchè non aveva figli ed era in potestà paterna, non di meno fu messa ad esecuzione interamente la sua ultima volontà, ebbe di Maria Ginevra degl' Alessandri un figliuolo chiamato Cosimo che morì di Novembre 1461. d' età di anni 9. in circa.

Cosimo nostro avolo uomo sapientissimo morì a Careggi a dì primo di Agosto 1464. d' età d' anni 76. in circa molto lacerato dalla vecchiezza, e dalla gotta, con grandissimo dolore, non solamente di noi, e di tutta la Città, ma generalmente di tutta Italia perchè fu uomo famosissimo ed ornato di molte, singolari virtù, morì in grandissimo stato quanto Cittadino Fiorentino, di cui sia memoria, fu seppellito in San Lorenzo, non volle far testamento nè volle pompa funebre, nondimeno tutti i Signori d' Italia mandarono ad onorarlo, e a condolersi della sua morte, e infra gli altri la Maestà del Re Luigi di Francia commisse fusse onorato della sua bandiera, che per rispetto di quanto aveva ordinato, di non voler pompa, non volle Piero nostro padre che si facesse.

Per decreto pubblico fu intitolato Pater Patriae, di che abbiamo in casa il privilegio o lettera patente.

Dopo la cui morte seguirono molte sedizioni nella Città, specialmente fu perseguitato per invidia nostro padre, e noi non senza gran pericolo, e degli amici, e dello Stato, e facoltà nostre. Da che nacque il Parlamento e novità del 1466. che furono relegati M. Agnolo Acciaiuoli, M. Dietisalvi, e Niccolò Soderini con altri, e riformossi lo Stato.

L' anno 1465. per la familiarità tenuta nostro avolo, e nostro padre con la casa di Francia, la Maestà del Re Luigi insignì e ornò l' Arme nostra di tre gigli d' oro nel campo azzurro, che portiamo al presente, di che abbiamo lettere patenti col suggello Reale pendente, che fu approvato, e confermato in Palazzo per 8. fave de' Priori.

Nº XII. L' anno 1467. di luglio ci venne il Duca Galeazzo di Milano ch' era in campo contro Bartolommeo da Bergamo in Romagna che vessava lo Stato nostro, e alloggiò in casa nostra, che così volle, benchè dalla Signoria gli fusse stato apparècchiato in Santa Maria Novella.

Il medesimo anno 1467. circa il Febbraio, e Marzo, si comprò Serezzana, e Serezzanello, e Castel-Nuovo da M. Lodovico, e M. Tommasino da Campo Fregosi per opera di Piero nostro padre, non ostante fussino nella guerra folta, e fecesi il pagamento a Siena per Francesco Sassetti nostro Ministro, e compagno in quel tempo degli Ufiziali del Monte.

Io Lorenzo tolsi Donna Clarice figliuola del Signore Iacopo Orsino, ovvero mi fu data, di Dicembre 1468. e feci le nozze in casa nostra a dì 4. di Giugno 1469 trovomi di lei insino a oggi due figliuoli una femmina chiamata Lucrezia d' età d' anni . . . e un maschio chiamato Piero di . . . . mesi, e lei gravida, Iddio ce li presti lungamente, e la guardi lungamente da ogni pericolo, sconciossi d' altri due figli maschi di mesi cinque in circa, e vissero infino al battesimo.

Di luglio 1469. à richiesta dell' Illustrissimo Duca Galeazzo di Milano andai a Milano e gli tenni a battesimo il suo primogenito, chiamato Giovanni Galeazzo a nome di Piero nostro padre, dovi fui molto onorato, e più ch' alcun' altro che vi fusse per simil cosa, benchè ve ne fussi de' più degni assai di me, e per fare il debito nostro donammo alla Duchessa una collano d' oro con un grosso Diamante che costò circa ducati tre mila. Donde è seguito ch' il prefato Signore ha voluto che battezzi tutti gli altri suoi figli.

Per eseguire e far' come gli altri giostrai in sulla piazza di Santa Croce con grande spesa, e gran sunto, nella quale trovo si spese circa fiorini 10. mila di suggello; e benchè d' anni, e di colpi non fussi molto strenue, mi fu giudicato il primo onore cioè un elmetto fornito d' ariento, con un marte per cimiero.

Piero nostro padre passò da questa vita alli 2. di Dicembre 1469. d' età di anni, . . . molto afflitto dalle gotte, non volle far testamento, ma fecesi l' inventario, e trovammoci allora il valsente di fiorini dugento trentasette mila novecento ottanta nove, come appare a un libro verde grande di mia mano in carta di capretto a c. 31. Fu sepellito in S. Lorenzo, e di continuo si fa la sua sepoltura, e di Gio. suo fratello, più degna che sappiamo per mettervi le loro ossa. Iddio abbia avuto misericordia delle anime. Fu molto pianto da tutta la Città, perchè era uomo intero, e di perfettissima bontà, e dai Signori d' Italia massimamente i principali fummo per lettere, e imbasciate, e condoglienze della sua morte, e così offerito lo Stato loro per la nostra difesa. N° XII.

Il secondo dì dopo la sua morte quantunque io Lorenzo fussi molto giovane, cioè di anni 21. vennono a noi a casa i Principali della Città, e dello Stato, a dolersi del caso, e confortarmi, che pigliassi la cura della Città, e dello Stato, come avevano fatto l'Avolo, e il padre mio, le quali cose per esser contro alla mia età, di gran carico, e pericolo, mal volentieri accettai, e solo per conservazione degli amici e sostanze nostre, perchè a Firenze si può mal vivere senza lo Stato, delle quali insino a quì siamo riusciti con onore, e grazia, reputando tutto, non da prudenza, ma per grazia di Dio, e per i buoni portamenti de' miei passati.

Gran somma di denari trovo abbiamo spesi dall' anno 1434. in quà, come appare per un quadernuccio in quarto da detto anno 1434 fino a tutto 1471. si vede somma incredibile, perchè ascende a fiorini 663755, tra muraglie limosine, e gravezze senza l' altre spese, di che non voglio dolermi, perchè quantunque molti giudicassero averne una parte in borsa, io giudico essere gran lume allo Stato nostro e pajommi ben collocati, e ne sono molto ben contento.

Di Settembre 1471, fui eletto Imbasciatore a Roma per l' incoronazione di Papa Sisto IV. dove fui molto onorato, e di quindi portai le due teste di marmo antiche dell' Immagine di Augusto, e di Agrippa, le quali mi donò detto Papa, e più portai la scodella nostra di Calcidonio intagliata con molti altri cammei, e medaglie, che si comprarono allora fra le altre il Calcidonio.

Ex

Nº XIII.

Ex Band. Spec. Lit. Flor. v. i. *p.* 111.

Christophori Landini Xandra, Liber secundus, ad Petrum Medicem.

Nº XIII. NOSTRI certa salus Medices, quo sospite, nunquam
Defuerunt sacris praemia virginibus,
Quo Duce Tyrrhenis deductum montibus Arnum
Praeferet Aoniis turba canora iugis.
Publica si quando cessant tibi munera, & audes
Instaurare brevi seria longa ioco,
Ne pudeat nostros percurrere Petre libellos,
Et nugas hilari fronte probare meas,
Magnos magna decent, fateor: tamen haec quoque fessos,
Quae reparent animos, ne fugienda putes.
Scipio nam quantus cessit, cui punica virtus,
Fortia cum Lybici contudit arma Ducis.
Hunc tamen in placido viderunt ocia ludo,
Ostrea Campano spargere lecta salo.
Tristius in terris, quam Stoica dicta Catonis,
Nil Danai, Latii nil meruere viri,
Hic tamen ad multam convivia ducere noctem.
Et solitus curas saepe levare mero.
Sic Tu, quo magni populi flectuntur habenae,
Dum legis haec sanctum pone supercilium.
Saepe tibi reditus Petre ad maiora dabuntur,
Si reparas mentem, qua geris illa, iocis.

Ad Petrum Medicem.

Carminibus nostris veniet tibi siqua voluptas,
Vt releves animum carmina nostra lege.
Quod si nec salibus poterunt, ullove lepore,
Te retinere Petre, tu tamen illa leges.
Sic Rex Peliacus quamvis non docta Poëtae
Suscepit laeta carmina fronte tamen,

Et

Et magis officium studiosi movit amici, N° XIII.
Quod tardum vatis laeserat ingenium.
Ergo non munus, sed dantis munera mentem
Inspice! sicque libens carmina nostra leges.
Non tam magnificus non est qui maxima donat,
Quam qui parva libens sumere dona potest.

Ad Petrum Medicem de suis, & Moecenatis laudibus.

Pvrpureis semper vernent tibi busta rosetis,
Inque tuum tellus sit levis usque caput,
Ulla nec Elysios passim celebrata per agros,
Quam tua Moecenas rideat umbra magis.
Moecenas, inopes quomdam miserate Poëtas,
Moecenas Phoebi, Pieridumque decus,
Te duce grandisonans consurgit in arma, virumque,
Olim qui denas vix cecinisset aves.
Alter erat tenuis pauper praeconis alumnus,
Cuius erat Lalagen dicere posse labor,
Hic ubi Campanos a te deductus in agros
Pauperiem verso sentit abire pede,
Protinus heroum Lesboo carmine laudes,
Et superum cecinit dulcia furta Deum;
Nec mirum tristi pulsis e pectore curis,
Libera si tantum mens agitabat opus.
Sed nunc Moecenas Tyrrhenis alter in oris
Conspicitur, claris qui favet ingeniis.
Vos modo sublimi vates consurgite versu,
Qui cupitis sacra cingere fronte caput.
Sive Sophocleis libet haec cantare cothurnis,
Seu iuvat Aonii ludere more senis.
Nam Medicum Fesulis stabunt dum fulta columnis
Atria magnanimis concelebrata viris
Nec vos materies, nec merces carminis unquam
Deseret, hoc virtus praestat utrumque Petri.
Ille colit musas, doctos colit ille Poëtas,
Unquam nec merita laude carere sinit.

Nam

N° XIII.

Nam novit quaecumque armis, quaecumque togata
Pace, gerant clari nobilitate viri,
Ni fuerint magno Musarum fulta favore,
Tendere in aeternum non reditura situm.
Ergo colit doctos, doctorum & carmina vatum,
Quae sint digna cani maxima fact gerit.
Nusquam magnanimo genitus fortique parente,
In coeptis gravibus degener ipse fuit.
Nam tantum emicuit iuvenili in pectore quondam
Consilium, quantum vix solet esse seni.
Inque dies crevit virtus crescentibus annis,
Seque tulit gradibus accumulata novis.
Unde & maturo gravior cum cesserat aetas,
Non cuncta ex usu mens meliora facit.
Quid mage iam sanctum, vel quid divinius unquam
Lydius Etrusca vidit in urbe Leo.
Ergo agite, o vates, sublimi insurgite versu,
Seu libeat natum dicere, sive patrem.
Iam canite altisono Medicum pia carmine facta,
Queis servata salus saepe fuit patriae.
Et si vos patriae pietas tenet ulla parentis,
Iam Patriam, versu concelebrate novo.

N° XIV.

Ex Monum. Ang. Fabronii.

Privilegium Ludovici XI. quo Mediceis concessit aurea Gallorum Regis Lilia in suorum stemmata inserere, extat in Filza VI. di documenti originali, *estque bujusmodi.*

N° XIV. LOYS par la grace de Dieu Roy de France. Savoir faisons à tous presens & advenir. Que nous ayans en mémoire la grande louable & recommandable renommée, que feu Cosme de'Medici a eue en son vivant en tous ses faits & affaires, les quels il a conduitz en si bonne vertu & prudence, que ses enfans & autres ses parens & amis en doivent éstre recommandez & eslevez en tout honneur. Pour ces causes & en obtemperant à la supplication & requéste, qui

qui faite nous être de la partie de notre ames, & leal Conseilleur Pierre de Medici filz de dit feu Cosme de Medici, avons de notre certaine science, grace especial, plaine puissance & auctorité Royal octroye & octroyons par ces presentes que le dit Pierre de Medici . . . . . . & ses heires & succeseurs nez & a naistre en loyal mariage puissent doresenevant à toûsjours perpetuellement avoir & porter en leurs armes trois fleurs de lis en la forme & maniere qu' elles sont ici portraictes . . . . Et Icelles armes leur avons données & donnons par ces dites presentes pour en user par tous les lieux & entre toutes les personnes que bon leur semblera & tant en temps de paix, que en temps de guerre sans que aucun empeschement leur puisse être mis ou donné ores ne pour les temps advenir en quelque maniere que ce faire au contraire. Et a fin que ce soit chose ferme & stable a tousjours nous avons fait mettre notre scel aux deux presentes sauf en autres choses notre droit, & l' autruy en toutes. Donné à Mont Lucon du moys de Mai l' an de grace 1465. & de notre Regne le quatriesme. N° XIV.

N° XV.

Ex codice XLII. membranaceo in 8. Plutei XXXIX. Bibliothecae Mediceae Laurentianae, qui continet Ugolini Verini Flammettam (pag. 41) *descriptum est sequens carmen elegiacum, quod est XLII. Libri II.*

Ad Lucretiam Donatam, ut amet
Laurentium Medicem.

GLORIA sis quamvis Tuscae, Lucretia, gentis, N° XV.
Aequiparesque ipsas nobilitate Deas;
Nec tua Tyndaridi concedat forma Lacaenae,
Aethereo tantum fulget in ore decus;
Sis nive candidior, sis formosissima tota,
Extet ut in toto pulchrius orbe nihil;
Sis facie insignis quamvis, & crine soluto
Ipse tuis pulcher cedat Apollo comis.
Sidereas quamvis vincant tua lumina flammas,
Et tua sint astris aemula labra poli;

N° XV.

Vincat ebur nitidum quamvis tua lactea cervix,
  Et superent roseae punica mala genae;
Os minimum, dentesque pares candore micantes,
  Et risum Juno vellet habere tuum;
Et Tyrio niveus perfusus rideat ostro
  Vultus, nativus sit color usque genis;
Et planae scapulae, nihil ut sit rectius illis,
  Brachia non tacta candidiora nive;
Parva mamillarum niveo sit pectore forma,
  Nec nimium pinguis, nec macilenta nimis;
Tyrrhenas collo superes tenus usque puellas,
  Nullaque ad exiguos vertice menda pedes;
Et quamvis victae cedant tibi voce Syrenae,
  Et Charites choreis, cedat & ipsa Venus;
Sit roseo vultu divina infusa venustas,
  Fecerit ut manibus Jupiter ipse suis;
Incessusque tuos quamvis soror ipsa Tonantis,
  Denique quidquid habes vellet habere tui;
Atque pudicitiae exemplar Lucretia cedat,
  Cujus habes nomen, moribus illa tuis;
Et quamvis omni penitus sis parte beata,
  Ut te felicem quisque vocare queat;
Non tamen idcirco talem contemnere amantem
  Debes, sed magis hic ultro petendus erat.
Si te divitiae capiunt, ditissimus hic est.
  Divitias moneo nulla puella velit.
Divitiis periere viri, periere puellae,
  Alcmeonis mater testis avara mihi est.
Si te nobilitas titulis insignis avorum
  Tangit, quis Medice est nobilitate prior?
Non fuit in populo generosior ulla Quiritum
  Stirps, neque tam claris nobilitata viris.
Si mores, si forma placet, juvenilis & aetas,
  Judice te, juvenis, pulcher, & ipse probus.
Quin age non alius tota praestantior urbe
  Est juvenis, si non saevus adesset amor.
Hunc quoque Castaliis Musae nutriere sub antris,
  Et totum hunc fovit Calliopea sinu.

Hunc,

Hunc, saeva, immiti patieris amore perire? N° XV.
Et quis te juvenis dignior alter erat?
Hic te dilexit, salvo Donata pudore;
Et famam laesit fabula nulla tuam.

N° XVI.

Inventiva d' una impositione di nuova gravezza, per Lodovico Ghetti.

Tratta da testo a penna del Secol. XV.

ACCIO che e sottoposti del magnifico commune di Firenze, et alcuni altri malivoli d' essa communità, et con doglenza e ramarichi non usino andare dicendo ne infamando che essi, con infinita gravezza, e stensioni incomportabili, sieno rubati et diserti da essa communità, in avere, et in persona; et con queste cose incitando e capitani et e tyranni di Italia, alchuna volta muoversi et fare imprese di guerra contro alla nostra città di Firenze, sperando di fare ribellioni negli agravati popoli, (et advengha dio che questa loro speranza sempre insino al dì doggi sia loro fallata, non resta perciò che la difesa sia suta sanza danni et pericoli et grande spesa della detta città e del suo paese,) et veduto che le terre d' Italia non sono atte a venire meno, ma di continuare, e crescere, et che la prefata nostra città sia posta in sito che per salute della nostra libertà, quasi a tutte le predette guerre ci bisogni porre mano, et participare et riparare; et che queste cose non si possino fare sanza continova spesa, la quale come detto è di sopra, per molti si dice con grande dogleuza non potersi sopportare, & che convenghono partirsi, le quali cose seguitando saria con grande danno, et biasimo, et pericolo della predetta nostra città—— N° XVI.

Adunque è da vedere, poiche la spesa è necessaria per salute della liberta e stato di Firenze, se si può porre questa gravezza in forma et in modo si ugualmente, che voluntaria da tutti possa essere sopportata, sanza biasimo, o lamento d' alchuna persona.

E perchè lo scriptore, avendo sopra di ciò facta alcuna imaginatione, dilibera dirne il suo pensiero; sempre siserbato migliore e più giustificato modo.

N° XVI. Et dicho così, acciochè ciaschuno participi generalmente alla detta gravezza, laquale conviene essere tanta che supplischa al bisogno del commune, che ella si pongha a perdere. Lo decimo, per stima, sopra tutti i fructi che frutta il terreno sottoposto al commune di Firenze, cioè sopra grano, et biade grosse, et minute, legume d' ogni ragione, lo decimo del vino, et sopra lo frutto del bestiame grosso, et minuto, dogni generatione, lo decimo dell olio, et lino, canape, safforano, guadi, robbia, di legne da fuoco, di fitti lavorj, et lo decimo di strame, di paschi d'erbe, et di fitti d' orti, et sopra la industria de detti che lavorano l' orta.

Ancora lo decimo de' fitti di mulina, o pigioni di case, di botteghe, et d' alberghi, et sopra ogni altra cosa che pagasse fitti e pigioni.

Ancora lo decimo sopra la rendità del monte.

Ancora lo decimo sopra e salari, e soldi degli ufficiali, dentro alla Città, e di fuori, et di loro giudici, et cavallieri, et sopra la pensioni de Castellani, tanto quegli che vanno di fuori della jurisdizione del commune di Firenze, quanto a quegli della Città et distretto; eccettuati gl' uffici forestieri quali non sieno tenuti a decimo.

Ancora porre lo decimo sopra alla industria et guadagno delle sette maggiori arti, tanto di fuori della Città et suggetti del commune, quanto dentro, et ancora sopra e salarj de' loro fattori grossi che avessono da Fl. 30 in su di salario, exceptuati quelli che lavorano di mano.

Similemente sopra lo decimo della industria et guadagno sopra queste delle quattordici minori arti, così di fuori come di dentro, et e loro fattori e lavoranti, sieno de loro prezzi e salarj franchi, concio sia cosa che lavorino di mano, e quasi sono tutte povere persone.

Et nota, che a tutti quanti questi decimi, verrieno a essere tenuti generalemente, ogni persona, tanto gli ecclesiastici, come e laici, et simile gl' assenti, e forestieri abitanti, conciosiacosachè ciascuno dessi possiede col favore del commune, et beneficio della pace, et della giustizia, et così debbono debitamente participare agl' affanni, et se pure alchuni clerici, o terre exenti si ricusassi,

ricusassi, la via et el modo e per le ragioni sopra dette a fargli acceptare voluntariamente. N° XVI,

Insino a qui, s'è detto di sopra, sopra a che sarebbe da mettere la impositione del decimo; resta ora a dichiarare quanto gittasse.

Et intorno a questo che a me pare, et per alcuni intendenti si dicie, che la Città di Firenze, col suo territorio, facci huomeni ottanta mila di guardia; che se cosl fusse, che si presume sia, seguiterebbe secondo naturale ragione, che ogni huomo di guardia, computata la sua persona, facessi l' uno per l' alto cinque boche, tra femmine, et fanciulli, et vecchj; che verrebbono a moltiplicare boche a quattro cento migliaja.

Arebbesi ora a vedere queste boche quanto pane, vino, olio, carne, vogliono l' anno; e per questa via si troverà quasi tutta la quantita de fructi, e quali, se non e qualche sterminata carestia, tutto eschono del territorio di Firenze, sicche appresso verro a dichiarare quanto vogliono le sopradette boche.

Dicho adunque che quattru cento milliaja di boche, aiutante la picholа colla grande, et el cittadino col contadino lavoratore, vuole Staja XIIII. per bocha l' anno, che monterà lo grano, dugento trenta due milliaja di moggia, lo quale stimo a Fior. . . . el moggio monta Fior. 111,815

Et pur stimo che le dette boche, ristorando l' una l' altra anchora del vino, avanza oltre all' anno, quantunque a molti ne manchi, tutto arbitro che voglieno, Cogna CCC. m. lo quale stimo quello d' allungie con quello d' appresso, e buoni co' mezzani et manuali, che l' uno per l' altro vaglia Fiorini tre e mezzo cioè Fl. 3½ che monta a una miglione di Fiorini—el decimo Fl. 100,000

Et stimo che voglino sopra dette boche, tra per ardere e per mangiare, olio orcia cento migliaja, a fior 1½ l' orcio, che monta lo decimo, fior. 15,000

E perche della carne non posso fare appunto per molti rispetti, nel conto piglo questo ordine, che io stimo che nel territorio di

Nº XVI. di Firenze sia pechore, fra mezzane, e basse, et grosse, et montanine, circa ad uno miglione, alle quali l' una per l' altra metto per decimo 2½ fl. fra l' agnello, lana, et caccio; et nota che tanto metto alle minute, et basse, quanto alle grosse, considerato che le grosse anno più spesa per l' andata di maremma et che monti questo decimo fior. 25,000

Et stimo che nello detto territorio, tra allevare a mano, et in selva, s' alievi porci quaranti migliaja a quali si debba mettere, cioè alli allevati a mano, et in casa, stimo sieno la meta grossi uno per porche, et agli della selva, considerato sta due anni a allevarsi, pure uno grosso per anno; montino a e decimi in tutto, ridotti in somma fior. 2500

A quegli che allevano e porci temporili, per rivendere, non gli metto per carne, ma per industria allarte inanzi.

Ancora stimo, che fra vache, bufoli, et cavalle, sia che figlino nel territorio di Firenze, capi ventimila, e più; alle quali per lo decimo del fructo, metto uno quarto di fior. per capo, che monta fior. 5000

Ancora stimo che oltre alle sopradette boche sia nella città, contado, et distretto di Firenze tra cortegiani, soldati a cavallo, et a pie, et marinai, et viandanti, et mendicanti, et altri forestieri, circa a boche XX m. le quali voglono molto più roba che l' ordinarie boche; stimo voglono l' uno per l' altro fior. XII. per uno, tra pane, vino, et carne, et oglo, che monti fior. 240,000 lo decimo sie fior. 24,000

Ancora fo, oltre al nostro bisogno, fornite tutte le sopradette boche, per uno anno che è detto, che avanzi sopra la spesa, grano per quattro mesi, che sarebbe alla ragione detta moggi ottanta mila di grano, lo decimo sarebbe otto mila che a fior. 5½ per moggio sono fior. 44,000

Ancora stimo che in Firenze, e nel paese, fra cortigiani, et soldati, et di cittadini, muli, cavagli, somieri da soma, circa a venti

venti quattro migliaja, cioè che mangino biada, le quali stimo l'una per l'altra mangino ⅛ di stajo el dì, che monta l'anno circa a cinquanta migliaja di moggia di biada grossa, che lo decimo sarebbe moggia 5000 a fiorini due et mezzo l'uno anno per l'altro el moggio, monta fior. 12,500

Ancora lo decimo del miglo, et saggina, e panicho, che stimo montera meglo che fior. 3000

Ancora lo decimo di fave, ceci, e d' altri lagumi fructi meglio che fior. 2000

Ancora lo decimo del lino, canape, guadi, robbia, zafferano, e fitti d' orti, fior. 3000

Ancora lo decimo di legname da edificj et d' altri lavori, e di quello da ardere, fior. 3000

Ancora lo decimo di strame, paglia, fieno, e paschi di montagne, e di marina, fior. 5000

Ancora lo decimo delle selve che si vendono, et ghiande, e lo decimo delle castagne, fior. 1000

Ancora stimo, che oltre al olio che è stimato adrieto, che bisogna per nostro uso, si tragha et consumi in arte di lana, che si fa nella città, e distretto, oltre accio, quello che avanza oltre al nostro uso, in tutto orcia sexanta migliaja che monte a fior. 1½ l' orcio fior. novanta migliaja—lo decimo, fior. 9000

Ancora stimo secondo lo macinato che voglono le boche in fitti de' Mulini collo decimo che guadagna il mugnaio, frutti a decimo tra el padrone et el mugnaio predetto, fior. cinquanta mila 5000

Ancora credo e tengho, che fructi la pigione delle case et di botteghe, et d' alberghi di Firenze, et del suo territorio, e distretto, lo decimo fior. 5000

Ancora

N° XVI. Ancora credo che frutti lo decimo de' salarj de capitani, vicarj, et podestà, e de loro giudici et cavalierj, e castellani, l' anno che sono uficj etiandio lo salario de gli ufici di dentro fior. . . . 5000

Ancora lo decimo della rendita del monte, chosi come detto abbiamo di interessi, cioè fior. dugento migliaja—fior. . . . 20,000

Ancora lo decimo della industria delle sette maggiori arti, e lo decimo de salarj de fattori loro—fior. 50,000

Ancora la industria delle quattordici minori arti, lo decimo fior. venticiuque migliaja. 25,000

Somma in tutto, fior. 475,815

Nota che io stimo per molti membri che anno le supradette arti, et maxime le minori, che si stendono nello distretto di fuori in grande numero, et sia molto maggiore quantita, che io non disegno di sopra.

Ora qui è una difficultà contraria a questo disegno, cioè che nel sopradetto disegno se a d' inchiudère lo decimo della meta di fructi a lavaratori che lavorano a mezzo, e quali essendo gravati di soldi tre di stimo per testa, non potrebbono sopportare ancora lo decimo.

A questo si dice non volendo guastare el numero delle taxe, in che entrano el sopradette soldi tre per testa, et cogli detti lavaratorj. Et nota che se del salario non fusse excettuato persona, et da altri non fussino e riagravati più che non potessono computare che si piglasse della sopradetta somma del decimo, tanto che si pagassi pegli detti contadini, la loro taxa, salvo et riservato a quegli che anno et lavorano lo terreno proprio, sicche abattuta la quantita che tocha a detti lavaratorj, et ancora a quello bischonto di non essere si grassa l' entrata del decimo come si disegna, che la detta somma resterebbe in su quattro cento migliaja netti di fiorini 400,000.

Et accio che questo decimo più pienamente gittasse le sopradetti quantità di fiorini, credo che sarebbe buono providemento di fare per le genti che a ciascuno persona habitante a Pisa o nel paese, fusse lecito di lavorare in ciascuno terreno sodo di quello di Pisa, sanza alchuna contraditione di padroni o d' altri d'altri, pagando egli a padroni de terreni l'usato convenevole araticho, et lavorando egli con quattro bestie, o bovine, o buffoline, o cavalline, et da indi in su potessi trarre per mare o per terra, la meta de grani o biade ricoglessi, pagando l' usata tracta, con questo inteso, che el grano non passasse a Firenze, soldi venti lo stajo, et passando non si posse trarre. N° XVI.

Seguiteranne che gli abitanti forestieri cresceranno a Pisa et nel contado; et miglioreranno le gabelle per la tracta, et entreranno danarj assai contanti di forestieri in paese, pero che gnuna cosa che empia di danari più maneschi uno paese quanto fa chi à a vendere grano. Ancora ne seguitera che sempre Pisa sara fornita per quello; restera che sara grande quantita di grano.

Ancora e da notare, che chi paghasse a ragione di fior. 5½ lo moggio del grano, per la sopradetta impositione del decimo, sara per questo necessario per la via della tratta, mantenere el grano in su soldi xx lo stajo, perche se valessi sol x per pagare lo detto decimo gli converrebbe vendere 2 stajo di grano per fare soldi xx, et a questo modo arebbe a pagare due decimi et cosi dell' olio et del vino. Non credo si potessi fare salvo, se non per una via cioè in tenerlo in su fior 5½; questo tengho in me per ora.

Avete veduto come il mio disegno delle impositione del decimo soprastato gitterebbe fior. 400,000 o più, e quali si vorebbono per più habilità pagare in tre termine, et questo è che quella parte che tochassi a lavoratori d' altrui, gl' osti loro ne fussono tenuti, accio che in su la ricolta la rechassono al loco, sicche questa sustanza rimanessi a l' oste e pagassi l' oste se detto lavoratore non pagasse al tempo.

De detti fiorini cccc. m. a chiarire per sperienza ciascuna persona che con CL. m. di fiorini l' anno, si puo mantenare et contentere cavagli 4000, fanti 1000 (*a*), siche abbi ad avvanzare della quantita fior CCL. m. e cosi con quegli si puo sdebitare el debito del monte, e poi resterebbono le rendite et el comune libero, colle quali si potra fare e mantenere più gente bisognando. Et non sara di bisogno ne prestanza, ne balzello. Et sarebbesi fuori d' una grande pistolenza e malattia. Et seguiterebbe che ci ritornerebbe assai cittadini.

(*a*) Più tosto, Cavagli 1000. Fanti 4000.

N° XVI. cittadini. Et molti danari uscirebbono fuori per ogni via. L' arti, el popolo, el paese, multiplicherebbe, e crescerebbe la riputatione, e non si direbbe pe' nostri vicini che fussimo falliti et in piegha. Et e tiranni non farebbono pensiero affare si leggiermente guerra, colle loro false speranze.

N° XVII.

Ex Oper. Ang. Politiani. Ed. Aldi. 1498.

Ad Laurent. Medicem.

N° XVII. CUM referam attonito Medices tibi carmina plectro,
Ingeniumque tibi serviat omne meum,
Quod tegor attrita ridet plebicula veste,
Tegmina quod pedibus sint recutita meis;
Quod digitos caligæ disrupto carcere nudos
Permittant cælo liberiore frui;
Intima bombycum vacua est quod stamine vestis,
Sectaque de cæsa vincula fallit ove;
Ridet, et ignavum sic me putat esse poetam,
Nec placuisse animo carmina nostra tuo.
Tu contra effusas toto sic pectore laudes
Ingeris, ut libris sit data palma meis;
Hoc tibi si credi cupis, et cohibere popellum,
Laurenti, vestes jam mihi mitte tuas.

Ad eundem, gratiarum actio.

Dum cupio ingentes numero tibi solvere grates,
Laurenti, ætatis gloria prima tuæ,
Excita jamdudum longo mihi murmure tandem
Astitit arguta Calliopeia lyra;
Astitit, inque meo preciosas corpore vestes
Ut vidit, pavidum rettulit inde pedem;

Nec

Nec potuit culti faciem dea nosse poetæ, N° XVII.
Corporaque in tyrio conspicienda sinu:
Si minus ergo tibi meritas ago carmine grates,
Frustrata est calamum diva vocata meum;
Mox tibi sublato modulabor pectine versus,
Cultibus assuerit cum mea muse novis.

N° XVIII.

Aloysius Laurentio de' Medicis.

MAGNIFICE vir affinis noster carissime. Non possumus non laetari summopere, cum bene valere vos & vestra omnia bene esse sentimus. Redivit nuper ad nos e Roma, dilectus consiliarius noster magister Ludovicus de Ambasia, qui cum iter per Florentiam fecerit, abunde retulit prospera vobis omnia succedere, quod profecto nobis admodum voluptati fuit: addiditque quantum a vobis perhumaniter exceptus fuerit, quamve interrogatus diligenter & summo cordis affectu de his quae nostra sunt, & nostra & regni nostri commoda concernunt. Quod etsi factum sciamus non praeter solitum, habemus tamen, quas possumus, gratias ingentiores praestantiae vestrae, quae ita omni tempore solicitam se praebeat rerum nostrarum, quas sibi & amicis cordi non dubitamus, tametsi quis hortatus fuerit nos, ut rem majori experimento comprobaremus: sed sinentes eum in sua sententia credimus contrarium, & nobis & vobis notum satis, experientia docente. De vobis erga nos integram illam servabimus opinionem, quam gessimus semper, & verba & rerum effectus comprobarunt. N° XVIII.

Caeterum facit illa, quam semper erga nos gessistis, benevolentia, ut quae nostra intersunt libenter vobiscum communicemus. Relatum fuit nobis superioribus mensibus Regem Ferdinandum tractasse, ut filia sua primogenita matrimonio jungeretur moderno Duci Subaudiae, cum dote trecentum millium ducatorum, sed rem adhuc esse imperfectam: ex quo mente revolventibus nobis quid potius bono & commodo ipsius Regis & nostro conveniret, illud videtur potissimum, ut invicem nos & illum ligaret aliquod matrimonii vinculum: quocirca in hanc sententiam & deliberationem venimus, quod contenti essemus, quod filia sua Delphino Viennensi primogenito nostro nuberet: quod per vos eidem Regi notum fieri vellemus, & fieri inde certiores

Nº XVIII. de mente sua circa hoc, & si negocium aggredi intendit quam dotem filiae se daturum dicet; quamvis ab ipso potius quam dotis summam quantitatem, cujus rei loco & tempore vestromet verbo stabimus, veram amicitiam & confederationem perpetuam expeteremus, quae sibi contra quoscumque inimicos suos ac praesertim contra domum Andegavensem, quae nobis etiam infida fuit & est, adjumento & favori erit. Speramus etiam, quod hac conventione mediante Rex ipse contra Regem Aragonum nobis praestabit auxilium & favorem, & amicus erit amicis nostris, & inimicus inimicis. Quae omnia nobis aperienda duximus his nostris tantum, ut quamprimum habita communicatione horum omnium cum Rege ipso, vestro medio, aut illorum, quibus onus per vos demandatum erit, quantocius fieri poterit, certiores fiamus de his, quae intendit & sentit Rex ipse super haec, quae si Majestati suae convenire videbuntur, ut executioni mandentur, dabitur opera, & Oratores nostros Florentiam mittemus vel in regnum suum pro conclusione terminanda, qua habita, poterit & ipse suos transmittere ad nos visum filium nostrum primogenitum, & ad alia exequenda quae occurrunt. Et gratum esset quod tam pro his, quam pro aliis nonnullis negociis, quae nobiscum communicanda saepe veniunt, ad nos aliquem ex vestris mitteretis, qui saltem certo tempore apud nos esset, qui habebit opportunitatem adeundi & redeundi. Sed hunc vellemus praemonitum, ne alicui se committat ex Magnatibus & Dominis de sanguine nostro, sed nobis tantum. Postremo quae oblectant non omittemus. Rogamus igitur vos, ut aliquem canem ex vestris a vobis dono habeamus, & etiamsi unum mittatis, satis erit, dummodo pulcher sit & magnus, quem apud personam nostram & cameram servari faciemus. Scriptum Ambasiae decima nona die mensis Junii 1473.

Ferdinandus

N° XIX.

Ferdinandus Rex Siciliae

Laurentio de' Medicis.

MAGNIFICE vir amice noster carissime. Etsi tanto in nos amore esse jampridem vos intellexerimus, ut nulla praeterea testificatione opus sit, quin exaltationem nostri status & nominis semper optaveritis, tamen litterae eae quas nuperrime accepimus, & ea quae Augustinus Biliottus retulit, ita nobis amorem ipsum significarunt, ut omnino difficillimum nunc quidem videatur judicare, utrum ab Alfonso ipso filio nostro magis vel amemur vel veneremur, quam a Laurentio, qui & amantissimus nostri est, & officii plenissimus. Facitis itaque, ut amicum amicissimum decet, qui nobis conditionem proponatis, quae honori & commodo nostro factura sit maximam accessionem, dum foedus feriendum, & iniendam esse affinitatem cum Rege Maximo Francorum, dandamque filiam nostram filio ejus primogenito uxorem suadetis, ut ipse suis ad vos litteris scribit. Qua de re nos vobis debere profitemur, quantum ut cupimus persolvere ita posse optamus. Sed ut meam mentem aliquando intelligatis, esset sane nobis non modo gratum, sed optatissimum etiam cum Rege ipso foedus percutere, inireque affinitatem, quem ut nobilissimo genere, ita amplissimo regno primum esse in toto orbe non ignoramus. Sed quando iis conditionibus res ipsa proponitur, quam cum integritate honoris nostri accipere nullo modo possumus, caussa est cur molestissime feramus. Etenim non modo adversus Serenissimum Regem Aragonum patruum nostrum nos unquam colligare, sed ipsi deesse tam iniquum putamus, ut prius mori statuamus, quam id simus facturi, vel quod ita ejus in nos beneficia postulant, vel quod pietas nostra in illum tanta est, ut nobis ipsis deesse, quam illi aequius putemus; neque movere nos debet, quod Rex ipse pollicetur, si conditionem acceperimus, futurum se hostem familiae Andegavensis. Ille enim jure optimo & posset & deberet id facere propter Andegavensium ipsorum perfidiam, eorumdemque in eum inimicitias. At ego immanitate ac potius feritate adductus videbor, si patruo defuero, cum adesse saltem ratione familiae, quando cetera arctiora vincula deessent, semper debebo, nisi is esse voluerim, qui meis desim, ut adsim externis. Quamobrem quod ad iniendam affinitatem, foedusque Rex ipse paciscitur, ut ego patruo meo adverser atque sibi foveam, aequius sanctiusque fuisset, si se affinitatis ipsius gratia fautorem mecum patruo meo dixisset; visusque esset cum pro sua humanitate agere, tum affinitatem hanc familiae meae commodo

2 potius

N° XIX. potius quam ejusdem incommodo desiderare, et honoris mei habere rationem. Impedit etiam haec non minus ictum foedus & societas, quae nobis est cum Illmo Burgundiae Duce, quam ut optatissimum fuit inire, ita nunc tueri esse debet jucundissimum. Ex quo fit ut nisi Rex ipse cum illo etiam Principe in pace victurus sit, perducere quo velle se ostendit negotium non poterimus. Ita enim aequitatis amatores, fidei nostrae observatores sumus, ut hanc omnibus nostris commodis praeponamus. Honorem autem nostrum tanti facimus, ut non modo res caeteras, verum etiam regnum universum nostrum ammittere, & capitis subire periculum malimus, quam ex eo ipso honore quidquid imminui patiamur. Verum si Rex ipse facturus est, quod ejus alioqui humanitatis officium fuerit, ut neque in patruum nostrum, neque in Ducem, amicum socium & fratrem bellum sit habiturus, sed vires suas in fidei hostes versurus, ex quibus gloriam atque triumphum honestius possit referre, non modo affinitatem societatemque annuemus, sed pollicebimur nos omnia facturos, quae vel honori, vel commodo ei futura intelligamus. Neque vero Regi ipsi aegre ferendum est, si fidem datam honoremque ac familiae nostrae imperium non minui aut labefactari velimus: quandoquidem si aliter faceremus, neque ipsi in nobis spem reponere, aut fidem habere conveniens foret, quem scimus etiam non ignorare gerenda esse bella in eos, a quibus injuriam acceperit. Nos autem qua injuria provocemur, aut ab rege patruo nostro, aut ab Illmo Burgundiae Duce, quis est qui ignoret? Quod si regnum ipse habere potest tranquillum & otiosum, simul Deo immortali gratias agere, eumdemque precari, ut tale semper habere liceat, simul eo contentus esse debet; ne si aliud appetat, non suum, violare jus videatur humanae societatis. Quamobrem suadere vos Regi poterit is honestissimas condiriones, quas si accepturus est, accipiemus nos quas ille nobis proponit. Proinde date operam, ut persuadeatis, ita enim nos vobis obligaveritis, ut qui nunc magnum quoddam vobis debemus, infinitum simus debituri. Reliquum est, si quid vestra caussa efficere possumus, licet utamini facultate nostra, quoad nostrae vires patientur. Datum in Castello Novo Neapolis die IX. Augusti 1473.

N° XX.

Marsilius Ficinus Flor. Martino Uranio Amico Unico S. D.

NIHIL a me justius postulare poteras, quam quod per Ioannem Straeler N° XX. congermanum tuum, iam saepe requiris, amicorum videlicet nostrorum catalogum, non ex quovis commercio, vel contubernio confluentium, sed in ipsa duntaxat liberalium disciplinarum communione convenientium. Quum enim absque amicorum meorum praesentia esse nusquam aut debeam, aut velim, ipseque sim, non in Italia solum in me ipso, sed in te etiam in Germania, merito amicos hic meos, istic etiam mihi adesse desidero. Omnes quidem ingenio, moribusque probatos esse scito: nullos enim habere umquam amicos statui, nisi quos judicaverim litteras, una cum honestate morum, quasi cum Iove Mercurium, conjunxisse. Plato enim noster in epistolis, integritatem vitae veram inquit esse Philosophiam; litteras autem, quasi externum Philosophiae nuncupat ornamentum. Idem in epistolis ait, philosophicam communionem, omni alia non solum benevolentia, sed etiam necessitudine praestantiorem stabilioremque existere. Sed ut mox veniam ad catalogum, cunctos summatim amicos ita laudatos accipito. At si proprias cujusque laudes singulatim narrare voluero, opus inceptavero longe prolixum; si quos praetermisero, non aeque laudatos, prorsus invidiosum. Omnino vero absurdum fuerit, si dum amicos ordine disponere tento, interim comparationibus omnia perturbavero, odium pro benevolentia postremo reportans. Primum summumque inter amicos locum patroni nostri Medices Jure optimo sibi vindicant. Magnus Cosmus, gemini Cosmi filii, viri praestantes, Petrus, atque Ioannes, gemini quoque Petri nati, magnus Laurentius, et inclitus Iulianus; tres Laurentii liberi, magnanimus Petrus, Ioannes Cardinalis plurimum venerandus, Iulianus egregia indole praeditus. Ac ne in longum singulorum laudes prosequar, una Medices omnes communi laude complectar; Genus heroicum. Praeter Patronos, duo sunt nobis amicorum genera. Alii enim, non auditores quidem omnes, nec omnino discipuli, sed consuetudine familiares, ut ita loquar, confabulatores, atque ultro citroque consiliorum, disciplinarumque liberalium communicatores. Alii autem, praeter hos quos dixi, nos quandoque legentes, et quasi docentes audiverunt, etsi ipsi quidem quasi discipuli, non tamen revera discipuli; non enim tantum mihi adrogo, ut docuerim aliquos, aut doceam, sed Socratico potius more sciscitor omnes, atque hortor, foecundaque familiarium meorum ingenia, ad partum adsidue provoco.

In

N° XX. In primo genere sunt Naldus Naldius, a tenera statim aetate mihi familiaris; post hunc in adolescentia nostra Peregrinus Allius, Christophorus Landinus, Baptista Leo Albertus, Petrus Pactius, Benedictus Accoltus Arretinus, Bartolomaeus Valor, Antonius Canisianus; paullo post Io. Cavalcantes, Dominicus Galectus, Antonius Calderinus, Hieronymus Rossius, Amerigus et Thomas, ambo Bencii, Cherubinus Quarqualius Geminianensis, Antonius Seraphicus, Michael Mercatus, ambo Miniatenses, Franciscus Bandinus, Laurentius Lippius Collensis, Bernardus Nuthius, Comandus, Baccius Ugolinus, Petrus Fannius Presbyter. Horum plurimi, exceptis Landino, et Baptista Leone, et Benedicto Accolto, primas lectiones nostras nonnumquam audiverunt. In aetate vero mea jam matura familiares, non auditores, Antonius Allius, Ricciardus Anglariensis, Bartolomaeus Platina, Oliverius Arduinus, Sebastianus Salvinus Amitinus noster, Laurentius Bonincontrius, Benedictus Biliottus, Georgius Ant. Vespuccius, Io. Baptista Boninsegnius, Demetrius Byzantius, Io. Victorius Soderinus, Angelus Politianus, Pierleonus Spoletinus, Io. Picus Mirandula. In secundo genere, idest in ordine auditorum, sunt Carolus Marsuppinus; Petri quinque, Nerus, Guicciardinus, Soderinus, Compagnius, Parentus; Philippi duo, Valor scilicet, et Carduccius; Ioannes quattuor, Canacius, Nesius, Guicciardinus, Rosatus; Bernardi quattuor, Victorius, Medices, Canisianus, Micheloctius; Francisci quattuor, Berlingherius, Rimicinus, Gaddus, Petrasancta; Amerigus Cursinus, Antonius Lanfredinus, Bindaccius Ricasulanus, Alamannus Donatus, Nicolaus Micheloctius, Matthaeus Rabatta, Alexander Albitius, Fortuna Ebraeus, Sebastianus Presbyter, Angelus Carduccius, Andreas Cursus, Alexander Borsius, Blasius Bibienius, Franc. Diaccetus, Nicolaus Valor.

ANGELI

N° XXI.

ANGELI POLITIANI CONJURATIONIS PACTIANÆ ANNI M.CCCC. LXXVIII. COMMENTARIUM.

Juxta Edit. Joannis Adimari ex Marchionibus Bumbae. Neapoli, 1769.

PACTIANAM conjurationem paucis describere instituo; nam id in primis memorabile facinus tempestate mea accidit, parumque abfuit, quin Florentinam omnem Rempublicam penitus everteret. N° XXI.

Cum is igitur esset ejus Urbis status, ut omnes boni a Laurentio, & Juliano fratribus, reliquaque Medicum familia starent; Pactiorum una gens, ac Salviatorum nonnulli coepere praesentibus rebus clam primo, mox etiam palam adversari. Invidebant enim Medicae familiae; ejusque summam nostra in Republica auctoritatem, & privatum decus, quantum in eis esset, obterebant.

Erat Pactiorum familia civibus, plebique juxta invisa: nam, praeterquam quod avarissimi essent omnes, neque eorum contumax, atque insolens ingenium satis aequo animo tolerari poterat: ejus familiae princeps Jacobus Pactius Equestris ordinis vir, diem noctemque aleae vacabat; sicubi male jactus caderet, Deos, atque homines diris agebat: nonnunquam vero & alveolum tesserarium, aut quod aliud irato offerretur, temere in proximum quemque jaculabatur: saepe & ad ipsum alveolum furiosi instar frontem allidebat. Ipse pallidus, & exanguis, caput jactare semper, & quod levitatis maximum foret argumentum, nunquam ore, nunquam oculis, nunquam manibus consistere. Duo in homine ingentia vitia, eaque, quod mirum esset, maxime inter se contraria eminebant: multa avaritia, multa ambitio. Domum paternam magnifice exstructam a fundamentis diruit: novam exaedificare aggressus est; mercenarias ibi operas conducere solitus, neque tamen integrum solvere; pauperculosque homines misere sibi vix manuum mercede in diem victum parantes defraudabat; quare omnibus erat invisus. Non ipse, non ejus majores gratiosi populo unquam fuerant. Erat praeterea sine legitima prole: quapropter & a suis necessariis, quippe qui hereditatem hominis captarent, praeter caeteros colebatur. Incuria in homine maxima, maximaque rei familiaris negligentia: cumque hi essent hominis mores, facile rem facturus videbatur, quod ipsi ad maturandum facinus calcar maximum,

Nº XXI. mum, facesque subdidit. Non enim sperabat homo insolens, & ambitiosus decoctoris ignominiam non iniquissimo se laturum animo: studebat itaque uno incendio sese, suamque omnem patriam concremare.

Franciscus autem Salviatus homo repente fortunatus, quippe qui Pisanum haud multo antea Archiepiscopatum esset adeptus, vix ipse sese, suamque fortunam capiens, coeperat, supra quam dici potest, secundis rebus, insolescere; nihilque non sibi de sese, suaque fortuna polliceri. Is Franciscus homo fuit (id quod Dii, atque homines sicunt) omnis divini, atque humani juris ignarus, & contemptor; omnibus flagitiis, & facinoribus coopertus; luxuria perditus, & lenociniis infamis. Aleae & ipse studiosissimus: maximus praeterea adulator: multae levitatis, ac vanitatis: idem audax, promptus, callidus, & impudens; Quibus artibus (adeo fortunam nihil puduit) & Archiepiscopatum est adeptus, & coelum ipsum votis captabat.

Hic una cum Francisco Pactio, quod propter insitam animo vanitatem ingentes spes sibi proposuerat, consilium Laurentii, ac Juliani necandi, occupandaeque Reipublicae multo antea Romae dicitur agitasse. Tandem in suburbana Jacobi Pactii Villa, quod Montughium dicitur, una omnis factio in facinus conjurant. Ejus conjurationis formulam Salviatus ipse praescribit. Franciscus ex Antonio Jacobi fratre erat natus, qui cum contumacis homo ingenii esset, magnos sibi spiritus, magnam arrogantiam sumpserat. Mirifice indignari, praeferri sibi Medicam familiam: semper Laurentio, semper Juliano obtrectare; eosque passim traducere: nulli maledicto parcere, nullis contumeliis, nihil pensi habere, dum illis, quantum in se esset, injuriam faceret. Romae plurimum ad nummariam ipsam Pactiorum mensam aetatem agere: nam Florentiae nihili suam esse auctoritatem sentiebat, propter eam, quam sibi Medices germani pietate, & bonis moribus vendicarant. Erat autem & ipse (id quod Pactiis omnibus peculiare fuit) supra quam dici potest, ad excandescentiam proclivis. Statura fuit brevi, gracili corpusculo, colore sublivido, candida coma, cujus & in cultu nimium ferebatur occupatus. Is vero ejus corporis, vultusque habitus, ii gestus erant, ut facile intelligeres hominis incredibilem insolentiam, quam tamen ipse primis maxime congressibus magnopere obtegere conabatur. Neque id satis ex sententia succedebat. Sanguinarius praeterea homo erat, & qui, dum rem quamcunque ipse animo volveret, expeditum iret, nulloque honestatis, nullo religionis, nullo famae, aut nominis respectu detineretur.

Jacobus

Jacobus dein Salviatus homo ad captandos hominum animos maxime factus, semper iis arridere modis omnibus, laute omnes accipere, scortis, & comessationibus intentus agere: mercaturae tamen studiosus, & gnarus ferebatur. N° XXI.

In his erat & Jacobus tertius, Poggii illius eloquentissimi viri filius. Hic & ob angustiam rei familiaris, aesque alienum, quod grande conflaverat, & ob ingenitam quandam sibi vanitatem, rerum novarum cupidus erat. Ejus praecipua in maledicendo virtus, in qua vel patrem maledicentissimum referebat. Semper ille aut Principes insectari passim, aut in mores hominum sine ullo discrimine invehi, aut cujusque docti scripta lacessere; nemini parcere. Ipse ex multa historiarum memoria, magnaque loquendi copia mirifice superbus esse: eas omnibus circulis, coronisque, vel ad satietatem audientium ingerere. Patrimonium, quod ipsi amplum ex hereditate paterna obvenerat, totum paucis annis profuderat: quare & egestate coactus, Pactiis, Salviatoque se totum addixerat: Erat enim id, quod semper fuerat, cuicunque emptori venalis.

Fuit in his & quartus Jacobus, Archiepiscopi frater, omnino vir obscurus, ac sordidus.

Bernardus praeterea Bandinus perditus homo, audax, impavidus, quem & ipsum dilapidata res familiaris in omne flagitium praecipitem ageret.

Septem ii fuere cives, qui facinus susciperint; additi his Joannes Baptista ex oppido Montesicco, ac Hieronymi Comitis familiaris, Antonius Volaterranus, quem vel patrium odium, vel facilis quaedam hominis, levisque ad obsequendum natura in facinus sollicitabat. Stephanus praeterea Sacerdos Jacobi Pactii scriba, homo impudens, & male audiens omni crimine, qui & in Jacobi domo haud satis honeste versari ferebatur: ejus enim unicam filiam adulterio conceptam literas docebat.

Conjurationis hujus & Renatum, & Gulielmum Pactios non ignaros fuisse compertum est. Gulielmus ipse Blancam Laurentii Medicis sororem in matrimonium duxerat, eque ea amplam jam sobolem susceperat; quare & duabus (quod dicitur) sellis sedere putabatur. Hic ejus, quem saepe dicimus, Francisci major natu erat germanus. Renatus autem ex Petro Equestris ordinis viro, Jacobi, atque Antonii fratre genitus, Gulielmi & Francisci

 patruelis.

Nº XXI. patruelis. Erat hic homo haud incallidus, maximusque odii, atque injuriae dissimulator: Animi vero maximi neque tamen audax, sed qui rem maturius quamcunque is animo agitasset, expeditum iret. Tenax idem, & pecuniae avidus: quapropter & multitudini minime charus.

Cliens praeterea Gulielmi Neapoleo Francesius non ultimas partes in eo negotio assumpserat.

Interfuere ei facinori & nonnulli obscuriores, patrim ex Archiepiscopi, partim ex familia Pactiorum. Hos inter & Brigliainus quidam homo extremae conditionis, & Nannes Notarius Pisanus vir sceleratus & factiosus.

Sed qui ex peregrinis primas partes susceperat, is erat, quem diximus, Joannes Baptista Hieronymi familiaris. Hic rem totum biennium jam ante agitatam, in quintum kalend. Majas anni a Christiana salute octavi & septuagesimi supra mille & quadringentos, inque ipsum Dominicum ante Ascensionem diem rejecerat. Erat is magni vir ingenii, multi consilii, & sagacis animi, ad obeundas res maxime dexter; neque vero in iis non saepe exercitatus. Magnam in eo fidem Salviatus, magnam conjurati omnes habuerant. Res ipsa jam postulat uti conjurationis consilium explicemus.

Medicum familia cum plerisque in rebus splendida semper, magnificentissimaque est, tum vel maxime in claris hospitibus accipiendis. Nemo unquam vir clarus aut Florentiam, aut Florentinum agrum petiit, in quem non illa domus hoc magnificentiae genere usa sit. Cum igitur in suburbano illo Jacobi rure, ubi supra, conjurationem factam ostendimus, Raphael forte Cardinalis, ex Hieronymi Comitis sorore natus, haud multo antea divertisset, hanc tanti facinoris ansam conjurati occupant. Nunciant Cardinalis nomine geminis fratribus, uti se Fesulis, quae ipsorum suburbana Villa est accipiant. Eo Laurentius, atque egomet cum puero etro Laurentii filio accedimus. Julianus, quod valetudine impediretur, domi restitit: id, quod rem in ipsum, quem diximus, diem extraxit. Iterum familiarius homini nunciant cupere Cardinalem & Florentiae convivio accipi. Urbanae domus ornamenta, vestem, aulea, gemmas, argentum, pretiosam omnem supellectilem inspicere. Nullum optimi juvenes dolum suspicantur. Domum parant, ornamenta depromunt, vestem explicant, argentum, signa, toreumata in propatulo conlocant, producunt gemmas in promptuarium: magnificentissime convivium adparatur.

Ecce

Ecce tibi ante tempus conjuratorum manus scitantur, *ubi Laurentius? ubi Julianus?* Dicunt, in Templo Divae Reparatae esse ambos; eo contendunt. Cardinalis in suggestum Chori de more subducitur. Dumque Eucharistiae Mysteria celebrantur, Archiepiscopus cum Jacobo Poggio, & duobus Jacobis Salviatis, aliisque nonnullis comitibus in Curiam contendit, uti Dominos Florentinos arce deturbet, ipse Curiam occupat: Reliqui in Templo ad facinus obeundum remanent. Destinatus ad Laurentii caedem Johannes Baptista, negotium detrectarat; Antonius Volaterranus, Stephanusque susceperant: Reliqui in Julianum tendebant. Nº XXI.

Ibi primum peracta Sacerdotis communicatione, signo dato, Bernardus Bandinus, Franciscus Pactius, aliique ex conjuratis, orbe facto, Julianum circumveniunt. Princeps Bandinus, ense per pectus adacto, juvenem transverberat. Ille moribundus aliquot passus fugitare; illi insequi. Juvenis, cum jam sanguis eum viresque defecissent, terrae concidit. Jacentem Franciscus repetito saepe ictu, pugione trajecit. Ita pium juvenem neci dedunt. Qui Julianum sequebatur famulus, terrore exanimatus in latebras se turpiter conjecerat.

Interim & Laurentium delecti sicarii invadunt; ac primo quidem Antonius Volaterranus sinistram ejus humero injicit, ictum in jugulum destinat. Ille imperterritus humeralem amictum exuit, laevoque advolvit brachio; simul gladium vagina liberat, uno tantum ictu petitur: nam dum sese expedit, vulnus in collo accipit. Mox se homo acer, & animosus stricto gladiolo ad sicarios vertere, circumspectare se caute, & tueri. Illi exterriti fugam capiunt. Neque vero segnis in eo tuendo Andreae, & Laurentii Cavalcantis (quibus ille pedissequis utebatur) opera fuit. Cavalcantis brachium vulneratur. Andreas integer superat.

Videre erat, tumultuantem populum, viros, mulierculas, Sacerdotes, pueros fugitantes passim quo pedes vocarent. Omnia fremitu plena, & gemitu: nihil exaudiri tamen expressae vocis. Fuere & qui crederent Templum corruere.

Qui Julianum trucidarat Bernardus Bandinus, non contentus suis partibus, ad Laurentium contendit. Ille se commodum cum paucis in Sacrarium conjecerat. Bernardus obiter Franciscum Norium prudentem virum, & mercaturis Medicae familiae praefectum, ense per stomachum adacto uno

vulnere

Nº XXI. vulnere perimit. Ejus cadaver spirans adhuc idem in sacrarium, quo se Laurentius receperat, invectum est.

Tum ego, qui eodem me contuleram, aliique nonnulli, fores, quae aheneae essent, occlusimus. Ita periculum, quod a Bandino ingrueret, propulsavimus. Dum fores servamus, trepidare intus alii, de Laurentii vulnere sollicití esse. Ibi Antonius Rodulphus Jacobi filius honestus adolescens Laurentii vulnus exugere. Ipse nullam suae salutis rationem ducere; sed rogitare continenter: Ecquid Julianus valeat. Interdum vero & indignabundus minitari querique, quod a quibus minime aequum fuerat, sua vita peteretur. Continuo juvenum globus, qui Medicae domui fidi essent, ad sacrarii fores cum telis constipantur. Clamant unanimes amicos sese, & necessarios. *Exeat, exeat Laurentius, priusquam adversa factio robur capiat.* Nos trepidi intus ambigere, hostes, an amici forent; rogitare tamen an incolumis Julianus. Ipsi ad ea nihil respondere. Tum Sismundus Stupha egregius juvenis, & qui Laurentio jam inde a puero miro amore, mira pietate esset conjunctus, scalas conscendit, speculam, quae in Templum despiceret, ubi & organa essent musica, festinans petit. Facinus continuo ex Juliani cadavere, quod prostratum viderat, intelligit. Qui prae foribus adstabant, videt esse amicos; jubet aperiri: illi frequentes Laurentium in armatorum globum adcipiunt. Domum per dispendia, ne in Juliani cadaver incideret, perducunt.

Ego recta domum perrexi; Julianumque multis confectum vulneribus, multo cruore foedatum miserabiliter jacentem offendi. Ibi titubans, & prae doloris magnitudine, vix satis animi compos, a quibusdam amicis sublevatus, domumque sum deductus.

Omnia ibi armatorum plena erant, omnia faventiam clamoribus personabant: strepitu, & vocibus tectum omne resultabat. Videres pueros, senes, juvenes, sacros, & prophanos viros arma capere: Domum Medicam quasi publicam omnium salutem defensare.

Interim Pisanus Praesul Caesarem Petrucium Vexilliferum, quod ajunt, Justitiae, remotis arbitris in colloquium vocat, eo consilio, ut hominem trucidet. Velle se, ait, nonnulla Pontificis referre nomine. Quidam ex Perusinis proscriptis, qui hominem facinoris conscii in Curiam comitabantur, in publici cubiculum Scribae se conjiciunt, ubi locum idoneum teneant.

Fores

Fores concludunt cubiculi, neque eas, ubi res postulat, aperire queunt, ita neque sibi, neque suis auxilio esse. At Caesar ubi titubantem Salviatum contemplatur, dolum suspicatus, lictores ad arma concitat: Salviatus metu perturbatus, e cubiculo se proripit. Ille in Jacobum Poggii filium incidit, eumque, ut est homo ingentis animi, capillo correptum humi deturbat, custodibusque servandum mandat: mox ad summam turrim cum Dominorum manu festinus evadit. Ibi quantum in se est, correpto e culina veru (nam id ei telum metus, atque ira obtulerant) fores tuetur; suam atque publicam salutem magna animi praesentia acerrime defensat. Idem alii pro se quisque viriliter agunt. N° XXI.

Crebrae in Florentina curia sunt januae: Eae a lictoribus occlusae, capita conjuratorum separant. Ita illi in multos diducti rivulos impetum perdunt. Interea omnis curia intus fremere, paucique ex civibus eo convenire.

Jacobus autem Pactius, ubi spem necandi Laurentii se fefellisse intellexit, haud ignarus quantum sceleris in se admisisset, utraque palma suam ipse faciem ceciderat. Mox dum se domum corriperet priusquam de templo egrederetur, ad terram prae angustia conlapsus est. Tandem ubi rem in angusto esse vidit, fortunam periclitari deliberans, cum paucis ex necessariis recta in forum contendit: populum ad arma convocat. Nihil succedere illi; verum omnes hominem scelestum, & tum prae formidine vix sonum vocis, qui exaudiretur, erumpentem, contemptui habere facinusque detestari. Is ubi nihil in populo auxilii videt, trepidare, animoque destitui.

Qui in summam curiae arcem receperant se, saxa ingentia, telaque in Jacobum jaculantur: Homo pavitans domum se refert. Eodem & Franciscus, acceptis in eo tumultu gravibus vulneribus, repente confugerat.

Interim Laurentiani curiam recipiunt. Perusini effracto ostio trucidantur: Tum & in reliquos saevitum. Jacobum Poggii e fenestris suspendunt; Cardinalem comprehensum magno praesidio in curiam subducunt, aegreque hominem a populi impetu tuentur. Qui eum assectari consueverant, plerique a plebe occisi; omnia direpta, cadavera ipsa foede lacerata. Jam ante Laurentii fores caput humanum lanceae praefixum, jam humeri partem adtulerant. Nihil tamen undique magis exaudiri quam populi voces: *Pilas, Pilas*; id enim Medicae familiae insigne est, clamitantes.

At

N° XXI. At Jacobus Pactius desperatis rebus fugâ sibi consulit: portam, quae ad Crucis dicitur, cum armatorum manu petit; inde erumpit.

Interim ad Medicum aedes miro studio, miro favore populus confluere; proditores ad supplicium flagitare; nulli maledicto, nullis minis parcere, dum ad poenam sceleratos rapi cogerent. Ibi Jacobi Pactii domus vix a direptione defensa, Franciscus nudus, ac saucius ex ipsis patrui aedibus a Petro Corsino, qui magna clientum manu stipatus eo accurrerat, ad laqueum rapitur pene semivivus: non enim facile, aut pronum erat furenti populò temperare. Mox & Pisanus Praesul ex ea, qua & Franciscus Pactius fenestra pendebat, supra ipsum exanimum corpus suspenditur. Cum dejiceretur (id, quod mirum omnibus visum iri arbitror) nemini tamen ignotum eo tempore extitit, sive id casus aliquis, seu rabies dederit, ipsum illud Francisci cadaver dentibus invadit; alteramque ejus mamillam vel cum laqueo suffocatus, apertis furialiter oculis mordicus detinebat. Post hunc & duo Jacobi ex Salviatorum familia laqueo guttur franguntur. Memini me tum venire in forum (nam domi quieta jam res erat) ibique multa cadavera foede lacerata passim videre projecta: Multa in ea populi ludibria, multae detestationes.

Erat enim Medica domus multis causis populo grata. Tum Juliani caedem detestari omnes, indignum facinus clamitare. Juvenem egregium, delicias Florentinae juventutis, per scelus, per dolum, ac proditionem, a quibus minime oportuit, interemptum; familiam impotentem, ac sacrilegam, Diis hominibusque infestam, tantum facinus perpetrasse. Stimulabat plebem & memoria recens ejus virtutis. Nam cum paucis ante annis equestre illud cataphractorum equitum certamen celebraretur, mira virtus Juliani extiterat, palmamque, & spolia domum reportaverat; quae res magnopere vulgi animos conciliat. Ad haec & facinoris indignitas accedebat. Neque enim quicquam tam scelestum dici, aut excogitari poterat, quod hujus atrocitatem sceleris adaequaret. Fremebant omnes, Juvenem pium, innocentem, in templo, inter aras, & sacra crudeliter trucidatum; violatum hospitium, violata sacra, pollutum humano sanguine templum: Ipsum autem Laurentium, in quem unum Florentina omnis Respublica recumberet, ipsum illum Laurentium, in quo spes omnes, opesque populi sitae forent, ferro petitum, id vero indignissimum clamitabant.

Jam

Jam ex omnibus municipiis, ut quaeque Urbi proxima essent, magna vis armatorum in forum, in trivia, in Medicam praecipue domum confluere; ostentare pro se quisque suum studium: Cives catervatim cum liberis, & clientibus polliceri suam operam, suas vires, atque opes: omnes ex uno Laurentio, & publicam, & privatam pendere ipsorum salutem, dictitare. Videre erat continuos aliquot dies, undique in domum Laurentianam arma convehi, importari carnes, & panes, quaeque essent victui opportuna. Ipse Laurentius non vulnere, non metu, non dolore, quem ex fratris nece maximum coeperat, impediri quo minus rebus suis prospiceret: prehensare cives omnes; gratiam se singulis habere, ipsis omnibus suam dicere salutem referre acceptam; populo se se de ipsius salute anxio, nonnunquam e fenestris ostentare: Ibi adclamare omnis populus; manus ad coelum tollere; gratulari ejus saluti, exultare gaudio. Ipse rebus omnibus intentus agere, neque animo, neque consilio destitui. N° XXI.

Dum haec aguntur, nuntiatum est Johannem Franciscum Tollentinatem Fori Cornelii praefectum cum delecta equitum manu, in nostrum agrum ex ipsis Fori Cornelii finibus irrupisse. Idem mox & Tiphernatem fecisse Laurentium, qua parte Senensium fines Florentinum discriminant agrum, multorum nunciis, litterisque admonemur. Tum utcumque a nostris pulsum domum suam recepisse se. Nocte atra, vigiliae per urbem dispositae; domus Laurentiana diligenter custodita: stationes armatorum in quadriviis, in foro, tota urbe. Postridie ejus diei Johannes Bentivolus Bononiensis eques, suaeque princeps reipublicae, vir multis officiis familiae Medicum conjunctissimus in Mugellanum cum aliquot equitum turmis, multisque peditum cohortibus auxilio venerat. Jamque tota urbs peditibus oppleri coepta. Sed veriti octoviri, quorum princeps Dionysius Puccius, nequid milites praedae avidi tumultuarentur, delectis qui custodiae urbis praeessent, reliquos, ut primum in urbem venerant, suam quemque domum, aut sicubi usu fore decernerent, regredi jubent.

Renatus interim Pactius, qui pridie ejus diei, quo facinus gestum est, in Villam Mugellanam se receperat, ibique milites cogebat, cum duobus fratribus Joanne, & Nicolao captus ducitur. Guilielmi, ac Francisci frater, Joannes Pactius, in horto quodam suae domui contiguo deprehenditur. Qui Jacobum sequuti sunt, ab omnibus jam destitutum in Castaneo Vico comprehendunt. Qui primus hominem adsequutus est, is fuit Alexander quidam Agricola annis plurimum XX, natus; ipse homini manum injicit. At Jacobus

 septem

N° XXI. septem prolatis aureis obsecrare rusticum incipit, uti se neci dedat; neque vero id homini persuadet. Ut vero magis hoc, magisque precibus contendit, a fratre Alexandri Scipione verberatur. Tum intellexit homo pavitans, verum esse quod dicitur: *Ducunt volentem fata, nolentem trahunt*. Ibi Florentiam cum praesidio octovirum, ne a plebe laniaretur, in curiam prolatus, expressa nullo tormento totius facinoris confessione, paucis post horis laqueo poenas luit. Hic homo jam letho vicinus, haudquaquam sui illius rabidi furiosique ingenii obliviscitur? manes suos adverso Daemoni dedere se clamat. Post eum & de Renato supplicium sumptum. Reliqui fratres in vincula conjecti: Eorum minimus natu Galeottus, impubes adhuc muliebri stola amictus, fugam trepidus moliebatur: ibi agnitus in eundem carcerem conjicitur: Eodemque haud multo post & Andream Pactium Renati fratrem ex fuga retractum obtrudunt.

Bandinus fugitans in Tiphernatem incidit, a quo in aciem receptus Senas pervasit. Neapoleo a Petro Vespuccio adjutus, fuga sibi salutem petiit. Aliquot post dies & de Joanne Baptista supplicium sumptum.

Qui Laurentium percusserant Antonius Volaterranus, & Stephanus, in Florentina Abbatia aliquot dies latuere. Id ubi rescitum, continuo gregatim eo populus convolat; vixque ab ipsis monachis, quod religione prohibiti, non eos indicassent, manum abstinent; abreptos sicarios foede lacerant: ibi demum mutilato naso, truncis auribus, multis colaphis contusi, ad laqueum post confessionem sceleris rapiuntur. Praemia deinde publice his decreta, ac per praeconem denunciata, qui Bandinum, & Neapoleonem aut occiderent, aut viventes agerent capti vos. Guilielmus Pactius, qui affinitate fretus in Laurentianam domum confugerat, una cum liberis ejus vigesimum trans quintum ab urbe lapidem proscribitur. Multae praeterea insequutae caedes, atque omnes conscii partim caesi, partim in vinculis habiti, aut proscripti sunt.

Romae ubi nunciatum est, maximus dolor, mira omnium de Laurentii incolumitate exultatio.

Funus Juliano magnifice ductum, & justa manibus in Divi Laurentii templo persoluta. Pleraque juventus vestem mutavit. Ipse undeviginti vulneribus perfossus erat. Annos vixerat quinque & viginti.

Ubi

Ubi rescitum est a Petro Vespuccio Neapoleonem adjutum, continuo & ipsum capiunt. Hic homo prodigus jam inde a pueritia bona paterna dilapidaverat: quamobrem & hereditatis jure parentis testamento mox cecidit. Domi erat illi summa inopia, foris grande aes alienum: quare & praesenti republica offendebatur, & rerum novarum cupiens erat. Atque is, ut primum Juliani caedes patrata est, coepit, ut erant hominis subita, ac repentina consilia, Paciorum facinus verbis adtollere: Mox, ut omnem populum, omnes cives videt a Laurentio stare, confestim se ad diripiendam Paciorum domum corripuit; nactusque praedam inhiantes milites parum absfuit (nisi Petrus Corsinus egregius juvenis ejus ferociae occurrisset) quin civitatem omnem, bona, fortunasque civium in summum periculum adduceret; adeo homo praeceps ac furiosus, populum, militesque omnes ad praedam animaverat. Demum & ipse in carcerem conjectus, & Marcus filius, ad quintum ab urbe lapidem proscriptus. N° XXI.

Paucis post diebus cum juges pluviae essent insequutae, repente ex omnibus agris magna vis hominum in urbem confluit. Nefas esse clamitant Jacobi Pactii corpus in sacro conditum. Ideo tandiu perpluisse, quod hominem nefarium, & qui ne in morte quidem religionis ullam, aut Dei, rationem habuerit, contra jus, fasque in templo condiderint. Officere id (quae vetus est rusticorum superstitio) lactentibus adhuc frumentis; idem & plebs omnis, ut in tali re assolet, passim dictitare. Mox vero ad ipsum sepulcri locum conveniunt frequentes, effossumque hominis cadaver, in pomerio defodiunt: Statimque foedatus nubibus aer (adeo plebis opinioni fortuna favebat) Solis fulgorem coepit ostendere.

Postridie ejus diei, id quod monstri simile visum est, puerorum ingens multitudo, velut quibusdam furiarum arcanis facibus accensa, conditum rursus cadaver effodiunt; prohibentem nescio quem, parum abfuit, quin lapidibus necarent. Eum, quo fuerat suffocatus laqueo adprehendunt, multis convitiis ac ludibriis per omnes urbis vicos raptant. Alii enim perridiculum praecuntes, decedere viae obvios jubere, quod se equitem insignem dicerent adducere; alii baculis, stimulisque increpitantes monere hominem, ne praestolantibus se in foro civibus esset in mora: Mox ad suas adductum aedes, januam capite pulsare subigunt, simul exclamant: ecquis intus familiarium sit, ecquis redeuntem magno comitatu domum excipiat. In forum venire prohibiti, ad Arni flumen contendunt, eoque cadaver abjiciunt. Id cum supernataret, magna vis rusticorum convitia fundentes subsequebantur. Unde

Nº XXI. de & quidam non irridicule dixisse fertur; fuisse illi omnia ex sententia successura, si quem extinctus habuit populi comitatum, & vivens habuisset.

Multa praeterea jocularia carmina in Jacobi Pactii contumeliam, inque omnium conjuratorum detestationem passim per urbem a pueris cantitata; multi undique famosi libelli in eosdem conscripti.

Bona eorum in publicum adducta; factumque Senatusconsultum ne quis post eam diem ejus nomen familiae usurparet; ne qua usquam Pactiorum insignia remanerent: neve quis nostra in Rep. affinitatem cum ipsis contraheret: qui contra faceret, eum contra Remp. contraque Senatus auctoritatem facere.

Ex hac tanta rerum commutatione, saepe ego de humanae fortunae instabilitate sum admonitus, maximeque admiratus incredibilem omnium de Juliani interitu dolorem. Cujus quae forma corporis, quive habitus, qui mores fuerint, paucis absolvam. Statura fuit procera, quadrato corpore, magno, & prominenti pectore; teretibus, ac musculosis brachiis, validis articulis, compressa alvo, amplis femoribus, suris aliquanto plenioribus, venegetis, nigrisque oculis, acri visu, subnigro colore, multa coma, capillo nigro, & promisso, atque in occiput a fronte rejecto: equitandi, jaculandique gnarus: saltu et palaestra excellens: venatu mirum in modum delectari solitus: vigiliae, atque inediae juxta patiens: potionis adeo exigue, ut ea aliquando vel integrum diem sponte abstinuerit. Magni erat animi; maximae constantiae; religionis, & bonorum morum cultor; picturam maxime amplectebatur, & musicam, atque omne munditiarum genus: ingenio erat ad Poesin non inepto. Scripsit nonnulla Etrusca carmina, mire gravia, & sententiarum plena: amatoria carmina libens lectitabat. Facundus erat, & prudens, minime tamen promptus. Idem & urbanitatum mirus amator, & ipse non inurbanus: mendaces magnopere oderat, & injuriarum memores. In cultu corporis mediocris; mire vero elegans, & lautus. Gravis decorusque erat ejus incessus; atque omnino dignitatis plenus. Obsequii erat multi, multae humanitatis. Magnae in fratrem pietatis, atque observantiae; magni roboris, et virtutis. Haec illa, atque alia charum populo, charum suis, dum vixit, reddebant. Haec eadem nobis omnibus luctuosam egregii Juvenis, atque acerbissimam memoriam relinquunt. Deum tamen optimum, maximumque ne prohibeat precamur:

Hunc saltem everso Juvenem succurrere saeclo.

Anno MCCCCLXXVIII.

Jacopo

Nº XXII.

Jacopo de' Pazzi Laurentio Medici Florentiae.

MAGNIFICO Lorenzo. Io mi raccomando sempre alla tua buona gratia. Sono avizato del nuovo ordine della gravezza preso, e della electione degli uomini, la qualcosa io lodo e commendo, non volendo entrare in nuova distributione, che havesse a dare lungo travaglio alla città. Così sono informato da quei di casa haverti parlato del caso mio, e risposta tua essere stata tanto gratiosa e benigna, quanto dire si può; il che, non che mi sia facile a crederlo, ma mil tengo per decto per molti rispecti, maxime considerando alle tue supreme virtù e bontà, sapiendo tu essere informato in buona parte de' danni grandi ricevuti e del disordine e travaglio grande in che mi trovo, che è di qualità, chel caso mio non ha bisogno nè di piagha nè di scarpello, ma di pichoni; e però ti prego strettissimamente, Magnifico Lorenzo mio, tu voglia essere contento volermi havere per raccomandato, e mettermi nel numero delle tue prime spetialità in forma, che io possa stare a Firenze, che se Dio m' ajuti, se la necessità non mi stringnesse, mi verghognerei a supplicarti o richiederti di quello non fusse la verità, o che t' avesse a dare alchuno charicho. In effecto ogni mia fede e speranza è in te, e sapiendo io che le parole teco sono superflue, farò sanza più, dire raccommandandomi di nuovo a te, che Iddio in felicissimo stato ti conservi. In Avignone a dì 21. di Dicembre 1474. Nº XXII.

Idem.

Magnifico Lorenzo. Io mi raccommando sempre alla tua buona gratia. Sono avisato della tua valetudine per lo Dio gratia, e mediante l' acqua della Poretta, essere sanza più dubio di febre, e ne se ito a Pisa per pigliare aria, di che ricevo singularissimo piacere, & a Dio piaccia in buona felicità lungo tempo prosperarti. Intendo al sì del nuovo ordine di gravezza e electione degli huomeni; il che lodo e commendo, non volendo maxime intrare in nuova gravezza, che havesse a dare maggiore confusione alla citta. Per lo simile mi dicevono quei di casa haverti parlato del caso mio, e la risposta tua non potrebbe essere stata più amorevole nè più gratiosa, di che mi rendono certissimo per infiniti rispecti, maxime sendo tu informato in buona parte del disordine e travaglio in che mi truovo. Il perchè ti priego, Magnifico Lorenzo mio, ti voglia placare, mettermi nel numero dei principali, & chi

tu

Nº XXII. tu abbi a prestare il favore tuo, e volere che io possa riputarmi per Dio & per te potere stare a Firenze. Certificandoti, che il caso mio non ha bisogno di pialla, ma di grosso pichone. E piacessi a Dio non dicessi il vero, come dico. Ma sapiendo io, che teco mi bisogni spendere poche parole, farò sanza più dirti, se non di nuovo pregarti tu mi vogli in detto numero porre: che l'Altissimo in felicità ti salvi. In Avignone a dì 23. Dicembre 1474.

Nº XXIII.

Ex Codice 170. Provisionum Reipublicae Florentinae.

Nº XXIII. IN Dei nomine Amen, anno Incarnationis Domini nostri Jesu Christi millesimo quadringentesimo septuagesimo octavo Indictione XI. die vigesimo tertio mensis Maii, in Consilio populi civitatis Florentiae mandato Magnificorum & Excelsorum Dominorum Dominorum Priorum Libertatis & Vexilliferi Justitiae populi Florentini, &c.

Novum & omnibus saeculis pene inauditum scelus in pernitiem Reipublicae Florentinae plures annos machinatum, & jam prope peractum proximis diebus cuncti cognovistis. Conjurarunt enim in patriam, Pactii, & Salviatus Pisanus Archiepiscopus in primis, & externi fautores nonnulli, qui nulla religione praediti, rerum novarum cupidi, & ambitione maxime ducti foeda crudeliaque in cives facinora fecere, majora & molituri. Nam assueti privatim & publice omnia rapere, delubra spoliare, sacra profanaque omnia polluere, summo quidem Magistratui tendere insidias per Archiepiscopum non dubitarunt, opportuna loca armatis militibus obsederunt; ipsi cum telis erant intenti paratique ad omne facinus, nihil magis quam tempus rei gerendae spectantes, nullis neque vigiliis, neque laboribus fatigati: tandem V. Kal. Maii in Basilica Virginis Matris post Eucharistiae consecrationem, assistente Cardinali, quem cum dicto Archiepiscopo & primoribus civibus, & nonnullis ex conjuratis, Laurentius & Julianus Medices eo die lautissime ac magnificentissime convivio erant accepturi, ausi sunt Pactii optimos cives affines suos & de Republica optime meritos armis impetere plurimis satellitibus nequissimis ac perditis hominibus constipati, & occidere sunt eos enisi. Non successit res ad votum. Evasit enim illorum manus quamvis saucius Laurentius, lumen civitatis nostrae, vivitque incolumis, Deoque vindice, caedes, quam aliis Reipublicae malo paraverant, in necis auctores magistrosque conversa est. Maxima profecto gratia est habenda Deo, quando referri non potest, qui misericorditer, non severe nobiscum agens nobis hunc optimum virum clementissimum & Reipublicae conservavit, cujus salus ex illius viri salute pendebat eo praesertim tempore, quippe tantum luminis & gratiae cunctis civibus infudit, ut cum primum scelus innotuit, armati omnis ordinis aetatisque ad tutandam patriae libertatem, & Reipublicae dignitatem conservandam subito accurrerint, Palatium receperint, loca opportuna urbis armatis complerint, cuncta communierint. O mira adversus patriam caritas, o ineffabilis Dei misericordia, cujus nutu incruenta fuit victoria! Nullus (mirabile dictu!) vulnus accepit, exceptis tantum parricidis, eorumque satellitibus. Cuncti fere sontes eodem die poenam, fracta laqueo gula, dederunt, vel capti venere in potestatem Magistratus, cui curae fuit, ne quid Respublica detrimenti caperet. Ita Deo volente proceres urbis experrecti Rempublicam capesserunt, libertatem & civium animas, quae in dubio erant, vigilando & bene consulendo conservarunt. Conjurati vero, nullo adhibito tormento, confessi se se caedem, status mutationem, aliaque foeda atque crudelia facinora in cives patriamque paravisse, militum manus locis opportunis, unde celeriter adesse possent, non sine magnis sumptibus, & suis, & externorum fautorum disposuisse (& jam adventabant hostes) prope parem sceleri exitum invenerunt. Spectavitque populus frequens eorum supplicium, partimque gaudio & laetitia gestiebat, sontes suspendi cernens, partim luctu & moerore tenebatur, recordatus acerbi crudelissimique casus optimi & gratiosi Juliani civis sui. Visa est eo tempore Florentina Respublica multo magis miserabilis. Mirabantur cum tam late propagati fines essent imperii, domique otium ac divitiae abunde essent, quae prima mortales putant, inventos esse cives rebus omnibus affluentes, qui se remque publicam obstinatis animis perditum irent. Haec omnia repetentes tristi animo Magnifici & Excelsi Domini D. P. Libertatis & Vexillifer Justitiae populi Florentini primorum civium judicio & suo censuerunt indignum esse pati illorum memoriam extare, qui libertatem patriae oppugnaverunt, & in eo fuerunt, ut Florentinum nomen extinguerent. Immo sanciendum lege fore, ut Pactiorum insignia, nomenque decusque privatim & publice supprimatur & extinguatur, nec nisi per ignominiam, cum de paricidis & conjuratis in patriam meminisse oportuerit, memorentur. Ideo habita primo super infrascriptis omnibus & singulis die 22. mensis Maii an. Domini 1478. indictione XI. inter se ipsos Dominos Priores & Vexilliferum Justitiae in sufficienti numero congregatos in Palatio populi Florentini deliberatione solemni, & inter eosdem facto solemni & secreto scruptinio & misso partito ad fabas nigras & albas . . . . . providerunt, N° XXIII.

N° XXIII. providerunt, ordinaverunt, & deliberaverunt, quod insignia Pactiorum, quae nostri arma domus appellant, ubicumque sculpta, ficta, caelata, vel picta reperiuntur in locis publicis seu sacris, seu profanis, dejiciantur, tollantur, eoque loco signa populi Florentini figantur, pingantur, aptentur; ubi vero in aliis essent locis, penitus deleantur, supponanturque illorum insignia, quorum talia loca fieut. Quam rem cum primum licebit, eritque otium, rebellium Offitiales curent effici. Quadrivium autem sive angulus Pactiorum non ita amplius nominetur, verum, mutato nomine, nuncupetur, uti Priores Libertatis & Vexillifer Justitiae instituerint atque declaraverint. Si quis deinde decreti negligens aut temere pristino vocabulo nominaverit, ad arbitrium Octovirorum custodiae civitatis mulctetur. Currus ignis sacri, qui ad Pactiorum aedes omnibus annis per urbem duci consuevit a templo D. Jo. Baptistae Sabati S. die non fiat amplius, sed provideant Consules callis mali, ut eo die quotannis idem ad templum ante fores loco aperto & commodo is adsit ignis, ita ut inde sumi a volentibus possit, & Pactiorum decus, non mos sublatus videatur. Si qua alia restant, quae ad Pactiorum decus spectent, quaeque ad eorum honorem fieri consuerint, cuncta ex nostrorum hominum memoria deleantur & sint extincta, idque curent Octoviri.

Quicumque superant ex ipsa familia, & quot quot ejus nominis sunt, intra Florentini fines imperii debeant intra bimestre tempus, quot quot autem extra eos fines reperiuntur, saltem intra sex menses proximos, mutasse signa sive arma, & nomen domus, quomodo sibi quisque voluerit, idque significari ac notum fieri curasse intra dicta temporum spatia Octoviris, aut eorum Scribae, atque ita in eorum libro, in quo apud eos & relegati et rebelles descripti sunt, de praedictis diligens fiat scriptura, & nova familiae nomina signaque sumpta notentur, curentque Octoviri, ut nota sint haec, uti convenientius judicarint ne hoc ignorent hi, ad quos spectare potest; ex iis Pactiis quicumque haec neglexerit, sed post factam talem commutationem, ea non observaverit, ipso facto rebellis intelligatur, absque alia solemnitate servanda. Praeterea nulli sculptorum, pictorum, aurificum, fusorum, fictorum, aut aliorum opificum liceat in jurisdictione populi Florentini sculpere, caelare, pingere aut facere aliquo loco, vase, panno, vel re Pactiorum insignia sive arma, sed omnes homines, qui ea domi quoquo more vel loco haberent, delevisse aut mutasse oporteat saltem intra quatuor menses proxime futuros post conclusionem praesentis Provisionis. Sub poena florenorum quinquaginta largorum cuilibet contrafacienti aut praedicta non observanti auferenda, & Communi Florentiae applicanda, pro qua sint supposita Officio

ac

ac Magistratui Octovirorum. Eandem quoque poenam incurrat quicumque faciet, aut fieri curaret, vel uteretur aliqua re de vetitis supradictis, & ob eam poenam sit suppositus ut supra, & semper notificator lucretur quartam partem; & insuper quicumque capiet uxorem natam seu nascituram per lineam masculinam ab aliquo descendenti per lineam masculinam Domini seu a Domino Andrea Guglielmini de Pazzis, vel nuptui traderet cuipiam ex talibus descendentibus aliquam suam filiam, intelligatur ipso facto, & ipsemet & omnes sui descendentes per lineam masculinam admonitus in perpetuum, privatusque omnibus officiis & dignitatibus tum Communis, tum pro Communi Florentiae, ac sic perpetuo observetur. Intelligantur autem contrafacere, seu contrafecisse huic capitulo, quo ad uxorem capiendam maritus tantum & ipsi & suis descendentibus, sit apposita dicta poena. In locanda autem & in matrimonium tradenda aliqua puella vel foemina cuipiam ex talibus descendentibus, sit pena apposita & praejudicia supradicta: praedicta omnia & singula sane & recte intelligendo, & referendo cuilibet personae ac rei quantum & quomodo congruit convenitque. N° XXIII.

Qua Provisione lecta & recitata, ut supradictum est, Magnificus vir Jacobus Domini Alexandri de Alexandris Vexillifer Justitiae & tunc Praepositus dicti Officii de voluntate, consilio, et consensu suorum collegarum in dicto Consilio praesentium in numero opportuno proposuit eam, & contenta in ea inter Consiliarios dicti Consilii, & super ea Consiliariorum rogata sententia, &c.

N° XXIV.

LUIGI per la gratia di Dio Re di Francia.

CARISSIMI & grandi amici. Noi abbiamo di presente saputo el grande & inhumano oltraggio, opprobrio, ingiuria, che, non è molto, furono facti tanto a Vostre Signorie, come alle persone de nostri carissimi & amati cugini Lorenzo & Giuliano de' Medici, & a loro amici & parenti, servidori & allegati per quegli del Bancho & delle alleganze de' Pazzi; & così la morte del nostro decto cugino Giuliano de' Medici, donde noi siamo stati & siamo così dolenti come di cosa, che ci potessi advenire; & perciò che lo honore vostro & il nostro ve stato tanto grandemente offeso; & perchè e Medici sono nostri parenti, amici & collegati, & perchè noi reputiamo el decto oltraggio & N° XXIV.

N° XXIV. la morte del decto nostro cugino Giuliano essere di tale effecto, che se fusse fatto & commesso nella nostra propria persona, & per questo tutti e decti Pazzi criminosi laesae Majestatis; noi che per niente vorremo sofferire, che la cosa restasse impunita, ma desideriamo de tucto nostro cuore ne sia facto punitione & correctione per exemplo di tutti gli altri. Et habbiamo pensato di mandare verso Vostre Signorie il nostro amato e fedele Consigliere & Cameriere el Signore d' Argentona Siniscalco del nostro paese de Poetous, che è oggi uno degli uomini che noi habbiamo, nel quale habbiamo maggior fidanza, per farvi sapere bene a lungo la nostra intentione, che vi dirà & exporrà più cose toccanti questa materia. Preghiam voi che di tucto quello vi dirà da nostra parte, che gli vogliate credere, & prestargli altrettanta fede, quanta voi fareste alla nostra propria persona, perchè con questa intentione ve lo mandiamo. Pregando Iddio, carissimi & grandi amici, che vi tenga in sua guardia. Dat. 12. Maii 1478.

Laur. Med. Ludovico Franciae Regi.

Serenissime Rex & Domine mi singularissime. Litterae Majestatis Vestrae, quas illa ad me super infelici nostro casu dignata est scribere, incredibilem quemdam in me amorem & paternam charitatem prae se ferunt; nam & quam ipsa acerbe calamitatem nostram tulerit, & quam egregio in nos animo sit, facile iis litteris certior sum factus. Quod si velim nunc ei gratias pro merito agere, ineptus profecto, tantique beneficii ignarus sim judicandus. Tanta enim amoris benevolentiaeque significatio in humilem servulum a Regia Majestate profecta nullis certe aut rebus aut verbis nostris pensari potest. Est tamen magnanimitatis Regiae, vestraeque praesertim animum hunc meum fide plenum saltem pignoris, aut arrhabonis loco accipere. Residuum nostri debiti speramus Majestati Vestrae Deum saltem persoluturum. Quod autem tam sapienter vestra eadem Majestas me consolatur, ut tantam calamitatem forti animo feram, sic pro certo habeat me non tam hoc tempore meam ipsius vicem quam Christiani nominis indignitatem dolere; unde enim maximum auxilium mihi in tam acerbo casu sperabam, in eo potissimum totius mali caput fontemque deprehendo. Nam & se se unum, multis praesentibus, fateri ultro est ausus, ejus facinoris caussam extitisse, & in me meosque filiolos, successores, complices & benevolos excommunicationem iniquissimam promulgavit. Nec contentus eo etiam arma contra hanc Rempublicam parat, etiam Ferdinandum Regem in nos concitavit, etiam Ferdinandi primogenitum cum magna militum multitudine, cum

cum infestis armis contra hanc Rempublicam venire compulit, ut quos dolo & fraude non penitus delevit, vi & armis deleat. Ego enim mihi sum conscius, Deus autem testis adest, nihil me commisisse contra Pontificem nisi quod vivam, quod me interfici non sim passus, quod Omnipotentis Dei gratia me protexit; hoc meum est peccatum, hoc scelus, ob hoc unum exterminari excommunicarique sum meritus. Deum tamen optimum cordium scrutatorem, justissimum judicem, meae innocentiae testem, minime permissurum credo, ut quem illemet inter suas aras & sacra, ante sui corporis sacramentum a sacrilegis illis non ab hac etiam injustissima calumnia defensum velit. Nobiscum faciunt Canonicae leges, nobiscum jus naturale & politicum, nobiscum veritas & innocentia, nobiscum Deus atque homines sunt: ille haec omnia uno tempore violat, & nos secum volutari percupit. Haec ego ad Majestatem vestram tanquam ad pium parentem scribenda decrevi, a qua procul dubio propter suam bonitatem, innocentiam, animique magnitudinem multum auxilii, multum favoris ac praesidii, ubi opus fuerit, expectamus: Neminem enim bonum passurum arbitramur, ut qui se in haec facinora praecipitem jaciat, in idem secum praecipitium & Christianum nomen protrahat. Valeat V. S. M. cui me semper humillime commendo. Florentiae die 19. Junii 1478. N° XXIV.

Laur. Med. Hispaniarum Regi.

Serenissime & Excellentissime Domine mi rex: post humilem commendationem, &c. Nunciatum mihi est superioribus diebus Majestatem vestram in acerbissimo illo tempore, quo mihi dulcissimus frater meus Julianus tam crudeliter in medio templo ereptus est, ego vulnere petitus sum, scripsisse ad me quasdam litteras plenas amoris & charitatis; quae tamen nescio qua caussa mihi redditae non fuerunt. Atque utinam redditae forent! Mirifice enim tanti Regis commotio dolorem illum recentem adhuc meum, qui me pene obruit, lenisset. Quod si vel tunc saltem & a Majestate vestra missas, & in itinere detentas scivissem, non medioeri mihi solatio & hoc ipsum extitisset. Egissemque jam tunc gratias Majestati vestrae pro sua hac tam egregii in me animi significatione: & nunc profecto quam maximas possum ago, meque ipsi magnopere devinctum obligatumque profiteor. Neque quicquam malim hoc tempore, quam dari occasionem mihi, qua meam erga Majestatem vestram devotionem aliquo argumento ostendere possim. Sed cum non ipsae modo litterae, sed vel nutus tanti Regis omnes meas superet vires, quando, re ipsa, mihi nequeo satisfacere, animo certe meo vestrae

N° XXIV. semper Majestati devotissimo uberrime mihi satisfaciam. Commendo autem me semper Majestati Vestrae, Domine mi Rex, eamque rogo, ut me sub umbra alarum suarum accipiat. Res nostras Majestati vestrae scio esse notissimas. Nos quantam possumus ad bellum accingimur, damusque operam, ut viribus saltem hostium resistamus. Et resistemus procul dubio, ut spero; nam & ipsi nobis non desumus, & affuturum Deum meliori caussae speramus. Iterum me Vestrae Serenissimae Majestati commendo, quam Deus perpetuo felicissimam conservet. Florentiae die 3. Aprilis 1479. Ejusdem Serenissimae Majestatis Vestrae

Devotissimus Servitor
Laurentius de' Medicis.

N° XXV.

N° XXV. *Hujus Epistolae Exemplar extat inter Acta Synodi Florentinae. V. App. XXVII.*

N° XXVI.

SIXTUS PAPA IV.

Ad futuram rei memoriam.

N° XXVI. INIQUITATIS filius & perditionis alumnus Laurentius de' Medicis, & nonnulli alii cives Florentini, ejus in hac parte complices & fautores, superioribus annis reprobi sensus, ac perversae & damnatae conditionis filio Nicolao de Vitellis, ut ejusdem Romanae Ecclesiae Civitatem Castelli nobis rebellem faceret, eamque per tyrannidem occuparet, & detineret occupatam, consulere, favere & auxiliari, etiam postquam per litteras & nuncios nostros Laurentium, & complices praedictos paterne monueramus, atque ut a praestandis dicto Nicolao auxiliis hujusmodi desisterent, charitative requisiveramus, quibus potuere viribus non expaverunt, quinimmo tanquam aspis surda nostris hujusmodi requisitionibus aures claudentes pertinaces, etiam postquam dilectus filius noster Julianus tituli S. Petri ad Vincula Presbyter Cardinalis in partibus illis Apostolicae Sedis Legatus, quem cum exercitu,

 ut

N° XXVI.

ut ipsam civitatem Castelli ad ejusdem Ecclesiae obedientiam & devotionem reduceret, transmiseramus, se illuc contulerat, ac exercitus hujusmodi noster apud civitatem antedictam castra metaretur, & illam teneret obsessam, Laurentius & complices praedicti, non ignari etiam gravium aliarum censurarum & poenarum, quas per certas alias nostras speciales litteras publicatas ipso facto erant incursuri quicumque dicto Nicolao & ejus gentibus auxilium darent, consilium vel favorem, quodque omnes & singulos, qui ipsi Nicolao quovis modo obligati ad ejus defensionem censeri poterant, quamquam contra dictam Romanam Ecclesiam ad eumdem Nicolaum ipsius Ecclesiae subditum & vassallum, praesertim in hujusmodi rebellione defendendum nemo potuit, ut notorium est, se obligare, ad cautelam tamen ab omni foederis, ligae, & juramenti vinculo quemcumque ad hujusmodi effectum tendente absolveramus, eidem Nicolao, quantum in eis per amplius favere & auxiliari non destiterunt, usque adeo, ut cum Nicolaus antedictus, omnipotenti Deo caussam Ecclesiae suae curante, a praedicta civitate ejectus extitisset, nosque in ea arcem pro potiori illius tutela, construi & aedificari mandavissemus, idem Laurentius & complices praedicti Nicolao praedicto, ut contra fidem per eum nobis datam, civitatem praenominatam per proditionem reingredi, & iterum occupare, praedictam Romanam Ecclesiam spoliando, valeret, rursus assistere ac postmodum ipse Nicolaus hujusmodi perfido suo proposito, adnitentibus in contrarium & contra eos, qui dictae arci per nos propositi erant, deceptus remansisset, eamdem, cum suis receptare, plerasque simultates & conspirationes cum eo adversus eamdem Romanam Ecclesiam facere, mala malis addendo, similiter non formidaverint.

His quoque non contenti, cum dicta civitate ipsam Romanam Ecclesiam, ut cupiebant, spoliare non possent, ut adversus eamdem, a qua tot honores & commoda, ac etiam in eorum opportunitatibus auxilia consecuti esse dignoscuntur, conceptum virus diffusius evomerent suis pravis & dolosis machinationibus, ut quidam Carolus de Montone Perusinam etiam civitatem a nostrae & praedictae Romanae Ecclesiae obedientia & devotione, quibus subest, subtraheret, ac suae tyrannidi subjiceret, solicitatis ad id etiam nonnullis dictae civitatis civibus, procurarunt, propter quae non minus graves impensas subire, quam de aliquorum subditorum nostrorum fide dubitare, & in nonnullos, qui culpabiles reperti fuerunt, animadvertere coacti sumus. Quinimo deinceps cum praedictum Carolum vana spe in hujusmodi negotio & tractatu illusum videret, ne ab incoeptis ob inopiam desistere cogeretur, Laurentius antedictus non advertens, quod Italiae pace turbata, & debilitatis dictae

N° XXVI. dictae Ecclesiae Romanae viribus, atrocissimo Turcorum Principi immanissimo Fidei Orthodoxae hosti, facilior ad Italiam ipsam aditus aperiebatur, praedictum Carolum, ut congregato facinorosorum hominum exercitu in Senensem agrum incursiones faceret, ipsumque depopularetur, & in praedam daret, ac plurima inibi nefanda perpetraret, induxit, ad finem etiam, ut substentato pro tempore ejus exercitu, nec intermissa interim proditione, solicitatione, Perusinam civitatem praedictam Carolus ipse de improviso ingredi, & ea per fraudem potiri valeret. Quod quidem cum per Dei potentiam minus eis ad votum similiter, successisset, & nos pro conservanda Italiae pace Castrum Montonis a dicto Carolo in territorio Perusino per antea possessum, qui his scandalis occasionem praebuerat, & in dies praebere posse videbatur, prout poterat, verisimiliter, formidari, ad jus & proprietatem ejusdem Romanae Ecclesiae, data prius pro eo recompensa, reduci curaremus, idem Laurentius & complices, etsi nulla injuria per nos, aut per nostros lacessiti fuissent, in suo pravo animo contra Romanam Ecclesiam praedictam improbe perseverantes, ne hujusmodi Castrum ad eamdem Ecclesiam deveniret, neve scandalorum materia tolleretur, destinatis ad id armigeris, quorum nonnulli ductores a nostris postea intercepti sunt, exquisitis & damnatis viis impedire tentarunt.

Insuper ut eamdem Romanam Ecclesiam, cumulatis contra eamdem improbis favoribus, magis opprimere conarentur, Deiphebum de Anguillaria quondam Aversi etiam de Anguillaria Comitis filium per felicis recordationis Paullum secundum Praedecessorem nostrum, exigentibus ejus demeritis, olim a detentione terrarum, castrorum & locorum, qui in territorio ipsius Romanae Ecclesiae per tyrannidem possidebat, amotum, & a terris ejusdem Romanae Ecclesiae exulem factum, ut se Carolo praedicto cum armata manu conjungeret, quo praedicta Ecclesia Romana a duobus fortius lacesseretur, evocari, venientemque in territoriis Dominii Florentini recipi, ac per plures dies ibidem commorari procurarunt.

Praeterea ad Castra ejusdem Ecclesiae anhelantes, & apertis faucibus inhiantes, Castrum Citernae Civitatis Castelli Dioecesis, quod ad eandem Ecclesiam pertinere dignoscitur, per insidias nocturnas clam invadere, & dato ad id nonnullis armigeris negotio, tyrannidi eorum subjicere, quamvis temerariis eorum ausibus fidelium dicti Castri custodum opera & diligentia obstiterit, minime erubuerunt, nec minus sententias & censuras per Praedecessores nostros, & nos successive in Bulla, quae in Coena Domini singulis annis

annis legitur & publicatur, in eos latas, qui ad Sedem Apostolicam venientes, vel recedentes ab eadem, temeritate propria capiunt, detinent, aut talia fieri mandant, nec non qui Romipetas & peregrinos ad Urbem caussa peregrinationis & devotionis accedentes capiunt, detinent, seu depraedantur, aut aliis super his auxilium praestant, consilium & favorem, pariformiter & per piratas & latrunculos maritimos, & illos praecipue, qui mare nostrum a monte Argentario usque ad Terracinam discurrere, & navigantes in illo depraedari, vulnerare, interficere, & rebus ac bonis suis spoliare praesumpserint, receptant, aut eis auxilium dant, consilium, vel favorem. Simul etiam, qui victualia, vel alia ad usum Romanae Curiae necessaria deducentes, ne ad Curiam ipsam deducantur, vel deferantur, impediunt, invadunt, seu perturbant, & qui talia facientes receptant, vel defendunt, idem Laurentius, & complices sui praedicti parvipendentes, & elevata cervice atque animo more Pharaonis indurato contemnentes & spernentes, multos ad ipsam Curiam Romanam caussa prosequendi negotia sua venientes & novissime dilectos filios Bernardum Sculteti de Luniborgo, Thimoholui de Leytzhau, & Henricum Brandis Clericum Lubicens. Romipetas & peregrinos, qui ad Urbem eandem caussa devotionis accedebant, capere, bonis spoliare, & carceri mancipare, nec non quasdam triremes remigiis & aliis navalibus instrumentis abunde munitas in mare nostrum praefatum discurrentes & navigantes, in illo depraedantes, bonisque & rebus eorum spoliantes, vulnerantes & interficientes, nec non & victualia, quae ad usum dictae Curiae Romanae necessaria ad eandem pro tempore deferebantur, invadentes, receptare, defendare, favoribus prosequi, alimenta eisdem non denegando, ut (quod deterius est) etiam stipendiis ordinariis conducere & adjuvare praesumpserunt, contumaciter in hujusmodi censuris & poenis, etiam per diuturna tempora insordescentes. N° XXVI.

Porro ne quid sceleris intentatum aut inausum relinquerent, non immemores aut ignari censurarum & poenarum in sacris canonibus contra violatores Ecclesiasticae libertatis & dictae Sedis auctoritatis per eosdem Praedecessores nostros diversis temporibus successive promulgatarum & contentarum, cum nos dudum Ecclesiae Pisanae certo modo vacanti, de venerabilium Fratrum nostrorum S. R. E. Cardinalium consilio, de persona bonae memoriae Francisci Archiepiscopi Pisani eumdem illi in Archiepiscopum praeficiendo providissemus, Laurentius & complices sui praedicti, ne provisio hujusmodi debitum sortiretur effectum, per plura tempora prohibere mandatis nostris palam resistendo non formidarunt. Deindeque cum per Omnipotentis Dei gratiam dictae Sedis praevaluisset auctoritas, idemque Franciscus Archiepiscopus,

Nº XXVI. copus, qui etiam ex insigni familia Salviatorum optimorum civium Florentinorum existebat, mandatorum uostrorum vigore regiminis & administrationis dictae Pisanae Ecclesiae pacificam possessionem consecutus fuisset, idem Laurentius pravo & maligno animo tam in eum, quam in multos alios dictae civitatis Florentinae etiam primarios & optimates cives odia exercens continue, dicti Archiepiscopi auctoritatem conculcare, & in iis, quae ad eum spectabant, indebite se immiscere, ac ipsius Archiepiscopi, sicut et tyrannide quadam Florentini populi, omnem auctoritatem sibi vendicare & usurpare non cessavit.

Cum nos Salvatoris nostri exemplo, cujus proprium est misereri semper & parcere, sperantes eosdem Laurentium & complices tot & tantorum excessuum per eos contra nos & praefatam Romanam Ecclesiam impie commissorum poenitere, & illatas injurias atque damna hujusmodi bene operando in dies recompensare debere, haec omnio pro Italiae praesertim pace & quiete aequo animo tolerare dovovissemus, eosdemque Laurentium & complices paterna charitate, ac si nunquam talia commisissent, prosequeremur, & pro posse non cessaremus in cunctis complacere eisdem, contrarium spei nostrae hujusmodi nobis ex directo successit, nam cum ex eo, quia Laurentius ipse novissime multos ex dictis civibus Florentinis primariis partim relegare, partim de medio tollere, & occidere, sicut fertur, intendens, ut latior sibi ad vindictam & crudelitatem hujusmodi campus pateret, se se in unum ex Octo civibus Florentinis de Balia nuncupatis, assumi & eligi procuraverat, aegre hoc ferentibus civibus, ad aliquas civiles & privatas inter eos dissensiones deventum esset, Laurentius praedictus & tunc Priores Libertatis, ac Vexillifer Justitiae dictae civitatis Florentinae, assistentibus eisdem complicibus reliquis ex dictis Octo de Balia nuncupatis, & nonnullis aliis civibus dictae civitatis, Dei timore penitus abjecto furore succensi, & diabolica suggestione vexati, ac tanquam canes ad efferam rabiem ducti, ut tandem sua libidine potiti, in Ecclesiasticas personas, quantum possent, ignominiosius saevirent, (proh dolor, & inauditum scelus!) in Archiepiscopum praedictum manus violentas injicere, & captum per plures horas in publico Palatio residentiae eorumdem Priorum & Vexilliferi detinere, ac tandem communicato invicem desuper consilio, eum publice in fenestris dicti Palatii eminentibus coram populo in die Dominico laqueo turpiter suspendi fecere; cumque vitam finivisset, laqueum scindi, ut corpus ipsius in terram caderet quemadmodum cecidit (quod nedum' referre, sed meminisse horremus) procurare minime erubuerunt; multosque deinde alios Presbyteros & Ecclesiasticos viros bonae conditionis

conditionis & famae, quorum aliqui erant ex dilecti filii nostri Raphaelis S. Georgii ad Velum aureum Diaconi Cardinalis in Provincia nostra Ducatus Spoletani, & nonnullis aliis civitatibus, terris & locis praedictae Romanae Ecclesiae dictae Sedis Legati, & aliqui ex dictis Archiepiscopi familiaribus, partim suspendi, partim gladiis & fustibus confodi & necari palam & publice in Ecclesiasticae dignitatis opprobrium fecerint, & deterrima prioribus aggrediendo Raphaelem Cardinalem & Legatum praedictum in dicta civitate Florentina in Ecclesia Cathedrali, dum ibidem divinis Officiis & Missarum solemniis eadem die Dominica interesset, capere & capi mandare, capturamque ipsam ratam habentes, eumdem sub fida custodia in praedicto Palatio teneri curarunt & curant, & dum venerabilis frater Nicolaus Episcopus Modrusensis noster, & ejusdem Sedis Nuncius ad hoc specialiter destinatus, praedictos Laurentium, Priores, Vexilliferum, ac complices, ut Raphaelem Cardinalem, & Legatum praelibatum in sua libertate reponerent, nostro nomine requisivisset, illud negare, & se eumdem Cardinalem dimittere nolle pertinaciter affirmare non dubitarunt in Clericalis Ordinis & Pastoralis Officii vituperium. Quae omnia in Raphaelem Cardinalem, & Legatum ac Archiepiscopum, Presbyteros & Clericos praedictos perpetrata, communi omnium de eis notitiam habentium judicio damnata, publica omnium fama id attestante, & facti notorietate approbante, adeo referuntur, & eorumdem de illis notitiam habentium animi in hoc suspensi & oculi pendentes esse asserantur, & expectent quid a nobis in tales pro tantorum scelerum ultione statuatur. N° XXVI.

Nos igitur praemissis omnibus debita meditatione pensatis, quamvis immensam scelestissimorum hominum crudelitatem, feritatemque immanissimam, ac flagitiosissimum & ignominiosum universae Ecclesiae Sanctae Dei dedecus turpiter illatum videamus, & a Praedecessoribus nostris in magnos Principes ob minora facinora acriter saevitum esse conspiciamus, *& infra*, habito super his cum eisdem fratribus nostris S. R. E. Cardinalibus matura deliberatione, de illorum unanimi consilio, & assensu, auctoritate Apostolica tenore praesentium declaramus iniquitatis filios Laurentium, Priores Vexilliferum, Octo de Balia antedictos, tunc & qui illis in eorum Prioratus & Vexilliferatus, ac Octo de Balia Officiis successerunt nunc existentes, ac omnes & singulos Ecclesiasticos & saeculares, qui eis in praemissis in Archiepiscopum & Raphaelem Cardinalem, Presbyteros & Clericos praefatos commissis praestiterunt & praestant auxilium, consilium vel favorem, detentionemque Raphaelis Cardinalis praefati continuant, quorum nomina & cognomina ac si exprimerentur, volumus haberi pro expressis, cujuscumque status, gradus, ordinis

N° XXVI. vel conditionis existant, & quacumque Ecclesiastica vel mundana dignitate fungantur, propter praemissa in Raphaelem Cardinalem Franciscum Archiepiscopum, Presbyteros & Clericos praefatos commissa, juxta bonae memoriae Bonifacii Papae Octavi similiter Praedecessoris nostri, & Viennensis Concilii, ac aliorum Praedecessorum nostrorum Constitutiones & Decreta criminis laesae Majestatis reos, sacrilegos, excommunicatos, anathematizatos, infames, diffidatos, intestabiles. Et ut publica repulsa confusi nullum inveniant suae militiae successorem, cujuslibet haereditates esse ab intestato incapaces, feudis insuper ac locationibus, officiis & bonis spiritualibus & temporalibus, qui singuli eorum a praefatis Romana & Pisana Ecclesiis, nec non dictorum Laurentii, Priorum, Vexilliferi, Octo de Balia, & aliorum complicum filios & nepotes per rectam lineam descendentes, quibuscumque beneficiis Ecclesiasticis, quae quomodolibet tempore perpetrationis excessuum praedictorum obtinebant, qualiacumqne forent, spe promotionis in futurum omnino sublata, privatos, nec non feuda ad bona locata hujusmodi, ad Ecclesias ipsas, ita ut ii, ad quos spectant, de illis pro sua voluntate disponant, reversa esse. Et cuncta eorumdem Laurentii, Priorum, Vexilliferi, & Octo de Balia, ac auxilium, consilium vel favorem praestantium, complicum, & adhaerentium hujusmodi aedificia in ruinam dari debere, ita ut eorum habitationes desertae fiant, & non sit qui eas inhabitet in posterum. Et ut perpetuam notam infamiae perpetua ruina testetur, nullo unquam tempore reparentur, nullum eis debita reddere, nullumve in judicio respondere teneri: nulli quoque filiorum aut nepotum praedictorum per virilem sexum descendentium ab eisdem, alicujus aperiri debere januam dignitatis aut honoris Ecclesiatici vel mundani, & ad alicujus loci regimen ascendere omnino posse, postulandi facultatem eis negatam Notariatus, Judicatus, & quodlibet aliud officium, seu ministerium publicum interdictum; ad Ordinis ascensum inhibitum, ad beneficia & officia Ecclesiastica denegatum ascensum existere. Et ut magis sit famosa eorum infamia, ad actus legitimos nullum eis aditum, nullamve portam patere. Quidquid in bonis tunc inveniebatur, eorumdem Fisci & Reipublicae dominio applicatum fore, ita ut ex illis nil transmittatur ad posteros, sed potius cum eis, & sua damnata existant. Florentinam praeterea & Fesulanam ac Pistoriensem illi propinquiores dominio subjectas Civitates & Dioceses Ecclesiastico & strictissimo interdicto suppositas esse, & praeter has poenas, eosdem Laurentium, Priores, Vexilliferum, Octo de Balia, auxiliatores, consultores, fautores, complices & adhaerentes omnes, & singulas alias excommunicationis, anathematis, & aeternae maledictionis sententias, censuras & poenas in tam gravia crimina & excessus perpetrantes tam

tam a jure, quam per extravagantes constitutiones & litteras Praedecessorum praedictorum, & nostras inflictas incurrisse; ipsam quoque civitatem Florentinam, si infra mensem ei a jure statutum Laurentium, Priores, Vexilliferum, Octo, auxiliatores, consultores, complices, fautores, & adhaerentes praedictos, prout tanti facinoris exigit enormitas, & ei facultas affuerit, non duxerit puniendos, Pontificali, Archiepiscopali, qua decoratur, dignitate privatam fore, & nihilominus interdictam remanere, &c. Denique Laurentium Mediceum ac Magistratus solemni ritu diebus festis anathemate percelli jussit, atque cum iis eorumque sectatoribus ac sociis quodvis genus commercii haberi vetuit. Datum Romae apud S. Petrum anno Incarnationis Dominicae millesimo quadringentesimo septuagesimo octavo Kal. Junii Pontificatus nostri anno VII. N° XXVI.

N° XXVII.

FLORENTINA Synodus in luce illa Spiritus Sancti congregata, quae illuminat omnem hominem venientem in hunc mundum, & revelat abscondita tenebrarum ad perpetuum veritatis testimonium, & Sixtianae caliginis dissipationem. Infallibilis summi Patris praescientia, qua nobis clamavit ab initio, *judicate matrem vestram, judicate quoniam uxor mea non est*, facit, ut rejectam in faciem filiorum pudibunda ejus operientium crapulam salva conscientia extergamus. Dies enim venere comminationis illius, *nudabo ignominiam tuam, destruent lupanar tuum, demoliantur prostibulum adulterii tui, & desines fornicari, mercedesque ultra non dabis amatoribus tuis.* N° XXVII.

Nam Sixtus leno matris suae oblitae jam dierum adolescentiae suae, quando erat nuda, operuit confusione faciem suam, ingressus vineam Domini Sabaoth bonos palmites extirpavit, malos inseruit, turrim aedificatam disjecit, maceriem opposuit pro muro Hierusalem, hortum conclusum dissipavit, locustas & brucos in agrum Domini convocavit. Quam celestis sponsus formosam suam unicam & columbam sine macula appellabat, hic adulterorum minister deformam meretricem & corvum sordibus plenum reddidit: emptam in templo profanis vendidit, & ex ejus pretio porcos auratis glandibus enutrivit. Successor inde Petri filium interemit, & diaboli Vicarius christianissimum quemque adortus est. Gubernator naviculae in solam Circis insulam enavigavit, & ejecto Joanne & Andrea, Tyresias tantum & Hieronymos transportavit. Claviger Superorum inferis omnibus ostium aperuit,

Nº XXVII. aperuit, & funiculo illo, quo Dominus ex Ecclesia vendentes & ementes columbas de templo ejecit, sicariis suis laqueum fecit. Pastor infectus sanas oves persecutus est, & suos solos, in quorum gregem Salvator immundos spiritus abire jussit, in caulis ejus congregavit. Propterea, dicit Dominus, *congregabo omnes quos dilexisti cum universis quos odisti, ut videant turpitudinem tuam, & denudent te vestimentis tuis.* Turpitudo ejus nova, quam Dominus per nos universis ejus fidelibus ostendi voluit, Sixti ascensus est, aliunde quam per ostium in Florentinum ovile; homicidium est innocentis agni Juliani de Medicis, quem tamquam fur & latro ante altare Domini mactavit & perdidit: illud per Salviatum Archiepiscopum Pisanum molitus est, hoc per Raphaelem perfecit Riarium, quem quia puerum ad Cardinalatum evexerat, voluit, ut his primitiis, & per sanguinem Christianum defectum suppleret aetatis. Commisit haec praeterea inter Missarum solemnia, dum corpus Domini a Sacerdote sumeretur, ut Christum quoque, cujus se Vicarium dicit, traderet, ac secum faceret proditorem. Et clamat in suis censuris, proh dolor! *suspenderunt Archiepiscopum;* Archiepiscopum, qui nunquam fuit Christianus, Archiepiscopum molientem seditionem, occupantem Palatium publicum, & suspensurum Priores patriae libertatis, nisi se defendissent: excommunicat Magnificum Laurentium sanctissimum civem, quod se mactari ut frater non permiserit, Dominos urbis quod se dejici de fenestris noluerint. O excommunicatam excommunicationem! O maledictam maledictionem damnatissimi judicis! *cujus maledictione os plenum est, & amaritudine & dolo, sub lingua ejus labor & dolor, sedet in insidiis cum divitibus, ut interficiat innocentem.*

Permittitur etiam diabolo defensio, nec vim vi repellere natura unquam aut leges ullae vetuerunt. Et pro poenitentia commissi sceleris, pro dissimulatione, quam etiam per castigationem suorum perferre potuit, pro aliqua commiseratione, quae ab eo fusi sanguinis expectabatur, subdit interdicto civitatem, quod libertatem suam tutata sit, pro remuneratione servati Cardinalis, quem aut homicidii participem ob tam familiarem conjurationem, aut nimium adolescentem fateri oportet, saevit in animas, litterisque necat, quos ferro non potuit.

Reos sanguinis, ne particeps fiat sanguinis, defendit Ecclesia. Hic quia Sanctae Reparatae templum cruentavit, fuso se immiscet sanguini, maledicit mortuo, vulneratum persequitur; nam, ne alteram quoque gladium contineat, armat Ferdinandum Regem, qui aperto marte perficiat, quod ipse occulte & per proditionem molitus est; sic, ut fuit, scelus scelere tegitur, & mendacium

mendacium mendacio excusatur. Nec unquam parcit malus, qui semel bonum offendit. Stimulabat primum ambitiosa malignitas; nunc & conscientia & detecta proditio faciunt, ut declaret quod intelligi non vult, quo opprimatur, aut auctoritati detur, si nequit rationi, quod intelligitur. N° XXVII.

II. Sed priusquam suis litteris respondeamus, modum tam nefandae conjurationis percurramus, & modum, quem nos non fingimus, aut arbitramur, sed quem sui deprehensi sine tortura scripsere, & Praetor alienigena, ac sex viri religiosi a sanctioribus nostrae civitatis praesentes subscripsere: neve minus credatur purae veritati nostrae, quam figmentis illius, ob cujus honorem tacebamus, inseremus propria verba Jo. Baptistae Montesecco, qui mandatum Sixti acceperat, excerpta fideli manu, ex confessione ipsius, quam vir gravis, verus, & tantum proditor, ne Domino suo esset proditor, reliquit. Caussam vero tam insolentis odii, & inexpectatae retributionis in familiam de Medicis, quae semper ei & Sedi Apostolicae servierat, nullam invenimus, nisi quamdam perditam carnis & sanguinis revelationem, qua ob Comitem illum suum Hieronymum, in cujus manibus nunc Ecclesia Dei est, delirat, furit & insanit. Habet hic suus Imolam S. Romanae Ecclesiae urbem, quam, ejecto Taddeo Manfredo, se tenere post mortem sui Pontificis posse diffidebat, nisi vicinum dominium Florentinum aliquo foedere amicitiae obligaret. Major autem obligatio inveniri posse non videbatur, quam si suo beneficio praeessent, qui in ea Republica primates essent; fieri autem id sine status mutatione non poterat, mutari autem status sine morte Laurentii & Juliani de Medicis impossibile videbatur: nullus enim pene in ea civitate patricius est, qui hac promovente domo, patricius non sit; nullus plebejus, qui Cosmianis opibus & pane Laurentiano pastus aliquando non fuerit. Hac igitur impellente rabie, Comes oblitus omnis humani, divinique juris, oblitus beneficiorum, oblitus conditionis suae, qui cerdo fuerat, stirpem Cosmianam delere aggreditur, Pactiam subrogare, ex qua etiam Franceschinum libidinum socium inter familiares habebat. Hunc, ac Salviatum Archiepiscopum, ut omnia ex suorum ore referamus, ita primum secum locutos Johannes Baptista moriturus scripsit. « Noi determiniamo mutar lo stato di
« Firenze, e vogliamo l' ajuto tuo. Io gli risposi, che per loro faria ogni
« cosa, ma essendo soldato del Papa e del Conte, non ci poteria intervenire:
« l' Arcivescovo mi rispose; come credi tu facciamo questa cosa senza con-
« sentimento del Conte? Immo ciò che si ricerca e che si fa, è per sua
« sicurtà, ed esaltar più lui, che noi, e per mantenerlo nello stato suo.
« Avvisandoti se questa cosa non si fa, io non ti daria del suo stato una
« fava,

N° XXVII. " sarà, perchè Lorenzo de' Medici, che gli vuol male, dopo la morte del " Papa non cercherà mai altro che torli quel poco di stato, e farlo mal capitare. Et infra: e in quanto pericolo era lo stato del Conte dopo la morte " del Papa, e che mutandosi detto stato saria istabilito di non potere il sud- " detto Conte aver più male, e che per questo si voleva fare ogni cosa."

Sed haec quantum ad caussam, & primam facem incendii, ut intelligatur nulla lacessitum injuria Comitem Hieronymum, sed ut tutius possideret, quod male occupaverat, in familiam conspirasse de Medicis. Mensum vero cum a suo animum Laurentii & intentionem ex his, quae sequuntur, apparet.

" E summo insieme con Lorenzo, nè altrimenti mi rispose, che se fosse " stato padre al Conte, nè con altro amore, in modo che a fè maravigliare. " Et infra: io me ne andai a Imola, dove stetti pochi giorni, perchè così " aveva in commissione per la espedizione di detta causa, e nel tornare ad- " dietro fui a Cafaggiolo, dove trovai la Magnificenza di Lorenzo e di Giu- " liano, e avendo riferito al Magnifico Lorenzo come aveva trovato le cose " del Conte, mi consigliò con le più cordiali parole ed amorevoli del mondo"

Nonne ex his colligitur Comitem statui suo fulcrum removisse, quaesisse laqueum *(in margine)* ab ejus infirmitate abegisse Medicos, advocasse insanos: nam ipsum sic mandasse huic suorum militum ductori tum ex multis ejus ad Archiepiscopum & Pazzios litteris, tum ex his verbis, cum essent ante Pontificem, & de morte istorum tractaretur, suadente Pontifice, ut si fieri posset, status sine caede mutaretur, deprehenditur. " E quest' ordine " ci fu dato tutto per il Sig. Conte in Roma." Item *(in margine)* tanquam sine sanguine tanta mutatio fieri posset, retulit sic Comitem respondisse: " se farà quanto se poderà non intervengha; pure quando intervenisse, la " Vostra Santità perdonerà a chi il fesse. Rispose il Papa al Conte: tu sei " una bestia" tamquam vellet dicere a domandarmene, nam & ipsum Pontificem consensisse caedi subsecuta verba satis plane demonstrant. " Con " questo ci levassimo da S. Santità, facendo conclusione esser contento dare " ogni favore & ajuto di gente d' arme, o d' altro, che a ciò fosse necessario. " l' Arcivescovo rispose e disse. Padre Santo siate contento, che guidiamo " noi questa barca, che la guideremo bene; e Nostre Signore rispose, io sono " contento; & con questo ci levassimo da' suoi piedi. Et infra: dicendo " imperò sempre, che l' onore di N. Santità e del Conte ci fosse raccoman- " dato,

" dato, e con quest' ordine la Domenica mattina a dì 26. d' Aprile 1478. si N° XXVII.
" fe in S. Reparata quanto è pubblico a tutto il mondo, &c."

Eat nunc Sixtus, & se Pontificem dicat, justum bellum movisse praedicet, recte censuras promulgasse clamet; sed quid probationis opus est? Fassus est, & hoc ipsemet post detectam conjurationem. Sed nolumus, nisi quae vidimus, & manus nostrae contractaverunt, in testimonium rei afferre; scribit tamen ad eum Philelphus vir non minoris doctrinae, quam aetatis istud idem audivisse se Mediolani his verbis: " at audio abs te, quo nibil est " absurdius, magisque indignum sanctissimo ore tuo id jactitatum esse tui " consilio & jussu, &c."

Videte quam obcaecatus, quam perditus sit senex, conjurat ob Comitem, omnia vult patiatur prius Sedes Apostolica, quam Comes; nec erubescit, qui modo panem vicatim mendicabat, fateri se voluisse per proditionem statum antiquissimae Reipublicae reformare, quo melius aut omnem sui Comitis in se culpam transferret, aut ambitionem dissimulet. Haec enim prima ejus in eumdem conjurationis ratio fuit, ut ex his verbis ejus colligitur. " E " così ti dico Gio. Batista, che io desidero assai, che lo stato di Fiorenza si " muti, &c. che ogni volta che ne fusse Lorenzo fuora, faressimo di quella " Repubblica quello volessimo, e saria a un gran proposito nostro. Il Conte " e l' Arcivescovo, che erano presenti, dissero: La Santità Vostra dice il " vero, che quando aviate Fiorenza in vostro arbitrio, e poterne disporre, " come potrete, la S. V. metterà legge a mezza Italia, e ognuno avrà caro " esservi amico, &c." Sed quid Florentinis cum Papa in his quae Spiritus non sunt, & quo saeculo, & qua pera hanc arrogantiam prompsit, ut cogitaret vir religiosus de invadenda Republica Florentina?

Mittitur denique Pisas Archiepiscopus Salviatus, Florentiam Franceschinus Pazzius, Imolam Joannes hic Baptista, qui suo nobis hanc digito veritatem ostendit, & Tiphernum Laurentius Eques Castellanus, qui praesto essent cum expeditis militibus ad diem caedis; alios non habebat Comes, quos Consiliarios suos appellaret, & hi omnes pariter in negotio palam deprehensi. Creatur interea Cardinalis in Studio nostro Pisano suus hic adolescens nepos Comitis. Venit Montughium Pazziorum villam, tamquam profecturus Perusiam suae jam legationis Provinciam; secum erat Archiepiscopus Salviatus; visitatur publico privatoque nomine a civibus universis. Invitatur Fesulas a Magnifico Laurentio, ubi etiam quantum postea percepimus, si Julianus

Nº XXVII. lianus adfuisset, inter epulas homicidium commisissent; adesse autem non potuit, quia erat infirmus, & ut omnia nude referamus, ancha, id est sanguinis tumore tenebatur. Alterum sine altero aggredi periculosum existimabant. Nam alias perducere illum Romam tentavere, quo securius disjunctis ab invicem fratribus homicidia diversis in locis committerentur. Non creditis Romam solitam esse asylum omnibus etiam sontibus, non fuisse tutam homini christianissimo? Legite quam ipsemet quoque Joannes Baptista admiratus sit. " E domandandolo io che modo era questo, mi disse Lorenzo " di venire questa Pasqua, e quanto prima si senta la sua partita, Franceaco " partirà ancor lui, & anderà a spedirsi, e farà il servizio a quello rimarrà, " & all' altro innanzi che torni, ec.

" Domandai il Conte; sa Nostro Signore questo medesimo, madio sì " dico. Diavolo egli è gran fatto, che il consenti. Mi rispose, non sai tu, " che gli facciamo fare quello vogliamo noi? Basta, che le cose anderanno " bene. E stettesi in queste trame parecchi dì del suo venire, o no. Da poi " veduto che non veniva, deliberammo ad ogni modo cavarne le mani."

Proponitur itaque, dum essent Fesulis, desiderium visendae Florentiae; offert Laurentius se refacturum libenter in urbe, quod ruri omiserat. Acceptatur, venitur. Die Dominica XXVI. Aprilis itur ad Ecclesiam, solemniter Missa celebratur.

Domi interea parabatur convivium, quantum nunquam alias magnificum: videte quam diversa hospitum & convivarum intentio. Deambulabat circa Chorum Laurentius; Julianus, quia claudus erat, stabat, reducturi ambo domum Cardinalem, qui quod venerat saeptus armatis pedissequis, & pluribus stipatoribus, quam ejusmodi soleant dignitates, multis reprehensioni fuit, suspicioni nulli; quis enim unquam Cardinalem, dum res divina ageretur, necaturum hospites suos, si non legisset illud, *qui comedunt tecum, ponent insidias*, credidisset? Archiepiscopus simulata salutatione matris, relicto in Ecclesia Cardinale, domum se contulerat. Conventum enim erat inter eos, ut auditis campanis in elevatione corporis Christi, Emissarii in Ecclesia genuflexos & adorantes fratres trucidarent, Archiepiscopus in Palatio civitatis curia, Dominos verbis, ac aditus armatis occuparet, Jacobus Eques Pazzius commissa a sicariis in templo caede, cum manu armatorum populum convocans invasoribus Palatii succurreret. Ingressi enim jam erant tanquam familia Cardinalis Urbem lecti sub Johanne Baptista milites, de quibus

quibus in confessione sua "& a me ordinò me ne andassi a Imola con cento "provigionati." Agrum quoque Aretinum Laurentius Castellanus, Mugellam Tolentinus, Imolae Gubernator cum exercitu Sixtiano intraverant. Evenit autem, ut in Ecclesia ab Elevatione ad Communionem res differretur. Voluit nam Dominus, arbitramur, aut in hoc secum sanguine novam sponsam descendentem de caelo communicare, aut a sua hujus innocentiam mortis ostendere. Ut enim Sacerdos in ejus memoriam calicem sumpsit, ambi inermes & sine ulla suspicione ab armatis sicariis invaduntur, occiditur statim Julianus a Franceschino Pazzio, Bernardoque Bandino lateri ejus haerentibus, infirmus quidem, & qui ea die praeter morem gladiolum, qui ei ulceratum crus quatiebat, domi reliquerat, sicque innocens juvenis, gaudium universae terrae, filius ac nepos eorum, qui semper erexere Ecclesias, in Ecclesia trucidatur inter Missarum solemnia, qui mille paverat Sacerdotes, & in oculis novi Cardinalis, qui eum erat convivio excepturus, immolatur. Vere martyr patriae suae, qui nulla sua culpa, sed quod sine ejus morte nec frater, nec illa subjici poterat, interficitur. Laurentius, sive quod pluris faciens Dominus ejus eleemosinas, quam symonias Comitis Hieronymi. *obumbravit caput ejus in die belli*, sive quod strenue manu & clamore populi se defenderet, uno tamen vulnere accepto sospes in Sacrarium se recipit. It tamen rumor per urbem utrumque esse mortuum, ac superatum Palatium, arcem civitatis. Intraverat enim jam illud Salviatus sub praesentandi Brevis Apostolici nomine, portamque ac aditus supremos tenebat. Nullus tamen victores secutus est; arma capit Patritius quisque ac Plebejus. Locum alii caedis, alii aedes Laurentianas, Forum majus multi petiere: civitas universa consurgit: ploratus auditur eorum, qui arma capere non possunt, sublatos e medio patres pauperum, propugnacula libertatis, panem patriae. Magistratus interea, qui tenebatur verbis Archiepiscopi quo adveniret Eques Pazzius, cognito dolo, arreptis candelabris, arreptis verubus, cum alia arma non haberet, invasores detrudit, turrim ascendit, venientemque in subsidium Jacobum saxis e campo subjecto repellit: tenebant tamen inferiorem Palatii partem Salviatani hanc ingressi per fractam ariete portam cives capiunt, suspendunt, praecipitant. Juventus interea, quae ad locum caedis concurrerat, jacentem Julianum offendit, ululat, amplectitur, Laurentium a Sacrario domum reducit, vulnus, quod ei inflictum collo fuerat, ob suspicionem veneni sugit labiis, parricidas insequitur. Mirum quam brevi tantum incendium extinctum sit, quam nullus e tot proditoribus evaserit. Solus Cardinalis opera Laurentii, qui etiam in tanta clade amissi optimi fratris, & propriae vitae periculo suae erga illam dignitatem reverentiae est recordatus, a

N° XXVII.

N° XXVII. furore populi liberatus est. Hunc Laurentiani in Palatium vix deduxerunt, reliquos omnes sanguis ille innocens aut suspensos vidit laqueo, aut discerptos unguibus.

III. Sic se res habuit, Christiani lectores, hac de caussa, hoc ordine, his mediis tentata eversio Florentina est. Per haec vestigia eum, *qui venit, ut vitam habeant, & abundantius habeant*, Sixtus secutus est. Sanguis optime de Christiana religione meritus per Principem religionis fusus, violata per Pontificem Ecclesia, polluta per summum Sacerdotem sacra sunt. Et haec nequis ignoret aut excusare possit, confirmat aperto bello & promulgatis censuris coeptam conjurationem sequitur. Eam mulierculam imitatur, quae vento detectum calvitium, ut posteriori veste retegeret, nates detexit. In cubiculo suo, ut vidistis, tractata res est: suus Comes Pactios ad necem armavit, suus cardinalis familiam caedi, presentiam sceleri praestitit, suus exercitus fideles fines nostros pro Turcis ingressus est. Quis jam non videat delirum senem his suis promulgatis censuris voluisse notam macula, lutum stercore lavare? Ecquis fidelis non moveatur ad tam sceleratam machinationem, studeatque saluti suae per nostrum periculum providere? Non enim pro sua, sed Domini caussa claves expediunt, qui ligandi atque solvendi auctoritatem habent. Non adimunt defensionem, qui judices esse volunt, non imprimunt censuras, qui officio satisfacturi sunt, non evaginant gladium, qui nolunt mortem peccatoris, sed ut magis convertatur & vivat. Non jubent, solvat nemo, exigant omnes, qui suum unicuique tribuunt, cum hi praesertim quos ad decoctionem compellere cupiebat, suis creditis non receptis, debitis omnibus persolutis, sic excommunicati & lacessiti dispensatori ejus non invenienti Romae, qui illi suas pecunias crederet de quadringentis aureis in quotidianas expensas subvenerit, quae omnia tam vobis timenda sunt, quam nobis deploranda. Sed ad refellendam sententiam ejus (*in margine*, quamquam rem exposuisse superasse sit) ut factis, non verbis, rationibus non querelis caussam nostram tueamur, veniamus.

Hic quidem undecim capita rerum objicit Sixtus Laurentio Medici, ut multis vincat, quem una ratione non potuit: adjutum Vitellium: tentatam Perusiam: defensum Montonium: vocatum Deiphaebum: Tyfernum expetitam: captos Romipetas: Pyratas immissos: negatam Salviato Pisano sacram possessionem: suspensionem ejusdem familiarium: denique mortem Archiepiscopi, ac detentionem Cardinalis.

Quae

Quae omnia tam vera sunt, quam falsum suis machinationibus Julianum non esse occisum. Bone Deus, quam toties labitur, qui semel offendit ad lapidem pedem suum (*in margine*. Quam vera ea vox Pauli: *quoniam & ipse circundatus est infirmitate*). Non satis est Solium illud Pontificium prostituisse; vult etiam censuras in contemptum, & eamdem turpitudinem adducere (*in margine*. Plenitudinem potestatis, quae ad criminalia non extenditur evacuat auctoritate dum replet injustitia). Vocat filium iniquitatis Laurentium, qui non iniqua tunc egit, cum pristinae paupertatis suae victum subministravit, cum postmodum assumpto ad Pontificatum, primus omnium obedientiam praestitit, & semper fuit aequissimus. Vocat perditionis alumnum, quia perditum cupiebat, at secundum Dominum, qui eum e tot gladiis eripuit, salutis fuit alumnus, quod etiam is, qui eum occisurus erat, praemonuit. « Non « me gli fate dare in Chiesa, che quelli Santi l' ajuteranno ;" religiosior sicarius, quam theologus Pontifex. Declarat excommunicatum, ut boni omnes intelligant extra communionem esse malorum juxta illud: *odivi Ecclesiam malignantium, & cum impiis non sedebo*. Maledicit, ut super maledictionem ipsius Dominus inducat benedictionem. Et monuimus, inquit, prius, immo necare voluit, prius gladium, prius adegit jugulo, quam verbum auri. Nunc conclamat post infectam rem, ut verbis conficiat quem ferro non potuit.

IV. Dicit sensisse cum Laurentio quosdam complices ejus. Interroget Cardinalem suum Sancti Georgii ad Velabrum, populusne, an complices isti erant, qui in illo tumultu capiti suo enses intentabant? Populusne an complices illud remiserunt? Partem ne civitatis an totam vidit pro Laurentio in parricidas insurgere? Raptavit ne per urbem cadaver Pactii, qui animam suam moriens diabolo commendavit, multitudo complicum an puerorum? Cujus erat illud threatrale carmen, « Muoja il Papa, muoja il Cardinale, « viva Lorenzo, che ci dà del pane" a complicibus ejusmodi aegre repressum. Vidit ille omnia, audivit, tetigit; modo sinatur ingenue loqui, nec prius Hieronymum adeat, quam Vicarium ejus Sixtum. Magnus certe fuit is complicum numerus, qui clamante Pazzio libertatem, mortuos esse Laurentium & Julianum, palatium, cessisse victoribus, neminem reliquerit vel affinem, qui eum sequeretur; mitis ea tyrannis, quae plures habuit mortua defensores, quam vivens ac victrix libertas sectatores: illud quoque quam ridiculum est, quam falsi, & imperiti judicii argumentum, voluisse Laurentium creari se ex Octo viris Baliae, ut aliquos cives e Republica ejiceret. Per alios faciunt, Sixte Pontifex, per alios Principes civitatum, cum quid ejusmodi

Nº XXVII.

modi est agendum. Auctores tamen haberi voluit eorum, quae populo sint placitura; & ne longe exempla petantur, cum primum in hos parricidas animadvertendum fuit, Magistratu se Laurentius abdicavit, acceptarat id, ut nimiam illius dignitatis in se licentiam corrigeret, & ut extorres quidam per eum in patriam revocarentur, non novi proscriberentur. Nunc vis eum omnia posse in Florentina Republica, quo melius communibus jaculis privatam simultatem ferias, nunc adeo debilem effingis, ut esse in Magistratu indigeat, quo aliquid in ea pro arbitrio statuere possit. Sistas, Sixte, oportet, si vis hanc tuam declarationem, non confusionem appellari. Sed quid verba singula repellimus? Cuperemus pro honore Romanae Sedis, ut una saltem clausula praeter illam (licet immeriti) in tam longo processu, vel excessu potius veritate niteretur, nam illa de fratrum nostrorum consensu quid mendacius, quid impudentius! Verius dixisset de filii nostri Hieronymi sinu, nam fratres illi sui viri sanctissimi nunquam tot mendaciis consenserunt: vivi sunt, possunt interrogari; sed credite, fideles; Monacho ad ultimum ad summum gradum provecto nihil frontosius, nihil privati appetitus pertinacius, publici honoris negligentius.

I. Quantum autem ad Nicolaum Vitellium, juvere hominem Florentini, ne sua patria ejiceretur, dum is praesertim nec rebellabat, nec unquam alias tam obediens Ecclesiae fuit, qui ita ex foedere icto de voluntate Pauli Pontificis per Sixtum quoque alioquin confirmato tenebatur. Revocari autem id subito lege ulla non permittebatur, cum hoc quod Tifernates cum Florentinis contraxerant, liberum esset, duraret & per conservationem sua cum Ecclesia initum esset & concessum, illa enim perturbatis, & in media eorum obedientia ac pace Italiae exercitus immissis, quid sibi voluit, quid subesse caussae poterat, quid externos, ne dum conjunctos exire in occursum non deberet? Utendum quidem fuit licentia, ne dum concesso foedere, quod saltem intelligeretur Pontifex ne, an militaris excursio improvisam illam calamitatem inferret. Nam patuit postea quid statui Florentino illius civitatis motus portendebat, quanquam multarum caedium & perturbationum fomes erat & initium. Fuit insuper auxilium illud ejusmodi, ut fidem Ligae servaret, Pontificis mentem offendere non posset: nam Legati copialas tam verum est alioquin fuisse lacessitas, quam falsum Florentinos eam solvere obsidionem non potuisse, si voluissent. Hujus rei testem alium nolumus, quam nepotem suum, ipsum scilicet Cardinalem S. Petri ad Vincula, quem is falso in testimonium suum Bullis inseruit. Fatetur hic ingenue palam se nunquam in ea legatione aut Laurentium, aut aliquid Laurentii contra Ecclesiam vidisse;

vidisse; dignior nepos thiara, quam patruus pileo. Fuit absolutus praeterea jam tertio Laurentius ab omni, si quem, ob missos a principio milites fines defensuros, in canonem incidisset. Nam quartus hic est annus hujus rei, cujus nunc judicium repetit, immemor, quod Dominus bis in idipsum non judicat, immemor quod Salvator dixit, *si peccaverit in te frater tuus, vade & corripe eum inter te & ipsum solum*, immemor, quod subjunxit etiam, *septuagies septies*, immemor illius ad Petrum, cujus tam vices gerit, quam monitum servat, *mitte gladium tuum in vaginam, nam qui gladio ferit, gladio perit.* N° XXVII.

At queritur revocatum post ope Laurentii in patriam Vitellium tanquam ea imprudentia sint Florentini, ut malint jacentem erigere, quam stantem non tueri. Durasset Vitellius, permansisset Tiferni Vitellius, si Florentinus manum apposuisset; quid enim obstabat, quo minus, capta urbe, arx quoque imperfecta caperetur, nisi quod deficientibus externis amicis, defecere & interni qui eum revocaverant. Nam Joannem Vitelli Vitellii filium, qui eorum stipendiis militabat, nedum reliquos tenuerunt Praetores Florentini, ne patrem contra Ecclesiam sequeretur, ita ut ejectum se Tiferno Vitellius a Florentinis non revocatum quereretur. Laurentium vero postmodum revocasse Nicolajum ex agro patriae suae vicino, & praeter auctoritatem Florentinae Libertatis transtulisse Pisas, quo pacatus Sixtus civitate illa poti-retur, non dicit. Subticet beneficia, offensas derivat in crimina, suspiciones affert pro commissis, in non subditos, non confessos, non convinctos, non citatos sententiam profert excommunicationis. Sic redditur pro bono malum, sic fratilis gratitudo pro custodito sublatum Tifernum queritur. Sic quod tumultuarie coepit, tumultuarie & nullo servato juris ordine prosequitur.

II. Sunt juncti foedere Florentini cum Perusinis, & his Perusinis, qui Comiti Carolo adversantur, Pontifici favent, & culpat Vicarius veritatis Laurentium, quod per Comitem Carolum, quaesierit abducere Perusiam ab Ecclesiae reverentia. Vanum omnino & ridiculum mendacium, & quod se ipsum solvat, sociasque calumnias apud recta judicia mentitas demonstret. Nam hi quoque Perusini, qui Caroli partes sequebantur, cum Florentiae exularent in Pactiana conjuratione deprehensi cum reliquis, qui Archiepiscopum ad occupandum Palatium secuti sunt, periere. Et, inquit, ut subdat Perusiam per Carolum suae tyrannidi. Subditur ne per reditum unius civis tam facile populosissima civitas nunquam verum jugum passa servitutis? Erat ne insuper Comes Carolus tam servus, ut praestaret ei secum pa-

N° XXVII. triam alienae subdere ditioni? Tyrannus praeterea Laurentius ne est, qui suo exercitu potuerit rem tantam aggredi? At forsan discessus Caroli a Venetis fuit adeo ignotus, ut simulatus putari posset. Pudet respondere tam puerilibus verbis & impudenti mendacio verecundam apponere veritatem. Credimus eum congerere in hanc Bullam voluisse quidquid adversi in suo Pontificatu, quidquid poenarum offenderit; tot enim pene execrationes in suis litteris conglutinat, quot vulnera Juliano etiam jacenti sicarius ejus inflixit, ut idem judex videretur & occisor. Unam tamen injustam juste poenam adhibuit. Privavit Pisanos dignitate Archiepiscopali, qui nihil aliud egerunt, quam quod cives duos in eo suspendio amisere, & id fecit, putamus, quia voluit etiam habere partem cum his, qui illos privarunt Archiepiscopos, & sentire in aliquo cum Presbytericidis, ut senserat cum homicidis. Verius quidem privarat eos (*in margine*, tam antiqua dignitate) cum Pisanae eorum Ecclesiae Simoniacum praefecit lenonem hereticum. Sed hanc novam excogitavit privationem, ut cognosceretis a multitudine poenarum ejus tam odii copiam, quam justitiae paupertatem (*in margine*, Florentinae quoque Ecclesiae tam justus fuit quam pius. Interdixit illam prius armis quam censuris, prius vetuit homicidio, quam interdicto divinum in ea celebrari officium, & id etiam credimus, ut intelligeretis praecedere in eo diabolum, subseqni Angelum, mucronem spiritualem temporalis esse ministrum. At inquit Paulus; *si quis templum Dei violaverit, disperdet illum Deus*).

III. Objicit tertio loco obsessum a se Montonium adjutum fuisse a populo Florentino, & ad fidem faciendam quosdam interceptos milites subsidiarios adducit. Deus immortalis! quam fulcimus pluribus, quod debilius videmus! Ipse, qui Comitem Carolum in Senenses pepulerat, Florentinos, qui hominem abscedere jusserunt, accusat. Nos jure ne, an injuria nobilis Senex ad propria rediens sua sede spoliatus fuerit, unde illi incubuit post necessitas, ut vivere posset, sua a Senensibus repetere, non requirimus. Nolumus enim quae nostri judicii non sunt, ut Sixtus nobis affirmare. Sed ob aliud quam Montonium, ob aliud venisse illuc castra Sixtiana ostendemus. Legite hanc sui Joannis Baptistae narrationem, non extortam cruciatu, nec ad ejus rei fidem exactam: cognoscetis Sixtum proditionem proditione voluisse occulere, imitatum eas mulierculas, quae cum ipsae meretrices sint, alias fornicarias appellant. Haec sunt verba Jo. Baptistae, mendacium illud, dum aliud narrat, aperientia. « Dipoi comenzò andare per il tavolero fatto del « Conte Carlo, e per dicta cagione bisognò mettere insieme ognuno, che « l' hebbero molto caro, & essendo il campo del Conte Carlo in quello di « Siena,

N° XXVII.

" Siena, e comprendendosi chiaramente la cosa non potere aver durata, fu " fatta deliberatione d' andare a campo a Montone, e tenere in tempo l' as- " sedio più che si posseva, acciochè chostoro havessero tempo a dare ordine " alla espedizione, e per decta cagione venne Francesco de' Pazzi in quello " tempo quì in Fiorenza con dimostratione di fuggire l' aere, &c. *Et infra.* " E da parte del Conte gli sollecitai assai a decta espedizione prima ch' el " campo si dividesse. Loro me resposero, che non bisognava speroni, ma " morso, & ad omne modo vederà spedirla in questo tempo, e che io stesse " parato, che sperava avvisarme presto quello havesse a fare, e che al suo " avviso non preterisse niente, & io dissi di farlo, e con questo me n' andai; " & non trovando chostoro comodità di farlo in quello tempo, deliberarono " lasciare stare sin a tempo nuovo, & avvisò che se deviasse il campo."

Et scribit in suis censuris bonus Pontifex ad pacem Italiae conservandam se illuc suas copias misisse. Pax ne Italiae erat, an perturbatio? An aditus Turcorum per eversionem Florentinae civitatis, commotio omnium Christianorum? Sunt ociosi Veneti pugnantes tot annos contra Turcos pro universa Christianitate; quid eos abducere a muro Hierusalem in auxilium sociorum quaerit? Est bonus Auditor spiritus prophetici *Orfano tu eris adjutor*; quid puerum Ducem Mediolani bellis implicare conatur? Est Florentinis forsan foedus cum eo, qui irritat Turcum in Christianos, qui eorum agrum diripit, incendit oppida, civitatem premit? Nunc intelligimus cur vendebat Ecclesias. Habebat unde simoniam excusare posset: in propugnatores fidei: in pupillum & viduam: in eos qui semper Ecclesiae partes secuti sunt. Credebatis omnia Tyresianas crepidas obligurisse. Restabat & quod in hoc sanctum opus exponere posset. Appellat bellum pacem noster hic Vicarius veritatis, ut omnia ei inversa sunt, & a contrario sensu interpretata. In cervices Florentinorum, in jugulum hujus populi, qui toties sanguinem suum pro dignitate Pontificum fudit, vicinus ille ad Montonium exercitus cogebatur, ut cum primum conjurati in urbe homicidium commisissent, externa haec auxilia ad fovendam proditionem, vel diripiendam potius opulentissimam civitatem convolarent. Nam is exercitus nonne illius Sixti erat, qui Spoletum, Tudertumque Apostoli Petri urbes sine caussa diripuit? Et quid pietatis in alienas sperari poterat, si in suas, dum longa processione Legatum excipiunt, tam crudeliter saevitum est? Quod si Montonio opem ferre voluissent Florentini, non erat ea vis obsidionis, non tam male munitum oppidum, ut propinqua hyeme, nec loci domino, duce fortissimo absente, defendi non posset. Sed facies ejus mendacii, ut ostendimus, tam deformis est,

quam

N° XXVII. quam vultus male compositus. Nam nec illud quoque huic purgationi deest, quod in omnibus suis rebus abunde semper subministratur, repugnantia scilicet, & sui ipsius redargutio. Immemor enim omnium, praeter quam dolosae intentionis crimen nunc appellat, quod olim innocentiam nominavit. Hoc ejus ad Laurentium Breve est. Legite cognituri quam alius posito, alius sumpto cucullo sit Monachus.

Dilecte fili salutem & Apostolicam benedictionem. Intelleximus ex litteris venerabilis Fratris Fr. Archiepiscopi Pisani Referendarii nostri te vehementer animo angi, quod processus contra Carolum de Fortebraccis facti, in quibus tui nominis mentio fit missi vulgatique fuerint. Non est, fili dilecte, quod moleste id feras; nos enim optime de tua devotione sentimus, innocentiamque tuam exploratam habemus. Nec idcirco processus hujusmodi misimus, ut te notare, sed ut purgare vellemus. Verba litterarum nostrarum, in quibus processus inclusimus, ita sonant, ut ille mentitus esse, si forte apud alios jactasset, & vir os magnae auctoritatis falso nominando, perfidiae suae favorem quaerere voluisse videatur. Nos nihil sinistri suspicari de tua in nos spectata caritate possumus, neque unquam suspicati sumus. Quare hortamur, ut omnem animi molestiam deponas, ubique persuadeas nos te unice diligere, & ad paternum nostrum in te amorem nihil addi posse, quemadmodum ex litteris dilecti filii nobilis viri Hieronymi nostri secundum carnem nepotis notum tibi esse potest. Datum Romae apud S. Petrum sub annulo Piscatoris die XXVII. Pontificatus nostri an. VII. L. Grifus.

Quid dicitis, Christiani Lectores? Idem ne est hic, qui ob Montonium excommunicat, an latet anguis in herba, & est hamus, non amor, quem paternum appellat? Nam eo potissimum tempore Breve hoc redditum est, quo, soluta Montoniana obsidione, Romam Laurentium attrahere cupiebat. Utrum capiatis dolum ne an contradictionem, Sixtianum est. (*In margine.* Nam egregie hic juxta Prophetam *mentita est iniquitas sibi.*)

IV. De vocato in Thusciam Deiphaebo mala pro bonis recipiunt Florentini. Scit enim Sixtus, scit sua conscientia bis hunc venientem ad stipendia Florentinorum, bis sua caussa fuisse rejectum. Recitaremus hic litteras, quibus & interrogatus est Sixtus, & respondit, nisi tribuere nimium evidenti mendacio videremur, praesertim cum vivat Deiphaebus, qui testis esse potest, locupletissimus, & apud illos militet, quam Florentinos. Sed dicat, precamur, Deiphaebi pecuniae nonne apud suos Pactios erant? Nonne per eos

ad

ad paternum regnum aspirabat? Si aspirabat, Florentini praeterea cur minus Christiani sunt, quam Veneti, quibus Deiphaebum militare conceditur? At vicini terris Ecclesiae non sunt, ut Florentini, Viciniores Senenses sunt Florentinis, & ad hos divertit bis Deiphaebus ut ad Florentinos: cur his crimen est, quod illis meritum? Nisi quia noverca non mater, ira non ratio hanc sententiam promulgavit. Sed hanc calliditatem quis Sixtum nostrum, qui tam simplex haberi vult, docuit ut omnem culpam, omnem caussam censurarum & belli in solum Laurentium rejiceret, quo dempto intestinis odiis capite, facilius reliquum civitatis corpus invaderet. Verum altius radices suas agit Laurus. Nimis sua illa viriditas, dum fulmina & hyemes contempsit; nimis ante oculos omnium caedes illa versatur; nimis cognitum Laurentium potius fuisse vulneratum, & unicum, quem habebat, amisisse fratrem ob patriam, quam patriam ob ejus ullam in aliquem injuriam fuisse lacessitam. Nam haec, quae objicit Sixtus, aut publico, aut privato nomine sunt gesta. Si publico, auget Laurentio commiserationem & gratiam, quia solus pro omnibus patiatur, cum solus praesertim, praeter locum relictum sibi a majoribus suis, nihil publici commodi capiat, omnia substineat. Si privato, quod fieri nequit in urbe libera, acquirit haec insecutio tam Sixto odium, quia innocentem pro nocente puniat, quam Laurentio auctoritatem, quia unus tot obierit, ut rempublicam & communem reliquis patriam augeret. Nihil enim Sixtianam versutiam tam puerilem demonstrat, quam fundatum super illato homicidio bellum: hoc Petrum, qui sedem erexit, ne dum hunc, qui illam dejecit, damnaret.

V. Ut ad Citernam oppidum insidiis petitum veniamus, & haec multo post reperitur querela tam fulcta veritate quam superior. Non occupant per insidias nocturnas alienas urbes Respublicae, Sixte Pontifex. Tyrannorum ea ars est, & eorum, qui non per comitia, sed cubicula res suas gubernant. Ignota cordis peccata castigas, qui manus & oris manifestam injuriam intulisti. Centurionis puerum sepelis, qui Lazarum in tua sede foetentem non excitas. Sed hujus tuae calumniae quam vel saltem conjecturam affers? Nonne tua Citerna est? Nimium tuis verbis tribui vis, qui contra evidens factum sola auctoritate niteris, & auctoritate, cui sine probatione, in terris, quae Ecclesiae sunt, credi non debet. Dominus certe, qui est scrutator cordium, suum Adam saltem citavit, tu alienum ne audias opprimis. Si tunc praeterea peccavit Laurentius, cur non tunc excommunicatus est? Cur in eum solum saevitur? Certe nulla fuit culpa, quae nullam tunc ab irato judice poenam substinuit. Quod si clementiae suae id dari contendat, con-

N° XXVII. tendemus & nos verisimile non esse ut verbis clemens sit, qui sanguini non pepercerit. Sed statera dolosa calumniam dilexit, & ut trabem suam aliena festuca excluderet, laborare fecit Dominum in sermonibus suis, quos etiam ne timeamus sanctae nos Scripturae monuerunt. *A verbis viri peccatoris ne timueritis, quia gloria ejus stercus, & vermis est, hodie extollitur, & cras non invenitur, quia conversus est in terram suam, & cogitatio ejus peribit* (in margine: *verba oris ejus iniquitas & dolus noluit intelligere ut bene ageret*).

Peregrinorum similiter objectionem non possumus non mirari, cum & Laurentius semper paverit pauperes, exceperit peregrinos, liberaverit obnoxios, & Florentini hoc apprime intelligant, nihil eis esse Romipetis utilius. Quod si quis mercator in eorum patria spoliatus ipsos transeuntes apud judicem de licentia Pontificis hic convenerit, ac etiam sine solutione dimiserit, non propterea arbitramur post tantam dilationem, aut civitatem hanc debuisse sacris interdici, aut Laurentium, ad quem parum ea res pertinuit, excommunicari, aut praedatores propterea debuisse ablata non restituere: subjiceremus hic fidem oblatorum nisi id melius ipsi testarentur, subjiceremus Bullam facultatis in eos concessae, nisi longior esset quam nostra haec defensiuncula capere possit. Registrum tamen Romae est; tam possumus nos mentiri, quam ipse non erubescere.

VI. De pyratis etiam Florentinis videre potius libet quam respondere. Quis enim unquam audivit Florentinos pyraticam exercuisse? Utinam non fuissent semper pyratarum praeda, quam nunquam ejusmodi artificium exercuere. Quod si aliquem ejus generis hominem ad defensionem suarum triremium conduxere, & is aliquid ex se commiserit, num propterea innocens pro nocente plectendus erat: num tam atrox sententia aliam non requirebat caussae cognitionem? Sed repetita tam longo intervallo memoria, tam impudens fuit precipitanda sententia. Judicaret saltem quod sentit; aliquam saltem judicii formam praeferret: toleraremus. At contra eam innocentiam, quae etiam ipsi judici exploratissima est, contra omnem stilum justitiae, omnem ordinem juris sub pretextu notorii, ignoti, nedum non probati damnari, non possumus non contemnere.

VII. Negatam vero a principio Salviato Pisani Archiepiscopatus possessionem tam excusamus, ut doleamus aliquando postmodum fuisse concessam. Si perstitissemus in ea inobedientia, nostrae nunc obedientiae retributionem non lugeremus. Per eum enim Sixtus, ut vidistis, omnem proditionem istam

istam machinatus est. Zelo domus Domini, & ut aliquid videretur habere gustus populus Florentinus, hunc eo anno promotum, quo aurato vultu per urbem in bacchanalibus & camelo vectus est, recusavit primum, acceptavit post ne obstinatus videretur, qui jam ostenderat, non sua electione, sed ejus, qui hominem propriis manibus consecravit, dignissimae Ecclesiae male esse provisum: si igitur ante obedientiam nihil contra renitentes factum est, ad quid post in Laurentium, cujus opera est data possessio, reddita spolia, receptus honorifice fertur censura? Quid bilis imperfecti homicidii pro justitia vomitur? N° XXVII.

VIII. At dicet, suspensus fuit, & per vos laqueo necatus. Suspensus leno suspensus parricida, suspensus lusor, suspensus proditor; & id in ipsa enormitate criminis dum fureret populus in proditores patriae, quorum hic erat caput, dum cives primarii de salute patriae trepidabant. Archiepiscopus non erat, quem popularis ille furor, dum palatium suum defendit, suspendit. Archiepiscopi enim talia non faciunt; armatus scuto & ense captus est; invasor Curiae retentus. Et quis hunc pro Archiepiscopo cognovisset, aut cognitum sacerdotaliter tractasset? Noluissemus ipsum Sixtum sic inventum fuisse a Savonensibus suis. Quod si injiciens manum quocumque modo in Clericum excommunicandus sit, cur non hi, qui manus injecerunt, excommunicantur? Quid miser Laurentius vulneratus & confectus dolore interempti fratris juxta illud, *ulula abies, quia cecidit cedrus*, de sua vita, de suo statu, de salute patriae anxius impetitur? Quid additur afflicto afflictio, & pro medela illati vulneris vulnus adjungitur? Est ne haec illa manifesta & rationabilis caussa, pro qua tantam ferri censuram sacri Canones statuerunt? Est hic gladius ille bis acutus ex ore sedentis in throno procedens, ut laudetur peccator in desideriis animae suae, & iniquis benedicatur? Maledicitur innocens, qui pene occisus est, occisor & proditor patriae, bonae memoriae filius appellatur. Haeccine memoria, Sixte Pontifex, tuae bonitatis & justitiae! Parricidarum ne patrem te Cardinales isti creaverunt! Hinc forsan cum hunc solus, & per saltum promovisti, hi vota sua reddere noluerunt, qui tam bonae memoriae partem omnem tibi relinquere statuerunt. Perfidia fidem, nocentia innocentiam, scelus bonitatem perdidit, & vis ad nomen censurarum benedictum maledictum existimemus? Non sic impii, non sic, sed tanquam pulvis, quem projicit ventus a facie terrae, frustraque jacitur rete ante oculos pennatorum. Vah qui dicis amarum dulce, & dulce amarum, ponens tenebras lucem, & lucem tenebras, nam sicut avis in incertum volans, & passer quolibet vadens, sic maledictum frustra prolatum venit super eo, qui misit illud; propiores enim sunt ligationi manus habentis potesta-

 tem

Nº XXVII. tem ligandi, quam ejus, qui ligandus sit, aut solvendus. Idem & de reliquis Cardinalis familiaribus, qui armati inventi sunt, referemus Clericos non esse, qui Domini sorte relicta arma capiunt & daemones sequuntur; ait enim Scriptura de ejusmodi Clericis. *Clericatus eorum non proderunt eis.* Quis viros graves, nedum furentem multitudinem requirat, ut ad pectus manus contineant, si videant capi arcem suae civitatis, opprimi libertatem, occupari patriam per proditionem?

Excommunicet eos, qui contra omnem religionem, contra omnem aequitatem, contra omnem humanitatem benemeritos de se cives & hospites offenderunt, non eos, qui se defenderunt, & pro patria dimicaverunt. Ceterum libenter hic intelligeremus ab eo, qui tot tam constanter proponit unde nunc maledicat, quod modo benedixit. Nonne illa sua vox fuit, cum audivit suspensum fuisse ob proditionem Archiepiscopum & Stipatores: "Benedicti vos "a Domino, qui hominem suspendistis; nunquam voluissemus praefecisse "eum illi Ecclesiae." Nonne etiam mentionem habuit de mittendo Florentiam Legato, qui afflictos consolaretur? Et unde post tam repens exorta in contrarium sententia? Tam subito mutata in crudelitatem commiseratio? Nondum erat forsan captus Jo. Baptista, qui, sua confessione, Sixti occultam voluntatem in apertam necessitatem converteret, vel pendet ab alio, & est Vicarius alicujus hostis nobis ignoti, & hominis, utinam boni, non ejus, qui Ecclesiam suam super firmam petram fundavit: utinam boni diximus, utinam non ejus, qui fines sibi extendere non potest, nisi suos minuat Ecclesia ejus, qui suum alienis stipendiis bellum gerit, ejus qui non tam pii Pontificis opera Romanae sedi erat obnoxius, quam hunc suo commodo nunc sibi mancipium fecit. Nam credit ne Sixtus ad minimum usque quadrantem stipendia haec illi se non soluturum? Urbes Ecclesiae nunc emuntur, dum exhausti Pontificis mala coepta foventur. Percurrimus haec singultuoso stilo & abrupto, quia dolor orationem mutilat. Quis enim magis vulnera sentit Ecclesiae, quam Florentinus? Si tam Hispanum aut Ligurem ejus calamitas tangeret, non adeo dolenter cladem illius & nostram intueremur. Privigni matrem in filios armaverunt, & ubera, quae replevimus, in amaritudinem nobis & venenum converterunt.

IX. Sed ad captum Cardinalem veniamus, in cujus oculis caedes illa nefandissima, & sacrilegium commissum est. Qua in re si pro bono opere lapidatum Laurentium videbitis, credetis & reliquas purgationes ejus non minori dignas esse commiseratione, quam fide. Hoc litterarum ipsius Cardinalis

nalis ad Pontificem exemplum est: ipse de se testimonium perhibeat, qui scit, an caperetur, an a furore populi Laurentii opera liberaretur. Paucis "ante diebus, Beatissime Pater, Sanctitati Vestrae significavi liberam mihi "abeundi facultatem fuisse concessam. Declaravi praeterea, quantum huic "Senatui, & praesertim Laurentio Medici ob mirificam in me pietatem es- "sem obnoxius. Postremo Sanctitatem Vestram suppliciter obsecrabam, "ut pro beneficiis in me suo nomine collatis, beneficio aliquo Florentinos "afficeret; verum longe me mea fefellit opinio, siquidem nuntiatum, popu- "lo Florentino & Laurentio praesertim sacris interdictum fuisse, & quibus "bona desiderabam expectabamque, mala nunc (heu miser!) video conti- "gisse: mirabitur forte Sanctitas Vestra, quod me modo miserum nuncu- "parim. Quid mirum? Exprimere non possum, Beatissime Pater, quanto "dolore premar, quod vel parum apud Sanctitatem Vestram meae preces "valuisse putentur, vel in eos ingratus existimer, quibus usque adeo gratus "esse percupio, ut non prius abire hinc meo quidem judicio decere videatur, "quam lata in eos sententia retractetur. Si pietas de Medicis huic populo "manifestissima Beatitudini Vestrae satis nota esset, nunquam tanquam im- "pios eos execraretur. Quantum laetatus sum, quando me Vestra Sanctitas "Cardineis titulis declaravit, tantum certe, multoque magis gaudebo, cum "sensero meo nomine hos optimates optime de nobis meritos, aliquando mu- "neribus gratitudinis ornavisse. Tunc maxime Beatitudini Vestrae me "commendatum esse cognoscam, cum Senatum hunc Laurentiumque nos- "trum imprimis intelligam commendatum. E Monasterio Annunciatae "Florentiae; die 10. Junii 1478." Quid igitur captum Cardinalem queritur Sixtus, si ipse se liberum & debitorem Laurentio profitetur? Si honorifice ac etiam prestitis in sumptus itineris pecuniis remissus, si redditum illi bonum pro malo contra morem Sixtianum est? Quod de superioribus, quae tam recentem & manifestam redargutionem non habeant credendum, si in hoc tam evidenti mendacio non verum deprehenditur: nam ipse quoquemet Sixtus per Episcopum Modrusiensem gratias retulit Magistratui Florentino, quod roganti Cardinali suo & exigenti deductio in Palatium concessa fuerit, quod a furore populi liberatus, quod honorifice tractatus. Sed prostituta mulier, ut diximus, & extra Monasterium Monachus ejusdem frontis sunt. Nos vulnera & necem ostendimus, ille verba & fictas calumnias adducit: nos eversam pene ipsam Rempublicam proponimus, ille pro remedio tam enormis injuriae Oratorem nostrum & mercatores Florentinos, qui Romae versabantur, capi jubet: nos Cardinalem servatum remittimus, ille civitatem sacris interdicit, parat exercitum, ut corpora simul, & animas bonus

N° XXVII.

pastor

N° XXVII. pastor interimat. *Ob necatos* inquit, *Clericus:* non dicit armati erant, palatium capiebant, seditionem moverant, janitorem Curiae, abreptis clavibus, tenebant, gladios in jugulum Dominorum vibrabant, Julianum occiderant. Accersendi ne erat tempus Joannem Andreae, qui cap. Si quis suadente diabolo declararet? Suasit id Dominus, suasit natura, suasit ratio; privilegio privatur, qui privilegio abutitur: nec ideo Ecclesiastica dignitas permissa est, ut clericus grassari in Ecclesia permittatur.

Sed quis judicem eum existimet, qui gestae rei partem unam tantum, & illam multo aliter, quam gesta sit, in sua sententia exprimat? Trucidati in Ecclesia, sine caussa vulnerati inter Missarum solemnia sine ullo Dei respectu impetimur. A proditore, ab hoste aperto judicamur. Et quis hanc censuram timeat? Quis non clamet in coelum? Quis non premat calcibus omnem religionem, omne execrationum genus, nedum hanc venientem a tam iniqua proditione sententiam. Nescimus quidem utro major sit, Sixti ne temeritas, an injustitia, qui censuris & armis credat commissum homicidium & seditionem justificare. (*In margine.* Pugnant sane inter se vis & censura; qui utrumque adhibet, utroque indiget. Vim prohibuit Dominus Pastoribus, cum jussit Petro, ut etiam pro se Christo gladium non educeret.) Censuram quoque aliter alius Sixtus, qnam hic noster exerceat, instituit. Scribit enim hic Hispanis Episcopis. Incerta nemo Pontificum judicare praesumat, & quamvis vera sint, non tamen credenda, nisi cum certis indiciis comprobantur, nisi cum manifesto judicio convincantur, nisi quae judiciario ordine publicantur. Hic Christianior Christo, Sixtior omni Sixto vim & arma in Christianos, censuras contra omnem ordinem juris exercet. Sed qui nec Christum audit, nec Secundum Sixtum & se ipsum judicat, jam a quibus audiendus sit vos judicate, qui & illum & nos audistis.

X. Duo haec sunt capita suarum censurarum: detentio Cardinalis, & suspensio Archiepiscopi; reliqua omnia pro fulcris istorum congeruntur. Cardinalem non hostiliter, sed reverenter, non temere, sed sapienter fuisse servatum per ejus litteras, reditum per rem ipsam probavimus. Quem si etiam vi, nedum precibus & sumptibus publicis in privata custodia, nedum Palatio publico Florentini, postquam audierunt suos Romae esse conjectos in arcem Adriani, tenuissent, a sacris canonibus ob rerum suarum defensionem non discessissent. Liber enim erat servatus, sedato jam populo, Cardinalis, cum auditur Romae captos esse Florentinos, ac eorum bona omnia pene esse direpta. Quo factum est, ut Cardinalis non tanquam obses, sed intercessor servaretur,

servaretur, illisque redditis redderetur. Archiepiscopum quoque non fuisse N° XXVII.
nedum suum Episcopum, quem Florentini suspenderunt, at Salviatum indicat Innocentius, qui diffidatum appellat, excommunicatum, & sine alia declaratione omni dignitate privatum eum, qui per assassinium hominem Christianum occideret. Direptionem domus Laurentii promiserat occisori Laurentii, & licet laqueus contritus sit, non minus tamen ipse degradatus est. Nec dicat habito etiam consilio id factitatum esse; aliud enim illi Palatii liberatores non consuluere, nisi ut subito, & priusquam id Laurentius intelligeret, suspenderetur; timebant enim ne ob religionem id in Archiepiscopo statueret, quod in Cardinale mandaverat. Repentinus fuit tumultus, repentina, & nullo Priorum rite communicato consilio, adhibita sunt remedia. Notum praeterea adhuc non erat his, qui se defendebant, quo in statu civitas esset, quamquam serperet in familias Pazziorum factio. Sciebant autem solere in seditionibus, demptis capitibus, & reliquos conjuratos arma deponere. Erat enim adhuc in armis eques Pactius. Veniebant hinc Tiferno per Senenses, hinc Foro Cornelio per agrum Mugellanum in auxilium conjuratorum copiae Sixtianae, quas verisimile erat subsistere audito eum, qui Palatium capturus erat, esse suspensum. Nonne licebat nascentem flammam, vel natam potius, priusquam invalesceret, extinguere? Hinc Salviatum, non Archiepiscopum absque ulla quaestione, vix scelus confessum e fenestris precipitarunt, nec Cardinali igitur, nec Archiepiscopo injuria illata est. Tam canonice nobiscum egissent ipsi, tam Christiane, tam ex lege vixissent, quam eos clementius quam decuit tractavimus. Quid enim hi sunt aut virtute aut nobilitate ad Julianum Medicem, quem nobis occiderunt? Sed videat Cardinalis, ne plus injuriae ejus restitutio suis intulerit, sublata belli caussa, quam detentio: ut enim dignitatem illam homicidio praeposuerat, sic materiem belli & ansam esse cupiebant.

XI. Restat itaque, ut sententia nulla sit, quae nullam habuit judicandi caussam, falsum sit judicium, quod mendacio nititur. Excommunicatus non sit, qui alios excommunicare vult violenter & injuste. Acceperit Spiritum Sanctum, non simoniace sit creatus, qui vocem suam veri Pastoris, non haeretici hominis vult haberi. Praeveniat citatio oportet ex jure Divino, & alibi quam Romae in faucibus hostium, ut Laurentius recte excommunicetur, ob id enim potissimum Clemens sententiam Henrici Imperatoris in Robertum Regem non revocavit, qui cum ad locum suspectum citaverat. Moveat aliud opus est quam perficiendi homicidii desiderium, ut injustitia, non odium videatur. Vulnera enim fasciolis, non gladiis, offensae indulgentiis,

Nº XXVII. gentiis, non censuris leniri solent. At Sixtus venenum vulneri, hastam gladio, exercitum sicario addidit, & quando obducta jam erat cicatrix, muris Hierusalem admovit machinas, censuras publicavit. Peccarit sane Laurentius quam dicit, commiserit quae congerit, num propterea erat a religioso Pontifice necandus in Ecclesia, num mittendus exercitus in eos, qui Laurentii non sunt? *(In margine:* quae enim utilitas in sanguine peccatoris? non infernus confitebitur Deo, neque mors laudabit eum.) Sentimus, quod nusquam legimus, expugnationes urbium, direptiones templorum, vestalium, puerorumque raptus, sanctum omne & innocens concedi praedae militari, baculum esse & disciplinam Pontificis in eos maxime, quibus, si interrogetur cur bellum intulerit, nesciat ipsemet vel unam caussam assignare, nisi dicat, ut Florentinos pro Comite Hieronymo, occisos pro homicida puniam. Excommunicationis enim aliqua praetendi a Pontifice caussa potuit; belli contra eos, qui semper juri paruerunt *(in margine:* nisi sanctior Nicolao, qui scribit, sancta Dei Ecclesia gladium non habet nisi spiritualem, quo non occidit, sed vivificat) nescimus aliam quam imperfectum in Ecclesia homicidium. Execrationem quoque in Laurentium latam, ex Sexto quantum videmus excerpsit, ubi disciplinans non eradicans jubetur esse censura.

Hinc illam imprimi fecit, non contentus calamo, illam vendi in campo Florae, non contentus valvis Ecclesiarum, ut ejus disciplina ad eos prius perveniens, ad eos quos non pertinebat, eradicans esset non emendans. Hinc etiam mandat populo, ut Priorum ac Octo virorum aedes tam publicas quam privatas demoliatur. Prudens sane, grata ac religiosa sententia; credit eos, qui defenderunt esse offensuros. Provocat in servatores Cardinalis eos qui discerpere Cardinalem voluerunt. Praecipit contra Jus Divinum ac praeceptum Domini, ne occidas, ut ejus videatur Vicarius, qui animam suam posuit pro ovibus suis, non contentus caede una totam urbem involvere eadem ruina contendit; quis enim tam inops mentis est, ut credat, sine caede multorum & sanguine sex & triginta domos optimatum posse subverti? Virum autem sanguinum & dolosum quomodo patietur Dominus illud subjicere justam vel injustam Pastoris sententiam esse timendam? Nam illud quoque sacri Canones addidere contra notoriam & manifestam caussam sententiam non valere. Si praeterea dixit timendam, non jussit observandam *(in margine:* nam praevidens hoc flagitium Spiritus Sanctus praedixerat per Prophetam; considerat peccator justum, & quaerit interficere eum: Dominus autem non derelinquet eum in manibus ejus, nec damnabit eum, cum judicabitur illi), maluntque boni judicio falsi Pastoris damnari, quam in minimam

nimam Evangelii litteram impingere; sed hanc quoque suam hujusmodi sententiam, constans sibi Pontifex, quodammodo paullo post abrogavit. Scripsit enim mox eidem populo, quem sacris interdixerat Breve in haec verba. " Si qui sunt, qui existiment nos defecisse a desiderio juvandae Reipublicae " Christianae, & arma adversus civitatem istam movere, errant quidem ve" hementer, nam neque publicae saluti nunquam decrimus, neque adversus " civitatem Florentinam, quam semper ex corde dileximus, quicquam sinis" tri cogitamus. Abeit a nobis haec cogitatio." N° XXVII.

Quomodo autem quis diligatur & interdicatur, nihil sinistri in eum cogitetur, & militum direptioni detur, hi judicent, qui noverunt quam differat in hyprocrita manus ab ore, ab opere verbum. Et audebit etiam aliquando dicere se ad libertatem Ecclesiae defendendam bellum Florentinis movisse, qui fecit eam servam omnium saecularium: qui prius eam lavit sanguine innocentis, quam suis purgavit sacrilegiis; qui eam speluncam latronum reddidit, omnique immunitate spoliavit; qui denudavit femur virginis in confusione; qui sedem, quam nunquam intulit Italiae, prius libidini unius juveni, prius militari praedae quam transalpinis nationibus concessit. Deus, qui absconditorum es cognitor, qui nostri omnia antequam fiant, tu scis, quia falsum testimonium tulit contra nos, nec oblitus es scabelli pedum tuorum in die furoris tui.

In tam manifesta itaque innocentia lacessiti, non servata forma, non servato jure, damnati, ad quem recurremus? Ad Pastorem animarum nostrarum? At is pro remedio perturbatae pacis, tentatae tyrannidis, invasi Palatii, afflictae civitatis, vulnerati Laurentii, occisi in Ecclesia per proditionem Juliani excommunicat, interdicit, & Curiam ac domos Principum civitatis solo aequari jubet, obsidet oppida nostra, diripit segetes, urit villas, sugentes ubera & omnem moventem feras aetatem militum suorum furori exponit. Oh Pastor! Oh idolum derelinquens gregem! Gladium super brachium ejus, & super oculum dextrum ejus: brachium ejus ariditate siccabitur, & oculus dexter ejus tenebrescens obscurabitur. Ad alterum igitur lumen, ipsum scilicet Caesarem semper Augustum confugiemus; id enim Dominus, ut huic nocti praeesset creavit; Christianissimum Regem Francorum, in cujus tutela Christi Ecclesia est, sub cujus alarum umbra populus Florentinus semper protectus est, invocabimus; omnes Principes & populos Christianos implorabimus, ut quando jam vident simoniace creatum Pontificem, templa, Cardinales, Missas ad homicidia fidelium exercere, Concilium (*in margine*, ad

Nº XXVII. quod appellavimus) amplius non differant, sponsam illius, in cujus sanguine baptizati sunt, a tanta turpitudine liberent: dicimus Ecclesiae, ut qui Ecclesia sunt per Evangelium, quod ita praecipit nos obdurato huic inauditus audiant. Dolenter, & eo impellente, id facimus. Sed cum Deo resistat, qui veritatem reprimit, turbinem metat, qui ventum seminavit (*in margine:* minoris enim peccati est, inquit Hieronymus, sequi malum quod bonum putaris, quam non audere defendere quod bonum pro certo noveris: & Bernardus; melius est ut scandalum oriatur, quam veritas relinquatur). Abeat itaque leno, casta erit mater, angularem lapidem non premat petra scandali, & non erit ultra offendiculum amaritudinis, nec spina dolorem inferens. Stuporem enim dentium, & omnem hunc nobis infidelium morsum acerbae uvae paternae pepererunt. Novistis multi Julianum Medicem, bonitatem ejus & virtutem pene omnes audistis. Cedri non fuerunt altiores illo in paradiso Dei, & tamen in templo per proditionem Pontificiam tam crudeliter occisus est, sanguinem ejus de manu Sixtiana requirens Dominus, non potest & eorum, qui haec patiuntur, consensum non requirere. Mercenarium jam pro Pastore habitum alieno sanguine cognoscite. Fructus ejus obscuri non sunt. Simonia, luxus, homicidium, proditio, haeresis, jam siquid aliud expectatis, quod mentita vestimenta, & quid intrinsecus sit declaret apertius, similem aliquam nostrae proditionem, & insuper bellum expectatis.

Columnae & vos aureae super bases argenteas, lapidem, quem dedistis offensionis, excutite. Non negate suos cardines templo, cujus vectes is jam demolitus est. Turbatur navicula Petri, quod in ea erat Judas (*in margine,* intus est qui concitat tempestatem). Dicite illi erranti cum Domino. *Vade post Sathana, scandalum nobis es; non sapis quae Dei sunt. Infatuatum sal foras mittite, priusquam conculcetur ab hominibus.* Minatur enim vobis Dominus in matre, si pudori illius non consulitis. Oblita es, inquit, legis Dei tui, obliviscar filiorum tuorum, auferat fornicationes a facie sua, & adulteria sua de medio uberum suorum, ne forte expoliem eam nudam, & statuam eam secundum diem nativitatis suae.

Dominus Deus noster, cujus manus est super omnes, qui quaerunt eum in bonitate, custodiat corda vestra, & intelligentias vestras liberet vos a falsis Pastoribus, qui veniunt in vestimentis ovium, intrinsece autem sunt lupi rapaces.

Datum in Ecclesia nostra Cathedrali Sanctae Reparatae 23. Julii 1478.

Excusatio

Nº XXVIII.

Excusatio Florentinorum per D. Bartholomaeum Scalam ex MS. Codice Bibliothecae Strozzianae.

SINGULIS atque universis, in quos haec scripta inciderint, Priores Libertatis, & Vexillifer Justitiae & Populus Florentinus salutem. Nº XXVIII.

Rem sumus narraturi inauditam & novam, adeo alienam ab omni humana natura & consuetudine vivendi, ut nihil dubitemus omnes qui audierint, vehementer tantam atrocitatem, atque immanitatem rei admiraturos. Movet autem nos non caussa modo nostra, ut haec scriberemus, & nota faceremus, sed Christiana etiam & publica, quae profecto his gubernatoribus his moribus dilabatur brevi, & funditus dispereat necesse est. Dum enim Religionis nostrae hostis post tot tantasque de bonis claras victorias in limine insultat, Italiae superbissimus atque formidabilissimus, dum imminet cervicibus nostris, & comminatur Romae, & nomini Christiano excidium, Sixtus Romanus Pontifex, & illi sui praeclari rerum administratores proditionibus dant operam sceleratissimis; insidiantur vitae & libertati populorum; incessunt maledictis cunctos bonos; Interdicunt sacris admodum execrabiliter, ac bellum inferunt Christianis; & direptionibus & praedae atque incendiis, quocumque arma convertunt, pro viribus involvunt; nihil penai aut habentes, sed foedantes omnia divina atque humana, barbaro potius quodam & ferino, quam aliquo humano more. Certo scimus non facile fuisse nos assensionem adepturos ob tam nefarii facinoris magnitudinem; sed fama rei gestae jam per universum fere orbem vulgata, patrocinatur vero, & fidem scriptis his pulcherrime procurat. Quod si ex primis quoque scelerum Ministris audientur ea, quae ipsi cum in nostras devenissent manus morituri fassi sunt, & chirographo suo tradiderunt nobis, erit profecto apud vos omni ex parte corroborata & stabilita veritas. Igitur visum est, ut ordinem omnem rei ipsi edoceant. Ex ipsis ergo Johannem Baptistam de Montesicco audiamus; ipse rem omnem ordine aperiet, cujus attestationis exemplar hoc est, videlicet.

Questa serà la confessione, la quale farà Giovambatista da Montesicco de sua mano propria, in la quale farà chiaro a omne uno l' ordine, & el modo dato per mutar lo stato della città de Fiorenza, comentiando dal principio insino alla fine, nè lasciando cosa alcuna inderietro, imo in narrando tutte le persone, con chi lui n' aveva auto colloquio, & particolarmente narrando le

 puntali

N° XXVIII.

puntali parole auto con tutti quelli, con chi n' ha parlato; e prima con l' Arcivescovo e Francesco de' Pazzi ne parlai in Roma in la camera del detto Arcivescovo, dicendome volerme revelare un suo secreto & pensiero, che avevono più tempo auto in core, e qui con sacramento volse, che io gli promettessi tenerli secreti, nè de questa cosa parlarne, nè non parlarne se non quanto saria il bisognio, e quanto porteria, e vorria a loro, & io così gli promissi.

L' Arcivescovo cominciò a parlare, facendome entendere, como lui e Francesco avevono el modo di mutare lo Stato di Fiorenza, e che determinavono ad omne modo farlo, & che ci voleva l' ajuto mio. Io glie rispuosi, che per loro faria ogni cosa, ma essendo soldato del Papa e del Conte, io non ci podeva intervenire; loro mi rispuoson: como credi tu che noi faremo questa cosa senza consentimento del Conte; imo ciò che si cerca, e che si fa per esaltario e magnificario così lui, come noi, è per mantenerlo nello Stato suo, avvisandoti, che se questa cosa non si fa, non ghe daria del suo Stato una fava, perchè Lorenzo de' Medici gli vuol mal di morte, nè crede che sia uomo al mondo, che gli voglia peggio; e dopo la morte del Papa non cercherà mai altro che torli quel poco Stato, e farlo mal capitare della persona, perchè da lui se sente grandemente ingiuriato. Et volendo lo entendere el perchè & la cagione Lorenzo era così inimico del Conte, mi disse cose assai sopra questa parte e della Depositeria e dell' Arcivescovato di Pisa, & più cose, che sareano longhe a scrivere; e in fine fo fatto questa conclusione, che dove concorreva l' onore, e utole del Conte, & el loro, io mi sforzeria a fare *juxta posse* tutto quel, che pel Conte mi sarà comandato; & tutte queste cose furono comune frallo Arcivescovo & Francesco, & che un altro dì se devesse essere insieme & con il Conte proprio, e pigliare determinazione de quello s' aveva da fare, & così se remase, &c. La cosa remase così per parecchi giorni, nè me fo detto altro, ma so bene, che fra l' Arcivescovo e Francesco & el Signor Conte ne fo in questo tempo parlato più volte.

Dapoi un giorno fui chiamato dal Signor Conte in camera sua, dove era l' Arcivescovo, e cominziò a parlarsi de novo di questa cosa, dicendome el Conte: l' Arcivescovo me dice, che t' hanno parlato d' una faccenda, che avemo alle mani: que te ne pare? Io gli rispuosi: Signore, non so que me ne dire di questa cosa, perchè non la intendo ancora; quando l' averò intesa, dirò el mio parere. L' Arcivescovo: como non t' ho io ditto, che volemo

mutare

mutare lo Stato in Fiorenza? Madiasì che me l' avete detto, ma non m' avete detto el modo; che non avendo inteso el modo, non so que ne parlare. Allora e l' uno e l' altro ussinno fuora, e cominciorno a dire della malivolenza e mal animo, che 'l Magnifico Lorenzo aveva contro de loro, e 'n quanto pericolo era lo Stato del Conte dopo la morte del Papa, & che mutandosi ditto Stato saria uno stabilire el Sig. Conte da non possere avere mai più male, e che per questo si voleva fare ogni cosa. E domandandoglie io del modo e del favore, mi dissero: noi averemo questo modo, che in Fiorenza è la casa de' Pazzi e de' Salviati, che si tirano dietro mezzo la città di Fiorenza. Bene; avete voi pensato el modo? El modo lassa io pensare a costoro, che dicono non potersi fare per altra via, che tagliare a pezzi Lorenzo e Giuliano, & aver poi preparato le genti d' arme, & andarsene a Fiorenza, e che bisogna accumulare queste genti d' arme in modo, che non se ne dia sospetto: che non dandose suspetto, ogni cosa verria ben fatta. Io gli rispuosi: Signore, vedete quel che voi fate: io vi certifico, che questa è una gran cosa; nè so como costoro se lo possono fare, perchè Fiorenza è una gran cosa; e la Magnificenza di Lorenzo ci ha una grande benevolenza, secondo io intendo. El Conte disse: dicono costoro el contrario; che ci ha poca grazia, & è malissimo voluto, & che morti loro, ognuno giungerà le mani al Cielo. L' Arcivescovo usì fuora, e disse: Giovambatista, tu non sei mai stato a Fiorenza: le cose de là, & la cognizione di Lorenzo noi lo 'ntendiamo meglio di voi, e sappiamo la benevolenza e la malevolenzia, che egli ha in nel popolo, e de questo non dubitare, che la reussirà, como noi siamo quì. Tutto el facto è, che ce resolviamo del modo. Bene; que modo ci è? El modo ci è riscaldar Messer Jacomo, che è più freddo che una ghiaccia; e como aviamo lui, la cosa è spacciata, nè n' è da dubitar punto. Bene; a Nostro Signore como piacerà questa cosa? E' me respuosoro: Nostro Signore li faremo far sempre quello vorrimo noi, & ancora la Sua Santità vuol male a Lorenzo; desidera questo più che altro che sia. Aveteneglie voi parlato? Madiasì, e faremo che te ne dirà ancora a te, e te farà intendere la sua intenzione. Pensiamo pure in que modo possiamo mettere le genti d' arme insieme senza suspetto, che l' altre cose passaranno tutte bene. Fo preso el modo di far far la mostra, e de mutare le genti d' arme da stanzia a stanzia, e mandare quelli del Signor Napolione in quello di Todi e de Perusia, e così el Signor Giovanfrancesco da Gonzaga; e così fo dato ordine. Da poi cominciò andar per il tavoliero el fatto del Conte Carlo, e per ditta casione bisognò mettere insieme ognuno, che l' ebbero molto caro: & essendo il campo del Conte Carlo in quello di Siena, & comprendendose chiaramente la cosa non avere du- N° XXVIII.

N° XXVIII.

rata, fu fatta deliberazione d' andare a campo a Montone, e tenere in tempo l' assedio più che se posseva, a cagion che costoro avesser tempo a dare ordine alla spedizione della faccienda; e per detta occasione venne Francesco de' Pazzi in quel tempo quì in Fiorenza con demostrazione di fuggir l' aiere, & fo a questo effetto; & essendo stato detto Francesco per alcuni giorni, scrisse a Roma all' Arcivescovo, como passavano le cose, & che bisognava riscaldare e pungere Messer Jacomo, e farghe intendere tutti li favori se arà in questa cosa, &c. Et il modo delle genti d' arme, e tutto quello favore se podeva avere, fargliclo intendere chiaramente, & inteselo se lassasse poi il pensiero a lui, che a tutto daria buon ordene; & aceadendo in quello medesimo tempo la malattia del Sig. Carlo di Faenza, & essendo stato longo tempo ammalato, venne in pericolo de morte, & dubitandose assai della morte sua, parse al Conte & allo Arcivescovo avere scusa licita di mandarme quì con intenzione, che io vedesse i modi di questa città & ancora del Magnifico Lorenzo, e che io parlasse con seco, & intendesse da lui, volendo el Conte cercare de aravere el suo stato, cioè Valdeseno, que favor se podeva avere de Sua Magnificenza e da questa Repubblica per suo mezzo, & che glie fesse intendere, che il Sig. Conte sperava più in sua Magnificenza, che persona del mondo, e che in questo io intendesse il consiglio & el parere suo, e che gli fesse ancora intendere, che non ostante alcune cose fossero state fra loro e 'l Conte, le voleva buttare tutte da parte, & in omne cosa desponerse a compiacerlo, & averlo in loco de patre; & con molte altre buone parole appresso, quali erono la maggior parte simulate. Et arrivando quì tardi la sera, non potì parlare con Sua Magnificenzia. La mattina andai a trovarlo, e se ne venne di sotto vestito a nero per la morte dell' Orsino, & fommo insieme, nè altramente me respuose, che si fosse stato patre del Conte, nè con altro amore, in modo che a me fe maravigliare, avendo inteso da altri, & poi ritrovandolo così ben disposto in le cose del Conte, che veramente non s'averia possuto parlore per niuno fratello più amorevolmente, che me parlò, dicendome: Tu te ne girai a Imola, e vederrai come trovi le cose, e daraimene avviso de quello te parerà s' abbia a fare dal canto nostro, che tutto si farà senza mancare de niente per satisfare alla Signoria del Conte, al quale e in questo & in omne altra cosa me sforzerò sempre a satisfarlo . . . . con li più amorevoli ricordi, che possesse mai patre a figliolo, li quali ricordi li tacerò per bene: la sua Magnificenzia gli deve bene avere a memoria: pur quando gli parrà, che io gli chiarisca, pensece bene, e diamene avviso, che io gli chiarirò.

Dipoi me ne andai all' ostaria della Campana a desinare; et avendo a parlare

parlare a Francesco de' Pazzi, & con Messer Jacomo pur de' Pazzi, ai quali avevo lettere di credenza del Sig. Conte e dello Arcivescovo, infin che si desinò, mandai ad intendere que n' era de loro: me fo detto, che Francesco era andato a Lucca, e non c' essendo, mandai a dire a Messer Jacomo predetto, che io aveva bisogno de parlarli, & de cose de 'mportanza, & che se voleva, che io andassi a casa sua, che io anderia, & se lui voleva venire all' ostaria, che io l' aspettaria. Messer Jacomo predetto venne all' ostaria della Campana, dove lui & mi ci ritirassimo in una camera in segreto, & per parte del Nostro Signore el confortai, e salutai, & così da parte del Sig. Conte Jeronimo e dell' Arcivescovo, de' quali Conte & Arcivescovo io avevo una lettera credenzial per uno: le appresentai; le lesse, e lette disse: che avemo noi a dire, Giovambatista? Avemo noi a parlare de Stato? Dissi madiasì. Mi rispuose: io non ti voglio intendere per niente, perchè costoro si vanno rompendo il cervello, & voglion deventare Signori de Fiorenza, & io intendo meglio queste cose nostre de loro: non me ne parlate per niente, che non ne voglio ascoltare. E persuadendolo io pure all' ascoltarme, se contentò d' intendermi. Que vuoi tu dire? Io vi conforto da parte di Nostro Signore, con el quale prima che io partissi, gli parlai, & presente el Conte e l' Arcivescovo me disse Sua Santità, che io vi confortasse a spedire questa causa de Fiorenza, perchè lui non sa in que tempo possa accadere un altro assedio de Montone da tenere sospese & insieme tante gente d' arme e così appresso al vostro terreno; & essendo pericoloso lo indusiare, ve conforta a far questo. Madiasì che Sua Santità dice, che vorria seguisse la mutazione della Stato, ma senza morte de persona. E dicendoli io, presente el Conte e l' Arcivescovo, Padre Santo queste cose se potranno forse mal fare senza morte di Lorenzo e di Giuliano, e forse delli altri; Sua Santità mi disse: io non voglio la morte di niuno per niente, perchè non è offizio nostro acconsentire alla morte di persona; e benchè Lorenzo sia un villano, & con noi si porte male, pure io non vorria la morte sua per niente, ma la mutazione dello Stato sì. Et el Conte respuose: se farà quanto se poderà, acciò non intervenga; pure quando intervenisse, la Vostra Santità perdonerà bene a chi 'l fesse. El Papa respuose al Conte: tu sii una bestia. Io te dico: non voglio la morte de niuno, ma la mutazione dello Stato sì. E così ti dico, Giovambatista, che io disidero assai, che lo Stato di Fiorenza se mute, & che se leve delle mani de Lorenzo, che elli è un villano, & un cattivo uomo, & non fa stima de noe, e tuttavolta ched c' fosse fuor de Fiorenza lui, farissimo de quella Repubblica quello vorressimo, & saria ad un gran preposito nostro. E 'l Conte e l' Arcivescovo, che erano presenti, dissero: la Santità Vostra dice il vero;

N° XXVIII.

Nº XXVIII.

vero; che quando aviate Fiorenza in vostro arbitrio, & posserne desponere, come porrete, si serà in mano de costoro, la Santità Vostra metterà legge a mezza Italia, & omne una averà caro esserve amico; sicchè siate contento si faccia ogni cosa per venire a questo effetto. Sua Santità disse; io ti dico che non voglio. Andate e fate quello volete voi, purchè non v' intervenga morte. Et con questo ci levassimo dinanzi da Sua Santità, facendo poi conclusione essere contento dare omne favore & ajuto de gente d' arme, o d' altro, che acciò fosse necessario. L' Arcivescovo rispuose & disse; Padre Santo, siate contento, che guidiamo noi questa barca, che la guideremo bene. Et Nostro Signore disse; io son contento. E con questo ci levassimo da' suoi piedi, e reducessemonce in camera del Conte, dove fo poi discussa la cosa particolarmente, e concluso che questa cosa non se poteva fare per niun modo senza la morte de' costoro, cioè del Magnifico Lorenzo e del fratello. Et dicendo io essere mal fatto, mi rispuosero, che le cose grandi non si possevano fare altramente; & sopra de ciò fo dato molti esempli, che seria lungo a scriverli; & finaliter fo concluso, che per intendere e modo, bisognava essere qui, & parlar con Francesco & Messer Jacomo, e intendere appunto quello era da fare, & intesolo mandare ad effetto. Io foi qui, e non trovando Francesco, non vulsi fare altra conclusione; se non che mi disse: vattene a Imola, e alla tornata tua sarà qui Francesco, & delibererasse tutto quello sarà da fare. Io me ne andai a Imola, dove stetti pochi giorni, perchè così aveva io in commissione per la espedizione di detta causa, e in nel tornare e dietro foi a Casaggiolo, dove trovai la Magnificenza di Lorenzo e de Giuliano, e avendo referte al detto Magnifico Lorenzo como aveva trovate le cose del Conte, me consigliò con le più cordiali & amorevoli parole del mondo, dicendome che per il Signor Conte aveva deliberato fare ogne cosa per farli intendere che gli voleva essere buono amico; & avendo Sua Magnificenzia deliberato tornare a Fiorenza, ce ne venissimo di compagnia, dove per la via mi fe intendere ancora più chiaramente quanto era el suo buon animo verso del Conte, che lo tacerò, perchè seria longo lo scrivere. Arrivai in Fiorenza, e fui con Francesco, con il quale presi ordine di non partire quel dì, acciocchè la notte ce retrovassimo con Messer Jacomo; & così fo fatto. La notte ditto Francesco venne per me, & condusseme in camera de M. Jacomo, dove fo parlato assai di questa cosa, & la conclusione fo questa, che per la espedizione bisognava più cose; una che l' Arcivescovo fosse de quà, & che vedesse venirci con qualche scusa licita in modo non desse suspetto, & a questo lassava pensarlo al Conte, e a lui, & che alla sua venuta si piglieria poi forma de quello s' avesse a fare, e che si fosse cifre, per le quali si potesse scrivere bene, & che

che non dubitava, avendo el favore delle genti del Papa ec. che la cosa non venissi fatta, ma che per farla netta, bisognava, che detti doi fratelli fossero fora, & che immediate, che la cosa avesse questo, di certo la spacciariamo, & che tra 'l Magnifico Lorenzo e 'l Signor di Piombino si trattava parentado per Giuliano, e seguendo, saria necessario uno de loro andasse là, el quale andava; la cosa era spacciata, ma essendo totti dua in la città, per niente non voleva fare, perchè non gli pareva posser riuscirlo; & Francesco diceva altramente, che ad omne modo si faria, & sempre gli andò per la mente in Chiesa, o a giuoco di carte o a nozze, purchè fossino tutti dua in un luogo, gli basteria l' animo di farlo, & che non ci voleva se non pochi con seco, & recercommene a me, che io volessi quello, che mai el volsi fare. Lui disse trovaria bene il modo a far questo, & che se desse pur più tempo che se poteva, e mandassesi l' Arcivescovo in quà, che a tutto se daria bene espedizione, & che de tutto quello s' avesse a fare, si avviseria. Intesa la conclusione, me n' andai a Roma, e referii el tutto al Conte & all' Arcivescovo, & subito fu presa per il Conte deliberazione de mandare l' Arcivescovo sotto colore delle cose di Favenza, &c. & a me ordinò che me n' andassi a Imola con cento provisionati, & con quelle poche genti d' arme, che gli erono state preparate ad omne requisizione de costoro, & etiam con i suoi popoli, &c. Io me partii, & andamene a Imola, & poi a Montugi; e fui una notte con Messer Jacomo e con Francesco, e fegli intendere l' ordine dato da ogni banda, e che questa cosa bisognava espedizione, & da parte, &c. del Conte gli sollicitai assai a detta espedizione prima che il campo si dividesse loro; me rispuosero, che non bisognava sproni, ma morso, & che ad omne modo vederia espedirlo in questo tempo, & che io stesse preparato, che sperava avvisarne presto quello avessi a fare, e che al suo avviso non preterisse niente; & io dissi di farlo, e con questo me ne andai, & non trovando costoro comodità di farlo in quel tempo per essere la persona del Conte Carlo quì, e alloggiato in casa de' Martelli, deliberorno lassarlo stare per fine a tempo nuovo, & avvisò, che si devidessa il campo, & così fo fatto, nè di questa cosa fo parlato più per un pezzo, &c. Et essendo stato a Imola per la recuperazione di Valdiseno, & essendosi recuperato, me n' andai a Roma questo Marzo, dove trovai la Signoria del Conte, e Giovanfrancesco da Tolentino, e Messer Lorenzo da Castello e Francesco de' Pazzi, &c. fra i quali molte volte si parlava de queste cose, & che se cominciava adesso approssimar il tempo d' espedir detta causa; & domandando io que modo era questo, me disse: Lorenzo deve venire quì per questa Pasqua, & quamprimum se senta la sua partita, Francesco se partirà ancora lui, & anderà a spedirsi; & farse il servizio a quello remanerà, & all'

Nº XXVIII.

N° XXVIII. all' altro, innanzi che torni, se penserà quello si doverrà fare di lui, & terrassi con esso tal modo, che la cosa sarà bene assettata innanzi che se parta da noi. Io gli dissi: Faretelo morire? Mi rispuose: madianò, che questo non voglio per niente, che quì abbia alcuno dispiacere; ma innanzi che parta, le cose saranno bene assettate in forma, che staranno bene. Domandai il Conte: Nostro Signore sa questo? Me disse: madiasì. Dico; Diavolo, egli è gran fatto che 'l consenta! Me respuose: non sai tu, che 'l fammo fare quello volemo noi? Basta che le cose anderanno bene. Et stettesi in queste trame parecchi dì del suo venire, o no. Dappoi veduto che non veniva, deliberarono ad ogni modo cavarne le mani prima che fosse fora Maggio, &c. Et como ho detto di questo più e più volte ne fo parlato in camera del Conte, & como mancava materia, se tornava su questo, e chi prima si trovava insieme con loro, ne parlava, dicendo, che per niente la cosa podeva durare così, che non venissi a palese, e questo per essere in tante lingue, & che ad ogni modo bisognava darli spedizione, onde che per detta casione fu preso per partito, che Francesco se ne venisse quì; e Giovanfrancesco da Tolentino & io ce ne andassimo a Imola, & Messer Lorenzo da Castello, &c. per dare ordene quello s' avesse da fare, e poi se ne tornasse a Castello, & omne uno con le preparazioni fatte stesse apparecchiato a tutto quello, che da Messer Jacomo, l' Arcivescovo e Francesco fosse ordinato et che ad omne sua requesta onneuno fosse presto a far quanto per loro saria comandato. Et quest' ordene ce fu dato tutto per el Signor Conte in Roma.

Da poi venne ultimamente il Vescovo de Lion, el quale ce comandò de nuovo, che ad omne requisizion de' sopradetti fussemo apparecchiati sanza fare una difficoltà al mondo; & così s' è fatto, nè mai se 'ntese niuno loro ordene, se non lo Sabato a doi ore di notte, e poi la Domenica mutorno ancora proposito; & in questa forma sono state governate queste cose diciendo imperò sempre, che l' onor de Nostro Signore e del Conte ci fosse raccomandato. Et con questo ordene la Domenica mattina a dì 26. d' Aprile 1478, si fece in Santa Liberata quanto è pubblico a tutto el mondo.

Item che tornando di Romagna, & andando a Roma, quando fu lì, & parlando con Nostro Signorè d' altre cose me disse: poi Giovambatista dell' Arcivescovo & de Francesco, che diceva voler far tante cose, e non savessero mutare uno Stato come quello de Fiorenza; ma non credo s'avesse pure accozzare tre ove in un bacile, se non con cianciatori; triati chi s'empaccia con loro.

Item

Item che 'l Signor Conte mi ha ditto molte volte, che Nostro Signore ha così gran desiderio della mutazione di questo Stato come noi, & se tu intendesse quello dice, quando semo lui e mi, diresti quello che dico io. N° XXVIII.

Io Giovan Batista da Montesicco confesso e fo fede essere vere tutte le predette cose scritte in un foglio intero & in un altro mezzo, e quì di sopra, e quanto io ho scritto avere detto a Messer Jacomo quì in Fiorenza della mente & voluntà della Santità del Papa, & queste cose sono verissime, & io mi trovai presente, quando la Sua Santità lo disse, & tutto questo è scritto, è di mia mano propria.

Io Matteo Tuscano da Milano Cavaliero e presentemente Podestà della Magnifica Città di Fiorenza sono stato presente insema colli Reverendi Patri infrascritti *(ut infra)* che 'l prefato Joanne Baptista ha detto, che quanto è scritto sopra in un foglio intero, e in un altro mezzo, e in questo, che tutti s' allegheranno inseme, sono ne sua propria mano, & confessò essere vero quanto de sopra è scritto, & così ne fazzo fede de mia propria mano, che gli è la propria verità quanto in esse scritto se contene: a dì 4 di Maggio 1478, in Fiorenza. *(Omittimus alias aliorum subscriptiones.)*

Noti jam sunt Conjuratores, atque eorum omnia consilia ex ipsis conjuratis. Nos modo quid inde secutum sit, brevi perstringemus. Cum dies advenisset Aprilis vigesimus sextus, qui destinatus erat facinori, in Libertae Templum conjurati tectis gladiis convenerunt, horam caedi constitutam expectantes. Convenerat eodem & frequentissimus populus ad sacrorum apparatiora spectacula. Raphael enim Cardinalis ex nepte natus Sixti Pontificis sacris solemnioribus praesidebat, accipiendus convivio a Laurentio Julianoque Medicibus post peracta sacra, quod proditores de industria curaverant, ut eos si in Templo perfici res non posset, domi inter epulandum obtruncarent. Aderant igitur in primis Laurentius Julianusque fratres, ut Cardinalem & convivas domum reducerent. Conjurati autem ad fractionem Eucharistiae, id enim datum signum erat, strictis gladiis Julianum confodiunt ante aras, caeduntque: atque eodem tempore altera manus, ut diversa spatia circum Altare faciebat, Laurentium adoritur, & sub aurem dextram in collo vulnerat. Deus, suo clementissimo beneficio, ex tam diro infortunio salvum reddidit. Ipse quoque suae saluti fortiter est opitulatus, & gladiolo, quem ex consuetudine Florentinae juventutis ad ornatum gerebat, stricto, dantibus viam proditoribus, in Sacrarium confugit.

 Eodem

Nº XXVIII. Eodem tempore, quo id negotii susceperat Franciscus Salviatus Archiepiscopus Pisanus, cum ad id delectis armatis satellitibus Palatium occupat Status nostri & Florentinae Libertatis domicilium: Magistratus cum circumveniri se improvisum sensisset, in deambulacra conscendit, & illic aditibus clausis se tutatur; atque inde Jacobum Pazium Equitem Florentinum immanissimum patricidam cum globo armatorum accurrentem & ferentem conjuratis auxilium, lapidibus ex deambulatris magnis jactibus deturbat, arcetque Palatio. Habet in summo aedificii Palatium duas quasi porticus, tectam alteram, sine tegumento alteram, in modum duplicis coronae ad deambulandi usum fabricatas, unde & deambulacri nomen est. Ea non modo ornatius faciunt Palatium, & commoditatem deambulandi & sub tecto & sub dio praebent, sed belligerandi & arcendi, unde unde veniat, invasorem pulcherrime faciunt facultatem. Dum igitur Magistratus hinc repugnat atque insectatur lapidibus parricidas, populus, caede cognita civium suorum, & Laurentii vulnere, & vim inferri Magistratui, percitus furore incredibili & dolore arma capit, in Curiam, ut Magistratui succurrerent, convolarunt. Principes quoque civitatis, atque optimates cuncti idem factitant. Ad aedes Mediceas sugendo vulneri ob veneni suspicionem amici dant operam. Ad Palatium ad effringendum trabalibus crebris ictibus atque igni appositis accensis facibus fores acerrimis insudatur studiis. Vix integram horam occupatores sustinuerunt impetum. Victi ergo, partim primo impetu caesi, partim vivi capti & conjecti in vincula, post quaestiones breves perierunt. Johannes Baptista de Montesicco erutus tandem e latebris, per quas paucos dies diffugerat, quae supra sunt posita, cum sua manu perscripsisset, & se ita scripsisse, & vera esse quae scripsisset, pluribus clarorum virorum attestationibus corroboratum, ut fieri ipse voluit, vidisset, quamquam in suprascripta confessione ejus quaedam bonis de causis subtracta sint, & ea tantum apposita, quae ad Sixtum Pontificem, atque Ecclesiae Gubernatores pertinent, capitis est damnatus. Sic Cives Civitasque, & Libertas, proditorum manus effugerunt. Nam & Johannes Franciscus Tolentinas, qui Imola absens, cum expeditis Sixti Papae militibus, jussus ad destinatum caedi diem ferre conjuratis auxilium, quique jam in Mugellanum agrum descenderat, re cognita, unde abierat, revertitur. Idem facit & Laurentius Tiphernas, qui alia parte eadem de caussa a Civitate Castelli movens, & per agrum discurrens nostrum ad Senenses fines accurrerat. Raphael Cardinalis, quem praeesse sacris supra diximus, sic procurantibus pluribus civibus & Laurentio Medice imprimis, qui in tanto periculo suo, in tot tantisque negotiis & tumultibus, atque omni confusione rerum, hujus quoque officii

officii non est oblitus, in Palatium perductus, vix furentes populi manus evasit. Moverat scilicet Laurentium Cardinalatus dignitas & Sanctae Romanae Ecclesiae reverentia, ut eum intactum inviolatumque curaret; ubi cum paucos dies publicis sumptibus honorificentissime fuisset, quoad populi furor elanguesceret & fieret remissior, Romam abiit incolumis. Quae tamen vel in primis praetenditur caussa, cur interdicamur sacris, & communio fidelium separemur? Ita de bono opere lapidamur, & ubi gratias reportasse oportuit, immeritissime damnamur. Tandem quod foeda proditione non successit, tentatur Ecclesiasticis censuris atque armis. Bellum infertur a Sixto Pontifice Maximo & praeclaris illis, quos gubernationi Status Ecclesiae proposuit, non aliam ob caussam, nisi quod trucidari nos non sivimus; nam id quoque accusat in interdictis, & de proditoribus, atque Archiepiscopo Pisano sumptum esse supplicium moleste fert; quae altera caussa est interdicti & censurarum. Quamvis quam juste, quam pie, quam religiose, & Pontificaliter factum sit, plurium est doctissimorum Jurisconsultorum & Collegiorum declaratum testimonio, & publicis eorum scriptis in aperto positum, & quod Palatium, Statumque & Libertatem nostram, quae vita quoque est carior, defendimus. Sic Pontificis Christianorum maximus exercitus in populum religiosissimum, & illius Pontificalis fastigii semper observantissimum, infestissimus insurgit, jamque agrum vastat, Castella diripit atque incendit; foeminas, maresque & sacra & profana loca militari licentiae & libidini elargitur. Deus bone quandiu tantam iniquitatem sustinebis? Quando laborantis gregis tui misereberis, & confirmabis populum tuum? Ad te quoque ad te confugimus, Federice Serenissime Imperator semper Auguste. Meminens rogamus fidelissimae urbis tuae Florentiae & populi hujus isti Sacratissimae Majestati Imperatoriae semper devotissimi. In nobis, ni fallimur, caussa agitur publica Christianae Religionis, quae dum Sixtus suis bellum infert, versatur in periculo manifestissimo victoriosissimis & potentissimis hostibus in limine Italiae ita insultantibus. Tua est in primis rerum omnium Christianarum cura. Tu quoque, Ludovice Francorum invictissime Rex & Christianissime, virtutem ut excites tuam admodum necesse est, & succurras rebus Christianis periclitantibus. Idem nisi caeteri quoque Principes & Populi Christiani fecerint, multum de salute Christianarum rerum dubitare cogimur. Agite igitur, agite omnes, expergiscimini jam, & capessite rem communem; & cum Christo Optimo Maximo Redemptore & Salvatore nostro, qui caussam suam profecto non deseret, in commune consulite. Ex Florentia die X. Mensis Augusti MCCCCLXXVIII.

Bartholomaeus Scala Cancel. Florentinus.

N° XXVIII.

Philelphus

Nº XXIX.

Philelphus Laurentio Medici Florentiae.

Nº XXIX. MAGNIFICE clarissimeque vir tanquam frater honorande. Quanto sia stato el dispiacere ho ricevuto del vostro acerbissimo caso per due altre mie lettere lo havete potuto comprendere. Delle cose passate & inrecuperabili bisogna haver patientia, e ben provvedere per lo advenire, il che, come prudentissimo che voi siete, sono certo el dovete fare, al che sommamente ve conforto & priego.

Harei carissimo essere advisato del fundamento & processo de tanto tradimento, & a cui petitione & a che fine se faceva, acciocchè una perpetua memoria per me scripta fusse, avisandove che a niuno la sparmierò & sia chi si vuole.

In quanto a Vostra Magnificentia paresse, io harei caro essere rebandito: potreste tenere quella via volle tenere il vostro Magnifico avolo Cosmo, il quale, come me significò per Messer Angelo Acciajolo & per Messer Nicodemo Tranchedino, per non aprire la via alli altri rubelli ordenò, chel Duca Francesco scrivesse una lettera a cotesta Illustr. Comunitate, demandando de gratia che io fosse rebandito, & così a contemplatione de quello io come forestiere fusse messo a partito. Ma il prefato Signore per tema de perderme entorbidò el tucto. De questo fatene quello a voi pare. Ben ve aviso, che io ve sarei così utile in Firenze quanto pochi amici voi habiate. Io ve ho dedicato el corpo e l'anima.

Farebbe molto per Vostra Magnificentia havere in Milano Aciarito, il quale è amato, & è di grande reputatione in Corte e tra tutti i Milanesi, e lui solo ha la pratica e l'usanza. Vale ex Mediolano 20. Maii 1478.

Nº XXX.

Nº XXX. BARTHOLOMÆUS SCALA Laurentio Medici salutem dicit. Succenseo tibi ad longa tempora, mi Laurenti, meum columen, idest donec redieris.

redieris. Quid enim potest esse longius? Non possum vero non admirari istam fortitudinem animi tui atque constantiam. Reviviscit in te illa antiqua virtus & magnitudo animi, quae quanto magis nova est, magisque aliena ab his modis & consuetudine vitae, tanto est admirabilior tantoque ornatior. De me fatebor id quod est. Non possum esse fortis, nec solum non admirari istam deliberationem tuam, sed etiam non valde timere. Sum vero aliquot dies exanimatus metu, & vix apud me sum: si collegero animum, poteris habere saniores litteras. Decemviri collegae tui oratorem te post discessum tuum ad Neapolitanum Regem statuerunt. Idem novi quoque Decemviri decreverunt. Putabam autem posse id fieri a Centumviris honoratius, sed quibusdam amicis id attentare non est visum: in quorum ego sententiam facile concessi, quod in tanta suspensione animorum atque expectatione rerum quid melius factu sit, non est facile cognoscere. N° XXX.

Calles nostros mores. Qui novas res cupiunt, si qui sunt, qui his minime contenti sint, oblatam occasionem confundendarum rerum avide accipiunt.

Rogavi ergo & scripsi Decemvirorum mandatum, quam potui, elegantius: & ut esse magis credidi in rem communem & tuam, si separari tua a nostra, idest a publica potest, ut ego non posse certe scio, & sum aperte saepe testificatus. Si tu adfuisses, non ita in condenda laborassem.

Cui vero mirum est si sine meo sole obcaecatus .... sine duce vager, & sine mea Arcto etiam naufragem. Si scire quid expectas a me de rebus nostris, animum in pacem intenderunt, & fieri eam per te posse honoratam & dignam civitate putant: ab omni nota, quae vel quid minimum obscurare antiquam Florentinae gentis gloriam queat, plurimum abhorrent. Si tu eam nobis confeceris e sententia, redibis totus aureus, beabisque nos. Magna spes est in tua prudentia & auctoritate.

Regis quoque mentem non ex praesenti rerum conditione pensant, sed paullo altius res ab eo gestas & paterna in nos studia meritaque recensent.

Quid multa dixerim? Linguis atque animis huic fortissimo incoepto tuo plerique favemus. Me tibi plurimum commendo. Vale. Ex Florentia die V. Dec. 1479.

Ferdinandus

Nº XXXI.

Ferdinandus Rex Siciliae Laurentio Medici.

Nº XXXI. MAGNIFICO LORENZO heri alle 20. hore hebbemo per cavallaro aposta lettera del Magnifico Messer Lorenzo de Castello Oratore della Santità de Nostro Signore, quale ve mandamo intro la presente; & videndo quello ne scrivea, como ancora vui vederite, ne parse per non disturbare tanto bene quanto delle conclusione, delle cose agitate se spera, scriver a quisti nostri supra sedessero fin ad altro nostro mandato: & poco spacio da poi venne ipso Messere Lorenzo, & licet per lettera de Messere Anello havessemo visto quanto de bona voluntà la Santità de Nostro Signore era condescesa a tutte quelle conditione della pace, che ultimamente erano state mandate de voluntà vostra & de' quisti Magnifici Oratori Ducali, tamen dicto Messer Lorenzo lo have dicto con tanta majore efficacia, quanto più lo have inteso per altre lettere have havute così dalla dicta Santità como dal Conte Hieronimo. Et perchè lo possate vedere, ve mandamo con la presente copia de quanto Messer Anello ne ha scripto. Benchè heri la donassemo al vostro Ser Nicolò, & credimo ve la habbia mandata. Da po venne el cavallaro con le lettere de Messere Princevallo, per le quale intesimo la ragione e cagione, per le quale a vui non parea dever retornar secondo Messer Lorenzo havea scripto & mandato dicendo. El che inteso per ipso Messer Lorenzo, se ne è mostrato mal contento, dicendo, che havendo la Santità de Nostro Signore acceptato tutto quello per nui li è stato scripto per grandissimo desiderio e voluntà, che have de questa pace, dubita grandemente, che non retornando vui, e dilatandose questa conclusione per qualsevoglia respecto, porranno facilmente seguir inconvenienti, che non solamente serranno causa de disturbar questa pace, ma de far malcontenti tutti quelli la desiderano. Et respondendoseli, che la partuta vostra era stata non voluntaria, ma necessaria per le cose de Fiorenza star in grandissimo periculo de trabuccar a camino contrario a quello desidera la Santità de Nostro Signore; & nui resposse, che considerato el tempo non era disposto a navigare, & considerato a Fiorenza omne homo averà là inteso vui esserve partuto, & che el tempo contrario ve ha impedito, & che tra quisto mezzo essendo supra venuta da Nostro Signore la resposta con la conclusione, quale per tucti se desiderava, site retornato, acciocchè alla conclusione della pace non se havesse de dar dilatione: & circa questo ve porrissivo allargar quanto ve paresse, & etiam porrissivo scrivere alli amici vostri

che

che bisognando per qualsevoglia respecto per tener le cose della Comunità vostra quiete, se poteno ajutare delle gente de Nostro Signore e nostre. Non solamente quella Comunità, & li amici vostri non haveranno dispiacere della vostra retornata quà, ma ne pigliaranno grandissimo conforto e consolatione praesertim che vui ancora li possite scrivere, che la conclusione se farrà de continente, & al più tardo alla resposta, che venerà da Milano, che ne serà tra secte dì, & che etiam se li po scriver, che immediate chel tempo serrà disposto, vui continuarete vostro camino, concludendo che quando vui non retornassivo, lui se parteria immediate, & serrà in tucto exclusa questa pratica; el quale ragionamento ne piacque grandemente, & simo certi non meno piacerà a vui. Et parendone le ragione de Messer Lorenzo bone & efficace, & pensando, che della vostra tornata quà son per seguire infiniti beneficii senza alcuno vostro sconcio, & del contrario infiniti mali, ve pregamo quanto ne è possible vogliate omnino disponerve e per terra o per mare, como più ve piacerà a tornare, acciocchè ultra li altri beneficii son per seguire a vui & a tucti per la conclusione de questa pace e lega, quale indubitatamente se concluderà vui retornando, se possa dir vui esserne causa, che non solamente li misi passati per fare quello effecto venissivo quà con tanta liberalità, non perdonando a pericoli della persona nè dello stato, ma da poi con non minor voluntà e promptezza siate retornato, & quisto acto a judicio nostro è de tal natura, che credimo lo animo della Santità de Nostro Signore ne restarà tanto placato & satisfacto, che con alcuna altra cosa non lo porrissivo più satisfare; demostrarasse la grandissima sincerità & optima voluntà vostra alla pace, & alla obedientia de Nostro Signore, disturbarite le pratiche de qualunca ha travagliato e travaglia alienar Nostro Signor da queste conclusione, che questa vostra retornata cancellerà in tucto queste persuasione & suspecti, & asserenerà lo animo de Nostro Signore non solum verso nui & vui, ma ancora verso quilli Illustrissimi Signori de Milano, adeo, che simo certi nulla cosa, che a proposito vostro sia & vui desiderate, ne porrà essere denegata; avisandove, che non simo fora de speranza, tornando vui, questi Magnifici Ambasciadori Ducali non debiano differir la stipulatione delli contracti, perchè alloro non è prohibito la stipulatione ma solamente li è comandato, che non concludendose la pace tra otto dì & poi tra quattro altri, se debiano partire, & se cosa alcuna li ha de indurre a stipulare de continente serrà la presentia vostra per lo beneficio certo, che de quella conclusione se vede have de seguire a tutti questi stati: & non dubitamo con ragione se mostrarà loro possono & devono far questa conclusione. Ma la più viva ragione serrà la presentia & lo conforto vostro; & praesertim perchè, N° XXXI.

Nº XXXI. perchè, statim fatta la conclusione, possate partire & tornare a Fiorenza con tanta gloria e stabilità delle cose di quella Excelsa Repubblica. A nui pare soverchio scrivere altre ragione & cause per persuaderve la vostra retornata, che essendo vui de tanta prudentia & intellecto, ne intendite multo più che nui. Solamente ve dirimo, che in satisfactione de quanto havessemo possuto, o porrimo fare tucta nostra vita in vostro beneficio, vogliate retornare per fare questa conclusione, la quale a judicio nostro importa tanto alli comuni stati, che non dubitamo, per fuggire li contrarj effecti, che possono seguire del vostro non tornare, se fussivo in Pisa, non che a Cajeta retornarissivo, & ve pregamo non vogliate mostrare de farla si non allegramente como certamente possite e devite, ancorchè ultra lo effecto de tanto bene è per seguire de la vostra retornata, la Santità de Nostro Signore habia de intendere lo havite facto con jocondissimo animo. Datum in Castello novo Neap. 1. Martii 1480.

Nº XXXII.

Al mio caro quanto fratello Albino,

Segretario dello Illustrissimo Sig. Duca di Calabria.

Nº XXXII. ALBINO mio caro quanto buon fratello. Io non so ancora giudicare, se le vostre de' 2 & 8. del presente mi hanno portato maggiore piacere che dispiacere, producendomi insieme nello animo uno sviscerato desiderio della gloria del nostro Sig. Duca, a che si è dato grandissimo principio per la profligatione di cotesti cani Turchi a di 8.; & uno stemperamento che io ho, che al Signore non venga per la animosità sua qualche sinistro caso. Quelle zerbottane, di che me scrivete, in mezzo delle quali spesso si trova il Signore, me hanno più d' una volta impallidito, perchè più d' una volte ho letta la vostra lettera ad mia maggior satisfactione: se è possible, Albino mio, mandateci spesso di queste nuove non miste da tanto suspetto, & confortate il Signore ad haversi cura alla persona. Non voglio dire più, perchè mi stempero mentre che ci penso. Conservesi per Dio a se, & a noi altri sui servitori, & facci quello medesimo col pericolo d' altri non suo. Voi che le siete appresso, dovete procurare questo innanzi alla vita vostra, e se non lo volete fare per vostro conto, fatelo per mio, se mi volete bene, & raccommandatemi al Signore, & io aspetto la risposta vostra ad questa con sommo desiderio per

per intendere, che questo mio amorevole ricordo habbi giovato senza diminuzione alcuna di quello che io tengo per constantissimo, & questo è che presto el Signore habbi ad reportare la laurea di cotesta expugnatione: oreu aspetto esserne ragguagliato alla giornata da voi. Florentiae die 18 Maii 1481. N° XXXII.

Laurentius de' Medicis.

N° XXXIII.

M. Anselmo Calderoni, Araldo della Signoria di Firenze mandato a Cosmo de' Medici.

Da testo a penna della Libreria Laurenziana.

SONETTO.

O LUME de' terrestri cittadini, N° XXXIII.
O chiaro specchio d' ogni mercatante,
O vero amico a tuct' opere sante,
O speranza de' grandi, & de piccini;
* * *
O soccorso d' ognun che bisognante,
O de' popilli, e vedovi aitante,
O forte scudo de' Toscan confini;
O sopra ogn' altro a Dio caritativo,
Prudente, temperato, giusto, e forte,
O padre al buono & padrigno al cattivo,
O di somma pietate largho porte,
O adversario d' ogn' acto lascivo;
O tu che rende per mal buone sorte!
Dobbiam fino alla morte,
Per Cosimo & Lorenzo tucti noi
Pover, pregare Iddio sempre per voi.

Di Maestro Niccolo Circo per epso Cosimo de' Medici.

SONETTO.

O DELLA nostra Italia unico lume,
O Cicerone in arti oratorie,
O nuovo Tito Livio all' alte historie,
O fior d' ogni poetico volume!

O voi

N° XXXIII.

O voi che'l fonte pegaseo consume,
O albergo di tucte le memorie,
O ch' alle muse hai dato eterne glorie,
O di philosophia lecto de piume!
Io corro a voi come cervo a chiar fonte,
A tormi sete, & viver piu contento.
Perchè la patria è sì ingrata al suo nato!
E'l nato exalta lei con voglie pronte;
Et chi ne sostien morte, & chi tormenti,
Et io ne so parlar che l' ho provato.

N° XXXIV.

Rime del Burchiello,

Da testo a penna del sec. XV.

N° XXXIV.

DI tutto el centro che la Europia cigne,
Italia n' è Reina incoronata,
Secundo che pe' savi si distingue:
Il frutto che la ciba, et tiene ornata,
E' la porpora vesta di Toscana,
Di fior' d' alisi, et gigli seminata:
Lo specchio in che costei si mira, e vana,
Si è *Fiorenza* terra sopra marte,
Che strigne ogni terrena etai lontana.
Perchè egliè guida, et fuor di molte parte
Si manda per rifar lo studio athene,
Molta sua imbasceria, con libri, et carte;
O quanta nobil gente si mantiene
In questa vaga et bella imbasceria,
Con poco senno le lor menti piene.
Se ti piacessi lettor, pregheria
Cho ti agustassi d' esta gente el nome,
Se vuoi avere alquanta giulleria. &c.

* * *

N° XXXIV.

Maestro mio se a dirmi non se' lasso,
  Io te prieghо per dio che ancor mi dica,
  E nomi di questi altri apasso apasso.
Et egli a me: e' non mi fia faticha,
  Et presto ti farò da loro contento,
  Villano è quello ch' a te nulla disdicha.
Rivoglanci diss' egli al nostro armento,
  Et mostrerotti uno nuovo pesce medicho,
  Grande di carne, e di poco sentimento;
Ne altrimente a chi teme il solleticho,
  Chi lo tocha per motti lo fa ridere,
  Tal fecie a me quel maestro farneticho.
Com io lo vidi, credetti dividere,
  Le mia mascella, per troppo letitia,
  Tal che Ser Gigi disse, non ti uccidere;
Et fa di tanto ridere masseritia,
  Che tu vedrai venire dirieto a lui,
  Gente che riderai più ch' a divizia
Se vuoi sapere el nome di costui,
  Maestro *Antonio Falcucci* egl' è chiamato,
  Ch'a ogni sole gli paion tempi buoi;
Costui è si perfetto smemorato,
  Che se toccasse el polso al campanile,
  Sonando a' festa non l'aria trovato.
Et non ostante che sia tanto vile,
  Egl' ha morti più huomini a suoi giorni,
  Che la spada d'Orlando signorile.
Dagli licenza, et di che non si torni;
  Però che dove sta vifa moria,
  Con suoi nuovi sciloppi, et masusomi.
Et io al medico, trovate la via,
  Quanto piu tosto meglio siate atene,
  Et fate a noi di voi gran carestia.
Quale colui che dal capo alle reno
  Porta gran peso, et lui fa gire in archo,
  Così fe quel medico di sene:
Cosi sen gia di vergogna carco,
  Et noi agli altri a rimirar ci demmo,
  Che cinspettavan per valere il varcho, &c.

Do

Nº XXXV.

Da Testo a penna della Libreria Laurenziana.

Bernardo Pulci a Lor. de' Medici.

SONETTO.

Nº XXXV.

NATURA per se fa il verso gentile,
Studio le rime, & ricche le 'nvenzioni;
Vere scienze solvon le quistioni,
El dilectarsi poi fa il dolce stile;
Amor l'ingegno sempre fa soctile,
Dote dal Cielo, privilegii, & doni,
Son questi: benche sien molte cagioni,
Che fanno un dir superbo, l'altrui humile.
Diversi casi fanno il dir diverso;
Quando amor, & fortuna, a dir ti strigne,
E colori temperrai con discretione:
Chi pensa il vero e poi compone il verso,
Eterno con la penna si dipgine,
Che poi morendo ha più riputatione.

SONETTO.

NUOVA influenza dalle Muse piove,
Novellamente & ho cangiato stile,
Cagion di quel Signor, vagho et gentile,
Che per Calisto fè transformar Giove.
Così amore d'un esser me rinuove,
Libero sendo: in acto hora servile,
Et tant' è in se crudel, quant' io humile,
Colei che favellando i sassi muove.
Sonetto mio, a *Cafaggiuolo* andrai,
Paese bel, che siede nel mugello,
Dove tu troverai *Lorenzo* nostro;
Et con gran riverenza porgi a quello
Questi altri tuo consorti; & sol dirai
Questi presenta a voi *Bernardo* vostro.

N° XXXVI.

Al Sig. Jacopo Facciolati, a Padova.

Venezia, 30. *Maggio* 1742.

LA Lettera al Principe Federigo d'Aragona mi ha dato lume, per venire in chiaro dell' essere e del nome del compilatore della vostra Raccolta di Rimatori antichi, e del tempo, in cui ella fu fatta. E quanto al tempo, si dice quasi nel cominciamento di essa, che trovandosi Federigo nella *Pisana Città nel passato anno*, ed essendo entrato col raccoglitore in ragionamento intorno a quegli, che nella volgar lingua aveano scritto, mostrò d'aver desiderio, che per opera di lui *tutti quegli Scrittori lo fossero insieme in un medesimo volume raccolti*. Il tempo in cui Federigo andò in Toscana, fu nel 1464. come si ha da Scipione Ammirato nell' Istoria Fiorentina *tom.* III. *pag.* 93. nè si trova, che in altro tempo egli facesse quel viaggio. La raccolta dunque ne fu fatta l' anno seguente, cioè nel 1465. Un anno fu impiegato nel farla, e non senza molta fatica, da chi si prese il carico di soddisfare alle instanze di quel Signore. Dell' essere del raccoglitore, due indizj mi porge la medesima Lettera: l'uno che e' fosse persona di qualità e d' alto rango, poichè l' espressioni, con le quali tratta con un Principi figliuolo e fratello di Re, e che poscia fu Re di Napoli anch' egli, non converrebbono a persona privata e di bassa sfera, ma bensì ad una, cho non conosce superiore, e che parla da grande e per nascità e per fortuna. L'altro indizio si è, che questi fosse Toscano, poichè parlando quivi dei Rimatori di quella nazione, li nomina semplicemente con l' aggiunto di *nostri*. Tutte queste però non sarebbono, se non semplici conghietture, e lontane per farci credere, che il raccoglitore fosse stato *Lorenzo de' Medici* il *Magnifico*, il quale era, come si sa, di quell' alta famiglia e grandezza in Firenze sua patria, e che nel 1465. era d'anni 17. o 18. stante l'esser lui nato nel Gennajo del 1448. Ciò che mi ha indotto a dirlo francamente, qual precedentemente vel dissi, per Lorenzo de' Medici, si è quel tanto che si legge nel fine della suddetta sua lettera al Principe d'Aragona. *Hobbiamo nello* ESTREMO *del libro (perchè così ne pare te piacesse) aggiunti alcuni delli* NOSTRI SONETTI *e* CANZONE, *acciò che quelli leggendo se rinnovelli nella tua mente la mia fede, e amore insieme verso la tua Signoria.* Ripigliato adunque per mano il vostro bel Codice, ed esaminatelo ben bene verso il fine, ho ritrovato, che l'ultimo componimento con nome di autore era alla *pag.* 2?3. 2. un Sonetto del

N° XXXVI.

N° XXXVI. del *Notaro Jacopo da Lentino*, Poeta notissimo Siciliano, vivuto però dugent' anni almeno prima dell' anno 1464. onde conclusi, che questi non poteva esser l' autore d'una Raccolta, dove stavano registrati i nomi, e i componimenti di tanti Poeti vivuti ne' due secoli susseguenti. Piacciavi ora dare un' attenta occhiata alla *pag.* 284. e anche alle susseguenti sino alla fine del Codice, e vedrete, che le Rime quivi trascritte sono tutte di un anonimo raccoglitore, che a veruna de esse non ha voluto apporre il suo nome, come nè pur l'avea apposto alla sua Lettera proemiale: onde alla *pag.* 285. 2. malamente è stato riempiuto un picciol vacuo, con recente inchiostro, col nome di *Notar Jacomo*, il quale sarà bene che nel facciate radere interamente. Dopo ciò messomi a leggere i componimenti del predetto anonimo raccoglitore, venni subito in sospetto, che questi esser potessero del suddetto Lorenzo; e però tolto per mano il volume delle sue *Poesie volgari*, stampate *in Vinegia in casa de' figliuoli di Aldo nel* 1554. *in ottavo*, vi ritrovai tutti quasi i componimenti, cioè i Sonetti e la Canzone, che stanno nel Manoscritto, toltone le cinque ultime Ballate, o sia Canzoni a ballo, che saran forse in altro volume con quelle del Poliziano e di altri stampate: di che non mi son potuto accertare, per esserne senza. Dopo ciò credo che non vi rimarrà dubbio alcuno intorno a quanto vi scrissi. Può essere, che io mi risolva a dirne qualche cosa, se mel permette, in una delle mie Annotazioni all' Eloquenza Italiana del fu Monsig. Fontanini, le quali a quest' ora sarebbono terminate, se le mie frequenti e lunghe indisposizioni non mi avesser costretto a sospenderne il lavoro. Vi ho recato un lungo tedio, e però senz' altro passo a dirvi, che di vero cuore sono e sarò sempre....

N° XXXVII.

Rispetti del Politiano.

N° XXXVII. O TRIOFANTE sopra ogni altra bella,
Gentile, onesta, & gratiosa Dama,
Ascolta el canto, con che ti favella
Colui, che sopra ogni altra cosa t' ama;
Perchè tu sei la sua lucente stella;
Et giorno, e notte il tuo bel nome chiama,
Principalmente a salutar ti manda,
Poi mille volte ti si raccomanda.

Et

Nº XXXVII.

Et priegati umilmente, che tu degni
Considerar la sua perfetta fede,
Et che qualche pietà nel tuo cuor regni,
Come a tanta bellezza si richiede;
Egli ha veduto mille, e mille segni
Della tuo gentilezza, & ogn' or vede,
Or non chiede altro el tuo fedel suggetto,
Se non veder di quei segni l'effetto.
Sa ben, che non è degno, che tu l'ami
Non n'è degno vedere i tuoi belli ochi,
Massime avendo tu tanti bei dami,
Che par che ognun solo el tuo bel viso adochi;
Ma perchè sa, che onore, & gloria t' ami,
E stimi poco altre frasche, o finochi,
Et lui sempremai cerca farti onore,
Spera per questo entrarti un dì nel core.
Quel che non si conosce, e non si vede,
Chi l'ami, o chi l' aprezi mai non trouva,
E di quì nasce, che tanto suo fede,
Non sendo conosciuta, non gli giova,
Che troverìa ne' belli occhi merzede,
Se tu facessi di lui qualche pruova;
Ognun zimbella, ognun guata, e vagheggia,
I' sol per fedeltà esco di greggia.
E se potessi un dì solo soletto
Trovarsi teco sanza gelosia,
Sanza paura, sanza niun sospetto,
E raccontarti la sua pena ria;
Mille, e mille sospiri uscir dal petto,
E i tuo begli occhi lagrimar faria,
E se sapessi ben aprire il suo cuore
Ne crederebbe acquistare el tuo amore.
Tu sei de' tuoi begli anni ora in sul fiore,
Tu sei nel colmo della tua bellezza,
Se di donarla non ti fai onore,
Te la torrà per forza la vecchiezza,
Che 'l tempo vola, e non si arreston l'ore,
E la rosa sfiorita non si apprezza,

 Dunque

Nº
XXXVII.

Dunque allo amante tuo fanne un presente,
Chi non fa, quando può, tardi si pente.
Il tempo fugge, e tu fuggir lo lassi,
Che non ha el mondo la più cara cosa,
E se tu aspetti ch'l Maggio trapassi,
Invan cercherai poi di cor la rosa;
Quel che non si fa presto, mai poi fassi,
Or che tu puoi, non istar più pensosa,
Piglia il tempo che fugge pel ciuffetto,
Prima che nasca qualche stran sospetto.
Egli è nello infra due pur troppo stato,
Et non sa, se si dorme, o se s' è desto,
O segli è sciolto, o segli è pur legato,
Deh fa un colpo, Dama, e sie pel resto,
Hai tu piacer di tenerlo impiccato?
O tu l'affoga, o tu taglia il capresto;
Non più per dio, questa ciriegia abocca;
O tu stendi omai l'arco, o tu lo scocca.
Tu lo pasci di frasche, e di parole,
Di risi, e cenni, e di vesciche, e vento,
E dì, che gli vuoi bene, e che ti duole
Di non poterlo far, Dama, contento;
Ogni cosa è possibile a chi vuole,
Purche 'l fuoco lavori un poco drento,
Non più pratiche, omai facciasi l'opera,
Prima che affatto questo amor si scuopra.
Ch' egli ha deliberato, e posto in sodo,
Se gli dovessi esser cavato il cuore,
Di cercare ogni via, ogni arte, e modo,
Per corre i frutti un dì di tanto amore;
Scior gli conviene, o tagliar questo nodo,
Pur sempre intende salvarti l'onore,
Ma e' conviene, Dama, che anche tu agussi
Pervenire ad effetto i tuoi [illegible].
E se tu pur restassi per paura
Di non perder la tua perfetta fama,
Usa quì l'arte, e poi molto ben cura,
Che ingegno, o che cervello ha quel che t' ama;

S' egli

N°
XXXVII.

S' egli è discreto, non istar più dura,
Che più si scuopre, quanto più si brama;
Cerca de' modi, truova qualche mezo,
E non tenere troppo il caval rezo.
Se tu guardissi a parole di frati,
Io direi, Dama, che tu fossi sciocca,
E' sanno ben riprendere e peccati,
Ma non si accorda il resto colla bocca;
E tutti siam d'una pece macchiati,
Io ho cantato pur, zara a chi tocca,
Poi quel proverbio del Diavolo è vero,
Che non è come si dipigne nero.
E non ti diè tanta bellezza Iddio,
Perchè la tenga sempre ascosa in seno,
Ma perchè ne contenti al parer mio
El servo tuo di fede, e d'amor pieno;
Nè creder tu, che sia peccato rio,
Per esser d'altrui, uscir un pò del freno,
Che se ne dai a lui quanto è bastanza,
Non si vuol gittar via, quel che t'avanza.
Egli è pur meglio, & più a Dio accetto
Far qualche bene al povero affamato,
Che ha presentato nei divin conspetto,
Cento per un ti fia remunerato;
Datti tre volte della man nel petto,
Et di tuo colpa, di questo peccato,
E non vuol troppo, e basta che raguzoli
Sotto la mensa tua di que' minuzoli.
Et però, Donna, rompi un tratto il ghiaccio,
Assaggia anche tu el frutto dell' amore;
Quando l'amante tuo ti arà poi in braccio,
D' aver tanto indugiato arai dolore;
Questi mariti non ne sanno straccio,
Perchè non hanno sì infiammato el cuore;
Cosa desiderata assai più giova,
E se nol credi, fanne pur la prova.
Questo mio ragionare è un Vangelo,
Io t' ho contato apertamente tutto;

 So

Nº XXXVII.

So che nell' uovo tu conosci il pelo,
E sapranne ben trarre el ver construtto;
E s' io arò punto di favor dal cielo,
Forse ne nascerà qualche buon frutto;
Fatti con Dio, che 'l troppo dire offende,
Chi è savia, e discreta, presto intende.

Nº XXXVIII.

Stanze di Francesco Berni,

Orlando Innamorato. lib. iii. *canto* 7.

Nº XXXVIII.

QUIVI era non so come capitato
Un certo buon compagno Fiorentino,
Fu Fiorentino e nobil, ben che nato
Fusse il padre e nutrito in Casentino,
Dove il padre di lui gran tempo stato
Sendo, si fece quasi cittadino,
Et tolse moglie e s' accasò in Bibbiena
Ch' una Terra è sopr' Arno molto amena.
Costui chi'o dico all' Amporecchio nacque,
Che' è famoso castel per quel Masetto,
Poi fu condotto in Firenze, ove giacque
Fin à diciannove anni poveretto,
A Roma andò da poi com' à Dio piacque
Pien di molta speranza & di concetto
D'un certo suo parente Cardinale,
Che non gli fece mai ne ben ne male.
Morto lui, stette con un suo Nipote
Dal qual trattato fu come dal Zio,
Onde le bolge trovandosi vote
Di mutar cibo gli venne disio,
Et sendo all'hor le laudi molto note
D'un che serviva al Vicario di Dio

In certo officio che chiaman Datario,
Si pose à star con lui per Secretario. N° XXXVIII.

* * *

Di persona era grande, magro & schietto,
Lunghe & sottil le gambe forte haveva,
E'l naso grande, e'l viso largo, & stretto
Lo spatio che le ciglia divideva,
Concavo l'occhio haveva azurro & netto,
La barba folta quasi il nascondeva
Se l'havesse portata, ma il padrone
Haveva con le barbe aspra quistione.
Nessun di servitù già mai si dolse
Ne piu ne fu nimico di costui,
Et pure à consumarlo il Diavol tolse,
Sempre il tenne fortuna in forza altrui,
Sempre che comandargli il padron volse
Di non servirlo venne voglia à lui,
Voleva far da se non comandato,
Com' un gli comandava era spacciato.
Cacce, musiche, feste, suoni, & balli,
Gioche, nessuna sorte di piacere
Troppo il movea, piacevangli i cavalli
Assai, ma si pasceva del vedere,
Che modo non havea da comperalli,
Onde il suo sommo bene era in jacere
Nudo, lungo, disteso, e'l suo diletto
Era non far mai nulla, & starsi in letto.
Tanto era dallo scriver stracco & morto,
Si i membri e i sensi haveva strutti & arsi,
Che non sapeva in piu tranquillo porto
Da cosi tempestoso mar ritarsi,
Ne piu conforme antidoto & conforto
Dar à tante fatiche, che lo starsi,
Che starsi in letto & non far mai niente,
Et cosi il corpo rifare & la mente.

Stanze

Nº XXXIX.

Stanze di Lor. de' Medici.

LA NENCIA DA BARBERINO.

Nº XXXIX.

ARDO d' amore, e conviemmi cantare
Per una dama che mi strugge il core,
Ch' ogn' otta ch' io la sento ricordare
El cuor mi brilla, e par che gli esca fore.
Ella non trova di bellezza pare
Con gl' occhi getta fiaccole d' amore,
Io sono stato in città e castella
Et mai non vidi gnuna tanto bella.

Io sono stato a Empoli al mercato,
A Prato, a Monticelli, a san Casciano:
A Colle, a Poggibonzi, a San Donato;
Et quinamonte insino a Dicomano:
Figline, Castelfranco ho ricercato,
San Pier, el Borgo, Montagna, e Gagliano:
Più bel mercato che nel mondo sia,
E' a Barberin dov' è la Nencia mia.

Non vidi mai fanciulla tanto honesta,
Nè tanto saviamente rilevata;
Non vidi mai la più pulita testa,
Nè si lucente, nè si ben quadrata:
Ell ha due occhi che pare una festa
Quando ella gl' alza; e che ella ti guata:
Et in quel mezo ha el naso tanto bello,
Che par proprio bucato col succhiello.

Le labbra rosse paion di corallo,
E havvi drento duo filar di denti,
Che son più bianchi che quei di cavallo,
Et d' ogni lato ella n' ha più di venti:
Le gote bianche paion di cristallo,
Senz' altri lisci ovver scorticamenti;
Et in quel mezzo ell' è come una rosa
Nel mondo non fu mai si bella cosa,

Ben

N° XXXIX.

Ben si potrà tener avventurato,
Che sia marito di sì bella moglie;
Ben si potrà tener in buon dì nato
Chi arà quel Fioraliso senza foglie:
Ben si potrà tenersi consolato,
Che si contenti tutte le sue voglie
D' aver la Nencia e tenersela in braccio,
Morbida, e bianca, che pare un sugnaccio.
Io t' ho agguagliata alla Fata Morgana
Che mena seco tanta baronia;
Io t'assomiglio alla stella diana,
Quando apparisce alla capanna mia;
Più chiara se' che acqua di fontana
Et se' più dolce che la Malvagia
Quando ti sguardo da sera, o mattina,
Piu bianca se' che'l fior della farina.
Ell' ha due occhi tanto rubacuori
Ch' ella trafigere' con essi un muro:
Chiunche la vede convien che s' innamori;
Ell' ha il suo cuore più ch'un ciottol duro:
Et sempre ha seco un migliajo d'amadori
Che da quegli occhi tutti presi furo:
Ma ella guarda sempre questo & quello,
Per modo tal che mi struggo il cervello.

* * *

Nenciozza mia chi' vo sabato andare
Fino a Firenza, a vender duo somelle
Di scheggie che mi posi ieri a tagliare,
In mentre che pascevan le vitelle.
Procura ben se ti posso arrecare,
O se tu vuoi ch' io t'arrechi cavelle,
O liscio, ò biacca drento un cartoccino,
O di spilletti, o d'agora un quattrino.
Ell' è direttamente ballerina:
Ch' ella si lancia com'una capretta;
Et gira più che ruota di mulina,
Et dassi delle man nella scarpetta,
Quand' ella compie el ballo ella s'inchina,
Poi torna indrieto e duo tratti scambietta;

N° XXXIX.

Ella fa le più belle riverenze
Che gnuna cittadina di Firenze.
Che non mi chiedi qualche zacherella,
Che so n' adopri di cento ragioni;
O uno intaglio per la tua gonnella
O uncinegli, o magliette, o bottoni,
O pel tuo camiciotto una scarsella,
O cintolin per legar gli scuffioni,
O voi per ammagliar la gammurrina
Una cordella a seta cilestrina.
Se tu volessi per portare al collo
Un corallin di que' bottoncin rossi
Con un dondol nel mezzo, arrecherollo,
Ma dimmi se gli vuoi piccoli, o grossi,
E s' so dovessi trargli dal midollo
Del fusol della gamba, o degli altr' ossi,
E s' io dovessi impegnar la gonnella,
I' te gli arrecherò, Nencia mia bella.
Se mi dicessi, quando Sieve è grossa,
Gettati dentro, i' mi vi getteria;
E s' io dovessi morir di percossa,
Il capo al muro per te batteria;
Comandami, se vuoi, cosa ch' i' possa,
E non ti peritar de' fatti mia:
Io so che molta gente ti promette,
Fanne la prova d' un pa' di scarpette.
Io mi sono avveduto, Nencia bella,
Ch' un altro ti gaveggia a mio dispetto;
E s' io dovessi trargli le budella,
E poi gittarle tutte inturun tetto;
Tu sai, ch' io porto allato la coltella,
Che taglia, e pugne, che par un diletto,
Che s' io el trovassi nella mia capanna,
Io gliele caccerei più d' una spanna.

N° XL.

TRIONFO DI BACCO E ARIANNO,

Di Lor. de' Medici.

N° XL.

QUANT' è bella giovinezza,
Che si fugge tuttavia;
Chi vuol' esser lieto sia,
Di doman non ci è certezza.
Quest' è Bacco, e Arianna,
Belli, e l'un dell' altro ardenti;
Perchè 'l tempo fugge, e'nganna,
Sempre insieme stan contenti:
Queste Ninfe, e altre genti
Sono allegre tuttavia:
Chi vuol' esser lieto sia,
Di doman non ci è certezza.
Questi lieti Satiretti,
Delle Ninfe innamorati;
Per caverne, e per boschetti
Han lor posto cento aguati:
Hor da Bacco riscaldati,
Ballon saltan tuttavia:
Chi vuol' esser lieto sia:
Di doman non ci è certezza.
Queste Ninfe hanno ancor caro,
Da loro essere ingannate;
Non puon far' à Amor riparo,
Se non genti rozze, e' ngrate:
Hora insieme mescolate,
Fanno festa tuttavia:
Chi vuol' esser lieto sia,
Di doman non ci è certezza.
Questa soma, che vien dreto,
Sopra l' Asino, è Sileno,
Cosi vecchio, è ebro, e lieto,
Gia di carne, e d' anni pieno:
Se non puo star ritto, almeno

N° XL.

Ride, e gode tuttavia:
Chi vuol' esser lieto, sia,
Di doman non ci è certezza.
Mida vien, dopo costoro,
Cio che tocca, oro diventa;
E che giova haver tesoro,
Poi che l'huom non si contenta?
Che dolcezza vuoi che senta,
Chi ha sete tuttavia?
Chi vuol' esser lieto sia,
Di doman non ci è certezza.
Ciascuno apra ben gli orecchi,
Di doman nessun si paschi;
Oggi siam giovani, e vecchi,
Lieti ognun femmine, e maschi:
Ogni tristo pensier caschi,
Facciam festa tuttavia:
Chi vuol' esser lieto sia
Di doman non ci è certezza.
Donne, e giovanetti Amanti,
Viva Bacco, e viva amore;
Ciascun suoni, balli, e canti,
Arda di dolcezza il core:
Non fatica, non dolore,
Quel c'hà esser, convien sia:
Chi vuol' esser lieto sia,
Di doman, non ci è certezza;
Quant' è bella giovinezza
Che is fugge tuttavia?

Nº XLI.

CANZONE A BALLO.

Di Lor. De' Medici.

Nº XLI.

BEN venga maggio,
E'l gonfalon selvaggio.
Ben venga Primavera,
Ch' ognun par che innamori;
E voi donzelle a schiera
Con li vostri amadori,
Che di rose, e di fiori
Vi fate belle il maggio.
Venite alla frescura
Delli verdi arbuscelli:
Ogni bella è sicura
Fra tanti damigelli;
Che le fiere, e gl' uccelli
Ardon d'amor il maggio.
Chi è giovane, e bella,
Deh non sie punto acerba
Che non si rinnovella
L'età come fa l' herba.
Nessuna stia superba,
All' amadore il maggio.
Ciascuna balli e canti
Di questa schiera nostra:
Ecco e dodici amanti,
Che per voi vanno in giostra
Qual dura allor si mostra
Farà sfiorire il maggio.
Per prender le donzelle
Si son gl'amanti armati;
Arrendetevi belle
A' vostri innamorati;
Rendete e cuor furati,
Non fate guerra il maggio.

N° XLI.

Chi l' altrui cuore invola
  Ad altri doni el core:
  Ma chi è, quel che vola?
  E' l' Angiolel d'amore,
  Che viene à fare honore
  Con voi donzelle al maggio.
Amor ne vien ridendo
  Con rose, e gigli in testa:
  E vien di voi caendo,
  Fategli o belle festa:
  Qual sarà la più presta
  A dargli el fior del maggio.
Ben venga il peregrino,
  Amor che ne comandi?
  Che al suo amante il crino
  Ogni bella ingrillandi;
  Che le zitelle, e grandi;
  S' innamoran di maggio.

N° XLII.

Joannes Picus Miran. Laurentio Medici.

N° XLII. LEGI, Laurenti Medice, Rhythmos tuos, quos tibi vernaculæ musæ per ætatem teneram suggesserunt. Agnovi musarum & gratiarum legitimam fœturam, ætatis teneræ opus non agnovi. Quis enim in tuis Rhythmis & numerosa versuum junctura saltantes ad numerum gratias non peresenser.t? quis in canoro dicendi genere & modulato canentes musas non audiat? quis in lepore non affectato, hilari argutia, mellitis salibus, aptis illecebris, miro candore in prudenti dispositione, in gravissimis sensibus ex penetralibus philosophiæ erutis, adolescentem hominem agnoscat? Scio profecto me non esse in hoc albo, nec eum qui huc ascendam, idest, ad judicium rerum. Sed vellem dici posse extra suspicionem adulationis quod de illis sentio. Dicerem profecto non esse veterem scriptorem, quem in hoc genere dicendi longo intervallo non antecesseris. Quod ne putes dictum ob gratiam, afferam

3

ram tibi hujusce sensus rationes meas. Sunt apud vos duo præcipue celebrati poetæ Florentinæ linguæ, Franciscus Petrarcha, & Dantes Aligerius; de quibus illud in universum sim præfatus esse ex eruditis, qui res in Francisco, verba in Dante desiderent; in te qui mentem habeat & aures neutrum desideraturum, in quo non sit videre, an res oratione, an verba sententiis magis illustrentur. Sed expendamus velut in librili particulatim uniuscujusque merita. Franciscus quidem si reviviscat, quod attinet ad sensus, quis eum dubitet ultro herbam tibi daturum? adeo tu & acutus semper, gravis & subtilis, ille vero de medio plurimum arripiens, sententias colorat verbis, & quæ sunt gregaria egregia facit genere dicendi: in quo videamus quid tibi ille, quid tu illi præstes. In quibusdam dulcior apparuerit, sed mihi illius dulcedo (ut ita dixerim) dulciter acida & suaviter austera. Ille fusus & æquabiliter deliniens, tu majestate, & quadam vivaci luce orationis animos perstringens. In illo ambitiosa & nimis, in te neglecta potius quam affectata diligentia. Ille tener & mollis, tu masculus & torosus. Ille volubilis & canorus, tu pressus, plenus, firmus, & modulatus. Ille forte lepidior, tu certe amplior & erectior. Ille fucatior, sed tu nervosior. In illo est, quod amputes, in te nihil redundans & nihil curtum. Sed forte audaculus, qui tollendum aliquid de illo dixerim. At ita est certe, ita multis videtur, quorum judicio confido: nam meo nihil; cum sæpe sit videre peccantem illum, quod Asiatici peccabant, idest infarcientem verba quasi rimas expleat, adhibentemque, voces plenas & concinnas, non ut exornent, sed ut sustineant quasi tibicines, carmen ne claudicet. In te omnia verba non minus in re necessaria, quam in ornatu grata, ita ut qui ex te demat, mutilet; qui ex illo, tondat & repurget. Quod si demus (quod nunquam dabo) lepidiora esse quæ ille scripserit, & comptiora tuis, facile id fuit præstare hominem, cui non esset cum ipsis sensibus labor & pugna. At tuæ illæ acres, subtiles, & (ut uno dixerim verbo) Laurentianæ sententiæ, vix dici potest, ut calamistros respuant, & istos fucos non libenter admittant. Quas ille tractandas si habuisset, quem mollem legimus, nitidum & jucundum, legeremus equidem spinosum, squalidum & ingratum; cum sit videre illum, quoties aliquid tale aggreditur, acutum implicitum vel nodosum, tam stylo cadere, quam sensu surgit. Cum vero illam suam verborum ostentat supellectilem, sua unguenta, cincinnos & flores admoneret sæpe siades set Castritius, quod admonuit in Graccho, ne falleremur rotundato sono, & versuum cursu, sed inspiceremus quidnam subesset, quæ sedes, quod firmamentum, quis fundus verbis: quod si facias illic, videas Epicuri quandoque vacuum, ita aut nullum subesse sensum, aut frigidum & levem.

N° XLII. levem. Qua parte (quamvis est maxima) etiam illi si non præstes, non video omnino, cur præstet ille tibi dicendi gratia: cum & verba apud te esse non possint illustriora, & collocatio illorum ita sit apta, ut nec cohærere melius, nec fluere rotundius, nec cadere numerosius ullo modo possint. Sed jam Dantem tecum pensiculimus, de quo fortasse plures controversiam sint facturi. Sunt enim multi, qui in scriptorum collatione non tam expendant merita, quam annos numerent, jubentque alios, ut priscos legant cum reverentia, coætaneos ipsi legere non possunt sine invidia. Primas, certe, quod ad stylum spectat, denegaturum tibi neminem puto, ita est Dantes nonnunquam horridus, asper & strigosus, ut multum rudis & impolitus: hoc ejus etiam aurarii fatentur; sed in ætatem & sæculum illud, id quod sit ita, culpam rejiciunt; omnino tu oratione cultior, & non ille grandior. At sensibus (inquient) grandior & sublimior. Quæso, quid mirum in philosophica re illum philosophari, ipsa natura ad hoc cogente, atque ultro suppeditante sententias? Si de Deo, de anima, de beatitudine agitur, affert quæ Thomas, quæ Augustinus de his scripserunt; & fuit ille in his tractandis meditandisque tam frequens quam assiduus, tu in obeundis maximis negotiis publicis & privatis. Non fuit tam præclarum in Dante hoc fecisse, quam non fecisse turpe fuerat: at fuit dubio procul summi ingenii opus, quod ipse præstas, philosophica facere, quæ sunt amatoria, & quæ sunt sua severitate austerula, superinducta venere facere amabilia. Ita in tuis versibus amantium lusibus, Philosophorum seria sunt admixta, ut & illa hinc dignitatem, & hæc illinc hilaritatem gratiamque lucrifecerint; ut ambo hac copula & retinuerint quod erat proprium, & mutuo se sibi ita participaverint, ut habeant utraque singulatim quæ prius erant simul amborum. Sed non est hoc tam admirandum, quam illud, quod me maxime movit: ita hæc a te invecta, ut non invecta, sed de materiæ ipsius (de qua agis) eruta gremio, & ex illa ipsa (ut ita dixerim) te irrigante solum, efflorescere videantur, ut appareant nativa, non adventitia; necessaria, non comportata; genuina omnino, non insititia, hoc est quod admirari satis non possum, quo mihi videris Dantem exsuperasse. Nam et si ille sublimis volat, materiæ alis attollitur; tu repugnante illa & deorsum trahente tolleris in altum alis ingenii, atque ita tolleris, ut a materia non discedas, sed illam tecum simul attollas, tantum de ipsa tu, quantum de Dante ipsa fuit benemerita. Jam videre licet quid te inter, Franciscumque & Dantem intersit, de quibus hoc addiderim, Franciscum quandoque non respondere pollicitis, habentem quod allectet in prima specie, sed ulterius non satisfaciat: Dantem habere quod in occursu quandoque offendat, sed juvet magis intima pervadentem.

Tua

Tua non minus habent in recessu quod detineat, quam habeant in prima fronte quod capiat. Adde quod illi suas poeses in secessibus, in umbra, in summa studiorum tranquillitate: tu tuas inter tumultus, curiæ strepitus, fori clamores, maximas curas, turbulentissimas tempestates, occupatissimus cecinisti. Illis erant Musæ ordinarium negotium, & principale: tibi ludus, & a curis quædam relaxatio. Illis summa defatigatio, tibi defatigatio otium. Denique eo animum remittens pertigisti, quo illi omnes animi neruos contendentes fortasse non pertigerunt. Sed quid dicam de mea paraphrasi? meam enim cur non appellem vel hujus, quæ mea est, appellationis jure? demum cur non meam, quam etsi veneror ut tuam, amo tamen ut meam? admiror profecto illam, & te in illa; ex qua conjicio quantum ego aberam a vera laude tuorum versuum, in quibus quæ erant maxima, quæque maxime illustria, quibus sum noctuinis oculis, non introspexeram, vidi deinde per te revelata, qui id solus & poteras & debebas; debebas autem tibi & nobis, ne multa & te gloria, & nos voluptate fraudares. Lego (deum testor) maxime Laurenti eam, non tam ad delectationem, quam ad doctrinam. Quot enim ibi ex Aristotele, auditu scilicet physico, ex libris de Anima, de Moribus, de Cælo, ex Problematis? Quot ex Platonis Protagora, ex Republica, ex Legibus, ex Symposio? quæ omnia quamquam alias apud illos legi, lego tamen apud te ut nova, ut meliora, & in nescio quam a te faciem transformata, ut tua videantur esse, & non illorum; & legens discere mihi aliquid videar, quod maximo est indicio, hæc te sapere non tam ex commentario, quam ex te ipso. Solent enim plurimi majore in literis sophisteia quam opera, cum quid scripturi sunt, philosophos habere velut pragmaticos, eis dogmata quædam suggerentes, quæ ingerant suis libellis, ut videantur philosophi. Sed facile hos deprehendas, nam videas illa nec recte disposita, nec cohærentia, & ab ipsis non explicata, sed implicata. Atque homines alioquin eloquentes, in illis dicendis apparent infantissimi. At te quis non videat ea non tenere precario, sed ut in quæ jus habeas & potestatem pro arbitrio versare, agere, tractare? Hæc tu (proh felix ingenium) in æstu Reip. in actuosa vita es assecutus, quæ nos philosophorum non discipuli, sed inquilini, in umbratili vita & cellularia, sequimur potius quam consequimur. Sed quid dicam de paraphraseos tuæ suavissimo stylo? is mihi videtur penitus, qui Cæsaris in Romana lingua. Est enim oratio non manu facta, non bracteata, non torta; sed suo ingenio erecta, candida, & quadrata, nec temere excurrens, sed pedem servans, nec luxurians, nec jejuna, nec lasciviens, nec ingrata, dulciter gravis, graviter amabilis, verba electa & non captata; illustria, non fucata; necessaria, non quæsita; non explicantia

N° XLII.

N° XLII. explicantia rem, sed ipsis oculis subjicientia. Prætereo quam tuæ personæ semper memineris, quam sint ubique tuæ illius prudentiæ impersa passim semina atque vestigia. Hæc ego & cum multis, & alius quisquam longe potiora. Sed duo præcipua præter hæc vidi, quæ videant forte non multi quamquam oculatiores. Primum est illud, ut illa suas divitias dissimulet, ut invidiam fugiat, flores in sinu habeat, non ostentet, non exurgat in plantas, sed subsidat in genua, ut minor appareat. Alterum quid sit non video, neque enim tam solers, sed video esse nescio quid (ut dicam signatissime) Laurentianum. Quod si quis videat Laurentii dotes, ingenium, præstantiam, Laurentium totum videat graphice effigiatum. Sed hæc nimis fortasse multa, quæ dixi etiam invitus, ipsa me transversum (ut dicunt) trahente in verba animi sententia. Illud non præteribo, hortari te quanto possum opere maximo, ut aliquod quandoque a moderanda republica otiolum suffuratus, absolvendæ paraphrasi impartiaris, tibi quidem & linguæ patriæ ad honorem, civibus tuis & nobis omnibus futuræ ad usum & voluptatem. Florentiæ idibus Julii MCCCCLXXXIV.

END OF THE FIRST VOLUME.

www.ingramcontent.com/pod-product-compliance
Lightning Source LLC
Chambersburg PA
CBHW032022110726
47901CB00004B/1168
9783743435636